The Complete Max Carrados

Volume I

The
Complete
Max Carrados

Volume I

by
Ernest Bramah

Edited by
David Marcum

ISBN Hardback 978-1-78705-779-2
ISBN Paperback 978-1-78705-780-8
AUK ePub ISBN 978-1-78705-781-5
AUK PDF ISBN 978-1-78705-782-2

These works are in the Public Domain in Great Britain

Published by
MX Publishing
335 Princess Park Manor, Royal Drive,
London, N11 3GX
www.mxpublishing.co.uk

David Marcum can be reached at:
thepapersofsherlockholmes@gmail.com

Cover design by Brian Belanger
www.belangerbooks.com and *www.redbubble.com/people/zhahadun*

CONTENTS
Volume I

Introductions

Adventures

Max Carrados

The Eyes of Max Carrados

The Specimen Case

The Following Stories
Appear in Volume II

Max Carrados Mysteries

The Bravo of London (A Novel)

Some of these stories originally
appeared in the following locations:

Volume I

Volume II

Meet Max Carrados
by David Marcum

In his little-known first mystery anthology, *Challenge to the Reader* (1938), author, editor, and detective Ellery Queen offered something new: Twenty-five mysteries featuring well-known detectives, but with their names changed so that part of the fun for the reader, along with playing armchair detective and trying to solve the mystery, was figuring out the identity of the detective in each story.

In the book, this challenge initially occurs as Ellery is discussing mystery stories with his friend, J..J. McC (who was likely Judge J.J. McCue, who provided forewords to a number of the early Queen novels). Each evening, over nearly one month, Ellery reads a carefully chosen story from his vast mystery collection, and J.J. attempts to figure out the sleuth's identity from internal clues. There are a lot of detectives that will be completely unknown to modern readers – Dr. Hailey and Jim Hanvey and Henry Poggioli. Then there are those that have remained familiar to the present. Ben Knott is the disguised name used for Sam Spade. M. Apollodore Pimpant is Hercule Poirot. Pharoah Jones is Sherlock Holmes. And Hilary King is substituted for Ellery Queen. (Ellery had used this alias in one of his own adventures, *The Devil to Pay* – also published in 1938, but occurring the year before.)

After reading "The Vanished Crown", (adapted from Ernest Bramah's "The Adventure of the Vanished Petition Crown"), Ellery asks J.J., *"What – or perhaps I should say whom – do you make of Mr. Stephen McCaulay,"* – for that is the altered name of that evening's featured detective.

"I make the only blind detective there is," replies J.J., seizing on the most memorable aspect of Mr. McCaulay. *"Max Carrados is the only one I ever heard of."* And then he and Ellery go on to discuss the other unaltered clues within the story that helped to identify McCaulay's true identity: There's the presence of Carrados' friend, private inquiry agent Louis Carlyle. *"McCaulay"* a numismatist specializing in Greek tetradrachms – that can only be Carrados. Finally, he's a financially independent dilettante who refuses to investigate cases for money.

J.J. has only heard of one blind detective, but Ellery – a formidable master of detective literature along with his brilliant sleuthing skills, says there's at least one other: Thornley Colton, who appeared respectively in a volume of short stories and a novel in 1915 and 1916 by Clinton H. Stagg. But Carrados appeared before Colton by over year, and he was the first of several dozen handicapped detectives appearing in subsequent years who more than made up for the limits of a missing sense or limb.

The first Max Carrados story appeared in *News of the World* (August 17, 1913), under the title "The Master Coiner Unmasked". For book publication a year later, it was retitled "The Coin of Dionysius". Between mid-August and December 28th of 1913, at a rate of two or three stories per month, a dozen Max Carrados adventures appeared in the same famed weekly British tabloid. In 1914, eight of these stories were collected in *Max Carrados*, but the other four languished for nearly a decade, until 1923, when they – along with five new tales – were published in *The Eyes of Max Carrados*. The following year, Bramah published a general short story collection with one Carrados story, "The Bunch of Violets", subtitled "An Episode in the War-time Activities of Max Carrados". Sometime later, Bramah wrote eight more final short stories, published in 1927 as *Max Carrados Mysteries*. He then concluded the series in 1934 with the full-length novel, *The Bravo of London*.

Meanwhile, the door had been opened to the curious originality of featuring handicapped detectives. While previous literary detectives had displayed eccentricities, these were simply aspects of their genius and personality. Sherlock Holmes, the greatest detective of all time without possibility of argument, had a horror of destroying documents and kept his tobacco in a Persian slipper. He pinned his correspondence to the mantel with a jack-knife, and he once fired a patriotic *V.R.* into the wall of his Baker Street sitting room with a hair-trigger gun. In seven adventures, his low-dose use of cocaine is referenced either directly mentioned or inferred – giving false hope to all of those readers who *need* Holmes to be a broken, hopeless, and helpless addict in order for them to connect with the stories.

Auguste Dupin preferred working at night by candlelight and smoking a meerschaum pipe. Hercule Poirot, whose first literary appearance was in 1920, had an interest in tidiness and order and similar-sized breakfast eggs and maintaining his mustache. Barker, Holmes's *"hated rival upon the Surrey shore"*, wore dark glasses and a Masonic tiepin. But Carrados was the first detective to be *blind* – and as such, he honed his other senses to a remarkable degree.

To reveal more about how this is presented would be to spoil the enjoyment of discovery. Additionally, it's better to find out about Carrados' friends, associates, relatives, and formidable reputation by way of reading the series, instead of having all the surprises spoiled beforehand.

Author Ernest Bramah – real name Ernest Bramah *Smith* – wrote an introduction for *The Eyes of Max Carrados*, the second Carrados collection, in which he discusses Carrados' initial introduction to the world, and then justifies all of the amazing skills that Carrados demonstrates during the course of his investigations. I considered moving this essay out of *The Eyes* and making it Bramah's foreword to these complete volumes, but I realized that, written as it was, nearly a decade *after* the publication of the first volume of Carrados stories, the essay simply gives away too much about Carrados and his world in its looking-back summary that should be discovered naturally by way of reading the stories.

As usual when reading these or any other stories, I studied carefully as I went and took notes, and I was able to build something of a Carrados chronology – which always adds layers of enjoyment if one wants to play that type of game. There are subtle clues. One story says that it occurs about a month after another – so the order of those two can be determined. The careful reader can work out Carrados' general age and approximate birthdate from another character's comment. Several stories can be specifically tied to dates around the first World War. The same attentive reading gives information about Carrados' other "Untold Cases".

In assembling this foreword, I started to provide a whole segment about what I'd constructed from my notes – when this or that event happened in Carrados' life, and the correct order in which to read the cases – but again, having everything laid out beforehand like that would spoil the fun. (I refuse to read book jackets because they intentionally reveal so much of the story. Additionally, I first discovered Sherlock Holmes at age ten, in 1975, with an abridged copy of *The Adventures* and a paperback of *The Return.* I read "The Empty House" before ever finding "The Final Problem", and thus I learned how Holmes survived his battle with Professor Moriarty atop the Reichenbach Falls before I ever knew that he'd supposedly died there. So I understand about reading in the correct manner.)

Despite being mostly unknown now, Carrados was popular in his heyday – even though there weren't an overwhelming number of stories in the Carrados Canon. For example, "The Bunch of Violets" appeared in the July 1924 issue of *The Strand* along with chapters from popular historical author Arthur Conan Doyle's serialized autobiography *Memories and Adventures* – and Carrados got higher billing than Doyle. (Such, however, would not have been the case if a new Holmes tale was being published that month, instead of nuggets about Watson's Literary Agent.)

The last Carrados short story collection, *Max Carrados Mysteries*, was published in 1927, and then – except for the sole novel, *The Bravo of London*'s appearance in 1934, there was nothing. Carrados essentially faded from view, except for mystery aficionados like Ellery Queen who kept the flame barely alive.

Carrados had an obscure appearance in August 1942 – just two months after Ernest Bramah's death – as portrayed on little-known American radio series called *Murder Clinic* by Alfred Shirley in "The Holloway Flat Tragedy". Then, for nearly thirty years, he had a truly slow glide into obscurity.

But in 1970, Hugh Green edited the first of four anthologies featuring *The Rivals of Sherlock Holmes*. In the first book, he included one of the most exciting Carrados tales, "The Game Played in the Dark". Next, Green used "The Tragedy at Brookbend Cottage" in *The Crooked Counties: Further Rivals of Sherlock Holmes* (1973). From the influence of these books, Thames Television produced *The Rivals of Sherlock Holmes*, with "The Missing Witness Sensation" being broadcast in late 1971. Robert

Stephens (who had portrayed Holmes in *The Private Life of Sherlock Holmes* the year before) was cast as Carrados.

Robert Stephens as Max Carrados (1971)

After that lone bow, Carrados again vanished until November 1995, when Bert Coules, most famous for adapting the complete Sherlock Holmes Canon for the BBC, and the first to do so with the same actors as Holmes and Watson in all sixty adventures, wrote *The Eyes of Max Carrados* – not an adaptation of every story in that book, but instead a sole episode starring Simon Callow. As described on the BBC website: "*1923. A desperate girl tries to clear her father, and only the celebrated blind detective Max Carrados can do it.*"

Between 2011 and 2016, BBC4 Radio aired sixteen episodes (in four series) of *The Rivals*. Dramatized by Chris Harrald, the program had the brilliant idea of having Inspector Lestrade working with a number of Sherlock Holmes's rivals in their cases. The series included three Carrados tales – more than any other detective represented in the series. These episodes were: "The Game Played in the Dark", The Knight's Cross Signal Problem", and "The Secret of Dunstan's Tower". They are well worth seeking out, and Lestrade's participation is a welcome adaptation.

5

Most recently, Carrados has appeared in "The Baffling Absence of Augustus Pickering" by Derrick Belanger, included in *The Consultations of Sherlock Holmes* (2023), in which Carrados and Sherlock Holmes finally work together. And Carrados is mentioned in two stories in my own recent collection, *The Singular Papers of Solar Pons*: "The Curious Affair of the Thumbless Jesus" and "The Subversive Drama". I can assure you that, now that I've met him, Carrados will return.

How This Book Came To Be

While I was aware of Max Carrados by way of *The Rivals* radio show, and his appearance in Ellery Queen's *Challenge to the Reader*, I had no great need to find out any more about him. But then a couple of things happened, one of them tragic, which led to this new Carrados collection.

The first was that from 2019 to 2021, I edited *The Complete Dr. Thorndyke*, nine massive volumes collecting all the Thorndyke novels and short stories. About this time, Sherlockian Mike Foy was producing a number of wonderfully researched oversize volumes for MX Publishing, wherein he tracked down ever-more obscure illustrations for the original Sherlock Holmes Canon. (These volumes are *Sherlock Holmes: A Study in Illustrations*, Volumes I through IV. Mike also assembled *The Curious Book of Sherlock Holmes Characters*.) I was increasingly amazed at how he was able to winkle out such obscure images that no modern Sherlockians had ever seen.

Mike, a Brit who had relocated to Florida, contacted me, asking if there was a possibility of producing such a volume of lost Thorndyke illustrations, but I had to tell him that sadly there had been very few original illustrations to go with those stories – certainly not enough to fill one of the gigantic books he'd been producing.

Meanwhile, after wrapping up *The Complete Dr. Thorndyke*, I was looking for another similar project, wherein the mostly forgotten adventures of other Rivals of Sherlock Holmes could be published for modern readers, and I stumbled upon the Carrados stories. *Perhaps,* I thought, *this would be something worthwhile.*

I ran the idea by Steve Emecz, the best and most influential Sherlockian Publisher in the World, who informed me that Mike was already thinking of working on the same thing. Letting the idea go, I moved on to other projects.

But then, in April 2024, the second thing happened: We found out that Mike had died unexpectedly. It was some time after that when Steve and I discussed the possibility of going forward with the Carrados project, and now here it is – dedicated to Mike, who did such an incredible job assembling those amazing Holmes illustration volumes, and who would have done wonderfully at compiling *The Complete Max Carrados*, if he'd had the chance.

> *"Of course, I could only stammer out my thanks."*
> *– The unhappy John Hector McFarlane,*
> "The Norwood Builder" – *The Return of Sherlock Holmes*

As always when any new project is finished, I want to first thank with all my heart my incredible, patient, brilliant, kind, and beautiful wife of nearly thirty-eight years, Rebecca – every day I'm luckier than the day before, and I'm wise enough to know it! – and our amazing, funny, creative, and wonderful son, and my friend, Dan. I love you both, and you are everything to me!

Special *Thank you*'s go to:

☐ *Steve Emecz* – From my first association with MX in 2013, I saw that MX (under Steve Emecz's leadership) was *the* fast-rising superstar of the Sherlockian publishing world. Connecting with MX and Steve Emecz was personally an amazing life-changing event for me, as it has been for countless other Sherlockian authors. It has led me to write many more stories, and then to edit books, along with unexpected additional Holmes Pilgrimages to England – none of which might have happened otherwise. By way of my first email with Steve, I've had the chance to make some incredible Sherlockian friends and play in the Holmesian Sandbox in ways that I would have never dreamed possible.

Through it all, Steve has been one of the most positive and supportive people that I have ever known.

From the beginning, Steve has let me explore various Sherlockian projects and open up my own personal possibilities in ways that otherwise would have never happened. Thank you, Steve, for every opportunity!

☐ *Brian Belanger* –I initially became acquainted with Brian when he took over the duties of creating the covers for MX Books, and I found him to be a great collaborator, and wonderfully creative too. I've worked with him on many projects with MX and Belanger Books, which he co-founded with his brother Derrick Belanger, also a good friend. Along with MX Publishing, Derrick and Brian have absolutely

7

locked up the Sherlockian publishing field with a vast amount of amazing material. The old dinosaurs must be trembling to see every new and worthy Sherlockian project, one after another after another, that these two companies create. Luckily MX and Belanger Books work closely with one another, and I'm thrilled to be associated with both of them. Many thanks to Brian for all he does for both publishers, and for all he's done for me personally.

And last but certainly *not* least, **Ernest Bramah Smith**: Founder of the Feast.

David Marcum
September 8th,, 2025

*Questions, comments, or story submissions
may be addressed to David Marcum at*

thepapersofsherlockholmes@gmail.com

Dedication

This collection is
dedicated to
Mike Foy
who would have been
The Editor

Editor's *Caveat*

These stories have been prepared using modern text-converting software, and as such, occasional deviations in punctuation have occurred. Those who absolutely must have the original version, down to each jot and dash, should understand that this version was created in order to present Max Carrados' adventures to a modern audience, and not to preserve an absolute pristine model for the historical archives.

Similarly, these stories were written in a time when racial prejudice and stereotypes were much more common than today. While some of these stereotypes must be unfortunately maintained within the story in order to accurately reflect the plot and the characters of those times, there are some words that were used in the original stories – vile racial epithets that have no business being repeated or perpetuated anywhere – that I have cheerfully removed. (There weren't many of them, but *any* are *too many*.)

If readers find that they want to experience the original versions as they were first written, with those hateful and ignorant words included, then they would be advised to seek out the original books. These versions celebrate Max Carrados, and as such, I felt no need whatsoever to include objectionable and offensive material simply for the sake of honoring or archiving the historical record.

David Marcum
Editor

The
Complete
Max Carrados

Volume I

Max Carrados

The Coin of Dionysius

It was eight o'clock at night and raining, scarcely a time when a business so limited in its clientele as that of a coin dealer could hope to attract any customer, but a light was still showing in the small shop that bore over its window the name of *Baxter*, and in the even smaller office at the back the proprietor himself sat reading the latest *Pall Mall*. His enterprise seemed to be justified, for presently the doorbell gave its announcement, and throwing down his paper Mr. Baxter went forward.

As a matter of fact, the dealer had been expecting someone, and his manner as he passed into the shop was unmistakably suggestive of a caller of importance. But at the first glance towards his visitor the excess of deference melted out of his bearing, leaving the urbane, self-possessed shopman in the presence of the casual customer.

"Mr. Baxter, I think?" said the latter. He had laid aside his dripping umbrella and was unbuttoning overcoat and coat to reach an inner pocket. "You hardly remember me, I suppose? Mr. Carlyle – two years ago I took up a case for you – "

"To be sure. Mr. Carlyle, the private detective – "

"Inquiry agent," corrected Mr. Carlyle precisely.

"Well," smiled Mr. Baxter, "for that matter I am a coin dealer and not an antiquarian or a numismatist. Is there anything in that way that I can do for you?"

"Yes," replied his visitor. "It is my turn to consult you." He had taken a small wash-leather bag from the inner pocket and now turned something carefully out upon the counter. "What can you tell me about that?"

The dealer gave the coin a moment's scrutiny.

"There is no question about this," he replied. "It is a Sicilian *tetradrachm* of Dionysius."

"Yes, I know that – I have it on the label out of the cabinet. I can tell you further that it's supposed to be one that Lord Seastoke gave two-hundred-and-fifty pounds for at the Brice sale in '94."

"It seems to me that you can tell me more about it than I can tell you," remarked Mr. Baxter. "What is it that you really want to know?"

"I want to know," replied Mr. Carlyle, "whether it is genuine or not."

"Has any doubt been cast upon it?"

"Certain circumstances raised a suspicion – that is all."

The dealer took another look at the *tetradrachm* through his magnifying glass, holding it by the edge with the careful touch of an expert. Then he shook his head slowly in a confession of ignorance.

17

"Of course I could make a guess – "

"No, don't," interrupted Mr. Carlyle hastily. "An arrest hangs on it and nothing short of certainty is any good to me."

"Is that so, Mr. Carlyle?" said Mr. Baxter, with increased interest. "Well, to be quite candid, the thing is out of my line. Now if it was a rare Saxon penny or a doubtful noble I'd stake my reputation on my opinion, but I do very little in the classical series."

Mr. Carlyle did not attempt to conceal his disappointment as he returned the coin to the bag and replaced the bag in the inner pocket.

"I had been relying on you," he grumbled reproachfully. "Where on earth am I to go now?"

"There is always the British Museum."

"Ah, to be sure, thanks. But will anyone who can tell me be there now?"

"Now? No fear!" replied Mr. Baxter. "Go round in the morning – "

"But I must know tonight," explained the visitor, reduced to despair again. "Tomorrow will be too late for the purpose."

Mr. Baxter did not hold out much encouragement in the circumstances.

"You can scarcely expect to find anyone at business now," he remarked. "I should have been gone these two hours myself only I happened to have an appointment with an American millionaire who fixed his own time." Something indistinguishable from a wink slid off Mr. Baxter's right eye. "Offmunson he's called, and a bright young pedigree-hunter has traced his descent from Offa, King of Mercia. So he – quite naturally – wants a set of Offas as a sort of collateral proof."

"Very interesting," murmured Mr. Carlyle, fidgeting with his watch. "I should love an hour's chat with you about your millionaire customers – some other time. Just now – look here, Baxter, can't you give me a line of introduction to some dealer in this sort of thing who happens to live in town? You must know dozens of experts."

"Why, bless my soul, Mr. Carlyle, I don't know a man of them away from his business," said Mr. Baxter, staring. "They may live in Park Lane or they may live in Petticoat Lane for all I know. Besides, there aren't so many experts as you seem to imagine. And the two best will very likely quarrel over it. You've had to do with 'expert witnesses', I suppose?"

"I don't want a witness. There will be no need to give evidence. All I want is an absolutely authoritative pronouncement that I can act on. Is there no one who can really say whether the thing is genuine or not?"

Mr. Baxter's meaning silence became cynical in its implication as he continued to look at his visitor across the counter. Then he relaxed.

18

"Stay a bit. There is a man – an amateur – I remember hearing wonderful things about some time ago. They say he really does know."

"There you are," exclaimed Mr. Carlyle, much relieved. "There always is someone. Who is he?"

"Funny name," replied Baxter. "Something Wynn or Wynn something." He craned his neck to catch sight of an important motor car that was drawing to the kerb before his window. "Wynn Carrados! You'll excuse me now, Mr. Carlyle, won't you? This looks like Mr. Offmunson."

Mr. Carlyle hastily scribbled the name down on his cuff.

"Wynn Carrados, right. Where does he live?"

"Haven't the remotest idea," replied Baxter, referring the arrangement of his tie to the judgment of the wall mirror. "I have never seen the man myself. Now, Mr. Carlyle, I'm sorry I can't do any more for you. You won't mind, will you?"

Mr. Carlyle could not pretend to misunderstand. He enjoyed the distinction of holding open the door for the transatlantic representative of the line of Offa as he went out, and then made his way through the muddy streets back to his office. There was only one way of tracing a private individual at such short notice – through the pages of the directories, and the gentleman did not flatter himself by a very high estimate of his chances.

Fortune favoured him, however. He very soon discovered a Wynn Carrados living at Richmond, and, better still, further search failed to unearth another. There was, apparently, only one householder at all events of that name in the neighbourhood of London. He jotted down the address and set out for Richmond.

The house was some distance from the station, Mr. Carlyle learned. He took a taxicab and drove, dismissing the vehicle at the gate. He prided himself on his power of observation and the accuracy of the deductions which resulted from it – a detail of his business. "It's nothing more than using one's eyes and putting two and two together," he would modestly declare, when he wished to be deprecatory rather than impressive, and by the time he had reached the front door of "The Turrets", he had formed some opinion of the position and tastes of the man who lived there.

A manservant admitted Mr. Carlyle and took in his card – his private card with the bare request for an interview that would not detain Mr. Carrados for ten minutes. Luck still favoured him. Mr. Carrados was at home and would see him at once. The servant, the hall through which they passed, and the room into which he was shown, all contributed something to the deductions which the quietly observant gentleman was half-unconsciously recording.

"Mr. Carlyle," announced the servant.

19

The room was a library or study. The only occupant, a man of about Carlyle's own age, had been using a typewriter up to the moment of his visitor's entrance. He now turned and stood up with an expression of formal courtesy.

"It's very good of you to see me at this hour," apologized the caller.

The conventional expression of Mr. Carrados's face changed a little.

"Surely my man has got your name wrong?" he exclaimed. "Isn't it Louis Calling?"

The visitor stopped short, and his agreeable smile gave place to a sudden flash of anger or annoyance.

"No, sir," he replied stiffly. "My name is on the card which you have before you."

"I beg your pardon," said Mr. Carrados, with perfect good-humour. "I hadn't seen it. But I used to know a Calling some years ago – at St. Michael's."

"St Michael's!" Mr. Carlyle's features underwent another change, no less instant and sweeping than before. "St Michael's! Wynn Carrados? Good Heavens! It isn't Max Wynn – Old 'Winning' Wynn?"

"A little older and a little fatter – yes," replied Carrados. "I have changed my name, you see."

"Extraordinary thing meeting like this," said his visitor, dropping into a chair and staring hard at Mr. Carrados. "I have changed more than my name. How did you recognize me?"

"The voice," replied Carrados. "It took me back to that little smoke-dried attic den of yours where we – "

"My God!" exclaimed Carlyle bitterly, "don't remind me of what we were going to do in those days." He looked round the well-furnished, handsome room and recalled the other signs of wealth that he had noticed. "At all events, you seem fairly comfortable, Wynn."

"I am alternately envied and pitied," replied Carrados, with a placid tolerance of circumstance that seemed characteristic of him. "Still, as you say, I am fairly comfortable."

"Envied, I can understand. But why are you pitied?"

"Because I am blind," was the tranquil reply.

"Blind!" exclaimed Mr. Carlyle, using his own eyes superlatively. "Do you mean – literally blind?"

"Literally . . . I was riding along a bridle-path through a wood about a dozen years ago with a friend. He was in front. At one point a twig sprang back – you know how easily a thing like that happens. It just flicked my eye – nothing to think twice about."

"And that blinded you?"

"Yes, ultimately. It's called *amaurosis*."

"I can scarcely believe it. You seem so sure and self-reliant. Your eyes are full of expression – only a little quieter than they used to be. I believe you were typing when I came . . . Aren't you having me?"

"You miss the dog and the stick?" smiled Carrados. "No. It's a fact."

"What an awful infliction for you, Max. You were always such an impulsive, reckless sort of fellow – never quiet. You must miss such a fearful lot."

"Has anyone else recognized you?" asked Carrados quietly.

"Ah, that was the voice, you said," replied Carlyle.

"Yes, but other people heard the voice as well. Only I had no blundering, self-confident eyes to be hoodwinked."

"That's a rum way of putting it," said Carlyle. "Are your ears never hoodwinked, may I ask?"

"Not now. Nor my fingers. Nor any of my other senses that have to look out for themselves."

"Well, well," murmured Mr. Carlyle, cut short in his sympathetic emotions. "I'm glad you take it so well. Of course, if you find it an advantage to be blind, old man – " He stopped and reddened. "I beg your pardon," he concluded stiffly.

"Not an advantage perhaps," replied the other thoughtfully. "Still, it has compensations that one might not think of. A new world to explore, new experiences, new powers awakening. Strange new perceptions. Life in the fourth dimension. But why do you beg my pardon, Louis?"

"I am an ex-solicitor, struck off in connexion with the falsifying of a trust account, Mr. Carrados," replied Carlyle, rising.

"Sit down, Louis," said Carrados suavely. His face, even his incredibly living eyes, beamed placid good nature. "The chair on which you will sit, the roof above you, all the comfortable surroundings to which you have so amiably alluded, are the direct result of falsifying a trust account. But do I call you 'Mr. Carlyle' in consequence? Certainly not, Louis."

"I did not falsify the account," cried Carlyle hotly. He sat down, however, and added more quietly: "But why do I tell you all this? I have never spoken of it before."

"Blindness invites confidence," replied Carrados. "We are out of the running – human rivalry ceases to exist. Besides, why shouldn't you? In my case the account was falsified."

"Of course that's all bunkum, Max," commented Carlyle. "Still, I appreciate your motive."

"Practically everything I possess was left to me by an American cousin, on the condition that I took the name of Carrados. He made his fortune by an ingenious conspiracy of doctoring the crop reports and

21

unloading favourably in consequence. And I need hardly remind you that the receiver is equally guilty with the thief."

"But twice as safe. I know something of that, Max . . . Have you any idea what my business is?"

"You shall tell me," replied Carrados.

"I run a private inquiry agency. When I lost my profession, I had to do something for a living. This occurred. I dropped my name, changed my appearance, and opened an office. I knew the legal side down to the ground, and I got a retired Scotland Yard man to organize the outside work."

"Excellent!" cried Carrados. "Do you unearth many murders?"

"No," admitted Mr. Carlyle. "Our business lies mostly on the conventional lines among divorce and defalcation."

"That's a pity," remarked Carrados. "Do you know, Louis, I always had a secret ambition to be a detective myself. I have even thought lately that I might still be able to do something at it if the chance came my way. That makes you smile?

"Well, certainly, the idea – "

"Yes, the idea of a blind detective – the blind tracking the alert – "

"Of course, as you say, certain faculties are no doubt quickened," Mr. Carlyle hastened to add considerately, "but, seriously, with the exception of an artist, I don't suppose there is any man who is more utterly dependent on his eyes."

Whatever opinion Carrados might have held privately, his genial exterior did not betray a shadow of dissent. For a full minute he continued to smoke as though he derived an actual visual enjoyment from the blue sprays that travelled and dispersed across the room. He had already placed before his visitor a box containing cigars of a brand which that gentleman keenly appreciated but generally regarded as unattainable, and the matter-of-fact ease and certainty with which the blind man had brought the box and put it before him had sent a questioning flicker through Carlyle's mind.

"You used to be rather fond of art yourself, Louis," he remarked presently. "Give me your opinion of my latest purchase – the bronze lion on the cabinet there." Then, as Carlyle's gaze went about the room, he added quickly: "No, not that cabinet – the one on your left."

Carlyle shot a sharp glance at his host as he got up, but Carrados's expression was merely benignly complacent. Then he strolled across to the figure.

"Very nice," he admitted. "Late Flemish, isn't it?"

"No. It is a copy of Vidal's 'Roaring Lion'."

"Vidal?"

"A French artist." The voice became indescribably flat. "He, also, had the misfortune to be blind, by the way."

"You old humbug, Max!" shrieked Carlyle, "you've been thinking that out for the last five minutes." Then the unfortunate man bit his lip and turned his back towards his host.

"Do you remember how we used to pile it up on that obtuse ass Sanders and then roast him?" asked Carrados, ignoring the half-smothered exclamation with which the other man had recalled himself.

"Yes," replied Carlyle quietly. "This is very good," he continued, addressing himself to the bronze again. "How ever did he do it?"

"With his hands."

"Naturally. But, I mean, how did he study his model?"

"Also with his hands. He called it 'seeing near'."

"Even with a lion – handled it?"

"In such cases he required the services of a keeper, who brought the animal to bay while Vidal exercised his own particular gifts . . . You don't feel inclined to put me on the track of a mystery, Louis?"

Unable to regard this request as anything but one of old Max's unquenchable pleasantries, Mr. Carlyle was on the point of making a suitable reply when a sudden thought caused him to smile knowingly. Up to that point he had, indeed, completely forgotten the object of his visit. Now that he remembered the doubtful Dionysius and Mr. Baxter's recommendation, he immediately assumed that some mistake had been made. Either Max was not the Wynn Carrados he had been seeking or else the dealer had been misinformed. For although his host was wonderfully expert in the face of his misfortune, it was inconceivable that he could decide the genuineness of a coin without seeing it. The opportunity seemed a good one of getting even with Carrados by taking him at his word.

"Yes," he accordingly replied, with crisp deliberation, as he recrossed the room. "Yes, I will, Max. Here is the clue to what seems to be a rather remarkable fraud." He put the *tetradrachm* into his host's hand. "What do you make of it?"

For a few seconds Carrados handled the piece with the delicate manipulation of his finger-tips while Carlyle looked on with a self-appreciative grin. Then with equal gravity the blind man weighed the coin in the balance of his hand. Finally he touched it with his tongue.

"Well?" demanded the other.

"Of course I have not much to go on, and if I was more fully in your confidence I might come to another conclusion – "

"Yes, yes," interposed Carlyle, with amused encouragement.

"Then I should advise you to arrest the parlourmaid, Nina Brun, communicate with the police authorities of Padua for particulars of the career of Helene Brunesi, and suggest to Lord Seastoke that he should return to London to see what further depredations have been made in his cabinet."

Mr. Carlyle's groping hand sought and found a chair, on to which he dropped blankly. His eyes were unable to detach themselves for a single moment from the very ordinary spectacle of Mr. Carrados's mildly benevolent face, while the sterilized ghost of his now forgotten amusement still lingered about his features.

"Good Heavens!" he managed to articulate, "how do you know?"

"Isn't that what you wanted of me?" asked Carrados suavely.

"Don't humbug, Max," said Carlyle severely. "This is no joke." An undefined mistrust of his own powers suddenly possessed him in the presence of this mystery. "How do you come to know of Nina Brun and Lord Seastoke?"

"You are a detective, Louis," replied Carrados. "How does one know these things? By using one's eyes and putting two and two together."

Carlyle groaned and flung out an arm petulantly.

"Is it all bunkum, Max? Do you really see all the time – though that doesn't go very far towards explaining it.

"Like Vidal, I see very well – at close quarters," replied Carrados, lightly running a forefinger along the inscription on the *tetradrachm*. "For longer range, I keep another pair of eyes. Would you like to test them?"

Mr. Carlyle's assent was not very gracious. It was, in fact, faintly sulky. He was suffering the annoyance of feeling distinctly unimpressive in his own department, but he was also curious.

"The bell is just behind you, if you don't mind," said his host. "Parkinson will appear. You might take note of him while he is in."

The man who had admitted Mr. Carlyle proved to be Parkinson.

"This gentleman is Mr. Carlyle, Parkinson," explained Carrados the moment the man entered. "You will remember him for the future?"

Parkinson's apologetic eye swept the visitor from head to foot, but so lightly and swiftly that it conveyed to that gentleman the comparison of being very deftly dusted.

"I will endeavour to do so, sir," replied Parkinson. Turning again to his master.

"I shall be at home to Mr. Carlyle whenever he calls. That is all."

"Very well, sir."

"Now, Louis," remarked Mr. Carrados briskly, when the door had closed again, "you have had a good opportunity of studying Parkinson. What is he like?"

"In what way?"

"I mean as a matter of description. I am a blind man – I haven't seen my servant for twelve years – what idea can you give me of him? I asked you to notice."

"I know you did, but your Parkinson is the sort of man who has very little about him to describe. He is the embodiment of the ordinary. His height is about average – "

"Five-feet-nine," murmured Carrados. "Slightly above the mean."

"Scarcely noticeably so. Clean-shaven. Medium brown hair. No particularly marked features. Dark eyes. Good teeth."

"False," interposed Carrados. "The teeth – not the statement.

"Possibly," admitted Mr. Carlyle. "I am not a dental expert and I had no opportunity of examining Mr. Parkinson's mouth in detail. But what is the drift of all this?"

"His clothes?"

"Oh, just the ordinary evening dress of a valet. There is not much room for variety in that."

"You noticed, in fact, nothing special by which Parkinson could be identified?"

"Well, he wore an unusually broad gold ring on the little finger of the left hand."

"But that is removable. And yet Parkinson has an ineradicable mole – a small one, I admit – on his chin. And you a human sleuth-hound. Oh, Louis!"

"At all events," retorted Carlyle, writhing a little under this good-humoured satire, although it was easy enough to see in it Carrados's affectionate intention. " – At all events, I dare say I can give as good a description of Parkinson as he can give of me."

"That is what we are going to test. Ring the bell again."

"Seriously?"

"Quite. I am trying my eyes against yours. If I can't give you fifty out of a hundred I'll renounce my private detectorial ambition forever."

"It isn't quite the same," objected Carlyle, but he rang the bell.

"Come in and close the door, Parkinson," said Carrados when the man appeared. "Don't look at Mr. Carlyle again – in fact, you had better stand with your back towards him, he won't mind. Now describe to me his appearance as you observed it."

Parkinson tendered his respectful apologies to Mr. Carlyle for the liberty he was compelled to take, by the deferential quality of his voice.

"Mr. Carlyle, sir, wears patent leather boots of about size seven and very little used. There are five buttons, but on the left boot one button – the third up – is missing, leaving loose threads and not the more usual metal fastener. Mr. Carlyle's trousers, sir, are of a dark material, a dark grey line of about a quarter-of-an-inch width on a darker ground. The bottoms are turned permanently up and are, just now, a little muddy, if I may say so."

"Very muddy," interposed Mr. Carlyle generously. "It is a wet night, Parkinson."

"Yes, sir. Very unpleasant weather. If you will allow me, sir, I will brush you in the hall. The mud is dry now, I notice. Then, sir," continued Parkinson, reverting to the business in hand, "there are dark green cashmere hose. A curb-pattern key-chain passes into the left-hand trouser pocket.

From the visitor's nether garments the photographic-eyed Parkinson proceeded to higher ground, and with increasing wonder Mr. Carlyle listened to the faithful catalogue of his possessions. His fetter-and-link albert of gold and platinum was minutely described. His spotted blue ascot, with its gentlemanly pearl scarfpin, was set forth, and the fact that the buttonhole in the left lapel of his morning coat showed signs of use was duly noted. What Parkinson saw he recorded but he made no deductions. A handkerchief carried in the cuff of the right sleeve was simply that to him and not an indication that Mr. Carlyle was, indeed, left-handed.

But a more delicate part of Parkinson's undertaking remained. He approached it with a double cough.

"As regards Mr. Carlyle's personal appearance, sir – "

"No, enough!" cried the gentleman concerned hastily. "I am more than satisfied. You are a keen observer, Parkinson.

"I have trained myself to suit my master's requirements, sir," replied the man. He looked towards Mr. Carrados, received a nod, and withdrew.

Mr. Carlyle was the first to speak.

"That man of yours would be worth five pounds a week to me, Max," he remarked thoughtfully. "But, of course – "

"I don't think that he would take it," replied Carrados, in a voice of equally detached speculation. "He suits me very well. But you have the chance of using his services – indirectly."

"You still mean that – seriously?"

"I notice in you a chronic disinclination to take me seriously, Louis. It is really – to an Englishman – almost painful. Is there something inherently comic about me or the atmosphere of The Turrets?"

"No, my friend," replied Mr. Carlyle, "but there is something essentially prosperous. That is what points to the improbable. Now what is it?"

"It might be merely a whim, but it is more than that," replied Carrados. "It is, well, partly vanity, partly *ennui*, partly – " Certainly there was something more nearly tragic in his voice than comic now. " – partly hope."

Mr. Carlyle was too tactful to pursue the subject.

"Those are three tolerable motives," he acquiesced. "I'll do anything you want, Max, on one condition."

"Agreed. And it is?

"That you tell me how you knew so much of this affair." He tapped the silver coin which lay on the table near them. "I am not easily flabbergasted," he added.

"You won't believe that there is nothing to explain – that it was purely second-sight?"

"No," replied Carlyle tersely. "I won't.

"You are quite right. And yet the thing is very simple."

"They always are – when you know," soliloquized the other. "That's what makes them so confoundedly difficult when you don't."

"Here is this one then. In Padua, which seems to be regaining its old reputation as the birthplace of spurious antiques, by the way, there lives an ingenious craftsman named Pietro Stelli. This simple soul, who possesses a talent not inferior to that of Cavino at his best, has for many years turned his hand to the not unprofitable occupation of forging rare Greek and Roman coins. As a collector and student of certain Greek colonials and a specialist in forgeries, I have been familiar with Stelli's workmanship for years. Latterly he seems to have come under the influence of an international crook called – at the moment – Dompierre, who soon saw a way of utilizing Stelli's genius on a royal scale. Helene Brunesi, who in private life is – and really is, I believe – Madame Dompierre, readily lent her services to the enterprise."

"Quite so," nodded Mr. Carlyle, as his host paused.

"You see the whole sequence, of course?"

"Not exactly – not in detail," confessed Mr. Carlyle.

"Dompierre's idea was to gain access to some of the most celebrated cabinets of Europe and substitute Stelli's fabrications for the genuine coins. The princely collection of rarities that he would thus amass might be difficult to dispose of safely, but I have no doubt that he had matured his plans. Helene, in the person of Nina Bran, an Anglicised French parlourmaid – a part which she fills to perfection – was to obtain wax impressions of the most valuable pieces and to make the exchange when the counterfeits reached her. In this way it was obviously hoped that the fraud would not come to light until long after the real coins had been sold, and I gather that she has already done her work successfully in several houses. Then, impressed by her excellent references and capable manner, my housekeeper engaged her, and for a few weeks she went about her

27

duties here. It was fatal to this detail of the scheme, however, that I have the misfortune to be blind. I am told that Helene has so innocently angelic a face as to disarm suspicion, but I was incapable of being impressed and that good material was thrown away. But one morning my material fingers – which, of course, knew nothing of Helene's angelic face – discovered an unfamiliar touch about the surface of my favourite Euclideas, and, although there was doubtless nothing to be seen, my critical sense of smell reported that wax had been recently pressed against it. I began to make discreet inquiries, and in the meantime, my cabinets went to the local bank for safety. Helene countered by receiving a telegram from Angiers, calling her to the death-bed of her aged mother. The aged mother succumbed. Duty compelled Helene to remain at the side of her stricken patriarchal father, and doubtless The Turrets was written off the syndicate's operations as a bad debt."

"Very interesting," admitted Mr. Carlyle. "But at the risk of seeming obtuse – " His manner had become delicately chastened. " – I must say that I fail to trace the inevitable connexion between Nina Brun and this particular forgery – assuming that it is a forgery."

"Set your mind at rest about that, Louis," replied Carrados. "It is a forgery, and it is a forgery that none but Pietro Stelli could have achieved. That is the essential connexion. Of course, there are accessories. A private detective coming urgently to see me with a notable *tetradrachm* in his pocket, which he announces to be the clue to a remarkable fraud – well, really, Louis, one scarcely needs to be blind to see through that."

"And Lord Seastoke? I suppose you happened to discover that Nina Brun had gone there?"

"No, I cannot claim to have discovered that, or I should certainly have warned him at once when I found out – only recently – about the gang. As a matter of fact, the last information I had of Lord Seastoke was a line in yesterday's *Morning Post* to the effect that he was still at Cairo. But many of these pieces – " He brushed his finger almost lovingly across the vivid chariot race that embellished the reverse of the coin, and broke off to remark: "You really ought to take up the subject, Louis. You have no idea how useful it might prove to you some day."

"I really think I must," replied Carlyle grimly. "Two-hundred-and-fifty pounds the original of this cost, I believe.

"Cheap, too. It would make five-hundred pounds in New York today. As I was saying, many are literally unique. This gem by Kimon is – here is his signature, you see. Peter is particularly good at lettering – and as I handled the genuine *tetradrachm* about two years ago, when Lord Seastoke exhibited it at a meeting of our society in Albemarle Street, there is nothing at all wonderful in my being able to fix the locale of your mystery. Indeed, I feel that I ought to apologize for it all being so simple."

"I think," remarked Mr. Carlyle, critically examining the loose threads on his left boot, "that the apology on that head would be more appropriate from me."

The Knight's Cross
Signal Problem

"Louis," exclaimed Mr. Carrados, with the air of genial gaiety that Carlyle had found so incongruous to his conception of a blind man, "you have a mystery somewhere about you! I know it by your step."

Nearly a month had passed since the incident of the false Dionysius had led to the two men meeting. It was now December. Whatever Mr. Carlyle's step might indicate to the inner eye it betokened to the casual observer the manner of a crisp, alert, self-possessed man of business. Carlyle, in truth, betrayed nothing of the pessimism and despondency that had marked him on the earlier occasion.

"You have only yourself to thank that it is a very poor one," he retorted. "If you hadn't held me to a hasty promise – "

"To give me an option on the next case that baffled you, no matter what it was – "

"Just so. The consequence is that you get a very unsatisfactory affair that has no special interest to an amateur and is only baffling because it is – well – "

"Well, baffling?"

"Exactly, Max. Your would-be jest has discovered the proverbial truth. I need hardly tell you that it is only the insoluble that is finally baffling and this is very probably insoluble. You remember the awful smash on the Central and Suburban at Knight's Cross Station a few weeks ago?"

"Yes," replied Carrados, with interest. "I read the whole ghastly details at the time."

"You *read?*" exclaimed his friend suspiciously.

"I still use the familiar phrases," explained Carrados, with a smile. "As a matter of fact, my secretary reads to me. I mark what I want to hear and when he comes at ten o'clock we clear off the morning papers in no time."

"And how do you know what to mark?" demanded Mr. Carlyle cunningly.

Carrados's right hand, lying idly on the table, moved to a newspaper near. He ran his finger along a column heading, his eyes still turned towards his visitor.

"'*The Money Market. Continued from page two. British Railways*'," he announced.

"Extraordinary," murmured Carlyle.

"Not very," said Carrados. "If someone dipped a stick in treacle and wrote '*Rats*' across a marble slab you would probably be able to distinguish what was there, blindfold."

"Probably," admitted Mr. Carlyle. "At all events, we will not test the experiment."

"The difference to you of treacle on a marble background is scarcely greater than that of printers' ink on newspaper to me. But anything smaller than *pica* I do not read with comfort, and below long primer I cannot read at all. Hence the secretary. Now the accident, Louis."

"The accident: Well, you remember all about that. An ordinary Central and Suburban passenger train, non-stop at Knight's Cross, ran past the signal and crashed into a crowded electric train that was just beginning to move out. It was like sending a garden roller down a row of handlights. Two carriages of the electric train were flattened out of existence. The next two were broken up. For the first time on an English railway, there was a good stand-up smash between a heavy steam-engine and a train of light cars, and it was 'bad for the coo'."

"Twenty-seven killed, forty something injured, eight died since," commented Carrados.

"That was bad for the Company," said Carlyle. "Well, the main fact was plain enough. The heavy train was in the wrong. But was the engine driver responsible? He claimed, and he claimed vehemently from the first and he never varied one iota, that he had a 'clear' signal – that is to say, the green light, it being dark. The signalman concerned was equally dogged that he never pulled off the signal – that it was at 'danger' when the accident happened and that it had been for five minutes before. Obviously, they could not both be right."

"Why, Louis?" asked Mr. Carrados smoothly.

"The signal must either have been up or down – red or green."

"Did you ever notice the signals on the Great Northern Railway, Louis?"

"Not particularly. Why?"

"One winterly day, about the year when you and I were concerned in being born, the engine driver of a Scotch express received the 'clear' from a signal near a little Huntingdon station called Abbots Ripton. He went on and crashed into a goods train, and into the thick of the smash a down express mowed its way. Thirteen killed and the usual tale of injured. He was positive that the signal gave him a 'clear'. The signalman was equally confident that he had never pulled it off the 'danger'. Both were right, and yet the signal was in working order. As I said, it was a winterly day. It had been snowing hard and the snow froze and accumulated on the upper edge

31

of the signal arm until its weight bore it down. That is a fact that no fiction writer dare have invented, but to this day every signal on the Great Northern pivots from the centre of the arm instead of from the end, in memory of that snowstorm."

"That came out at the inquest, I presume?" said Mr. Carlyle. "We have had the Board of Trade inquiry and the inquest here and no explanation is forthcoming. Everything was in perfect order. It rests between the word of the signalman and the word of the engine driver – not a jot of direct evidence either way. Which is right?"

"That is what you are going to find out, Louis?" suggested Carrados.

"It is what I am being paid for finding out," admitted Mr. Carlyle frankly. "But so far we are just where the inquest left it, and, between ourselves, I candidly can't see an inch in front of my face in the matter."

"Nor can I," said the blind man, with a rather wry smile. "Never mind. The engine driver is your client, of course?"

"Yes," admitted Carlyle. "But how the deuce did you know?"

"Let us say that your sympathies are enlisted on his behalf. The jury were inclined to exonerate the signalman, weren't they? What has the company done with your man?"

"Both are suspended. Hutchins, the driver, hears that he may probably be given charge of a lavatory at one of the stations. He is a decent, bluff, short-spoken old chap, with his heart in his work. Just now you'll find him at his worst – bitter and suspicious. The thought of swabbing down a lavatory and taking pennies all day is poisoning him."

"Naturally. Well, there we have honest Hutchins: Taciturn, a little touchy perhaps, grown grey in the service of the company, and manifesting quite a bulldog-like devotion to his favourite 538."

"Why, that actually was the number of his engine – How do you know it?" demanded Carlyle sharply.

"It was mentioned two or three times at the inquest, Louis," replied Carrados mildly.

"And you remembered – with no reason to?"

"You can generally trust a blind man's memory, especially if he has taken the trouble to develop it."

"Then you will remember that Hutchins did not make a very good impression at the time. He was surly and irritable under the ordeal. I want you to see the case from all sides."

"He called the signalman – Mead – a 'lying young dog', across the room, I believe. Now, Mead, what is he like? You have seen him, of course?"

32

"Yes. He does not impress me favourably. He is glib, ingratiating, and distinctly 'greasy'. He has a ready answer for everything almost before the question is out of your mouth. He has thought of everything."

"And now you are going to tell me something, Louis," said Carrados encouragingly.

Mr. Carlyle laughed a little to cover an involuntary movement of surprise

"There is a suggestive line that was not touched at the inquiries," he admitted. "Hutchins has been a saving man all his life, and he has received good wages. Among his class he is regarded as wealthy. I daresay that he has five-hundred pounds in the bank. He is a widower with one daughter, a very nice-mannered girl of about twenty. Mead is a young man, and he and the girl are sweethearts – have been informally engaged for some time. But old Hutchins would not hear of it. He seems to have taken a dislike to the signalman from the first and latterly he had forbidden him to come to his house or his daughter to speak to him."

"Excellent, Louis!" cried Carrados in great delight. "We shall clear your man in a blaze of red and green lights yet and hang the glib, 'greasy' signalman from his own signal-post."

"It is a significant fact, seriously?"

"It is absolutely convincing."

"It may have been a slip, a mental lapse on Mead's part which he discovered the moment it was too late, and then, being too cowardly to admit his fault, and having so much at stake, he took care to make detection impossible. It may have been that, but my idea is rather that probably it was neither quite pure accident nor pure design. I can imagine Mead meanly pluming himself over the fact that the life of this man who stands in his way, and whom he must cordially dislike, lies in his power. I can imagine the idea becoming an obsession as he dwells on it. A dozen times with his hand on the lever he lets his mind explore the possibilities of a moment's defection. Then one day he pulls the signal off in sheer bravado – and hastily puts it at danger again. He may have done it once or he may have done it oftener before he was caught in a fatal moment of irresolution. The chances are about even that the engine driver would be killed. In any case he would be disgraced, for it is easier on the face of it to believe that a man might run past a danger signal in absentmindedness, without noticing it, than that a man should pull off a signal and replace it without being conscious of his actions."

"The fireman was killed. Does your theory involve the certainty of the fireman being killed, Louis?"

"No," said Carlyle. "The fireman is a difficulty, but looking at it from Mead's point of view – whether he has been guilty of an error or a crime

33

– it resolves itself into this: First, the fireman may be killed. Second, he may not notice the signal at all. Third, in any case he will loyally corroborate his driver and the good old jury will discount that."

Carrados smoked thoughtfully, his open, sightless eyes merely appearing to be set in a tranquil gaze across the room.

"It would not be an improbable explanation," he said presently. "Ninety-nine men out of a hundred would say: 'People do not do these things.' But you and I, who have in our different ways studied criminology, know that they sometimes do, or else there would be no curious crimes. What have you done on that line?"

To anyone who could see, Mr. Carlyle's expression conveyed an answer.

"You are behind the scenes, Max. What was there for me to do? Still I must do something for my money. Well, I have had a very close inquiry made confidentially among the men. There might be a whisper of one of them knowing more than had come out – a man restrained by friendship, or enmity, or even grade jealousy. Nothing came of that. Then there was the remote chance that some private person had noticed the signal without attaching any importance to it then, one who would be able to identify it still by something associated with the time. I went over the line myself. Opposite the signal the line on one side is shut in by a high blank wall. On the other side are houses, but coming below the butt-end of a scullery the signal does not happen to be visible from any road or from any window."

"My poor Louis!" said Carrados, in friendly ridicule. "You were at the end of your tether?"

"I was," admitted Carlyle. "And now that you know the sort of job it is, I don't suppose that you are keen on wasting your time over it."

"That would hardly be fair, would it?" said Carrados reasonably. "No, Louis, I will take over your honest old driver and your greasy young signalman and your fatal signal that cannot be seen from anywhere."

"But it is an important point for you to remember, Max, that although the signal cannot be seen from the box, if the mechanism had gone wrong, or anyone tampered with the arm, the automatic indicator would at once have told Mead that the green light was showing. Oh, I have gone very thoroughly into the technical points, I assure you."

"I must do so too," commented Mr. Carrados gravely.

"For that matter, if there is anything you want to know, I dare say that I can tell you," suggested his visitor. "It might save your time."

"True," acquiesced Carrados. "I should like to know whether anyone belonging to the houses that bound the line there came of age or got married on the twenty-sixth of November."

Mr. Carlyle looked across curiously at his host.

34

"I really do not know, Max," he replied, in his crisp, precise way. "What on earth has that got to do with it, may I inquire?"

"The only explanation of the Pont St. Lin swing-bridge disaster of '75 was the reflection of a green bengal light on a cottage window."

Mr. Carlyle smiled his indulgence privately.

"My dear chap, you mustn't let your retentive memory of obscure happenings run away with you," he remarked wisely. "In nine cases out of ten, the obvious explanation is the true one. The difficulty, as here, lies in proving it. Now, you would like to see these men?"

"I expect so. In any case, I will see Hutchins first."

"Both live in Holloway. Shall I ask Hutchins to come here to see you – say tomorrow? He is doing nothing."

"No," replied Carrados. "Tomorrow I must call on my brokers and my time may be filled up."

"Quite right. You mustn't neglect your own affairs for this – experiment," assented Carlyle.

"Besides, I should prefer to drop in on Hutchins at his own home. Now, Louis, enough of the honest old man for one night. I have a lovely thing by Eumenes that I want to show you. Today is – Tuesday. Come to dinner on Sunday and pour the vials of your ridicule on my want of success."

"That's an amiable way of putting it," replied Carlyle. "All right, I will."

Two hours later Carrados was again in his study, apparently, for a wonder, sitting idle. Sometimes he smiled to himself, and once or twice he laughed a little, but for the most part his pleasant, impassive face reflected no emotion and he sat with his useless eyes tranquilly fixed on an unseen distance. It was a fantastic caprice of the man to mock his sightlessness by a parade of light, and under the soft brilliance of a dozen electric brackets the room was as bright as day. At length he stood up and rang the bell.

"I suppose Mr. Greatorex isn't still here by any chance, Parkinson?" he asked, referring to his secretary.

"I think not, sir, but I will ascertain," replied the man.

"Never mind. Go to his room and bring me the last two files of *The Times*. Now – " when he returned " – turn to the earliest you have there. The date?"

"November the second."

"That will do. Find the Money Market. It will be in the *Supplement*. Now look down the columns until you come to British Railways."

"I have it, sir."

"Central and Suburban. Read the closing price and the change."

"'*Central and Suburban Ordinary, 66-1/2-67-1/2, fall 1/8. Preferred Ordinary, 81-81-1/2, no change. Deferred Ordinary, 27-1/2-27-3/4, fall 1/4.*' That is all, sir."

"Now take a paper about a week on. Read the Deferred only."

"'*27-27-1/4, no change.*'"

"Another week."

"'*29-1/2-30, rise 5/8.*'"

"Another."

"'*31-1/2-32-1/2, rise 1.*'"

"Very good. Now on Tuesday the twenty-seventh November."

"'*31-7/8-32-3/4, rise 1/2.*'"

"Yes. The next day."

"'*24-1/2-23-1/2, fall 9.*'"

"Quite so, Parkinson. There had been an accident, you see."

"Yes, sir. Very unpleasant accident. Jane knows a person whose sister's young man has a cousin who had his arm torn off in it – torn off at the socket, she says, sir. It seems to bring it home to one, sir."

"That is all. Stay – in the paper you have, look down the first money column and see if there is any reference to the Central and Suburban."

"Yes, sir. '*City and Suburbans, which after their late depression on the projected extension of the motor bus service, had been steadily creeping up on the abandonment of the scheme, and as a result of their own excellent traffic returns, suffered a heavy slump through the lamentable accident of Thursday night. The Deferred in particular at one time fell eleven points as it was felt that the possible dividend, with which rumour has of late been busy, was now out of the question.*'"

"Yes. That is all. Now you can take the papers back. And let it be a warning to you, Parkinson, not to invest your savings in speculative railway deferreds."

"Yes, sir. Thank you, sir, I will endeavour to remember." He lingered for a moment as he shook the file of papers level. "I may say, sir, that I have my eye on a small block of cottage property at Acton. But even cottage property scarcely seems safe from legislative depredation now, sir."

The next day Mr. Carrados called on his brokers in the city. It is to be presumed that he got through his private business quicker than he expected, for after leaving Austin Friars he continued his journey to Holloway, where he found Hutchins at home and sitting morosely before his kitchen fire. Rightly assuming that his luxuriant car would involve him in a certain amount of public attention in Klondyke Street, the blind man dismissed it some distance from the house, and walked the rest of the way, guided by the almost imperceptible touch of Parkinson's arm.

"Here is a gentleman to see you, Father," explained Miss Hutchins, who had come to the door. She divined the relative positions of the two visitors at a glance.

"Then why don't you take him into the parlour?" grumbled the ex-driver. His face was a testimonial of hard work and general sobriety but at the moment one might hazard from his voice and manner that he had been drinking earlier in the day."

"I don't think that the gentleman would be impressed by the difference between our parlour and our kitchen," replied the girl quaintly, "and it is warmer here."

"What's the matter with the parlour now?" demanded her father sourly. "It was good enough for your mother and me. It used to be good enough for you."

"There is nothing the matter with it, nor with the kitchen either." She turned impassively to the two who had followed her along the narrow passage. "Will you go in, sir?"

"I don't want to see no gentleman!" cried Hutchins noisily. "Unless – " His manner suddenly changed to one of pitiable anxiety. " – unless you're from the Company, sir, to – to – "

"No. I have come on Mr. Carlyle's behalf," replied Carrados, walking to a chair as though he moved by a kind of instinct.

Hutchins laughed his wry contempt.

"Mr. Carlyle!" he reiterated. "Mr. Carlyle! Fat lot of good he's been. Why don't he do something for his money?"

"He has," replied Carrados, with imperturbable good-humour. "He has sent me. Now, I want to ask you a few questions."

"A few questions!" roared the irate man. "Why, blast it, I have done nothing else but answer questions for a month. I didn't pay Mr. Carlyle to ask me questions. I can get enough of that for nixes. Why don't you go and ask Mr. Herbert Ananias Mead your few questions – then you might find out something."

There was a slight movement by the door and Carrados knew that the girl had quietly left the room.

"You saw that, sir?" demanded the father, diverted to a new line of bitterness. "You saw that girl – my own daughter, that I've worked for all her life?"

"No," replied Carrados.

"The girl that's just gone out – she's my daughter," explained Hutchins.

"I know, but I did not see her. I see nothing. I am blind."

37

"Blind!" exclaimed the old fellow, sitting up in startled wonderment. "You mean it, sir? You walk all right and you look at me as if you saw me. You're kidding surely."

"No," smiled Carrados. "It's quite right."

"Then it's a funny business, sir – you what are blind expecting to find something that those with their eyes couldn't," ruminated Hutchins sagely.

"There are things that you can't see with your eyes, Hutchins."

"Perhaps you are right, sir. Well, what is it you want to know?"

"Light a cigar first," said the blind man, holding out his case and waiting until the various sounds told him that his host was smoking contentedly. "The train you were driving at the time of the accident was the six-twenty-seven from Notcliff. It stopped everywhere until it reached Lambeth Bridge, the chief London station of your line. There it became something of an express, and leaving Lambeth Bridge at seven-eleven, should not stop again until it fetched Swanstead on Thames, eleven miles out, at seven-thirty-four. Then it stopped on and off from Swanstead to Ingerfield, the terminus of that branch, which it reached at eight-five."

Hutchins nodded, and then, remembering, said, "That's right, sir."

"That was your business all day – running between Notcliff and Ingerfield?"

"Yes, sir. Three journeys up and three down mostly."

"With the same stops on all the down journeys?"

"No. The seven-eleven is the only one that does a run from the Bridge to Swanstead. You see, it is just on the close of the evening rush, as they call it. A good many late business gentlemen living at Swanstead use the seven-eleven regular. The other journeys we stop at every station to Lambeth Bridge, and then here and there beyond."

"There are, of course, other trains doing exactly the same journey – a service, in fact?"

"Yes, sir. About six."

"And do any of those – say, during the rush – do any of those run non-stop from Lambeth to Swanstead?"

Hutchins reflected a moment. All the choler and restlessness had melted out of the man's face. He was again the excellent artisan, slow but capable and self-reliant.

"That I couldn't definitely say, sir. Very few short-distance trains pass the junction, but some of those may. A guide would show us in a minute, but I haven't got one."

"Never mind. You said at the inquest that it was no uncommon thing for you to be pulled up at the 'stop' signal east of Knight's Cross Station. How often would that happen – only with the seven-eleven, mind."

"Perhaps three times a week. Perhaps twice."

"The accident was on a Thursday. Have you noticed that you were pulled up oftener on a Thursday than on any other day?"

A smile crossed the driver's face at the question.

"You don't happen to live at Swanstead yourself, sir?" he asked in reply.

"No," admitted Carrados. "Why?"

"Well, sir, we were always pulled up on Thursday – practically always, you may say. It got to be quite a saying among those who used the train regular. They used to look out for it."

Carrados's sightless eyes had the one quality of concealing emotion supremely. "Oh," he commented softly, "always. And it was quite a saying, was it? And why was it always so on Thursday?"

"It had to do with the early closing, I'm told. The suburban traffic was a bit different. By rights we ought to have been set back two minutes for that day, but I suppose it wasn't thought worthwhile to alter us in the time-table, so we most always had to wait outside Three Deep Tunnel for a west-bound electric to make good."

"You were prepared for it then?"

"Yes, sir, I was," said Hutchins, reddening at some recollection, "and very down about it was one of the jury over that. But, mayhap once in three months, I did get through even on a Thursday, and it's not for me to question whether things are right or wrong just because they are not what I may expect. The signals are my orders, sir – *Stop! Go on!* – and it's for me to obey, as you would a general on the field of battle. What would happen otherwise! It was nonsense what they said about going cautious, and the man who started it was a barber who didn't know the difference between a 'distance' and a 'stop' signal down to the minute they gave their verdict. My orders, sir, given me by that signal, was 'Go right ahead and keep to your running time!'"

Carrados nodded a soothing assent. "That is all, I think," he remarked.

"All!" exclaimed Hutchins in surprise. "Why, sir, you can't have got much idea of it yet."

"Quite enough. And I know it isn't pleasant for you to be taken along the same ground over and over again."

The man moved awkwardly in his chair and pulled nervously at his grizzled beard.

"You mustn't take any notice of what I said just now, sir," he apologized. "You somehow make me feel that something may come of it, but I've been badgered about and accused and cross-examined from one to another of them these weeks till it's fairly made me bitter against everything. And now they talk of putting me in a lavatory – Me that has

39

been with the company for five and forty years and on the foot-plate thirty-two! – a man suspected of running past a danger signal."

"You have had a rough time, Hutchins. You will have to exercise your patience a little longer yet," said Carrados sympathetically.

"You think something may come of it, sir? You think you will be able to clear me? Believe me, sir, if you could give me something to look forward to it might save me from – " He pulled himself up and shook his head sorrowfully. "I've been near it," he added simply.

Carrados reflected and took his resolution.

"Today is Wednesday. I think you may hope to hear something from your general manager towards the middle of next week."

"Good God, sir! You really mean that?"

"In the interval show your good sense by behaving reasonably. Keep civilly to yourself and don't talk. Above all – " He nodded towards a quart jug that stood on the table between them, an incident that filled the simple-minded engineer with boundless wonder when he recalled it afterwards. " – above all, leave that alone."

Hutchins snatched up the vessel and brought it crashing down on the hearthstone, his face shining with a set resolution.

"I've done with it, sir. It was the bitterness and despair that drove me to that. Now I can do without it."

The door was hastily opened and Miss Hutchins looked anxiously from her father to the visitors and back again

"Oh, whatever is the matter?" she exclaimed. "I heard a great crash."

"This gentleman is going to clear me, Meg, my dear," blurted out the old man irrepressibly. "And I've done with the drink forever."

"Hutchins! Hutchins!" said Carrados warningly.

"My daughter, sir. You wouldn't have her not know?" pleaded Hutchins, rather crest-fallen. "It won't go any further."

Carrados laughed quietly to himself as he felt Margaret Hutchins's startled and questioning eyes attempting to read his mind. He shook hands with the engine driver without further comment, however, and walked out into the commonplace little street under Parkinson's unobtrusive guidance.

"Very nice of Miss Hutchins to go into half-mourning, Parkinson," he remarked as they went along. "Thoughtful, and yet not ostentatious."

"Yes, sir," agreed Parkinson, who had long ceased to wonder at his master's perceptions.

"The Romans, Parkinson, had a saying to the effect that gold carries no smell. That is a pity sometimes. What jewellery did Miss Hutchins wear?"

"Very little, sir. A plain gold brooch representing a merry-thought – the merry-thought of a sparrow, I should say, sir. The only other article was a smooth-backed gun-metal watch, suspended from a gun-metal bow."

"Nothing showy or expensive, eh?"

"Oh dear no, sir. Quite appropriate for a young person of her position."

"Just what I should have expected." He slackened his pace. "We are passing a hoarding, are we not?"

"Yes, sir."

"We will stand here a moment. Read me the letterpress of the poster before us."

"This '*Oxo*' one, sir?"

"Yes."

"'*Oxo*', sir."

Carrados was convulsed with silent laughter. Parkinson had infinitely more dignity and conceded merely a tolerant recognition of the ludicrous.

"That was a bad shot, Parkinson," remarked his master when he could speak. "We will try another."

For three minutes, with scrupulous conscientiousness on the part of the reader and every appearance of keen interest on the part of the hearer, there were set forth the particulars of a sale by auction of superfluous timber and builders' material.

"That will do," said Carrados, when the last detail had been reached. "We can be seen from the door of No. 107 still?"

"Yes, sir."

"No indication of anyone coming to us from there?"

"No, sir."

Carrados walked thoughtfully on again. In the Holloway Road they rejoined the waiting motor car. "Lambeth Bridge Station," was the order the driver received.

From the station the car was sent on home and Parkinson was instructed to take two first-class singles for Richmond, which could be reached by changing at Stafford Road. The "evening rush" had not yet commenced and they had no difficulty in finding an empty carriage when the train came in.

Parkinson was kept busy that journey describing what he saw at various points between Lambeth Bridge and Knight's Cross. For a quarter-of-a-mile Carrados's demands on the eyes and the memory of his remarkable servant were wide and incessant. Then his questions ceased. They had passed the "stop" signal, east of Knight's Cross Station.

41

The following afternoon they made the return journey as far as Knight's Cross. This time, however, the surroundings failed to interest Carrados. "We are going to look at some rooms," was the information he offered on the subject, and an imperturbable "Yes, sir" had been the extent of Parkinson's comment on the unusual proceeding. After leaving the station, they turned sharply along a road that ran parallel with the line, a dull thoroughfare of substantial, elderly houses that were beginning to sink into decrepitude. Here and there a corner residence displayed the brass plate of a professional occupant, but for the most part they were given up to the various branches of second-rate apartment letting.

"The third house after the one with the flagstaff," said Carrados.

Parkinson rang the bell, which was answered by a young servant, who took an early opportunity of assuring them that she was not tidy, as it was rather early in the afternoon. She informed Carrados, in reply to his inquiry, that Miss Chubb was at home, and showed them into a melancholy little sitting room to await her appearance."

"I shall be 'almost' blind here, Parkinson," remarked Carrados, walking about the room. "It saves explanation."

"Very good, sir," replied Parkinson.

Five minutes later, an interval suggesting that Miss Chubb also found it rather early in the afternoon, Carrados was arranging to take rooms for his attendant and himself for the short time that he would be in London, seeing an oculist.

"One bedroom, mine, must face north," he stipulated. "It has to do with the light."

Miss Chubb replied that she quite understood. Some gentlemen, she added, had their requirements, others their fancies. She endeavoured to suit all. The bedroom she had in view from the first did face north. She would not have known, only the last gentleman, curiously enough, had made the same request.

"A sufferer like myself?" inquired Carrados affably.

Miss Chubb did not think so. In his case she regarded it merely as a fancy. He had said that he could not sleep on any other side. She had had to turn out of her own room to accommodate him, but if one kept an apartment house one had to be adaptable, and Mr. Ghoosh was certainly very liberal in his ideas.

"Ghoosh? An Indian gentleman, I presume?" hazarded Carrados.

It appeared that Mr. Ghoosh was an Indian. Miss Chubb confided that at first she had been rather perturbed at the idea of taking in "a black man", as she confessed to regarding him. She reiterated, however, that Mr. Ghoosh proved to be "quite the gentleman". Five minutes of affability put Carrados in full possession of Mr. Ghoosh's manner of life and movements – the dates of his arrival and departure, his solitariness and his daily habits.

"This would be the best bedroom," said Miss Chubb.

It was a fair-sized room on the first floor. The window looked out on to the roof of an outbuilding. Beyond, the deep cutting of the railway line. Opposite stood the dead wall that Mr. Carlyle had spoken of.

Carrados "looked" round the room with the discriminating glance that sometimes proved so embarrassing to those who knew him.

"I have to take a little daily exercise," he remarked, walking to the window and running his hand up the woodwork. "You will not mind my fixing a 'developer' here, Miss Chubb – a few small screws?"

Miss Chubb thought not. Then she was sure not. Finally she ridiculed the idea of minding with scorn.

"If there is width enough," mused Carrados, spanning the upright critically. "Do you happen to have a wooden foot-rule convenient?"

"Well, to be sure!" exclaimed Miss Chubb, opening a rapid succession of drawers until she produced the required article. "When we did out this room after Mr. Ghoosh, there was this very ruler among the things that he hadn't thought worth taking. This is what you require, sir?"

"Yes," replied Carrados, accepting it, "I think this is exactly what I require." It was a common new white-wood rule, such as one might buy at any small stationer's for a penny. He carelessly took off the width of the upright, reading the figures with a touch, and then continued to run a finger-tip delicately up and down the edges of the instrument.

"Four-and-seven-eighths," was his unspoken conclusion.

"I hope it will do, sir."

"Admirably," replied Carrados. "But I haven't reached the end of my requirements yet, Miss Chubb."

"No, sir?" said the landlady, feeling that it would be a pleasure to oblige so agreeable a gentleman. "What else might there be?"

"Although I can see very little I like to have a light, but not any kind of light. Gas I cannot do with. Do you think that you would be able to find me an oil lamp?"

"Certainly, sir. I got out a very nice brass lamp that I have specially for Mr. Ghoosh. He read a good deal of an evening and he preferred a lamp."

"That is very convenient. I suppose it is large enough to burn for a whole evening?"

"Yes, indeed. And very particular he was always to have it filled every day."

"A lamp without oil is not very useful," smiled Carrados, following her towards another room, and absentmindedly slipping the foot-rule into his pocket."

Whatever Parkinson thought of the arrangement of going into second-rate apartments in an obscure street, it is to be inferred that his devotion to his master was sufficient to overcome his private emotions as a self-respecting "man". At all events, as they were approaching the station he asked, and without a trace of feeling, whether there were any orders for him with reference to the proposed migration.

"None, Parkinson," replied his master. "We must be satisfied with our present quarters."

"I beg your pardon, sir," said Parkinson, with some constraint. "I understood that you had taken the rooms for a week certain."

"I am afraid that Miss Chubb will be under the same impression. Unforeseen circumstances will prevent our going, however. Mr. Greatorex must write tomorrow, enclosing a cheque, with my regrets, and adding a penny for this ruler which I seem to have brought away with me. It, at least, is something for the money."

Parkinson may be excused for not attempting to understand the course of events.

"Here is your train coming in, sir," he merely said.

"We will let it go and wait for another. Is there a signal at either end of the platform?"

"Yes, sir. At the further end."

"Let us walk towards it. Are there any of the porters or officials about here?"

"No, sir. None."

"Take this ruler. I want you to go up the steps – there are steps up the signal, by the way?"

"Yes, sir."

"I want you to measure the glass of the lamp. Do not go up any higher than is necessary, but if you have to stretch, be careful not to mark on the measurement with your nail, although the impulse is a natural one. That has been done already."

Parkinson looked apprehensively around and about. Fortunately the part was a dark and unfrequented spot and everyone else was moving towards the exit at the other end of the platform. Fortunately, also, the signal was not a high one.

"As near as I can judge on the rounded surface, the glass is four-and-seven-eighths across," reported Parkinson.

"Thank you," replied Carrados, returning the measure to his pocket. "Four-and-seven-eighths is quite near enough. Now we will take the next train back."

Sunday evening came, and with it Mr. Carlyle to The Turrets at the appointed hour. He brought to the situation a mind poised for any eventuality and a trenchant eye. As the time went on and the impenetrable Carrados made no allusion to the case, Carlyle's manner inclined to a waggish commiseration of his host's position. Actually, he said little, but the crisp precision of his voice when the path lay open to a remark of any significance left little to be said.

It was not until they had finished dinner and returned to the library that Carrados gave the slightest hint of anything unusual being in the air. His first indication of coming events was to remove the key from the outside to the inside of the door.

"What are you doing, Max?" demanded Mr. Carlyle, his curiosity overcoming the indirect attitude.

"You have been very entertaining, Louis," replied his friend, "but Parkinson should be back very soon now and it is as well to be prepared. Do you happen to carry a revolver?"

"Not when I come to dine with you, Max," replied Carlyle, with all the aplomb he could muster. "Is it usual?"

Carrados smiled affectionately at his guest's agile recovery and touched the secret spring of a drawer in an antique bureau by his side. The little hidden receptacle shot smoothly out, disclosing a pair of dull-blued pistols.

"Tonight, at all events, it might be prudent," he replied, handing one to Carlyle and putting the other into his own pocket. "Our man may be here at any minute, and we do not know in what temper he will come."

"Our man!" exclaimed Carlyle, craning forward in excitement. "Max! You don't mean to say that you have got Mead to admit it?"

"No one has admitted it," said Carrados. "And it is not Mead."

"Not Mead . . . Do you mean that Hutchins –?"

"Neither Mead nor Hutchins. The man who tampered with the signal – for Hutchins was right and a green light was exhibited – is a young Indian from Bengal. His name is Drishna and he lives at Swanstead."

Mr. Carlyle stared at his friend between sheer surprise and blank incredulity.

"You really mean this, Carrados?" he said.

"My fatal reputation for humour!" smiled Carrados. "If I am wrong, Louis, the next hour will expose it."

45

"But why – why – why? The colossal villainy, the unparalleled audacity!" Mr. Carlyle lost himself among incredulous superlatives and could only stare.

"Chiefly to get himself out of a disastrous speculation," replied Carrados, answering the question. "If there was another motive – or at least an incentive – which I suspect, doubtless we shall hear of it."

"All the same, Max, I don't think that you have treated me quite fairly," protested Carlyle, getting over his first surprise and passing to a sense of injury. "Here we are and I know nothing, absolutely nothing, of the whole affair."

"We both have our ideas of pleasantry, Louis," replied Carrados genially. "But I dare say you are right and perhaps there is still time to atone." In the fewest possible words he outlined the course of his investigations. "And now you know all that is to be known until Drishna arrives."

"But will he come?" questioned Carlyle doubtfully. "He may be suspicious."

"Yes, he will be suspicious."

"Then he will not come."

"On the contrary, Louis, he will come because my letter will make him suspicious. He is coming. Otherwise Parkinson would have telephoned me at once and we should have had to take other measures."

"What did you say, Max?" asked Carlyle curiously.

"I wrote that I was anxious to discuss an Indo-Scythian inscription with him, and sent my car in the hope that he would be able to oblige me."

"But is he interested in Indo-Scythian inscriptions?"

"I haven't the faintest idea," admitted Carrados, and Mr. Carlyle was throwing up his hands in despair when the sound of a motor car wheels softly kissing the gravel surface of the drive outside brought him to his feet.

"By Gad, you are right, Max!" he exclaimed, peeping through the curtains. "There is a man inside."

"Mr. Drishna," announced Parkinson, a minute later.

The visitor came into the room with leisurely self-possession that might have been real or a desperate assumption. He was a slightly built young man of about twenty-five, with black hair and eyes, a small, carefully trained moustache, and a dark olive skin. His physiognomy was not displeasing, but his expression had a harsh and supercilious tinge. In attire he erred towards the immaculately spruce.

"Mr. Carrados?" he said inquiringly.

Carrados, who had risen, bowed slightly without offering his hand.

46

"This gentleman," he said, indicating his friend, "is Mr. Carlyle, the celebrated private detective."

The Indian shot a very sharp glance at the object of this description. Then he sat down.

"You wrote me a letter, Mr. Carrados," he remarked, in English that scarcely betrayed any foreign origin, "a rather curious letter, I may say. You asked me about an ancient inscription. I know nothing of antiquities, but I thought, as you had sent, that it would be more courteous if I came and explained this to you."

"That was the object of my letter," replied Carrados.

"You wished to see me?" said Drishna, unable to stand the ordeal of the silence that Carrados imposed after his remark.

"When you left Miss Chubb's house you left a ruler behind." One lay on the desk by Carrados and he took it up as he spoke.

"I don't understand what you are talking about," said Drishna guardedly. "You are making some mistake."

"The ruler was marked at four-and-seven-eighths inches – the measure of the glass of the signal lamp outside."

The unfortunate young man was unable to repress a start. His face lost its healthy tone. Then, with a sudden impulse, he made a step forward and snatched the object from Carrados's hand.

"If it is mine I have a right to it," he exclaimed, snapping the ruler in two and throwing it on to the back of the blazing fire. "It is nothing."

"Pardon me, I did not say that the one you have so impetuously disposed of was yours. As a matter of fact, it was mine. Yours is – elsewhere."

"Wherever it is, you have no right to it if it is mine," panted Drishna, with rising excitement. "You are a thief, Mr. Carrados. I will not stay any longer here."

He jumped up and turned towards the door. Carlyle made a step forward, but the precaution was unnecessary.

"One moment, Mr. Drishna," interposed Carrados, in his smoothest tones. "It is a pity, after you have come so far, to leave without hearing of my investigations in the neighbourhood of Shaftesbury Avenue."

Drishna sat down again.

"As you like," he muttered. "It does not interest me."

"I wanted to obtain a lamp of a certain pattern," continued Carrados. "It seemed to me that the simplest explanation would be to say that I wanted it for a motor car. Naturally I went to Long Acre. At the first shop I said: 'Wasn't it here that a friend of mine, an Indian gentleman, recently had a lamp made with a green glass that was nearly five inches across?' No, it was not there, but they could make me one. At the next shop the same. At the third, and fourth, and so on. Finally my persistence was rewarded. I found the place where the lamp had been made, and at the cost of ordering another, I obtained all the details I wanted. It was news to them, the shopman informed me, that in some parts of India green was the danger colour and therefore tail lamps had to show a green light. The incident made some impression on him and he would be able to identify their customer – who paid in advance and gave no address – among a thousand of his countrymen. Do I succeed in interesting you, Mr. Drishna?"

"Do you?" replied Drishna, with a languid yawn. "Do I look interested?"

"You must make allowance for my unfortunate blindness," apologized Carrados, with grim irony.

"Blindness!" exclaimed Drishna, dropping his affectation of unconcern as though electrified by the word. "Do you mean – really blind – that you do not see me?"

"Alas, no," admitted Carrados.

The Indian withdrew his right hand from his coat pocket and with a tragic gesture flung a heavy revolver down on the table between them.

"I have had you covered all the time, Mr. Carrados, and if I had wished to go and you or your friend had raised a hand to stop me, it would have been at the peril of your lives," he said, in a voice of melancholy triumph. "But what is the use of defying fate, and who successfully evades his destiny? A month ago I went to see one of our people who reads the future and sought to know the course of certain events. 'You need fear no human eye,' was the message given to me. Then she added: 'But when the sightless sees the unseen, make your peace with Yama.' And I thought she spoke of the Great Hereafter!"

"This amounts to an admission of your guilt," exclaimed Mr. Carlyle practically.

"I bow to the decree of fate," replied Drishna. "And it is fitting to the universal irony of existence that a blind man should be the instrument. I don't imagine, Mr. Carlyle," he added maliciously, "that you, with your eyes, would ever have brought that result about."

"You are a very cold-blooded young scoundrel, sir!" retorted Mr. Carlyle. "Good Heavens! Do you realize that you are responsible for the death of scores of innocent men and women?"

"Do you realise, Mr. Carlyle, that you and your Government and your soldiers are responsible for the death of thousands of innocent men and women in my country every day? If England was occupied by the Germans who quartered an army and an administration with their wives and their families and all their expensive paraphernalia on the unfortunate country until the whole nation was reduced to the verge of famine, and the appointment of every new official meant the callous death sentence on a thousand men and women to pay his salary, then if you went to Berlin and wrecked a train you would be hailed a patriot. What Boadicea did and – and Samson – so have I. If they were heroes, so am I."

"Well, upon my word!" cried the highly scandalized Carlyle, "what next! Boadicea was a – er – semi-legendary person, whom we may possibly admire at a distance. Personally, I do not profess to express an opinion. But Samson, I would remind you, is a Biblical character. Samson was mocked as an enemy. You, I do not doubt, have been entertained as a friend."

"And haven't I been mocked and despised and sneered at every day of my life here by your supercilious, superior, empty-headed men?" flashed back Drishna, his eyes leaping into malignity and his voice trembling with sudden passion. "Oh! how I hated them as I passed them in the street and recognized by a thousand petty insults their lordly English contempt for me as an inferior being – a nigger. How I longed with Caligula that a nation had a single neck that I might destroy it at one blow. I loathe you in your complacent hypocrisy, Mr. Carlyle – despise and utterly abominate you from an eminence of superiority that you can never even understand."

"I think we are getting rather away from the point, Mr. Drishna," interposed Carrados, with the impartiality of a judge. "Unless I am misinformed, you are not so ungallant as to include everyone you have met here in your execration?"

"Ah, no," admitted Drishna, descending into a quite ingenuous frankness. "Much as I hate your men, I love your women. How is it possible that a nation should be so divided – its men so dull-witted and offensive, its women so quick, sympathetic and capable of appreciating?"

"But a little expensive, too, at times?" suggested Carrados.

Drishna sighed heavily.

"Yes. It is incredible. It is the generosity of their large nature. My allowance, though what most of you would call noble, has proved quite inadequate. I was compelled to borrow money and the interest became overwhelming. Bankruptcy was impracticable because I should have then been recalled by my people, and much as I detest England, a certain reason made the thought of leaving it unbearable."

"Connected with the Arcady Theatre?"

"You know? Well, do not let us introduce the lady's name. In order to restore myself, I speculated on the Stock Exchange. My credit was good through my father's position and the standing of the firm to which I am attached. I heard on reliable authority, and very early, that the Central and Suburban, and the Deferred especially, was safe to fall heavily, through a motor bus amalgamation that was then a secret. I opened a bear account and sold largely. The shares fell, but only fractionally, and I waited. Then, unfortunately, they began to go up. Adverse forces were at work and rumours were put about. I could not stand the settlement, and in order to carry over an account I was literally compelled to deal temporarily with some securities that were not technically my own property."

"Embezzlement, sir," commented Mr. Carlyle icily. "But what is embezzlement on the top of wholesale murder!"

"That is what it is called. In my case, however, it was only to be temporary. Unfortunately, the rise continued. Then, at the height of my despair, I chanced to be returning to Swanstead rather earlier than usual one evening, and the train was stopped at a certain signal to let another pass. There was conversation in the carriage and I learned certain details. One said that there would be an accident some day, and so forth. In a flash – as by an inspiration – I saw how the circumstance might be turned to account. A bad accident and the shares would certainly fall and my position would be retrieved. I think Mr. Carrados has somehow learned the rest."

"Max," said Mr. Carlyle, with emotion, "is there any reason why you should not send your man for a police officer and have this monster arrested on his own confession without further delay?"

"Pray do so, Mr. Carrados," acquiesced Drishna. "I shall certainly be hanged, but the speech I shall prepare will ring from one end of India to the other. My memory will be venerated as that of a martyr, and the emancipation of my motherland will be hastened by my sacrifice."

"In other words," commented Carrados, "there will be disturbances at half-a-dozen disaffected places, a few unfortunate police will be clubbed to death, and possibly worse things may happen. That does not suit us, Mr. Drishna."

"And how do you propose to prevent it?" asked Drishna, with cool assurance.

"It is very unpleasant being hanged on a dark winter morning – very cold, very friendless, very inhuman. The long trial, the solitude and the confinement, the thoughts of the long sleepless night before, the hangman and the pinioning and the noosing of the rope, are apt to prey on the imagination. Only a very stupid man can take hanging easily."

"What do you want me to do instead, Mr. Carrados?" asked Drishna shrewdly.

Carrados's hand closed on the weapon that still lay on the table between them. Without a word he pushed it across.

"I see," commented Drishna, with a short laugh and a gleaming eye. "Shoot myself and hush it up to suit your purpose. Withhold my message to save the exposures of a trial, and keep the flame from the torch of insurrectionary freedom."

"Also," interposed Carrados mildly, "to save your worthy people a good deal of shame, and to save the lady who is nameless the unpleasant necessity of relinquishing the house and the income which you have just settled on her. She certainly would not then venerate your memory."

"What is that?"

"The transaction which you carried through was based on a felony and could not be upheld. The firm you dealt with will go to the courts, and the money, being directly traceable, will be held forfeit as no good consideration passed."

"Max!" cried Mr. Carlyle hotly. "You are not going to let this scoundrel cheat the gallows after all?"

"The best use you can make of the gallows is to cheat it, Louis," replied Carrados. "Have you ever reflected what human beings will think of us a hundred years hence?"

"Oh, of course I'm not really in favour of hanging," admitted Mr. Carlyle.

"Nobody really is. But we go on hanging. Mr. Drishna is a dangerous animal who for the sake of pacific animals must cease to exist. Let his barbarous exploit pass into oblivion with him. The disadvantages of spreading it broadcast immeasurably outweigh the benefits."

"I have considered," announced Drishna. "I will do as you wish."

"Very well," said Carrados. "Here is some plain notepaper. You had better write a letter to someone saying that the financial difficulties in which you are involved make life unbearable."

"But there are no financial difficulties – now."

"That does not matter in the least. It will be put down to an hallucination and taken as showing the state of your mind."

"But what guarantee have we that he will not escape?" whispered Mr. Carlyle.

"He cannot escape," replied Carrados tranquilly. "His identity is too clear."

"I have no intention of trying to escape," put in Drishna, as he wrote. "You hardly imagine that I have not considered this eventuality, do you?"

"All the same," murmured the ex-lawyer, "I should like to have a jury behind me. It is one thing to execute a man morally. It is another to do it almost literally."

"Is that all right?" asked Drishna, passing across the letter he had written.

Carrados smiled at this tribute to his perception.

51

"Quite excellent," he replied courteously. "There is a train at nine-forty. Will that suit you?"

Drishna nodded and stood up. Mr. Carlyle had a very uneasy feeling that he ought to do something but could not suggest to himself what.

The next moment he heard his friend heartily thanking the visitor for the assistance he had been in the matter of the Indo-Scythian inscription, as they walked across the hall together. Then a door closed.

"I believe that there is something positively uncanny about Max at times," murmured the perturbed gentleman to himself."

The Tragedy at Brookbend Cottage

"**M**ax," said Mr. Carlyle, when Parkinson had closed the door behind him, "this is Lieutenant Hollyer, whom you consented to see."

"To *hear*," corrected Carrados, smiling straight into the healthy and rather embarrassed face of the stranger before him. "Mr. Hollyer knows of my disability?"

"Mr. Carlyle told me," said the young man, "but, as a matter of fact, I had heard of you before, Mr. Carrados, from one of our men. It was in connexion with the foundering of the *Ivan Saratov*."

Carrados wagged his head in good-humoured resignation.

"And the owners were sworn to inviolable secrecy!" he exclaimed. "Well, it is inevitable, I suppose. Not another scuttling case, Mr. Hollyer?"

"No, mine is quite a private matter," replied the lieutenant. "My sister, Mrs. Creake – but Mr. Carlyle would tell you better than I can. He knows all about it."

"No, no. Carlyle is a professional. Let me have it in the rough, Mr. Hollyer. My ears are my eyes, you know."

"Very well, sir. I can tell you what there is to tell, right enough, but I feel that when all's said and done it must sound very little to another, although it seems important enough to me."

"We have occasionally found trifles of significance ourselves," said Carrados encouragingly. "Don't let that deter you."

This was the essence of Lieutenant Hollyer's narrative:

"I have a sister, Millicent, who is married to a man called Creake. She is about twenty-eight now and he is at least fifteen years older. Neither my mother (who has since died), nor I, cared very much about Creake. We had nothing particular against him, except, perhaps, the moderate disparity of age, but none of us appeared to have anything in common. He was a dark, taciturn man, and his moody silence froze up conversation. As a result, of course, we didn't see much of each other."

"This, you must understand, was four or five years ago, Max," interposed Mr. Carlyle officiously.

Carrados maintained an uncompromising silence. Mr. Carlyle blew his nose and contrived to impart a hurt significance into the operation. Then Lieutenant Hollyer continued.

"Millicent married Creake after a very short engagement. It was a frightfully subdued wedding – more like a funeral to me. The man

53

professed to have no relations and apparently he had scarcely any friends or business acquaintances. He was an agent for something or other and had an office off Holborn. I suppose he made a living out of it then, although we knew practically nothing of his private affairs, but I gather that it has been going down since, and I suspect that for the past few years they have been getting along almost entirely on Millicent's little income. You would like the particulars of that?"

"Please," assented Carrados.

"When our father died about seven years ago, he left three-thousand pounds. It was invested in Canadian stock and brought in a little over a hundred a year. By his will my mother was to have the income of that for life, and on her death it was to pass to Millicent, subject to the payment of a lump sum of five-hundred pounds to me. But my father privately suggested to me that if I should have no particular use for the money at the time, he would propose my letting Millicent have the income of it until I did want it, as she would not be particularly well off. You see, Mr. Carrados, a great deal more had been spent on my education and advancement than on her. I had my pay, and, of course, I could look out for myself better than a girl could."

"Quite so," agreed Carrados.

"Therefore I did nothing about that," continued the lieutenant. "Three years ago I was over again but I did not see much of them. They were living in lodgings. That was the only time since the marriage that I have seen them until last week. In the meanwhile, our mother had died and Millicent had been receiving her income. She wrote me several letters at the time. Otherwise we did not correspond much, but about a year ago she sent me their new address – Brookbend Cottage, Mulling Common – a house that they had taken. When I got two months' leave I invited myself there as a matter of course, fully expecting to stay most of my time with them, but I made an excuse to get away after a week. The place was dismal and unendurable, the whole life and atmosphere indescribably depressing." He looked round with an instinct of caution, leaned forward earnestly, and dropped his voice. "Mr. Carrados, it is my absolute conviction that Creake is only waiting for a favourable opportunity to murder Millicent."

"Go on," said Carrados quietly. "A week of the depressing surroundings of Brookbend Cottage would not alone convince you of that, Mr. Hollyer."

"I am not so sure," declared Hollyer doubtfully. "There was a feeling of suspicion and – before me – polite hatred that would have gone a good way towards it. All the same, there was something more definite. Millicent told me this the day after I went there. There is no doubt that a few months ago Creake deliberately planned to poison her with some weed-killer. She told me the circumstances in a rather distressed moment, but afterwards she refused to speak of it again – even weakly denied it – and, as a matter of fact, it was with the greatest difficulty that I could get her at any time to talk about her husband or his affairs. The gist of it was that she had the strongest suspicion that Creake doctored a bottle of stout which he expected she would drink for her supper when she was alone. The weed-killer, properly labelled, but also in a beer bottle, was kept with other miscellaneous liquids in the same cupboard as the beer but on a high shelf. When he found that it had miscarried he poured away the mixture, washed out the bottle and put in the dregs from another. There is no doubt in my mind that if he had come back and found Millicent dead or dying he would have contrived it to appear that she had made a mistake in the dark and drunk some of the poison before she found out."

"Yes," assented Carrados. "The open way. The safe way."

"You must understand that they live in a very small style, Mr. Carrados, and Millicent is almost entirely in the man's power. The only servant they have is a woman who comes in for a few hours every day. The house is lonely and secluded. Creake is sometimes away for days and nights at a time, and Millicent, either through pride or indifference, seems to have dropped off all her old friends and to have made no others. He might poison her, bury the body in the garden, and be a thousand miles away before anyone began even to inquire about her. What am I to do, Mr. Carrados?"

"He is less likely to try poison than some other means now," pondered Carrados. "That having failed, his wife will always be on her guard. He may know, or at least suspect, that others know. No . . . The common-sense precaution would be for your sister to leave the man, Mr. Hollyer. She will not?"

"No," admitted Hollyer, "she will not. I at once urged that." The young man struggled with some hesitation for a moment and then blurted out: "The fact is, Mr. Carrados, I don't understand Millicent. She is not the girl she was. She hates Creake and treats him with a silent contempt that eats into their lives like acid, and yet she is so jealous of him that she will let nothing short of death part them. It is a horrible life they lead. I stood it for a week and I must say, much as I dislike my brother-in-law, that he has something to put up with. If only he got into a passion like a man and killed her, it wouldn't be altogether incomprehensible."

"That does not concern us," said Carrados. "In a game of this kind, one has to take sides and we have taken ours. It remains for us to see that our side wins. You mentioned jealousy, Mr. Hollyer. Have you any idea whether Mrs. Creake has real ground for it?"

55

"I should have told you that," replied Lieutenant Hollyer. "I happened to strike up with a newspaper man whose office is in the same block as Creake's. When I mentioned the name he grinned. 'Creake,' he said. 'Oh, he's the man with the romantic typist, isn't he?' 'Well, he's my brother-in-law,' I replied. 'What about the typist?' Then the chap shut up like a knife. 'No, no,' he said, 'I didn't know he was married. I don't want to get mixed up in anything of that sort. I only said that he had a typist. Well, what of that? So have we. So has everyone.' There was nothing more to be got out of him, but the remark and the grin meant – well, about as usual, Mr. Carrados."

Carrados turned to his friend.

"I suppose you know all about the typist by now, Louis?"

"We have had her under efficient observation, Max," replied Mr. Carlyle, with severe dignity.

"Is she unmarried?"

"Yes. So far as ordinary repute goes, she is."

"That is all that is essential for the moment. Mr. Hollyer opens up three excellent reasons why this man might wish to dispose of his wife. If we accept the suggestion of poisoning – though we have only a jealous woman's suspicion for it – we add to the wish the determination. Well, we will go forward on that. Have you got a photograph of Mr. Creake?"

The lieutenant took out his pocket-book.

"Mr. Carlyle asked me for one. Here is the best I could get."

Carrados rang the bell.

"This, Parkinson," he said, when the man appeared, "is a photograph of a Mr. – What first name, by the way?"

"Austin," put in Hollyer, who was following everything with a boyish mixture of excitement and subdued importance.

" – of a Mr. Austin Creake. I may require you to recognize him."

Parkinson glanced at the print and returned it to his master's hand.

"May I inquire if it is a recent photograph of the gentleman, sir?" he asked.

"About six years ago," said the lieutenant, taking in this new actor in the drama with frank curiosity. "But he is very little changed."

"Thank you, sir. I will endeavour to remember Mr. Creake, sir."

Lieutenant Hollyer stood up as Parkinson left the room. The interview seemed to be at an end.

"Oh, there's one other matter," he remarked. "I am afraid that I did rather an unfortunate thing while I was at Brookbend. It seemed to me that as all Millicent's money would probably pass into Creake's hands sooner or later, I might as well have my five-hundred pounds, if only to help her

56

with afterwards. So I broached the subject and said that I should like to have it now as I had an opportunity for investing."

"And you think?"

"It may possibly influence Creake to act sooner than he otherwise might have done. He may have got possession of the principal even and find it very awkward to replace it."

"So much the better. If your sister is going to be murdered, it may as well be done next week as next year so far as I am concerned. Excuse my brutality, Mr. Hollyer, but this is simply a case to me and I regard it strategically. Now Mr. Carlyle's organization can look after Mrs. Creake for a few weeks but it cannot look after her forever. By increasing the immediate risk, we diminish the permanent risk."

"I see," agreed Hollyer. "I'm awfully uneasy, but I'm entirely in your hands."

"Then we will give Mr. Creake every inducement and every opportunity to get to work. Where are you staying now?"

"Just now with some friends at St. Albans."

"That is too far." The inscrutable eyes retained their tranquil depth but a new quality of quickening interest in the voice made Mr. Carlyle forget the weight and burden of his ruffled dignity. "Give me a few minutes, please. The cigarettes are behind you, Mr. Hollyer." The blind man walked to the window and seemed to look out over the cypress-shaded lawn. The lieutenant lit a cigarette and Mr. Carlyle picked up *Punch*. Then Carrados turned round again"

"You are prepared to put your own arrangements aside?" he demanded of his visitor.

"Certainly."

"Very well. I want you to go down now – straight from here – to Brookbend Cottage. Tell your sister that your leave is unexpectedly cut short and that you sail tomorrow."

"*The Martian?*"

"No, no. *The Martian* doesn't sail. Look up the movements on your way there and pick out a boat that does. Say you are transferred. Add that you expect to be away only two or three months and that you really want the five-hundred pounds by the time of your return. Don't stay in the house long, please."

"I understand, sir."

"St. Albans is too far. Make your excuse and get away from there today. Put up somewhere in town, where you will be in reach of the telephone. Let Mr. Carlyle and myself know where you are. Keep out of Creake's way. I don't want actually to tie you down to the house, but we

57

may require your services. We will let you know at the first sign of anything doing, and if there is nothing to be done we must release you."

"I don't mind that. Is there nothing more that I can do now?"

"Nothing. In going to Mr. Carlyle you have done the best thing possible – you have put your sister into the care of the shrewdest man in London." Whereat the object of this quite unexpected eulogy found himself becoming covered with modest confusion.

"Well, Max?" remarked Mr. Carlyle tentatively when they were alone.

"Well, Louis?"

"Of course it wasn't worthwhile rubbing it in before young Hollyer, but, as a matter of fact, every single man carries the life of any other man – only one, mind you – in his hands, do what you will."

"Provided he doesn't bungle," acquiesced Carrados.

"Quite so."

"And also that he is absolutely reckless of the consequences."

"Of course."

"Two rather large provisos. Creake is obviously susceptible to both. Have you seen him?"

"No. As I told you, I put a man on to report his habits in town. Then, two days ago, as the case seemed to promise some interest – for he certainly is deeply involved with the typist, Max, and the thing might take a sensational turn any time – I went down to Mulling Common myself. Although the house is lonely, it is on the electric tram route. You know the sort of market garden rurality that about a dozen miles out of London offers – alternate bricks and cabbages. It was easy enough to get to know about Creake locally. He mixes with no one there, goes into town at irregular times but generally every day, and is reputed to be devilish hard to get money out of. Finally I made the acquaintance of an old fellow who used to do a day's gardening at Brookbend occasionally. He has a cottage and a garden of his own with a greenhouse, and the business cost me the price of a pound of tomatoes."

"Was it – a profitable investment?"

"As tomatoes, yes. As information, no. The old fellow had the fatal disadvantage from our point of view of labouring under a grievance. A few weeks ago, Creake told him that he would not require him again as he was going to do his own gardening in future."

"That is something, Louis."

"If only Creake was going to poison his wife with hyoscyamine and bury her, instead of blowing her up with a dynamite cartridge and claiming that it came in among the coal."

"True, true. Still – "

58

"However, the chatty old soul had a simple explanation for everything that Creake did. Creake was mad. He had even seen him flying a kite in his garden where it was bound to get wrecked among the trees. 'A lad of ten would have known better,' he declared. And certainly the kite did get wrecked, for I saw it hanging over the road myself. But that a sane man should spend his time 'playing with a toy' was beyond him."

"A good many men have been flying kites of various kinds lately," said Carrados. "Is he interested in aviation?"

"I dare say. He appears to have some knowledge of scientific subjects. Now what do you want me to do, Max?"

"Will you do it?"

"Implicitly – subject to the usual reservations."

"Keep your man on Creake in town and let me have his reports after you have seen them. Lunch with me here now. 'Phone up to your office that you are detained on unpleasant business and then give the deserving Parkinson an afternoon off by looking after me while we take a motor run round Mulling Common. If we have time, we might go on to Brighton, feed at the 'Ship', and come back in the cool."

"Amiable and thrice lucky mortal," sighed Mr. Carlyle, his glance wandering round the room.

But, as it happened, Brighton did not figure in that day's itinerary. It had been Carrados's intention merely to pass Brookbend Cottage on this occasion, relying on his highly developed faculties, aided by Mr. Carlyle's description, to inform him of the surroundings. A hundred yards before they reached the house, he had given an order to his chauffeur to drop into the lowest speed and they were leisurely drawing past when a discovery by Mr. Carlyle modified their plans.

"By Jupiter!" that gentleman suddenly exclaimed, "there's a board up, Max. The place is to be let."

Carrados picked up the tube again. A couple of sentences passed and the car stopped by the roadside, a score of paces past the limit of the garden. Mr. Carlyle took out his notebook and wrote down the address of a firm of house agents.

"You might raise the bonnet and have a look at the engines, Harris," said Carrados. "We want to be occupied here for a few minutes."

"This is sudden. Hollyer knew nothing of their leaving," remarked Mr. Carlyle.

"Probably not for three months yet. All the same, Louis, we will go on to the agents and get a card to view, whether we use it today or not."

A thick hedge, in its summer dress effectively screening the house beyond from public view, lay between the garden and the road. Above the hedge showed an occasional shrub. At the corner nearest to the car a chestnut flourished. The wooden gate, once white. Which they had passed, was grimed and rickety. The road itself was still the unpretentious country lane that the advent of the electric car had found it. When Carrados had taken in these details there seemed little else to notice. He was on the point of giving Harris the order to go on when his ear caught a trivial sound.

"Someone is coming out of the house, Louis," he warned his friend. "It may be Hollyer, but he ought to have gone by this time."

"I don't hear anyone," replied the other, but as he spoke a door banged noisily and Mr. Carlyle slipped into another seat and ensconced himself behind a copy of *The Globe*.

"Creake himself," he whispered across the car, as a man appeared at the gate. "Hollyer was right. He is hardly changed. Waiting for a car, I suppose."

But a car very soon swung past them from the direction in which Mr. Creake was looking and it did not interest him. For a minute or two longer he continued to look expectantly along the road. Then he walked slowly up the drive back to the house.

"We will give him five or ten minutes," decided Carrados. "Harris is behaving very naturally."

Before even the shorter period had run out they were repaid. A telegraph-boy cycled leisurely along the road, and, leaving his machine at the gate, went up to the cottage. Evidently there was no reply, for in less than a minute he was trundling past them back again. Round the bend an approaching tram clanged its bell noisily, and, quickened by the warning sound, Mr. Creake again appeared, this time with a small portmanteau in his hand. With a backward glance he hurried on towards the next stopping-place, and, boarding the car as it slackened down, he was carried out of their knowledge.

"Very convenient of Mr. Creake," remarked Carrados, with quiet satisfaction. "We will now get the order and go over the house in his absence. It might be useful to have a look at the wire as well."

"It might, Max," acquiesced Mr. Carlyle a little dryly. "But if it is, as it probably is, in Creake's pocket, how do you propose to get it?"

"By going to the post office, Louis."

"Quite so. Have you ever tried to see a copy of a telegram addressed to someone else?"

"I don't think I have ever had occasion yet," admitted Carrados. "Have you?"

"In one or two cases I have perhaps been an accessory to the act. It is generally a matter either of extreme delicacy or considerable expenditure."

"Then for Hollyer's sake we will hope for the former here." And Mr. Carlyle smiled darkly and hinted that he was content to wait for a friendly revenge.

A little later, having left the car at the beginning of the straggling High Street, the two men called at the village post office. They had already visited the house agent and obtained an order to view Brookbend Cottage, declining, with some difficulty, the clerk's persistent offer to accompany them. The reason was soon forthcoming. "As a matter of fact," explained the young man, "the present tenant is under our notice to leave."

"Unsatisfactory, eh?" said Carrados encouragingly.

"He's a corker," admitted the clerk, responding to the friendly tone. "Fifteen months and not a doit of rent have we had. That's why I should have liked – "

"We will make every allowance," replied Carrados.

The post office occupied one side of a stationer's shop. It was not without some inward trepidation that Mr. Carlyle found himself committed to the adventure. Carrados, on the other hand, was the personification of bland unconcern.

"You have just sent a telegram to Brookbend Cottage," he said to the young lady behind the brasswork lattice. "We think it may have come inaccurately and should like a repeat." He took out his purse. "What is the fee?"

The request was evidently not a common one. "Oh," said the girl uncertainly, "wait a minute, please." She turned to a pile of telegram duplicates behind the desk and ran a doubtful finger along the upper sheets. "I think this is all right. You want it repeated?"

"Please." Just a tinge of questioning surprise gave point to the courteous tone.

"It will be fourpence. If there is an error the amount will be refunded." Carrados put down a coin and received his change.

"Will it take long?" he inquired carelessly, as he pulled on his glove.

"You will most likely get it within a quarter-of-an-hour," she replied.

"Now you've done it," commented Mr. Carlyle, as they walked back to their car. "How do you propose to get that telegram, Max?"

"Ask for it," was the laconic explanation.

And, stripping the artifice of any elaboration, he simply asked for it and got it. The car, posted at a convenient bend in the road, gave him a warning note as the telegraph-boy approached. Then Carrados took up a convincing attitude with his hand on the gate while Mr. Carlyle lent himself to the semblance of a departing friend. That was the inevitable impression when the boy rode up.

61

"Creake, Brookbend Cottage?" inquired Carrados, holding out his hand, and without a second thought the boy gave him the envelope and rode away on the assurance that there would be no reply.

"Some day, my friend," remarked Mr. Carlyle, looking nervously towards the unseen house, "your ingenuity will get you into a tight corner."

"Then my ingenuity must get me out again," was the retort. "Let us have our 'view' now. The telegram can wait."

An untidy workwoman took their order and left them standing at the door. Presently a lady whom they both knew to be Mrs. Creake appeared.

"You wish to see over the house?" she said, in a voice that was utterly devoid of any interest. Then, without waiting for a reply, she turned to the nearest door and threw it open.

"This is the drawing room," she said, standing aside.

They walked into a sparsely furnished, damp-smelling room and made a pretence of looking round, while Mrs. Creake remained silent and aloof.

"The dining room," she continued, crossing the narrow hall and opening another door.

Mr. Carlyle ventured a genial commonplace in the hope of inducing conversation. The result was not encouraging. Doubtless they would have gone through the house under the same frigid guidance had not Carrados been at fault in a way that Mr. Carlyle had never known him fail before. In crossing the hall he stumbled over a mat and almost fell.

"Pardon my clumsiness," he said to the lady. "I am, unfortunately, quite blind. But," he added, with a smile, to turn off the mishap, "even a blind man must have a house."

The man who had eyes was surprised to see a flood of colour rush into Mrs. Creake's face.

"Blind!" she exclaimed. "Oh, I beg your pardon. Why did you not tell me? You might have fallen."

"I generally manage fairly well," he replied. "But, of course, in a strange house – "

She put her hand on his arm very lightly.

"You must let me guide you, just a little," she said.

The house, without being large, was full of passages and inconvenient turnings. Carrados asked an occasional question and found Mrs. Creake quite amiable without effusion. Mr. Carlyle followed them from room to room in the hope, though scarcely the expectation, of learning something that might be useful.

"This is the last one. It is the largest bedroom," said their guide. Only two of the upper rooms were fully furnished and Mr. Carlyle at once saw, as Carrados knew without seeing, that this was the one which the Creakes occupied.

"A very pleasant outlook," declared Mr. Carlyle.

"Oh, I suppose so," admitted the lady vaguely. The room, in fact, looked over the leafy garden and the road beyond. It had a French window opening on to a small balcony, and to this, under the strange influence that always attracted him to light, Carrados walked.

"I expect that there is a certain amount of repair needed?" he said, after standing there a moment.

"I am afraid there would be," she confessed.

"I ask because there is a sheet of metal on the floor here," he continued. "Now that, in an old house, spells dry rot to the wary observer."

"My husband said that the rain, which comes in a little under the window, was rotting the boards there," she replied. "He put that down recently. I had not noticed anything myself."

It was the first time she had mentioned her husband. Mr. Carlyle pricked up his ears.

"Ah, that is a less serious matter," said Carrados. "May I step out on to the balcony?"

"Oh yes, if you like to." Then, as he appeared to be fumbling at the catch, "Let me open it for you."

But the window was already open, and Carrados, facing the various points of the compass, took in the bearings.

"A sunny, sheltered corner," he remarked. "An ideal spot for a deck-chair and a book."

She shrugged her shoulders half-contemptuously.

"I dare say," she replied, "but I never use it."

"Sometimes, surely," he persisted mildly. "It would be my favourite retreat. But then – "

"I was going to say that I had never even been out on it, but that would not be quite true. It has two uses for me, both equally romantic. I occasionally shake a duster from it, and when my husband returns late without his latchkey he wakes me up and I come out here and drop him mine."

Further revelation of Mr. Creake's nocturnal habits was cut off, greatly to Mr. Carlyle's annoyance, by a cough of unmistakable significance from the foot of the stairs. They had heard a trade cart drive up to the gate, a knock at the door, and the heavy-footed woman tramp along the hall.

"Excuse me a minute, please," said Mrs. Creake.

"Louis," said Carrados, in a sharp whisper, the moment they were alone, "stand against the door."

With extreme plausibility Mr. Carlyle began to admire a picture so situated that while he was there it was impossible to open the door more than a few inches. From that position he observed his confederate go through the curious procedure of kneeling down on the bedroom floor and for a full minute pressing his ear to the sheet of metal that had already engaged his attention. Then he rose to his feet, nodded, dusted his trousers, and Mr. Carlyle moved to a less equivocal position.

"What a beautiful rose-tree grows up your balcony," remarked Carrados, stepping into the room as Mrs. Creake returned. "I suppose you are very fond of gardening?"

"I detest it," she replied.

"But this Glorie, so carefully trained –?"

"Is it?" she replied. "I think my husband was nailing it up recently." By some strange fatality, Carrados's most aimless remarks seemed to involve the absent Mr. Creake. "Do you care to see the garden?"

The garden proved to be extensive and neglected. Behind the house was chiefly orchard. In front, some semblance of order had been kept up. Here it was lawn and shrubbery, and the drive they had walked along. Two things interested Carrados: The soil at the foot of the balcony, which he declared on examination to be particularly suitable for roses, and the fine chestnut-tree in the corner by the road.

As they walked back to the car Mr. Carlyle lamented that they had learned so little of Creake's movements.

"Perhaps the telegram will tell us something," suggested Carrados. "Read it, Louis."

Mr. Carlyle cut open the envelope, glanced at the enclosure, and in spite of his disappointment could not restrain a chuckle.

"My poor Max," he explained. "You have put yourself to an amount of ingenious trouble for nothing. Creake is evidently taking a few days' holiday and prudently availed himself of the Meteorological Office forecast before going. Listen: '*Immediate prospect for London warm and settled. Further outlook cooler but fine.*' Well, well. I did get a pound of tomatoes for my fourpence."

"You certainly scored there, Louis," admitted Carrados, with humorous appreciation. "I wonder," he added speculatively, "whether it is Creake's peculiar taste usually to spend his week-end holiday in London."

"Eh?" exclaimed Mr. Carlyle, looking at the words again. "By Gad, that's rum, Max. They go to Weston-super-Mare. Why on earth should he want to know about London?"

"I can make a guess, but before we are satisfied I must come here again. Take another look at that kite, Louis. Are there a few yards of string hanging loose from it?"

"Yes, there are."

"Rather thick string – unusually thick for the purpose?"

"Yes, but how do you know?"

As they drove home again Carrados explained, and Mr. Carlyle sat aghast, saying incredulously: "Good God, Max, is it possible?"

An hour later he was satisfied that it was possible. In reply to his inquiry, someone in his office telephoned him the information that "they" had left Paddington by the four-thirty for Weston.

It was more than a week after his introduction to Carrados that Lieutenant Hollyer had a summons to present himself at The Turrets again. He found Mr. Carlyle already there and the two friends awaiting his arrival.

"I stayed in all day after hearing from you this morning, Mr. Carrados," he said, shaking hands. "When I got your second message, I was all ready to walk straight out of the house. That's how I did it in the time. I hope everything is all right?"

"Excellent," replied Carrados. "You'd better have something before we start. We probably have a long and perhaps an exciting night before us."

"And certainly a wet one," assented the lieutenant. "It was thundering over Mulling way as I came along.

"That is why you are here," said his host. "We are waiting for a certain message before we start, and in the meantime, you may as well understand what we expect to happen. As you saw, there is a thunderstorm coming on. The Meteorological Office morning forecast predicted it for the whole of London if the conditions remained. That was why I kept you in readiness. Within an hour it is now inevitable that we shall experience a deluge. Here and there damage will be done to trees and buildings. Here and there a person will probably be struck and killed."

"Yes."

"It is Mr. Creake's intention that his wife should be among the victims."

"I don't exactly follow," said Hollyer, looking from one man to the other. "I quite admit that Creake would be immensely relieved if such a thing did happen, but the chance is surely an absurdly remote one."

"Yet unless we intervene it is precisely what a Coroner's Jury will decide has happened. Do you know whether your brother-in-law has any practical knowledge of electricity, Mr. Hollyer?"

"I cannot say. He was so reserved, and we really knew so little of him – "

"Yet in 1896, an Austin Creake contributed an article on 'Alternating Currents' to the *American Scientific World*. That would argue a fairly intimate acquaintanceship."

"But do you mean that he is going to direct a flash of lightning?"

"Only into the minds of the doctor who conducts the *post-mortem*, and the coroner. This storm, the opportunity for which he has been waiting for weeks, is merely the cloak to his act. The weapon which he has planned to use – scarcely less powerful than lightning but much more tractable – is the high voltage current of electricity that flows along the tram wire at his gate."

"Oh!" exclaimed Lieutenant Hollyer, as the sudden revelation struck him.

"Some time between eleven o'clock tonight – about the hour when your sister goes to bed – and one-thirty in the morning – the time up to which he can rely on the current – Creake will throw a stone up at the balcony window. Most of his preparation has long been made. It only remains for him to connect up a short length to the window handle and a longer one at the other end to tap the live wire. That done, he will wake his wife in the way I have said. The moment she moves the catch of the window – and he has carefully filed its parts to ensure perfect contact – she will be electrocuted as effectually as if she sat in the executioner's chair in Sing Sing Prison."

"But what are we doing here!" exclaimed Hollyer, starting to his feet, pale and horrified. "It is past ten now and anything may happen."

"Quite natural, Mr. Hollyer," said Carrados reassuringly, "but you need have no anxiety. Creake is being watched, the house is being watched, and your sister is as safe as if she slept tonight in Windsor Castle. Be assured that whatever happens, he will not be allowed to complete his scheme. But it is desirable to let him implicate himself to the fullest limit. Your brother-in-law, Mr. Hollyer, is a man with a peculiar capacity for taking pains.

"He is a damned cold-blooded scoundrel!" exclaimed the young officer fiercely. "When I think of Millicent five years ago – "

"Well, for that matter, an enlightened nation has decided that electrocution is the most humane way of removing its superfluous citizens," suggested Carrados mildly. "He is certainly an ingenious-minded gentleman. It is his misfortune that in Mr. Carlyle he was fated to be opposed by an even subtler brain – "

"No, no! Really, Max!" protested the embarrassed gentleman.

"Mr. Hollyer will be able to judge for himself when I tell him that it was Mr. Carlyle who first drew attention to the significance of the abandoned kite," insisted Carrados firmly. "Then, of course, its object

66

became plain to me – as indeed to anyone. For ten minutes, perhaps, a wire must be carried from the overhead line to the chestnut-tree. Creake has everything in his favour, but it is just within possibility that the driver of an inopportune tram might notice the appendage. What of that? Why, for more than a week he has seen a derelict kite with its yards of trailing string hanging in the tree. A very calculating mind, Mr. Hollyer. It would be interesting to know what line of action Mr. Creake has mapped out for himself afterwards. I expect he has half-a-dozen artistic little touches up his sleeve. Possibly he would merely singe his wife's hair, burn her feet with a red-hot poker, shiver the glass of the French window, and be content with that to let well alone. You see, lightning is so varied in its effects that whatever he did or did not do would be right. He is in the impregnable position of the body showing all the symptoms of death by lightning shock and nothing else but lightning to account for it – a dilated eye, heart contracted in systole, bloodless lungs shrunk to a third the normal weight, and all the rest of it. When he has removed a few outward traces of his work, Creake might quite safely 'discover' his dead wife and rush off for the nearest doctor. Or he may have decided to arrange a convincing alibi, and creep away, leaving the discovery to another. We shall never know. He will make no confession."

"I wish it was well over," admitted Hollyer. "I'm not particularly jumpy, but this gives me a touch of the creeps."

"Three more hours at the worst, Lieutenant," said Carrados cheerfully. "A-ha – something is coming through now."

He went to the telephone and received a message from one quarter. Then made another connection and talked for a few minutes with someone else.

"Everything working smoothly," he remarked between times over his shoulder. "Your sister has gone to bed, Mr. Hollyer."

Then he turned to the house telephone and distributed his orders.

"So we," he concluded, "must get up."

By the time they were ready, a large closed motor car was waiting. The lieutenant thought he recognized Parkinson in the well-swathed form beside the driver, but there was no temptation to linger for a second on the steps. Already the stinging rain had lashed the drive into the semblance of a frothy estuary. All round the lightning jagged its course through the incessant tremulous glow of more distant lightning, while the thunder only ceased its muttering to turn at close quarters and crackle viciously.

"One of the few things I regret missing," remarked Carrados tranquilly. "But I hear a good deal of colour in it."

The car slushed its way down to the gate, lurched a little heavily across the dip into the road, and, steadying as it came upon the straight, began to hum contentedly along the deserted highway.

"We are not going direct?" suddenly inquired Hollyer, after they had travelled perhaps half-a-dozen miles. The night was bewildering enough but he had the sailor's gift for location.

"No – through Hunscott Green and then by a field-path to the orchard at the back," replied Carrados. "Keep a sharp look out for the man with the lantern about here, Harris," he called through the tube.

"Something flashing just ahead, sir," came the reply, and the car slowed down and stopped.

Carrados dropped the near window as a man in glistening waterproof stepped from the shelter of a lich-gate and approached.

"Inspector Beedel, sir," said the stranger, looking into the car.

"Quite right, Inspector," said Carrados. "Get in."

"I have a man with me, sir."

"We can find room for him as well."

"We are very wet."

"So shall we all be soon."

The lieutenant changed his seat and the two burly forms took places side by side. In less than five minutes the car stopped again, this time in a grassy country lane.

"Now we have to face it," announced Carrados. "The inspector will show us the way."

The car slid round and disappeared into the night, while Beedel led the party to a stile in the hedge. A couple of fields brought them to the Brookbend boundary. There a figure stood out of the black foliage, exchanged a few words with their guide, and piloted them along the shadows of the orchard to the back door of the house.

"You will find a broken pane near the catch of the scullery window," said the blind man.

"Right, sir," replied the inspector. "I have it. Now who goes through?"

"Mr. Hollyer will open the door for us. I'm afraid you must take off your boots and all wet things, Lieutenant. We cannot risk a single spot inside."

They waited until the back door opened, then each one divested himself in a similar manner and passed into the kitchen, where the remains of a fire still burned. The man from the orchard gathered together the discarded garments and disappeared again"

Carrados turned to the lieutenant.

"A rather delicate job for you now, Mr. Hollyer. I want you to go up to your sister, wake her, and get her into another room with as little fuss as possible. Tell her as much as you think fit and let her understand that her very life depends on absolute stillness when she is alone. Don't be unduly hurried, but not a glimmer of a light, please."

Ten minutes passed by the measure of the battered old alarum on the dresser shelf before the young man returned.

"I've had rather a time of it," he reported, with a nervous laugh, "but I think it will be all right now. She is in the spare room."

"Then we will take our places. You and Parkinson come with me to the bedroom. Inspector, you have your own arrangements. Mr. Carlyle will be with you."

They dispersed silently about the house. Hollyer glanced apprehensively at the door of the spare room as they passed it but within was as quiet as the grave. Their room lay at the other end of the passage.

"You may as well take your place in the bed now, Hollyer," directed Carrados when they were inside and the door closed. "Keep well down among the clothes. Creake has to get up on the balcony, you know, and he will probably peep through the window, but he dare come no farther. Then when he begins to throw up stones slip on this dressing-gown of your sister's. I'll tell you what to do after."

The next sixty minutes drew out into the longest hour that the lieutenant had ever known. Occasionally he heard a whisper pass between the two men who stood behind the window curtains, but he could see nothing. Then Carrados threw a guarded remark in his direction.

"He is in the garden now."

Something scraped slightly against the outer wall. But the night was full of wilder sounds, and in the house the furniture and the boards creaked and sprung between the yawling of the wind among the chimneys, the rattle of the thunder, and the pelting of the rain. It was a time to quicken the steadiest pulse, and when the crucial moment came, when a pebble suddenly rang against the pane with a sound that the tense waiting magnified into a shivering crash, Hollyer leapt from the bed on the instant.

"Easy, easy," warned Carrados feelingly. "We will wait for another knock." He passed something across. "Here is a rubber glove. I have cut the wire but you had better put it on. Stand just for a moment at the window, move the catch so that it can blow open a little, and drop immediately. Now."

Another stone had rattled against the glass. For Hollyer to go through his part was the work merely of seconds, and with a few touches Carrados spread the dressing-gown to more effective disguise about the extended form. But an unforeseen and in the circumstances rather horrible interval followed, for Creake, in accordance with some detail of his never-revealed plan, continued to shower missile after missile against the panes until even the unimpressionable Parkinson shivered.

"The last act," whispered Carrados, a moment after the throwing had ceased. "He has gone round to the back. Keep as you are. We take cover now." He pressed behind the arras of an extemporized wardrobe, and the spirit of emptiness and desolation seemed once more to reign over the lonely house.

From half-a-dozen places of concealment ears were straining to catch the first guiding sound. He moved very stealthily, burdened, perhaps, by some strange scruple in the presence of the tragedy that he had not feared to contrive, paused for a moment at the bedroom door, then opened it very quietly, and in the fickle light read the consummation of his hopes.

"At last!" they heard the sharp whisper drawn from his relief. "At last!"

He took another step and two shadows seemed to fall upon him from behind, one on either side. With primitive instinct a cry of terror and surprise escaped him as he made a desperate movement to wrench himself free, and for a short second he almost succeeded in dragging one hand into a pocket. Then his wrists slowly came together and the handcuffs closed.

"I am Inspector Beedel," said the man on his right side. "You are charged with the attempted murder of your wife, Millicent Creake."

"You are mad," retorted the miserable creature, falling into a desperate calmness. "She has been struck by lightning."

"No, you blackguard, she hasn't," wrathfully exclaimed his brother-in-law, jumping up. "Would you like to see her?"

"I also have to warn you," continued the inspector impassively, "that anything you say may be used as evidence against you."

A startled cry from the farther end of the passage arrested their attention.

"Mr. Carrados," called Hollyer. "Oh, come at once."

At the open door of the other bedroom stood the lieutenant, his eyes still turned towards something in the room beyond, a little empty bottle in his hand.

"Dead!" he exclaimed tragically, with a sob. "With this beside her. Dead just when she would have been free of the brute."

The blind man passed into the room, sniffed the air, and laid a gentle hand on the pulseless heart.

"Yes," he replied. "That, Hollyer, does not always appeal to the woman, strange to say."

70

The Clever Mrs. Straithwaite

M r. Carlyle had arrived at The Turrets in the very best possible spirits. Everything about him, from his immaculate white spats to the choice gardenia in his buttonhole, from the brisk decision with which he took the front-door steps to the bustling importance with which he had positively brushed Parkinson aside at the door of the library, proclaimed consequence and the extremely good terms on which he stood with himself.

"Prepare yourself, Max," he exclaimed. "If I hinted at a case of exceptional delicacy that will certainly interest you by its romantic possibilities –?"

"I should have the liveliest misgivings. Ten to one it would be a jewel mystery," hazarded Carrados, as his friend paused with the point of his communication withheld, after the manner of a quizzical youngster with a promised bon-bon held behind his back. "If you made any more of it I should reluctantly be forced to the conclusion that the case involved a society scandal connected with a priceless pearl necklace."

Mr. Carlyle's face fell.

"Then it is in the papers, after all?" he said, with an air of disappointment.

"What is in the papers, Louis?."

"Some hint of the fraudulent insurance of the Honourable Mrs. Straithwaite's pearl necklace," replied Carlyle.

"Possibly," admitted Carrados. "But so far I have not come across it."

Mr. Carlyle stared at his friend, and marching up to the table brought his hand down on it with an arresting slap.

"Then what in the name of goodness are you talking about, may I ask?" he demanded caustically. "If you know nothing of the Straithwaite affair, Max, what other pearl necklace case are you referring to?"

Carrados assumed the air of mild deprecation with which he frequently apologized for a blind man venturing to make a discovery.

"A philosopher once made the remark – "

"Had it anything to do with Mrs. Straithwaite's – the Honourable Mrs. Straithwaite's – pearl necklace? And let me warn you, Max, that I have read a good deal both of Mill and Spencer at odd times."

"It was neither Mill nor Spencer. He had a German name, so I will not mention it. He made the observation, which, of course, we recognize as an obvious commonplace when once it has been expressed, that in order to have an accurate knowledge of what a man will do on any occasion it is only necessary to study a single characteristic action of his."

71

"Utterly impracticable," declared Mr. Carlyle.

"I therefore knew that when you spoke of a case of exceptional interest to me, what you really meant, Louis, was a case of exceptional interest to you."

Mr. Carlyle's sudden thoughtful silence seemed to admit that possibly there might be something in the point.

"By applying, almost unconsciously, the same useful rule, I became aware that a mystery connected with a valuable pearl necklace and a beautiful young society belle would appeal the most strongly to your romantic imagination."

"Romantic! I, romantic? Thirty-five and a private inquiry agent! You are – positively feverish, Max."

"Incurably romantic – or you would have got over it by now: The worst kind."

"Max, this may prove a most important and interesting case. Will you be serious and discuss it?"

"Jewel cases are rarely either important or interesting. Pearl necklace mysteries, in nine cases out of ten, spring from the miasma of social pretence and vapid competition and only concern people who do not matter in the least. The only attractive thing about them is the name. They are so barren of originality that a criminological Linnæus could classify them with absolute nicety. I'll tell you what – we'll draw up a set of tables giving the solution to every possible pearl necklace case for the next twenty-one years."

"We will do any mortal thing you like, Max, if you will allow Parkinson to administer a bromo-seltzer and then enable me to meet the officials of the Direct Insurance without a blush."

For three minutes Carrados picked his unerring way among the furniture as he paced the room silently but with irresolution in his face. Twice his hand went to a paper-covered book lying on his desk, and twice he left it untouched.

"Have you ever been in the lion house at feeding-time, Louis?" he demanded abruptly.

"In the very remote past, possibly," admitted Mr. Carlyle guardedly.

"As the hour approaches, it is impossible to interest the creatures with any other suggestion than that of raw meat. You came a day too late, Louis." He picked up the book and skimmed it adroitly into Mr. Carlyle's hands. "I have already scented the gore, and tasted in imagination the joy of tearing choice morsels from other similarly obsessed animals.

"'*Catalogue des monnaies grecques et romaines,*'" read the gentleman. "'*To be sold by auction at the Hotel Drouet, Paris, salle 8,*

72

April the 24th, 25th, etc.' Hmm." He turned to the plates of photogravure illustration which gave an air to the volume. "This is an event, I suppose?"

"It is the sort of dispersal we get about once in three years," replied Carrados. "I seldom attend the little sales, but I save up and then have a week's orgy."

"And when do you go?"

"Today. By the afternoon boat – Folkestone. I have already taken rooms at Mascot's. I'm sorry it has fallen so inopportunely, Louis."

Mr. Carlyle rose to the occasion with a display of extremely gentlemanly feeling – which had the added merit of being quite genuine.

"My dear chap, your regrets only serve to remind me how much I owe to you already. *Bon voyage*, and the most desirable of *Eu – Eu –* well, perhaps it would be safer to say, of Kimons, for your collection."

"I suppose," pondered Carrados, "this insurance business might have led to other profitable connexions?"

"That is quite true," admitted his friend. "I have been trying for some time – but do not think any more of it, Max."

"What time is it?" demanded Carrados suddenly.

"Eleven-twenty-five."

"Good. Has any officious idiot had anyone arrested?"

"No, it is only – "

"Never mind. Do you know much of the case?"

"Practically nothing as yet, unfortunately. I came – "

"Excellent. Everything is on our side. Louis, I won't go this afternoon – I will put off till the night boat from Dover. That will give us nine hours."

"Nine hours?" repeated the mystified Carlyle, scarcely daring to put into thought the scandalous inference that Carrados's words conveyed.

"Nine full hours. A pearl necklace case that cannot at least be left straight after nine hours' work will require a column to itself in our chart. Now, Louis, where does this Direct Insurance live?"

Carlyle had allowed his blind friend to persuade him into – as they had seemed at the beginning – many mad enterprises. But none had ever, in the light of his own experience, seemed so foredoomed to failure as when, at eleven-thirty, Carrados ordered his luggage to be on the platform of Charing Cross Station at eight-fifty and then turned light-heartedly to the task of elucidating the mystery of Mrs. Straithwaite's pearl necklace in the interval.

The head office of the Direct and Intermediate Insurance Company proved to be in Victoria Street. Thanks to Carrados's speediest car, they entered the building as the clocks of Westminster were striking twelve, but for the next twenty minutes they were consigned to the general office while Mr. Carlyle fumed and displayed his watch ostentatiously. At last a clerk slid off his stool by the speaking-tube and approached them.

"Mr. Carlyle?" he said. "The General Manager will see you now, but as he has another appointment in ten minutes, he will be glad if you will make your business as short as possible. This way, please."

Mr. Carlyle bit his lip at the pompous formality of the message, but he was too experienced to waste any words about it, and with a mere nod he followed, guiding his friend until they reached the Manager's room. But, though subservient to circumstance, he was far from being negligible when he wished to create an impression."Mr. Carrados has been good enough to give us a consultation over this small affair," he said, with just the necessary touches of deference and condescension that it was impossible either to miss or to resent. "Unfortunately he can do little more, as he has to leave almost at once to direct an important case in Paris."

The General Manager conveyed little, either in his person or his manner, of the brisk precision that his message seemed to promise. The name of Carrados struck him as being somewhat familiar – something a little removed from the routine of his business and a matter therefore that he could unbend over. He continued to stand comfortably before his office fire, making up by a tolerant benignity of his hard and bulbous eye for the physical deprivation that his attitude entailed on his visitors.

"Paris, egad?" he grunted. "Something in your line that France can take from us since the days of – What's-his-name – Vidocq, eh? Clever fellow, that, what? Wasn't it about him and the Purloined Letter?"

Carrados smiled discreetly.

"Capital, wasn't it?" he replied. "But there is something else that Paris can learn from London, more in your way, sir. Often when I drop in to see the principal of one of their chief houses or the head of a Government department, we fall into an entertaining discussion of this or that subject that may be on the tapis. 'Ah, Monsieur,' I say, after perhaps half-an-hour's conversation, 'it is very amiable of you and sometimes I regret our insular methods, but it is not thus that great businesses are formed. At home, if I call upon one of our princes of industry – a railway director, a merchant, or the head of one of our leading insurance companies – nothing will tempt him for a moment from the stern outline of the business in hand. You are too complaisant. The merest gossip takes advantage of you.'"

"That's quite true," admitted the General Manager, occupying the revolving chair at his desk and assuming a serious and very determined expression. "Slackers, I call them. Now, Mr. Carlyle, where are we in this business?"

"I have your letter of yesterday. We should naturally like all the particulars you can give us."

The Manager threw open a formidable-looking volume with an immense display of energy, sharply flattened some typewritten pages that had ventured to raise their heads, and lifted an impressive finger.

"We start here, the 27th of January. On that day Karsfeld, the Princess Street jeweller, y'know, who acted as our jewellery assessor, forwards a proposal of the Hon. Mrs. Straithwaite to insure a pearl necklace against theft. Says that he has had an opportunity of examining it and passes it at five-thousand pounds. That business goes through in the ordinary way: The premium is paid and the policy taken out.

"A couple of months later Karsfeld has a little unpleasantness with us and resigns. Resignation accepted. We have nothing against him, you understand. At the same time, there is an impression among the directors that he has been perhaps a little too easy in his ways, a little too – let us say, *expansive*, in some of his valuations and too accommodating to his own clients in recommending to us business of a – well – speculative basis. Business that we do not care about and which we now feel is foreign to our traditions as a firm. However – " The General Manager threw apart his stubby hands as though he would shatter any fabric of criminal intention that he might be supposed to be insidiously constructing. " – that is the extent of our animadversion against Karsfeld. There are no irregularities and you may take it from me that the man is all right."

"You would propose accepting the fact that a five-thousand-pound necklace was submitted to him?" suggested Mr. Carlyle.

"I should," acquiesced the Manager, with a weighty nod. "Still – this brings us to April the third – this break, so to speak, occurring in our routine, it seemed a good opportunity for us to assure ourselves on one or two points. Mr. Bellitzer – you know Bellitzer, of course. Know of him, I should say – was appointed vice. Karsfeld and we wrote to certain of our clients, asking them – as our policies entitled us to do – as a matter of form to allow Mr. Bellitzer to confirm the assessment of his predecessor. Wrapped it up in silver paper, of course. Said it would certify the present value and be a guarantee that would save them some formalities in case of ensuing claim, and so on. Among others, wrote to the Hon. Mrs. Straithwaite to that effect – April fourth. Here is her reply of three days later. Sorry to disappoint us, but the necklace has just been sent to her bank for custody as she is on the point of leaving town. Also scarcely sees that it is necessary in her case as the insurance was only taken so recently."

"That is dated April the seventh?" inquired Mr. Carlyle, busy with pencil and pocket-book.

"April seventh," repeated the Manager, noting this conscientiousness with an approving glance and then turning to regard questioningly the indifferent attitude of his other visitor. "That put us on our guard – naturally. Wrote by return regretting the necessity and suggesting that a line to her bankers, authorizing them to show us the necklace, would meet the case and save her any personal trouble. Interval of a week. Her reply, April sixteenth. Thursday last. Circumstances have altered her plans and she has returned to London sooner than she expected. Her jewel-case has been returned from the bank, and will we send our man round – 'our man', Mr. Carlyle! – on Saturday morning not later than twelve, please."

The Manager closed the record book, with a sweep of his hand cleared his desk for revelations, and leaning forward in his chair fixed Mr. Carlyle with a pragmatic eye.

"On Saturday, Mr. Bellitzer goes to Luneburg Mansions and the Hon. Mrs. Straithwaite shows him the necklace. He examines it carefully, assesses its insurable value up to five-thousand, two-hundred-and-fifty pounds, and reports us to that effect. But he reports something else, Mr. Carlyle. It is *not* the necklace that the lady had insured.

"Not the necklace?" echoed Mr. Carlyle.

"No. In spite of the number of pearls and a general similarity, there are certain technical differences, well known to experts, that made the fact indisputable. The Hon. Mrs. Straithwaite has been guilty of misrepresentation. Possibly she has no fraudulent intention. We are willing to pay to find out. That's your business."

Mr. Carlyle made a final note and put away his book with an air of decision that could not fail to inspire confidence.

"Tomorrow," he said, "we shall perhaps be able to report something."

"Hope so," vouchsafed the Manager. "Morning."

From his position near the window, Carrados appeared to wake up to the fact that the interview was over.

"But so far," he remarked blandly, with his eyes towards the great man in the chair, "you have told us nothing of the theft."

The Manager regarded the speaker dumbly for a moment and then turned to Mr. Carlyle.

"What does he mean?" he demanded pungently.

But for once Mr. Carlyle's self-possession had forsaken him. He recognized that somehow Carrados had been guilty of an appalling lapse, by which his reputation for prescience was wrecked in that quarter forever, and at the catastrophe his very ears began to exude embarrassment.

In the awkward silence Carrados himself seemed to recognize that something was amiss.

"We appear to be at cross-purposes," he observed. "I inferred that the disappearance of the necklace would be the essence of our investigation."

"Have I said a word about it disappearing?" demanded the Manager, with a contempt-laden raucity that he made no pretence of softening. "You don't seem to have grasped the simple facts about the case, Mr. Carrados. Really, I hardly think – Oh, come in!"

There had been a knock at the door, then another. A clerk now entered with an open telegram.

"Mr. Longworth wished you to see this at once, sir."

"We may as well go," whispered Mr. Carlyle with polite depression to his colleague.

"Here, wait a minute," said the Manager, who had been biting his thumb-nail over the telegram. "No, not you – " to the lingering clerk. "You clear." Much of the embarrassment that had troubled Mr. Carlyle a minute before seemed to have got into the Manager's system. "I don't understand this," he confessed awkwardly. "It's from Bellitzer. He wires: '*Have just heard alleged robbery Straithwaite pearls. Advise strictest investigation.*'"

Mr. Carlyle suddenly found it necessary to turn to the wall and consult a highly coloured lithographic inducement to insure. Mr. Carrados alone remained to meet the Manager's constrained glance.

"Still, he tells us really nothing about the theft," he remarked sociably.

"No," admitted the Manager, experiencing some little difficulty with his breathing, "he does not."

"Well, we still hope to be able to report something tomorrow. Goodbye."

It was with an effort that Mr. Carlyle straightened himself sufficiently to take leave of the Manager. Several times in the corridor he stopped to wipe his eyes.

"Max, you unholy fraud," he said, when they were outside. "You knew all the time."

"No. I told you that I knew nothing of it," replied Carrados frankly. "I am absolutely sincere."

"Then all I can say is, that I see a good many things happen that I don't believe in."

Carrados's reply was to hold out a coin to a passing newsboy and to hand the purchase to his friend who was already in the car.

"There is a slang injunction to 'keep your eyes skinned'. That being out of my power, I habitually 'keep my ears skinned'. You would be surprised to know how very little you hear, Louis, and how much you miss. In the last five minutes up there I have had three different newsboys' account of this development."

"By Jupiter, she hasn't waited long!" exclaimed Mr. Carlyle, referring eagerly to the headlines. "'*Pearl Necklace Sensatoin. Society Lady's £5,000 Trinket Disappears.*' Things are moving. Where next, Max?"

"It is now a quarter-to-one," replied Carrados, touching the fingers of his watch. "We may as well lunch on the strength of this new turn. Parkinson will have finished packing. I can telephone him to come to us at Merrick's in case I require him. Buy all the papers, Louis, and we will collate the points."

The undoubted facts that survived a comparison were few and meagre, for in each case a conscientious journalist had touched up a few vague or doubtful details according to his own ideas of probability. All agreed that on Tuesday evening – it was now Thursday – Mrs. Straithwaite had formed one of a party that had occupied a box at the new Metropolitan Opera House to witness the performance of *La Pucella*, and that she had been robbed of a set of pearls valued in round figures at five-thousand pounds. There agreement ended. One version represented the theft as taking place at the theatre. Another asserted that at the last moment the lady had decided not to wear the necklace that evening and that its abstraction had been cleverly effected from the flat during her absence. Into a third account came an ambiguous reference to Markhams, the well-known jewellers, and a conjecture that their loss would certainly be covered by insurance.

Mr. Carlyle, who had been picking out the salient points of the narratives, threw down the last paper with an impatient shrug.

"Why in Heaven's name have we Markhams coming into it now?" he demanded. "What have they to lose by it, Max? What do you make of the thing?"

"There is the second genuine string – the one Bellitzer saw. That belongs to someone."

"By Gad, that's true – only five days ago, too. But what does our lady stand to make by that being stolen?"

Carrados was staring into obscurity between an occasional moment of attention to his cigarette or coffee.

"By this time the lady probably stands to wish she was well out of it," he replied thoughtfully. "Once you have set this sort of stone rolling and it has got beyond you – " He shook his head.

"It has become more intricate than you expected?" suggested Carlyle, in order to afford his friend an opportunity of withdrawing.

Carrados pierced the intention and smiled affectionately.

"My dear Louis," he said, "one-fifth of the mystery is already solved."

"One-fifth? How do you arrive at that?"

"Because it is one-twenty-five and we started at eleven-thirty."

He nodded to their waiter, who was standing three tables away, and paid the bill. Then with perfect gravity he permitted Mr. Carlyle to lead him by the arm into the street, where their car was waiting, Parkinson already there in attendance.

"Sure I can be of no further use?" asked Carlyle. Carrados had previously indicated that after lunch he would go on alone, but, because he was largely sceptical of the outcome, the professional man felt guiltily that he was deserting. "Say the word?"

Carrados smiled and shook his head. Then he leaned across.

"I am going to the opera house now. Then, possibly, to talk to Markham a little. If I have time I must find a man who knows the Straithwaites, and after that I may look up Inspector Beedel if he is at the Yard. That is as far as I can see yet, until I call at Luneburg Mansions. Come round on the third anyway."

"Dear old chap," murmured Mr. Carlyle, as the car edged its way ahead among the traffic. "Marvellous shots he makes!"

In the meanwhile, at Luneburg Mansions, Mrs. Straithwaite had been passing anything but a pleasant day. She had awakened with a headache and an overnight feeling that there was some unpleasantness to be gone on with. That it did not amount to actual fear was due to the enormous self-importance and the incredible ignorance which ruled the butterfly brain of the young society beauty – for in spite of three years' experience of married life, Stephanie Straithwaite was as yet on the enviable side of two-and-twenty.

Anticipating an early visit from a particularly obnoxious sister-in-law, she had remained in bed until after lunch in order to be able to deny herself with the more conviction. Three journalists who would have afforded her the mild excitement of being interviewed had called and been in turn put off with polite regrets by her husband. The objectionable sister-in-law postponed her visit until the afternoon and for more than an hour Stephanie "suffered agonies". When the visitor had left and the martyred hostess announced her intention of flying immediately to the consoling society of her own bridge circle, Straithwaite had advised her, with some significance, to wait for a lead. The unhappy lady cast herself bodily down upon a couch and asked whether she was to become a nun. Straithwaite merely shrugged his shoulders and remembered a club engagement. Evidently there was no need for him to become a monk: Stephanie followed him down the hall, arguing and protesting. That was how they came jointly to encounter Carrados at the door.

79

"I have come from the Direct Insurance in the hope of being able to see Mrs. Straithwaite," he explained, when the door opened rather suddenly before he had knocked. "My name is Carrados – Max Carrados."

There was a moment of hesitation all round. Then Stephanie read difficulties in the straightening lines of her husband's face and rose joyfully to the occasion.

"Oh yes. Come in, Mr. Carrados," she exclaimed graciously. "We are not quite strangers, you know. You found out something for Aunt Pigs. I forget what, but she was most frantically impressed."

"Lady Poges," enlarged Straithwaite, who had stepped aside and was watching the development with slow, calculating eyes. "But, I say, you are blind, aren't you?"

Carrados's smiling admission turned the edge of Mrs. Straithwaite's impulsive, "Teddy!"

"But I get along all right," he added. "I left my man down in the car and I found your door first shot, you see."

The references reminded the velvet-eyed little mercenary that the man before her had the reputation of being quite desirably rich, his queer taste merely an eccentric hobby. The consideration made her resolve to be quite her nicest possible, as she led the way to the drawing room. Then Teddy, too, had been horrid beyond words and must be made to suffer in the readiest way that offered.

"Teddy is just going out and I was to be left in solitary bereavement if you had not appeared," she explained airily. "It wasn't very compy only to come to see me on business by the way, Mr. Carrados, but if those are your only terms I must agree."

Straithwaite, however, did not seem to have the least intention of going. He had left his hat and stick in the hall and he now threw his yellow gloves down on a table and took up a negligent position on the arm of an easy-chair.

"The thing is, where do we stand?" he remarked tentatively.

"That is the attitude of the insurance company, I imagine," replied Carrados.

"I don't see that the company has any standing in the matter. We haven't reported any loss to them and we are not making any claim, so far. That ought to be enough."

"I assume that they act on general inference," explained Carrados. "A limited liability company is not subtle, Mrs. Straithwaite. This one knows that you have insured a five-thousand-pound pearl necklace with it, and when it becomes a matter of common knowledge that you have had one answering to that description stolen, it jumps to the conclusion that they are one and the same."

"But they aren't – worse luck," explained the hostess. "This was a string that I let Markhams send me to see if I would keep."

"The one that Bellitzer saw last Saturday?"

"Yes," admitted Mrs. Straithwaite quite simply.

Straithwaite glanced sharply at Carrados and then turned his eyes with lazy indifference to his wife.

"My dear Stephanie, what are you thinking of?" he drawled. "Of course those could not have been Markhams' pearls. Not knowing that you are much too clever to do such a foolish thing, Mr. Carrados will begin to think that you have had fraudulent designs upon his company."

Whether the tone was designed to exasperate or merely fell upon a fertile soil, Stephanie threw a hateful little glance in his direction.

"I don't care," she exclaimed recklessly. "I haven't the least little objection in the world to Mr. Carrados knowing exactly how it happened."

Carrados put in an instinctive word of warning, even raised an arresting hand, but the lady was much too excited, too voluble, to be denied.

"It doesn't really matter in the least, Mr. Carrados, because nothing came of it," she explained. "There never were any real pearls to be insured. It would have made no difference to the company, because I did not regard this as an ordinary insurance from the first. It was to be a loan."

"A loan?" repeated Carrados."

"Yes. I shall come into heaps and heaps of money in a few years' time under Prin-Prin's will. Then I should pay back whatever had been advanced."

"But would it not have been better – simpler – to have borrowed purely on the anticipation?"

"We have," explained the lady eagerly. "We have borrowed from all sorts of people, and both Teddy and I have signed heaps and heaps of papers, until now no one will lend any more."

The thing was too tragically grotesque to be laughed at. Carrados turned his face from one to the other and by ear, and by even finer perceptions, he focussed them in his mind – the delicate, feather-headed beauty, with the heart of a cat and the irresponsibility of a kitten, eye and mouth already hardening under the stress of her frantic life, and, across the room, her debonair consort, whose lank pose and nonchalant attitude towards the situation Carrados had not yet categorized.

Straithwaite's dry voice, with its habitual drawl, broke into his reflection.

"I don't suppose for a moment that you either know or care what this means, my dear girl, but I will proceed to enlighten you. It means the extreme probability that unless you can persuade Mr. Carrados to hold his tongue, you, and – without prejudice – I also, will get two years' hard. And yet, with unconscious but consummate artistry, it seems to me that you have perhaps done the trick, for, unless I am mistaken, Mr. Carrados will find himself unable to take advantage of your guileless confidence, whereas he would otherwise have quite easily found out all he wanted."

"That is the most utter nonsense, Teddy!" cried Stephanie, with petulant indignation. She turned to Carrados with the assurance of meeting understanding. "We know Mr. Justice Enderleigh very well indeed, and if there was any bother I should not have the least difficulty in getting him to take the case privately and in explaining everything to him. But why should there be? Why indeed?" A brilliant little new idea possessed her. "Do you know any of these insurance people at all intimately, Mr. Carrados?"

"The General Manager and I are on terms that almost justify us in addressing each other as 'silly ass'," admitted Carrados.

"There you see, Teddy, you needn't have been in a funk. Mr. Carrados would put everything right. Let me tell you exactly how I had arranged it. I dare say you know that insurances are only too pleased to pay for losses: It gives them an advertisement. Freddy Tantroy told me so, and his father is a director of hundreds of companies. Only, of course, it must be done quite regularly. Well, for months and months we had both been most frightfully hard up, and, unfortunately, everyone else – at least all our friends – seemed just as stony. I had been absolutely racking my poor brain for an idea when I remembered papa's wedding present. It was a string of pearls that he sent me from Vienna, only a month before he died – not real, of course, because poor papa was always quite utterly on the verge himself, but very good imitation and in perfect taste. Otherwise, I am sure papa would rather have sent a silver penwiper, for although he had to live abroad because of what people said, his taste was simply exquisite and he was most romantic in his ideas. What do you say, Teddy?"

"Nothing, dear. It was only my throat ticking."

"I wore the pearls often and millions of people had seen them. Of course our own people knew about them, but others took it for granted that they were genuine for me to be wearing them. Teddy will tell you that I was almost babbling in delirium, things were becoming so ghastly, when an idea occurred. Tweety – she's a cousin of Teddy's, but quite an aged person – has a whole coffer full of jewels that she never wears and I knew that there was a necklace very like mine among them. She was going almost immediately to Africa for some shooting, so I literally flew into the wilds of Surrey and begged her on my knees to lend me her pearls for the Lycester House dance. When I got back with them I stamped on the clasp and took it at once to Karsfeld in Princess Street. I told him they were only

82

paste but I thought they were rather good and I wanted them by the next day. And of course he looked at them, and then looked again, and then asked me if I was certain they were imitation, and I said, Well, we had never thought twice about it, because poor papa was always rather chronic, only certainly he did occasionally have fabulous streaks at the tables, and finally, like a great owl, Karsfeld said:

"'I am happy to be able to congratulate you, Madam. They are undoubtedly Bombay pearls of very fine Orient. They are certainly worth five-thousand pounds.'"

From this point Mrs. Straithwaite's narrative ran its slangy, obvious course. The insurance effected – on the strict understanding of the lady with herself that it was merely a novel form of loan, and after satisfying her mind on Freddy Tantroy's authority that the Direct and Intermediate could stand a temporary loss of five-thousand pounds – the genuine pearls were returned to the cousin in the wilds of Surrey and Stephanie continued to wear the counterfeit. A decent interval was allowed to intervene and the plot was on the point of maturity when the company's request for a scrutiny fell like a thunderbolt. With many touching appeals to Mr. Carrados to picture her frantic distraction, with appropriate little gestures of agony and despair, Stephanie described her absolute prostration, her subsequent wild scramble through the jewel stocks of London to find a substitute. The danger over, it became increasingly necessary to act without delay, not only to anticipate possible further curiosity on the part of the insurance, but in order to secure the means with which to meet an impending obligation held over them by an inflexibly obdurate Hebrew.

The evening of the previous Tuesday was to be the time. The opera house, during the performance of *La Pucella*, the place. Straithwaite, who was not interested in that precise form of drama, would not be expected to be present, but with a false moustache and a few other touches which his experience as an amateur placed within his easy reach, he was to occupy a stall, an end stall somewhere beneath his wife's box. At an agreed signal Stephanie would jerk open the catch of the necklace, and as she leaned forward the ornament would trickle off her neck and disappear into the arena beneath. Straithwaite, the only one prepared for anything happening, would have no difficulty in securing it. He would look up quickly as if to identify the box, and with the jewels in his hand walk deliberately out into the passage. Before anyone had quite realized what was happening he would have left the house.

Carrados turned his face from the woman to the man.

"This scheme commended itself to you, Mr. Straithwaite?"

"Well, you see, Stephanie is so awfully clever that I took it for granted that the thing would go all right."

"And three days before, Bellitzer had already reported misrepresentation and that two necklaces had been used!"

"Yes," admitted Straithwaite, with an air of reluctant candour, "I had a suspicion that Stephanie's native ingenuity rather fizzled there. You know, Stephanie dear, there is a difference, it seems, between Bombay and Californian pearls."

"The wretch!" exclaimed the girl, grinding her little teeth vengefully. "And we gave him champagne!"

"But nothing came of it, so it doesn't matter?" prompted Straithwaite.

"Except that now Markhams' pearls have gone and they are hinting at all manner of diabolical things," she wrathfully reminded him.

"True," he confessed. "That is by way of a sequel, Mr. Carrados. I will endeavour to explain that part of the incident, for even yet Stephanie seems unable to do me justice."

He detached himself from the arm of the chair and lounged across the room to another chair, where he took up exactly the same position.

"On the fatal evening I duly made my way to the theatre – a little late, so as to take my seat unobserved. After I had got the general hang I glanced up occasionally until I caught Stephanie's eye, by which I knew that she was there all right and concluded that everything was going along quite jollily. According to arrangement, I was to cross the theatre immediately the first curtain fell and standing opposite Stephanie's box twist my watch chain until it was certain that she had seen me. Then Stephanie was to fan herself three times with her programme. Both, you will see, perfectly innocent operations, and yet conveying to each other the intimation that all was well. Stephanie's idea, of course. After that, I would return to my seat and Stephanie would do her part at the first opportunity in Act II.

"However, we never reached that. Towards the end of the first act something white and noiseless slipped down and fell at my feet. For the moment I thought they were the pearls gone wrong. Then I saw that it was a glove – a lady's glove. Intuition whispered that it was Stephanie's before I touched it. I picked it up and quietly got out. Down among the fingers was a scrap of paper – the corner torn off a programme. On it were pencilled words to this effect:

Something quite unexpected. Can do nothing tonight. Go back at once and wait. May return early. Frightfully worried.

– S.

"You kept the paper, of course?"

"Yes. It is in my desk in the next room. Do you care to see it?"

"Please."

Straithwaite left the room and Stephanie flung herself into a charming attitude of entreaty.

"Mr. Carrados, you will get them back for us, won't you? It would not really matter, only I seem to have signed something and now Markhams threaten to bring an action against us for culpable negligence in leaving them in an empty flat."

"You see," explained Straithwaite, coming back in time to catch the drift of his wife's words, "except to a personal friend like yourself, it is quite impossible to submit these clues. The first one alone would raise embarrassing inquiries. The other is beyond explanation. Consequently I have been obliged to concoct an imaginary burglary in our absence and to drop the necklace case among the rhododendrons in the garden at the back, for the police to find."

"Deeper and deeper," commented Carrados.

"Why, yes. Stephanie and I are finding that out, aren't we, dear? However, here is the first note. Also the glove. Of course I returned immediately. It was Stephanie's strategy and I was under her orders. In something less than half-an-hour I heard a motor car stop outside. Then the bell here rang.

"I think I have said that I was alone. I went to the door and found a man who might have been anything standing there. He merely said: 'Mr. Straithwaite?' and on my nodding handed me a letter. I tore it open in the hall and read it. Then I went into my room and read it again. This is it:

Dear T.,

Absolutely ghastly. We simply must put off tonight. Will explain that later. Now what do you think? Bellitzer is here in the stalls and young K. D. has asked him to join us at supper at the Savoy. It appears that the creature is Something and I suppose the D's want to borrow off him. I can't get out of it and I am literally quaking. Don't you see, he will spot something? Send me the M. string at once and I will change somehow before supper. I am scribbling this in the dark. I have got the Willoughby's man to take it. Don't, don't fail.

– S.

"It is ridiculous, preposterous," snapped Stephanie. "I never wrote a word of it – or the other. There was I, sitting the whole evening. And Teddy – oh, it is maddening!"

"I took it into my room and looked at it closely," continued the unruffled Straithwaite. "Even if I had any reason to doubt, the internal evidence was convincing, but how could I doubt? It read like a continuation of the previous message. The writing was reasonably like Stephanie's under the circumstances, the envelope had obviously been obtained from the box-office of the theatre and the paper itself was a sheet of the programme. A corner was torn off. I put against it the previous scrap and they exactly fitted." The gentleman shrugged his shoulders, stretched his legs with deliberation and walked across the room to look out of the window. "I made them up into a neat little parcel and handed it over," he concluded.

Carrados put down the two pieces of paper which he had been minutely examining with his finger-tips and still holding the glove addressed his small audience collectively.

"The first and most obvious point is that whoever carried out the scheme had more than a vague knowledge of your affairs, not only in general but also relating to this – well, loan, Mrs. Straithwaite."

"Just what I have insisted," agreed Straithwaite. "You hear that, Stephanie?"

"But who is there?" pleaded Stephanie, with weary intonation. "Absolutely no one in the wide world. Not a soul."

"So one is liable to think offhand. Let us go further, however, merely accounting for those who are in a position to have information. There are the officials of the insurance company who suspect something. There is Bellitzer, who perhaps knows a little more. There is the lady in Surrey from whom the pearls were borrowed, a Mr. Tantroy who seems to have been consulted, and, finally, your own servants. All these people have friends, or underlings, or observers. Suppose Mr. Bellitzer's confidential clerk happens to be the sweetheart of your maid?"

"They would still know very little."

"The arc of a circle may be very little, but, given that, it is possible to construct the entire figure. Now your servants, Mrs. Straithwaite? We are accusing no one, of course."

"There is the cook, Mullins. She displayed alarming influenza on Tuesday morning, and although it was most frightfully inconvenient I packed her off home without a moment's delay. I have a horror of the influ. Then Fraser, the parlourmaid. She does my hair – I haven't really got a maid, you know."

"Peter," prompted Straithwaite.

"Oh yes, Beta. She's a daily girl and helps in the kitchen. I have no doubt she is capable of any villainy."

"And all were out on Tuesday evening?"

"Yes. Mullins gone home. Beta left early as there was no dinner, and I told Fraser to take the evening after she had dressed me so that Teddy could make up and get out without being seen."

Carrados turned to his other witness.

"The papers and the glove have been with you ever since?"

"Yes, in my desk."

"Locked?"

"Yes."

"And this glove, Mrs. Straithwaite? There is no doubt that it is yours?"

"I suppose not," she replied. "I never thought. I know that when I came to leave the theatre one had vanished and Teddy had it here."

"That was the first time you missed it?"

"Yes."

"But it might have gone earlier in the evening – mislaid or lost or stolen?"

"I remember taking them off in the box. I sat in the corner farthest from the stage – the front row, of course – and I placed them on the support."

"Where anyone in the next box could abstract one without much difficulty at a favourable moment."

"That is quite likely. But we didn't see anyone in the next box."

"I have half-an-idea that I caught sight of someone hanging back," volunteered Straithwaite.

"Thank you," said Carrados, turning towards him almost gratefully. "That is most important – that you think you saw someone hanging back. Now the other glove, Mrs. Straithwaite: What became of that?"

"An odd glove is not very much good, is it?" said Stephanie. "Certainly I wore it coming back. I think I threw it down somewhere in here. Probably it is still about. We are in a frantic muddle and nothing is being done."

The second glove was found on the floor in a corner. Carrados received it and laid it with the other.

"You use a very faint and characteristic scent, I notice, Mrs. Straithwaite," he observed.

"Yes. It is rather sweet, isn't it? I don't know the name because it is in Russian. A friend in the Embassy sent me some bottles from Petersburg."

"But on Tuesday you supplemented it with something stronger," he continued, raising the gloves delicately one after the other to his face.

"Oh, eucalyptus. Rather," she admitted. "I simply drenched my handkerchief with it."

87

"You have other gloves of the same pattern?"

"Have I? Now let me think! Did you give them to me, Teddy?"

"No," replied Straithwaite from the other end of the room. He had lounged across to the window and his attitude detached him from the discussion. "Didn't Whitstable?" he added shortly.

"Of course. Then there are three pairs, Mr. Carrados, because I never let Bimbi lose more than that to me at once, poor boy."

"I think you are rather tiring yourself out, Stephanie," warned her husband.

Carrados's attention seemed to leap to the voice. Then he turned courteously to his hostess.

"I appreciate that you have had a trying time lately, Mrs. Straithwaite," he said. "Every moment I have been hoping to let you out of the witness box – "

"Perhaps tomorrow – " began Straithwaite, recrossing the room.

"Impossible. I leave town tonight," replied Carrados firmly. "You have three pairs of these gloves, Mrs. Straithwaite. Here is one. The other two –?"

"One pair I have not worn yet. The other – good gracious, I haven't been out since Tuesday! I suppose it is in my glove-box."

"I must see it, please."

Straithwaite opened his mouth, but as his wife obediently rose to her feet to comply he turned sharply away with the word unspoken.

"These are they," she said, returning.

"Mr. Carrados and I will finish our investigation in my room," interposed Straithwaite, with quiet assertiveness. "I should advise you to lie down for half-an-hour, Stephanie, if you don't want to be a nervous wreck tomorrow."

"You must allow the culprit to endorse that good advice, Mrs. Straithwaite," added Carrados. He had been examining the second pair of gloves as they spoke and he now handed them back again. "They are undoubtedly of the same set," he admitted, with extinguished interest, "and so our clue runs out."

"I hope you don't mind," apologized Straithwaite, as he led his guest to his own smoking room. "Stephanie," he confided, becoming more cordial as two doors separated them from the lady, "is a creature of nerves and indiscretions. She forgets. Tonight she will not sleep. Tomorrow she will suffer." Carrados divined the grin. "So shall I!"

"On the contrary, pray accept my regrets," said the visitor. "Besides," he continued, "there is nothing more for me to do here, I suppose . . . ."

"It is a mystery," admitted Straithwaite, with polite agreement. "Will you try a cigarette?"

"Thanks. Can you see if my car is below?" They exchanged cigarettes and stood at the window lighting them

"There is one point, by the way, that may have some significance." Carrados had begun to recross the room and stopped to pick up the two fictitious messages. "You will have noticed that this is the outside sheet of a programme. It is not the most suitable for the purpose. The first inner sheet is more convenient to write on, but there the date appears. You see the inference? The programme was obtained before – "

"Perhaps. Well –?" for Carrados had broken off abruptly and was listening.

"You hear someone coming up the steps?"

"It is the general stairway."

"Mr. Straithwaite, I don't know how far this has gone in other quarters. We may only have a few seconds before we are interrupted."

"What do you mean?"

"I mean that the man who is now on the stairs is a policeman or has worn the uniform. If he stops at your door – "

The heavy tread ceased. Then came the authoritative knock.

"Wait," muttered Carrados, laying his hand impressively on Straithwaite's tremulous arm. "I may recognize the voice."

They heard the servant pass along the hall and the door unlatched. Then caught the jumble of a gruff inquiry.

"Inspector Beedel of Scotland Yard!" The servant repassed their door on her way to the drawing room. "It is no good disguising the fact from you, Mr. Straithwaite, that you may no longer be at liberty. But I am. Is there anything you wish done?"

There was no time for deliberation. Straithwaite was indeed between the unenviable alternatives of the familiar proverb, but, to do him justice, his voice had lost scarcely a ripple of its usual sang-froid.

"Thanks," he replied, taking a small stamped and addressed parcel from his pocket. "You might drop this into some obscure pillar-box, if you will."

"The Markham necklace?"

"Exactly. I was going out to post it when you came."

"I am sure you were."

"And if you could spare five minutes later – if I am here – "

Carrados slid his cigarette-case under some papers on the desk.

"I will call for that," he assented. "Let us say about half-past-eight."

"I am still at large, you see, Mr. Carrados – though after reflecting on the studied formality of the inspector's business here, I imagine that you will scarcely be surprised."

"I have made it a habit," admitted Carrados, "never to be surprised."

"However, I still want to cut a rather different figure in your eyes. You regard me, Mr. Carrados, either as a detected rogue or a repentant ass?"

"Another excellent rule is never to form deductions from uncertainties."

Straithwaite made a gesture of mild impatience.

"You only give me ten minutes. If I am to put my case before you, Mr. Carrados, we cannot fence with phrases . . . Today you have had an exceptional opportunity of penetrating into our mode of life. You will, I do not doubt, have summed up our perpetual indebtedness and the easy credit that our connexion procures. Stephanie's social ambitions and expensive popularity. Her utterly extravagant incapacity to see any other possible existence, and my tacit acquiescence. You will, I know, have correctly gauged her irresponsible, neurotic temperament, and judged the result of it in conflict with my own. What possibly has escaped you, for in society one has to disguise these things, is that I still love my wife.

"When you dare not trust the soundness of your reins you do not try to pull up a bolting horse. For three years I have endeavoured to guide Stephanie round awkward corners with as little visible restraint as possible. When we differ over any project upon which she has set her heart, Stephanie has one strong argument."

"That you no longer love her?"

"Well, perhaps, but more forcibly expressed. She rushes to the top of the building – there are six floors, Mr. Carrados, and we are on the second – and climbing on to the banister she announces her intention of throwing herself down into the basement. In the meanwhile, I have followed her and drag her back again. One day I shall stay where I am and let her do as she intends."

"I hope not," said Carrados gravely.

"Oh, don't be concerned. She will then climb back herself. But it will mark an epoch. It was by that threat that she obtained my acquiescence to this scheme – that and the certainty that she would otherwise go on without me. But I had no intention of allowing her to land herself – to say nothing of us both – behind the bars of a prison if I could help it. And, above all, I wished to cure her of her fatuous delusion that she is clever, in the hope that she may then give up being foolish.

"To fail her on the occasion was merely to postpone the attempt. I conceived the idea of seeming to cooperate and at the same time involving us in what appeared to be a clever counter-fraud. The thought of the real loss will perhaps have a good effect. The publicity will certainly prevent her from daring a second 'theft'. A sordid story, Mr. Carrados," he concluded. "Do not forget your cigarette-case in reality."

The paternal shake of Carrados's head over the recital was neutralized by his benevolent smile.

"Yes, yes," he said. "I think we can classify you, Mr. Straithwaite. One point – the glove?"

"That was an afterthought. I had arranged the whole story and the first note was to be brought to me by an attendant. Then, on my way, in my overcoat pocket I discovered a pair of Stephanie's gloves which she had asked me to carry the day before. The suggestion flashed – how much more convincing if I could arrange for her to seem to drop the writing in that way. As she said, the next box was empty. I merely took possession of it for a few minutes and quietly drew across one of her gloves. And that reminds me – of course there was nothing in it, but your interest in them made me rather nervous."

Carrados laughed outright. Then he stood up and held out his hand.

"Goodnight, Mr. Straithwaite," he said, with real friendliness. "Let me give you the quaker's advice: Don't attempt another conspiracy – but if you do, don't produce a 'pair' of gloves of which one is still suggestive of scent, and the other identifiable with eucalyptus!"

"Oh – !" said Straithwaite.

"Quite so. But at all hazard suppress a second pair that has the same peculiarity. Think over what it must mean. Goodbye."

Twelve minutes later Mr. Carlyle was called to the telephone.

"It is eight-fifty-five and I am at Charing Cross," said a voice he knew. "If you want local colour, contrive an excuse to be with Markham when the first post arrives tomorrow." A few more words followed, and an affectionate valediction.

"One moment, my dear Max, one moment. Do I understand you to say that you will post me on the report of the case from Dover?"

"No, Louis," replied Carrados, with cryptic discrimination. "I only said that I will post you on a report of the case from Dover."

The Last Exploit of
Harry the Actor

The one insignificant fact upon which turned the following incident in the joint experiences of Mr. Carlyle and Max Carrados was merely this: That having called upon his friend just at the moment when the private detective was on the point of leaving his office to go to the safe deposit in Lucas Street, Piccadilly, the blind amateur accompanied him, and for ten minutes amused himself by sitting quite quietly among the palms in the centre of the circular hall while Mr. Carlyle was occupied with his deed-box in one of the little compartments provided for the purpose.

The Lucas Street depository was then (it has since been converted into a picture palace) generally accepted as being one of the strongest places in London. The front of the building was constructed to represent a gigantic safe door, and under the colloquial designation of "The Safe" the place had passed into a synonym for all that was secure and impregnable. Half of the marketable securities in the west of London were popularly reported to have seen the inside of its coffers at one time or another, together with the same generous proportion of family jewels. However exaggerated an estimate this might be, the substratum of truth was solid and auriferous enough to dazzle the imagination. When ordinary safes were being carried bodily away with impunity or ingeniously fused open by the scientifically equipped cracksman, nervous bond-holders turned with relief to the attractions of an establishment whose modest claim was summed up in its telegraphic address: "Impregnable." To it went also the jewel-case between the lady's social engagements, and when in due course "the family" journeyed north – or south, east or west – whenever, in short, the London house was closed, its capacious storerooms received the plate-chest as an established custom. Not a few traders also – jewellers, financiers, dealers in pictures, antiques, and costly *bijouterie*, for instance – constantly used its facilities for any stock that they did not requite immediately to hand.

There was only one entrance to the place, an exaggerated keyhole, to carry out the similitude of the safe-door alluded to. The ground floor was occupied by the ordinary offices of the company. All the strong rooms and safes lay in the steel-cased basement. This was reached both by a lift and by a flight of steps. In either case the visitor found before him a grille of massive proportions. Behind its bars stood a formidable commissionaire who never left his post, his sole duty being to open and close the grille to arriving and departing clients. Beyond this, a short passage led into the round central hall where Carrados was waiting. From this part, other passages radiated off to the vaults and strong rooms, each one barred from the hall by a grille scarcely less ponderous than the first one. The doors of the various private rooms put at the disposal of the company's clients, and that of the manager's office, filled the wall-space between the radiating passages. Everything was very quiet, everything looked very bright, and everything seemed hopelessly impregnable.

"But I wonder?" ran Carrados's dubious reflection as he reached this point.

"Sorry to have kept you so long, my dear Max," broke in Mr. Carlyle's crisp voice. He had emerged from his compartment and was crossing the hall, deed-box in hand. "Another minute and I will be with you."

Carrados smiled and nodded and resumed his former expression, which was merely that of an uninterested gentleman waiting patiently for another. It is something of an attainment to watch closely without betraying undue curiosity, but others of the senses – hearing and smelling, for instance – can be keenly engaged while the observer possibly has the appearance of falling asleep.

"Now," announced Mr. Carlyle, returning briskly to his friend's chair, and drawing on his grey suede gloves.

"You are in no particular hurry?"

"No," admitted the professional man, with the slowness of mild surprise. "Not at all. What do you propose?"

"It is very pleasant here," replied Carrados tranquilly. "Very cool and restful with this armoured steel between us and the dust and scurry of the hot July afternoon above. I propose remaining here for a few minutes longer."

"Certainly," agreed Mr. Carlyle, taking the nearest chair and eyeing Carrados as though he had a shrewd suspicion of something more than met the ear. "I believe some very interesting people rent safes here. We may encounter a bishop, or a winning jockey, or even a musical comedy actress. Unfortunately it seems to be rather a slack time."

"Two men came down while you were in your cubicle," remarked Carrados casually. "The first took the lift. I imagine that he was a middle-aged, rather portly man. He carried a stick, wore a silk hat, and used spectacles for close sight. The other came by the stairway. I infer that he arrived at the top immediately after the lift had gone. He ran down the steps, so that the two were admitted at the same time, but the second man, though the more active of the pair, hung back for a moment in the passage and the portly one was the first to go to his safe."

Mr. Carlyle's knowing look expressed: "*Go on, my friend. You are coming to something.*" But he merely contributed an encouraging, "Yes?"

"When you emerged just now, our second man quietly opened the door of his pen a fraction. Doubtless he looked out. Then he closed it as quietly again. You were not his man, Louis."

"I am grateful," said Mr. Carlyle expressively.

"What next, Louis?"

"That is all. They are still closeted."

Both were silent for a moment. Mr. Carlyle's feeling was one of unconfessed perplexity. So far the incident was utterly trivial in his eyes, but he knew that the trifles which appeared significant to Max had a way of standing out like signposts when the time came to look back over an episode. Carrados's sightless faculties seemed indeed to keep him just a move ahead as the game progressed.

"Is there really anything in it, Max?" he asked at length.

"Who can say?" replied Carrados. "At least we may wait to see them go. Those tin deed-boxes now. There is one to each safe, I think?"

"Yes, so I imagine. The practice is to carry the box to your private lair and there unlock it and do your business. Then you lock it up again and take it back to your safe."

"Steady! Our first man," whispered Carrados hurriedly. "Here, look at this with me." He opened a paper – a prospectus – which he pulled from his pocket, and they affected to study its contents together.

"You were about right, my friend," muttered Mr. Carlyle, pointing to a paragraph of assumed interest. "Hat, stick, and spectacles. He is a clean-shaven, pink-faced old boy. I believe – yes, I know the man by sight. He is a bookmaker in a large way, I am told."

"Here comes the other," whispered Carrados.

The bookmaker passed across the hall, joined on his way by the manager whose duty it was to counterlock the safe, and disappeared along one of the passages. The second man sauntered up and down, waiting his turn. Mr. Carlyle reported his movements in an undertone and described him. He was a younger man than the other, of medium height, and passably well dressed in a quiet lounge suit, green Alpine hat, and brown shoes. By the time the detective had reached his wavy chestnut hair, large and rather ragged moustache, and sandy, freckled complexion, the first man had completed his business and was leaving the place.

"It isn't an exchange lay, at all events," said Mr. Carlyle. "His inner case is only half the size of the other and couldn't possibly be substituted."

"Come up now," said Carrados, rising. "There is nothing more to be learned down here."

They requisitioned the lift and on the steps outside the gigantic keyhole stood for a few minutes discussing an investment as a couple of trustees or a lawyer and a client who were parting there might do. Fifty yards away, a very large silk hat with a very curly brim marked the progress of the bookmaker towards Piccadilly.

The lift in the hall behind them swirled up again and the gate clashed. The second man walked leisurely out and sauntered away without a backward glance.

"He has gone in the opposite direction," exclaimed Mr. Carlyle, rather blankly. "It isn't the 'lame goat' nor the 'follow-me-on', nor even the homely but efficacious sand-bag."

"What colour were his eyes?" asked Carrados.

"Upon my word, I never noticed," admitted the other.

"Parkinson would have noticed," was the severe comment.

"I am not Parkinson," retorted Mr. Carlyle, with asperity, "and, strictly as one dear friend to another, Max, permit me to add, that while cherishing an unbounded admiration for your remarkable gifts, I have the strongest suspicion that the whole incident is a ridiculous mare's nest, bred in the fantastic imagination of an enthusiastic criminologist."

Mr. Carrados received this outburst with the utmost benignity. "Come and have a coffee, Louis," he suggested. "Mehmed's is only a street away."

Mehmed proved to be a cosmopolitan gentleman from Mocha whose shop resembled a house from the outside and an Oriental divan when one was within. A turbaned Arab placed cigarettes and cups of coffee spiced with saffron before the customers, gave *salaam*, and withdrew.

"You know, my dear chap," continued Mr. Carlyle, sipping his black coffee and wondering privately whether it was really very good or very bad, "speaking quite seriously, the one fishy detail – our ginger friend's watching for the other to leave – may be open to a dozen very innocent explanations."

"So innocent that tomorrow I intend taking a safe myself."

"You think that everything is all right?"

"On the contrary, I am convinced that something is very wrong."

"Then why –?"

"I shall keep nothing there, but it will give me the entrée. I should advise you, Louis, in the first place to empty your safe with all possible speed, and in the second to leave your business card on the manager."

Mr. Carlyle pushed his cup away, convinced now that the coffee was really very bad.

"But, my dear Max, the place – 'The Safe' – is impregnable!"

"When I was in the States, three years ago, the head porter at one hotel took pains to impress on me that the building was absolutely fireproof. I at once had my things taken off to another hotel. Two weeks later the first place was burnt out. It was fireproof, I believe, but of course the furniture and the fittings were not and the walls gave way."

"Very ingenious," admitted Mr. Carlyle, "but why did you really go? You know you can't humbug me with your superhuman sixth sense, my friend."

Carrados smiled pleasantly, thereby encouraging the watchful attendant to draw near and replenish their tiny cups"

"Perhaps," replied the blind man, "because so many careless people were satisfied that it was fireproof."

"A-ha, there you are – the greater the confidence the greater the risk. But only if your self-confidence results in carelessness. Now do you know how this place is secured, Max?"

"I am told that they lock the door at night," replied Carrados, with bland malice.

"And hide the key under the mat to be ready for the first arrival in the morning," crowed Mr. Carlyle, in the same playful spirit. "Dear old chap! Well, let me tell you – "

"That force is out of the question. Quite so," admitted his friend.

"That simplifies the argument. Let us consider fraud. There again, the precautions are so rigid that many people pronounce the forms a nuisance. I confess that I do not. I regard them as a means of protecting my own property and I cheerfully sign my name and give my password, which the manager compares with his record-book before he releases the first lock of my safe. The signature is burned before my eyes in a sort of crucible there, the password is of my own choosing and is written only in a book that no one but the manager ever sees, and my key is the sole one in existence."

"No duplicate or master-key?"

"Neither. If a key is lost it takes a skilful mechanic half-a-day to cut his way in. Then you must remember that clients of a safe-deposit are not multitudinous. All are known more or less by sight to the officials there, and a stranger would receive close attention. Now, Max, by what combination of circumstances is a rogue to know my password, to be able to forge my signature, to possess himself of my key, and to resemble me personally? And, finally, how is he possibly to determine beforehand whether there is anything in my safe to repay so elaborate a plant?" Mr. Carlyle concluded in triumph and was so carried away by the strength of his position that he drank off the contents of his second cup before he realized what he was doing.

"At the hotel I just spoke of," replied Carrados, "there was an attendant whose one duty in case of alarm was to secure three iron doors. On the night of the fire he had a bad attack of toothache and slipped away for just a quarter-of-an-hour to have the thing out. There was a most up-to-date system of automatic fire alarm. It had been tested only the day before and the electrician, finding some part not absolutely to his satisfaction, had taken it away and not had time to replace it. The night watchman, it turned out, had received leave to present himself a couple of hours later on that particular night, and the hotel fireman, whose duties he took over, had missed being notified. Lastly, there was a big riverside blaze at the same time and all the engines were down at the other end of the city."

Mr. Carlyle committed himself to a dubious monosyllable. Carrados leaned forward a little.

"All these circumstances formed a coincidence of pure chance. Is it not conceivable, Louis, that an even more remarkable series might be brought about by design?"

"Our tawny friend?"

"Possibly. Only he was not really tawny." Mr. Carlyle's easy attitude suddenly stiffened into rigid attention. "He wore a false moustache."

"He wore a false moustache!" repeated the amazed gentleman. "And you cannot see! No, really, Max, this is beyond the limit!"

"If only you would not trust your dear, blundering old eyes so implicitly, you would get nearer that limit yourself," retorted Carrados. "The man carried a five-yard aura of spirit gum, emphasized by a warm, perspiring skin. That inevitably suggested one thing. I looked for further evidence of making-up and found it – these preparations all smell. The hair you described was characteristically that of a wig – worn long to hide the joining and made wavy to minimize the length. All these things are trifles. As yet we have not gone beyond the initial stage of suspicion. I will tell you another trifle. When this man retired to a compartment with his deed-box, he never even opened it. Possibly it contains a brick and a newspaper. He is only watching."

"Watching the bookmaker."

"True, but it may go far wider than that. Everything points to a plot of careful elaboration. Still, if you are satisfied – "

"I am quite satisfied," replied Mr. Carlyle gallantly. "I regard 'The Safe' almost as a national institution, and as such, I have an implicit faith in its precautions against every kind of force or fraud." So far Mr. Carlyle's attitude had been suggestive of a rock, but at this point he took out his watch, hummed a little to pass the time, consulted his watch again, and continued: "I am afraid that there were one or two papers which I

97

overlooked. It would perhaps save me coming again tomorrow if I went back now – ”

“Quite so,” acquiesced Carrados, with perfect gravity. “I will wait for you.”

For twenty minutes he sat there, drinking an occasional tiny cup of boiled coffee and to all appearance placidly enjoying the quaint atmosphere which Mr. Mehmed had contrived to transplant from the shore of the Persian Gulf

At the end of that period Carlyle returned, politely effusive about the time he had kept his friend waiting but otherwise bland and unassailable. Anyone with eyes might have noticed that he carried a parcel of about the same size and dimensions as the deed-box that fitted his safe.

The next day Carrados presented himself at the safe-deposit as an intending renter. The manager showed him over the vaults and strong rooms, explaining the various precautions taken to render the guile or force of man impotent: The strength of the chilled-steel walls, the casing of electricity-resisting concrete, the stupendous isolation of the whole inner fabric on metal pillars so that the watchman, while inside the building, could walk above, below, and all round the outer walls of what was really – although it bore no actual relationship to the advertising device of the front – a monstrous safe, and, finally, the arrangement which would enable the basement to be flooded with steam within three minutes of an alarm. These details were public property. “The Safe” was a showplace and its directors held that no harm could come of displaying a strong hand.

Accompanied by the observant eyes of Parkinson, Carrados gave an adventurous but not a hopeful attention to these particulars. Submitting the problem of the tawny man to his own ingenuity, he was constantly putting before himself the question: *How shall I set about robbing this place?* and he had already dismissed force as impracticable. Nor, when it came to the consideration of fraud, did the simple but effective safeguards which Mr. Carlyle had specified seem to offer any loophole.

“As I am blind I may as well sign in the book,” he suggested, when the manager passed to him a gummed slip for the purpose. The precaution against one acquiring particulars of another client might well be deemed superfluous in his case.

But the manager did not fall into the trap.

“It is our invariable rule in all cases, sir,” he replied courteously. “What word will you take?” Parkinson, it may be said, had been left in the hall.

“Suppose I happen to forget it? How do we proceed?”

"In that case I am afraid that I might have to trouble you to establish your identity," the manager explained. "It rarely happens."

"Then we will say 'Conspiracy'."

The word was written down and the book closed.

"Here is your key, sir. If you will allow me – your key-ring – "

A week went by and Carrados was no nearer the absolute solution of the problem he had set himself. He had, indeed, evolved several ways by which the contents of the safes might be reached, some simple and desperate, hanging on the razor-edge of chance to fall this way or that – others more elaborate, safer on the whole, but more liable to break down at some point of their ingenious intricacy. And setting aside complicity on the part of the manager – a condition that Carrados had satisfied himself did not exist – they all depended on a relaxation of the forms by which security was assured. Carrados continued to have several occasions to visit the safe during the week, and he "watched" with a quiet persistence that was deadly in its scope. But from beginning to end there was no indication of slackness in the business-like methods of the place, nor during any of his visits did the "tawny man" appear in that or any other disguise. Another week passed. Mr. Carlyle was becoming inexpressibly waggish, and Carrados himself, although he did not abate a jot of his conviction, was compelled to bend to the realities of the situation. The manager, with the obstinacy of a conscientious man who had become obsessed with the pervading note of security, excused himself from discussing abstract methods of fraud. Carrados was not in a position to formulate a detailed charge. He withdrew from active investigation, content to await his time.

It came, to be precise, on a certain Friday morning, seventeen days after his first visit to "The Safe". Returning late on the Thursday night, he was informed that a man giving the name of Draycott had called to see him. Apparently the matter had been of some importance to the visitor for he had returned three hours later on the chance of finding Mr. Carrados in. Disappointed in this, he had left a note. Carrados cut open the envelope and ran a finger along the following words:

Dear Sir,

I have today consulted Mr. Louis Carlyle, who thinks that you would like to see me. I will call again in the morning, say at nine o'clock. If this is too soon or otherwise inconvenient I entreat you to leave a message fixing as early an hour as possible. to leave a message fixing as early an hour as possible.

Yours faithfully,

Herbert Draycott. "

P.S. – I should add that I am the renter of a safe at the Lucas Street depository. H. D.

A description of Mr. Draycott made it clear that he was not the West End bookmaker. The caller, the servant explained, was a thin, wiry, keen-faced man. Carrados felt agreeably interested in this development, which seemed to justify his suspicion of a plot.

At five-minutes-to-nine the next morning Mr. Draycott again presented himself.

"Very good of you to see me so soon, sir," he apologized, on Carrados at once receiving him. "I don't know much of English ways – I'm an Australian – and I was afraid it might be too early."

"You could have made it a couple of hours earlier as far as I am concerned," replied Carrados. "Or you either for that matter, I imagine," he added, "for I don't think that you slept much last night."

"I didn't sleep at all last night," corrected Mr. Draycott. "But it's strange that you should have seen that. I understood from Mr. Carlyle that you – excuse me if I am mistaken, sir – but I understood that you were blind."

Carrados laughed his admission lightly.

"Oh yes," he said. "But never mind that. What is the trouble?"

"I'm afraid it means more than just trouble for me, Mr. Carrados." The man had steady, half-closed eyes, with the suggestion of depth which one notices in the eyes of those whose business it is to look out over great expanses of land or water. They were turned towards Carrados's face with quiet resignation in their frankness now. "I'm afraid it spells disaster. I am a working engineer from the Mount Magdalena district of Coolgardie. I don't want to take up your time with outside details, so I will only say that about two years ago I had an opportunity of acquiring a share in a very promising claim – gold, you understand, both reef and alluvial. As the work went on, I put more and more into the undertaking – you couldn't call it a venture by that time. The results were good, better than we had dared to expect, but from one cause and another the expenses were terrible. We saw that it was a bigger thing than we had bargained for and we admitted that we must get outside help."

So far Mr. Draycott's narrative had proceeded smoothly enough under the influence of the quiet despair that had come over the man. But

100

at this point a sudden recollection of his position swept him into a frenzy of bitterness.

"Oh, what the blazes is the good of going over all this again!" he broke out. "What can you or anyone else do anyhow? I've been robbed, rooked, cleared out of everything I possess." And tormented by recollections and by the impotence of his rage the unfortunate engineer beat the oak table with the back of his hand until his knuckles bled.

Carrados waited until the fury had passed.

"Continue, if you please, Mr. Draycott," he said. "Just what you thought it best to tell me is just what I want to know."

"I'm sorry, sir," apologized the man, colouring under his tanned skin. "I ought to be able to control myself better. But this business has shaken me. Three times last night I looked down the barrel of my revolver, and three times I threw it away . . . Well, we arranged that I should come to London to interest some financiers in the property. We might have done it locally or in Perth, to be sure, but then, don't you see, they would have wanted to get control. Six weeks ago I landed here. I brought with me specimens of the quartz and good samples of extracted gold, dust, and nuggets, the clearing up of several weeks' working, about two-hundred-and-forty ounces in all. That includes the Magdalena Lodestar, our lucky nugget, a lump weighing just under seven pounds of pure gold.

"I had seen an advertisement of this Lucas Street safe-deposit and it seemed just the thing I wanted. Besides the gold, I had all the papers to do with the claims – plans, reports, receipts, licences, and so on. Then when I cashed my letter of credit I had about one-hundred-and-fifty pounds in notes. Of course I could have left everything at a bank but it was more convenient to have it, as it were, in my own safe, to get at any time, and to have a private room that I could take any gentlemen to. I hadn't a suspicion that anything could be wrong. Negotiations hung on in several quarters – it's a bad time to do business here, I find. Then, yesterday, I wanted something. I went to Lucas Street, as I had done half-a-dozen times before, opened my safe, and had the inner case carried to a room . . . Mr. Carrados, it was empty!"

"Quite empty?"

"No." He laughed bitterly. "At the bottom was a sheet of wrapper paper. I recognized it as a piece I had left there in case I wanted to make up a parcel. But for that I should have been convinced that I had somehow opened the wrong safe. That was my first idea."

"It cannot be done."

"So I understand, sir. And, then, there was the paper with my name written on it in the empty tin. I was dazed. It seemed impossible. I think I stood there without moving for minutes – it was more like hours. Then I closed the tin box again, took it back, locked up the safe, and came out."

"Without notifying anything wrong?"

"Yes, Mr. Carrados." The steady blue eyes regarded him with pained thoughtfulness. "You see, I reckoned it out in that time that it must be someone about the place who had done it."

"You were wrong," said Carrados.

"So Mr. Carlyle seemed to think. I only knew that the key had never been out of my possession and I had told no one of the password. Well, it did come over me rather like cold water down the neck, that there was I alone in the strongest dungeon in London and not a living soul knew where I was."

"Possibly a sort of up-to-date Sweeney Todd's?"

"I'd heard of such things in London," admitted Draycott. "Anyway, I got out. It was a mistake. I see it now. Who is to believe me as it is – it sounds a sort of unlikely tale. And how do they come to pick on me? To know what I had? I don't drink, or open my mouth, or hell 'round. It beats me."

"They didn't pick on you – you picked on them," replied Carrados. "Never mind how. You'll be believed all right. But as for getting anything back – " The unfinished sentence confirmed Mr. Draycott in his gloomiest anticipations.

"I have the numbers of the notes," he suggested, with an attempt at hopefulness. "They can be stopped, I take it?"

"Stopped? Yes," admitted Carrados. "And what does that amount to? The banks and the police stations will be notified and every little public house between here and Land's End will change one for the scribbling of '*John Jones*' across the back. No, Mr. Draycott, it's awkward, I dare say, but you must make up your mind to wait until you can get fresh supplies from home. Where are you staying?"

Draycott hesitated.

"I have been at the Abbotsford, in Bloomsbury, up to now," he said, with some embarrassment. "The fact is, Mr. Carrados, I think I ought to have told you how I was placed before consulting you, because I – I see no prospect of being able to pay my way. Knowing that I had plenty in the safe, I had run it rather close. I went chiefly yesterday to get some notes. I have a week's hotel bill in my pocket, and – " He glanced down at his trousers. " – I've ordered one or two other things unfortunately."

"That will be a matter of time, doubtless," suggested the other encouragingly.

Instead of replying Draycott suddenly dropped his arms on to the table and buried his face between them. A minute passed in silence.

102

"It's no good, Mr. Carrados," he said, when he was able to speak. "I can't meet it. Say what you like, I simply can't tell those chaps that I've lost everything we had and ask them to send me more. They couldn't do it if I did. Understand, sir. The mine is a valuable one. We have the greatest faith in it, but it has gone beyond our depth. The three of us have put everything we own into it. While I am here they are doing labourers' work for a wage, just to keep going . . . Waiting – Oh, my God! Waiting for good news from me!"

Carrados walked round the table to his desk and wrote. Then, without a word, he held out a paper to his visitor.

"What's this?" demanded Draycott, in bewilderment. "It's – it's a cheque for a hundred pounds."

"It will carry you on," explained Carrados imperturbably. "A man like you isn't going to throw up the sponge for this set-back. Cable to your partners that you require copies of all the papers at once. They'll manage it, never fear. The gold . . . must go. Write fully by the next mail. Tell them everything and add that in spite of all you feel that you are nearer success than ever."

Mr. Draycott folded the cheque with thoughtful deliberation and put it carefully away in his pocket-book.

"I don't know whether you've guessed as much, sir," he said in a queer voice, "but I think that you've saved a man's life today. It's not the money, it's the encouragement . . . and faith. If you could see you'd know better than I can say how I feel about it."

Carrados laughed quietly. It always amused him to have people explain how much more he would learn if he had eyes.

"Then we'll go on to Lucas Street and give the manager the shock of his life," was all he said. "Come, Mr. Draycott, I have already rung up the car."

But, as it happened, another instrument had been destined to apply that stimulating experience to the manager. As they stepped out of the car opposite "The Safe", a taxicab drew up and Mr. Carlyle's alert and cheery voice hailed them.

"A moment, Max," he called, turning to settle with his driver, a transaction that he invested with an air of dignified urbanity which almost made up for any small pecuniary disappointment that may have accompanied it. "This is indeed fortunate. Let us compare notes for a moment. I have just received an almost imploring message from the manager to come at once. I assumed that it was the affair of our colonial friend here, but he went on to mention Professor Holmfast Bulge. Can it really be possible that he also has made a similar discovery?"

"What did the manager say?" asked Carrados.

"He was practically incoherent, but I really think it must be so. What have you done?"

"Nothing," replied Carrados. He turned his back on "The Safe" and appeared to be regarding the other side of the street. "There is a tobacconist's shop directly opposite?"

"There is."

"What do they sell on the first floor?"

"Possibly they sell 'Rubbo'. I hazard the suggestion from the legend 'Rub in Rubbo for Everything' which embellishes each window."

"The windows are frosted?"

"They are, to halfway up, mysterious man."

Carrados walked back to his motor car.

"While we are away, Parkinson, go across and buy a tin, bottle, box, or packet of 'Rubbo'."

"What is 'Rubbo', Max?" chirped Mr. Carlyle with insatiable curiosity.

"So far we do not know. When Parkinson gets some, Louis, you shall be the one to try it."

They descended into the basement and were passed in by the grille-keeper, whose manner betrayed a discreet consciousness of something in the air. It was unnecessary to speculate why. In the distance, muffled by the armoured passages, an authoritative voice boomed like a sonorous bell heard under water.

"What, however, are the facts?" it was demanding, with the causticity of baffled helplessness. "I am assured that there is no other key in existence, yet my safe has been unlocked. I am given to understand that without the password it would be impossible for an unauthorized person to tamper with my property. My password, deliberately chosen, is 'anthropophaginian', sir. Is it one that is familiarly on the lips of the criminal classes? But my safe is empty! What is the explanation? Who are the guilty persons? What is being done? Where are the police?"

"If you consider that the proper course to adopt is to stand on the doorstep and beckon in the first constable who happens to pass, permit me to say, sir, that I differ from you," retorted the distracted manager. "You may rely on everything possible being done to clear up the mystery. As I told you, I have already telephoned for a capable private detective and for one of my directors."

"But that is not enough," insisted the professor angrily. "Will one mere private detective restore my #6000 Japanese 4-½-per-cent bearer bonds? Is the return of my irreplaceable notes on 'Polyphyletic Bridal Customs Among the mid-Pleistocene Cave Men' to depend on a solitary director? I demand that the police shall be called in – as many as are available. Let Scotland Yard be set in motion. A searching inquiry must be made. I have only been a user of your precious establishment for six months, and this is the result."

"There you hold the key of the mystery, Professor Bulge," interposed Carrados quietly.

"Who is this, sir?" demanded the exasperated professor at large.

"Permit me," explained Mr. Carlyle, with bland assurance. "I am Louis Carlyle, of Bampton Street. This gentleman is Mr. Max Carrados, the eminent amateur specialist in crime."

"I shall be thankful for any assistance towards elucidating this appalling business," condescended the professor sonorously. "Let me put you in possession of the facts – "

"Perhaps if we went into your room," suggested Carrados to the manager, "we should be less liable to interruption."

"Quite so, quite so," boomed the professor, accepting the proposal on everyone else's behalf. "The facts, sir, are these: I am the unfortunate possessor of a safe here, in which, a few months ago, I deposited – among less important matter – sixty bearer bonds of the Japanese Imperial Loan – the bulk of my small fortune – and the manuscript of an important projected work on '*Polyphyletic Bridal Customs Among the mid-Pleistocene Cave Men*'. Today I came to detach the coupons which fall due on the fifteenth, to pay them into my bank a week in advance, in accordance with my custom. What do I find? I find the safe locked and apparently intact, as when I last saw it a month ago. But it is far from being intact, sir. It has been opened – ransacked, cleared out. Not a single bond. Not a scrap of paper remains."

It was obvious that the manager's temperature had been rising during the latter part of this speech and now he boiled over.

"Pardon my flatly contradicting you, Professor Bulge. You have again referred to your visit here a month ago as your last. You will bear witness of that, gentlemen. When I inform you that the professor had access to his safe as recently as on Monday last, you will recognize the importance that the statement may assume."

The professor glared across the room like an infuriated animal, a comparison heightened by his notoriously hircine appearance.

"How dare you contradict me, sir!" he cried, slapping the table sharply with his open hand. "I was not here on Monday."

The manager shrugged his shoulders coldly.

"You forget that the attendants also saw you," he remarked. "Cannot we trust our own eyes?"

"A common assumption, yet not always a strictly reliable one," insinuated Carrados softly.

"I cannot be mistaken."

"Then can you tell me, without looking, what colour Professor Bulge's eyes are?"

There was a curious and expectant silence for a minute. The professor turned his back on the manager and the manager passed from thoughtfulness to embarrassment.

"I really do not know, Mr. Carrados," he declared loftily at last. "I do not refer to mere trifles like that."

"Then you can be mistaken," replied Carrados mildly yet with decision.

"But the ample hair, the venerable flowing beard, the prominent nose and heavy eyebrows – "

"These are just the striking points that are most easily counterfeited. They 'take the eye'. If you would ensure yourself against deception, learn rather to observe the eye itself, and particularly the spots on it, the shape of the fingernails, the set of the ears. These things cannot be simulated."

"You seriously suggest that the man was not Professor Bulge – that he was an impostor?"

"The conclusion is inevitable. Where were you on Monday, Professor?"

"I was on a short lecturing tour in the Midlands. On Saturday I was in Nottingham. On Monday in Birmingham. I did not return to London until yesterday."

Carrados turned to the manager again and indicated Draycott, who so far had remained in the background.

"And this gentleman? Did he by any chance come here on Monday?"

"He did not, Mr. Carrados. But I gave him access to his safe on Tuesday afternoon and again yesterday."

Draycott shook his head sadly.

"Yesterday I found it empty," he said. "And all Tuesday afternoon I was at Brighton, trying to see a gentleman on business."

The manager sat down very suddenly.

"Good God, another!" he exclaimed faintly.

"I am afraid the list is only beginning," said Carrados. "We must go through your renters' book."

The manager roused himself to protest.

"That cannot be done. No one but myself or my deputy ever sees the book. It would be – unprecedented."

"The circumstances are unprecedented," replied Carrados.

"If any difficulties are placed in the way of these gentlemen's investigations, I shall make it my duty to bring the facts before the Home

Secretary," announced the professor, speaking up to the ceiling with the voice of a brazen trumpet.

Carrados raised a deprecating hand.

"May I make a suggestion?" he remarked. "Now, I am blind. If, therefore —?"

"Very well," acquiesced the manager. "But I must request the others to withdraw."

For five minutes Carrados followed the list of safe-renters as the manager read them to him. Sometimes he stopped the catalogue to reflect a moment. Now and then he brushed a finger-tip over a written signature and compared it with another. Occasionally a password interested him. But when the list came to an end he continued to look into space without any sign of enlightenment.

"So much is perfectly clear and yet so much is incredible," he mused. "You insist that you alone have been in charge for the last six months?"

"I have not been away a day this year."

"Meals?"

"I have my lunch sent in."

"And this room could not be entered without your knowledge while you were about the place?"

"It is impossible. The door is fitted with a powerful spring and a feather-touch self-acting lock. It cannot be left unlocked unless you deliberately prop it open."

"And, with your knowledge, no one has had an opportunity of having access to this book?"

"No," was the reply.

Carrados stood up and began to put on his gloves.

"Then I must decline to pursue my investigation any further," he said icily.

"Why?" stammered the manager.

"Because I have positive reason for believing that you are deceiving me."

"Pray sit down, Mr. Carrados. It is quite true that when you put the last question to me a circumstance rushed into my mind which — so far as the strict letter was concerned — might seem to demand 'Yes' instead of 'No'. But not in the spirit of your inquiry. It would be absurd to attach any importance to the incident I refer to."

"That would be for me to judge."

"You shall do so, Mr. Carrados. I live at Windermere Mansions with my sister. A few months ago she got to know a married couple who had recently come to the opposite flat. The husband was a middle-aged, scholarly man who spent most of his time in the British Museum. His

107

wife's tastes were different. She was much younger, brighter, gayer – a mere girl in fact, one of the most charming and unaffected I have ever met. My sister Amelia does not readily – "

"Stop!" exclaimed Carrados. "A studious middle-aged man and a charming young wife! Be as brief as possible. If there is any chance it may turn on a matter of minutes at the ports. She came here, of course?"

"Accompanied by her husband," replied the manager stiffly. "Mrs. Scott had travelled and she had a hobby of taking photographs wherever she went. When my position accidentally came out one evening she was carried away by the novel idea of adding views of a safe-deposit to her collection – as enthusiastic as a child. There was no reason why she should not. The place has often been taken for advertising purposes."

"She came, and brought her camera – under your very nose!"

"I do not know what you mean by 'under my very nose'. She came with her husband one evening just about our closing time. She brought her camera, of course – quite a small affair."

"And contrived to be in here alone?"

"I take exception to the word 'contrived'. It – it happened. I sent out for some tea, and in the course – "

"How long was she alone in here?"

"Two or three minutes at the most. When I returned she was seated at my desk. That was what I referred to. The little rogue had put on my glasses and had got hold of a big book. We were great chums, and she delighted to mock me. I confess that I was startled – merely instinctively – to see that she had taken up this book, but the next moment I saw that she had it upside down."

"Clever! She couldn't get it away in time. And the camera, with half-a-dozen of its specially sensitized films already snapped over the last few pages, by her side!"

"That child!"

"Yes. She is twenty-seven and has kicked hats off tall men's heads in every capital from Petersburg to Buenos Aires! Get through to Scotland Yard and ask if Inspector Beedel can come up."

The manager breathed heavily through his nose.

"To call in the police and publish everything would ruin this establishment – confidence would be gone. I cannot do it without further authority."

"Then the professor certainly will."

"Before you came I rang up the only director who is at present in town and gave him the facts as they then stood. Possibly he has arrived by this. If you will accompany me to the boardroom we will see."

They went up to the floor above, Mr. Carlyle joining them on the way.

"Excuse me a moment," said the manager.

Parkinson, who had been having an improving conversation with the hall porter on the subject of land values, approached."

"I am sorry, sir," he reported, "but I was unable to procure any 'Rubbo'. The place appears to be shut up."

"That is a pity. Mr. Carlyle had set his heart on it."

"Will you come this way, please?" said the manager, reappearing.

In the boardroom they found a white-haired old gentleman who had obeyed the manager's behest from a sense of duty, and then remained in a distant corner of the empty room in the hope that he might be overlooked. He was amiably helpless and appeared to be deeply aware of it.

"This is a very sad business, gentlemen," he said, in a whispering, confiding voice. "I am informed that you recommend calling in the Scotland Yard authorities. That would be a disastrous course for an institution that depends on the implicit confidence of the public."

"It is the only course," replied Carrados.

"The name of Mr. Carrados is well known to us in connexion with a delicate case. Could you not carry this one through?"

"It is impossible. A wide inquiry must be made. Every port will have to be watched. The police alone can do that." He threw a little significance into the next sentence. "I alone can put the police in the right way of doing it."

"And you will do that, Mr. Carrados?"

Carrados smiled engagingly. He knew exactly what constituted the great attraction of his services.

"My position is this," he explained. "So far my work has been entirely amateur. In that capacity I have averted one or two crimes, remedied an occasional injustice, and now and then been of service to my professional friend, Louis Carlyle. But there is no reason at all why I should serve a commercial firm in an ordinary affair of business for nothing. For any information I should require a fee, a quite nominal fee of, say, one-hundred pounds."

The director looked as though his faith in human nature had received a rude blow.

"A hundred pounds would be a very large initial fee for a small firm like this, Mr. Carrados," he remarked in a pained voice.

"And that, of course, would be independent of Mr. Carlyle's professional charges," added Carrados.

"Is that sum contingent on any specific performance?" inquired the manager.

"I do not mind making it conditional on my procuring for you, for the police to act on, a photograph and a description of the thief."

The two officials conferred apart for a moment. Then the manager returned.

"We will agree, Mr. Carrados, on the understanding that these things are to be in our hands within two days. Failing that – "

"No, no!" cried Mr. Carlyle indignantly, but Carrados good-humouredly put him aside.

"I will accept the condition in the same sporting spirit that inspires it. Within forty-eight hours or no pay. The cheque, of course, to be given immediately the goods are delivered?"

"You may rely on that."

Carrados took out his pocket-book, produced an envelope bearing an American stamp, and from it extracted an unmounted print.

"Here is the photograph," he announced. "The man is called Ulysses K. Groom, but he is better known as 'Harry the Actor'. You will find the description written on the back."

Five minutes later, when they were alone, Mr. Carlyle expressed his opinion of the transaction.

"You are an unmitigated humbug, Max," he said, "though an amiable one, I admit. But purely for your own private amusement you spring these things on people."

"On the contrary," replied Carrados, "people spring these things on me."

"Now this photograph. Why have I heard nothing of it before?"

Carrados took out his watch and touched the fingers.

"It is now three-minutes-to-eleven. I received the photograph at twenty-past-eight."

"Even then, an hour ago you assured me that you had done nothing."

"Nor had I – so far as result went. Until the keystone of the edifice was wrung from the manager in his room, I was as far away from demonstrable certainty as ever."

"So am I – as yet," hinted Mr. Carlyle.

"I am coming to that, Louis. I turn over the whole thing to you. The man has got two clear days' start and the chances are nine-to-one against catching him. We know everything, and the case has no further interest for me. But it is your business. Here is your material.

"On that one occasion when the 'tawny' man crossed our path, I took from the first a rather more serious view of his scope and intention than you did. That same day I sent a cipher cable to Pierson of the New York service. I asked for news of any man of such and such a description – merely negative – who was known to have left the States: An educated man, expert in the use of disguises, audacious in his operations, and a specialist in 'dry' work among banks and strong rooms."

110

"Why the States, Max?"

"That was a sighting shot on my part. I argued that he must be an English-speaking man. The smart and inventive turn of the modern Yank has made him a specialist in ingenious devices, straight or crooked. Unpickable locks and invincible lock-pickers, burglar-proof safes and safe-specializing burglars, come equally from the States. So I tried a very simple test. As we talked that day and the man walked past us, I dropped the words 'New York' – or, rather, 'Noo Y'rk' – in his hearing."

"I know you did. He neither turned nor stopped."

"He was that much on his guard, but into his step there came – though your poor old eyes could not see it, Louis – the 'psychological pause', an absolute arrest of perhaps a fifth of a second, just as it would have done with you if the word 'London' had fallen on your ear in a distant land. However, the *why*'s and the *wherefore*'s don't matter. Here is the essential story:

"Eighteen months ago 'Harry the Actor' successfully looted the office safe of M'Kenkie, J. F. Higgs and Company, of Cleveland, Ohio. He had just married a smart but very facile third-rate vaudeville actress – English by origin – and wanted money for the honeymoon. He got about five-hundred pounds, and with that they came to Europe and stayed in London for some months. That period is marked by the Congreave Square post office burglary, you may remember. While studying such of the British institutions as most appealed to him, the 'Actor's' attention became fixed on this safe-deposit. Possibly the implied challenge contained in its telegraphic address grew on him until it became a point of professional honour with him to despoil it. At all events, he was presumedly attracted by an undertaking that promised not only glory but very solid profit. The first part of the plot was, to the most skilful criminal 'impersonator' in the States, mere skittles. Spreading over those months he appeared at 'The Safe' in twelve different characters and rented twelve safes of different sizes. At the same time he made a thorough study of the methods of the place. As soon as possible he got the keys back again into legitimate use, having made duplicates for his own private ends, of course. Five he seems to have returned during his first stay. One was received later, with profuse apologies, by registered post. One was returned through a leading Berlin bank. Six months ago he made a flying visit here, purely to work off two more. One he kept from first to last, and the remaining couple he got in at the beginning of his second long residence here, three or four months ago.

"This brings us to the serious part of the cool enterprise. He had funds from the Atlantic and South-Central Mail-car coup when he arrived here last April. He appears to have set up three establishments: A home, in the guise of an elderly scholar with a young wife, which, of course, was next

111

door to our friend the manager. An observation point, over which he plastered the inscription '*Rub in Rubbo for Everything*' as a reason for being, and, somewhere else, a dressing room with essential conditions of two doors into different streets.

"About six weeks ago he entered the last stage. Mrs. Harry, with quite ridiculous ease, got photographs of the necessary page or two of the record-book. I don't doubt that for weeks before then everyone who entered the place had been observed, but the photographs linked them up with the actual men into whose hands the 'Actor's' old keys had passed – gave their names and addresses, the numbers of their safes, their passwords and signatures. The rest was easy."

"Yes, by Jupiter. Mere play for a man like that," agreed Mr. Carlyle, with professional admiration. "He could contrive a dozen different occasions for studying the voice and manner and appearance of his victims. How much has he cleared?"

"We can only speculate as yet. I have put my hand on seven doubtful callers on Monday and Tuesday last. Two others he had ignored for some reason. The remaining two safes had not been allotted. There is one point that raises an interesting speculation."

"What is that, Max?"

"The 'Actor' has one associate, a man known as 'Billy the Fondant', but beyond that – with the exception of his wife, of course – he does not usually trust anyone. It is plain, however, that at least seven men must latterly have been kept under close observation. It has occurred to me – "

"Yes, Max?"

"I have wondered whether Harry has enlisted the innocent services of one or other of our clever private inquiry offices."

"Scarcely," smiled the professional. "It would hardly pass muster."

"Oh, I don't know. Mrs. Harry, in the character of a jealous wife or a suspicious sweetheart, might reasonably – "

Mr. Carlyle's smile suddenly faded.

"By Jupiter!" he exclaimed. "I remember – "

"Yes, Louis?" prompted Carrados, with laughter in his voice.

"I remember that I must telephone to a client before Beedel comes," concluded Mr. Carlyle, rising in some haste.

At the door he almost ran into the subdued director, who was wringing his hands in helpless protest at a new stroke of calamity.

"Mr. Carrados," wailed the poor old gentleman in a tremulous bleat, "Mr. Carrados, there is another now – Sir Benjamin Gump. He insists on seeing me. You will not – you will not desert us?"

112

"I should have to stay a week," replied Carrados briskly, "and I'm just off now. There will be a procession. Mr. Carlyle will support you, I am sure."

He nodded, "Good morning" straight into the eyes of each, and found his way out with the astonishing certainty of movement that made so many forget his infirmity. Possibly he was not desirous of encountering Draycott's embarrassed gratitude again, for in less than a minute they heard the swirl of his departing car.

"Never mind, my dear sir," Mr. Carlyle assured his client, with impenetrable complacency. "Never mind. I will remain instead. Perhaps I had better make myself known to Sir Benjamin at once."

The director turned on him the pleading, trustful look of a cornered dormouse.

"He is in the basement," he whispered. "I shall be in the boardroom – if necessary."

Mr. Carlyle had no difficulty in discovering the centre of interest in the basement. Sir Benjamin was expansive and reserved, bewildered and decisive, long-winded and short-tempered, each in turn and more or less all at once. He had already demanded the attention of the manager, Professor Bulge, Draycott, and two underlings to his case and they were now involved in a babel of inutile reiteration. The inquiry agent was at once drawn into a circle of interrogation that he did his best to satisfy impressively while himself learning the new facts.

The latest development was sufficiently astonishing. Less than an hour before, Sir Benjamin had received a parcel by district messenger. It contained a jewel-case which ought at that moment to have been securely reposing in one of the deposit safes. Hastily snatching it open, the recipient's incredible forebodings were realized. It was empty – empty of jewels, that is to say, for, as if to add a sting to the blow, a neatly inscribed card had been placed inside, and on it the agitated baronet read the appropriate but at the moment rather gratuitous maxim: "*Lay not up for yourselves treasures upon earth –* "

The card was passed round and all eyes demanded the expert's pronouncement.

"' *– where moth and rust doth corrupt and where thieves break through and steal.*' Hmm," read Mr. Carlyle with weight. "This is a most important clue, Sir Benjamin – "

"Hey, what? What's that?" exclaimed a voice from the other side of the hall. "Why, damme if I don't believe you've got another! Look at that, gentlemen, look at that. What's on, I say? Here now, come. Give me my safe. I want to know where I am."

113

It was the bookmaker who strode tempestuously in among them, flourishing before their faces a replica of the card that was in Mr. Carlyle's hand.

"Well, upon my soul this is most extraordinary," exclaimed that gentleman, comparing the two. "You have just received this, Mr. – Mr. Berge, isn't it?"

"That's right, Berge – 'Iceberg' on the course. Thank the Lord Harry, I can take my losses coolly enough, but this – this is a facer. Put into my hand half-an-hour ago inside an envelope that ought to be here and as safe as in the Bank of England. What's the game, I say? Here, Johnny, hurry and let me into my safe."

Discipline and method had for the moment gone by the board. There was no suggestion of the boasted safeguards of the establishment. The manager added his voice to that of the client, and when the attendant did not at once appear he called again.

"John, come and give Mr. Berge access to his safe at once."

"All right, sir," pleaded the harassed key-attendant. Hurrying up with the burden of his own distraction. "There's a silly fathead got in what thinks this is a left-luggage office, so far as I can make out – a foreigner."

"Never mind that now," replied the manager severely. "Mr. Berge's safe: *No. 01724.*"

The attendant and Mr. Berge went off together down one of the brilliant colonnaded vistas. One or two of the others who had caught the words glanced across and became aware of a strange figure that was drifting indecisively towards them. He was obviously an elderly German tourist of pronounced type – long-haired, spectacled, outrageously garbed and involved in the mental abstraction of his philosophical race. One hand was occupied with the manipulation of a pipe, as markedly Teutonic as its owner. The other grasped a carpet-bag that would have ensured an opening laugh to any low comedian.

Quite impervious to the preoccupation of the group, the German made his way up to them and picked out the manager.

"This was a safety deposit, *nicht wahr?*"

"Quite so," acquiesced the manager loftily, "but just now – "

"Your fellow was dense of gomprehension." The eyes behind the clumsy glasses wrinkled to a ponderous humour. "He forgot his own business. Now this goot bag – "

Brought into fuller prominence, the carpet-bag revealed further details of its overburdened proportions. At one end a flannel shirt cuff protruded in limp dejection. At the other an ancient collar, with the grotesque attachment known as a "dickey", asserted its presence. No wonder the manager frowned his annoyance. "The Safe" was in low

114

enough repute among its patrons at that moment without any burlesque interlude to its tragic hour.

"Yes, yes," he whispered, attempting to lead the would-be depositor away, "but you are under a mistake. This is not – "

"It was a safety deposit? Goot. Mine bag – I would deposit him in safety till the time of mine train. *Ja?*"

"*Nein, nein!*" almost hissed the agonized official. "Go away, sir, go away! It isn't a cloakroom. John, let this gentleman out."

The attendant and Mr. Berge were returning from their quest. The inner box had been opened and there was no need to ask the result. The bookmaker was shaking his head like a baffled bull.

"Gone, no effects," he shouted across the hall. "Lifted from 'The Safe', by crumb!"

To those who knew nothing of the method and operation of the fraud it seemed as if the financial security of the Capital was tottering. An amazed silence fell, and in it they heard the great grille door of the basement clang on the inopportune foreigner's departure. But, as if it was impossible to stand still on that morning of dire happenings, he was immediately succeeded by a dapper, keen-faced man in severe clerical attire who had been let in as the intruder passed out.

"Canon Petersham!" exclaimed the professor, going forward to greet him.

"My dear Professor Bulge!" reciprocated the canon. "You here! A most disquieting thing has happened to me. I must have my safe at once." He divided his attention between the manager and the professor as he monopolized them both. "A most disquieting and – and outrageous circumstance. My safe, please – Yes, yes, Reverend Henry Noakes Petersham. I have just received by hand a box, a small box of no value but one that I thought, yes, I am convinced that it was the one, a box that was used to contain certain valuables of family interest which should at this moment be in my safe here. No. 7436? Very likely, very likely. Yes, here is my key. But not content with the disconcerting effect of that, Professor, the box contained – and I protest that it's a most unseemly thing to quote any text from the Bible in this way to a clergyman of my position – well, here it is. '*Lay not up for yourselves treasures upon earth –* ' Why, I have a dozen sermons of my own in my desk now on that very verse. I'm particularly partial to the very needful lesson that it teaches. And to apply it to me! It's monstrous!"

"No. 7436, John," ordered the manager, with weary resignation.

The attendant again led the way towards another armour-plated aisle. Smartly turning a corner, he stumbled over something, bit a profane exclamation in two, and looked back.

"It's that bloomin' foreigner's old bag again," he explained across the place in aggrieved apology. "He left it here after all."

"Take it upstairs and throw it out when you've finished," said the manager shortly.

"Here, wait a minute," pondered John, in absent-minded familiarity. "Wait a minute. This is a funny go. There's a label on that wasn't here before. 'Why not look inside?'"

"'Why not look inside?'" repeated someone.

"That's what it says."

There was another puzzled silence. All were arrested by some intangible suggestion of a deeper mystery than they had yet touched. One by one they began to cross the hall with the conscious air of men who were not curious but thought that they might as well see.

"Why, curse my crumpet," suddenly exploded Mr. Berge, "if that ain't the same writing as these texts!"

"By Gad, but I believe you are right," assented Mr. Carlyle. "Well, why not look inside?"

The attendant, from his stooping posture, took the verdict of the ring of faces and in a trice tugged open the two buckles. The central fastening was not locked, and yielded to a touch. The flannel shirt, the weird collar and a few other garments in the nature of a "top-dressing" were flung out and John's hand plunged deeper . . . .

Harry the Actor had lived up to his dramatic instinct. Nothing was wrapped up. Nay, the rich booty had been deliberately opened out and displayed, as it were, so that the overturning of the bag, when John the keybearer in an access of riotous extravagance lifted it up and strewed its contents broadcast on the floor, was like the looting of a smuggler's den, or the realization of a speculator's dream, or the bursting of an Aladdin's cave, or something incredibly lavish and bizarre. Bank-notes fluttered down and lay about in all directions, relays of sovereigns rolled away like so much dross, bonds and scrip for thousands and tens of thousands clogged the downpouring stream of jewellery and unset gems. A yellow stone the size of a four-pound weight and twice as heavy dropped plump upon the canon's toes and sent him hopping and grimacing to the wall. A ruby-hilted kris cut across the manager's wrist as he strove to arrest the splendid rout. Still the miraculous cornucopia deluged the ground, with its pattering, ringing, bumping, crinkling, rolling, fluttering produce until, like the final tableau of some spectacular ballet, it ended with a golden rain that masked the details of the heap beneath a glittering veil of yellow sand.

"My dust!" gasped Draycott.

"My fivers, by golly!" ejaculated the bookmaker, initiating a plunge among the spoil.

116

"My Japanese bonds, coupons and all, and – Yes, even the manuscript of my work on '*Polyphyletic Bridal Customs Among the mid-Pleistocene Cave Men*'. Ha!" Something approaching a cachinnation of delight closed the professor's contribution to the pandemonium, and eyewitnesses afterwards declared that for a moment the dignified scientist stood on one foot in the opening movement of a can-can.

"My wife's diamonds, thank Heaven!" cried Sir Benjamin, with the air of a schoolboy who was very well out of a swishing.

"But what does it mean?" demanded the bewildered canon. "Here are my family heirlooms – a few decent pearls, my grandfather's collection of camei and other trifles – but who –?"

"Perhaps this offers some explanation," suggested Mr. Carlyle, unpinning an envelope that had been secured to the lining of the bag. "It is addressed '*To Seven Rich Sinners*'. Shall I read it for you?"

For some reason the response was not unanimous, but it was sufficient. Mr. Carlyle cut open the envelope.

My dear Friends,

Aren't you glad? Aren't you happy at this moment? Ah yes – but not with the true joy of regeneration that alone can bring lightness to the afflicted soul. Pause while there is yet time. Cast off the burden of your sinful lusts, for what shall it profit a man if he shall gain the whole world and lose his own soul? (Mark, Chap. VIII., V. 36.)

"Oh, my friends, you have had an all-fired narrow squeak. Up till the Friday in last week I held your wealth in the hollow of my ungodly hand and rejoiced in my nefarious cunning, but on that day as I with my guilty female accomplice stood listening with worldly amusement to the testimony of a converted brother at a meeting of the Salvation Army on Clapham Common, the gospel light suddenly shone into our rebellious souls and then and there we found salvation. Hallelujah!

What we have done to complete the unrighteous scheme upon which we had laboured for months has only been for your own good, dear friends that you are, though as yet divided from us by your carnal lusts. Let this be a lesson to you. Sell all you have and give it to the poor – through the organization of the Salvation Army by preference – and thereby lay up for yourselves treasures where neither moth nor rust doth corrupt and where thieves do not break through and steal. (Matthew, Chap, VI., V. 20.)

Yours in good works,

Private Henry, the Salvationist

P.S. (in haste). I may as well inform you that no crib is really uncrackable, though the Cyrus J. Coy Co.'s Safe Deposit on West 24th Street, N.Y. comes nearest the kernel. And even that I could work to the bare rock if I took hold of the job with both hands – that is to say I could have done in my sinful days. As for you, I should recommend you to change your T. A. to "Peanut".

U. K. G.

"There sounds a streak of the old Adam in that postscript, Mr. Carlyle," whispered Inspector Beedel, who had just arrived in time to hear the letter read.

The Tilling Shaw Mystery

"**I** will see Miss George now," assented Carrados. Parkinson retired and Greatorex looked round from his chair. The morning "clearing-up" was still in progress.

"Shall I go?" he inquired.

"Not unless the lady desires it. I don't know her at all."

The secretary was not unobservant and he had profited from his association with Mr. Carrados. Without more ado, he began to get his papers quietly together.

The door opened and a girl of about twenty came eagerly yet half-timorously into the room. Her eyes for a moment swept Carrados with an anxious scrutiny. Then, with a slight shade of disappointment, she noticed that they were not alone.

"I have come direct from Oakshire to see you, Mr. Carrados," she announced, in a quick, nervous voice that was evidently the outcome of a desperate resolution to be brave and explicit. "The matter is a dreadfully important one to me and I should very much prefer to tell it to you alone."

There was no need for Carrados to turn towards his secretary. That discriminating young gentleman was already on his way. Miss George flashed him a shy look of thanks and filled in the moment with a timid survey of the room.

"Is it something that you think I can help you with?"

"I had hoped so. I had heard in a roundabout way of your wonderful power – Ought I to tell you how? – does it matter?"

"Not in the least if it has nothing to do with the case," replied Carrados.

"When this dreadful thing happened I instinctively thought of you. I felt sure that I ought to come and get you to help me at once. But I – I have very little money, Mr. Carrados, only a few pounds, and I am not so childish as not to know that very clever men require large fees. Then when I got here my heart sank, for I saw at once from your house and position that what seemed little even to me would be ridiculous to you – that if you did help me it would be purely out of kindness of heart and generosity."

"Suppose you tell me what the circumstances are," suggested Carrados cautiously. Then, to afford an opening, he added: "You have recently gone into mourning, I see."

"See!" exclaimed the girl almost sharply. "Then you are not blind?"

"Oh yes," he replied, "only I use the familiar expression, partly from custom, partly because it sounds unnecessarily pedantic to say, 'I deduce from certain observations.'"

"I beg your pardon. I suppose I was startled not so much by the expression as by your knowledge. I ought to have been prepared. But I am already wasting your time and I came so determined to be business-like. I got a copy of the local paper on the way, because I thought that the account in it would be clearer to you than I could tell it. Shall I read it?"

"Please, if that was your intention."

"It is *The Stinbridge Herald*," explained the girl, taking a closely folded newspaper from the handbag which she carried. "Stinbridge is our nearest town – about six miles from Tilling Shaw, where we live. This is the account:

Mysterious Tragedy at Tillin
Well-known Agriculturalist Attempts Murder and Commits Suicide

The districts of Great Tilling, Tilling Shaw, and the immediate neighbourhood were thrown into a state of unusual excitement on Thursday last by the report of a tragedy in their midst such as has rarely marked the annals of our law-abiding country-side.

A Herald *representative was early on the scene, and his inquiries elucidated the fact that it was only too true that in this case rumour had not exaggerated the circumstances, rather the reverse indeed.*

On the afternoon of the day in question, Mr. Frank Whtmarsh, of High Barn, presented himself at Barony, the residence of his uncle, Mr. William Whitmarsh, with the intention of seeing him in reference to a dispute that was pending between them. This is understood to be connected with an alleged trespass in pursuit of game, each relative claiming exclusive sporting rights over a piece of water known as Hunstan Mere.

On this occasion the elder gentleman was not at home and Mr. Frank Whitmarsh, after waiting for some time, departed, leaving a message to the effect that he would return, and, according to one report, "have it out with Uncle William," later in the evening.

This resolution he unfortunately kept. Returning about eight-forty-five p.m. he found his uncle in and for some time

120

the two men remained together in the dining room. What actually passed between them has not yet transpired, but it is said that for half-an-hour, there had been nothing to indicate to the other occupants of the house that anything unusual was in progress when suddenly two shots rang out in rapid succession. Mrs. Lawrence, the housekeeper at Barony, and a servant were the soonest on the spot, and, conquering the natural terror that for a moment held them outside the now silent room, they summoned up courage to throw open the door and to enter. The first thing that met their eyes was the body of Mr. Frank Whitmarsh lying on the floor almost at their feet. In their distressed state it was immediately assumed by the horrified women that he was dead, or at least seriously wounded, but a closer examination revealed the fact that the gentleman had experienced an almost miraculous escape. At the time of the tragedy he was wearing a large old-fashioned silver watch, and in this the bullet intended for his heart was found, literally embedded deep in the works. The second shot had, however, effected its purpose, for at the other side of the room, still seated at the table, was Mr. William Whitmarsh, already quite dead, with a terrible wound in his head and the weapon, a large-bore revolver of obsolete pattern, lying at his feet.

Mr. Frank Whitmarsh subsequently explained that the shock of the attack, and the dreadful appearance presented by his uncle when, immediately afterwards, he turned his hand against himself, must have caused him to faint.

Readers of The Herald *will join in our expression of sympathy for all members of the Whitmarsh family, and in our congratulations to Mr. Frank Whitmarsh on his providential escape.*

The inquest is fixed for Monday and it is anticipated that the funeral will take place on the following day.

"That is all," concluded Miss George.

"All that is in the paper," amended Carrados.

"It is the same everywhere – '*Attempted murder and suicide*' – that is what everyone accepts as a matter of course," went on the girl quickly. "How do they know that my father tried to kill Frank, or that he killed himself? How can they know, Mr. Carrados?"

"Your father, Miss George?"

121

"Yes. My name is Madeline Whitmarsh. At home everyone looks at me as if I was an object of mingled pity and reproach. I thought that they might know the name here, so I gave the first that came into my head. I think it is a street I was directed along. Besides, I don't want it to be known that I came to see you in any case."

"Why?"

Much of the girl's conscious nervousness had stiffened into an attitude of unconscious hardness. Grief takes many forms, and whatever she had been before, the tragic episode had left Miss Whitmarsh a little hurt and cynical.

"You are a man living in a town and can do as you like. I am a girl living in the country and have therefore to do largely as my neighbours like. For me to set up my opinion against popular feeling would constitute no small offence. To question its justice would be held to be adding outrageous insult to enormous injury."

"So far I am unable to go beyond the newspaper account. On the face of it, your father – with what provocation of course I do not know – did attempt this Mr. Frank Whitmarsh's life and then take his own. You imply another version. What reason have you?"

"That is the terrible part of it," exclaimed the girl, with rising distress. "It was that which made me so afraid of coming to you, although I felt that I must, for I dreaded that when you asked me for proofs and I could give you none you would refuse to help me. We were not even in time to hear him speak, and yet I know, know with absolute conviction, that my father would not have done this. There are things that you cannot explain, Mr. Carrados, and – well, there is an end of it."

Her voice sank to an absent-minded whisper.

"Everyone will condemn him now that he cannot defend himself, and yet he could not even have had the revolver that was found at his feet."

"What is that?" demanded Carrados sharply. "Do you mean that?"

"Mean what?" she asked, with the blankness of one who has lost the thread of her own thoughts.

"What you said about the revolver – that your father could not have had it?"

"The revolver?" she repeated half-wearily. "Oh yes. It was a heavy, old-fashioned affair. It had been lying in a drawer of his desk for more than ten years because once a dog came into the orchard in broad daylight light and worried half-a-dozen lambs before anyone could do anything."

"Yes, but why could he not have it on Thursday?"

"I noticed that it was gone. After Frank had left in the afternoon I went into the room where he had been waiting, to finish dusting. The paper says the dining room, but it was really Papa's business room and no one

122

else used it. Then when I was dusting the desk I saw that the revolver was no longer there."

"You had occasion to open the drawer?"

"It is really a very old bureau and none of the drawers fit closely. Dust lies on the ledges and you always have to open them a little to dust properly. They were never kept locked."

"Possibly your father had taken the revolver with him."

"No. I had seen it there after he had gone. He rode to Stinbridge immediately after lunch and did not return until nearly eight. After he left I went to dust his room. It was then that I saw it. I was doing the desk when Frank knocked and interrupted me. That is how I came to be there twice."

"But you said that you had no proof, Miss Whitmarsh," Carrados reminded her, with deep seriousness. "Do you not recognize the importance – the deadly importance – that this one shred of evidence may assume?"

"Does it?" she replied simply. "I am afraid that I am rather dull just now. All yesterday I was absolutely dazed. I could not do the most ordinary things. I found myself looking at the clock for minutes together, yet absolutely incapable of grasping what time it was. In the same way I know that it struck me as being funny about the revolver, but I always had to give it up. It was as though everything was there but things would not fit in."

"You are sure, absolutely sure, that you saw the revolver there after your father had left, and missed it before he returned?"

"Oh yes," said the girl quickly. "I remember realizing how curious it was at the time. Besides, there is something else. I so often had things to ask papa about when he was out of the house that I got into the way of making little notes to remind me later. This morning I found on my dressing-table one that I had written on Thursday afternoon."

"About this weapon?"

"Yes – to ask him what could have become of it."

Carrados made a further inquiry, and this was Madeline Whitmarsh's account of affairs existing between the two branches of the family:

Until the time of William Whitmarsh, father of the William Whitmarsh just deceased, the properties of Barony and High Barn had formed one estate, descending from a William Senior to a William Junior down a moderately long line of yeomen Whitmarshes. Through the influence of his second wife, this William senior divided the property, leaving Barony with its four-hundred acres of good land to William Junior, and High Barn, with which went three-hundred acres of poor land, to his other son, father of the Frank implicated in the recent tragedy. But though

123

divided, the two farms still had one common link. Beneath their growing corn and varied pasturage lay, it was generally admitted, a seam of coal at a depth and of a thickness that would render its working a paying venture. Even in William the Divider's time, when the idea was new, money in plenty would have been forthcoming, but he would have none of it, and when he died his will contained a provision restraining either son from mining or exploiting his land for mineral without the consent and co-operation of the other.

This restriction became a legacy of hate. The brothers were only half-brothers and William having suffered unforgettably at the hands of his step-mother had old scores to pay off. Quite comfortably prosperous on his own rich farm, and quite satisfied with the excellent shooting and the congenial life, he had not the slightest desire to increase his wealth. He had the old dour, peasant-like instinct to cling to the house and the land of his forefathers. From this position no argument moved him.

In the meanwhile, on the other side of the new boundary fence, Frank Senior was growing poorer year by year. To his periodical entreaties that William would agree to shafts being sunk on High Barn he received an emphatic "Never in my time!" The poor man argued, besought, threatened, and swore. The prosperous one shook his head and grinned. Carrados did not need to hear the local saying: "half-brothers: Whole haters. Like the Whitmarshes," to read the situation.

"Of course I do not really understand the business part of it," said Madeline, "and many people blamed poor Papa, especially when Uncle Frank drank himself to death. But I know that it was not mere obstinacy. He loved the undisturbed, peaceful land just as it was, and his father had wished it to remain the same. Collieries would bring swarms of strange men into the neighbourhood, poachers and trespassers, he said. The smoke and dust would ruin the land for miles round and drive away the game, and in the end, if the work did not turn out profitable, we should all be much worse off than before."

"Does the restriction lapse now? Will Mr. Frank junior be able to mine?"

"It will now lie with Frank and my brother William, just as it did before with their fathers. I should expect Willie to be quite favourable. He is more – *modern*."

"You have not spoken of your brother."

"I have two. Bob, the younger, is in Mexico," she explained. "And Willie in Canada with an engineering firm. They did not get on very well with papa and they went away."

It did not require preternatural observation to deduce that the late William Whitmarsh had been "a little difficult".

124

"When Uncle Frank died, less than six months ago, Frank came back to High Barn from South Africa. He had been away about two years."

"Possibly he did not get on well with his father?"

Madeline smiled sadly.

"I am afraid that no two Whitmarsh men ever did get on well together," she admitted.

"Your father and young Frank, for instance?"

"Their lands adjoin. There were always quarrels and disputes," she replied. "Then Frank had his father's grievance over again."

"He wished to mine?"

"Yes. He told me that he had had experience of coal in Natal."

"There was no absolute ostracism between you then? You were to some extent friends?"

"Scarcely." She appeared to reflect. "Acquaintances . . . We met occasionally, of course, at people's houses."

"You did not visit High Barn?"

"Oh no."

"But there was no particular reason why you should not?"

"Why do you ask me that?" she demanded quickly, and in a tone that was quite incompatible with the simple inquiry. Then, recognizing the fact, she added, with shamefaced penitence: "I beg your pardon, Mr. Carrados. I am afraid that my nerves have gone to pieces since Thursday. The most ordinary things affect me inexplicably."

"That is a common experience in such circumstances," said Carrados reassuringly. "Where were you at the time of the tragedy?"

"I was in my bedroom, which is rather high up, changing. I had driven down to the village, to give an order, and had just returned. Mrs. Lawrence told me that she had been afraid there might be quarrelling, but no one would ever have dreamed of this, and then came a loud shot and then, after a few seconds, another not so loud, and we rushed to the door – she and Mary first – and everything was absolutely still."

"A loud shot and then another not so loud?"

"Yes. I noticed that even at the time. I happened to speak to Mrs. Lawrence of it afterwards and then she also remembered that it had been like that."

Afterwards Carrados often recalled with grim pleasantry that the two absolutely vital points in the fabric of circumstantial evidence that was to exonerate her father and fasten the guilt upon another had dropped from the girl's lips utterly by chance. But at the moment the facts themselves monopolized his attention.

"You are not disappointed that I can tell you so little?" she asked timidly.

125

"Scarcely," he replied. "A suicide who could not have had the weapon he dies by, a victim who is miraculously preserved by an opportune watch, and two shots from the same pistol that differ materially in volume, all taken together do not admit of disappointment."

"I am very stupid," she said. "I do not seem able to follow things. But you will come and clear my father's name?"

"I will come," he replied. "Beyond that who shall prophesy?"

It had been arranged between them that the girl should return at once, while Carrados would travel down to Great Tilling late that same afternoon and put up at the local fishing inn. In the evening he would call at Barony, where Madeline would accept him as a distant connexion of the family. The arrangement was only for the benefit of the domestics and any casual visitor who might be present, for there was no possibility of a near relation being in attendance. Nor was there any appreciable danger of either his name or person being recognized in those parts, a consideration that seemed to have some weight with the girl, for, more than once, she entreated him not to disclose to anyone his real business there until he had arrived at a definite conclusion.

It was nine o'clock, but still just light enough to distinguish the prominent features of the landscape, when Carrados, accompanied by Parkinson, reached Barony. The house, as described by the manservant, was a substantial grey stone building, very plain, very square, very exposed to the four winds. It had not even a porch to break the flat surface, and here and there in the line of its three solid storeys a window had been built up by some frugal, tax-evading Whitmarsh of a hundred years ago.

"Sombre enough," commented Carrados, "but the connexion between environment and crime is not yet capable of analysis. We get murders in brand-new suburban villas and the virtues, light-heartedness and good fellowship, in moated granges. What should you say about it, eh, Parkinson?"

"I should say it was damp, sir," observed Parkinson, with his wisest air.

Madeline Whitmarsh herself opened the door. She took them down the long flagged hall to the dining room, a cheerful enough apartment whatever its exterior might forebode.

"I am glad you have come now, Mr. Carrados," she said hurriedly, when the door was closed. "Sergeant Brewster is here from Stinbridge Police Station to make some arrangements for the inquest. It is to be held at the schools here on Monday. He says that he must take the revolver with him to produce. Do you want to see it before he goes?"

"I should like to," replied Carrados.

"Will you come into Papa's room then? He is there."

The sergeant was at the table, making notes in his pocket-book, when they entered. An old-fashioned revolver lay before him.

"This gentleman has come a long way on hearing about poor Papa," said the girl. "He would like to see the revolver before you take it, Mr. Brewster."

"Good evening, sir," said Brewster. "It's a bad business that brings us here."

Carrados "looked" round the room and returned the policeman's greeting. Madeline hesitated for a moment, and then, picking up the weapon, put it into the blind man's hand.

"A bit out of date, sir," remarked Brewster, with a nod. "But in good order yet, I find."

"An early French make, I should say – one of Lefaucheux's probably," said Carrados. "You have removed the cartridges?"

"Why, yes," admitted the sergeant, producing a matchbox from his pocket. "They're pin-fire, you see, and I'm not too fond of carrying a thing like that loaded in my pocket as I'm riding a young horse."

"Quite so," agreed Carrados, fingering the cartridges. "I wonder if you happened to mark the order of these in the chambers?"

"That was scarcely necessary, sir. Two, together, had been fired. The other four had not."

"I once knew a case – possibly I read of it – where a pack of cards lay on the floor. It was a murder case and the guilt or innocence of an accused man depended on the relative positions of the fifty-first and fifty-second cards."

"I think you must have read of that, sir," replied Brewster, endeavouring to implicate first Miss Whitmarsh and then Parkinson in his meaning smile. "However, this is straightforward enough."

"Then, of course, you have not thought it worthwhile to look for anything else?"

"I have noted all the facts that have any bearing on the case. Were you referring to any particular point, sir?"

"I was only wondering," suggested Carrados, with apologetic mildness, "whether you, or anyone, had happened to find a wad lying about anywhere."

The sergeant stroked his well-kept moustache to hide the smile that insisted, however, on escaping through his eyes"

"Scarcely, sir," he replied, with fine irony. "Bulleted revolver cartridges contain no wad. You are thinking of a shot-gun, sir."

"Oh," said Carrados, bending over the spent cartridge he was examining, "that settles it, of course."

"I think so, sir," assented the sergeant, courteously but with a quiet enjoyment of the situation. "Well, Miss, I'll be getting back now. I think I have everything I want."

"You will excuse me a few minutes?" said Miss Whitmarsh, and the two callers were left alone.

"Parkinson," said Carrados softly, as the door closed, "look round on the floor. There is no wad lying within sight?"

"No, sir."

"Then take the lamp and look behind things. But if you find one don't disturb it."

For a minute strange and gigantic shadows chased one another across the ceiling as Parkinson moved the table-lamp to and fro behind the furniture. The man to whom blazing sunlight and the deepest shade were as one sat with his eyes fixed tranquilly on the unseen wall before him.

"There is a little pellet of paper here behind the couch, sir," announced Parkinson.

"Then put the lamp back."

Together they drew the cumbrous old piece of furniture from the wall and Carrados went behind. On hands and knees, with his face almost to the floor, he appeared to be studying even the dust that lay there. Then with a light, unerring touch he carefully picked up the thing that Parkinson had found. Very gently he unrolled it, using his long, delicate fingers so skilfully that even at the end the particles of dust still clung here and there to the surface of the paper.

"What do you make of it, Parkinson?"

Parkinson submitted it to the judgment of a single sense.

"A cigarette-paper to all appearance, sir. I can't say it's a kind that I've had experience of. It doesn't seem to have any distinct watermark, but there is a half-inch of glossy paper along one edge."

"Amber-tipped. Yes?"

"Another edge is a little uneven. It appears to have been cut."

"This edge opposite the mouthpiece. Yes, yes."

"Patches are blackened, and little holes – like pinpricks – burned through. In places it is scorched brown."

"Anything else?"

"I hope there is nothing I have failed to observe, sir," said Parkinson, after a pause.

Carrados's reply was a strangely irrelevant question.

"What is the ceiling made of?" he demanded.

"Oak boards, sir, with a heavy cross-beam."

"Are there any plaster figures about the room?"

"No, sir."

"Or anything at all that is whitewashed?"

"Nothing, sir."

Carrados raised the scrap of tissue paper to his nose again, and for the second time he touched it with his tongue.

"Very interesting, Parkinson," he remarked, and Parkinson's responsive "Yes, sir" was a model of discreet acquiescence.

"I am sorry that I had to leave you," said Miss Whitmarsh, returning, "but Mrs. Lawrence is out and my father made a practice of offering everyone refreshment."

"Don't mention it," said Carrados. "We have not been idle. I came from London to pick up a scrap of paper, lying on the floor of this room. Well, here it is." He rolled the tissue into a pellet again and held it before her eyes.

"The wad!" she exclaimed eagerly. "Oh, that proves that I was right?"

"Scarcely 'proves', Miss Whitmarsh."

"But it shows that one of the shots was a blank charge, as you suggested this morning might have been the case."

"Hardly even that."

"What then?" she demanded, with her large dark eyes fixed in a curious fascination on his inscrutable face.

"That behind the couch we have found this scrap of powder-singed paper."

There was a moment's silence. The girl turned away her head.

"I am afraid that I am a little disappointed," she murmured.

"Perhaps better now than later. I wished to warn you that we must prove every inch of ground. Does your cousin Frank smoke cigarettes?"

"I cannot say, Mr. Carrados. You see . . . I knew so little of him."

"Quite so. There was just the chance. And your father?"

"He never did. He despised them."

"That is all I need ask you now. What time tomorrow shall I find you in, Miss Whitmarsh? It is Sunday, you remember."

"At any time. The curiosity I inspire doesn't tempt me to encounter my friends, I can assure you," she replied, her face hardening at the recollection. "But . . . Mr. Carrados – "

"Yes?"

"The inquest is on Monday afternoon . . . I had a sort of desperate faith that you would be able to vindicate Papa."

"By the time of the inquest, you mean?"

"Yes. Otherwise – "

"The verdict of a Coroner's Jury means nothing, Miss Whitmarsh. It is the merest formality."

"It means a very great deal to me. It haunts and oppresses me. If they say – if it goes out – that Papa is guilty of the attempt of murder, and of suicide, I shall never raise my head again."

Carrados had no desire to prolong a futile discussion.

"Good night," he said, holding out his hand.

"Good night, Mr. Carrados." She detained him a moment, her voice vibrant with quiet feeling. "I already owe you more than I can ever hope to express. Your wonderful kindness – "

"A strange case," moralized Carrados, as they walked out of the quadrangular yard into the silent lane. "Instructive, but I more-than-half wish I'd never heard of it."

"The young lady seems grateful, sir," Parkinson ventured to suggest.

"The young lady is the case, Parkinson," replied his master rather grimly.

A few score yards farther on a swing gate gave access to a field-path, cutting off the corner that the high road made with the narrow lane. This was their way, but instead of following the brown line of trodden earth, Carrados turned to the left and indicated the line of buildings that formed the back of one side of the quadrangle they had passed through.

"We will investigate here," he said. "Can you see a way in?"

Most of the buildings opened on to the yard, but at one end of the range Parkinson discovered a door, secured only by a wooden latch. The place beyond was impenetrably dark, but the sweet, dusty smell of hay, and, from beyond, the occasional click of a horse's shoe on stone and the rattle of a head-stall chain through the manger ring told them that they were in the chaff-pen at the back of the stable.

Carrados stretched out his hand and touched the wall with a single finger.

"We need go no farther," he remarked, and as they resumed their way across the field he took out a handkerchief to wipe the taste of whitewash off his tongue.

Madeline had spoken of the gradual decay of High Barn, but Carrados was hardly prepared for the poverty-stricken desolation which Parkinson described as they approached the homestead on the following afternoon. He had purposely selected a way that took them across many of young Whitmarsh's ill-stocked fields, fields in which sedge and charlock wrote an indictment of neglected drains and half-hearted tillage. On the land, the gates and hedges had been broken and unkempt. The buildings, as they passed through the farmyard, were empty and showed here and there a skeletonry of bare rafters to the sky.

"Starved," commented the blind man, as he read the signs. "The thirsty owner and the hungry land: They couldn't both be fed."

130

Although it was afternoon, the bolts and locks of the front door had to be unfastened in answer to their knock. When at last the door was opened a shrivelled little old woman, rather wicked-looking in a comic way, and rather begrimed, stood there.

"Mr. Frank Whitmarsh?" she replied to Carrados's polite inquiry. "Oh yes, he lives here. Frank," she called down the passage, "you're wanted."

"What is it, Mother?" responded a man's full, strong voice rather lazily.

"Come and see!" and the old creature ogled Carrados with her beady eyes as though the situation constituted an excellent joke between them.

There was the sound of a chair being moved and at the end of the passage a tall man appeared in his shirt sleeves.

"I am a stranger to you," explained Carrados, "but I am staying at the Bridge Inn and I heard of your wonderful escape on Thursday. I was so interested that I have taken the liberty of coming across to congratulate you on it."

"Oh, come in, come in," said Whitmarsh. "Yes . . . it was a sort of miracle, wasn't it?.

He led the way back into the room he had come from, half-kitchen, half-parlour. It at least had the virtue of an air of rude comfort, and some of the pewter and china that ornamented its mantelpiece and dresser would have rejoiced a collector's heart.

"You find us a bit rough," apologized the young man, with something of contempt towards his surroundings. "We weren't expecting visitors."

"And I was hesitating to come because I thought that you would be surrounded by your friends."

This very ordinary remark seemed to afford Mrs. Whitmarsh unbounded entertainment, and for quite a number of seconds she was convulsed with silent amusement at the idea.

"Shut up, Mother," said her dutiful son. "Don't take any notice of her," he remarked to his visitors. "She often goes on like that. The fact is," he added, "we Whitmarshes aren't popular in these parts. Of course that doesn't trouble me. I've seen too much of things. And, taken as a boiling, the Whitmarshes deserve it."

"Ah, wait till you touch the coal, my boy, then you'll see," put in the old lady, with malicious triumph.

"I reckon we'll show them then, eh, Mother?" he responded bumptiously. "Perhaps you've heard of that, Mr. –?"

"Carrados – Wynn Carrados. This is my man, Parkinson. I have to be attended because my sight has failed me. Yes, I had heard something about

131

coal. Providence seems to be on your side just now, Mr. Whitmarsh. May I offer you a cigarette?"

"Thanks, I don't mind for once in a way."

"They're Turkish. Quite innocuous, I believe."

"Oh, it isn't that. I can smoke cutty with any man, I reckon, but the paper affects my lips. I make my own and use a sort of paper with an end that doesn't stick."

"The paper is certainly a drawback sometimes," agreed Carrados. "I've found that. Might I try one of yours?

They exchanged cigarettes and Whitmarsh returned to the subject of the tragedy.

"This has made a bit of a stir, I can tell you," he remarked, with complacency.

"I am sure it would. Well, it was the chief topic of conversation when I was in London."

"Is that a fact?" Avowedly indifferent to the opinion of his neighbours, even Whitmarsh was not proof against the pronouncement of the metropolis. "What do they say about it up there?"

"I should be inclined to think that the interest centres round the explanation you will give at the inquest of the cause of the quarrel."

"There! What did I tell you?" exclaimed Mrs. Whitmarsh.

"Be quiet, Mother. That's easily answered, Mr. Carrados. There was a bit of duck shooting that lay between our two places. But perhaps you saw that in the papers?"

"Yes," admitted Carrados, "I saw that. Frankly, the reason seemed inadequate to so deadly a climax."

"What did I say?" demanded the irrepressible dame. "They won't believe it."

The young man cast a wrathful look in his mother's direction and turned again to the visitor.

"That's because you don't know Uncle William. Any reason was good enough for him to quarrel over. Here, let me give you an instance. When I went in on Thursday he was smoking a pipe. Well, after a bit I took out a cigarette and lit it. I'm damned if he didn't turn round and start on me for that. How does that strike you for one of your own family, Mr. Carrados?"

"Unreasonable, I am bound to admit. I am afraid that I should have been inclined to argue the point. What did you do, Mr. Whitmarsh?"

"I hadn't gone there to quarrel," replied the young man, half-sulky at the recollection. "It was his house. I threw it into the fireplace."

"Very obliging," said Carrados. "But, if I may say so, it isn't so much a matter of speculation why he should shoot you as why he should shoot himself."

"The gentleman seems friendly. Better ask his advice, Frank," put in the old woman in a penetrating whisper.

"Stow it, Mother!" said Whitmarsh sharply. "Are you crazy? Her idea of a coroner's inquest," he explained to Carrados, with easy contempt, "is that I am being tried for murder. As a matter of fact, Uncle William was a very passionate man, and, like many of that kind, he frequently went beyond himself. I don't doubt that he was sure he'd killed me, for he was a good shot and the force of the blow sent me backwards. He was a very proud man too, in a way – wouldn't stand correction or any kind of authority, and when he realized what he'd done and saw in a flash that he would be tried and hanged for it, suicide seemed the easiest way out of his difficulties, I suppose."

"Yes. That sounds reasonable enough," admitted Carrados.

"Then you don't think there will be any trouble, sir?" insinuated Mrs. Whitmarsh anxiously.

Frank had already professed his indifference to local opinion, but Carrados was conscious that both of them hung rather breathlessly on to his reply.

"Why, no," he declared weightily. "I should see no reason for anticipating any. Unless," he added thoughtfully, "some clever lawyer was instructed to insist that there must be more in the dispute than appears on the surface."

"Oh, them lawyers, them lawyers!" moaned the old lady in a panic. "They can make you say anything."

"They can't make me say anything." A cunning look came into his complacent face. "And, besides, who's going to engage a lawyer?"

"The family of the deceased gentleman might wish to do so."

"Both of the sons are abroad and could not be back in time."

"But is there not a daughter here? I understood so."

Whitmarsh gave a short, unpleasant laugh and turned to look at his mother.

"Madeline won't. You may bet your bottom tikkie it's the last thing she would want."

The little old creature gazed admiringly at her big showy son and responded with an appreciative grimace that made her look more humorously rat-like than ever.

"He! He! Missie won't," she tittered. "That would never do. He! He!" Wink succeeded nod and meaning smile until she relapsed into a state of quietness, and Parkinson, who had been fascinated by her contortions, was unable to decide whether she was still laughing or had gone to sleep.

Carrados stayed a few more minutes, and before they left he asked to see the watch.

"A unique memento, Mr. Whitmarsh," he remarked, examining it. "I should think this would become a family heirloom."

"It's no good for anything else," said Whitmarsh practically. "A famous time-keeper it was, too."

"The fingers are both gone."

"Yes. The glass was broken, of course, and they must have caught in the cloth of my pocket and ripped off."

"They naturally would. It was ten minutes past nine when the shot was fired."

The young man thought and then nodded.

"About that," he agreed.

"Nearer than 'about,' if your watch was correct. Very interesting, Mr. Whitmarsh. I am glad to have seen the watch that saved your life."

Instead of returning to the inn, Carrados directed Parkinson to take the road to Barony. Madeline was at home, and from the sound of voices it appeared that she had other visitors, but she came out to Carrados at once, and at his request took him into the empty dining room while Parkinson stayed in the hall.

"Yes?" she said eagerly.

"I have come to tell you that I must throw up my brief," he said. "There is nothing more to be done and I return to town tonight."

"Oh!" she stammered helplessly. "I thought – I thought – "

"Your cousin did not abstract the revolver when he was here on Thursday, Miss Whitmarsh. He did not at his leisure fire a bullet into his own watch to make it appear, later in the day, as if he had been attacked. He did not reload the cartridge with a blank charge. He did not deliberately shoot your father and then fire off the blank cartridge. He was attacked and the newspaper version is substantially correct. The whole fabric so delicately suggested by inference and innuendo falls to pieces."

"Then you desert me, Mr. Carrados?" she said, in a low, bitter voice.

"I have seen the watch – the watch that saved Whitmarsh's life," he continued, unmoved. "It would save it again if necessary. It indicates ten minutes past nine – the time to a minute at which it is agreed the shot was fired. By what prescience was he to know at what exact minute his opportunity would occur?"

"When I saw the watch on Thursday night the fingers were not there."

134

"They are not, but the shaft remains. It is of an old-fashioned pattern and it will only take the fingers in one position. That position indicates ten minutes past nine."

"Surely it would have been an easy matter to have altered that afterwards?"

"In this case, Fate has been curiously systematic, Miss Whitmarsh. The bullet that shattered the works has so locked the action that it will not move a fraction this way or that."

"There is something more than this – something that I do not understand," she persisted. "I think I have a right to know."

"Since you insist, there is. There is the wad of the blank cartridge that you fired in the outbuilding."

"Oh!" she exclaimed, in the moment of startled undefence, "how do you – how can you – "

"You must leave the conjurer his few tricks for effect. Of course you naturally would fire it where the precious pellet could not get lost – the paper you steamed off the cigarette that Whitmarsh threw into the empty fire-grate, and of course the place must be some distance from the house or even that slight report might occasion remark."

"Yes," she confessed, in a sudden abandonment to weary indifference, "it has been useless. I was a fool to set my cleverness against yours. Now, I suppose, Mr. Carrados, you will have to hand me over to justice.

"Well, why don't you say something?" she demanded impatiently, as he offered no comment.

"People frequently put me in this embarrassing position," he explained diffidently, "and throw the responsibility on me. Now a number of years ago a large and stately building was set up in London and it was beautifully called 'The Royal Palace of Justice'. That was its official name and that was what it was to be, but very soon people got into the way of calling it the Law Courts, and today, if you asked a Londoner to direct you to the Palace of Justice he would undoubtedly set you down as a religious maniac. You see my difficulty?"

"It is very strange," she said, intent upon her own reflections, "but I do not feel a bit ashamed to you of what I have done. I do not even feel afraid to tell you all about it, although of some of that I must certainly be ashamed. Why is it?"

"Because I am blind?"

"Oh no," she replied very positively.

Carrados smiled at her decision but he did not seek to explain that when he could no longer see the faces of men, the power was gradually given to him of looking into their hearts, to which some in their turn – strong, free spirits – instinctively responded.

"There is such a thing as friendship at first sight," he suggested.

"Why, yes, like quite old friends," she agreed. "It is a pity that I had no very trusty friend, since my mother died when I was quite little. Even my father has been – it is queer to think of it now – well, almost a stranger to me really."

She looked at Carrados's serene and kindly face and smiled.

"It is a great relief to be able to talk like this, without the necessity for lying," she remarked. "Did you know that I was engaged?"

"No, you had not told me that."

"Oh no, but you might have heard of it. He is a clergyman whom I met last summer. But, of course, that is all over now."

"You have broken it off?"

"Circumstances have broken it off. The daughter of a man who had the misfortune to be murdered might just possibly be tolerated as a vicar's wife, but the daughter of a murderer and suicide – it is unthinkable! You see, the requirements for the office are largely social, Mr. Carrados."

"Possibly your vicar may have other views."

"Oh, he isn't a vicar yet, but he is rather well-connected, so it is quite assured. And he would be dreadfully torn if the choice lay with him. As it is, he will perhaps rather soon get over my absence. But, you see, if we married he could never get over my presence. It would always stand in the way of his preferment. I worked very hard to make it possible, but it could not be."

"You were even prepared to send an innocent man to the gallows?"

"I think so, at one time," she admitted frankly. "But I scarcely thought it would come to that. There are so many well-meaning people who always get up petitions . . . No, as I stand here looking at myself over there, I feel that I couldn't quite have hanged Frank, no matter how much he deserved it . . . You are very shocked, Mr. Carrados?"

"Well," admitted Carrados, with pleasant impartiality, "I have seen the young man, but the penalty, even with a reprieve, still seems to me a little severe."

"Yet how do you know, even now, that he is, as you say, an innocent man?"

"I don't," was the prompt admission. "I only know, in this astonishing case, that so far as my investigation goes, he did not murder your father by the act of his hand."

"Not according to your Law Courts?" she suggested. "But in the great Palace of Justice? . . . Well, you shall judge."

136

She left his side, crossed the room, and stood by the square, ugly window, looking out, but as blind as Carrados to the details of the somnolent landscape.

"I met Frank for the first time after I was at all grown-up about three years ago, when I returned from boarding school. I had not seen him since I was a child, and I thought him very tall and manly. It seemed a frightfully romantic thing in the circumstances to meet him secretly – of course my thoughts flew to Romeo and Juliet. We put impassioned letters for one another in a hollow tree that stood on the boundary hedge. But presently I found out – gradually and incredulously at first and then one night with a sudden terrible certainty – that my ideas of romance were not his . . . I had what is called, I believe, a narrow escape. I was glad when he went abroad, for it was only my self-conceit that had suffered. I was never in love with him: Only in love with the idea of being in love with him.

"A few months ago Frank came back to High Barn. I tried never to meet him anywhere, but one day he overtook me in the lanes. He said that he had thought a lot about me while he was away, and would I marry him. I told him that it was impossible in any case, and, besides, I was engaged. He coolly replied that he knew. I was dumbfounded and asked him what he meant.

"Then he took out a packet of my letters that he had kept somewhere all the time. He insisted on reading parts of them up and telling me what this and that meant and what everyone would say it proved. I was horrified at the construction that seemed capable of being put on my foolish but innocent gush. I called him a coward and a blackguard and a mean cur and a sneaking cad and everything I could think of in one long breath, until I found myself faint and sick with excitement and the nameless growing terror of it.

"He only laughed and told me to think it over, and then walked on, throwing the letters up into the air and catching them.

"It isn't worthwhile going into all the times he met and threatened me. I was to marry him or he would expose me. He would never allow me to marry anyone else. And then finally he turned round and said that he didn't really want to marry me at all. He only wanted to force father's consent to start mining and this had seemed the easiest way."

"That is what is called blackmail, Miss Whitmarsh – a word you don't seem to have applied to him. The punishment ranges up to penal servitude for life in extreme cases."

"Yes, that is what it really was. He came on Thursday with the letters in his pocket. That was his last threat when he could not move me. I can guess what happened. He read the letters and proposed a bargain. And my father, who was a very passionate man, and very proud in certain ways,

137

shot him as he thought, and then, in shame and in the madness of despair, took his own life . . . Now, Mr. Carrados, you were to be my judge."

"I think," said the blind man, with a great pity in his voice, "that it will be sufficient for you to come up for Judgment when called upon."

Three weeks later a registered letter bearing the Liverpool postmark was delivered at The Turrets. After he had read it Carrados put it away in a special drawer of his desk, and once or twice in after years, when his work seemed rather barren, he took it out and read it. This is what it contained:

Dear Mr. Carrados,

> *Some time after you had left me that Sunday afternoon, a man came in the dark to the door and asked for me. I did not see his face for he kept in the shade, but his figure was not very unlike that of your servant Parkinson. A packet was put into my hands and he was gone without a word. From this I imagine that perhaps you did not leave quite as soon as you had intended.*
>
> *Thank you very much indeed for the letters. I was glad to have the miserable things, to drop them into the fire, and to see them pass utterly out of my own and everybody else's life. I wonder who else in the world would have done so much for a forlorn creature who just flashed across a few days of his busy life? And then I wonder who else could.*
>
> *But there is something else for which I thank you now far, far more, and that is for saving me from the blindness of my own passionate folly. When I look back on the abyss of meanness, treachery, and guilt into which I would have wilfully cast myself, and been condemned to live in all my life, I can scarcely trust myself to write*
>
> *I will not say that I do not suffer now. I think I shall for many years to come, but all the bitterness and I think all the hardness have been drawn out.*
>
> *You will see that I am writing from Liverpool. I have taken a second-class passage to Canada and we sail tonight. Willie, who returned to Barony last week, has lent me all the money I shall need until I find work. Do not be apprehensive. It is not with the vague uncertainty of an indifferent typist or a downtrodden governess that I go, but as an efficient domestic servant – a capable cook, housemaid, or "general",*

as need be. It sounds rather incredible at first, does it not, but such things happen, and I shall get on very well.

Goodbye, Mr. Carrados. I shall remember you very often and very gratefully.

Madeline Whitmarsh

P.S. – Yes, there is friendship at first sight.

The Comedy at
Fountain Cottage

Carrados had rung up Mr. Carlyle soon after the inquiry agent had reached his office in Bampton Street on a certain morning in April. Mr. Carlyle's face at once assumed its most amiable expression as he recognized his friend's voice.

"Yes, Max," he replied, in answer to the call, "I am here and at the top of form, thanks. Glad to know that you are back from Trescoe. Is there – anything?"

"I have a couple of men coming in this evening whom you might like to meet," explained Carrados. "Manoel the Zambesia explorer is one, and the other an East-End slum doctor who has seen a few things. Do you care to come round to dinner?"

"Delighted," warbled Mr. Carlyle, without a moment's consideration. "Charmed. Your usual hour, Max?" Then the smiling complacence of his face suddenly changed and the wire conveyed an exclamation of annoyance. "I am really very sorry, Max, but I have just remembered that I have an engagement. I fear that I must deny myself after all."

"Is it important?"

"No," admitted Mr. Carlyle. "Strictly speaking, it is not in the least important. This is why I feel compelled to keep it. It is only to dine with my niece. They have just got into an absurd doll's house of a villa at Groat's Heath and I had promised to go there this evening."

"Are they particular to a day?"

There was a moment's hesitation before Mr. Carlyle replied.

"I am afraid so, now it is fixed," he said. "To you, Max, it will be ridiculous or incomprehensible that a third to dinner – and he only a middle-aged uncle – should make a straw of difference. But I know that in their bijou way it will be a little domestic event to Elsie – an added anxiety in giving the butcher an order, an extra course for dinner, perhaps. A careful drilling of the one diminutive maid-servant, and she is such a charming little woman – eh? Who, Max? No! No! I did not say the maid-servant. If I did, it is the fault of this telephone. Elsie is such a delightful little creature that, upon my soul, it would be too bad to fail her now."

"Of course it would, you old humbug," agreed Carrados, with sympathetic laughter in his voice. "Well, come tomorrow instead. I shall be alone."

"Oh, besides, there is a special reason for going, which for the moment I forgot," explained Mr. Carlyle, after accepting the invitation. "Elsie wishes for my advice with regard to her next-door neighbour. He is an elderly man of retiring disposition and he makes a practice of throwing kidneys over into her garden."

"Kittens! Throwing kittens?"

"No, no, Max. Kidneys. Stewed *k-i-d-n-e-y-s*. It is a little difficult to explain plausibly over a badly vibrating telephone, I admit, but that is what Elsie's letter assured me, and she adds that she is in despair."

"At all events, it makes the lady quite independent of the butcher, Louis!"

"I have no further particulars, Max. It may be a solitary diurnal offering, or the sky may at times appear to rain kidneys. If it is a mania, the symptoms may even have become more pronounced and the man is possibly showering beef-steaks across by this time. I will make full inquiry and let you know."

"Do," assented Carrados, in the same light-hearted spirit. "Mrs. Nickleby's neighbourly admirer expressed his feelings by throwing cucumbers, you remember, but this man puts him completely in the shade."

It had not got beyond the proportions of a jest to either of them when they rang off – one of those whimsical occurrences in real life that sound so fantastic in outline. Carrados did not give the matter another thought until the next evening when his friend's arrival revived the subject.

"And the gentleman next door?" he inquired among his greetings. "Did the customary offering arrive while you were there?"

"No," admitted Mr. Carlyle, beaming pleasantly upon all the familiar appointments of the room, "it did not, Max. In fact, so diffident has the mysterious philanthropist become, that no one at Fountain Cottage has been able to catch sight of him lately, although I am told that Scamp – Elsie's terrier – betrays a very self-conscious guilt and suspiciously muddy paws every morning."

"Fountain Cottage?"

"That is the name of the toy villa."

"Yes, but Fountain something, Groat's Heath – Fountain Court: Wasn't that where Metrobe –?"

"Yes, yes, to be sure, Max. Metrobe the traveller, the writer and scientist – "

"Scientist!"

"Well, he took up spiritualism or something, didn't he? At any rate, he lived at Fountain Court, an old red-brick house in a large neglected garden there, until his death a couple of years ago. Then, as Groat's Heath

141

had suddenly become a popular suburb with a tube railway, a land company acquired the estate, the house was razed to the ground, and in a twinkling a colony of Noah's ark villas took its place. There is Metrobe Road here, and Court Crescent there, and Mansion Drive and what not, and Elsie's little place perpetuates another landmark."

"I have Metrobe's last book there," said Carrados, nodding towards a point on his shelves. "In fact, he sent me a copy. *The Flame Beyond the Dome* it is called – the queerest farrago of balderdash and metaphysics imaginable. But what about the neighbour, Louis? Did you settle what we might almost term 'his hash'?"

"Oh, he is mad, of course. I advised her to make as little fuss about it as possible, seeing that the man lives next door and might become objectionable, but I framed a note for her to send which will probably have a good effect."

"Is he mad, Louis?"

"Well, I don't say that he is strictly a lunatic, but there is obviously a screw loose somewhere. He may carry indiscriminate benevolence towards Yorkshire terriers to irrational lengths. Or he may be a food specialist with a grievance. In effect he is mad on at least that one point. How else are we to account for the circumstances?"

"I was wondering," replied Carrados thoughtfully.

"You suggest that he really may have a sane object?"

"I suggest it – for the sake of argument: If he has a sane object, what is it?"

"That I leave to you, Max," retorted Mr. Carlyle conclusively. "If he has a sane object, pray what is it?"

"For the sake of the argument, I will tell you that in half-a-dozen words, Louis," replied Carrados, with good-humoured tolerance. "If he is not mad in the sense which you have defined, the answer stares us in the face. His object is precisely that which he is achieving."

Mr. Carlyle looked inquiringly into the placid, unemotional face of his blind friend, as if to read there whether, incredible as it might seem, Max should be taking the thing seriously after all.

"And what is that?" he asked cautiously.

"In the first place, he has produced the impression that he is eccentric or irresponsible. That is sometimes useful in itself. Then what else has he done?"

"What else, Max?" replied Mr. Carlyle, with some indignation. "Well, whatever he wishes to achieve by it, I can tell you one thing else that he has done: He has so demoralized Scamp with his confounded kidneys that Elsie's neatly arranged flower-beds – and she took Fountain Cottage principally on account of an unusually large garden – are

142

hopelessly devastated. If she keeps the dog up, the garden is invaded night and day by an army of peregrinating feline marauders that scent the booty from afar. He has gained the everlasting annoyance of an otherwise charming neighbour, Max. Can you tell me what he has achieved by that?"

"The everlasting esteem of Scamp probably. Is he a good watch-dog, Louis?"

"Good Heavens, Max!" exclaimed Mr. Carlyle, coming to his feet as though he had the intention of setting out for Groat's Heath then and there, "is it possible that he is planning a burglary?"

"Do they keep much of value about the house?"

"No," admitted Mr. Carlyle, sitting down again with considerable relief. "No, they don't. Bellmark is not particularly well endowed with worldly goods – In fact, between ourselves, Max, Elsie could have done very much better from a strictly social point of view, but he is a thoroughly good fellow and idolizes her. They have no silver worth speaking of, and for the rest – well, just the ordinary petty cash of a frugal young couple."

"Then he probably is not planning a burglary. I confess that the idea did not appeal to me. If it is only that, why should he go to the trouble of preparing this particular succulent dish to throw over his neighbour's ground when cold liver would do quite as well?"

"If it is not only that, why should he go to the trouble, Max?"

"Because by that bait he produces the greatest disturbance of your niece's garden."

"And, if sane, why should he wish to do that?"

"Because in those conditions he can the more easily obliterate his own traces if he trespasses there at nights."

"Well, upon my word, that's drawing a bow at a venture, Max. If it isn't burglary, what motive could the man have for any such nocturnal perambulation?"

An expression of suave mischief came into Carrados's usually imperturbable face.

"Many imaginable motives surely, Louis. You are a man of the world. Why not to meet a charming little woman – "

"No, by Gad!" exclaimed the scandalized uncle warmly. "I decline to consider the remotest possibility of that explanation. Elsie – '

"Certainly not," interposed Carrados, smothering his quiet laughter. "The maid-servant, of course."

Mr. Carlyle reined in his indignation and recovered himself with his usual adroitness.

"But, you know, that is an atrocious libel, Max," he added. "I never said such a thing. However, is it probable?"

143

"No," admitted Carrados. "I don't think that in the circumstances it is at all probable."

"Then where are we, Max?"

"A little further than we were at the beginning. Very little . . . Are you willing to give me a roving commission to investigate?"

"Of course, Max, of course," assented Mr. Carlyle heartily. "I – well, as far as I was concerned, I regarded the matter as settled."

Carrados turned to his desk and the ghost of a smile might possibly have lurked about his face. He produced some stationery and indicated it to his visitor.

"You don't mind giving me a line of introduction to your niece?"

"Pleasure," murmured Carlyle, taking up a pen. "What shall I say?"

Carrados took the inquiry in its most literal sense and for reply he dictated the following letter:

My dear Elsie,

"If that is the way you usually address her," he parenthesized.

"Quite so," acquiesced Mr. Carlyle, writing.

> *The bearer of this is Mr. Carrados, of whom I have spoken to you.*

"You have spoken of me to her, I trust, Louis?" he put in.

"I believe that I have casually referred to you," admitted the writer.

"I felt sure you would have done. It makes the rest easier."

> *He is not in the least mad, although he frequently does things which to the uninitiated appear more or less eccentric at the moment. I think that you would be quite safe in complying with any suggestion he may make.*
>
> *Your affectionate uncle,*
> *Louis Carlyle*

He accepted the envelope and put it away in a pocket-book that always seemed extraordinarily thin for the amount of papers it contained.

"I may call there tomorrow," he added.

Neither again referred to the subject during the evening, but when Parkinson came to the library a couple of hours after midnight to know whether he would be required again, he found his master rather deeply immersed in a book and a gap on the shelf where *The Flame Beyond the Dome* had formerly stood.

It is not impossible that Mr. Carlyle supplemented his brief note of introduction with a more detailed communication that reached his niece by the ordinary postal service at an earlier hour than the other. At all events, when Mr. Carrados presented himself at the toy villa on the following afternoon, he found Elsie Bellmark suspiciously disposed to accept him and his rather gratuitous intervention among her suburban troubles as a matter of course.

When the car drew up at the bright green wooden gate of Fountain Cottage, another visitor, apparently a good-class working man, was standing on the path of the trim front garden, lingering over a reluctant departure. Carrados took sufficient time in alighting to allow the man to pass through the gate before he himself entered. The last exchange of sentences reached his ear.

"I'm sure, marm, you won't find anyone to do the work at less."

"I can quite believe that," replied a very fair young lady who stood nearer the house, "but, you see, we do all the gardening ourselves, thank you."

Carrados made himself known and was taken into the daintily pretty drawing room that opened on to the lawn behind the house.

"I do not need to ask if you are Mrs. Bellmark," he had declared.

"I have Uncle Louis's voice?" she divined readily.

"The niece of his voice, so to speak," he admitted. "Voices mean a great deal to me, Mrs. Bellmark."

"In recognizing and identifying people?" she suggested.

"Oh, very much more than that. In recognizing and identifying their moods – their thoughts even. There are subtle lines of trouble and the deep rings of anxious care quite as patent to the ear as to the sharpest eye sometimes."

Elsie Bellmark shot a glance of curiously interested speculation to the face that, in spite of its frank, open bearing, revealed so marvellously little itself.

"If I had any dreadful secret, I think that I should be a little afraid to talk to you, Mr. Carrados," she said, with a half-nervous laugh.

"Then please do not have any dreadful secret," he replied, with quite youthful gallantry. "I more than suspect that Louis has given you a very transpontine idea of my tastes. I do not spend all my time tracking murderers to their lairs, Mrs. Bellmark, and I have never yet engaged in a hand-to-hand encounter with a band of cut-throats."

"He told us," she declared, the recital lifting her voice into a tone that Carrados vowed to himself was wonderfully thrilling, "about this: He said that you were once in a sort of lonely underground cellar near the river with two desperate men whom you could send to penal servitude. The police, who were to have been there at a certain time, had not arrived, and you were alone. The men had heard that you were blind but they could hardly believe it. They were discussing in whispers which could not be overheard what would be the best thing to do, and they had just agreed that if you really were blind they would risk the attempt to murder you. Then, Louis said, at that very moment you took a pair of scissors from your pocket, and coolly asking them why they did not have a lamp down there, you actually snuffed the candle that stood on the table before you. Is that true?"

Carrados's mind leapt vividly back to the most desperate moment of his existence, but his smile was gently deprecating as he replied.

"I seem to recognize the touch of truth in the inclination to do anything rather than fight," he confessed. "But, although he never suspects it, Louis really sees life through rose-coloured opera glasses. Take the case of your quite commonplace neighbour – "

"That is really what you came about?" she interposed shrewdly.

"Frankly, it is," he replied. "I am more attracted by a turn of the odd and grotesque than by the most elaborate tragedy. The fantastic conceit of throwing stewed kidneys over into a neighbour's garden irresistibly appealed to me. Louis, as I was saying, regards the man in the romantic light of a humanitarian monomaniac or a demented food reformer. I take a more subdued view and I think that his action, when rightly understood, will prove to be something quite obviously natural."

"Of course it is very ridiculous, but all the same it has been desperately annoying," she confessed. "Still, it scarcely matters now. I am only sorry that it should have been the cause of wasting your valuable time, Mr. Carrados."

"My valuable time," he replied, "only seems valuable to me when I am, as you would say, wasting it. But is the incident closed? Louis told me that he had drafted you a letter of remonstrance. May I ask if it has been effective?"

Instead of replying at once she got up and walked to the long French window and looked out over the garden where the fruit-trees that had been spared from the older cultivation were rejoicing the eye with the promise of their pink and white profusion.

"I did not send it," she said slowly, turning to her visitor again. "There is something that I did not tell Uncle Louis, because it would only have distressed him without doing any good. We may be leaving here very soon."

146

"Just when you had begun to get it well in hand?" he said, in some surprise.

"It is a pity, is it not, but one cannot foresee these things. There is no reason why you should not know the cause, since you have interested yourself so far, Mr. Carrados. In fact," she added, smiling away the seriousness of the manner into which she had fallen, "I am not at all sure that you do not know already."

He shook his head and disclaimed any such prescience.

"At all events you recognized that I was not exactly light-hearted," she insisted. "Oh, you did not say that I had dark rings under my eyes, I know, but the cap fitted excellently . . . It has to do with my husband's business. He is with a firm of architects. It was a little venturesome taking this house – we had been in apartments for two years – but Roy was doing so well with his people and I was so enthusiastic for a garden that we did – scarcely two months ago. Everything seemed quite assured. Then came this thunderbolt. The partners – it is only a small firm, Mr. Carrados – required a little more capital in the business. Someone whom they know is willing to put in two-thousand pounds, but he stipulates for a post with them as well. He, like my husband, is a draughtsman. There is no need for the services of both, and so – "

"Is it settled?"

"In effect, it is. They are as nice as can be about it, but that does not alter the facts. They declare that they would rather have Roy than the new man and they have definitely offered to retain him if he can bring in even one-thousand pounds. I suppose they have some sort of compunction about turning him adrift, for they have asked him to think it over and let them know on Monday. Of course, that is the end of it. It may be – I don't know – I don't like to think, how long before Roy gets another position equally good. We must endeavour to get this house off our hands and creep back to our three rooms. It is . . . luck."

Carrados had been listening to her wonderfully musical voice as another man might have been drawn irresistibly to watch the piquant charm of her delicate face.

"Yes," he assented, almost to himself, "it is that strange, inexplicable grouping of men and things that, under one name or another, we all confess . . . just luck."

"Of course you will not mention this to Uncle Louis yet, Mr. Carrados?"

"If you do not wish it, certainly not."

"I am sure that it would distress him. He is so soft-hearted, so kind, in everything. Do you know, I found out that he had had an invitation to dine somewhere and meet some quite important people on Tuesday. Yet he came here instead, although most other men would have cried off, just because he knew that we small people would have been disappointed."

"Well, you can't expect me to see any self-denial in that," exclaimed Carrados. "Why, I was one of them myself."

Elsie Bellmark laughed outright at the expressive disgust of his tone.

"I had no idea of that," she said. "Then there is another reason. Uncle is not very well off, yet if he knew how Roy was situated he would make an effort to arrange matters. He would, I am sure, even borrow himself in order to lend us the money. That is a thing Roy and I are quite agreed on. We will go back – We will go under, if it is to be. – but we will not borrow money, not even from Uncle Louis."

Once, subsequently, Carrados suddenly asked Mr. Carlyle whether he had ever heard a woman's voice roll like a celestial kettle-drum. The professional gentleman was vastly amused by the comparison, but he admitted that he had not.

"So that, you see," concluded Mrs. Bellmark, "there is really nothing to be done."

"Oh, quite so. I am sure that you are right," assented her visitor readily. "But in the meanwhile, I do not see why the annoyance of your next-door neighbour should be permitted to go on."

"Of course: I have not told you that, and I could not explain it to uncle," she said. "I am anxious not to do anything to put him out because I have a hope – rather a faint one, certainly – that the man may be willing to take over this house."

It would be incorrect to say that Carrados pricked up his ears – if that curious phenomenon has any physical manifestation – for the sympathetic expression of his face did not vary a fraction. But into his mind there came a gleam such as might inspire a patient digger who sees the first speck of gold that justifies his faith in an unlikely claim.

"Oh," he said, quite conversationally, "is there a chance of that?"

"He undoubtedly did want it. It is very curious in a way. A few weeks ago, before we were really settled, he came one afternoon, saying he had heard that this house was to be let. Of course I told him that he was too late, that we had already taken it for three years."

"You were the first tenants?"

"Yes. The house was scarcely ready when we signed the agreement. Then this Mr. Johns, or Jones – I am not sure which he said – went on in a rather extraordinary way to persuade me to sublet it to him. He said that the house was dear and I could get plenty, more convenient, at less rent, and it was unhealthy, and the drains were bad, and that we should be pestered by tramps and it was just the sort of house that burglars picked on, only he had taken a sort of fancy to it and he would give me a fifty-pound premium for the term."

"Did he explain the motive for this rather eccentric partiality?"

"I don't imagine that he did. He repeated several times that he was a queer old fellow with his whims and fancies and that they often cost him dear."

"I think we all know that sort of old fellow," said Carrados. "It must have been rather entertaining for you, Mrs. Bellmark."

"Yes, I suppose it was," she admitted. "The next thing we knew of him was that he had taken the other house as soon as it was finished."

"Then he would scarcely require this?"

"I am afraid not." It was obvious that the situation was not disposed of. "But he seems to have so little furniture there and to live so solitarily," she explained, "that we have even wondered whether he might not be there merely as a sort of caretaker."

"And you have never heard where he came from or who he is?"

"Only what the milkman told my servant – our chief source of local information, Mr. Carrados. He declares that the man used to be the butler at a large house that stood here formerly, Fountain Court, and that his name is neither Johns nor Jones. But very likely it is all a mistake."

"If not, he is certainly attached to the soil," was her visitor's rejoinder. "And, apropos of that, will you show me over your garden before I go, Mrs. Bellmark?"

"With pleasure," she assented, rising also. "I will ring now and then I can offer you tea when we have been round. That is, if you –?"

"Thank you, I do," he replied. "And would you allow my man to go through into the garden – in case I require him?"

"Oh, certainly. You must tell me just what you want without thinking it necessary to ask permission, Mr. Carrados," she said, with a pretty air of protection. "Shall Amy take a message?"

He acquiesced and turned to the servant who had appeared in response to the bell.

"Will you go to the car and tell my man – Parkinson – that I require him here. Say that he can bring his book. He will understand."

"Yes, sir."

They stepped out through the French window and sauntered across the lawn. Before they had reached the other side, Parkinson reported himself.

"You had better stay here," said his master, indicating the sward generally. "Mrs. Bellmark will allow you to bring out a chair from the drawing room."

"Thank you, sir. There is a rustic seat already provided," replied Parkinson.

He sat down with his back to the houses and opened the book that he had brought. Let in among its pages was an ingeniously contrived mirror.

When their promenade again brought them near the rustic seat, Carrados dropped a few steps behind.

"He is watching you from one of the upper rooms, sir," fell from Parkinson's lips as he sat there without raising his eyes from the page before him.

The blind man caught up to his hostess again.

"You intended this lawn for croquet?" he asked.

"No, not specially. It is too small, isn't it?"

"Not necessarily. I think it is in about the proportion of four-by-five all right. Given that, size does not really matter for an unsophisticated game."

To settle the point, he began to pace the plot of ground, across and then lengthways. Next, apparently dissatisfied with this rough measurement, he applied himself to marking it off more exactly by means of his walking stick. Elsie Bellmark was by no means dull, but the action sprang so naturally from the conversation that it did not occur to her to look for any deeper motive.

"He has got a pair of field-glasses and is now at the window," communicated Parkinson.

"I am going out of sight," was the equally quiet response. "If he becomes more anxious, tell me afterwards."

"It is quite all right," he reported, returning to Mrs. Bellmark with the satisfaction of bringing agreeable news. "It should make a splendid little ground, but you may have to level up a few dips after the earth has set."

A chance reference to the kitchen garden by the visitor took them to a more distant corner of the enclosure where the rear of Fountain Cottage cut off the view from the next house windows.

"We decided on this part for vegetables because it does not really belong to the garden proper," she explained.

"When they build farther on this side, we shall have to give it up very soon. And it would be a pity if it was all in flowers."

With the admirable spirit of the ordinary Englishwoman, she spoke of the future as if there was no cloud to obscure its prosperous course. She had frankly declared their position to her uncle's best friend because in the circumstances it had seemed to be the simplest and most straightforward thing to do. Beyond that, there was no need to whine about it.

"It is a large garden," remarked Carrados. "And you really do all the work of it yourselves?"

"Yes. I think that is half the fun of a garden. Roy is out here early and late and he does all the hard work. But how did you know? Did Uncle tell you?"

"No. You told me yourself."

"I? Really?"

"Indirectly. You were scorning the proffered services of a horticultural mercenary at the moment of my arrival."

"Oh, I remember," she laughed. "It was Irons, of course. He is a great nuisance. He is so stupidly persistent. For some weeks now he has been coming time after time, trying to persuade me to engage him. Once when we were all out, he had actually got into the garden and was on the point of beginning work when I returned. He said he saw the milkmen and the grocers leaving samples at the door so he thought that he would too!"

"A practical jester evidently. Is Mr. Irons a local character?"

"He said that he knew the ground and the conditions round about here better than anyone else in Groat's Heath," she replied. "Modesty is not among Mr. Irons's handicaps. He said that he – How curious!"

"What is, Mrs. Bellmark?"

"I never connected the two men before, but he said that he had been gardener at Fountain Court for seven years."

"Another family retainer who is evidently attached to the soil."

"At all events, they have not prospered equally, for while Mr. Johns seems able to take a nice house, poor Irons is willing to work for half-a-crown a day, and I am told that all the other men charge four shillings."

They had paced the boundaries of the kitchen garden, and as there was nothing more to be shown, Elsie Bellmark led the way back to the drawing room. Parkinson was still engrossed in his book, the only change being that his back was now turned towards the high paling of clinker-built oak that separated the two gardens.

"I will speak to my man," said Carrados, turning aside.

"He hurried down and is looking through the fence, sir," reported the watcher.

"That will do then. You can return to the car."

"I wonder if you would allow me to send you a small hawthorn tree?" inquired Carrados among his felicitations over the teacups five minutes later. "I think it ought to be in every garden."

"Thank you – but is it worthwhile?" replied Mrs. Bellmark, with a touch of restraint. As far as mere words went, she had been willing to ignore the menace of the future, but in the circumstances the offer seemed singularly inept and she began to suspect that outside his peculiar gifts, the wonderful Mr. Carrados might be a little bit obtuse after all."

"Yes. I think it is," he replied, with quiet assurance.

151

"In spite of –?"

"I am not forgetting that unless your husband is prepared on Monday next to invest one-thousand pounds, you contemplate leaving here."

"Then I do not understand it, Mr. Carrados."

"And I am unable to explain as yet. But I brought you a note from Louis Carlyle, Mrs. Bellmark. You only glanced at it. Will you do me the favour of reading me the last paragraph?"

She picked up the letter from the table where it lay and complied with cheerful good humour.

"There is some suggestion that you want me to accede to," she guessed cunningly when she had read the last few words.

"There are some three suggestions which I hope you will accede to," he replied. "In the first place, I want you to write to Mr. Johns next door – let him get the letter tonight – inquiring whether he is still disposed to take this house."

"I had thought of doing that shortly."

"Then that is all right. Besides, he will ultimately decline."

"Oh," she exclaimed – it would be difficult to say whether with relief or disappointment – "do you think so? Then why – "

"To keep him quiet in the meantime. Next I should like you to send a little note to Mr. Irons – your maid could deliver it also tonight, I dare say?"

"Irons! Irons the gardener?"

"Yes," apologetically. "Only a line or two, you know. Just saying that, after all, if he cares to come on Monday you can find him a few days' work."

"But in any circumstances I don't want him."

"No. I can quite believe that you could do better. Still, it doesn't matter, as he won't come, Mrs. Bellmark. Not for half-a-crown a day, believe me. But the thought will tend to make Mr. Irons less restive also. Lastly, will you persuade your husband not to decline his firm's offer until Monday?"

"Very well, Mr. Carrados," she said, after a moment's consideration. "You are Uncle Louis's friend and therefore our friend. I will do what you ask."

"Thank you," said Carrados. "I shall endeavour not to disappoint you."

"I shall not be disappointed because I have not dared to hope. And I have nothing to expect because I am still completely in the dark."

"I have been there for nearly twenty years, Mrs. Bellmark."

"Oh, I am sorry!" she cried impulsively.

152

"So am I – occasionally," he replied. "Goodbye, Mrs. Bellmark. You will hear from me shortly, I hope. About the hawthorn, you know."

It was, indeed, in something less than forty-eight hours that she heard from him again. When Bellmark returned to his toy villa early on Saturday afternoon, Elsie met him almost at the gate with a telegram in her hand.

"I really think, Roy, that everyone we have to do with here goes mad," she exclaimed, in tragi-humorous despair. "First it was Mr. Johns or Jones – if he is Johns or Jones – and then Irons who wanted to work here for half of what he could get at heaps of places about, and now just look at this wire that came from Mr. Carrados half-an-hour ago."

This was the message that he read:

Please procure sardine tin opener, mariner's compass, and bottle of champagne. Shall arrive 6:45 bringing Crataegus Coccinea.

Carrados

"Could anything be more absurd?" she demanded.

"Sounds as though it was in code," speculated her husband. "Who's the foreign gentleman he's bringing?"

"Oh, that's a kind of special hawthorn – I looked it up. But a bottle of champagne, and a compass, and a sardine tin opener! What possible connexion is there between them?"

"A very resourceful man might uncork a bottle of champagne with a sardine tin opener," he suggested.

"And find his way home afterwards by means of a mariner's compass?" she retorted. "No, Roy dear, you are not a sleuth-hound. We had better have our lunch."

They lunched, but if the subject of Carrados had been tabooed the meal would have been a silent one.

"I have a compass on an old watch-chain somewhere," volunteered Bellmark.

"And I have a tin opener in the form of a bull's head," contributed Elsie.

"But we have no champagne, I suppose?"

"How could we have, Roy? We never have had any. Shall you mind going down to the shops for a bottle?"

"You really think that we ought?"

"Of course we must, Roy. We don't know what mightn't happen if we didn't. Uncle Louis said that they once failed to stop a jewel robbery because the jeweller neglected to wipe his shoes on the shop doormat, as

153

Mr. Carrados had told him to do. Suppose Johns is a desperate anarchist and he succeeded in blowing up Buckingham Palace because we – ”

“All right. A small bottle, eh?”

“No. A large one. Quite a large one. Don’t you see how exciting it is becoming?”

“If you are excited already you don’t need much champagne,” argued her husband.

Nevertheless he strolled down to the leading wine shop after lunch and returned with his purchase modestly draped in the light summer overcoat that he carried on his arm. Elsie Bellmark, who had quite abandoned her previous unconcern, in the conviction that “something was going to happen”, spent the longest afternoon that she could remember, and even Bellmark, in spite of his continual adjurations to her to “look at the matter logically”. smoked five cigarettes in place of his usual Saturday afternoon pipe and neglected to do any gardening.

At exactly six-forty-five a motor car was heard approaching. Elsie made a desperate rally to become the self-possessed hostess again. Bellmark was favourably impressed by such marked punctuality. Then a Regent Street delivery van bowled past their window and Elsie almost wept.

The suspense was not long, however. Less than five minutes later another vehicle raised the dust of the quiet suburban road, and this time a private car stopped at their gate.

“Can you see any policemen inside?” whispered Elsie.

Parkinson got down and opening the door took out a small tree which he carried up to the porch and there deposited. Carrados followed.

“At all events there isn’t much wrong,” said Bellmark. “He’s smiling all the time.”

“No, it isn’t really a smile,” explained Elsie. “It’s his normal expression.”

She went out into the hall just as the front door was opened.

“It is the ‘Scarlet-fruited thorn’ of North America,” Bellmark heard the visitor remarking. “Both the flowers and the berries are wonderfully good. Do you think that you would permit me to choose the spot for it, Mrs. Bellmark?”

Bellmark joined them in the hall and was introduced.

“We mustn’t waste any time,” he suggested. “There is very little light left.”

“True,” agreed Carrados. “And *Coccinea* requires deep digging.”

They walked through the house, and turning to the right passed into the region of the vegetable garden. Carrados and Elsie led the way, the blind man carrying the tree, while Bellmark went to his outhouse for the required tools.

"We will direct our operations from here," said Carrados, when they were halfway along the walk. "You told me of a thin iron pipe that you had traced to somewhere in the middle of the garden. We must locate the end of it exactly."

"My rosary!" sighed Elsie, with premonition of disaster, when she had determined the spot as exactly as she could. "Oh, Mr. Carrados!"

"I am sorry, but it might be worse," said Carrados inflexibly. "We only require to find the elbow-joint. Mr. Bellmark will investigate with as little disturbance as possible."

For five minutes Bellmark made trials with a pointed iron. Then he cleared away the soil of a small circle and at about a foot deep exposed a broken inch pipe.

"The fountain," announced Carrados, when he had examined it. "You have the compass, Mr. Bellmark?"

"Rather a small one," admitted Bellmark.

"Never mind. You are a mathematician. I want you to strike a line due east."

The reel and cord came into play and an adjustment was finally made from the broken pipe to a position across the vegetable garden.

"Now a point nine yards, nine feet, and nine inches along it."

"My onion bed!" cried Elsie tragically.

"Yes. It is really serious this time," agreed Carrados. "I want a hole a yard across, digging here. May we proceed?"

Elsie remembered the words of her uncle's letter – or what she imagined to be his letter – and possibly the preamble of selecting the spot had impressed her.

"Yes, I suppose so. Unless," she added hopefully, "the turnip bed will do instead? They are not sown yet."

"I am afraid that nowhere else in the garden will do," replied Carrados.

Bellmark delineated the space and began to dig. After clearing to about a foot deep he paused.

"About deep enough, Mr. Carrados?" he inquired.

"Oh, dear no," replied the blind man.

"I am two feet down," presently reported the digger.

"Deeper!" was the uncompromising response.

Another six inches were added and Bellmark stopped to rest.

"A little more and it won't matter which way up we plant *Coccinea*," he remarked.

"That is the depth we are aiming for," replied Carrados.

Elsie and her husband exchanged glances. Then Bellmark drove his spade through another layer of earth.

"Three feet," he announced, when he had cleared it.

Carrados advanced to the very edge of the opening.

"I think that if you would loosen another six inches with the fork we might consider the ground prepared," he decided.

Bellmark changed his tools and began to break up the soil. Presently the steel prongs grated on some obstruction.

"Gently," directed the blind watcher. "I think you will find a half-pound cocoa tin at the end of your fork."

"Well, how on earth you spotted that – !" was wrung from Bellmark admiringly, as he cleared away the encrusting earth. "But I believe you are about right." He threw up the object to his wife, who was risking a catastrophe in her eagerness to miss no detail. "Anything in it besides soil, Elsie?"

"She cannot open it yet," remarked Carrados. "It is soldered down."

"Oh, I say," protested Bellmark.

"It is perfectly correct, Roy. The lid is soldered on."

They looked at each other in varying degrees of wonder and speculation. Only Carrados seemed quite untouched.

"Now we may as well replace the earth," he remarked.

"Fill it all up again?" asked Bellmark.

"Yes. We have provided a thoroughly disintegrated subsoil. That is the great thing. A depth of six inches is sufficient merely for the roots."

There was only one remark passed during the operation.

"I think I should plant the tree just over where the tin was," Carrados suggested. "You might like to mark the exact spot." And there the hawthorn was placed.

Bellmark, usually the most careful and methodical of men, left the tools where they were, in spite of a threatening shower. Strangely silent, Elsie led the way back to the house and, taking the men into the drawing room, switched on the light.

"I think you have a tin opener, Mrs. Bellmark?"

Elsie, who had been waiting for him to speak, almost jumped at the simple inquiry. Then she went into the next room and returned with the bull-headed utensil.

"Here it is," she said, in a voice that would have amused her at any other time.

"Mr. Bellmark will perhaps disclose our find."

Bellmark put the soily tin down on Elsie's best table-cover without eliciting a word of reproach, grasped it firmly with his left hand, and worked the opener round the top.

156

"Only paper!" he exclaimed, and without touching the contents he passed the tin into Carrados's hands.

The blind man dexterously twirled out a little roll that crinkled pleasantly to the ear, and began counting the leaves with a steady finger.

"They're bank-notes!" whispered Elsie in an awestruck voice. She caught sight of a further detail. "Bank-notes for a hundred pounds each. And there are dozens of them!"

"Fifty, there should be," dropped Carrados between his figures. "Twenty-five, twenty-six – "

"Good God," murmured Bellmark. "That's five-thousand pounds!"

"Fifty," concluded Carrados, straightening the edges of the sheaf. "It is always satisfactory to find that one's calculations are exact." He detached the upper ten notes and held them out. "Mrs. Bellmark, will you accept one-thousand pounds as a full legal discharge of any claim that you may have on this property?"

"Me – I?" she stammered. "But I have no right to any in any circumstances. It has nothing to do with us."

"You have an unassailable moral right to a fair proportion, because without you the real owners would never have seen a penny of it. As regards your legal right – " He took out the thin pocket-book and extracting a business-looking paper spread it open on the table before them. "Here is a document that concedes it: '*In consideration of the valuable services rendered by Elsie Bellmark, etc., etc., in causing to be discovered and voluntarily surrendering the sum of five-thousand pounds deposited and not relinquished by Alexis Metrobe, late of, etc., etc., deceased, Messrs Binstead and Polegate, solicitors, of 77a Bedford Row, acting on behalf of the administrator and next-of-kin of the said etc., etc., do hereby*' – Well, that's what they do. Signed, witnessed, and stamped at Somerset House."

"I suppose I shall wake presently," said Elsie dreamily.

"It was for this moment that I ventured to suggest the third requirement necessary to bring our enterprise to a successful end," said Carrados.

"Oh, how thoughtful of you!" cried Elsie. "Roy, the champagne."

Five minutes later, Carrados was explaining to a small but enthralled audience.

"The late Alexis Metrobe was a man of peculiar character. After seeing a good deal of the world and being many things, he finally embraced spiritualism, and in common with some of its most pronounced adherents, he thenceforward abandoned what we should call 'the common-sense view'.

157

"A few years ago, by the collation of *The Book of Revelations*, a set of Zadkiel's *Almanacs*, and the complete works of Mrs. Mary Baker Eddy, Metrobe discovered that the end of the world would take place on the tenth of October 1910. It therefore became a matter of urgent importance in his mind to ensure pecuniary provision for himself for the time after the catastrophe had taken place."

"I don't understand," interrupted Elsie. "Did he expect to survive it?"

"You cannot understand, Mrs. Bellmark, because it is fundamentally incomprehensible. We can only accept the fact by the light of cases which occasionally obtain prominence. Metrobe did not expect to survive, but he was firmly convinced that the currency of this world would be equally useful in the spirit-land into which he expected to pass. This view was encouraged by a lady medium at whose feet he sat. She kindly offered to transmit to his banking account in the Hereafter, without making any charge whatever, any sum that he cared to put into her hands for the purpose. Metrobe accepted the idea but not the offer. His plan was to deposit a considerable amount in a spot of which he alone had knowledge, so that he could come and help himself to it as required."

"But if the world had come to an end –?"

"Only the *material* world, you must understand, Mrs. Bellmark. The spirit world, its exact impalpable counterpart, would continue as before and Metrobe's hoard would be spiritually intact and available. That is the prologue.

"About a month ago, there appeared a certain advertisement in a good many papers. I noticed it at the time, and three days ago I had only to refer to my files to put my hand on it at once. It reads:

> *Alexis Metrobe. Any servant or personal attendant of the late Alexis Metrobe of Fountain Court, Groat's Heath, possessing special knowledge of his habits and movements, may hear of something advantageous on applying to Binstead and Polegate, 77a Bedford Row, W.C.*

"The solicitors had, in fact, discovered that five-thousand pounds' worth of securities had been realized early in 1910. They readily ascertained that Metrobe had drawn that amount in gold out of his bank immediately after, and there the trace ended. He died six months later. There was no hoard of gold and not a shred of paper to show where it had gone, yet Metrobe lived very simply within his income. The house had meanwhile been demolished, but there was no hint or whisper of any lucky find.

158

"Two inquirers presented themselves at 77a Bedford Row. They were informed of the circumstances and offered a reward, varying according to the results, for information that would lead to the recovery of the money. They are both described as thoughtful, slow-spoken men. Each heard the story, shook his head, and departed. The first caller proved to be John Foster, the ex-butler. On the following day Mr. Irons, formerly gardener at the Court, was the applicant.

"I must now divert your attention into a side track. In the summer of 1910, Metrobe published a curious work entitled *The Flame Beyond the Dome*. In the main it is an eschatological treatise, but at the end he tacked on an epilogue, which he called *The Fable of the Chameleon*. It is even more curious than the rest and with reason, for under the guise of a speculative essay, he gives a cryptic account of the circumstances of the five-thousand pounds and, what is more important, details the exact particulars of its disposal. His reason for so doing is characteristic of the man. He was conscious by experience that he possessed an utterly treacherous memory and, having had occasion to move the treasure from one spot to another, he feared that when the time came his bemuddled shade would be unable to locate it. For future reference, therefore, he embodied the details in his book, and to make sure that plenty of copies should be in existence, he circulated it by the only means in his power – in other words, he gave a volume to everyone he knew and to a good many people whom he didn't.

"So far I have dealt with actualities. The final details are partly speculative but they are essentially correct. Metrobe conveyed his gold to Fountain Court, obtained a stout oak coffer for it, and selected a spot west of the fountain. He chose a favourable occasion for burying it, but by some mischance Irons came on the scene. Metrobe explained the incident by declaring that he was burying a favourite parrot. Irons thought nothing particular about it then, although he related the fact to the butler, and to others, in evidence of the general belief that 'the old cock was quite barmy'. But Metrobe himself was much disturbed by the accident. A few days later he dug up the box. In pursuance of his new plan, he carried his gold to the Bank of England and changed it into these notes. Then transferring the venue to one due east of the fountain, he buried them in this tin, satisfied that the small space it occupied would baffle the search of anyone not in possession of the exact location.

"But, I say!" exclaimed Mr. Bellmark. "Gold might remain gold, but what imaginable use could be made of bank-notes after the end of the world?"

"That is a point of view, no doubt. But Metrobe, in spite of his foreign name, was a thorough Englishman. The world might come to an end, but he was satisfied that somehow the Bank of England would ride through it all right. I only suggest that. There is much that we can only guess."

"That is all there is to know, Mr. Carrados?"

"Yes. Everything comes to an end, Mrs. Bellmark. I sent my car away to call for me at eight. Eight has struck. That is Harris announcing his arrival."

He stood up, but embarrassment and indecision marked the looks and movements of the other two.

"How can we possibly take all this money, though?" murmured Elsie, in painful uncertainty. "It is entirely your undertaking, Mr. Carrados. It is the merest fiction bringing me into it at all."

"Perhaps in the circumstances," suggested Bellmark nervously, "you remember the circumstances, Elsie? – Mr. Carrados would be willing to regard it as a loan – "

"No, no!" cried Elsie impulsively. "There must be no half-measures. We know that a thousand pounds would be nothing to Mr. Carrados, and he knows that a thousand pounds are everything to us." Her voice reminded the blind man of the candle-snuffing recital. "We will take this great gift, Mr. Carrados, quite freely, and we will not spoil the generous satisfaction that you must have in doing a wonderful and a splendid service by trying to hedge our obligation."

"But what can we ever do to thank Mr. Carrados?" faltered Bellmark mundanely.

"Nothing," said Elsie simply. "That is it."

"But I think that Mrs. Bellmark has quite solved that," interposed Carrados.

The Game Played
in the Dark

"It's a funny thing, sir," said Inspector Beedel, regarding Mr. Carrados with the pensive respect that he always extended towards the blind amateur. "It's a funny thing, but nothing seems to go on abroad now but what you'll find some trace of it here in London if you take the trouble to look."

"In the right quarter," contributed Carrados.

"Why, yes," agreed the inspector. "But nothing comes of it nine times out of ten, because it's no one's particular business to look here, or the thing's been taken up and finished from the other end. I don't mean ordinary murders or single-handed burglaries, of course, but – " A modest ring of professional pride betrayed the quiet enthusiast. " – real First-Class Crimes."

"The State Antonio Five-per-cent Bond Coupons?" suggested Carrados.

"Ah, you are right, Mr. Carrados." Beedel shook his head sadly, as though perhaps on that occasion someone ought to have looked. "A man has a fit in the inquiry office of the Agent-General for British Equatoria, and two-hundred-and-fifty-thousand pounds' worth of faked securities is the result in Mexico. Then look at that jade fylfot charm pawned for one-and-three down at the Basin, and the use that could have been made of it in the Kharkov 'ritual murder' trial."

"The West Hampstead Lost Memory puzzle and the Baripur bomb conspiracy that might have been smothered if one had known."

"Quite true, sir. And the three children of that Chicago millionaire – Cyrus V. Bunting, wasn't it? – kidnapped in broad daylight outside the New York Lyric and here, three weeks later, the dumb girl who chalked the wall at Charing Cross. I remember reading once in a financial article that every piece of foreign gold had a string from it leading to Threadneedle Street. A figure of speech, sir, of course, but apt enough, I don't doubt. Well, it seems to me that every big crime done abroad leaves a finger-print here in London – if only, as you say, we look in the right quarter."

"And at the right moment," added Carrados. "The time is often the present. The place the spot beneath our very noses. We take a step and the chance has gone forever."

The inspector nodded and contributed a weighty monosyllable of sympathetic agreement. The most prosaic of men in the pursuit of his ordinary duties, it nevertheless subtly appealed to some half-dormant streak of vanity to have his profession taken romantically when there was no serious work on hand.

"No. Perhaps not 'forever' in one case in a thousand, after all," amended the blind man thoughtfully. "This perpetual duel between the Law and the Criminal has sometimes appeared to me in the terms of a game of cricket, Inspector. Law is in the field. The Criminal at the wicket. If Law makes a mistake – sends down a loose ball or drops a catch – the Criminal scores a little or has another lease of life. But if he makes a mistake – if he lets a straight ball pass or spoons towards a steady man – he is done for. His mistakes are fatal. Those of the Law are only temporary and retrievable."

"Very good, sir," said Mr. Beedel, rising – the conversation had taken place in the study at The Turrets, where Beedel had found occasion to present himself. "Very apt indeed. I must remember that. Well, sir, I only hope that this 'Guido the Razor' lot will send a catch in our direction."

The 'this' delicately marked Inspector Beedel's instinctive contempt for Guido. As a craftsman he was compelled, on his reputation, to respect him, and he had accordingly availed himself of Carrados's friendship for a confabulation. As a man – he was a foreigner: Worse, an Italian, and if left to his own resources the inspector would have opposed to his sinuous flexibility those rigid, essentially Britannia-metal methods of the Force that strike the impartial observer as so ponderous, so amateurish and conventional, and, it must be admitted, often so curiously and inexplicably successful.

The offence that had circuitously brought "il Rasojo" and his "lot" within the cognizance of Scotland Yard outlines the kind of story that is discreetly hinted at by the society paragraphist of the day, politely disbelieved by the astute reader, and then at last laid indiscreetly bare in all its details by the inevitable princessly "Recollections" of a generation later. It centred round an impending royal marriage in Vienna, a certain jealous "Countess X" – (Here you have the discretion of the paragrapher.) – and a document or two that might be relied upon (the aristocratic biographer will impartially sum up the contingencies) to play the deuce with the approaching nuptials.

To procure the evidence of these papers the Countess enlisted the services of Guido, as reliable a scoundrel as she could probably have selected for the commission. To a certain point – to the abstraction of the papers, in fact – he succeeded, but it was with pursuit close upon his heels. There was that disadvantage in employing a rogue to do work that

162

implicated roguery, for whatever moral right the Countess had to the property, her accomplice had no legal right whatever to his liberty.

On half-a-dozen charges at least he could be arrested on sight in as many capitals of Europe. He slipped out of Vienna by the Nordbahn with his destination known, resourcefully stopped the express outside Czaslau and got away across to Chrudim. By this time the game and the moves were pretty well understood in more than one keenly interested quarter. Diplomacy supplemented justice, and the immediate history of Guido became that of a fox hunted from covert to covert with all the familiar earths stopped against him. From Pardubitz he passed on to Glatz, reached Breslau and went down the Oder to Stettin. Out of the liberality of his employer's advances he had ample funds to keep going, and he dropped and rejoined his accomplices as the occasion ruled. A week's harrying found him in Copenhagen, still with no time to spare, and he missed his purpose there. He crossed to Malmo by ferry, took the connecting night train to Stockholm, and the same morning sailed down the Saltsjon, ostensibly bound for Obo, intending to cross to Revel and so get back to central Europe by the less frequented routes.

But in this move again luck was against him and receiving warning just in time, and by the mysterious agency that had so far protected him, he contrived to be dropped from the steamer by boat among the islands of the crowded Archipelago, made his way to Helsingfors, and within forty-eight hours was back again on the Frihavnen with pursuit for the moment blinked and a breathing-time to the good.

To appreciate the exact significance of these wanderings it is necessary to recall the conditions. Guido was not zigzagging a course about Europe in an aimless search for the picturesque, still less inspired by any love of the melodramatic. To him every step was vital, each tangent or rebound the necessary outcome of his much-badgered plans. In his pocket reposed the papers for which he had run grave risks. The price agreed upon for the service was sufficiently lavish to make the risks worth taking time after time, but in order to consummate the transaction it was necessary that the booty should be put into his employer's hand. Halfway across Europe, that employer was waiting with such patience as she could maintain, herself watched and shadowed at every step. The Countess X was sufficiently exalted to be personally immune from the high-handed methods of her country's secret service, but every approach to her was tapped. The problem was for Guido to earn a long-enough respite to enable him to communicate his position to the Countess and for her to go or to reach him by a trusty hand. Then the whole fabric of intrigue could fall to pieces, but so far Guido had been kept successfully on the run and in the meanwhile, time was pressing.

163

"They lost him after the Hutola," Beedel reported, in explaining the circumstances to Max Carrados. "Three days later, they found that he'd been back again in Copenhagen, but by that time he'd flown. Now they're without a trace except the inference of these '*Orange peach blossom*' agonies in *The Times*. But the Countess has gone hurriedly to Paris, and Lafayard thinks it all points to London."

"I suppose the Foreign Office is anxious to oblige just now?"

"I expect so, sir," agreed Beedel, "but, of course, my instructions don't come from that quarter. What appeals to us is that it would be a feather in our caps – they're still a little sore up at the Yard about Hans the Piper."

"Naturally," assented Carrados. "Well, I'll see what I can do if there is real occasion. Let me know anything, and, if you see your chance yourself, come round for a talk if you like on – today's Wednesday? – I shall be in at any rate on Friday evening."

Without being a precisian, the blind man was usually exact in such matters. There are those who hold that an engagement must be kept at all hazard: Men who would miss a death-bed message in order to keep literal faith with a beggar. Carrados took lower, if more substantial, ground. "My word," he sometimes had occasion to remark, "is subject to contingencies, like everything else about me. If I make a promise it is conditional on nothing which seems more important arising to counteract it. That, among men of sense, is understood." And, as it happened, something did occur on this occasion.

He was summoned to the telephone just before dinner on Friday evening to receive a message personally. Greatorex, his secretary, had taken the call, but came in to say that the caller would give him nothing beyond his name – Brebner. The name was unknown to Carrados, but such incidents were not uncommon, and he proceeded to comply.

"Yes," he responded. "I am Max Carrados speaking. What is it?"

"Oh, it is you, sir, is it? Mr. Brickwill told me to get to you direct."

"Well, you are all right. Brickwill? Are you the British Museum?"

"Yes. I am Brebner in the Chaldean Art Department. They are in a great stew here. We have just found out that someone has managed to get access to the Second Inner Greek Room and looted some of the cabinets there. It is all a mystery as yet."

"What is missing?" asked Carrados.

"So far we can only definitely speak of about six trays of Greek coins – a hundred to a hundred-and-twenty, roughly."

"Important?"

The line conveyed a caustic bark of tragic amusement.

"Why, yes, I should say so. The beggar seems to have known his business. All fine specimens of the best period. Syracuse – Messana – Croton – Amphipolis. Eumenes – Evainetos – Kimons. The chief quite wept."

Carrados groaned. There was not a piece among them that he had not handled lovingly.

"What are you doing?" he demanded.

"Mr. Brickwill has been to Scotland Yard, and, on advice, we are not making it public as yet. We don't want a hint of it to be dropped anywhere, if you don't mind, sir."

"That will be all right."

"It was for that reason that I was to speak with you personally. We are notifying the chief dealers and likely collectors to whom the coins, or some of them, may be offered at once if it is thought that we haven't found it out yet. Judging from the expertness displayed in the selection, we don't think that there is any danger of the lot being sold to a pawnbroker or a metal-dealer, so that we are running very little real risk in not advertising the loss."

"Yes. Probably it is as well," replied Carrados. "Is there anything that Mr. Brickwill wishes me to do?"

"Only this, sir: If you are offered a suspicious lot of Greek coins, or hear of them, would you have a look – I mean ascertain whether they are likely to be ours, and if you think they are communicate with us and Scotland Yard at once."

"Certainly," replied the blind man. "Tell Mr. Brickwill that he can rely on me if any indication comes my way. Convey my regrets to him and tell him that I feel the loss quite as a personal one . . . I don't think that you and I have met as yet, Mr. Brebner?"

"No, sir," said the voice diffidently, "but I have looked forward to the pleasure. Perhaps this unfortunate business will bring me an introduction."

"You are very kind," was Carrados's acknowledgment of the compliment. "Any time . . . I was going to say that perhaps you don't know my weakness, but I have spent many pleasant hours over your wonderful collection. That ensures the personal element. Goodbye."

Carrados was really disturbed by the loss, although his concern was tempered by the reflection that the coins would inevitably in the end find their way back to the Museum. That their restitution might involve ransom to the extent of several thousand pounds was the least poignant detail of the situation. The one harrowing thought was that the booty might, through stress or ignorance, find its way into the melting-pot. That dreadful contingency, remote but insistent, was enough to affect the appetite of the blind enthusiast.

He was expecting Inspector Beedel, who would be full of his own case, but he could not altogether dismiss the aspects of possibility that Brebner's communication opened before his mind. He was still concerned with the chances of destruction and a very indifferent companion for Greatorex, who alone sat with him, when Parkinson presented himself. Dinner was over but Carrados had remained rather longer than his custom, smoking his mild Turkish cigarette in silence.

"A lady wishes to see you, sir. She said you would not know her name, but that her business would interest you."

The form of message was sufficiently unusual to take the attention of both men..

"You don't know her, of course, Parkinson?" inquired his master

For just a second the immaculate Parkinson seemed tongue-tied. Then he delivered himself in his most ceremonial strain.

"I regret to say that I cannot claim the advantage, sir," he replied.

"Better let me tackle her, sir," suggested Greatorex with easy confidence. "It's probably a sub."

The sportive offer was declined by a smile and a shake of the head. Carrados turned to his attendant.

"I shall be in the study, Parkinson. Show her there in three minutes. You stay and have another cigarette, Greatorex. By that time she will either have gone or have interested me."

In three minutes' time Parkinson threw open the study door.

"The lady, sir," he announced.

Could he have seen, Carrados would have received the impression of a plainly, almost dowdily, dressed young woman of buxom figure. She wore a light veil, but it was ineffective in concealing the unattraction of the face beneath. The features were swart and the upper lip darkened with the more than incipient moustache of the southern brunette. Worse remained, for a disfiguring rash had assailed patches of her skin. As she entered she swept the room and its occupant with a quiet but comprehensive survey.

"Please take a chair, Madame. You wished to see me?"

The ghost of a demure smile flickered about her mouth as she complied, and in that moment her face seemed less uncomely. Her eye lingered for a moment on a cabinet above the desk, and one might have noticed that her eye was very bright. Then she replied.

"You are Signor Carrados, in – in the person?"

Carrados made his smiling admission and changed his position a fraction – possibly to catch her curiously pitched voice the better.

"The great collector of the antiquities?"

"I do collect a little," he admitted guardedly.

"You will forgive me, Signor, if my language is not altogether good. When I live at Naples with my mother. we let boardings, chiefly to Inglish and Amerigans. I pick up the words, but since I marry and go to live in Calabria, my Inglish has gone all red – no, no, you say, rusty. Yes, that is it – quite rusty."

"It is excellent," said Carrados. "I am sure that we shall understand one another perfectly."

The lady shot a penetrating glance but the blind man's expression was merely suave and courteous. Then she continued.

"My husband is of name Ferraja – Michele Ferraja. We have a vineyard and a little property near Forenzana." She paused to examine the tips of her gloves for quite an appreciable moment. "Signor," she burst out, with some vehemence, "the laws of my country are not good at all."

"From what I hear on all sides," said Carrados, "I am afraid that your country is not alone."

"There is at Forenzana a poor labourer, Gian Verde of name," continued the visitor, dashing volubly into her narrative. "He is one day digging in the vineyard, the vineyard of my husband, when his spade strikes itself upon an obstruction. 'A-ha,' says Gian. 'What have we here?' And he goes down upon his knees to see. It is an oil jar of red earth, Signor, such as was anciently used, and in it is filled with silver money.

"Gian is poor but he is wise. Does he call upon the authorities? No, no. He understands that they are all corrupt. He carries what he has found to my husband, for he knows him to be a man of great honour.

"My husband also is of brief decision. His mind is made up. 'Gian,' he says, 'keep your mouth shut. This will be to your ultimate profit.' Gian understands, for he can trust my husband. He makes a sign of mutual implication. Then he goes back to the spade digging."

"My husband understands a little of these things but not enough. We go to the collections of Messina and Naples and even Rome and there we see other pieces of silver money, similar, and learn that they are of great value. They are of different sizes, but most would cover a lira and of the thickness of two. On the one side imagine the great head of a pagan deity. On the other – Oh, so many things I cannot remember what." A gesture of circumferential despair indicated the hopeless variety of design.

"A biga or quadriga of mules?" suggested Carrados. "An eagle carrying off a hare, a figure flying with a wreath, a trophy of arms? Some of those perhaps?"

"*Si, si bene,*" cried Madame Ferraja. "You understand, I perceive, Signor. We are very cautious, for on every side is extortion and an unjust law. See, it is even forbidden to take these things out of the country, yet if we try to dispose of them at home, they will be seized and we punished,

167

for they are *tesoro Trovato* – what you call treasure troven and belonging to the State – these coins which the industry of Gian discovered and which had lain for so long in the ground of my husband's vineyard."

"So you brought them to England?"

"Si, Signor. It is spoken of as a land of justice and rich nobility who buy these things at the highest prices. Also, my speaking a little of the language would serve us here."

"I suppose you have the coins for disposal then? You can show them to me?"

"My husband retains them. I will take you, but you must first give *parola d'onore* of an English Signor not to betray us, or to speak of the circumstance to another."

Carrados had already foreseen this eventuality and decided to accept it. Whether a promise exacted on the plea of treasure trove would bind him to respect the despoilers of the British Museum was a point for subsequent consideration. Prudence demanded that he should investigate the offer at once, and to cavil over Madame Ferraja's conditions would be fatal to that object. If the coins were, as there seemed little reason to doubt, the proceeds of the robbery, a modest ransom might be the safest way of preserving irreplaceable treasures, and in that case Carrados could offer his services as the necessary intermediary.

"I give you the promise you require, Madame," he accordingly declared.

"It is sufficient," assented Madame. "I will now take you to the spot. It is necessary that you alone should accompany me, for my husband is so distraught in this country, where he understands not a word of what is spoken, that his poor spirit would cry 'We are surrounded!' if he saw two strangers approach the house. Oh, he is become most dreadful in his anxiety, my husband. Imagine only, he keeps on the fire a cauldron of molten lead and he would not hesitate to plunge into it this treasure and obliterate its existence if he imagined himself endangered."

"So," speculated Carrados inwardly. "*A likely precaution for a simple vine-grower of Calabria!* Very well," he assented aloud, "I will go with you alone. Where is the place?"

Madame Ferraja searched in the ancient purse that she discovered in her rusty handbag and produced a scrap of paper.

"People do not understand sometimes my way of saying it," she explained. "Sette, Herringbone – "

"May I –?" said Carrados, stretching out his hand. He took the paper and touched the writing with his finger-tips. "Oh yes, 7 Heronsbourne Place. That is on the edge of Heronsbourne Park, is it not?" He transferred the paper casually to his desk as he spoke and stood up. "How did you come, Madame Ferraja?"

Madame Ferraja followed the careless action with a discreet smile that did not touch her voice.

"By motor bus – first one then another, inquiring at every turning. Oh, but it was interminable," sighed the lady.

"My driver is off for the evening – I did not expect to be going out – but I will 'phone up a taxi and it will be at the gate as soon as we are." He despatched the message and then, turning to the house telephone, switched on to Greatorex.

"I'm just going round to Heronsbourne Park," he explained. "Don't stay, Greatorex, but if anyone calls expecting to see me, they can say that I don't anticipate being away more than an hour."

Parkinson was hovering about the hall. With quite novel officiousness he pressed upon his master a succession of articles that were not required. Over this usually complacent attendant, the unattractive features of Madame Ferraja appeared to exercise a stealthy fascination, for a dozen times the lady detected his eyes questioning her face and a dozen times he looked guiltily away again. But his incongruities could not delay for more than a few minutes the opening of the door.

"I do not accompany you, sir?" he inquired, with the suggestion plainly tendered in his voice that it would be much better if he did.

"Not this time, Parkinson."

"Very well, sir. Is there any particular address to which we can telephone in case you are required, sir?"

"Mr. Greatorex has instructions."

Parkinson stood aside, his resources exhausted. Madame Ferraja laughed a little mockingly as they walked down the drive.

"Your manservant thinks I may eat you, Signor Carrados," she declared vivaciously.

Carrados, who held the key of his usually exact attendant's perturbation – for he himself had recognized in Madame Ferraja the angelic Nina Brun, of the Sicilian *tetradrachm* incident, from the moment she opened her mouth – admitted to himself the humour of her audacity. But it was not until half-an-hour later that enlightenment rewarded Parkinson. Inspector Beedel had just arrived and was speaking with Greatorex when the conscientious valet, who had been winnowing his memory in solitude, broke in upon them, more distressed than either had ever seen him in his life before, and with the breathless introduction: "It was the ears, sir! I have her ears at last!" poured out his tale of suspicion, recognition, and his present fears.

169

In the meanwhile, the two objects of his concern had reached the gate as the summoned taxicab drew up.

"Seven Heronsbourne Place," called Carrados to the driver.

"No, no," interposed the lady, with decision, "let him stop at the beginning of the street. It is not far to walk. My husband would be on the verge of distraction if he thought in the dark that it was the arrival of the police. Who knows?"

"Brackedge Road, opposite the end of Heronsbourne Place," amended Carrados.

Heronsbourne Place had the reputation, among those who were curious in such matters, of being the most reclusive residential spot inside the four-mile circle. To earn that distinction it was, needless to say, a cul-de-sac. It bounded one side of Heronsbourne Park but did not at any point of its length give access to that pleasance. It was entirely devoted to unostentatious little houses, something between the villa and the cottage, some detached and some in pairs, but all possessing the endowment of larger, more umbrageous gardens than can generally be secured within the radius. The local house agent described them as "delightfully old-world" or "completely modernized" according to the requirement of the applicant.

The cab was dismissed at the corner and Madame Ferraja guided her companion along the silent and deserted way. She had begun to talk with renewed animation, but her ceaseless chatter only served to emphasize to Carrados the one fact that it was contrived to disguise.

"I am not causing you to miss the house with looking after me – No. 7, Madame Ferraja?" he interposed.

"No, certainly," she replied readily. "It is a little farther. The numbers are from the other end. But we are there. *Ecco!*"

She stopped at a gate and opened it, still guiding him. They passed into a garden, moist and sweet-scented with the distillate odours of a dewy evening. As she turned to relatch the gate, the blind man endeavoured politely to anticipate her. Between them his hat fell to the ground.

"My clumsiness," he apologized, recovering it from the step. "My old impulses and my present helplessness, alas, Madame Ferraja!"

"One learns prudence by experience," said Madame sagely. She was scarcely to know, poor lady, that even as she uttered this trite aphorism, under cover of darkness and his hat, Mr. Carrados had just ruined his signet ring by blazoning a golden "7" upon her garden step to establish its identity if need be. A cul-de-sac that numbered from the closed end seemed to demand some investigation.

"Seldom," he replied to her remark. "One goes on taking risks. So we are there?"

Madame Ferraja had opened the front door with a latchkey. She dropped the latch and led Carrados forward along the narrow hall. The room they entered was at the back of the house, and from the position of the road it therefore overlooked the park. Again the door was locked behind them.

"The celebrated Mr. Carrados!" announced Madame Ferraja, with a sparkle of triumph in her voice. She waved her hand towards a lean, dark man who had stood beside the door as they entered. "My husband."

"Beneath our poor roof in the most fraternal manner," commented the dark man, in the same derisive spirit. "But it is wonderful."

"The even more celebrated Monsieur Dompierre, unless I am mistaken?" retorted Carrados blandly. "I bow on our first real meeting."

"You knew!" exclaimed the Dompierre of the earlier incident incredulously. "Stoker, you were right, and I owe you a hundred lire. Who recognized you, Nina?"

"How should I know?" demanded the real Madame Dompierre crossly. "This blind man himself, by chance.

"You pay a poor compliment to your charming wife's personality to imagine that one could forget her so soon," put in Carrados. "And you a Frenchman, Dompierre!"

"You knew, Monsieur Carrados," reiterated Dompierre, "and yet you ventured here. You are either a fool or a hero."

"An enthusiast – it is the same thing as both," interposed the lady. "What did I tell you? What did it matter if he recognized? You see?"

"Surely you exaggerate, Monsieur Dompierre," contributed Carrados. "I may yet pay tribute to your industry. Perhaps I regret the circumstance and the necessity, but I am here to make the best of it. Let me see the things Madame has spoken of, and then we can consider the detail of their price, either for myself or on behalf of others."

There was no immediate reply. From Dompierre came a saturnine chuckle and from Madame Dompierre a titter that accompanied a grimace. For one of the rare occasions in his life Carrados found himself wholly out of touch with the atmosphere of the situation. Instinctively he turned his face towards the other occupant of the room, the man addressed as "Stoker," whom he knew to be standing near the window.

"This unfortunate business has brought me an introduction," said a familiar voice.

For one dreadful moment the universe stood still round Carrados. Then, with the crash and grind of overwhelming mental tumult, the whole strategy revealed itself, like the sections of a gigantic puzzle falling into place before his eyes.

171

There had been no robbery at the British Museum! That plausible concoction was as fictitious as the intentionally transparent tale of treasure trove. Carrados recognized now how ineffective the one device would have been without the other in drawing him – how convincing the two together – and while smarting at the humiliation of his plight he could not restrain a dash of admiration at the ingenuity – the accurately conjectured line of inference – of the plot. It was again the familiar artifice of the cunning pitfall masked by the clumsily contrived trap just beyond it. And straightway into it he had blundered.

"And this," continued the same voice, "is Carrados, Max Carrados, upon whose perspicuity a government – only the present government, let me in justice say – depends to outwit the undesirable alien! My country – Oh my country!"

"Is it really Monsieur Carrados?" inquired Dompierre in polite sarcasm. "Are you sure, Nina, that you have not brought a man from Scotland Yard instead?"

"*Basta!* He is here – What more do you want? Do not mock the poor sightless gentleman," answered Madame Dompierre, in doubtful sympathy.

"That is exactly what I was wondering," ventured Carrados mildly. "I am here – What more do you want? Perhaps you, Mr. Stoker –?"

"Excuse me. 'Stoker' is a mere colloquial appellation based on a trifling incident of my career in connection with a disabled liner. The title illustrates the childish weakness of the criminal classes for nicknames, together with their pitiable baldness of invention. My real name is Montmorency, Mr. Carrados – Eustace Montmorency."

"Thank you, Mr. Montmorency," said Carrados gravely. "We are on opposite sides of the table here tonight, but I should be proud to have been with you in the stokehold of the *Benvenuto*."

"That was pleasure," muttered the Englishman. "This is business."

"Oh, quite so," agreed Carrados. "So far I am not exactly complaining. But I think it is high time to be told – and I address myself to you – why I have been decoyed here and what your purpose is."

Mr. Montmorency turned to his accomplice.

"Dompierre," he remarked, with great clearness, "why the devil is Mr. Carrados kept standing?"

"Ah, oh, Heaven!" exclaimed Madame Dompierre with tragic resignation, and flung herself down on a couch.

"*Scusi,*" grinned the lean man, and with burlesque grace he placed a chair for their guest's acceptance.

"Your curiosity is natural," continued Mr. Montmorency, with a cold eye towards Dompierre's antics, "although I really think that by this time you ought to have guessed the truth. In fact, I don't doubt that you have guessed, Mr. Carrados, and that you are only endeavouring to gain time. For that reason – because it will perhaps convince you that we have nothing to fear – I don't mind obliging you."

"Better hasten," murmured Dompierre uneasily.

"Thank you, Bill," said the Englishman, with genial effrontery. "I won't fail to report your intelligence to the Rasojo. Yes, Mr. Carrados, as you have already conjectured, it is the affair of the Countess X to which you owe this inconvenience. You will appreciate the compliment that underlies your temporary seclusion, I am sure. When circumstances favoured our plans and London became the inevitable place of meeting, you and you alone stood in the way. We guessed that you would be consulted and we frankly feared your intervention. You were consulted. We know that Inspector Beedel visited you two days ago and he has no other case in hand. Your quiescence for just three days had to be obtained at any cost. So here you are."

"I see," assented Carrados. "And having got me here, how do you propose to keep me?"

"Of course that detail has received consideration. In fact, we secured this furnished house solely with that in view. There are three courses before us. The first, quite pleasant, hangs on your acquiescence. The second, more drastic, comes into operation if you decline. The third – but really, Mr. Carrados, I hope you won't oblige me even to discuss the third. You will understand that it is rather objectionable for me to contemplate the necessity of two able-bodied men having to use even the smallest amount of physical compulsion towards one who is blind and helpless. I hope you will be reasonable and accept the inevitable."

"The inevitable is the one thing that I invariably accept," replied Carrados. "What does it involve?"

"You will write a note to your secretary explaining that what you have learned at 7 Heronsbourne Place makes it necessary for you to go immediately abroad for a few days. By the way, Mr. Carrados, although this is Heronsbourne Place, it is not No. 7."

"Dear, dear me," sighed the prisoner. "You seem to have had me at every turn, Mr. Montmorency."

"An obvious precaution. The wider course of giving you a different street altogether we rejected as being too risky in getting you here. To continue: To give conviction to the message, you will direct your man Parkinson to follow by the first boat-train tomorrow, with all the requirements for a short stay, and put up at Mascot's, as usual, awaiting your arrival there."

"Very convincing," agreed Carrados. "Where shall I be in reality?"

"In a charming though rather isolated bungalow on the south coast. Your wants will be attended to. There is a boat. You can row or fish. You will be run down by motor car and brought back to your own gate. It's really very pleasant for a few days. I've often stayed there myself."

"Your recommendation carries weight. Suppose, for the sake of curiosity, that I decline?"

"You will still go there, but your treatment will be commensurate with your behaviour. The car to take you is at this moment waiting in a convenient spot on the other side of the park. We shall go down the garden at the back, cross the park, and put you into the car – anyway."

"And if I resist?"

The man whose pleasantry it had been to call himself Eustace Montmorency shrugged his shoulders.

"Don't be a fool," he said tolerantly. "You know who you are dealing with and the kind of risks we run. If you call out or endanger us at a critical point, we shall not hesitate to silence you effectively."

The blind man knew that it was no idle threat. In spite of the cloak of humour and fantasy thrown over the proceedings, he was in the power of coolly desperate men. The window was curtained and shuttered against sight and sound, the door behind him locked. Possibly at that moment a revolver threatened him. Certainly weapons lay within reach of both his keepers.

"Tell me what to write," he asked, with capitulation in his voice.

Dompierre twirled his mustachios in relieved approval. Madame laughed from her place on the couch and picked up a book, watching Montmorency over the cover of its pages. As for that gentleman, he masked his satisfaction by the practical business of placing on the table before Carrados the accessories of the letter.

"Put into your own words the message that I outlined just now."

"Perhaps to make it altogether natural I had better write on a page of the notebook that I always use," suggested Carrados.

"Do you wish to make it natural?" demanded Montmorency, with latent suspicion.

"If the miscarriage of your plan is to result in my head being knocked – yes, I do," was the reply.

"Good!" chuckled Dompierre, and sought to avoid Mr. Montmorency's cold glance by turning on the electric table-lamp for the blind man's benefit. Madame Dompierre laughed shrilly.

"Thank you, Monsieur," said Carrados, "you have done quite right. What is light to you is warmth to me – heat, energy, inspiration. Now to business."

174

He took out the pocket-book he had spoken of and leisurely proceeded to flatten it down upon the table before him. As his tranquil, pleasant eyes ranged the room meanwhile, it was hard to believe that the shutters of an impenetrable darkness lay between them and the world. They rested for a moment on the two accomplices who stood beyond the table, picked out Madame Dompierre lolling on the sofa on his right, and measured the proportions of the long, narrow room. They seemed to note the positions of the window at the one end and the door almost at the other, and even to take into account the single pendent electric light which up till then had been the sole illuminant.

"You prefer pencil?" asked Montmorency.

"I generally use it for casual purposes. But not," he added, touching the point critically, "like this."

Alert for any sign of retaliation, they watched him take an insignificant penknife from his pocket and begin to trim the pencil. Was there in his mind any mad impulse to force conclusions with that puny weapon? Dompierre worked his face into a fiercer expression and touched reassuringly the handle of his knife. Montmorency looked on for a moment, then, whistling softly to himself, turned his back on the table and strolled towards the window, avoiding Madame Nina's pursuant eye.

Then, with overwhelming suddenness, it came, and in its form altogether unexpected.

Carrados had been putting the last strokes to the pencil, whittling it down upon the table. There had been no hasty movement, no violent act to give them warning. Only the little blade had pushed itself nearer and nearer to the electric light cord lying there . . . and suddenly and instantly the room was plunged into absolute darkness.

"To the door, Dom!" shouted Montmorency in a flash. "I am at the window. Don't let him pass and we are all right."

"I am here," responded Dompierre from the door.

"He will not attempt to pass," came the quiet voice of Carrados from across the room. "You are now all exactly where I want you. You are both covered. If either moves an inch, I fire – and remember that I shoot by sound, not sight."

"But – but what does it mean?" stammered Montmorency, above the despairing wail of Madame Dompierre

"It means that we are now on equal terms – three blind men in a dark room. The numerical advantage that you possess is counterbalanced by the fact that you are out of your element – I am in mine."

"Dom," whispered Montmorency across the dark space, "strike a match. I have none."

"I would not, Dompierre, if I were you," advised Carrados, with a short laugh. "It might be dangerous." At once his voice seemed to leap into a passion. "Drop that matchbox," he cried. "You are standing on the brink of your grave, you fool! Drop it, I say. Let me hear it fall."

A breath of thought – almost too short to call a pause – then a little thud of surrender sounded from the carpet by the door. The two conspirators seemed to hold their breath.

"That is right." The placid voice once more resumed its sway. "Why cannot things be agreeable? I hate to have to shout, but you seem far from grasping the situation yet. Remember that I do not take the slightest risk. Also please remember, Mr. Montmorency, that the action even of a hair-trigger automatic scrapes slightly as it comes up. I remind you of that for your own good, because if you are so ill-advised as to think of trying to pot me in the dark, that noise gives me a fifth of a second start of you. Do you by any chance know Zinghi's in Mercer Street?"

"The shooting gallery?" asked Mr. Montmorency a little sulkily.

"The same. If you happen to come through this alive and are interested, you might ask Zinghi to show you a target of mine that he keeps. Seven shots at twenty yards, the target indicated by four watches, none of them so loud as the one you are wearing. He keeps it as a curiosity."

"I wear no watch," muttered Dompierre, expressing his thought aloud.

"No, Monsieur Dompierre, but you wear a heart, and that not on your sleeve," said Carrados. "Just now it is quite as loud as Mr. Montmorency's watch. It is more central too – I shall not have to allow any margin. That is right. Breathe naturally – " For the unhappy Dompierre had given a gasp of apprehension. "It does not make any difference to me, and after a time holding one's breath becomes really painful."

"Monsieur," declared Dompierre earnestly, "there was no intention of submitting you to injury, I swear. This Englishman did but speak within his hat. At the most extreme, you would have been but bound and gagged. Take care: Killing is a dangerous game."

"For you – not for me," was the bland rejoinder. "If you kill me you will be hanged for it. If I kill you, I shall be honourably acquitted. You can imagine the scene – the sympathetic court – the recital of your villainies – the story of my indignities. Then with stumbling feet and groping hands the helpless blind man is led forward to give evidence. Sensation! No, no, it isn't really fair, but I can kill you both with absolute certainty and Providence will be saddled with all the responsibility. Please don't fidget with your feet, Monsieur Dompierre. I know that you aren't moving, but one is liable to make mistakes."

176

"Before I die – " said Montmorency – and for some reason laughed unconvincingly in the dark. " – before I die, Mr. Carrados, I should really like to know what has happened to the light. That, surely, isn't Providence?"

"Would it be ungenerous to suggest that you are trying to gain time? You ought to know what has happened. But as it may satisfy you that I have nothing to fear from delay, I don't mind telling you. In my hand was a sharp knife – contemptible, you were satisfied, as a weapon. Beneath my nose the 'flex' of the electric lamp. It was only necessary for me to draw the one across the other and the system was short-circuited. Every lamp on that fuse is cut off and in the distributing-box in the hall you will find a burned-out wire. You, perhaps – but Monsieur Dompierre's experience in plating ought to have put him up to simple electricity."

"How did you know that there is a distributing-box in the hall?" asked Dompierre, with dull resentment.

"My dear Dompierre, why beat the air with futile questions?" replied Max Carrados. "What does it matter? Have it in the cellar if you like."

"True," interposed Montmorency. "The only thing that need concern us now – "

"But it is in the hall – nine feet high," muttered Dompierre in bitterness. "Yet he, this blind man – "

"The only thing that need concern us," repeated the Englishman, severely ignoring the interruption, "is what you intend doing in the end, Mr. Carrados?"

"The end is a little difficult to foresee," was the admission. "So far, I am all for maintaining the *status quo*. Will the first grey light of morning find us still in this impasse? No, for between us we have condemned the room to eternal darkness. Probably about daybreak Dompierre will drop off to sleep and roll against the door. I, unfortunately mistaking his intention, will send a bullet through – Pardon, Madame, I should have remembered – but pray don't move."

"I protest, Monsieur – "

"Don't protest. Just sit still. Very likely it will be Mr. Montmorency who will fall off to sleep the first after all.

"Then we will anticipate that difficulty," said the one in question, speaking with renewed decision. "We will play the last hand with our cards upon the table if you like. Nina, Mr. Carrados will not injure you whatever happens – be sure of that. When the moment comes you will rise – "

"One word," put in Carrados with determination. "My position is precarious and I take no risks. As you say, I cannot injure Madame Dompierre, and you two men are therefore my hostages for her good behaviour. If she rises from the couch you, Dompierre, fall. If she advances another step Mr. Montmorency follows you."

"Do nothing rash, *Carissima*," urged her husband, with passionate solicitude. "You might get hit in place of me. We will yet find a better way."

"You dare not, Mr. Carrados!" flung out Montmorency, for the first time beginning to show signs of wear in this duel of the temper. "He dare not, Dompierre. In cold blood and unprovoked! No jury would acquit you!"

"Another who fails to do you justice, Madame Nina," said the blind man, with ironic gallantry. "The action might be a little high-handed, one admits, but when you, appropriately clothed and in your right complexion, stepped into the witness box and I said: 'Gentlemen of the jury, what is my crime? That I made Madame Dompierre a widow!' can you doubt their gratitude and my acquittal? Truly my countrymen are not all bats or monks, Madame." Dompierre was breathing with perfect freedom now, while from the couch came the sounds of stifled emotion, but whether the lady was involved in a paroxysm of sobs or of laughter it might be difficult to swear.

It was perhaps an hour after the flourish of the introduction with which Madame Dompierre had closed the door of the trap upon the blind man's entrance.

The minutes had passed but the situation remained unchanged, though the ingenuity of certainly two of the occupants of the room had been tormented into shreds to discover a means of turning it to their advantage. So far the terrible omniscience of the blind man in the dark and the respect for his markmanship with which his coolness had inspired them, dominated the group. But one strong card yet remained to be played, and at last the moment came upon which the conspirators had pinned their despairing hopes.

There was the sound of movement in the hall outside, not the first about the house, but towards the new complication Carrados had been strangely unobservant. True, Montmorency had talked rather loudly, to carry over the dangerous moments. But now there came an unmistakable step and to the accomplices it could only mean one thing. Montmorency was ready on the instant.

"Down, Dom!" he cried. "Throw yourself down! Break in, Guido. Break in the door. We are held up!"

There was an immediate response. The door, under the pressure of a human battering-ram, burst open with a crash. On the threshold the intruders – four or five in number – stopped starkly for a moment, held in astonishment by the extraordinary scene that the light from the hall, and of their own bull's-eyes, revealed.

Flat on their faces, to present the least possible surface to Carrados's aim, Dompierre and Montmorency lay extended beside the window and behind the door. On the couch, with her head buried beneath the cushions, Madame Dompierre sought to shut out the sight and sound of violence. Carrados – Carrados had not moved, but with arms resting on the table and fingers placidly locked together he smiled benignly on the new arrivals. His attitude, compared with the extravagance of those around him, gave the impression of a complacent modern deity presiding over some grotesque ceremonial of pagan worship
"So, Inspector, you could not wait for me, after all?" was his greeting.

The Eyes of
Max Carrados

Introduction
by Ernest Bramah

In offering a series of stories which continue the adventures of a group of characters already introduced to the reading public, a writer is inevitably at a certain disadvantage. In contriving their first appearance, he has been able to select both the occasion and the moment which lend themselves most effectively to his plan. He has begun at the beginning – or, at least, at what, so far as you and he and the tale he has to tell are concerned, must be accepted as the beginning. Buttonholing you at the intersection of these three lines of destiny he has, in effect, exclaimed: *My dear Reader! The very man I wished to see. I want to introduce rather a remarkable character to you – Max Carrados, whom you see approaching. You will notice that he is blind – quite blind, but so far from that crippling his interests in life or his energies, it has merely impelled him to develop those senses which in most of us lie half-dormant and practically unused. Thus you will understand that while he may be at a disadvantage when you are at an advantage, he is at an advantage when you are at a disadvantage. The alert, slightly spoffish gentleman with the knowing look, who accompanies him, is his friend Carlyle. He has a private inquiry business now. Formerly he was a solicitor, but. . .* (here the voice becomes discreetly inaudible) . . . *and having run up across Carrados again. . .* And so on.

This is well enough once, but it should not be repeated. One cannot begin at the beginning twice. In any case, it does not dispose of an obvious dilemma: Those among prospective readers who are acquainted with the first book do not need to be informed of the how, when, and wherefore of Carrados and his associates. Those who are not so acquainted (possibly even a larger class) do need to be informed, and may resent the omission. In the circumstances a word of explanation where it can conveniently be avoided seems to offer the least harmful course.

Max Carrados was published in the spring of 1914. It consisted of eight tales, each separate and complete in itself, but connected (as are the nine of the present volume) by the central figure of Carrados. The first story, "The Coin of Dionysius", cleared the necessary ground. Carlyle, a private inquiry agent, who has descended in the social scale owing to an irregularity – an indiscretion rather than a crime – is very desirous one evening of testing the genuineness of a certain rare and valuable Sicilian *tetradrachm*, for upon its authenticity an immediate arrest depends. It is too late at night for him to get in touch with expert professional opinion, but finally he is referred to a certain gifted amateur, a Mr. Max Carrados, who lives at Richmond. To Richmond he accordingly proceeds, and is at once recognised by Carrados as a former friend, Calling by name. The recognition is not at first mutual, for Carrados has also changed his name – he was formerly Max Wynn – in order to qualify for a considerable fortune, and he, like Carlyle, has altered in appearance with passing years. More to the point, he has become blind: "*Literally. . . I was riding along a bridle-path through a wood about a dozen years ago with a friend. He was in front. At one point a twig sprang back – you know how easily a thing like that happens. It just flicked my eye – nothing to think twice about . . . It is called* amaurosis."

Carlyle fails to recognise Carrados because the latter is an altered personality, with a different name, and living in unexpected circumstances, but to the blind man the change in Carlyle is negligible against the identity of a remembered voice. They talk of old times and of present times. Carlyle explains his business, and Carrados confesses that the idea of criminal investigation has always attracted him. Even yet, he thinks, he might not be entirely out at it, for blindness has unexpected compensations: "*A new world to explore, new experiences, new powers awakening. Strange new perceptions. Life in the fourth dimension.*"

Not regarding the suggestion of co-operation seriously, Carlyle puts the offer aside, but, later, Carrados returns to it again. Then the private detective remembers the object of his visit, the meanwhile forgotten coin, and to settle the matter, and to demonstrate to Carrados his helplessness (for the idea of the blind man being an expert must, of course, have been someone's blunder), he slyly offers to put his friend on the track of a mystery. "Yes," he accordingly replied, with crisp deliberation, as he recrossed the room. "Yes, I will, Max. Here is the clue to what seems to be a rather remarkable fraud." He put the *tetradrachm* into his host's hand. "What do you make of it?" For a few seconds Carrados handled the piece with the delicate manipulation of his finger-tips, while Carlyle looked on with a self-appreciative grin. Then with equal gravity the blind man weighed the coin in the balance of his hand. Finally he touched it with his tongue

"Well?" demanded the other

"Of course I have not much to go on, and if I was more fully in your confidence I might come to another conclusion ."

"Yes, yes," interposed Carlyle, with amused encouragement

"Then I should advise you to arrest the parlour maid, Nina Brun, communicate with the police authorities of Padua for particulars of the career of Helene Brunesi, and suggest to Lord Seastoke that he should return to London to see what further depredations have been made in his cabinet."

Mr. Carlyle's groping hand sought and found a chair, on which he dropped blankly. His eyes were unable to detach themselves for a single moment from the very ordinary spectacle of Mr. Carrados's mildly benevolent face, while the sterilised ghost of his now forgotten amusement still lingered about his features

"Good Heavens!" he managed to articulate. "How do you know?

"Isn't that what you wanted of me?" asked Carrados suavely

"Don't humbug, Max," said Carlyle severely. "This is no joke." An undefined mistrust of his own powers suddenly possessed him in the presence of this mystery. "How do you come to know of Nina Brun and Lord Seastoke?"

"You are a detective, Louis," replied Carrados. "How does one know these things?

The bottom having been thus knocked out of his objection, Carlyle has no option but to promise Carrados the reversion of "the next murder" that comes his way. Actually, it is a case involving thirty-five murders that redeems this pledge.

But in spite of every device of Carrados's perspicuity, there is still the cardinal deficiency that he cannot see. Whatever remains outside the range of four supertrained senses, aided by that subtle and elusive perception (every man in odd moments has surprised his own mind in the act of throwing out faint-spun and wholly forgotten tentacles of search towards it) called in vague ignorance the "sixth sense" – all beyond these must be forever a *terra incognita* to his knowledge. To remedy this he has a personal attendant called Parkinson. Carlyle ingenuously falls into a proposed test that Carrados suggests – his powers of observation against those of Parkinson. When it comes to actual specified details, the visitor finds that he only has a loose and general idea of the appearance of the man who has admitted him. On the other hand, when Parkinson is called up he is able to run off a precise and categorical description of Mr. Carlyle – although his period of observation had certainly not been the more favourable – from the size and material of the caller's boots, with a button missing from the left foot, to the fashion and fabric of his watch-chain. A very ordinary man of strictly limited ability, he has, in fact, trained this one faculty of detailed observation and retention to supply his master's need

These three men – Carrados, Carlyle, and Parkinson – are the only characters of any prominence who are carried over from the first book to the second. An Inspector Beedel makes an occasional and unimportant appearance in both. In the story called "The Mystery of the Poisoned Dish of Mushrooms" a Mrs. Bellmark (niece to Carlyle) will be met. She is the lady whose acquaintance Carrados formed in "The Comedy at Fountain Cottage", when a very opportune buried treasure was unearthed in her suburban garden. Every generation not unnaturally "fancies itself", and whatever is happening is therefore somewhat more wonderful than anything that has ever happened before. But for this present age there is, of course, a special reason why the exploits of the sightless obtain prominence, and why every inch won in the narrowing of the gulf between the seeing and the blind is hailed almost with the satisfaction of a martial victory. That the general condition of the blind is being raised – that they are, in the mass, more capable and infinitely less dependent than at any period of the past – is undeniable, and these things are plainly to the good, but when we think that blind men individually do more surprising feats and carry themselves more confidently in their blindness than has ever been done before, we deceive ourselves, in the superficiality that is common to the times. The higher capacity under blindness is a form of genius and, like other kinds of genius, it is not the prerogative of any century or of any system. Judged by this standard, Max Carrados is by no means a super-blind man, and although for convenience the qualities of more than one blind prototype may have been collected within a single frame, on the other hand literary licence must be judged to have its limits, and many of the realities of fact have been deemed too improbable to be transferred to fiction. Carrados's opening exploit, that of accurately deciding an antique coin to be a forgery, by the sense of touch, is far from being unprecedented

The curious and the incredulous may be referred to a little book, first published in 1820. This is entitled *Biography of the Blind, or the Lives of Such as Have Distinguished Themselves as Poets, Philosophers, Artists, etcetera,* and it is by James Wilson, "*Who has been Blind from his Infancy.*" From the authorities given (they are stated in every case), it is obvious that these lives and anecdotes are available elsewhere, but probably in no other single volume is so much that is informing and entertaining on this one subject brought together. The coin incident finds its warrant in the biography of Nicholas Saunderson, LL.D., F.R.S., who was born in Yorkshire in the year 1682. When about twelve months old, he lost not only his sight but the eyes themselves from an attack of small-pox. In 1707 he proceeded to Cambridge, where he appears to have made some stir. At all events he was given his M.A. in 1711 by a special process and immediately afterwards elected Lucasian Professor of Mathematics. Of his lighter qualities Wilson says: "*He could with great nicety and exactness perceive the smallest degree of roughness, or defect of polish, on a surface. Thus, in a set of Roman medals he distinguished the genuine from the false, though they had been counterfeited with such exactness as to deceive a connoisseur who had judged from the eye. By the sense of touch also, he distinguished the least variation, and he has been seen in a garden, when observations were making on the sun, to take notice of every cloud that interrupted the observation, almost as justly as others could see it. He could also tell when anything was held near his face, or when he passed by a tree at no great distance, merely from the different impulse of the air on his face. His ear was also equally exact. He could readily distinguish the fourth part of a note by the quickness of this sense, and could judge of the size of a room, and of his distance from the wall. And if he ever walked over a pavement in courts or piazzas which reflected sound, and was afterwards conducted thither again, he could tell in what part of the walk he had stood, merely by the note it sounded."*

Another victim to small-pox during infancy was Dr. Henry Moyes, a native of Fifeshire, born during the middle of the eighteenth century. *"He was the first blind man who had proposed to lecture on chemistry, and as a lecturer he acquired great reputation. His address was easy and pleasing, his language correct, and he performed his experiments in a manner which always gave great pleasure to his auditors . . . Being of a restless disposition, and fond of travelling, he, in 1785, visited America . . ."* The following paragraph respecting him appeared in one of the American newspapers of that day: *"The celebrated Dr. Moyes, though blind, delivered a lecture upon optics, in which he delineated the properties of light and shade, and also gave an astonishing illustration of the power of touch. A highly polished plate of steel was presented to him with the stroke of an etching tool so minutely engraved on it that it was invisible to the naked eye, and only discoverable by a powerful magnifying glass. With his fingers, however, he discovered the extent, and measured the length of the line. Dr. Moyes informed us that being overturned in a stage-coach one dark rainy evening in England, and the carriage and four horses thrown into a ditch, the passengers and drivers, with two eyes apiece, were obliged to apply to him, who had no eyes, for assistance in extricating the horses. 'As for me,' said he, 'I was quite at home in the dark ditch. . . now directing eight persons to haul here, and haul there with all the dexterity and activity of a man-of-war's boatswain. '"*

Thomas Wilson, "the blind bell-ringer of Dumfries," also owed his affliction to small-pox in childhood. At the mature age of twelve he was promoted to be chief ringer of Dumfries. Says our biographer: *"He moreover excelled in the culinary art, cooking his victuals with the greatest nicety, and priding himself on the architectural skill he displayed in erecting a good ingle or fire. In his domestic economy he neither had nor required an assistant. He fetched his own water, made his own bed,*

187

cooked his own victuals, planted and raised his own potatoes, and, what is more strange still, cut his own peats, and was allowed by all to keep as clean a house as the most particular spinster in the town. Among a hundred rows of potatoes he easily found the way to his own, and when turning peats walked as carefully among the hags of lochar moss as those who were in possession of all their faculties. At raising potatoes, or any other odd job, he was ever ready to bear a hand, and when a neighbour became groggy on a Saturday night, it was by no means an uncommon spectacle to see Tom conducting him home to his wife and children . . . At another time, returning home one evening a little after ten o'clock, he heard a gentleman, who had just alighted from the mail, inquiring the way to Colin, and Tom instantly offered to conduct him thither. His services were gladly accepted, and he acted his part so well that, although Colin is three miles from Dumfries, the stranger did not discover his guide was blind until they reached the end of their journey."

Music, indeed, in some form, would seem to be the natural refuge of the blind. Among the many who have made it their profession, John Stanley was one of the most eminent. Born in 1713, he lost his sight at the age of two, not from disease, but *"by falling on a marble hearth, with a china basin in his hand"*. At eleven he became organist of All-Hallows', Bread Street. At thirteen, he was chosen from among many candidates to fill a similar position at St. Andrew's, Holborn. Eight years later *"the Benchers of the Honourable Society of the Inner Temple elected him one of their organists"*. The following was written by one of Stanley's old pupils: *"It was common, just as the service of St. Andrew's Church, or the Temple, was ended, to see forty or fifty organists at the altar, waiting to hear his last voluntary, and even Handel himself I have frequently seen at both of those places. In short, it must be confessed that his extempore voluntaries were inimitable, and his taste in composition wonderful. I was his apprentice, and I remember, the first year I went to him, his occasionally playing (for his amusement only) at billiards, mississipie, shuffle-board, and skittles, at which games he constantly beat his competitors. To avoid prolixity I shall only mention his showing me the way, both on horseback and on foot, through the private streets in Westminster, the intricate passages of the city, and the adjacent villages, places at which I had never been before. I remember also his playing very correctly all Corelli's and Geminiani's twelve solos on the violin. He had so correct an ear that he never forgot the voice of any person he had once heard speak, and I myself have divers times been a witness of this. In April, 1779, as he and I were going to Pall Mall, to the late Dr. Boyce's auction, a gentleman met us who had been in Jamaica twenty years, and in a feigned voice said, 'How do you do, Mr. Stanley?' when he, after pausing*

188

a little, said, 'God bless me, Mr. Smith, how long have you been in England?' If twenty people were seated at a table near him, he would address them all in regular order, without their situations being previously announced to him. Riding on horseback was one of his favourite exercises, and towards the conclusion of his life, when he lived at Epping Forest, and wished to give his friends an airing, he would often take them the pleasantest road and point out the most agreeable prospects."

All the preceding, it will be noticed, became blind early in life, and this would generally seem to be a necessary condition towards the subject acquiring an exceptional mastery over his affliction. At all events, of the twenty-six biographies (including his own) in which Wilson provides the necessary data, only six lose their sight later than youth, and several of these – as Milton and Euler, for instance – are included for their eminence pure and simple and not because they are remarkable as blind men. Perhaps even Huber must be included in this category, for his marvellous research work among bees (he it was who solved the mystery of the queen bee's aerial "nuptial flight") seems to have been almost entirely conducted through the eyes of his wife, his son, and a trained attendant, and not to depend in any marked way on the compensatory development of other senses. Of the twenty youthful victims, the cause of blindness is stated in fourteen cases, and of these fourteen no fewer than ten owe the calamity to small-pox.

To this general rule of youthful initiation, Dr. Hugh James provides an exception. He was born at St. Bees in 1771, and had already been practising for several years when he became totally blind at the age of thirty-five. In spite of this, he continued his ordinary work as a physician, *"even with increased success"*. If Dr. James's record under this handicap is less showy than that of many others, it is remarkable for the mature age at which he successfully adapted himself to a new life. He died at forty-five, still practising. Indeed, he died of a disease contracted at the bedside of a needy patient

But for energy, resource and sheer bravado under blindness, no age and no country can show anything to excel the record of John Metcalf – "Blind Jack of Knaresborough" (1717-1810). At six he lost his sight through small-pox, at nine he could get on pretty well unaided, at fourteen he announced his intention of disregarding his affliction thenceforward and of behaving in every respect as a normal human being. It is true that immediately on this brave resolve, he fell into a gravel pit and received a serious hurt while escaping, under pursuit, from an orchard he was robbing, but fortunately this did not affect his self-reliance. At twenty he had made a reputation as a pugilist. Metcalf's exploits are too many and diverse to be more than briefly touched upon. In boyhood he became an expert swimmer, diver, horse-rider, and, indeed, an adept in country sports generally. While yet a boy he was engaged to find the bodies of two men who had been drowned in a local river and swept away into its treacherous depths. He succeeded in recovering one. He followed the hounds regularly, won some races, and had at that time an ambition to become a jockey. He was also a very good card-player (for stakes), a professional violinist, and a trainer of fighting-cocks. All through life there was a streak of jocosity, even of devilment, in his nature. Twenty-one found him very robust, just under six-feet-two high, and as ready with his tongue as with his hands and feet. The following year, he learned that his sweetheart was being married by her parents to a more eligible rival. Metcalf eloped with her on the night before the wedding and married her himself the next day. From Knaresborough, where they set up house, he walked to London and back, beating the coach on the return journey. On the outbreak of the '45, he started recruiting for the King, and in two days had enlisted one-hundred-and-forty men. Sixty-four of these, Metcalf playing at their head, marched into Newcastle, where they were drafted into Pulteney's regiment. With them, Metcalf took part in the Battle of Falkirk, and in other engagements down to Culloden. After Culloden, he returned to Knaresborough and became horse-dealer, cotton and worsted merchant, and general smuggler. A little later, he did well in army contract work, and then started to run a stage-coach between York and Knaresborough, driving it himself both summer and winter. His extensive journeyings and his coach work had made the blind man familiar, in a very special way, with the roads and the land between them, and in 1765, at the age of forty-eight, he came into his true vocation – that of road construction. It is unnecessary to follow his career in this development. It is enough to say that during the next twenty-seven years he constructed some one-hundred-and-eighty miles of road. Much of it was over very difficult country – some of it, indeed, over country which up to that time had been deemed impossible, but all of it was well made. His plans did not always commend themselves in advance to the authorities. For such a contingency Metcalf had a very reasonable proposal: *"Let me make the road my way, and if it is not perfectly satisfactory when finished I will pull it all to pieces and, without extra charge, make it your way."* He had been over the ground in his very special way. Of this a Dr. Bew, who knew him, wrote: *"With the assistance only of a long staff, I have several times met this man traversing roads, ascending steep and rugged heights, exploring valleys and investigating their extent, form and situation so as to answer his designs in the best manner . . . He was alone as usual."*

Remarkable to the end, John Metcalf reached his ninety-fourth year and left behind him ninety great-grandchildren.

It would be easy to multiply appropriate instances from Wilson's book, but bulk is not the object. Nor can his Anecdotes of the Blind be materially drawn upon, although it is impossible to resist alluding to two delightful cases where blind men detected blindness in horses after the animals had been examined and passed by ordinary experts. In one instance, suspicion arose from the sound of the horse's step while walking, *"which implied a peculiar and unusual caution in the manner of putting down his feet."* In the other case the blind man, relying solely on his touch, *"felt the one eye to be colder than the other."* These two anecdotes are credited to Dr. Abercrombie. Scott, in a note to Peveril of the Peak ("Mute Vassals"), recounts a similar case, where the blind man discovered the imperfection by touching the horse's eyes sharply with one hand, while he placed the other over its heart and observed that there was no increase of pulsation.

One point in the capacity of the blind is frequently in dispute – the power to distinguish colour. Even so ingenious a man as the Nicholas Saunderson already mentioned not only could gain no perception of colour himself, but used to say that "it was pretending to impossibilities." Mr. J. A. Macy, who edited Miss Helen Keller's book, *The Story of my Life* – an experience that ought surely to have effaced the word "impossible" from his mind in connection with the blind – makes the bold statement: *"No blind person can tell colour."*

Three instances of those for whom this power has been claimed are all that can be included here. The reader must attach so much credibility to them as he thinks fit:

1.   From *Wilson's Biography*, as ante:

The late family tailor (MacGuire) of Mr. M'Donald, of Clanronald, in Inverness-shire, lost his sight fifteen years before his death, yet he still continued to work for the family as before, not indeed with the same expedition, but with equal correctness. It is well known how difficult it is to make a tartan dress, because every stripe and colour (of which there are many) must fit each other with mathematical exactness. Hence even very few tailors who enjoy their sight are capable of executing that task . . . It is said that MacGuire could, by the sense of touch, distinguish all the colours of the tartan.

2.   From *The Dictionary of National Biography*:

M'Avoy, Margaret (1800-1820), blind lady, was born at Liverpool of respectable parentage on 28 June, 1800. She was of a sickly constitution,

191

and became totally blind in June 1816. Her case attracted considerable attention from the readiness with which she could distinguish by her touch the colours of cloth, silk, and stained glass. She could accurately describe, too, the height, dress, bearing, and other characteristics of her visitors, and she could even decipher the forms of letters in a printed book or clearly written manuscript with her fingers' ends, so as to be able to read with tolerable facility. Her needlework was remarkable for its extreme neatness. Within a few days of her death she wrote a letter to her executor. She died at Liverpool on 18 August, 1820.

3.   From *The Daily Telegraph*, 29th April, 1922:

American scientists are deeply interested in the discovery of a young girl of seventeen, Willetta Huggins, who, although totally blind and deaf, can *"see and hear"* perfectly through a supernormal sense of smell and touch. Miss Huggins, who has been quite deaf since she was ten years old, and totally blind since she was fifteen, demonstrated to the satisfaction of physicians and scientists that she can hear perfectly over the telephone by placing her finger-tips upon the receiver and listening to conversation with friends by placing her fingers on the speakers' cheeks. She attends lectures and concerts, and hears by holding a thin sheet of paper between her fingers directed broadside towards the volume of sound, and reads newspaper headlines by running her finger-tips over large type. She discerns colours by odours, and before the Chicago Medical Society recently she separated several skeins of wool correctly and declared their colours by smelling them, and also recognised the various colours in a neck-tie.

The case of Miss Helen Keller has already been referred to. In America that case has become classic. Indeed, in its way the life of Miss Keller is almost as remarkable as that of John Metcalf, but, needless to say, the way is a very different one. Her book, *The Story of My Life*, is a very full and engrossing account of her education (in this instance *"life"* and *"education"* are interchangeable) from *"the earliest time"* until shortly after her entry into Radcliffe College in 1900, she then being in her twenty-first year. The book consists of three parts: (1) her autobiography, (2) her letters, (3) her biography from external sources, chiefly by the account of Miss Sullivan, who trained her.

The difficulty here was not merely blindness. When less than two years old not only sight, but hearing, and with hearing speech, were all lost. Her people were well-to-do, and skilled advice was frequently obtained, but no improvement came. As the months and the years went on, intelligent communication between the child and the world grew less, while a naturally impulsive nature deepened into sullenness and passion in the face of a dimly realised *"difference"*, and of her inability to understand and to be understood. When Miss Sullivan came to live with the Kellers in 1887, on a rather forlorn hope of being able to do something with Helen, the child was six, and relapsing into primitive savagery. The first – and in the event the one and only – problem was that of opening up communication with the stunted mind, of raising or piercing the black veil that had settled around it four years before

A month after her arrival Miss Sullivan wrote as follows:

> *I must write you a line this morning because something very important has happened. Helen has taken the second great step in her education. She has learned that everything has a name, and that the manual alphabet is the key to everything she wants to know.*
>
> *In a previous letter I think I wrote you that* "mug" *and* "milk" *had given Helen more trouble than all the rest. She confused the nouns with the verb* "drink". *She didn't know the word for* "drink", *but went through the pantomime of drinking whenever she spelled* "mug" *or* "milk". *This morning, while she was washing, she wanted to know the name for* "water". *When she wants to know the name of anything, she points to it and pats my hand. I spelled* "w-a-t-e-r" *and thought no more about it until after breakfast. Then it occurred to me that with the help of this new word I might succeed in straightening out the* "mug-milk" *difficulty. We went out to the pump house, and I made Helen hold her mug under the spout while I pumped. As the cold water gushed forth, filling the mug, I spelled* "w-a-t-e-r" *in Helen's free hand. The word coming so close upon the sensation of cold water rushing over her hand seemed to startle her. She dropped the mug and stood as one transfixed. A new light came into her face. She spelled* "water" *several times. Then she dropped on the ground and asked for its name and pointed to the pump and the trellis, and suddenly turning round she asked for my name. I spelled* "teacher". *Just then the nurse brought Helen's little sister into the pump house, and Helen spelled* "baby" *and pointed to the nurse. All the way back to the house she was highly excited, and learned the name of every object she touched, so that in a few hours she had added thirty new words to her vocabulary.*

Here are some of them: Door, open, shut, give, go, come, *and a great many more.*

P.S. – I didn't finish my letter in time to get it posted last night, so I shall add a line. Helen got up this morning like a radiant fairy. She has flitted from object to object, asking the name of everything and kissing me for very gladness. Last night when I got in bed, she stole into my arms of her own accord and kissed me for the first time, and I thought my heart would burst, so full was it of joy.

Seven months later we have this characteristic sketch. It may not be very much to the point here, but it would be difficult to excel its peculiar quality:

We took Helen to the circus, and had "the time of our lives!" The circus people were much interested in Helen, and did everything they could to make her first circus a memorable event. They let her feel the animals whenever it was safe. She fed the elephants, and was allowed to climb up on the back of the largest, and sit in the lap of the "Oriental Princess" while the elephant marched majestically around the ring. She felt some young lions. They were as gentle as kittens, but I told her they would get wild and fierce as they grew older. She said to the keeper: "I will take the baby lions home and teach them to be mild." The keeper of the bears made one big black fellow stand on his hind legs and hold out his great paw to us, which Helen shook politely. She was greatly delighted with the monkeys and kept her hand on the star performer while he went through his tricks, and laughed heartily when he took off his hat to the audience. One cute little fellow stole her hair-ribbon, and another tried to snatch the flowers out of her hat. I don't know who had the best time, the monkeys, Helen, or the spectators. One of the leopards licked her hands, and the man in charge of the giraffes lifted her up in his arms so that she could feel their ears and see how tall they were. She also felt a Greek chariot, and the charioteer would have liked to take her round the ring, but she was afraid of "many swift horses". The riders and clowns and rope-walkers were all glad to let the little blind girl feel their costumes and follow their motions whenever it was possible, and she kissed them all, to show her gratitude. Some of them cried, and the Wild

Man of Borneo shrank from her sweet little face in terror. She has talked about nothing but the circus ever since.

So far there is nothing in this case very material to the purpose of this Introduction. The story of Helen Keller is really the story of the triumph of Miss Sullivan, showing how, with infinite patience and resource, she presently brought a naturally keen and versatile mind out of bondage and finally led it, despite all obstacles, to the full attainment of its originally endowed powers. But the last resort of the blind – some of them – is the undeterminate quality to which the expression "sixth sense" has often been applied. On this subject, Helen being about seven years old at this time, Miss Sullivan writes: *"On another occasion while walking with me she seemed conscious of the presence of her brother, although we were distant from him. She spelled his name repeatedly and started in the direction in which he was coming."*

When walking or riding she often gives the names of the people we meet almost as soon as we recognise them.

And a year later:

I mentioned several instances where she seemed to have called into use an inexplicable mental faculty, but it now seems to me, after carefully considering the matter, that this power may be explained by her perfect familiarity with the muscular variations of those with whom she comes into contact, caused by their emotions . . . One day, while she was walking out with her mother and Mr. Anagnos, a boy threw a torpedo, which startled Mrs. Keller. Helen felt the change in her mother's movements instantly, and asked, "What are we afraid of?" On one occasion, while walking on the Common with her, I saw a police officer taking a man to the station house. The agitation which I felt evidently produced a perceptible physical change, for Helen asked excitedly, "What do you see?"

A striking illustration of this strange power was recently shown while her ears were being examined by the aurists in Cincinnati. Several experiments were tried, to determine positively whether or not she had any perception of sound. All present were astonished when she appeared not only to hear a whistle, but also an ordinary tone of voice. She would turn her head, smile, and act as though she had heard what was said. I was then standing beside her, holding her hand. Thinking that she was receiving impressions from me, I put her hands upon the table, and withdrew to the opposite side of the room. The aurists then tried their experiments with quite different results. Helen remained motionless through them all, not once showing the least sign that she realised what was going on. At my suggestion, one of the gentlemen took her hand, and the tests were repeated. This time her countenance changed whenever she was spoken to, but there was not such a decided lighting up of the features as when I held her hand.

In the account of Helen last year it was stated that she knew nothing about death, or the burial of the body, yet on entering a cemetery for the first time in her life she showed signs of emotion – her eyes actually filling with tears . . . .

While making a visit at Brewster, Massachusetts, she one day accompanied my friend and me through the graveyard. She examined one stone after another, and seemed pleased when she could decipher a name. She smelt of the flowers, but showed no desire to pluck them, and, when I gathered a few for her, she refused to have them pinned on her dress. When her attention was drawn to a marble slab inscribed with the name Florence in relief, she dropped upon the ground as though looking for something, then turned to me with a face full of trouble, and asked, "Where is poor little Florence?" I evaded the question, but she persisted. Turning to my friend, she asked, "Did you cry loud for poor little Florence?" Then she added: "I think she is very dead. Who put her in big hole?" As she continued, to ask these distressing questions, we left the cemetery. Florence was the daughter of my friend, and was a young lady at the time of her death, but Helen had been told nothing about her, nor did she even know that my friend had had a daughter. Helen had been given a bed and carriage for her dolls, which she had received and used like any other gift. On her return to the house after her visit to the cemetery, she ran to the closet where these toys were kept, and carried them to my friend, saying, "They are poor little Florence's." This was true, although we were at a loss to understand how she guessed it.

"Muscular variation" would rather seem to be capable of explaining away most of the occult phenomena if this is it. But at all events the latest intelligence of Miss Keller is quite tangible and undeniably "in the

196

picture." According to *Who's Who in America*, she *"appears in moving picture-play,* Deliverance, *based on her autobiography."* This, doubtless, is another record in the achievements of the blind: Miss Keller has become a *"movie"*.

The *Virginiola* Fraud

If there was one thing more than another about Max Carrados that came as a continual surprise, even a mild shock, to his acquaintances, it was the wide and unrestricted scope of his amusements. Had the blind man displayed a pensive interest in chamber music, starred by an occasional visit to the opera, taken a daily walk in the park on his attendant's arm, and found his normal recreation in chess or in being read to, the routine would have seemed an eminently fit and proper one. But to call at The Turrets and learn that Carrados was out on the river punting, or to find him in his gymnasium, probably with the gloves on, outraged one's sense of values. The only extraordinary thing in fact about his recreations was their ordinariness. He frequently spent an afternoon at Lord's when there was the prospect of a good game being put up. He played golf, bowls, croquet, and cards. Fished in all waters, and admitted that he had never missed the University Boat Race since the great finish of '91. When he walked about the streets anywhere within two miles of his house, he was quite independent of any guidance, and on one occasion he had saved a mesmerised girl's life on Richmond Bridge by dragging her into one of the recesses just in time to escape an uncontrollable dray that had jumped the kerb.

This prelude is by way of explaining the attitude of a certain Mr. Marrable whom Carrados knew, as he knew a hundred strange and useful people. Marrable had chambers in the neighbourhood of Piccadilly which he furnished and decorated on a lavish and expensive scale. His bric-à-brac, pictures, books, and appointments, indeed, constituted the man's means of living, for he as one of the best all-round judges of art and the antique in London, and with a nonchalant air of indifference he very pleasantly and profitably lounged his way through life on the honey extracted from one facile transaction after another. Living on his wits in a strictly legitimate sense, he enjoyed all the advantages of being a dealer without the necessity of maintaining a place of business. It was not even necessary for him to find "bargains" in the general sense, for buying in the ordinary market and selling in a very special and restricted one disclosed a substantial margin. This commercial system, less rare than one might imagine, involved no misrepresentation: His wealthy and exclusive clients were quite willing to pay the difference for the cachet of Mr. Marrable's connoisseurship and also, perhaps, for the amiable reluctance with which he carried on his operations.

199

The business that took Carrados to the amateur dealer's rooms one day in April has nothing to do with this particular incident. It was quite friendly and satisfactory on both sides, but it was not until Carrados rose to leave that the tangent of the visit touched the circle of the *Virginiola*.

"I am due at Gurnard's at about three-thirty," remarked Marrable, glancing at a Louis XVI ormolu clock for which he had marked off a certain musical comedy countess at two-hundred-and-fifty guineas. "Your way at all?"

"Gurnard and Lane's – the auctioneer."

"Yes. They have a book sale on this afternoon."

"I hope I haven't been keeping you," apologised Carrados.

"Oh, not at all. There is nothing I want among the earlier lots." He picked up a catalogue from a satinwood desk in which Mademoiselle Mars had once kept her play-bills and glanced down the pages. "No. 191 is the first I have marked: '*An Account of the Newly Discovered Islands of Sir George Sommers, called* "Virginiola"'. You aren't a competitor, by the way?"

"No," replied Carrados. "But if you don't mind, I should like to go with you."

Marrable looked at him with slightly suspicious curiosity.

"You'd find it uncommonly dull, surely, seeing nothing," he remarked.

"I generally contrive to extract some interest from what is going on," said Carrados modestly. "And as I have never yet been at a book sale – "

"Oh, come, by all means," interposed the other. "I shall be very glad of your company. Only I was surprised for the moment at the idea. I should warn you, however, that it isn't anything great in the way of a dispersal – no Caxtons or first-folio Shakespeares. Consequently, there will be an absence of ducal bibliophiles and literary Cabinet ministers, and we shall have a crowd of more or less frowsy dealers."

They had walked down into the street as they conversed. Marrable held up a finger to the nearest taxicab on an adjacent rank, opened the door for Carrados, and gave the driver the address of the auction rooms of which he had spoken.

"I don't expect to get very much," he speculated, turning over the later pages of the catalogue, which he still carried in his hand. "I've marked a dozen lots, but I'm not particularly keen on half of them. But I should certainly like to land the *Virginiola*."

"It is rare, I suppose?" inquired Carrados. Indifferent to books from the bibliophile's standpoint, he was able to feel the interest that one collector is generally willing to extend to the tastes of another.

200

"Yes," assented Marrable with weighty consideration. "Yes. In a way it is extremely rare. But this copy is faulty – the Dedication and Address pages are missing. That will bring down the bidding enormously, and yet it is just the defect that makes it attractive to me."

For a moment he was torn between the secretiveness bred of his position and a human desire to expound his shrewdness. The weakness triumphed.

"A few months ago," he continued, "I came cross another copy of the *Virginiola* among the lumber of a Bristol second-hand book-dealer's stock. It was altogether a rotten specimen – both covers gone, scores of pages ripped away, and most of those that remained appallingly torn and dirty. It was a fragment in fact, and I was not tempted even at the nominal guinea that was put upon it. But now – "

"Quite so," agreed Carrados.

"The first few pages were just the scrap that was presentable. I have a wonderful memory for details like that. The pages I want were discoloured, but they were sound. Sunshine or a chloride of lime bath will restore them to condition. If I get this *Virginiola* I shall run down to Bristol tomorrow."

"I congratulate you," said Carrados. "Unless, of course, your Bristol friend runs up to London today!" Mr. Marrable started rather violently. Then he shook his head with a knowing look.

"No, he won't do that. He is only a little backstreet huckster. True, if he found out that a *Virginiola* short of the pages he possesses was being sold he might have written to a London dealer, but he won't find out. For some reason they have overlooked the defect in cataloguing. Of course every expert will spot the omission at once, as I did this morning, and the book will be sold as faulty, but if my Bristol friend, as you call him, did happen to see a catalogue, there would be nothing to suggest any profitable opening to him."

"Splendid," admitted the blind man. "What would a perfect *Virginiola* be worth?"

"Auction price? Oh, about five-hundred guineas."

"And today's copy?"

"Ah, that's more difficult ground. You see, every perfect copy is alike, but every imperfect copy is different. Well, say anything from a hundred-and-fifty to three-hundred, according to who wants it. I shall be very content to take it halfway."

"Two-hundred-and-twenty-five? Yes, I suppose so. Five-hundred, less two twenty-five plus one leaves two-hundred-and-seventy-four guineas to the good. You shall certainly pay for the taxi!"

201

"Oh, I don't mind standing the taxi," declared Mr. Marrable magniloquently. "But don't pin me down to five-hundred – that's the auction price. I should want a trifle above – if I decided to let the book go out of my own library, that is to say. Probably I should keep it. Well, here we are."

The cab had drawn to the kerb opposite the door of Messrs Gurnard's unpretentious frontage. Mr. Marrable piloted his friend into the sale room and to a vacant chair by the wall, and then went off to watch the fray at closer quarters. Carrados heard the smooth-tongued auctioneer referring to an item as No. 142, and for the next fifty lots he followed the strangely unexciting progress of the sale with his own peculiar speculative interest.

"Lot 191," announced the easy, untiring voice. "*An Account of the Newly Discovered Islands, etc.*" At last the atmosphere pulsed to a faint thrill of expectation. "Unfortunately we had not the book before us when the catalogue was drawn up. Lot 191 is imperfect and is sold not subject to return – very desirable volume all the same. What may I say for Lot 191, please? '*An Account, etc.*', in original leather, faulty, and not subject to return."

As Mr. Marrable had indicated, the defective *Virginiola* occupied a rather special position. *Did anyone else want it?* was in several minds, and if so, how much did he want it? Everyone waited until at last the question seemed to fine down into: *Did anyone want it?*

"May I say two-hundred guineas?" suggested the auctioneer persuasively.

A large, heavy-faced man, who might have been a cattle-dealer from the North by every indication that his appearance gave, opened the bidding. He, at any rate, could have dissipated the uncertainty and saved the room the waiting. Holding, as he did, two commissions, he was bound to make the price a point above the lower of the orders.

"A hundred-and-twenty-one pounds."

"Guineas," came back like a slap from across the tables.

"A-hundred-and-twenty-eight pounds."

"Guineas."

"A hundred-and-thirty-five."

"Guineas."

"A hundred-and-fifty."

"Guineas."

The duel began to resemble the efforts of some unwieldy pachyderm to shake off the attack of a nimble carnivore by fruitless twists and plunges. But now other voices, nods, and uplifted eyebrows joined in, complicating a direct issue, and the forked arithmetic played hi among pounds and guineas with bewildering iteration. Then, as suddenly as it had grown, the fusilade shrivelled away, leaving the two original antagonists like two doughty champions emerging from a melee.

"Two-hundred-and-thirty."

"Guineas."

"Two-hundred-and-fifty."

"Guineas."

"Two-hundred-and-seventy."

There was no response. The large man in the heavy ulster and pot-hat was to survive the attack after all, apparently: The elephant to outlast the jaguar.

"Two-hundred-and-seventy pounds?" The auctioneer swept a comprehensive inquiry at every participant in the fray and raised his hammer., "It's against you, sir. No advance? At two-hundred-and-seventy pounds . . .?"

The hammer began to fall. A score of pencils wrote "£270" against Lot 191.

"And eighty!"

The voice of the new bidder cut in crisp and businesslike. Without ostentation it conveyed the cheerful message: "Now we are just beginning. I feel uncommonly fit." It caught the hammer in mid-air and arrested it. It made the large man feel tired and discouraged. He pushed back his hat, shook his head slowly, with his eyes fixed on his catalogue, and remained in stolid meditation. Carrados smiled inwardly at the restraint and strategy of his friend.

"Two-hundred-and-eighty. Thank you, sir. Two-hundred-and-eighty pounds . . .?" He knew by intuition that the price was final and the hammer fell decisively. "Mr. Marrable. . . . Lot 192, '*History and Antiquities of the County, etc.*' Put it in the bidding, please. One pound . . .?"

After the sale Mr. Marrable came round to Carrados's chair in very good spirits. Certainly he had had to give a not insignificant price for the *Virginiola*, but the attendant circumstances had elated him. Then he had secured the greater part of the other lots he wanted, and at quite moderate valuations.

"I've paid my cheque and got my delivery note," he explained. "I shall send my men round for the books when I get back. What do you think of the business?"

"Vastly entertaining," replied Carrados. "I have enjoyed myself thoroughly."

"Oh, well . . . But they were out for the *Virginiola*, weren't they?"

"Yes," admitted Carrados. "I feel that it is my turn to stand a taxi. Can I drop you?"

Mr. Marrable assented graciously and they set out again.

203

"Look here," said that gentleman as they approached his door, "I think that I can put my hand on the Rimini cameo I told you about, if you don't mind coming up again. Do you care to, now that you are here?"

"Certainly," replied Carrados. "I should like to handle it."

"May as well turn off the taxi then. There is a stand quite near."

The cameo proved interesting and led to the display of one or two other articles of bijouterie. The host rang for tea and easily prevailed on Carrados – who could be entertained by anyone except the rare individual who had no special knowledge on any subject whatever – to remain. Thus it came about that the blind man was still there when the servant arrived with the books.

"I say, Carrados," called out Mr. Marrable. He had crossed the room to speak with his man, who had come up immediately on his return. The servant continued to explain, and it was evident that something annoying had happened. "Here's a devilish fine thing," continued Mr. Marrable, dividing his attention between the two. "Felix has just been to Gurnard's and they tell him that the *Virginiola* cannot be found!"

"'Mislaid for the moment,' the gentleman said," amplified Felix.

"They send me back my cheque pending the book's recovery, but did you ever hear of such a thing? I was going down to Bristol by an early train tomorrow. Now I don't know what the deuce to do."

"Why not go back and find out what has really happened?" suggested Carrados. "They will tell you more than they would tell your man. If the book is stolen, you may as well put off your journey. If it is mislaid – taken off by someone else in mistake, I expect they mean – it may be on its way back by now."

"Yes. I suppose I'd better go. You've had enough of it, I suppose?"

"On the contrary, I was going to ask you to let me accompany you. It may be getting interesting."

"I hope not," retorted Marrable. "Come if you can spare the time, but the very tamest ending will suit me the best."

Felix had called up another cab by the time they reached the door, and for the second time that afternoon they spun through the West End streets with the auction rooms for their destination.

"Your turn to pay again, I think," proposed Carrados when they arrived. "You take the odd numbers and I'll take the even!"

Inside, most of the staff were obviously distracted by the strain of the untoward event and it was very evident that barbed words had been on the wing. In the private office to which Mr. Marrable's card gained them immediate admittance, they found all those actually concerned in the loss engaged in saying the same things over to each other for the hundredth time.

"The book isn't on the shelves now and there's the number in the delivery note. That's all I know about it," a saleroom porter was reiterating with the air of an extremely reasonable martyr.

"Yes, yes," admitted the auctioneer who had conducted the sale, "no one – Oh, I'm glad you are here, Mr. Marrable. You've heard of our – er – eh – "

"My man came back with something about the book – the *Virginiola* – being mislaid," replied Mr. Marrable. "That is all I know so far."

"Well, it's very regrettable, of course, and we must ask your indulgence, but what has happened is simple enough and I hope it isn't serious."

"What concerns me," interposed Mr. Marrable, "is merely this: Am I to have the book, and when?"

"We hope to deliver it into your hands – Well, in a very short time. As I was saying, what has happened is this: Another purchaser bought certain lots. Among them was Lot 91. My sale clerk, in the stress of his duties, inadvertently filled in the delivery note as Lot 191." A gesture of despairing protest from the unfortunate young man referred to passed unheeded.

"Consequently, as this gentleman took away his purchases at the end of the sale, he carried off the *Virginiola* among them. When he comes to look into the parcel he will at once discover the substitution and – er – of course return the volume."

"I see," assented Mr. Marrable. "That seems straightforward enough, but the delay is unfortunate for me. Have you sent after the purchaser, by the way?"

"We haven't sent after the purchaser because he happens to live in Derbyshire," was the reply. "Here is his card. We are writing at once, but the probability is that he is staying in London overnight at least."

"You might wire."

"We will, of course, wire if you ask us to do so, Mr. Marrable, but it seems to indicate an attitude of distrust towards Mr. – er – Mr. Dillworthy of Cullington Grange that I see no reason to entertain."

"Assuming the whole incident to be accidental, I think you are doing quite right. But in order to save time, mayn't it perhaps be worthwhile anticipating that something else may have been at work?" They all looked at Mr. Carrados, who advanced this suggestion diffidently. The young man in the background breathed an involuntary "Ah!" of agreement and came a little more to the front.

"Do you suggest that Mr. Dillworthy of Cullington Grange would actually deny possession of the book?" inquired the auctioneer a little cuttingly.

"Pardon me," replied Carrados blandly, "but do you know Mr. Dillworthy of Cullington Grange?"

"No, certainly, I – "

"Nor, of course, the purchaser of Lot 91? That naturally follows. Then for the purpose of our hypothesis, I would suggest that we eliminate Mr. Dillworthy, who quite reasonably may not have been within a hundred miles of Charing Cross today. What remains? His visiting card, that would cost about a crown at the outside to reproduce, or might much more cheaply be picked up from a hundred halls or office tables."

The auctioneer smiled.

"An elaborate plant, eh? Have you any practical knowledge, sir, of the difficulty, the impossibility, that would attend the disposal of this imperfect copy the moment our loss is notified?"

"But suppose it should become a perfect copy in the meantime? That might throw dust in their eyes. Eh, Marrable?"

"I say!" exclaimed the virtuoso, with his ideas forcibly directed into a new channel. "Yes, there is that, you know, Mr. Trenchard."

"Even in that very unlikely event the *Virginiola* remains a white elephant. It cannot be got off today nor yet tomorrow. Any bookseller would require time in which to collate the volume. It dare not be offered by auction. It is like a Gainsborough or a Leonardo illegally come by – so much unprofitable lumber after it is stolen."

"Then," hazarded Carrados, "there is the alternative, which might suggest itself to a really intelligent artist, of selling it before it is stolen."

The conditions were getting a little beyond Mr. Trenchard's easy access. "Sell it before it is stolen?" he repeated. "Why?"

"Because of the extreme difficulty, as you have proved, of selling it after."

"But how, I mean?"

"I think," interposed a quiet voice from the doorway, "that we had better accept Mr. Carrados's advice, if he does us the great service of offering it, without discussion, Leonard. I have the pleasure of speaking to Mr. Max Carrados, have I not?" continued a white-haired old gentleman, advancing into the room. "My young friend Trenchard, in his jealousy for the firm's reputation, starts with the conviction that it is impossible for us to be victimised. You and I know better, Mr. Carrados. Now will you tell me – I am Mr. Ing, by the way – will you tell me what has really happened?"

"I wish I could," admitted Carrados frankly. "Unfortunately I know less of the circumstances than you do, and although I was certainly present during a part of the sale, I never even 'saw' the book – " He spread out the

206

fingers of a hand to illustrate. " – and probably I was not within several yards of it or its present holder."

"But you have some idea of the method adopted – some theory," persisted Mr. Ing. "You can tell us what to do."

"Even there, I can only put two and two together and suggest investigation on common-sense lines."

"It is necessary to go to an expert even for that sometimes," submitted the old gentleman with a very comical look. "Now, Mr. Carrados, pray enlighten us."

"May I put a few questions then?"

"By all means."

"Do you require me, sir?" inquired Mr. Trenchard distantly.

"Not if you will kindly leave the sale-book and papers, I think, thank you," replied Carrados. "This young gentleman, though." The sale clerk came forward eagerly. "You have the delivery note there? No, I don't want it. This gentleman, whom we will refer to as Mr. Dillworthy – 91 is the first thing he bought?"

"Yes, sir."

"The price?"

"Three-pounds-fifteen."

"Is that a good price or a bargain?"

The clerk looked towards Mr. Ing"

"It's Coulthorp's *Marvellous Recoveries*, sir. The edition of 1674," he explained.

"A fair price," commented the old gentleman. "Yes, quite a good auction figure."

"The *Virginiola* is folio, I believe. What size is *Marvellous Recoveries*?"

"It is folio also."

"What was the next lot that Dr. Dillworthy bought?"

"Lot 198."

"Any others?"

"Yes, sir. Lots 211, 217 and 234."

"And the prices of these four lots?"

"Lot 198, a guinea. 211, twelve-and-six. 217, fifteen shillings. 234, twenty-three shillings."

"Those must be very low prices?"

"They are books in no great demand. At every sale from mixed sources, there are a certain number of make-weight lots."

"We find, then, that Mr. Dillworthy bought 91 at a good price. After that he did nothing until 191 had passed. Then he at once secured four lots of cheap books. This gives a certain colour to suspicion, but it may be pure coincidence. Now," he continued, addressing himself to the clerk again, "after the delivery slip had been made out, did Mr. Dillworthy borrow a pen from you?"

The youth's ingenuous face suddenly flashed to a recollection.

"Suffering Moses!" he exclaimed irrepressibly.

"Well – "

"Then he did?" demanded Mr. Ing, too keenly interested to stop to reprove the manner.

"Not exactly, sir. He didn't borrow a pen, but I lent him one."

"Ah!" remarked Carrados. "That sounds even better. How did it come about?"

"His bill was six-pounds-twelve-and-six. He gave me seven pounds and I made out the delivery form and gave it to him with the change. Then he said: 'Could you do with a fiver instead of five ones, by the way? I may run short of change,' and he held out a banknote. 'Certainly, if you will kindly write your name and address on the back,' I replied, and I gave him a pen."

"The one you had been using?"

"Yes, it was in my hand. He turned away and I thought that he was doing what I asked, but before he would have had time to do that, he handed me the pen back and said: 'Thanks. After all, I'll leave it as it is.'"

"Who sent in the book for sale?"

"Described as '*the property of a gentleman*'," contributed Mr. Marrable. "I wondered."

"If you will excuse me for a moment," said Mr. Ing, "I will find out."

He returned from another office smiling amiably but shaking his head.

"'*The property of a gentleman*'," he repeated with senile deliberateness. "I find that the owner expressed a definite wish for the transaction to be treated confidentially. It is no unusual thing for a client to desire that. On certain points of etiquette, Mr. Carrados, I am just as jealous for the firm as Trenchard could be, so that until we can obtain consent, I am afraid that the gentleman must remain anonymous."

"The question is," volunteered Mr. Marrable, "where has the volume got to, rather than where has it come from?"

"Sometimes," remarked the blind man, "after looking in many unlikely places, one finds the key in the lock itself. At all events, we seem to have come to the end of our usefulness here. Unless one of your people happens to come forward with a real clue, Mr. Ing, I venture to predict that you will find more profit in investigating farther afield."

"But what are we to do?" exclaimed the old gentleman rather blankly, when he saw that Carrados was preparing to go. "We are absolute babes at this sort of thing – at least I know that I am."

"The remedy for that is quite simple. Put the case into the hands of the police."

"True, true, but it is not so absolutely simple to us. We have various interests and, yes, let us say, old-fashioned prejudices to consider. I suppose – " He became quite touchingly wistful. " – I suppose that you could not be persuaded, Mr. Carrados?"

"I'm afraid not," replied Carrados. "I have other irons in the fire just now. But before you do call in the police, by the way, there is Mr. Trenchard's view to be considered."

"You mean?"

"I mean that it would be as well to make sure that the *Virginiola* has been stolen."

"By wiring to Cullington Grange?"

"Assuming that there is a Cullington Grange. Then there is a harmless experiment in collateral proof that you might like to make in the meantime, if the reply is delayed, as it reasonably may be through a dozen causes."

"And what is that, Mr. Carrados?"

"Send up Charing Cross Road and find out among the second-hand shops whether the other books Mr. Dillworthy took away with him were sold there immediately after the sale. They were only bought to round off the operation. They would be a dangerous incubus to keep, but if our man is a cool hand he may contrive to realise a pound or so for them before anything is known. You might even learn something else in the process."

"Aye, aye, to be sure," acquiesced Mr. Ing. "We'll do that at once. And then, Mr. Carrados, just a parting hint: If you were taking up the case, what would you do then?"

The temptation to be oracular was irresistible. Carrados smiled inwardly.

"I should try to find a tall, short-sighted, Welsh book-dealer who smokes perique tobacco, suffers from a weak chest, wears thick-soled boots and always carries an umbrella," he replied with impressive gravity. Mr. Ing, the saleroom porter, the young clerk, and Mr. Marrable all looked at each other and then began to repeat the varied attributes of the required individual.

"There's that – what's his name? – old chap with a red waistcoat who's always here," hopefully suggested the porter in an aside. "He wears specs, and I've never seen him without an umbrella."

"He's a Scotchman and stands about five feet three, fathead!" whispered the clerk. "Isn't Mr. Powis Welsh, sir?"

"To be sure. Powis of Redmayne Street is the man," assented Mr. Ing. "Isn't that correct, Mr. Carrados?"

"I don't know," replied Carrados, "but if he answers to the description, it probably is."

"And then?"

"Then I think I should call and encourage him to talk to me – about Shakespeare."

"Why, dash it, Carrados!" cried Mr. Marrable. "You said that you knew nothing of book-collecting and yet you seem to be aware that Powis specialises Shakespeariana and to know that the *Virginiola* would interest him. I wonder how much you have been getting at me!"

"Oh, I suppose that I'm beginning to pick up a thing or two," admitted the blind man diffidently.

In the course of his experience of crime, fragments of many mysteries had been brought to Carrados's notice – detached chapters of chequered human lives to which the opening and the *finis* had never been supplied. Some had fascinated him and yet remained impenetrable to the end, yet the theft of the *Virginiola*, a mere coup of cool effrontery in which he felt no great interest after he had pierced the method, was destined to unfold itself before his mind without an effort on his part.

The sale at Gurnard's had taken place on a Wednesday. Friday brought Carrados a reminder of the stone that he had set rolling in the appearance of a visiting card bearing the name and address of Mr. Powis of Redmayne Street. Mr. Powis was shown in and proved to be a tall, mild-looking man with a chronic cough. He carried a moderate parcel in one hand and, despite the bright, settled condition of the weather, an umbrella in the other.

"I'm an antiquarian bookseller, Mr. Carrados," he remarked by way of introduction. "I haven't the honour of your custom that I know of, but I dare say you can guess what brings me here."

"You might tell me," replied Carrados.

"Oh yes, Mr. Carrados, I will tell you. Certainly I will tell you," retorted Mr. Powis, in a rather louder voice than was absolutely necessary. "Mr. Ing looked in at my place of pizzness yesterday. He said that he was 'just passing' – 'just passing', you understand."

Mr. Powis emphasised the futility of the subterfuge by laughing sardonically.

"A charming old gentleman," remarked Carrados pleasantly. "I don't suppose that he would deceive a rabbit."

"I don't suppose that he could," asserted Mr. Powis. "'By the way,' he said, 'did you see the *Virginiola* we sold yesterday?' 'By the way!' Yes, that was it."

Carrados nodded his smiling appreciation.

"'Oh-ho,' I thought, 'the *Virginiola*!' 'Yes, Mr. Ing,' I said, 'it was a nice copy parring the defect, but a week ago I could have shown you a nicer and a perfect one to poot."

"'You've got one too, have you?' he asked.

"'Certainly I have,' I replied, 'or I should not say so. At least I had, but it may be sold now. It has gone to a gentleman in Rutland."

"'Rutland. That's a little place,' he remarked thoughtfully. 'Have you any objection to mentioning your customer's name?"

"'Not in the least, Mr. Ing,' I told him. 'Why should I have? It has taken me five-and-twenty years to make my connection, but let all the trade have it. Sir Roland Chargrave of Densmore Hall is the gentleman."

"Now, look you, Mr. Carrados, I could see by the way Mr. Ing gasped when I told him that things are not all right. It seems to be your doing that I am brought into it, and I want to know where I stand."

"Have you any misgivings as to where you stand?" inquired Carrados.

"No, Mr. Carrados, I have not," exclaimed the visitor indignantly. "I pought my *Virginiola* three or four weeks ago and I paid a goot price for it."

"Then you certainly have nothing to trouble about."

"Put I have a goot deal to trouble about," vociferated Mr. Powis. "I have a copy of the *Virginiola* to dispose of."

"Oh, you still have it, then?"

"Yes, Mr. Carrados, I have. Thanks to what is peing said pehind my pack, the pook was returned to me this morning. My name has been connected with a stolen copy and puyers are very shy, look you, when they hear that. And word, it travels. Oh yes. You may not know how, but today they will be saying in Wales: 'Have you heard what is peing said of Mr. Powis of London?' And tomorrow in Scotland it will be: 'That old tamn rascal Powis has been caught at last!'"

In spite of Mr. Powis's desperate seriousness, Carrados could not restrain a laugh at the forcefulness of the recital. "Come, come, Mr. Powis," he said soothingly, "it isn't as bad as that, you know. In any case you have only to display your receipt."

"Oh, very goot, very goot indeed!" retorted the Welshman in an extremity of satire. "Show a buyer my receipt! Excellent! That would be a capital way to carry on the antiquarian pook pizzness! Besides," he added, rather lamely, "in this case it happens that I do not possess a receipt."

"Isn't that – rather an oversight?" suggested Carrados.

"No doubt I could easily procure one. Let me tell you the circumstances, Mr. Carrados. I only want to convince you that I have nothing to conceal."

With this laudable intention Mr. Powis's attitude became more and more amiable and his manner much less Welsh. He had, in fact, used up all the indignation that he had generated in anticipation of a wordy conflict – a species of protective mimicry common to mild-tempered men.

"I bought this book from the Reverend Mr. Winch, the vicar of Fordridge, in Leicestershire. A few weeks ago I received a registered parcel from Fordridge containing a fine copy of the *Virginiola*. The same post brought me a letter from Mr. Winch. I dare say I have it here. . . . No, never mind. It was to the effect that the book had been in the writer's family for many generations. Being something of a collector, he had never wished to sell it, but an unexpected misfortune now obliged him to raise a sum of money. He had contracted blood-poisoning in his hand and he had to come up to London for an operation. After that he would have to take a long sea voyage. He went on to say that he had heard of me as a likely buyer and would call on me in a day or two. In the meantime, he sent the book to give me full opportunity of examining it.

"Nothing could be more straightforward, Mr. Carrados. Two days later Mr. Winch walked into my place. We discussed the price, and finally we agreed upon – well, a certain figure."

"You can rely upon my discretion, Mr. Powis."

"I paid him £2 and 60."

"That would be a fair price in the circumstances?"

"I thought so, Mr. Carrados. I don't say that it wasn't a bargain, but it wasn't an outrageous bargain."

"You have occasionally done better?" smiled Carrados.

"Frequently. If I buy a book for threepence and sell it again for a shilling I do better, although it doesn't sound so well. Of course I am a dealer and I have to live on my profits and to pay for my bad bargains with my good bargains. Now if I had had an immediate customer in view, the book might have been worth a good deal more to me. I may say that Wednesday's price at Gurnard's surprised me. Prices have certainly been going up, but only five years ago it would have required a practically perfect copy to make that."

"At all events, Mr. Winch accepted?"

"I think I may say that he was perfectly satisfied," amended Mr. Powis. "You see, Mr. Carrados, he wanted the money at once, and, apart from the uncertainty and expense, he could not have waited for an auction. I was making out a cheque when he reminded me that his right hand was useless and asked me to initial it to '*Bearer*'. That is why I come to have no receipt."

"Yes," assented Carrados. "Yes, that is it. How was the letter signed?"

"It was typewritten, like the rest of it. You remember that his hand was bad when he wrote."

"True. Did you notice the postmark – was it Fordridge?"

"Yes. You should understand that Mr. Winch posted on the book before he left Fordridge for London." It seemed to the visitor that Mr. Carrados was rather slow, even for a blind man.

"I think I am beginning to grasp the position," said Carrados mildly. "Of course, you had no occasion to write to him at Fordridge?"

"Nothing whatever. Besides, he was coming to London almost immediately. If I wrote, it was to be to the Fitzalan Hotel, off the Strand. Now here is the book, Mr. Carrados. You saw – you examined, that is, the auction *Virginiola*?"

"No, unfortunately I did not."

"I am sorry. You would now have recognised how immeasurably superior my copy is, even apart from the missing pages."

"I can quite believe it." He was turning over the leaves of the book, which Mr. Powis had passed to him.

"But this writing on the dedication page?"

"Oh, that," said the dealer carelessly. "Some former owner has written his name there."

"I suppose it constitutes a blot?"

"Why, yes, in a small way it does," admitted Mr. Powis. "Had it been '*Wm. Shakespeare*,' it would have added a thousand guineas. As it's only '*Wm. Shoelack*', it knocks two or three off."

"Possibly," suggested Carrados, "it was this blemish that decided Sir Roland Chargrave against the book?"

"No, no," insisted Mr. Powis. "Someone has hinted something to him. I don't say that you are to blame, Mr. Carrados, but a suspicion has been created. It has got about."

"But Sir Roland is the one man whom it could not affect," pointed out Carrados. "He, at any rate, would know that this copy is unimpeachable, because when the other was being stolen this was actually in his hands and had been for – for how long?"

"Five or six days. He kept it for about a week. And that no doubt is true as a specific case, but a malicious rumour is wide, Mr. Carrados. So-and-so is unreliable. He deals in questionable property. Better be careful. It is enough. No, no. Mr. Chatton said nothing about any objection to the book, merely that Sir Roland had decided not to retain it."

213

"Mr. Chatton?"

"He is the secretary or the librarian there. I have frequently done business with him in the old baronet's time. This man is a nephew who succeeded only a few months ago. Well, Mr. Carrados, I hope I have convinced you that I came by this *Virginiola* in a legitimate manner?"

"Scarcely that."

"I haven't!" exclaimed Mr. Powis in blank astonishment.

"I never doubted it. At the sale, I happened to hear you remark to a friend that you had recently bought a copy. My suggestion to Mr. Ing was merely to hint that, with your exceptional knowledge, your unique experience, you would probably be able to put them on the right line as to the disposal of the stolen copy and so on. An unfortunate misunderstanding."

Mr. Powis stared and then nodded several times with an expression of acute resignation.

"That old man is past work," he remarked feelingly. "I might have saved myself a journey. Well, I'll go now, Mr. Carrados."

"Not yet," declared Carrados hospitably. "I am going to persuade you to stay and lunch with me, Mr. Powis. I want – " He was still fingering the early pages of the *Virginiola* with curious persistence. "I want you to explain to me the way in which these interesting old books were bound."

With the departure of Mr. Powis a few hours later, Carrados might reasonably conclude that he had heard the last of the *Virginiola* theft, for he was now satisfied that it would never reach publicity as a police court case. But, willy-nilly, the thing pursued him. Mr. Carlyle was to have dined with him one evening in the following week. It was a definite engagement, but during the day the inquiry agent telephoned his friend to know what he should do. A young gentleman who had been giving him some assistance in a case was thrown on his hands for the evening.

"You are the most amiable of men, Max," chirruped Mr. Carlyle. "But, really, I don't like to ask."

"Bring him by all means," assented the most amiable of men. "I expect two or three others to turn up tonight." So Mr. Carlyle brought him.

"Mr. Chatton, Max."

An unobtrusive young man, whose face wore a perpetual expression of docile willingness, shook hands with Carrados. Anything less like the sleek, competent self-assurance of the conventional private secretary it would be difficult to imagine. Mr. Chatton's manner was that of a well-meaning man who habitually blundered from a too-conscientious sense of duty, knew it all along, and was pained at the inevitableness of the recurring catastrophe.

"I have just taken up a case that might interest you, Max," said Mr. Carlyle, as the three of them stood together. "Simple enough, but it involves a valuable old book that has been stolen. Gurnard's called me in – " And he proceeded to outline the particulars of the missing *Virginiola*.

"And you went down yourself to Gurnard's to look into it, Mr. Chatton?" said Carrados, masking the species of admiration that he felt for his new acquaintance.

"Well, I don't know about looking into it," confessed Mr. Chatton. "You see, it doesn't really concern Sir Roland at all now. But I thought that I ought to offer them any information – a description or something of that sort might be wanted – when I heard of their loss. Of course," he added, with a deepening of his habitual look of rueful perturbation, "we can't help it, but it's very distressing to think of them losing so much money over our affair."

"Not a bit of it, not a bit of it," cried Mr. Carlyle heartily. "It's all in the way of business and Gurnard's won't feel a touch like that. Very good of you to take all the .trouble you have, I say." He turned his beaming, self-confident eye towards his host to explain. "I happened to meet Mr. Chatton there this morning and ever since he has been helping me to put about inquiries in likely quarters and so on. I haven't any doubt of pulling our man up in a week or two, unless it's the work of a secret bibliomaniac, and Gurnard's don't entertain that."

"Wednesday last, you say," pondered Carrados. "Aren't they rather late in turning it over to you?"

"Just what I complained of. Then it came out that they had been pinning their faith to the advice of some officious idiot who happened to be present at the sale. Nothing came of it, of course."

"They did not happen to mention the idiot's name?" inquired Max tentatively.

"No. The old gentleman – Mr. Ing – said that he had already got into hot water once through doing that." Mr. Carlyle began to laugh in his hearty way over a recollection of the incident. "Do you know what this genius's brilliant idea was? He put them on the track of a copy of this book that had been recently sold to a dealer, assuming that it must necessarily be the stolen copy. And so it had been recently sold, Max, but it happened to be before the other was stolen!"

"Very amusing," agreed Carrados.

"Do you know, I can't help thinking that I was somehow to blame for that," confessed Mr. Chatton in a troubled voice. "You remember, I told you."

"No, no," protested Mr. Carlyle encouragingly.

"How could it be your fault?"

215

"Well, it's very good of you to reassure me," continued the young man, relieved but not convinced. "But I really think I may have introduced a confusing element. I should like Mr. Carrados to judge. . . . When I learned from Sir Roland that he intended sending this *Virginiola* to Gurnard's, knowing that it was a valuable book, I saw the necessity of going over it carefully with another copy – 'collating' it is called – to find out whether anything was missing. The British Museum doesn't possess an example, and in any case, I could not well spare a day just then to come to London for the purpose. So I wrote to a few dealers, rather, I am afraid, giving them the impression that we wished to buy a copy. In this way I got what I wanted sent up on approval and I was able to go through the two thoroughly. At the moment I argued that my duty to my employer justified the subterfuge, but I don't know, I don't know. I really question whether it was quite legitimate."

"Oh, nonsense," remonstrated Mr. Carlyle, to whom the subtleties did not appeal. "Rather a smart way of getting what you wanted in the circumstances, don't you think, Max?"

Carrados paid a willing if equivocal tribute to the wider problem of Mr. Chatton's brooding conscientiousness

"Very ingenious altogether," he admitted.

Mr. Carlyle did not pull his man up in a few weeks. In fact, he never reached him at all. For the key to the disappearance of the *Virginiola* he had to wait two years. He was at The Turrets one day when his host was called away for a short time to see a man who had come on business.

Carlyle had picked up a newspaper when Carrados came back from the door and, opening one of the inner drawers of his desk, threw out a long envelope.

"There," he remarked as he went on again, "is something that may interest you more."

He was quite right. The inquiry agent cut open the envelope that was addressed to himself and read the following narrative:

> *In the year 1609 a seafaring gentleman called Somers –*
> *Sir George Somers – was wrecked on an island in the Atlantic.*
> *This island – one of a group – although destitute of human*
> *inhabitants, was overrun by pigs. During the first part of their*
> *enforced residence there, the shipwrecked mariners were*
> *much concerned by unearthly shrieks and wailings that filled*
> *the night. With the simple piety of the time these were*
> *attributed to the activity of witches, imps and demons. In fact,*
> *in addition to the varied appellations of Virginiola,*

216

*Bermoothes, Somers Islands, etc., the place was enticingly
called* "The He of Divels".

*In due course the castaways were rescued and returned
to England. In due course, also, there appeared a variety of
printed accounts of their adventures. (We are prone to think
that the tendency is modern, Louis, but it is not.) One of these
coming into the hands of a cynical, middle-aged playwright
on the look-out for a new plot to annex, was at once pressed
into his scheme. Doubtless he saw behind the shadowy
"divels" the substantial outlines of the noisy "hogges".
However, the idea was good enough for a background. He
wrote his play and called it* The Tempest. *This is the
explanation offered to me of the high and increasing value of
rare early works on Bermuda. They can be classed among the
Shakespeariana. There is also another reason: They can be
classed among the Americana.*

*About three-hundred years later, a certain young
gentleman who combined fairly expensive tastes with good
commercial ability succeeded to a title and its appendages.
Among the latter were a mansion in Rutlandshire, which he
determined was too expensive, a library in which he was not
vastly interested, and a private secretary whose services he
continued to retain. One day about six months after his
succession, Sir Roland Chargrave called in his secretary to
receive instructions.*

*"Look here, Chatton," he said, "I have decided to let this
place furnished for a time. See Turvey about the value and
then advertise it for something more than he advises. It ought
to bring in a decent rental. Then there are some valuable
things here that are no earthly good to me. I'll start with the
library."*

*"You intend to dispose of the library, Sir Roland?"
faltered the secretary.*

*"No. The library gives a certain distinction to a fellow
and the Chargraves have always had one. I'll keep the library,
but I'll weed out all the old stuff that will make high prices.
Uncle Vernon left a valuation list which appears to have been
made out about ten years ago. One book alone –* 'An Account
of Virginiola' *– he puts down at £300. Then there are a dozen
others that ought to bring another £200 among them. I require
£500 just now. Here is a list of the books I have picked out.
Send them off to Gurnard's to be sold as soon as possible.*

Don't have my name catalogued. I don't want it to be known that I'm selling anything. That's all."

The secretary withdrew with an accentuation of his unhappy manner. It was very distressing to him, this dispersal of the family heirlooms. It was also extremely inconvenient personally, because he had already sold the Virginiola himself only a week before. For he also had expenses. Perhaps he had fallen into the hands of the Jews. Perhaps it was the Jewesses. At all events, like Sir Roland, he required money, and again like Sir Roland, the Virginiola had seemed the most suitable method. He had quietly withdrawn the book about the time of his former master's death, and thus saved the new baronet quite an item in duty. He had secured Sir Vernon's valuation list and after six months had concluded that he was safe. He had taken extraordinary pains to cover his identity in selling the book and the old dotard appeared to have made two lists and to have deposited one elsewhere.

Like a wise man, Mr. Chatton set about discovering how he could retrieve himself. He had had charge of the library and he knew that it was too late to report the book as lost. In any case he would be dismissed. If inquiry was made at that stage he would be prosecuted. From the depths of his brooding melancholy Mr. Chatton evolved a scheme.

The first thing was to get back the Virginiola a little before the sale. By that time he had sent in the list, but not the books. Doubtless he still had some of the illicit funds in hand. Now the Virginiola had been valued at £300 by old Sir Vernon, but if at the sale it was discovered to be imperfect in an important detail then it might realise only a fraction of that sum. There was also another consideration. A name had been indelibly written on one of the early pages, and if Mr. Powis was not to recognise his property that page must be temporarily removed.

I think it was Chatton's undoubted intention to buy back the book if possible and run no further risk with it. What he had not taken into account was the enormous rise in the value of this class of work. What had been reasonably worth £300 ten years before, the market now apprised at nearly double. Even the imperfect copy reached nearly the original estimate and thereby Chatton's first string failed.

But this painstakingly conscientious young man had not been content to risk all on a single chance. What form his

218

second venture took it will be unnecessary to recall to you. He calculated on the chances of the saleroom, and he succeeded. The Virginiola *was recovered. The abstracted sheet was cunningly replaced, probably certain erasable marks that had been put in for fuller disguise were removed, and Mr. Powis received back his property with formal regrets.*

I anticipate an indignant question rising to your lips. I did not tell you this before, Louis, because of one curious fact: The story is entirely speculative on my part so far as demonstrable proof is concerned. Chatton, who is rather a remarkable young man, did not leave behind him one solitary shread of evidence that would stand before a jury. Time and Mr. Chatton's future career can alone bring my justification, but some day if we have the opportunity – (I am committing this to paper in case we should not) – we will go over the evidence together. In the meanwhile, Gurnard's can, as you said, stand the loss.

Here the typewritten account ended, but at the foot of the last page, Carrados had pasted a newspaper cutting. From it, Mr. Carlyle learned that *"Vernon Howard, alias Digby Skeffington, etc., etc., whose real name was said to be Chatton, well connected,"* had, the week before, been convicted, chiefly on the King's evidence of a female accomplice, of obtaining valuable jewellery under false pretences. Sentence had been deferred, pending further inquiries.

The Disappearance of
Marie Severe

"I wonder if you might happen to be interested in this case of Marie Severe, Mr. Carrados?"

If Carrados's eyes had been in the habit of expressing emotion, they would doubtless have twinkled as Inspector Beedel thus casually introduced the subject of the Swanstead on Thames schoolgirl whose inexplicable disappearance two weeks earlier had filled column upon column of every newspaper with excited speculation until the sheer impossibility of keeping the sensation going without a shred of actual fact had relegated Marie Severe to the obscurity of an occasional paragraph.

"If you are concerned with it, I am sure that I shall be interested, Inspector," said the blind man encouragingly. "It is still being followed, then?"

"Why, yes, sir, I have it in hand, but as for following it – well, 'following' is perhaps scarcely the word now."

"Ah," commented Carrados. "There was very little to follow. I remember."

"I don't think that I've ever known a case of the kind with less, sir. For all the trace she left, the girl might have melted out of existence, and from that day to this, with the exception of that printed communication received by her mother – you remember that, Mr. Carrados? – there hasn't been a clue worth wasting so much as shoe leather on."

"You have had plenty of hints all the same, I suppose?"

Inspector Beedel threw out a gesture of mild despair. It conveyed the patient exasperation of the conscientious and long-suffering man.

"I should say that the case 'took on' remarkably, Mr. Carrados. I doubt if there has been a more popular sensation of its kind for years. Mind you, I'm all in favour of publicity in the circumstances the photographs and description may bring important facts to light, but sometimes it's a bit trying for those who have to do the work at our end. *'Seen in Northampton,' 'Seen in Ealing,' 'Heard of in West Croydon,' 'Girl answering to the description observed in the waiting room at Charing Cross,' 'Suspicious-looking man with likely girl noticed about the Victoria Dock, Hull,' 'Seen and spoken to near Chorley, Lancs,' 'Caught sight of apparently struggling in a luxurious motor car on the Portsmouth Road,' 'Believed to have visited a Watford Picture Palace'* – They've all been gone into as carefully as though we believed that each one was the real thing at last."

"And you haven't, eh?"

The Inspector looked round. He knew well enough that they were alone in the study at The Turrets, but the action had become something of a mannerism with him.

"I don't mind admitting to you, sir, that I've never had any other opinion than that the father of the little girl went down that day and got her away. Where she is now, and whether dead or alive, I can't pretend to say, but that he's at the bottom of it I'm firmly convinced. And what's more," he added with slow significance, "I hope so."

"Why in particular?" inquired the other.

Beedel felt in his breast pocket, took out a formidable wallet, and from among its multitudinous contents selected a cabinet photograph sheathed in its protecting envelope of glazed transparent paper.

"If you could make out anything of what this portrait shows, you'd understand better what I mean, Mr. Carrados," he replied delicately.

Carrados shook his head but nevertheless held out his hand for the photograph.

"No good, I'm afraid," he confessed before he took it. "A print of this sort is one of the few things that afford no graduation to the sense of touch. No, no – " as he passed his finger-tips over the paper, " – a gelatino-chloride surface of mathematical uniformity, Inspector, and nothing more. Now had it been the negative – "

"I am sure that that could be procured if you wished to have it, Mr. Carrados. Anyway, I dare say that you've seen in some of the papers what this young girl is like. She is ten years old and big – at least tall – for her age. This picture is the last taken – some time this year – and I am told that it is just like her."

"How should you describe it, Inspector?"

"I am not much good at that sort of thing," said the large man with a shy awkwardness, "but it makes as sweet a picture as ever I've seen. She is very straight-set, and yet with a sort of gracefulness such as a young wild animal might have. It's a full-faced position, and she is looking straight out at you with an expression that is partly serious and partly amused, and as noble and gracious with it all as a young princess might be. I have children of my own, Mr. Carrados, and of course I think they're very nice and pretty, but this – this is quite a different thing. Her hair is curly without being in separate curls, and the description calls it black. Eyes dark brown with straight eyebrows, complexion a sort of glowing brown, small regular teeth. Of course we have a full description of what she was wearing and so forth."

"Yes, yes," assented Carrados idly. "The Van Brown Studio, Photographers, eh? These people are quite well off, then?"

"Oh yes. Very nice house and good position – Mrs. Severe, that is to say. You will remember that she obtained a divorce from her husband four or five years ago. I've turned up the particulars and it wasn't what you'd call a bad case as things go, but the lady seemed determined, and in the end Severe didn't defend. She had five- or six-hundred a year of her own, but he had nothing beyond his salary, and he threw his position up then, and ever since he has been going steadily down. He's almost on the last rung now and picks up his living casual."

"What's the case against him?"

"Well, it scarcely amounts to a case as yet because there is no evidence of his being seen with the child, nor is there anything to connect him with her after the disappearance. Still, it is a working hypothesis. If it was the act of a tramp or a maniac, experience goes to show that we should have found her, dead or alive, by now. Mrs. Severe is all for it being her husband. Of course the decree gave her the custody of Marie. Severe asked to be allowed to see her occasionally, and at first a servant took the child to have tea with him once a month. That was at his rooms. Then he asked to be met in one of the parks or at a gallery. He hadn't got so much as a room then, you see, sir. At last the servant reported that he had grown so shabby as to shame her that the child should be seen with him, though she did say that he was always sober and very kind to Marie, bringing her a little toy or something even when he didn't seem to have sixpence for himself. After that the visits were stopped altogether. Then about a month ago these two, husband and wife, met accidentally in the street. Severe said that he hoped to be doing a bit better soon, and asked for the visits to be continued. How it would have gone I cannot say, but Mrs. Severe happened to have a friend with her, an American lady called Miss Julp, who seems to be living with her now, and the middle-aged female – she's a hard sister, that Cornelia Julp, I should say – pushed her way into the conversation and gave her views on his conduct until Severe must have had some trouble with his hands. Finally Mrs. Severe had an unfortunate impulse to end the discussion by giving her husband a bank-note. She says she got the most awful look she ever saw on any face. Then Severe very deliberately tore up the note, dropped the pieces down a gutter grid that they were standing near, dusted his fingers on his handkerchief, raised his hat and walked away without another word. That was the last she saw of him, but she professes to have been afraid of something happening ever since.

"Then something happens, and so, of course, it must be Severe?" suggested Carrados.

222

"It does look a bit like that so far, I must admit, sir," assented the Inspector. "Still, Mrs. Severe's opinions aren't quite all. Severe's account of his movements on the afternoon in question – say between twelve-thirty and four in particular – are not satisfactory. Latterly he has been occupying a miserable room off Red Lion Street. He went out at twelve and returned about five – that he doesn't deny. Says he spent the time walking about the streets and in the Holborn newsroom, but can mention no one who saw him during those five hours. On the other hand, a porter at Swanstead station identifies him as a passenger who alighted there from the 1:17 that afternoon."

"From a newspaper likeness?"

"In the first instance, Mr. Carrados. Afterwards in person."

"Did they speak, or is it merely visual?"

"Only from what he saw of him."

"Struck, I suppose, by the remarkable fact that the passenger wore a hat and a tie – as shown in the picture, or inspired to notice him closely by something indescribably suggestive in the passenger's way of giving up his ticket? It may be all right, Beedel, I admit, but I heartily distrust the weight of importance that these casual identifications are being given on vital points nowadays. Are you satisfied with this yourself?"

"Only as corroborative, sir. Until we find the girl or some trace of her, we're bound to make casts in the hope of picking up a line. Well, then there's the letter Mrs. Severe received."

"Have you that with you?"

The Inspector took up the wallet that he had not yet returned to his pocket and selected another enclosure.

"It's a very unusual form," he commented as he handed the envelope to Mr. Carrados and waited for his opinion.

The blind man passed his finger-tips across the paper and at once understood the point of singularity. The lines were printed, but not in consecutive form, every letter being on a little separate square of paper. It was evident that they had been cut out from some other sheet and then pasted on the envelope to form the address.

"'*London, E. C., 5:30 p.m., 15ᵗʰ May*'," read Carrados from the postmark.

"The day of the kidnapping. There is a train from Swanstead arriving at Lambeth Bridge at 4:47," remarked Beedel.

"What was your porter doing when that left?"

"He was off duty, sir."

Carrados took out the enclosure and read it off as he had already done the envelope, but with a more deliberative touch, for the print was smaller.

The type and the paper were suggestive of a newspaper origin. In most cases whole words had been found available.

"*Do not be alarmed,*" ran the patchwork message. "*The girl is in good hands. Only risk lies in pressing search. Wait and she will return uninjured.*"

"You have identified the newspaper?"

"Yes. It is all cut from *The Times* of May the 13th. The printing on the back of the words fixes it absolutely. Premeditated, Mr. Carrados."

"The whole incident points to that. The date of the newspaper means little, but the deliberate selection of words, the careful way they have been cut out and aligned, taken in conjunction with the time the child disappeared and the time that this was posted – Yes, I think you may assume premeditation, Inspector."

"Stationery of the commonest description. Immediate return to London, and the method of a man who used this print because he feared that under any disguise his handwriting might be recognised."

Carrados nodded.

"Severe cannot hope to retain the child, of course," he remarked casually. "What motive do you infer?"

"Mrs. Severe is convinced that it is to distress her, out of revenge."

"And this letter is to reassure her?"

The inspector bit his lip as he smiled at the quiet thrust.

"It might also be to influence her towards suspending search," he suggested.

"At all events, I dare say that it has reassured her?"

"In a certain way, yes, it has. It has enabled us to establish that the act is not one of casual lust or vagabondage. There is an alternative that we naturally did not suggest to her."

"And that is?"

"Another Thelby Wood case, Mr. Carrados. The maniacal infatuation of someone who would be the last to be suspected. Some man of good position, a friend and neighbour possibly, who sees this beautiful young creature – the school friend of his own daughters or sitting before him in church it may be – and becomes the slave of his diseased imagination until he is prepared to risk everything for that one overpowering object. A primitive man for the time, one may say, or, even worse, a satyr or a gorilla."

"I wonder," observed Carrados thoughtfully, "if you also have ever felt that you would like to drop it and become a monk, Inspector. Or a Stylites on a pole."

Beedel laughed softly and then rubbed his chin in the same contemplative spirit.

"I think I know what you mean, sir," he admitted. "It's a black page. But," he added with wholesome philosophy, "after all, it is only a page in a longish book. And if I was in a monastery there'd be one or two more things done that I've helped to keep undone."

"Including the cracking of my head, Inspector? Very true. We must take the world as we find it and ourselves as we are. And I wish that I could agree with you about Severe. It would be a more endurable outlook: Spite and revenge are at least decent human motives. Unfortunately, the only hint I can offer is a negative one." He indicated the printed cuttings on the sheet that Beedel had submitted to him. "This photo-mountant costs about sixpence a pot, but you can buy a bottle of gum for a penny.

"Well, sir," said Beedel, "I did think of having that examined, but I waited for you to see the letter as it stood. After all, it didn't strike me as a point one could put much reliance on."

"Quite right," assented Mr. Carrados, "there is nothing personal or definite in it. It may suggest a photographer, amateur or professional, but it would be preposterous to assume so much from this alone. Severe, even, may have – There are hundreds of chances. I should disregard it for the moment."

"There is nothing more to be got from the letter?"

"There may be, but it is rather elusive at present. What has been done with it?"

"I received it from Mrs. Severe and it has been in my possession ever since."

"You haven't submitted it to a chemist for any purpose?"

"No, sir. I gave a copy of the wording to some newspaper gentlemen, but no one but myself has handled it."

"Very good. Now if you care to leave it with me for a few days."

Inspector Beedel expressed his immediate willingness and would have added his tribute of obligation for Mr. Carrados's service, but the blind man cut him short.

"Don't rely on anything, Inspector," he warned him. "I am afraid that this resolves itself into a game of chance. Just one touch of luck may give us a winning point, or it may go the other way. In any case, there is no reason why I should not motor round by Swanstead one of these days when I am out. If anything fresh turns up before you hear from me, you had better telephone me. Now exactly where did this happen?"

The actual facts surrounding the disappearance of Marie Severe constituted the real mystery of the case. Arling Avenue, Swanstead, was one of those leisurely suburban roads where it is impossible to imagine anything happening hurriedly, from the delivery of an occasional telegram to the activity of the local builder. Houses, detached houses each

225

surrounded by its rood or more of garden, had been built here and there along its length at one time or another, but even the most modern one had now become matured, and the vacant plots between them had reverted from the condition of "eligible sites" into very passable fields of buttercups and daisies again, so that Arling Avenue remained a pleasant and exclusive thoroughfare. One side of the road was entirely unbuilt on and afforded the prospect of a level meadow where hay was made and real animals grazed in due season. The inhabitants of Arling Avenue never failed to point out to visitors this evidence of undeniable rurality. It even figured in the prospectus of Homewood, the Arling Avenue day school for girls and little boys which the Misses Chibwell had carried on with equal success and inconspicuousness until the Severe affair suddenly brought them into the glare of a terrifying publicity.

Mrs. Severe's house, The Hollies, was the first in the road, as the road was generally regarded – that is to say, from the direction of the station. Beedel picked up a loose sheet of paper and scored it heavily with a plan of the neighbourhood as he explained the position with some minuteness. Next to The Hollies came Arling Lodge. After Arling Lodge there was one of the vacant plots of ground before the next house was reached, but between the Lodge and the vacant plot was a broad grassy opening, unfenced towards the road, and here the inspector's pencil underlined the deepest significance, culminating in an ominous X about the centre of the space. Originally the opening had doubtless marked the projection of another road, but the scheme had come to nothing. Occasionally a little band of exploring children with the fictitious optimism of youth pecked among its rank and tangled growth in the affectation of hoping to find blackberries there. Once in a while a passing chair-mender or travelling tinker regarded it favourably for the scene of his midday *siesta*, but its only legitimate use seemed to be that of affording access to the side door of Arling Lodge garden. The inspector pencilled in the garden door as an afterthought, with the parenthesis that it was seldom used and always kept locked. Then he followed out the Avenue as far as the school, indicating all the houses and other features. The whole distance traversed did not exceed two-hundred yards.

A few minutes before two o'clock on the afternoon of her disappearance, Marie Severe set out as usual for Miss Chibwell's school. Since the incident of the unfortunate encounter with her former husband, Mrs. Severe had considered it necessary to exercise a peculiar vigilance over her only child. Thenceforward, Marie never went out alone – never, with the exception of the short walk to school and back. That is to say, for in that quiet straight road, in the full light of day, it was ridiculous to imagine that anything could happen. It was ridiculous, but all the same the vaguely uneasy woman generally walked to the garden gate with the little girl and watched her until the diminished figure passed, with a last gay wave of hand or satchel, out of her sight into the school yard.

"That's how it would have been on this occasion," narrated Beedel, "only just as they got to the garden gate, a tradesman whom Mrs. Severe wanted to speak with drove up and passed in by the back way. The lady looked along the avenue, and as it happened at that moment Miss Chibwell was standing in the road by her gate. No one else was in sight, so it isn't to be wondered at that Mrs. Severe went back to the house immediately without another thought.

"That was the last that has been seen of Marie. As a matter of fact, Miss Chibwell turned back into her garden almost as soon as Mrs. Severe did. When the child did not appear for the afternoon school the mistress thought nothing of it. She is a little short-sighted, and although she had seen the two at their gate she concluded that they were going out together somewhere. Consequently it was not until four o'clock, when Marie did not return home, that the alarm was raised."

Continuous narration was not congenial to Inspector Beedel's mental attitude. He made frequent pauses as though to invite cross-examination. Sometimes Carrados ignored the opening, at others he found it more convenient to comply.

"The inference is that someone was waiting in this space just beyond Arling Lodge?" he now contributed.

"I think it is reasonable to assume that, sir. Premeditated, we both admit. Doubtless a favourable opportunity was being looked for and there it was. At all events there – " He tapped the X as the paper lay beneath Carrados's hand " – there is the very last trace that we can rely on."

"The scent, you mean?"

"Yes, Mr. Carrados. We got one of our dogs down the next morning and put him on the trail. We gave him the scent of a boot and from the gate he brought us without a pause to where I have marked this X. There the line ended. There can be no doubt that from that point the girl had been picked up and carried. That is a very remarkable thing. It could scarcely have been done openly past the houses. The fences on all sides are of such a nature that it is incredible for any man to have got an unwilling or insensible burden of that sort over without at least laying it down in the process. If our dog is to be trusted, it wasn't laid down. Some sort of a vehicle remains. We find no recent wheel-marks, and no one seems to have seen anything that would answer about at that time.

"You are determined to mystify me, Inspector," smiled Carrados.

"I'm that way myself, sir," said the detective.

"And I know you too well to ask if you have done this and that – "

"I've done everything," admitted Beedel modestly.

"Is this X spot commanded by any of the houses? Here is Arling Lodge There is one window overlooking, but now the trees are too much out for anything to be seen. Besides, it's only a passage window. Dr. Ellerslie took me up there himself to settle the point."

"Ellerslie – Dr. Ellerslie?"

"The gentleman who lives there. At least he doesn't live altogether there, as I understand that he has it for a week-end place. Boating, I believe, sir. His regular practice is in town."

"Harley Street? Prescott Ellerslie, do you know?"

"That is the same, Mr. Carrados."

"Oh, a very well-known man. He has a great reputation as an operator for peritonitis. Nothing less than fifty guineas a time, Inspector." Perhaps the fee did not greatly impress Mr. Carrados, but doubtless he judged that it would interest Inspector Beedel. "And this house on the other side – Lyncote?"

"A retired Indian army colonel lives there – Colonel Doige."

"I mean as regards overlooking the spot."

"No, it is quite cut off from there. It cannot be seen."

Carrados's interpreting finger stopped lightly over a detail of the plan that it was again exploring. The inspector's pencil had now added a line of dots leading from The Hollies gate to the X.

"The line the dog took," Beedel explained, following the other's movement. "You notice that the girl turned sharply out of the avenue into this opening at right angles."

"I was just considering that."

"Something took her attention suddenly or someone called her there – I wonder what, Mr. Carrados."

"I wonder," echoed the blind man, raising the anonymous letter to his face again.

Mr. Carrados frequently professed to find inspiration in the surroundings of light and brilliance to which his physical sense was dead, but when he wished to go about his work with everyone else at a notable disadvantage he not unnaturally chose the dark. It was therefore night when, in accordance with his promise to Beedel, he motored round by Swanstead – or, more exactly, it was morning, for the clock in the square ivied tower of the parish church struck two as the car switch-backed over the humped bridge from Middlesex into Surrey.

"This will do, Harris. Wait here," he said a little later. He knew that there were trees above and wide open spaces on both sides. The station lay just beyond, and from the station to Arling Avenue was a negligible step. Even at that hour, Arling Avenue might have been awake to the intrusion of an alien car of rather noticeable proportions. The adaptable Harris picked out Mr. Carrados's most substantial rug and went to sleep, to dream of a wayside cycle shop and tearooms where he could devote himself to pedigree Wyandottes. With Parkinson at his elbow, Carrados walked slowly on to Arling Avenue. What was lacking on Beedel's plan Parkinson's eyes supplied. On a subtler plane, in the moist, warm night, full of quiet sounds and earthy odours, other details were filled in like the work of a lightning cartoonist before the blind man's understanding.

They walked the length of the avenue once and then returned to the grassy opening where the last trace of Marie Severe had evaporated.

"I will stay here. You walk on back to the highroad and wait for me. I may be some time. If I want you, you will hear the whistle."

"Very good, sir." Parkinson knew of old that there were times when his master would have no human eye upon him as he went about his work, and with a magnificent stolidity the man had not a particle of curiosity. It did not even occur to him to wonder. But for nearly half-an-hour the more inquiring creatures of the night looked down – or up, according to their natures – to observe the strange attitudes and quiet persistence of the disturber of the solitude as he crossed and recrossed their little domain, studied its boundaries, and explored every corner of its miniature thickets. A single petal picked up near the locked door to the garden of Arling Lodge seemed a small return for such perseverance, but it is to be presumed that the patient search had not been in vain, for it was immediately after the discovery that Carrados left the opening, and with the cool effrontery that marked his methods, he opened the front gate of Dr. Ellerslie's garden and made his way with slow but unerring insight along the boundary wall.

"A blind man," he had once replied to Mr. Carlyle's nervous remonstrance, "a blind man carries on his face a sufficient excuse for every indiscretion."

It was nearly three o'clock when, by the light of the street lamp at the corner of the avenue and the highroad, Parkinson saw his master approaching. But to the patient and excellent servitor's disappointment, Carrados at that moment turned back and retraced his steps in the same leisurely manner. As a matter of fact, a new consideration had occurred to the blind man and he continued to pace up and down the footpath as he considered it.

"Oh, sir!"

He stopped at once, but betraying no surprise, without the start which few can restrain when addressed suddenly in the dark. It was always dark to him, but was it ever sudden? Was he indeed ignorant of the obscure figure that had appeared at the gate during his perambulation.

229

"I have seen you walking up and down at this hour and I wondered – I wondered whether you had any news."

"Who are you?" he asked.

"I am Mrs. Severe. My little girl Marie disappeared from here two weeks ago. You must surely know about it. Everybody does."

"Yes, I know," he admitted. "Inspector Beedel told me."

"Oh, Inspector Beedel!" There was obvious disappointment in her voice. "He is very kind and promises – but nothing comes of it, and the days go on, the days go on," she repeated tragically.

"Ida! Ida!" Someone was calling from one of the upper windows, but Carrados was speaking also and Mrs. Severe merely waved her hand back towards the house without responding.

"Your little girl was very fond of flowers?"

"Oh yes, indeed." The pleasant recollection dwarfed the poor lady's present sense of calamity and for a moment she was quite bright. "She loved them. She would bury her face in a bunch of flowers and drink their scent. She almost lived in the garden. They were more to her than toys or dolls, I am sure. But how do you know?

"I only guessed."

"Ida! Ida!" The rather insistent, nasally querulous voice was raised again and this time Mrs. Severe replied.

"Yes, dear, immediately," she called back, still lingering, however, to discover whether she had anything to hope from this outlandish visitant.

"Had Marie been ill recently?" Carrados detained her with the question.

"Ill! Oh no." The reply was instant and emphatic. It was almost – if one could credit a mother's pride in her child's health being carried to such a length – it was almost resentful.

"Nothing that required the services of a doctor?"

"Marie never requires the services of a doctor." The tone, distant and constrained, made it clear that Mrs. Severe had given up any expectations in this quarter. "My child, I am glad to say, does not know what illness means," she added deliberately.

"Ida! Oh, here you are." The very unromantically accoutred form of a keen-visaged, middle-aged female, padding heavily in bedroom slippers along the garden walk, gave its quietus to the situation.

"What a scare you gave me, dearie. Why, whoever – "

"Good night," said Mrs. Severe, turning from the gate.

Carrados raised his hat and resumed his interrupted stroll. He had not sought the interview and he made no effort to prolong it, for there was little to be got from that source.

"A strange flare of maternal pride," he remarked in his usual detached fashion as he rejoined Parkinson.

About five o'clock on the same day – five o'clock in the afternoon, let it be understood – Inspector Beedel was called to the telephone.

"Oh, nothing fresh so far, Mr. Carrados," he reported when he identified his caller. "I shan't forget to let you know whenever there – "

"But I think that possibly there is," replied Mr. Carrados. "Or at least there might be if you went down to Arling Lodge and insisted on seeing the child who slept there last night."

"Arling Lodge? Dr. Ellerslie's? You don't mean to say, sir – "

"That is for you to satisfy yourself. Dr. Ellerslie is a widower with no children. Marie Severe was drugged by phronolal on some flowers which she was given. Phronolal is a new anaesthetic which is practically unknown outside medical circles. She was carried into the garden of Arling Lodge and into the house. The bunch of flowers was thrown down temporarily inside the wall, probably while the door was relocked. The girl's hair caught on a raspberry cane six yards from the back door along the path leading there. Ellerslie had previously sent away the two people who look after the place – a housekeeper and her husband who sees to the garden. That letter, by the way, was associable with phronolal. Now you have all that I know, Inspector, and I hope to goodness that I am clear of it."

"But, good Heavens, Mr. Carrados, this is really terrible!" protested Beedel, moved to emotion in spite of his rich experience of questionable humanity. "A man in his position! Is he a maniac?"

"I don't know. To tell you frankly, Inspector, I haven't gone an inch further than I was compelled to go in order to be sure. Make use of the information as you like, but I don't want to have anything more to do with the case. It isn't a pleasant thing to have pulled down a man like Ellerslie – a callous, exacting machine in the operating room, one hears, but a man who was doing fine work – saving useful lives every day. I'm sick of it, Beedel, that's all."

"I understand, sir. Still, there's the other side, isn't there, after all? Of course I'll keep your name out of it as you wish, but I shall be given a good deal of credit that I oughtn't to accept. If you don't do anything for a few weeks the papers are always more complimentary when you do do it."

"I'm afraid that you will have to put up with that," replied Carrados drily.

There was an acquiescent laugh from the other end and a reference to the speaker's indebtedness. Then: "Well, I'll get the necessary authority and go down at once, sir."

"Yes. Goodbye," said Carrados. He hung up the receiver with the only satisfaction that he had experienced since he had fixed on Ellerslie – satisfaction to have done with it. The thing was unpalatable enough in itself, and to add another element of distaste, through one or two circumstances that had come his way in the past, he had an actual regard for the surgeon whom some called brutal, but who was universally admitted to be splendidly efficient. It would have been a much more congenial business to the blind man to clear him than to implicate. He betook himself to a tray of Sicilian coins of the autonomous period to get the taste out of his mouth and swore that he would not read a word of any stage of the proceedings.

"A Mr. Severe wishes to see you, sir."

So it happened that about an hour after he had definitely shelved his interest in the case, Max Carrados was again drawn into its complications. Had Severe been merely a well-to-do suppliant, perhaps . . . but the blind man had enough of the vagabond spirit to ensure his sympathy towards one whom he knew, on the contrary, to be extremely ill-to-do. In a flash of imagination he saw the outcast walking from Red Lion Street to Richmond, and, denied admission, from Richmond back to Red Lion Street again, because he hadn't sixpence to squander – the man who always bought a little toy."

"It is nearly seven, isn't it, Parkinson? Mr. Severe will stay and dine with me," were almost the first words the visitor heard.

"Very well, sir."

"I? Dine?" interposed Severe quickly. "No, no. I really – "

"If you will be so good as to keep me company," said Carrados with suave determination. Parkinson retired, knowing that the thing was settled. "I am quite alone, Mr. Severe, and my selfishness takes that form. If a man calls on me about breakfast-time he must stay to breakfast, at lunch-time to lunch, and so on."

"Your friends, doubtless," suggested Severe with latent bitterness. "Well, I am inclined to describe anyone who will lighten my darkness for an hour as a friend. You would yourself in the circumstances, you know." And then, quite unconsciously, under this treatment the years of degradation slipped from Severe and he found himself accepting the invitation in the conventional phrases and talking to his host just as though they were two men of the same world in the old times. Guessing what had brought him, and knowing that it mattered little or nothing then, Carrados kept his guest clear of the subject of the disappearance until they were alone again after dinner. Then, to be denied no longer, Severe tackled it with a blunt inquiry.

"Scotland Yard has been consulting you about Marie, Mr. Carrados?"

232

"Surely that is not in the papers?"

"I don't know," replied Severe, "but they aren't my authority. Among the people I have mostly to do with, many shrewd bits of information circulate that never get into The Press. Sometimes they are mere headwork, of course, but quite often they have ground. Just at present I am something of a celebrity in my usual haunts – I am 'Jones' in town, by the way, but my identity has come out – and everything to do with the notorious Severe affair comes round to me. I hear that Inspector Beedel, who has the case in hand, has just been to see you. Your co-operation is inferred."

"And if so?" queried Carrados.

"If so," continued his visitor, "I have a word to say. Beedel got it into his thick, unimaginative skull that I must be the kidnapper because, on the orthodox 'motive' lines, he couldn't fix on anyone else. As a matter of fact, Mr. Carrados, I have rather too much affection for my little daughter to have taken her out of a comfortable home. My unfortunate wife may have her faults – I don't mind admitting that she has – serious faults and a great many of them – but she would at least give Marie decent surroundings. When I heard of the child's disappearance – it was in the early evening papers the next morning – I was distracted. I dreaded every edition to see a placard announcing that the body had been found and to read the usual horrible details of insane or bestial outrage. I searched my pockets and found a shilling and a few coppers. Without any clear idea of what I expected to do, I tore off to the station and spent my money on a third single to Swanstead."

"Oh," interposed Carrados, "the 1:17 arrival?"

Severe laughed contemptuously.

"The station porter, you mean?" he said. "Yes. That bright youth merely predated his experience by twenty-four hours when he saw that there was bunce in it a few days later. Oh, I dare say he really thought it then. As for me, before I had got to Swanstead I had realised my mistake. What could I do in any case? Nothing that the least efficient local bobby could not do much better. Least of all did I wish to meet Ida – Mrs. Severe. No I walked out of the station, turned to the right instead of the left and padded back to town."

"And you have come now, a fortnight or more later, to tell me this, Mr. Severe?"

"Well, I have come to have small hopes of Beedel. At first I didn't care two straws what they thought, expecting every hour to hear the worst. But that may not have happened. Two weeks have passed without anything being found, so that the child may be alive somewhere. If you are taking it up there is a chance – provided only that you don't let them obsess you with the idea that I have had anything to do with it."

"I don't imagine that you have had anything to do with it, Mr. Severe, and I believe that Marie is still alive."

"Thank God for that," said Severe with sudden intensity. "I am very, very glad to hear you express that opinion, Mr. Carrados. I don't suppose that I shall see much of the girl as time goes on, or that she will be taught to regard the Fifth Commandment very seriously. All the same, the relief of hearing that makes me your debtor forever . . . Anxious as I am, I will be content with that. I won't worry you for your clues or your ideas . . . but I will tell you one thing. It may amuse you. My notion, a few days ago, of what might have happened – "

"Yes?" encouraged his host.

"It shows you the wild ideas one gets in such circumstances. My former wife is, if I may be permitted to say so, the most amiable and devoted creature in the world. Subject to that, I will readily concede that a more self-opinionated, credulous, dogmatically wrong-headed and crank-ridden woman does not exist. There isn't a silly fad that she hasn't taken up – and what's more tragic, absolutely believed in for the time – from ozonised milk to rhythmic yawning. Some time ago she was swept into Christian Science. An atrocious harpy called Julp – a professional 'healer' – fastened on her and has dominated her ever since. Well, fantastic as it seems now, I was actually prepared to believe that Marie had been ill and under their really sincere but grotesque 'healing' had died. Then to hide the failure of their creed or because they got panic-stricken – "

Then Carrados interrupted, an incivility he rarely committed.

"Yes, yes, I see," he said quickly. "But your daughter never is ill?"

"Never ill? Marie? Oh, isn't she! In the past six months I've – "

"But Mrs. Severe deliberately said – her words – that Marie 'does not know what illness means'."

"That's their jargon. They hold that illness does not exist and so it has no meaning. But I should describe Marie as a delicate child on the whole – bilious attacks and so on."

"Christian Scientists . . . gastric trouble . . . Prescott Ellerslie? Good Heavens! This comes of half-doing a thing," muttered Carrados.

"Nothing wrong, I hope?" ventured the visitor.

"Wait." Severe wondered what the deuce turn the business was taking, but there being no incentive to do anything else, he waited. Coffee, rather more fragrant that that purveyed at the nocturnal stall, and fat Egyptian cigarettes of a subtle aroma somehow failed nevertheless to make the time pass quickly. Yet five minutes would have covered Carrados's absence.

"Nothing wrong, but an unfortunate oversight," he remarked when he returned. "I was too late to catch Beedel, so we must try to mend matters at the other end if we can. I shall have to ask you to go with me. I have ordered the car and I can tell you how we stand on the way."

"I shall be glad if you can make any use of me," said Severe.

"I hope that I may. And as for anything being wrong," added Carrados with deliberation, "so far as Marie is concerned, I think we may find that the one thing necessary for her future welfare has been achieved."

"That's all I ask," said Severe.

"But it isn't all that I ask," retorted the blind man almost sharply. This time there was nothing clandestine about the visit to Arling Avenue. On the contrary, the pace they kept up made it necessary that the horn should give pretty continuous notice of their presence.

If it was a race, however, they had the satisfaction of being successful.

The manner – more suggestive of the trained nurse than the domestic servant – of the maid who came to the door of Arling Lodge made it clear to Carrados, apart from any other indication, that the catastrophe of Beedel's arrival had not yet been launched. When the young person at the door began conscientiously, but with obvious inexperience, to prevaricate with the truth, the caller merely accepted her statements and wrote a few words on his card.

"When Dr. Ellerslie does return, will you please give him this at once?" he said. "I will wait."

It is to be inferred that the great specialist's return had been providentially timed, for Carrados was scarcely seated when Prescott Ellerslie hurried into the room with the visiting card in his hand.

"Mr. Carrados?" he postulated. "Will you please explain this rather unusually worded request for an interview?

"Certainly I will," replied Carrados. "The wording is prompted by the necessity of compelling your immediate attention. The interview is the outcome of my desire to be of use to you."

"Thank you," said Ellerslie with non-committal courtesy. "And the occasion?"

"The occasion is the impending visit of Inspector Beedel from Scotland Yard – not, this time, to look out of your landing window, but to demand the surrender of the missing Marie Severe and, if you deny any knowledge of her, armed with authority to search your house."

"Oh," replied the doctor with astonishing composure. "And if the situation develops on the lines which you have so pointedly indicated, how do you propose to help me?"

"That depends a little on your explanation of the circumstances."

"Surely between Mr. Carrados and Scotland Yard there is nothing that remains to be explained!"

"Mr. Carrados can only speak for himself," replied the blind man with unmoved good humour. "And in his case, there are several things to be explained. There is probably not a great deal of time before the inspector's arrival, but there may be enough if you are disposed – "

"Very well," acquiesced Ellerslie. "You are quite right in assuming Marie Severe to be in this house. I had her brought here . . . out of revenge, to redress an old and very grievous injury. Perhaps you had guessed that?"

"Not in those terms," said Carrados mildly.

"Yet so it was. Ten years ago a very sweet and precious little child, my only daughter, was wantonly done to death by an ignorant and credulous woman who had charge of her, in the tenets of her faith. It is called Christian Science. The opportunity was put before me and today I stand convicted of having outraged every social and legal form by snatching Marie Severe from just that same fate."

Carrados nodded gravely.

"Yes," he assented. "That is the thing I missed."

"I used to see her on her way to school, whenever I was here," went on the doctor wistfully, "and soon I came to watch for her and to know the times at which she ought to pass. She was of all living creatures the gayest and the most vivid, glowing and vibrant with the compelling joy of life, a little being of wonderful grace, delicacy, and charm. She has, I found when I came to know her somewhat, that distinction of manner which one is prone to associate unreasonably only with the children of the great and wealthy – a young nobility. In much the reminded me constantly of my own lost child. In other ways she attracted me by her diversity. Such, Mr. Carrados, was the nature of my interest in Marie Severe.

"I don't know the Severes and I have never even spoken to the mother. I believe that she has only lived here about a year, and in any case I have no concern in the social life of Swanstead. But a few months ago my worthy old housekeeper struck up an acquaintance with one of Mrs. Severe's servants, a staid, middle-aged person who had gone into the family as Marie's nurse. The friendship begun down our respective gardens – they adjoin – developed to the stage of these two dames taking tea occasionally with one another. My Mrs. Glass is a garrulous old woman. Hitherto my difficulty had often been to keep her quiet. Now I let her talk and deftly steered the conversation. I learned that my neighbours were Christian Scientists and had a so-called 'healer' living with them. The information struck me with a sudden dread."

'I suppose they are never ill, then?' I inquired carelessly.

"Mrs. Severe had not been ill since she had embraced Christian Science, and Miss Julp was described in a phrase obviously of her own importing as being 'all selvage'. The servants were allowed to see a doctor if they wished, although they were strongly pressed to have done with such 'trickery' in dispelling a mere 'illusion'."

"And isn't there a child?' I asked.

"Marie, it appeared, had from time to time suffered from the 'illusion' that she had not felt well – had suffered pain. Under Miss Julp's spiritual treatment the 'hallucination' had been dispelled. Mrs. Glass had laughed, looked very knowing, and then given her friend away in her appreciation of the joke. The faithful nurse had accepted the situation and, as soon as her mistress's back was turned, had doctored Marie according to her own simple notions. Under this double influence the child had always picked up again, but the two women had ominously speculated what would happen if she fell 'really ill'. I led her on to details of the sicknesses – their symptoms, frequency, and so on. It was a congenial topic between the motherly old creature and the nurse and I could not have had a better medium. I learned a good deal from her chatter. It did not reassure me.

"From that time, without allowing my interest to appear, I sought better opportunities to see the child. I inspired Mrs. Glass to suggest to the nurse that Miss Marie might come and explore the garden here – it is a large and tangled place, such as an adventuring child would love to roam in, and this one, as I found, was passionately fond of flowers and growing things and birds and little animals. I got a pair of tame squirrels and turned them loose here. You can guess her enchantment when she discovered them. I went out with nuts for her to give them and we were friends at once. All the time I was examining her without her knowledge. I don't suppose it ever occurred to her that I might be a doctor. The result practically confirmed the growing suspicion that everything I had heard pointed to. And the tragic irony of the situation was that it had been appendicitis that my child – my child – had perished from!"

"Oh, so this was appendicitis, then?"

"Yes. It was appendicitis of that insidious and misleading type to which children are particularly liable. These apparently negligible turns at intervals of weeks were really inflammation of the appendix, and the condition was inevitably passing into one of general suppurative peritonitis. Very soon there would come another 'illusion' according to the mother and Miss Julp, another 'bilious turn' according to the nurse, similar to those already experienced, but apparently more obstinate. The Christian Scientists would argue with it, Hannah would surreptitiously dose it. This time, however, it would hang on. Still there would be no really very alarming symptoms to wring the natural affection of the mother, nothing

237

severe enough to have the nurse into mutiny. The pulse running at about 140 would be the last thing they would notice."

"And then?" Ellerslie was pacing the room in savage indignation, but Carrados had Beedel's impending visit continually before him.

"Then she would be dead. Quite suddenly and unceremoniously this fair young life, which in ten minutes I could render immune from this danger for all the future, would go clean out – extinguished to demonstrate that appendicitis does not exist and that Mind is All in All. If my diagnosis was correct, there could be no appeal, no shockful realisation of the true position to give the mother a chance. It would be inevitable, but it would be quite unlooked for.

"What was I to do, should you say, Mr. Carrados, in this emergency? I had dealt with these fanatics before, and I knew that if I took so unusual a course as to go to Mrs. Severe, I should at the best be met by polite incredulity and a text from Mrs. Mary Baker Eddy's immortal work. And by doing that, I should have made any other line of action risky, if not impossible. You, I believe, are a humane man. What was I to do?"

"What you did do," said his visitor, "was about the most dangerous thing that a doctor could be mixed up in.

"Oh, no," replied Ellerslie. "He does a much more dangerous thing whenever he operates on a septiferous subject, whenever he enters a fever-stricken house. To career and reputation, you would say. But believe me, Mr. Carrados, life is quite as important as livelihood, and every doctor does that sort of thing every day. Well, like many very ordinary men whom you may meet, I am something of a maniac and something of a mystic. Incredible as it will doubtless seem to the world tomorrow, I found that, at the risk of my professional career, at the risk, possibly, of a criminal conviction, the greatest thing that I should ever do would be to save this one exquisite young life. Elsewhere other men just as good could take my place, but here it was I and I alone."

"Well, you did it?" prompted Carrados. "I must remind you that the time presses and I want to know the facts.

"Yes I did it. I won't delay with the precautions I had taken in securing the child or with the scheme that I had worked out for returning her. I believed that I had a very good chance of coming through undiscovered and I infer that I have to thank you that I did not. Marie has not the slightest idea where she is and when I go into the room I am sufficiently disguised. She thinks that she has had an accident."

"Of course you must have had assistance?"

"I have had the devoted help of an assistant and two nurses, but the whole responsibility is mine. I managed to send off Mrs. Glass and her husband for a holiday so as to keep them out of it. That was after I had decided upon the operation. To justify what I was about to do, there had to be no mistake about the necessity. I contrived a final test.

"Less than three weeks ago I saw Hannah and the little girl come to the house one afternoon. Shortly afterwards, Mrs. Glass knocked at my door. Could she ask Hannah to tea and, as Mrs. Severe and her friend were being out until late, might Miss Marie also stay? There was, as she knew, no need for her to ask me, but my housekeeper is primitive in her ideas of duty. Of course I readily assented, but I suggested that Marie should have tea with me, and so it was arranged.

"Before tea, she amused herself about the garden. I told her to gather me a bunch of flowers and when she came in with them, I noticed that she had scratched her arm with a thorn. I hurried through the meal, for I had then determined what to do. When we had finished, without ringing the bell, I gave her a chair in front of the fire and sat down opposite her. There was a true story about a clever goose that I had promised her.

"'But you are going to sleep, Marie,' I said, looking at her fixedly. 'It is the heat of the fire.'

"'I think I must be,' she admitted drowsily. 'Oh, how silly. I can scarcely keep my eyes open.'

"'You are going to sleep,' I repeated. 'You are very, very tired.' I raised my hand and moved it slowly before her face. 'You can hardly see my hand now. Your eyes are closed. When I stop speaking you will be asleep.' I dropped my hand and she was fast asleep.

"I had made my arrangements and had everything ready. From her arm, where the puncture of the needle was masked by the scratch, I secured a few drops of blood. Then I applied a simple styptic to the place and verified by a more leisurely examination some of the symptoms I had already looked for. When I woke her, a few minutes later, she had no inkling of what had passed.

"'Why,' I was saying as she awakened, 'I don't believe that you have heard a word about old Solomon!'

"I applied the various laboratory tests to the blood which I had obtained without delay. The result, taken in conjunction with the other symptoms, was conclusive. I was resolved upon my course from that moment. The operation itself was simple and completely successful. The condition demonstrated the pressing necessity for what I did. Marie Severe will probably outlive her mother now – especially if the lady remains faithful to Christian Science. As for the sequel . . . I am sorry, but I don't regret."

* * * * *

239

"A surprise, eh, Inspector?"

Inspector Beedel, accompanied by Mrs. Severe and – if the comparative degree may be used to indicate her relative importance – even more accompanied by Miss Julp, had arrived at Arling Lodge and been given immediate admission. It was Carrados who thus greeted him.

Beedel looked at his friend and then at Dr. Ellerslie. With unconscious habit, he even noticed the proportions of the room, the position of the door and window, and the chief articles of furniture. His mind moved rather slowly, but always logically, and in cases where "sound intelligence" sufficed, he was rarely unsuccessful. He had brought Mrs. Severe to identify Marie, whom he had never seen, and his men remained outside within whistle-call in case of any emergency. He now saw that he might have to shift his ground and he at once proceeded cautiously.

"Well, sir," he admitted, "I did not expect to see you here."

"Nor did I anticipate coming. Mrs. Severe – " He bowed to her. "I think that we have already met informally. Your friend, Miss Julp, unless I am mistaken? It is a good thing that we are all here."

"That is my name, sir," struck in the recalcitrant Cornelia, "but I am not aware – "

"At the gate early – very early – this morning, Miss Julp. I recognise your step. But accept my assurance, my dear lady – " For Miss Julp had given a start of maidenly confusion at the recollection. " – that although I heard, I did not see you. Well, Inspector, I have since found that I misled you. The mistake was mine – a fundamental error. You were right. Mrs. Severe was right. Dr. Ellerslie is unassailably right. I speak for him because it was I who fastened an unsupportable motive on his actions. Marie Severe is in this house, but she was received here by Dr. Ellerslie in his professional capacity and strictly in the relation of doctor and patient . . . Mr. Severe has at length admitted that he alone is to blame. You see, you were right after all."

"Arthur! Oh!" exclaimed Mrs. Severe, deeply moved.

"But why," demanded the other lady hostilely, "why should the man want her here?"

"Mr. Severe was apprehensive on account of his daughter's health," replied Carrados gravely. "His story is that, fearing something serious, he submitted her to this eminent specialist, who found a dangerous – a critical – condition that could only be removed by immediate operation. Dr. Ellerslie has saved your daughter's life, Mrs. Severe."

"Fiddlesticks!" shouted Miss Julp excitedly. "It's an outrage – a criminal outrage. An operation! There was no danger – there couldn't be with me at hand. You've done it this time, Doctor Ellerslie. My gosh, but this will be a case!"

Mrs. Severe sank into a chair, pale and trembling.

"I can scarcely believe it," she managed to say. "It is a crime. Dr. Ellerslie – no doctor had the right. Mr. Severe has no authority whatever. The court gave me sole control of Marie."

"Excuse me," put in Carrados with the blandness of perfect self-control and cognisance of his point. "Excuse me, but have you ever informed Dr. Ellerslie of that ruling?"

"No," admitted Mrs. Severe with faint surprise. "No. Why should I?"

"Quite so. Why should you? But have you any knoedge that Dr. Ellerslie is acquainted with the details of your unhappy domestic differences?"

"I do not know at all. What do these things matter?"

"Only this: Why should Dr. Ellerslie question the authority of a parent who brings his child? It shows at least that he is the one who is concerned about her welfare. For all Dr. Ellerslie knew, you might be the unauthorised one, Mrs. Severe. A doctor can scarcely be expected to withhold a critical operation while he investigates the family affairs of his patients."

"But all this time – this dreadful suspense. He must have known." Carrados shrugged his shoulders and seemed to glance across the room to where their host had so far stood immovable.

"I did know, Mrs. Severe. I could not help knowing. But I knew something else, and to a doctor the interests of his patient must overrule every ordinary consideration. Should the occasion arise, I shall be prepared at any time to justify my silence."

"Oh, the occasion will arise and pretty sharp, don't you fear," chimed in the irrepressible Miss Julp. "There's a sight more in this business, Ida, than we've got at yet. A mighty cute idea putting up Severe now. I never did believe that he was in it. He's a piece too mean-spirited to have the nerve. And where is Arthur Severe now? Gone, of course. Quit the country and at someone else's expense."

"Not at all," said Carrados very obligingly. "Since you ask, Miss Julp – " He raised his voice. "Mr. Severe!"

The door opened and Severe strolled into the room with great sangfroid. He bowed distantly to his wife and nodded familiarly to the police official.

"Well, Inspector," he remarked, "you've cornered me at last, you see."

"I'm not so sure of that," retorted Beedel shortly.

241

"Oh, come now. You are too modest. My unconvincing alibi that you broke down. The printed letter so conclusively from my hand. And Grigson – your irrefutable, steadfast witness from the station here, Inspector. There's no getting round Grigson now, you know."

Beedel rubbed his chin helpfully but made no answer. Things seemed to have reached a momentary impasse.

"Perhaps we may at least all sit down," suggested Ellerslie, to break the silence. "There are rather a lot of us, but I think the chairs will go round."

"If I wasn't just dead tired, I would sooner drop than sit down in the house of a man calling himself a doctor," declared Miss Julp. Then she sat down rather heavily. Sharp on the action came a piercing yell, a deep – wrung "*Yag!*" of pain and alarm, and the lady was seen bounding to her feet, to turn and look suspiciously at the place she had just vacated.

"It was a needle, Cornelia," said Mrs. Severe, who sat next to her. "See, here it is."

"Dear me, how unfortunate," exclaimed Ellerslie, following the action. "One of my surgical needles. I do hope that it has been properly sterilised since the last operation."

"What's that?" demanded Miss Julp sharply.

"Well," explained the doctor slowly, "I mean that there is such a thing as blood-poisoning. At least," he amended, "for *me* there is such a thing as blood-poisoning. For you, fortunately, it does not exist. Any more than pain does," he added thoughtfully.

"Do you mean," demanded Miss Julp with slow precision, "that through your carelessness, your criminal carelessness, I run any risk of blood-poisoning?"

"Cornelia!" exclaimed Mrs. Severe in pale incredulity.

"Of course not," retorted the surgeon. "How can you, if such a thing does not exist?"

"I don't care whether it exists or not – "

"Cornelia !" repeated her faithful disciple in horror.

"Be quiet, Ida. This is my business. It isn't like an ordinary illness. I've always had a horror of blood-poisoning. I have nightmares about it. My father died of it. He had to have glass tubes put in his veins, and that night he died. Oh, I tell you I can't stand the thought of it. There's nothing else I believe in, but blood-poisoning – "

She shuddered. "I tell you, Doctor," she declared with a sudden descent to the practical, "if I get laid up from this, you'll have to stand the racket, and pretty considerable damages as well."

"But at the worst this is a very simple matter," protested Ellerslie. "If you will let me dress the place – "

Miss Julp went as red as a swarthy-complexioned lady of forty-five could be expected to go.

"How can I let you dress the place?" she snapped. "It is – "

"Oh, Cornelia, Cornelia!" exclaimed Mrs. Severe reproachfully, through her disillusioned tears, "would you really be so false to the great principles which you have taught me?"

"I have a trained nurse here," suggested the doctor. "She would do it as well as I could."

"Are you really going?" demanded Mrs. Severe, for there was no doubt that Miss Julp was going and going with alacrity.

"I don't abate one iota of my principles, Ida," she remarked. "But one has to discriminate. There are natural illnesses and there are unnatural illnesses. We say with truth that there can be no death, but no one will deny that Christian Scientists do, as a matter of fact, in the ordinary sense, die. Perhaps this is rather beyond you yet, dear, but I hope that some day you will see it in the light of its deeper mystery."

"Do you?" replied Mrs. Severe with cold disdain. "At present, I only see that there is one law of indulgence for yourself and another for your dupes."

"After all," interposed Ellerslie, "this embarrassing discussion need never have arisen. I now see that the offending implement is only one of Mrs. Glass's darning needles. How careless of her! You need have no fear, Miss Julp."

"Oh, you coward!" exclaimed Miss Julp breathlessly. "You coward! I won't stay here a moment longer. I will go home."

"I won't detain you," said Mrs. Severe as Cornelia passed her. "Your home is in Chicago, I believe? Ann will help you to pack."

Carrados rose and touched Beedel on the arm.

"You and I are not wanted here, Inspector," he whispered. "The bottom's dropped out of the case," and they slipped away together.

Mrs. Severe looked across the room towards her late husband, hesitated and then slowly walked up to him.

"There is a great deal here that I do not understand," she said, "but is not this so, that you were willing to go to prison to shield this man who has been good to Marie?"

Severe flushed a little. Then he dropped his deliberate reply.

"I am willing to go to Hell for this man for his goodness to Marie," he said curtly.

"Oh!" exclaimed Mrs. Severe with a little cry. "I wish you never said that you would go to Hell for me!"

The outcast stared. Then a curious look, a twisted smile of tenderness and half-mocking humour crossed his features.

"My dear," he responded gravely, "perhaps not. But I often thought it!"

Dr. Ellerslie, who had followed out the last two of his departing guests, looked in at the door.

"Marie is awake, I hear," he said. "Will you go up now, Mrs. Severe?"

With a shy smile the lady held out her hand towards the shabby man.

"You must go with me, Arthur," she stipulated.

The Secret of
Dunstan's Tower

It was a peculiarity of Mr. Carrados that he could drop the most absorbing occupation of his daily life at a moment's notice if need be, apply himself exclusively to the solution of some criminological problem, possibly a matter of several days, and at the end of the time return and take up the thread of his private business exactly where he had left it.

On the morning of the 3rd of September he was dictating to his secretary a monograph to which he had given the attractive title, "*The Portrait of Alexander the Great, as Jupiter Ammon, on an Unedited Octadrachm of Macedonia*" when a telegram was brought in. Greatorex, the secretary, dealt with such communications as a matter of course, and, taking the envelope from Parkinson's salver, he cut it open in the pause between a couple of sentences

"This is a private matter of yours, sir," he remarked, after glancing at the message. "Handed in at Netherhempsfield, 10:48 a.m. '*Repeated. One step higher. Quite baffled. Tulloch.*'"

"Oh yes. That's all right," said Carrados. "No reply, Parkinson. Have you got down '*the Roman supremacy*'?

"'. . . *the type of workmanship that still enshrined the memory of Spartan influence down to the era of Roman supremacy,*'" read the secretary.

"That will do. How are the trains for Netherhempsfield?"

Greatorex put down the notebook and took up an *ABC*.

"Waterloo departure eleven – " He cocked an eye towards the desk clock. "Oh, that's no good. 12:17, 2:11, 5:09, 7:25."

"The 5:09 should do," interposed Carrados. "Arrival?"

"6:48."

"Now what has *The Gazeteer* to say about the place?"

The yellow railway guide gave place to a weightier volume, and the secretary read out the following details:

> *Netherhempsfield, parish and village, popuplation 732, South Downshire. 2,728 acres land and twenty-seven water. Soil rich loam, occupied as arable, pasture, orchard and woodland. Subsoil various. The church of St. Dunstan (restored 1740) is Saxon and Early English. It possesses an oak roof with curious grotesque bosses, and contains brasses*

and other memorials (earliest thirteenth century) of the Aynosforde family. In the "Swinefield", one-and-a-half miles south-west of the village, are fifteen large stones, known locally as "The Judge and Jury", which constitute the remains of a Druidical circle and temple. Dunstan's Tower, a moated residence built in the baronial style, and probably dating from the fourteenth century, is the seat of the Aynosfordes.

"I can give three days easily," mused Carrados. "Yes, I'll go down by the 5:09."

"Do I accompany you, sir?" inquired Greatorex.

"Not this time, I think. Have three days off yourself. Just pick up the correspondence and take things easy. Send on anything to me, care of Dr. Tulloch. If I don't write, expect me back on Friday."

"Very well, Mr. Carrados. What books shall I put out for Parkinson to pack?"

"Say . . . Gessner's *Thesaurus* and – yes, you may as well add Hilarion's *Celtic Mythology*."

Six hours later, Carrados was on his way to Netherhempsfield. In his pocket was the following letter, which may be taken as offering the only explanation why he should suddenly decide to visit a place of which he had never even heard until that morning:

Dear Mr. Carrados ("Old Wynn", it used to be),

Do you remember a fellow at St. Michael's who used to own insects and the name of Tulloch – "Earwigs", they called him? Well, you will find it at the end of this epistle, if you have the patience to get there. I ran across Jarvis about six months ago on Euston platform – you'll recall him by his red hair and great feet – and we had a rapid and comprehensive pow-wow. He told me who you were, having heard of you from Lessing, who seems to be editing a high-class review. He always was a trifle eccentric, Lessing.

As for yours t., well, at the moment I'm local demon in a G-f-s little place that you'd hardly find on anything less than a four-inch ordnance. But I won't altogether say it mightn't be worse, for there's trout in the stream, and after half-a-decade of Cinder Moor, in the Black Country, a great and holy peace broods on the smiling land.

But you will guess that I wouldn't be taking up the time of a busy man of importance unless I had something to say, and you'd be right. It may interest you, or it may not, but here it is.

Living about two miles out of the village, at a sort of mediaeval stronghold known as Dunstan's Tower, there is an ancient county family called Aynosforde. And, for the matter of that, they are about all there is here, for the whole place seems to belong to them, and their authority runs from the power to charge you two-pence if you sell a pig between Friday night and Monday morning to the right to demand an exchange of scabbards with the reigning sovereign whenever he comes within seven bowshot flights of the highest battlement of Dunstan's Tower. (I don't gather that any reigning sovereign ever has come, but that isn't the Aynosfordes' fault.) But, levity apart, these Aynosfordes, without being particularly rich, or having any title, are accorded an extraordinary position. I am told that scarcely a living duchess could hold out against the moral influence old dame Aynosforde could bring to bear on social matters, and yet she scarcely ever goes beyond Netherhempsfield now.

My connection with these high-and-mighties ought to be purely professional, and so, in a manner, it is, but on the top of it I find myself drawn into a full-blooded, old haunted house mystery that takes me clean out of my depth.

Darrish, the man whose place I'm taking for three months, had a sort of arrangement that once a week he should go up to the Tower and amuse old Mrs. Aynosforde for a couple of hours under the pretence of feeling her pulse. I found that I was let in for continuing this. Fortunately the old dame was quite amiable at close quarters. I have no social qualifications whatever, and we got on very well together on those terms. I have heard that she considers me "thoroughly responsible".

For five or six weeks everything went on swimmingly. I had just enough to do to keep me from doing nothing. People have a delightful habit of not being taken ill in the night, and there is a comfortable cob to trot round on.

Tuesday is my Dunstan's Tower day. Last Tuesday I went as usual. I recall now that the servants about the place seemed rather wild and the old lady did not keep me quite as long as usual, but these things were not sufficiently noticeable to make any impression on me at the time. On Friday a groom rode over with a note from Swarbrick, the butler. Would I go up

247

that afternoon and see Mrs. Aynosforde? He had taken the liberty of asking me on his own responsibility, as he thought that she ought to be seen. Deuced queer it struck me, but of course I went

Swarbrick was evidently on the look-out. He is a regular family retainer, taciturn and morose rather than bland. I saw at once that the old fellow had something on his mind, and I told him that I should like a word with him. We went into the morning room.

"Now, Swarbrick," I said, "you sent for me. What is the matter with your mistress since Tuesday?"

He looked at me dourly, as though he was still in two minds about opening his mouth. Then he said slowly

"It isn't since Tuesday, sir. It was on that morning."

"What was?" I asked

"The beginning of it, Dr. Tulloch. Mrs. Aynosforde slipped at the foot of the stairs on coming down to breakfast."

"She did?" I said. "Well, it couldn't have been very serious at the time. She never mentioned it to me."

"No, sir," the old monument assented, with an appalling surface of sublime pride, "she would not."

"Why wouldn't she if she was hurt?" I demanded. "People do mention these things to their medical men, in strict confidence."

"The circumstances are unusual, sir," he replied, without a ruffle of his imperturbable respect. "Mrs. Aynosforde was not hurt, sir. She did not actually fall, but she slipped – on a pool of blood."

"That's unpleasant," I admitted, looking at him sharply, for an owl could have seen that there was something behind all this. "How did it come there? Whose was it?"

"Sir Philip Bellmont's, sir."

I did not know the name. "Is he a visitor here?" I asked.

"Not at present, sir. He stayed with us in 1662. He died here, sir, under rather unpleasant circumstances."

There you have it, Wynn. That is the keystone of the whole business. But if I keep to my conversation with the still reluctant Swarbrick, I shall run out of foolscap and into midnight. Briefly, then, the "unpleasant circumstances" were as follows: Just about two-and-a-half centuries ago, when Charles II was back, and things in England were rather gay, a certain Sir Philip Bellmont was a guest at Dunstan's Tower.

248

There were dice, and there was a lady – probably a dozen, but the particular one was the Aynosforde's young wife. One night there was a flare-up. Bellmont was run through with a rapier, and an ugly doubt turned on whether the point came out under the shoulder-blade, or went in there. Dripping onto every stair, the unfortunate man was carried up to his room. He died within a few hours, convinced, from the circumstances, of treachery all round, and with his last breath he left an anathema on every male and female Aynosforde as the day of their death approached. There are fourteen steps in the flight that Bellmont was carried up, and when the pool appears in the hall, some Aynosforde has just two weeks to live. Each succeeding morning the stain may be found one stair higher. When it reaches the top there is a death in the family. This was the gist of the story. As far as you and I are concerned, it is, of course, merely a matter as to what form our scepticism takes, but my attitude is complicated by the fact that my nominal patient has become a real one. She is seventy-two and built to be a nonagenarian, but she has gone to bed with the intention of dying on Tuesday week. And I firmly believe she will

"How does she know that she is the one?" I asked. There aren't many Aynosfordes, but I knew that there were some others.

To this Swarbrick maintained a discreet ambiguity. It was not for him to say, he replied, but I can see that he, like most of the natives round here, is obsessed with Aynosfordism.

"And for that matter," I objected, "your mistress is scarcely entitled to the distinction. She will not really be an Aynosforde at all – only one by marriage."

"No, sir," he replied readily, "Mrs. Aynosforde was also a Miss Aynosforde, sir – one of the Dorset Aynosfordes. Mr. Aynosforde married his cousin."

"Oh," I said, "do the Aynosfordes often marry cousins?"

"Very frequently, sir. You see, it is difficult otherwise for them to find eligible partners."

Well, I saw the lady, explaining that I had not been altogether satisfied with her condition on the Tuesday. It passed, but I was not able to allude to the real business. Swarbrick, in his respectful, cast-iron way, had impressed on me that Sir Philip Bellmont must not be mentioned, assuring me that even Darrish would not venture to do so. Mrs.

Aynosforde was certainly a little feverish, but there was nothing the matter with her. I left, arranging to call again on the Sunday.

When I came to think it over, the first form it took was: Now who is playing a silly practical joke, or working a deliberate piece of mischief? But I could not get any further on those lines, because I do not know enough of the circumstances. Darrish might know, but Darrish is cruising off Spitsbergen, suffering from a nervous breakdown. The people here are amiable enough superficially, but they plainly regard me as an outsider.

It was then that I thought of you. From what Jarvis had told me, I gathered that you were keen on a mystery for its own sake. Furthermore, though I understand that you are now something of a dook, you might not be averse to a quiet week in the country, jogging along the lanes, smoking a peaceful pipe of an evening, and yarning over old times. But I was not going to lure you down and then have the thing turn out to be a ridiculous and transparent hoax, no matter how serious its consequences. I owed it to you to make some reasonable investigation myself. This I have now done.

On Sunday when I went there, Swarbrick, with a very long face, reported that on each morning he had found the stain one step higher. The patient, needless to say, was appreciably worse. When I came down I had made up my mind.

"Look here, Swarbrick," I said, "there is only one thing for it: I must sit up here tonight and see what happens."

He was very dubious at first, but I believe the fellow is genuine in his attachment to the house. His final scruple melted when he learned that I should not require him to sit up with me. I enjoined absolute secrecy, and this, in a large rambling place like the Tower, is not difficult to maintain. All the maidservants had fled. The only people sleeping within the walls now, beyond those I have mentioned, are two of Mrs. Aynosforde's grandchildren (a girl and a young man whom I merely know by sight), the housekeeper, and a footman. All these had retired long before the butler admitted me by an obscure little door, about half-an-hour after midnight.

The staircase with which we are concerned goes up from the dining hall. A much finer, more-modern way ascends from the entrance hall. This earlier one, however, only gives access now to three rooms, a lovely oak-panelled chamber occupied by my patient and two small rooms, turned nowadays into a boudoir and a bathroom. When Swarbrick had left me in an easy-chair, wrapped in a couple of rugs, in a corner of the dark dining hall, I waited for half-an-hour and then proceeded to make my own preparations. Moving very quietly, I crept up the stairs, and at the top drove one drawing-pin into the lintel about a foot up, another at the same height into the baluster opposite, and across the stairs fastened a black thread, with a small bell hanging over the edge. A touch and the bell would ring, whether the thread broke or not. At the foot of the stairs I made another attachment and hung another bell.

"I think, my unknown friend," I said, as I went back to the chair. "You are cut off above and below now."

I won't say that I didn't close my eyes for a minute through the whole night, but if I did sleep it was only as a watchdog sleeps. A whisper or a creak of a board would have found me alert. As it was, however, nothing happened. At six o'clock Swarbrick appeared, respectfully solicitous about my vigil.

"We've done it this time, Swarbrick," I said in modest elation. "Not the ghost of a ghost has appeared. The spell is broken."

He had crossed the hall and was looking rather strangely at the stairs. With a very queer foreboding I joined him and followed his glance. By Heavens, Wynn, there, on the sixth step up, was a bright red patch! I am not squeamish – I cleared four steps at a stride, and stooping down I dipped my finger into the stuff and felt its slippery viscidity against my thumb. There could be no doubt about it – it was the genuine thing. In my baffled amazement I looked in every direction for a possible clue to human agency. Above, more than twenty feet above, were the massive rafters and boarding of the roof itself. By my side reared a solid stone wall, and beneath was simply the room we stood in, for the space below the stairway was not enclosed.

I pointed to my arrangement of bells.

"Nobody has gone up or down, I'll swear," I said a little warmly. Between ourselves, I felt a bit of an ass for my pains, before the monumental Swarbrick.

"No, sir," he agreed. "I had a similar experience myself on Saturday night.

"The deuce you did,"' I exclaimed. "Did you sit up then?"

"Not exactly, sir," he replied, "but after making all secure at night I hung a pair of irreplaceable Dresden china cups in a similar way. They were both still intact in the morning, sir."

Well, there you are. I have nothing more to say on the subject. "Hope not," you'll be muttering. If the thing doesn't tempt you, say no more about it. If it does, just wire a time and I'll be at the station. Welcome isn't the word.

Yours as of yore,
Jim Tulloch

P.S. – Can put your man up all right. J.T.

Carrados had "wired a time", and he was seized on the platform by the awaiting and exuberant Tulloch and guided with elaborate carefulness to the doctor's cart, which was, as its temporary owner explained, "knocking about somewhere in the lane outside."

"Splendid little horse," he declared. "Give him a hedge to nibble at and you can leave him to look after himself for hours. Motors? He laughs at them, Wynn, merely laughs."

Parkinson and the luggage found room behind, and the splendid little horse shook his shaggy head and launched out for home. For a mile the conversation was a string of, "Do you ever come across Brown now?"

"You know Sugden was killed flying?"

"Heard of Marling only last week. He's gone on the stage."

"By the way, that appalling ass Sanders married a girl with a pot of money and runs horses now," and doubtless it would have continued in a similar strain to the end of the journey if an encounter with a farmer's country trap had not interrupted its tenor. The lane was very narrow at that point and the driver of the trap drew into the hedge and stopped to allow the doctor to pass. There was a mutual greeting, and Tulloch pulled up also when their hubs were clear.

"No more sheep killed, I hope?" he called back.

"No, sir. I can't complain that we have," said the driver cheerfully. "But I do hear that Mr. Stone, over at Daneswood, lost one last night."

"In the same way, do you mean?"

"So I heard. It's a queer business, Doctor."

"It's a blackguardly business. It's a marvel what the fellow thinks he's doing."

252

"He'll get nabbed, never fear, sir. He'll do it once too often."

"Hope so," said the doctor. "Good day." He shook the reins and turned to his visitor. "One of our local 'Farmer Jarges'. It's part of the business to pass the time o' day with them all .and ask after the cow or the pig, if no other member of the family happens to be on the sick list."

"What is the blackguardly business?" asked Carrados.

"Well, that is a bit out of the common, I'll admit. About a week ago this man, Bailey, found one of his sheep dead in the field. It had been deliberately killed – head cut half-off. It hadn't been done for meat, because none was taken. But, curiously enough, something else had been taken. The animal had been opened and the heart and intestines were gone. What do you think of that, Wynn?"

"Revenge, possibly."

"Bailey declares that he hasn't got the shadow of an enemy in the world. His three or four labourers are quite content. Of course a thing like that makes a tremendous sensation in a place like this. You may see as many as five men talking together almost any day now. And here, on the top if it, comes another case at Stone's. It looks like one of those outbreaks that crop up from time to time for no obvious reason and then die out again."

"No reason, Jim?"

"Well, if it isn't revenge, and if it isn't food, what is there to be got by it?"

"What is there to be got when an animal is killed?"

Tulloch stared without enlightenment.

"What is there that I am here to trace?"

"Godfrey Dan'l, Wynn! You don't mean to say that there is any connection between?"

"I don't say it," declared Carrados promptly. "But there is very strong reason why we should consider it. It solves a very obvious question that faces us. A pricked thumb does not produce a pool. Did you microscope it?"

"Yes, I did. I can only say that it's mammalian. My limited experience doesn't carry me beyond that. Then what about the entrails, Wynn? Why take those?"

"That raises a variety of interesting speculations certainly."

"It may to you. The only thing that occurs to me is that it might be a blind."

"A very unfortunate one, if so. A blind is intended to allay curiosity – to suggest an obvious but fictitious motive. This, on the contrary, arouses curiosity. The abstraction of a haunch of mutton would be an excellent blind. Whereas now, as you say, what about the entrails?"

253

Tulloch shook his head.

"I've had my shot," he answered. "Can you suggest anything?"

"Frankly, I can't," admitted Carrados.

"On the face of it, I don't suppose anyone short of an oracle could. Pity our local shrine has got rusty in the joints." He levelled his whip and pointed to a distant silhouette that showed against the last few red streaks in the western sky a mile away. "You see that solitary old outpost of paganism – "

The splendid little horse leapt forward in indignant surprise as the extended whip fell sharply across his shoulders. Tulloch's ingenuous face seemed to have caught the rubicundity of the distant sunset.

"I'm beastly sorry, Wynn, old man," he muttered. "I ought to have remembered."

"My blindness?" contributed Carrados. "My dear chap, everyone makes a point of forgetting that. It's quite a recognised form of compliment among friends. If it were baldness I probably should be touchy on the subject. As it's only blindness, I'm not."

"I'm very glad you take it so well," said Tulloch. "I was referring to a stone circle that we have here. Perhaps you have heard of it?"

"The Druids' altar!" exclaimed Carrados with an inspiration. "Jim, to my everlasting shame, I had forgotten it.

"Oh, well, it isn't much to look at," confessed the practical doctor. "Now in the church there are a few decent monuments – all Aynosfordes, of course."

"Aynosfordes – naturally. Do you know how far that remarkable race goes back?"

"A bit beyond Adam, I should fancy," laughed Tulloch. "Well, Darrish told me that they really can trace to somewhere before the Conquest. Some antiquarian Johnny has claimed that the foundations of Dunstan's Tower cover a Celtic stronghold. Are you interested in that sort of thing?"

"Intensely," replied Carrados. "But we must not neglect other things. This gentleman who owned the unfortunate sheep, the second victim, now? How far is Daneswood away?"

"About a mile – mile-and-a-half at the most."

Carrados turned towards the back seat. "Do you think that in seven minutes' time you would be able to distinguish the details of a red mark on the grass, Parkinson?"

Parkinson took the effect of three objects, the sky above, the herbage by the roadside, and the back of his hand, and then spoke regretfully.

"I'm afraid not, sir. Not with any certainty," he replied.

254

"Then we need not trouble Mr. Stone tonight," said Carrados philosophically.

After dinner there was the peaceful pipe that Tulloch had forecast, and mutual reminiscences until the long clock in the corner, striking the smallest hour of the morning, prompted Tulloch to suggest retirement.

"I hope you have everything," he remarked tentatively, when he had escorted the guest to his bedroom. "Mrs. Jones does for me very well, but you are an unknown quantity to her as yet."

"I shall be quite all right, you may be sure," replied Carrados, with his engagingly grateful smile. "Parkinson will already have seen to everything. We have a complete system, and I know exactly where to find anything I require."

Tulloch gave a final glance round.

"Perhaps you would prefer the window closed?" he suggested.

"Indeed I should not. It is south-west, isn't it?"

"Yes."

"And a south-westerly breeze to bring the news. I shall sit here for a little time." He put his hand on the top rail of a chair with unhesitating precision and drew it to the open casement. "There are a thousand sounds that you in your arrogance of sight ignore, a thousand individual scents of hedge and orchard that come to me up here. I suppose it is quite dark to you now, Jim? What a lot you seeing people must miss!"

Tulloch guffawed, with his hand on the door knob. "Well, don't let your passion for nocturnal nature study lead you to miss breakfast at eight. My eyes won't, I promise you. Ta-ta."

He jigged off to his own room and in ten minutes was soundly asleep. But the oak clock in the room beneath marked the quarters one by one until the next hour struck, and then round the face again until the little finger stood at three, and still the blind man sat by the open window that looked out over the south-west, interpreting the multitudinous signs of the quiet life that still went on under the dark cover of the warm summer night.

"The word lies with you, Wynn," remarked Tulloch at breakfast the next morning – he was twelve minutes late, by the way, and found his guest interested in the titles of Dr. Darrish's excellent working library. "I am supposed to be on view here from nine to ten, and after that I am due at Abbot's Farm somewhere about noon. With those reservations, I am at your disposal for the day."

"Do you happen to go anywhere near the 'Swinefield' on your way to Abbot's Farm?" asked Carrados.

"The 'Swinefield'? Oh, the Druids' circle. Yes, one way – and it's as good as any other – passes the wheel-track that leads up to it."

"Then I should certainly like to inspect the site."

"There's really nothing to see, you know," apologised the doctor. "Only a few big rocks on end. They aren't even chiselled smooth."

"I am curious," volunteered Carrados, "to discover why fifteen stones should be called 'The Judge and Jury'."

"Oh, I can explain that for you," declared Tulloch. "Two of them are near together with a third block across the tops. That's the Judge. The twelve jurymen are scattered here and there. But we'll go, by all means."

"There is a public right of way, I suppose?" asked Carrados, when, in due course, the trap turned from the highway into a field track.

"I don't know about a right," said Tulloch, "but I imagine that anyone goes across who wants to. Of course it's not a Stonehenge, and we have very few visitors, or the Aynosfordes might put some restrictions. As for the natives, there isn't a man who wouldn't sooner walk ten miles to see a five-legged calf than cross the road to look at a Phidias. And for that matter," he added thoughtfully, "this is the first time I've been really up to the place myself."

"It's on Aynosforde property, then?"

"Oh yes. Most of the parish is, I believe. But this 'Swinefield' is part of the park. There is an oak plantation across there or Dunstan's Tower would be in sight."

They had reached the gate of the enclosure. The doctor got down to open it, as he had done the former ones.

"This is locked," he said, coming back to the step, "but we can climb over easy enough. You can get down all right?"

"Thanks," replied Carrados. He descended and followed Tulloch, stopping to pat the little horse's neck.

"He'll be all right," remarked the doctor with a backward nod. "I fancy Tommy's impressionable years must have been spent between the shafts of a butcher's cart. Now, Wynn, how do we proceed?"

"I should like to have your arm over this rough ground. Then if you will take me from stone to stone – "

They paced the broken circle leisurely, Carrados judging the appearance of the remains by touch and by the answers to the innumerable questions that he put. They were approaching the most important monument the Judge – when Tulloch gave a shout of delight.

"Oh, the beauty!" he cried with enthusiasm. "I must see you closer. Wynn, do you mind – a minute – "

"Lady, Jim?" murmured Carrados. "Certainly not. I'll stand like Tommy."

Tulloch shot off with a laugh and Carrados heard him racing across the grass in the direction of the trilithon. He was still amused when he returned, after a very short interval.

"No, Wynn, not a lady, but it occurred to me that you might have been farther off. A beautiful airy creature very brightly clad. A Purple Emperor, in fact. I haven't netted a butterfly for years, but the sight gave me all the old excitement of the chase."

"Tolerably rare, too, aren't they?"

"Generally speaking, they are. I remember waiting in an oak grove with a twenty-foot net for a whole day once, and not a solitary Emperor crossed my path."

"An oak grove. Yes, you said there was an oak plantation here."

"I didn't know the trick then. You needn't go to that trouble. His Majesty has rather peculiar tastes for so elegant a being. You just hang a piece of decidedly ripe meat anywhere near."

"Yes, Jim?"

"Do you notice anything?" demanded the doctor, with his face up to the wind.

"Several things," replied Carrados.

"Apropos of high meat? Do you know, Wynn, I lost that Purple Emperor here, round the blocks. I thought it must have soared, as I couldn't quite fathom its disappearance. This used to be the Druids' altar, they say. I don't know if you follow me, but it would be a devilish rum go if – eh?"

Carrados accepted the suggestion of following Jim's idea with impenetrable gravity.

"I haven't the least doubt that you are right," he assented. "Can you get up?"

"It's about ten feet high," reported Tulloch, "and not an inch of crevice to get a foothold on. If only we could bring the trap in here – "

"I'll give you a back," said Carrados, taking a position against one of the pillars. "You can manage with that?"

"Sure you can stand it?"

"Only be as quick as you can."

"Wait a minute," said Tulloch with indecision. "I think someone is coming."

"I know there is," admitted Carrados, "but it is only a matter of seconds. Make a dash for it."

"No," decided Tulloch. "One looks ridiculous. I believe it is Miss Aynosforde. We'd better wait."

A young girl with a long thin face, light hair, and the palest blue eyes that it would be possible to imagine had come from the wood and was approaching them hurriedly. She might have been eighteen, but she was "dressed young", and when she spoke she expressed the ideas of a child.

"You ought not to come in here," was her greeting. "It belongs to us."

"I am sorry if we are trespassing," apologised Tulloch, colouring with chagrin and surprise. "I was under the impression that Mrs. Aynosforde allowed visitors to inspect these ruins. I am Dr. Tulloch."

"I don't know anything about that," said the girl vaguely. "But Dunstan will be very cross if he sees you here. He is always cross if he finds that anyone has been here. He will scold me afterwards. And he makes faces in the night."

"We will go," said Tulloch quietly. "I am sorry that we should have unconsciously intruded." He raised his hat and turned to walk away, but Miss Aynosforde detained him.

"You must not let Dunstan know that I spoke to you about it," she implored him. "That would be as bad. Indeed," she added plaintively, "whatever I do always makes him cruel to me."

"We will not mention it, you may be sure," replied the doctor. "Good morning."

"Oh, it is no good!" suddenly screamed the girl. "He has seen us! He is coming!"

Tulloch looked round in the direction that Miss Aynosforde's frightened gaze indicated. A young man whom he knew by sight as her brother had left the cover of the wood and was strolling leisurely towards them. Without waiting to encounter him the girl turned and fled, to hide herself behind the farthest pillar, running with ungainly movements of her long, wispish arms and uttering a low cry as she went. As young Aynosforde approached, he courteously raised his hat to the two elder men. He appeared to be a few years older than his sister, and in him her colourless ovine features were moulded to a firmer cast.

"I am afraid that we are trespassing," said the doctor, awkward between his promise to the girl and the necessity of glossing over the situation. "My friend is interested in antiquities – "

"My unfortunate sister!" broke in Aynosforde quietly, with a sad smile. "I can guess what she has been saying. You are Dr. Tulloch, are you not?"

"Yes."

"Our grandmother has a foolish but amiable weakness that she can keep poor Edith's infirmity dark. I cannot pretend to maintain that appearance before a doctor . . . and I am sure that we can rely on the discretion of your friend?"

"Oh, certainly," volunteered Tulloch. "He is – "

"Merely an amateur," put in Carrados, suavely, but with the incisiveness of a scalpel.

"You must, of course, have seen that Edith is a little unusual in her conversation," continued the young man. "Fortunately, it is nothing worse than that. She is not helpless, and she is never violent. I have some hope, indeed, that she will outgrow her delusions. I suppose – " He laughed a little as he suggested it. "I suppose she warned you of my displeasure if I saw you here?"

"There was something of the sort," admitted Tulloch, judging that the circumstances nullified his promise. Aynosforde shook his head slowly.

"I am sorry that you have had the experience," he remarked. "Let me assure you that you are welcome to stay as long as you like under the shadows of these obsolete fossils, and to come as often as you please. It is a very small courtesy. The place has always been accessible to visitors."

"I am relieved to find that I was not mistaken," said the doctor.

"When I have read up the subject I should like to come again," interposed Carrados. "For the present we have gone all over the ground." He took Tulloch's arm, and under the insistent pressure the doctor turned towards the gate. "Good morning, Mr. Aynosforde."

"What a thing to come across!" murmured Tulloch when they were out of earshot. "I remember Darrish making the remark that the girl was simple for her years or something of that sort, but I only took it that she was backward. I wonder if the old ass knew more than he told me!"

They were walking without concern across the turf and had almost reached the gate when Carrados gave a sharp, involuntary cry of pain and wrenched his arm free. As he did so a stone of dangerous edge and size fell to the ground between them.

"Damnation!" cried Tulloch, his face darkening with resentment. "Are you hurt, old man?"

"Come on," curtly replied Carrados between his set teeth.

"Not until I've given that young cub something to remember," cried the outraged doctor truculently. "It was Aynosforde, Wynn. I wouldn't have believed it, but I just caught sight of him in time. He laughed and ran behind a pillar when you were hit.

"Come on," reiterated Carrados, seizing his friend's arm and compelling him towards the gate. "It was only the funny bone, fortunately. Would you stop to box the village idiot's ears because he puts out his tongue at you?

"Village idiot!" exclaimed Tulloch. "I may only be a thick-skulled, third-rate general practitioner of no social pretension whatever, but I'm blistered if I'll have my guests insulted by a long-eared pedigree blighter

259

without putting up a few plain words about it. An Aynosforde or not, he must take the consequences. He's no village idiot."

"No," was Carrados's grim retort. "He is something much more dangerous – the castle maniac."

Tulloch would have stopped in sheer amazement, but the recovered arm dragged him relentlessly on.

"Aynosforde! Mad!"

"The girl is on the borderline of imbecility. The man has passed beyond the limit of a more serious phase. The ground has been preparing for generations. Doubtless in him the seed has quietly germinated for years. Now his time has come."

"I heard that he was a nice, quiet young fellow, studious and interested in science. He has a workshop and a laboratory."

"Yes. Anything to occupy his mind. Well, in future he will have a padded room and a keeper."

"But the sheep killed by night and the parts exposed on the Druids' altar? What does it mean, Wynn?"

"It means madness, nothing more and nothing less. He is the receptacle for the last dregs of a rotten and decrepit stock that has dwindled down to mental atrophy. I don't believe that there is any method in his midnight orgies. The Aynosfordes are certainly a venerable line, and it is faintly possible that its remote ancestors were Druid priests who sacrificed and practised haruspicy on the very spot that we have left. I have no doubt that on that questionable foundation you would find advocates of a more romantic theory."

"Moral atavism?" suggested the doctor shrewdly.

"Yes – reincarnation. I prefer the simpler alternative. Aynosforde has been so fed up with pride of family and traditions of his ancient race that his mania takes this natural trend. You know what became of his father and mother?"

"No, I have never heard them mentioned."

"The father is in a private madhouse. The mother – another cousin, by the way – died at twenty-five."

"And the blood stains on the stairs? Is that his work?"

"Short of actual proof, I should say yes. It is the realisation of another family legend, you see. Aynosforde may have an insane grudge against his grandmother, or it may be simply apeish malignity, put into his mind by the sight of blood."

"What do you propose doing, then? We can't leave the man at large."

"We have nothing yet to commit him on. You would not sign for a reception order on the strength of seeing him throw a stone? We must contrive to catch him in the act tonight, if possible." Tulloch woke up the little horse with a sympathetic touch – they were ambling along the highroad again by this time – and permitted himself to smile.

"And how do you propose to do that, Excellency?" he asked.

"By sprinkling the ninth step with iodide of nitrogen. A warm night . . . it will dry in half-an-hour."

"Well, do you know, I never thought of that," admitted the doctor. "Certainly that would give us the alarm if a feather brushed it. But we don't possess a chemist's shop, and I very much doubt if I can put my hand on any iodine."

"I brought a couple of ounces," said Carrados with diffidence. "Also a bottle of 4880 ammonia to be on the safe side."

"You really are a bit of a *sine qua non*, Wynn," declared Tulloch expressively.

"It was such an obvious thing," apologised the blind man. "I suppose Brook Ashfield is too far for one of us to get over to this afternoon?"

"In Dorset?"

"Yes. Colonel Eustace Aynosforde is the responsible head of the family now, and he should be en the spot if possible. Then we ought to get a couple of men from the county lunatic asylum. We don't know what may be before us."

"If it can't be done by train, we must wire – or perhaps Colonel Aynosforde is on the telephone. We can go into that as soon as we get back. We are almost at Abbot's Farm now. I will cut it down to fifteen minutes at the outside. You don't mind waiting here?"

"Don't hurry," replied Carrados. "Few cases are matters of minutes. Besides, I told Parkinson to come on here from Daneswood on the chance of our picking him up."

"Oh, it's Parkinson, to be sure," said the doctor. "Thought I knew the figure crossing the field. Well, I'll leave you to him."

He hastened along the rutty approach to the farmhouse, and Tommy, under the pretext of being driven there by certain pertinacious flies, imperceptibly edged his way towards the long grass by the roadside. In a few minutes Parkinson announced his presence at the step of the vehicle.

"I found what you described, sir," he reported. "These are the shapes."

Tulloch kept to his time. In less than a quarter-of-an-hour he was back again, and gathering up the reins.

"That little job is soon worked off," he remarked with mild satisfaction. "Home now, I suppose, Wynn?"

"Yes," assented Carrados. "And I think that the other little job is morally worked off." He held up a small piece of note-paper, cut to a neat octagon, with two long sides and six short ones. "What familiar object would just about cover that plan, Jim?"

"If it isn't implicating myself in any devilment, I should say that one of our four-ounce bottles would be about the ticket," replied Tulloch.

"It very likely does implicate you to the extent of being one of your four-ounce bottles, then," said Carrados. "The man who killed Stone's sheep had occasion to use what we will infer to be a four-ounce bottle. It does not tax the imagination to suggest the use he put it to, nor need we wonder that he found it desirable to wash it afterwards – this small, flat bottle that goes conveniently into a waistcoat pocket. On one side of the field – the side remote from the road, Jim, but in the direct line for Dunstan's Tower – there is a stream. There he first washed his hands, carefully placing the little bottle on the grass while he did so. That indiscretion has put us in possession of a ground plan, so to speak, of the vessel."

"Pity it wasn't of the man instead."

"Of the man also. In the field the earth is baked and unimpressionable, but down by the water-side the conditions are quite favourable, and Parkinson got perfect reproductions of the footprints. Soon, perhaps, we may have an opportunity of making a comparison." The doctor glanced at the neat lines to which the papers Carrados held out had been cut.

"It's a moral," he admitted. "There's nothing of the hobnailed about those boots, Wynn."

Swarbrick had been duly warned and obedience to his instructions had been ensured by the note that conveyed them bearing the signature of Colonel Aynosforde. Between eleven and twelve o'clock, a light in a certain position gave the intelligence that Dunstan Aynosforde was in his bedroom and the coast quite clear. A little group of silent men approached the Tower, and four, crossing one of the two bridges that spanned the moat, melted spectrally away in a dark angle of the walls.

Every detail had been arranged. There was no occasion for whispered colloquies about the passages, and with the exception of the butler's sad and respectful greeting of an Aynosforde, scarcely a word was spoken. Carrados, the colonel, and Parkinson took up their positions in the great dining hall, where Dr. Tulloch had waited on the occasion of his vigil. A screen concealed them from the stairs and the chairs on which they sat did not creak – all the blind man asked for. The doctor, who had carried a small quantity of some damp powder wrapped in a saturated sheet of blotting-paper, occupied himself for five minutes distributing it minutely over the surface of the ninth stair. When this was accomplished he disappeared, and the silence of a sleeping house settled upon the ancient Tower. A party, however, is only as quiet as its most restless member, and the colonel soon discovered a growing inability to do nothing at all and to do it in absolute silence. After an exemplary hour, he began to breathe whispered comments on the situation into his neighbour's ear, and it required all Carrados's tact and good humour to repress his impatience. Two o'clock passed and still nothing had happened.

"I began to feel uncommonly dubious, you know," whispered the colonel, after listening to the third clock strike the hour. "We stand to get devilishly chaffed if this gets about. Suppose nothing happens?"

"Then your aunt will probably get up again," replied Carrados.

"True, true. We shall have broken the continuity. But, you know, Mr. Carrados, there are some things about this portent, visitation – call it what you will – that even I don't fully understand down to this day. There is no doubt that my grandfather, Oscar Aynosforde, who died in 1817, did receive a similar omen, or summons, or whatever it may be. We have it on the authority – "

Carrados clicked an almost inaudible sound of warning and laid an admonishing hand on the colonel's arm. "Something going on," he breathed.

The soldier came to the alert like a terrier at a word, but his straining ears could not distinguish a sound beyond the laboured ticking of the hall clock beyond.

"I hear nothing," he muttered to himself. He had not long to wait. Halfway up the stairs something snapped off like the miniature report of a toy pistol. Before the sound could translate itself to the human brain, another louder discharge had swallowed it up and out of its echo a crackling fusillade again marked the dying effects of the scattered explosive.

At the first crack, Carrados had swept aside the screen. "Light, Parkinson!" he cried.

An electric lantern flashed out and centred its circle of brilliance on the stairs opposite. Its radiance pierced the nebulous balloon of violet smoke that was rising to the roof and brought out every detail of the wall beyond.

"Good Heavens!" exclaimed Colonel Aynosforde, "there is a stone out. I knew nothing of this." As he spoke, the solid block of masonry slid back into its place and the wall became as blankly impenetrable as before.

"Colonel Aynosforde," said Carrados, after a hurried word with Parkinson, "you know the house. Will you take my man and get round to Dunstan's workroom at once? A good deal depends upon securing him immediately.

263

"Am I to leave you here without any protection, sir?" inquired Parkinson in mild rebellion.

"Not without any protection, thank you, Parkinson. I shall be in the dark, remember.."

They had scarcely gone when Dr. Tulloch came stumbling in from the hall and the main stairs beyond, calling on Carrados as he bumped his way past a succession of inopportune pieces of furniture.

"Are you there, Wynn?" he demanded, in high-strung irritation. "What the devil's happening? Aynosforde hasn't left his room, we'll swear, but hasn't the iodide gone off?"

"The iodide has gone off and Aynosforde has left his room, though not by the door. Possibly he is back in it by now."

"The deuce!" exclaimed Tulloch blankly. "What am I to do?"

"Return – " began Carrados, but before he could say more, there was a confused noise and a shout outside the window.

"We are saved further uncertainty," said the blind man. "He has thrown himself down into the moat."

"He will be drowned!"

"Not if Swarbrick put the drag-rake where he was instructed, and if those keepers are even passably expert," replied Carrados imperturbably. "After all, drowning . . . But perhaps you had better go and see, Jim."

In a few minutes men began to return to the dining hall as though where the blind man was constituted their headquarters. Colonel Aynosforde and Parkinson were the first, and immediately afterwards Swarbrick entered from the opposite side, bringing a light.

"They've got him out," exclaimed the colonel. "Upon my word, I don't know whether it's for the best or the worst, Mr. Carrados." He turned to the butler, who was lighting one after another of the candles of the great hanging centre-pieces. "Did you know anything of a secret passage giving access to these stairs, Swarbrick?" he inquired.

"Not personally, sir," replied Swarbrick, "but we always understood that formerly there was a passage and hiding chamber somewhere, though the positions had been lost. We last had occasion to use it when we were defeated at Naseby, sir."

Carrados had walked to the stairs and was examining the wall.

"This would be the principal stairway, then?" he asked.

"Yes, sir, until we removed the Elizabethan gallery when we restored in 1712."

"It is on the same plan as the 'Priest's Chamber' at Lapwood. If you investigate in the daylight, Colonel Aynosforde, you will find that you command a view of both bridges when the stone is open. Very convenient sometimes, I dare say."

"Very, very," assented the colonel absently. "Every moment," he explained, "I am dreading that Aunt Eleanor will make her appearance. She must have been disturbed."

"Oh, I took that into account," said Tulloch, catching the remark as he put his head in at the door and looked round. "I recommended a sleeping draught when I was here last – no, this evening. We have got our man in all right now," he continued, "and if we can have a dry suit – "

"I will accompany you, sir," said Swarbrick"

"Is he – violent?" asked the colonel, dropping his voice.

"Violent? Well," admitted Tulloch, holding out two dripping objects that he had been carrying, "we thought it just as well to cut his boots off." He threw them down in a corner and followed the butler out of the room"

Carrados took two pieces of shaped white paper from his pocket and ran his fingers round the outlines. Then he picked up Dunstan Aynosforde's boots and submitted them to a similar scrutiny.

"Very exact, Parkinson," he remarked approvingly.

"Thank you, sir," replied Parkinson with modest pride.

The Mystery of the
Poisoned Dish of Mushrooms

Some time during November of a recent year, newspaper readers who are in the habit of being attracted by curious items of quite negligible importance might have followed the account of the tragedy of a St. Abbots schoolboy which appeared in The Press under the headings, "*Fatal Dish of Mushrooms*", "*Are Toadstools Distinguishable?*", or some similarly alluring title.

The facts relating to the death of Charlie Winpole were simple and straightforward, and the jury sworn to the business of investigating the cause had no hesitation in bringing in a verdict in accordance with the medical evidence. The witnesses who had anything really material to contribute were only two in number: Mrs. Dupreen and Robert Wilberforce Slark, M.D. A couple of hours would easily have disposed of every detail of an inquiry that was generally admitted to have been a pure formality, had not the contention of an interested person delayed the inevitable conclusion by forcing the necessity of an adjournment.

Irene Dupreen testified that she was the widow of a physician and lived at Hazlehurst, Chesset Avenue, St. Abbots, with her brother. The deceased was their nephew, an only child and an orphan, and was aged twelve. He was a ward of Chancery and the Court had appointed her as guardian, with an adequate provision for the expenses of his bringing up and education. That allowance would, of course, cease with her nephew's death.

Coming to the particulars of the case, Mrs. Dupreen explained that for a few days the boy had been suffering from a rather severe cold. She had not thought it necessary to call in a doctor, recognising it as a mild form of influenza. She had kept him from school and restricted him to his bedroom. On the previous Wednesday, the day before his death, he was quite convalescent, with a good pulse and a normal temperature, but as the weather was cold she decided still to keep him in bed as a measure of precaution. He had a fair appetite, but did not care for the lunch they had, and so she had asked him, before going out in the afternoon, if there was anything that he would especially fancy for his dinner. He had thereupon expressed a partiality for mushrooms, of which he was always very fond.

"I laughed and pulled his ear," continued the witness, much affected at her recollection, "and asked him if that was his idea of a suitable dish for an invalid. But I didn't think that it really mattered in the least then, so

I went to several shops about them. They all said that mushrooms were over, but finally I found a few at Lackington's, the greengrocer in Park Road. I bought only half-a-pound. No one but Charlie among us cared for them, and I thought that they were already very dry and rather dear."

The connection between the mushrooms and the unfortunate boy's death seemed inevitable. When Mrs. Dupreen went upstairs after dinner she found Charlie apparently asleep and breathing soundly. She quietly removed the tray and without disturbing him turned out the gas and closed the door. In the middle of the night, she was suddenly and startlingly awakened by something. For a moment she remained confused, listening. Then a curious sound coming from the direction of the boy's bedroom drew her there. On opening the door, she was horrified to see her nephew lying on the floor in a convulsed attitude. His eyes were open and widely dilated. One hand clutched some bed-clothes which he had dragged down with him, and the other still grasped the empty water-bottle that had been by his side. She called loudly for help, and her brother and then the servant appeared. She sent the latter to a medicine cabinet for mustard leaves and told her brother to get in the nearest available doctor. She had already lifted Charlie on to the bed again. Before the doctor arrived, which was in about half-an-hour, the boy was dead.

In answer to a question, the witness stated that she had not seen her nephew between the time she removed the tray and when she found him ill. The only other person who had seen him within a few hours of his death had been her brother, Philip Loudham, who had taken up Charlie's dinner. When he came down again he had made the remark: "The youngster seems lively enough now."

Dr. Slark was the next witness. His evidence was to the effect that about three-fifteen on the Thursday morning, he was hurriedly called to Hazlehurst by a gentleman whom he now knew to be Mr. Philip Loudham. He understood that the case was one of convulsions and went provided for that contingency, but on his arrival he found the patient already dead. From his own examination and from what he was told, he had no hesitation in diagnosing the case as one of agaric poisoning. He saw no reason to suspect any of the food except the mushrooms, and all the symptoms pointed to bhurine, the deadly principle of *Amanita Bhuroides*, or the *Black Cap*, as it was popularly called, from its fancied resemblance to the head-dress assumed by a judge in passing death sentence, coupled with its sinister and well-merited reputation. It was always fatal.

Continuing his evidence, Dr. Slark explained that only after maturity did the Black Cap develop its distinctive appearance. Up to that stage, it had many of the characteristics of *Agaricus campestris*, or common mushroom. It was true that the gills were paler than one would expect to

267

find, and there were other slight differences of a technical kind, but all might easily be overlooked in the superficial glance of the gatherer. The whole subject of edible and noxious fungi was a difficult one, and at present very imperfectly understood. He, personally, very much doubted if true mushrooms were ever responsible for the cases of poisoning which one occasionally saw attributed to them. Under scientific examination, he was satisfied that all would resolve themselves into poisoning by one or other of the many noxious fungi that could easily be mistaken for the edible varieties. It was possible to prepare an artificial bed, plant it with proper spawn, and be rewarded by a crop of mushroom-like growth of undoubted virulence. On the other hand, the injurious constituents of many poisonous fungi passed off in the process of cooking. There was no handy way of discriminating between the good and the bad except by the absolute identification of species. The salt test and the silver-spoon test were all nonsense, and the sooner they were forgotten the better. Apparent mushrooms that were found in woods or growing in the vicinity of trees or hedges should always be regarded with the utmost suspicion.

Dr. Slark's evidence concluded the case so far as the subpoenaed witnesses were concerned, but before addressing the jury the coroner announced that another person had expressed a desire to be heard. There was no reason why they should not accept any evidence that was tendered, and as the applicant's name had been mentioned in the case, it was only right that he should have the opportunity of replying publicly.

Mr. Lackington thereupon entered the witness box and was sworn. He stated that he was a fruiterer and greengrocer, carrying on a business in Park Road, St. Abbots. He remembered Mrs. Dupreen coming to his shop two days before. The basket of mushrooms from which she was supplied consisted of a small lot of about six pounds, brought in by a farmer from a neighbouring village, with whom he had frequent dealings. All had been disposed of and in no other case had illness resulted. It was a serious matter to him as a tradesman to have his name associated with a case of this kind. That was why he had come forward – not only with regard to mushrooms, but as a general result, people would become shy of dealing with him if it was stated that he sold unwholesome goods.

The coroner, intervening at this point, remarked that he might as well say that he would direct the jury that, in the event of their finding the deceased to have died from the effects of the mushrooms or anything contained among them, there was no evidence other than that the occurrence was one of pure mischance.

Mr. Lackington expressed his thanks for the assurance, but said that a bad impression would still remain. He had been in business in St. Abbots for twenty-seven years and during that time, he had handled some tons of mushrooms without a single complaint before. He admitted, in answer to the interrogation, that he had not actually examined every mushroom of the half-pound sold to Mrs. Dupreen, but he weighed them, and he was confident that if a toadstool had been among them he would have detected it. Might it not be a cooking utensil that was the cause?

Dr. Slark shook his head and was understood to say that he could not accept the suggestion.

Continuing, Mr. Lackington then asked whether it was not possible that the deceased, doubtless an inquiring, adventurous boy and as mischievous as most of his kind, feeling quite well again and being confined to the house, had got up in his aunt's absence and taken something that would explain this sad affair? They had heard of a medicine cabinet. What about tablets of trional or veronal or something of that sort that might perhaps look like sweets? It was all very well for Dr. Slark to laugh, but this matter was a serious one for the witness.

Dr. Slark apologised for smiling – he had not laughed – and gravely remarked that the matter was a serious one for all concerned in the inquiry. He admitted that the reference to trional and veronal in this connection had, for the moment, caused him to forget the surroundings. He would suggest that in the circumstances perhaps the coroner would think it desirable to order a more detailed examination of the body to be made.

After some further discussion the coroner, while remarking that in most cases an analysis was quite unnecessary, decided that in view of what had transpired it would be more satisfactory to have a complete autopsy carried out. The inquest was accordingly adjourned.

A week later, most of those who had taken part in the first inquiry assembled again in the room of the St. Abbots Town Hall which did duty for the Coroner's Court. Only one witness was heard and his evidence was brief and conclusive.

Dr. Herbert Ingpenny, consulting pathologist to St. Martin's Hospital, stated that he had made an examination of the contents of the stomach and viscera of the deceased. He found evidence of the presence of the poison bhurine in sufficient quantity to account for the boy's death, and the symptoms, as described by Dr. Slark and Mrs. Dupreen in the course of the previous hearing, were consistent with bhurine poisoning. Bhurine did not occur naturally except as a constituent of *Amanita Bhuroides*. One-fifth of a grain would be fatal to an adult. In other words, a single fungus in the dish might poison three people. A child, especially if experiencing the effects of a weakening illness, would be even more susceptible. No other harmful substance was present.

Dr. Ingpenny concluded by saying that he endorsed his colleague's general remarks on the subject of mushrooms and other fungi, and the jury, after a plain direction from the coroner, forthwith brought in a verdict in accordance with the medical evidence.

It was a foregone conclusion with anyone who knew the facts or had followed the evidence. Yet five days later, Philip Loudham was arrested suddenly and charged with the astounding crime of having murdered his nephew.

It is at this point that Max Carrados makes his first appearance in the Winpole tragedy.

A few days after the arrest, being in a particularly urbane frame of mind himself, and having several hours with no demands on them that could not be fitly transferred to his subordinates, Mr. Carlyle looked 'round for some social entertainment and, with a benevolent condescension, very opportunely remembered the existence of his niece living at Groat's Heath.

"Elsie will be delighted," he assented to the suggestion. "She is rather out of the world up there, I imagine. Now if I get there at four, put in a couple of hours – "

Mrs. Bellmark was certainly pleased, but she appeared to be still more surprised, and behind that lay an effervescence of excitement that even to Mr. Carlyle's complacent self-esteem seemed out of proportion to the occasion. The reason could not be long withheld.

"Did you meet anyone, Uncle Louis?" was almost her first inquiry.

"Did I meet anyone?" repeated Mr. Carlyle with his usual precision. "Um, no, I cannot say that I met anyone particular. Of course – "

"I've had a visitor and he's coming back again for tea. Guess who it is? But you never will. Mr. Carrados."

"Max Carrados!" exclaimed her uncle in astonishment. "You don't say so. Why, bless my soul, Elsie, I'd almost forgotten that you knew him. It seems years ago. What on earth is Max doing in Groat's Heath?"

"That is the extraordinary thing about it," replied Mrs. Bellmark. "He said that he had come up here to look for mushrooms."

"Mushrooms?"

"Yes. That was what he said. He asked me if I knew of any woods about here that he could go into and I told him of the one down Stonecut Lane."

"But don't you know, my dear child," exclaimed Mr. Carlyle, "that mushrooms growing in woods or even near trees are always to be regarded with suspicion? They may look like mushrooms, but they are probably poisonous."

"I didn't know," admitted Mrs. Bellmark. "But if they are, I imagine Mr. Carrados will know."

"It scarcely sounds like it – going to a wood, you know. As it happens, I have been looking up the subject lately. But, in any case, you say that he is coming back here?"

"He asked me if he might call on his way home for a cup of tea, and of course I said, 'Of course.'"

"Of course," also said Mr. Carlyle. "Motoring, I suppose."

"Yes, a big grey car. He had Mr. Parkinson with him."

Mr. Caryle was slightly puzzled, as he frequently was by his friend's proceedings, but it was not his custom to dwell on any topic that involved an admission of inadequacy. The subject of Carrados and his eccentric quest was therefore dismissed until the sound of a formidable motor car dominating the atmosphere of the quiet suburban road was almost immediately followed by the entrance of the blind amateur. With a knowing look towards his niece Carlyle had taken up a position at the farther end of the room, where he remained in almost breathless silence.

Carrados acknowledged the hostess's smiling greeting and then nodded familiarly in the direction of the playful guest.

"Well, Louis," he remarked, "we've caught each other."

Mrs. Bellmark was perceptibly startled, but rippled musically at the failure of the conspiracy.

"Extraordinary," admitted Mr. Carlyle, coming forward.

"Not so very," was the dry reply. "Your friendly little maid – " to Mrs. Bellmark " – mentioned your visitor as she brought me in."

"Is it a fact, Max," demanded Mr. Carlyle, "that you have been to – er – Stonecut Wood to get mushrooms?"

"Mrs. Bellmark told you?"

"Yes. And did you succeed?"

"Parkinson found something that he assured me looked just like mushrooms."

Mr. Carlyle bestowed a triumphant glance on his niece.

"I should very much like to see these so-called mushrooms. Do you know, it may be rather a good thing for you that I met you."

"It is always a good thing for me to meet you," replied Carrados. "You shall see them. They are in the car. Perhaps I shall be able to take you back to town?"

"If you are going very soon. No, no, Elsie – " in rèsponse to Mrs. Bellmark's protesting "Oh!"

"I don't want to influence Max, but I really must tear myself way the moment after tea. I still have to clear up some work on a rather important case I am just completing. It is quite appropriate to the occasion, too. Do you know all about the Winpole business, Max?"

271

"No," admitted Carrados, without any appreciable show of interest. "Do you, Louis?"

"Yes," responded Mr. Carlyle with crisp assurance, "yes, I think that I may claim I do. In fact, it was I who obtained the evidence that induced the authorities to take up the case against Loudham."

"Oh, do tell us all about it," exclaimed Elsie. "I have only seen something in *The Indicator*."

Mr. Carlyle shook his head, hemmed and looked wise, and then gave in.

"But not a word of this outside, Elsie," he stipulated. "Some of the evidence won't be given until next week and it might be serious."

"Not a syllable," assented the lady. "How exciting! Go on."

"Well, you know, of course, that the Coroner's Jury – very rightly, according to the evidence before them – brought in a verdict of accidental death. In the circumstances, it was a reflection on the business methods or the care or the knowledge or whatever one may decide of the man who sold the mushrooms, a greengrocer called Lackington. I have seen Lackington, and with a rather remarkable pertinacity in the face of the evidence he insists that he could not have made this fatal blunder – that in weighing so small a quantity as half-a-pound, at any rate, he would at once have spotted anything that wasn't quite all right."

"But the doctor said, Uncle Louis – "

"Yes, my dear Elsie, we know what the doctor said, but, rightly or wrongly, Lackington backs his experience and practical knowledge against theoretical generalities. In ordinary circumstances, nothing more would have come of it, but it happens that Lackington has for a lodger a young man on the staff of the local paper, and for a neighbour a pharmaceutical chemist. These three men talked things over more than once – Lackington restive under the damage that had been done to his reputation, the journalist stimulating and keen for a newspaper sensation, the chemist contributing his quota of practical knowledge. At the end of a few days, a fabric of circumstance had been woven which might be serious or innocent according to the further development of the suggestion and the manner in which it could be met. These were the chief points of the attack.

"Mrs. Dupreen's allowance for the care and maintenance of Charlie Winpole ceased with his death, as she had told the jury. What she did not mention was that the deceased boy would have come into an inheritance of some fifteen-thousand pounds at age, and that this fortune now fell in equal shares to the lot of his two nearest relatives – Mrs. Dupreen and her brother, Philip.

"Mrs. Dupreen was by no means in easy circumstances. Philip Loudham was equally poor and had no assured income. He had tried several forms of business and now, at about thirty-five, was spending his time chiefly in writing poems and painting watercolours, none of which brought him any money so far as one could learn.

"Philip Loudham, it was admitted, took up the food round which the tragedy centred.

"Philip Loudham was shown to be in debt and urgently in need of money. There was supposed to be a lady in the case – I hope I need say no more, Elsie."

"Who is she?" asked Mrs. Bellmark with poignant interest.

"We do not know yet. A married woman, it is rumoured, I regret to say. It scarcely matters – certainly not to you, Elsie. To continue:

"Mrs. Dupreen got back from her shopping in the afternoon before her nephew's death at about three o'clock. In less than half-an-hour, Loudham left the house and going to the station took a return ticket to Euston. He went by the 3:41 and was back in St. Abbots at 5:43. That would give him barely an hour in town for whatever business he transacted. What was that business?

"The chemist next door supplied the information that although bhurine only occurs in nature in this one form, it can be isolated from the other constituents of the fungus and dealt with like any other liquid poison. But it was a very exceptional commodity, having no commercial uses and probably not half-a-dozen retail chemists in London had it on their shelves. He himself had never stocked it and never been asked for it."

"With this suggestive but by no means convincing evidence," continued Mr. Carlyle, "the young journalist went to the editor of *The Morning Indicator*, to which he acted as St. Abbots correspondent, and asked him whether he cared to take up the inquiry as a 'scoop'. The local trio had carried it as far as they were able. The editor of *The Indicator* decided to look into it and asked me to go on with the case. This is how my connection with it arose."

"Oh, that's how newspapers get to know things?" commented Mrs. Bellmark. "I often wondered."

"It is one way," assented her uncle.

"An American development," contributed Carrados. "It is a little overdone there."

"It must be awful," said the hostess. "And the police methods! In the plays that come from the States – " The entrance of the friendly hand-maiden, bringing tea, was responsible for the platitudinous wave. The conversation, in deference to Mr. Carlyle's scruples, marked time until the door closed on her departure.

"My first business," continued the inquiry agent, after making himself useful at the table, "was naturally to discover among the chemists in London whether a sale of bhurine coincided with Philip Loudham's hasty visit. If this line failed, the very foundation of the edifice of hypothetical guilt gave way. If it succeeded . . . Well, it did succeed. In a street off Caistor Square, Tottenham Court Road – Trenion Street – we found a man called Lightcraft, who at once remembered making such a sale. As bhurine is a specified poison, the transaction would have to be entered, and Lightcraft's book contained this unassailable piece of evidence. On Wednesday, the sixth of this month, a man signing his name as '*J. D. Williams*', and giving '*25 Chalcott Place*' as the address, purchased four drachms of bhurine. Lightcraft fixed the time as about half-past-four. I went to 25 Chalcott Place and found it to be a small boarding house. No one of the name of Williams was known there."

If Mr. Caryle's tone of finality went for anything, Philip Loudham was as good as pinioned. Mrs. Bellmark supplied the expected note of admiration.

"Just fancy!" was the form it took.

"Under the Act, the purchaser must be known to the chemist?" suggested Carrados.

"Yes," agreed Mr. Carlyle. "And there our friend Lightcraft may have let himself in for a little trouble. But, as he says – and we must admit that there is something in it – who is to define what 'known to' actually means? A hundred people are known to him as regular or occasional customers and he has never heard their names. A score of names and addresses represent to him regular or occasional customers whom he has never seen. This '*J. D. Williams*' came in with an easy air and appeared at all events to know Lightcraft. The face seemed not unfamiliar, and Lightcraft was perhaps a little too facile in assuming that he did know him. Well, well, Max, I can understand the circumstances. Competition is keen – especially against the private chemist – and one may give offence and lose a customer. We must all live."

"Except Charlie Winpole," occurred to Max Carrados, but he left the retort unspoken. "Did you happen to come across any inquiry for bhurine at other shops?" he asked instead.

"No," replied Carlyle, "no, I did not. It would have been an indication then, of course, but after finding the actual place the others would have no significance. Why do you ask?"

"Oh, nothing. Only don't you think that he was rather lucky to get it first shot if our St. Abbots authority was right?"

"Yes, yes. Perhaps he was. But that is of no interest to us now. The great thing is that a peculiarly sinister and deliberate murder is brought home to its perpetrator. When you consider the circumstances, upon my soul, I don't know that I have ever unmasked a more ingenious and cold-blooded ruffian."

"Then he has confessed, Uncle?"

"Confessed, my dear Elsie," said Mr. Carlyle, with a tolerant smile. "No, he has not confessed – men of that type never do. On the contrary, he asserted his outraged innocence with a considerable show of indignation. What else was he to do? Then he was asked to account for his movements between 4:15 and five o'clock on that afternoon. Egad, the fellow was so cocksure of the safety of his plans that he hadn't even taken the trouble to think that out. First he denied that he had been away from St. Abbots at all. Then he remembered. He had run down to town in the afternoon for a few things. – What things? – Well, chiefly stationery. – Where had he bought it? – At a shop in Oxford Street. He did not know the name. – Would he be able to point it out? – He thought so. – Could he identify the attendant? – No, he could not remember him in the least. – Had he the bill? – No, he never kept small bills. – How much was the amount? – About three or four shillings. – And the return fare to Euston was three-and-eightpence. Was it not rather an extravagant journey? – He could only say that he did so. – Three or four shillings' worth of stationery would be a moderate parcel. Did he have it sent? – No, he took it with him. – Three or four shillings' worth of stationery in his pocket? – No, it was in a parcel. – Too large to go in his pocket? – Yes. – Two independent witnesses would testify that he carried no parcel. They were townsmen of St. Abbots who had travelled. down in the same carriage with him. Did he still persist that he had been engaged in buying stationery? Then he declined to say anything further – about the best thing he could do."

"And Lightcraft identifies him?"

"Um, well, not quite so positively as we might wish. You see, a fortnight has elapsed. The man who bought the poison wore a moustache – put on, of course – but Lightcraft will say that there is a resemblance and the type of the two men the same."

"I foresee that Mr. Lightcraft's accommodating memory for faces will come in for rather severe handling in cross-examination," said Carrados, as though he rather enjoyed the prospect.

"It will balance Mr. Philip Loudham's unfortunate forgetfulness for localities, Max," rejoined Mr. Carlyle, delivering the thrust with his own inimitable aplomb.

Carrados rose with smiling acquiescence to the shrewdness of the riposte.

"I will be quite generous, Mrs. Bellmark," he observed. "I will take him away now, with the memory of that lingering in your ears – all my crushing retorts unspoken."

"Five-thirty, egad!" exclaimed Mr. Carlyle, displaying his imposing gold watch. "We must – or, at all events, I must. You can think of them in the car, Max."

"I do hope you won't come to blows," murmured the lady. Then she added: "When will the real trial come on, Uncle Louis?"

"The Sessions? Oh, early in January."

"I must remember to look out for it." Possibly she had some faint idea of Uncle Louis taking a leading part in the proceedings. At any rate Mr. Carlyle looked pleased, but when *adieux* had been taken and the door was closed Mrs. Bellmark was left wondering what the enigma of Max Carrados's departing smile had been.

Before they had covered many furlongs Mr. Carlyle suddenly remembered the suspected mushrooms and demanded to see them. A very moderate collection was produced for his inspection. He turned them over sceptically

"The gills are too pale for true mushrooms, Max," he declared sapiently. "Don't take any risk. Let me drop them out of the window?"

"No." Carrados's hand quietly arrested the threatened action. "No, I have a use for them, Louis, but it is not culinary. You are quite right: They are rank poison. I only want to study them for – a case I am interested in."

"A case! You don't mean to say that there is another mushroom poisoner going?"

"No, it is the same."

"But – but you said – "

"That I did not know all about it? Quite true. Nor do I yet. But I know rather more than I did then."

"Do you mean that Scotland Yard – "

"No, Louis." Mr. Carrados appeared to find something rather amusing in the situation. "I am for the other side."

"The other side! And you let me babble out the whole case for the prosecution! Well, really, Max!"

"But you are out of it now? The Public Prosecutor has taken it up?"

"True, true. But, for all that, I feel devilishly bad."

"Then I will give you all the whole case for the defence and so we shall be quits. In fact, I am relying on you to help me with it."

"With the defence? I – after supplying the evidence that the Public Prosecutor is acting on?"

"Why not? You don't want to hang Philip Loudham – specially if he happens to be innocent – do you?"

"I don't want to hang anyone," protested Mr. Carlyle. "At least – not – as a private individual."

"Quite so. Well, suppose you and I between ourselves find out the actual facts of the case and decide what is to be done. The more usual course is for the prosecution to exaggerate all that tells against the accused and to contradict everything in his favour, for the defence to advance fictitious evidence of innocence, and to lie roundly on everything that endangers his client, while on both sides witnesses are piled up to bemuse the jury into accepting the desired version. That does not always make for impartiality or for justice . . . Now you and I are two reasonable men, Louis — "

"I hope so," admitted Mr. Carlyle. "I hope so."

"You can give away the case for the prosecution and I will expose the weakness of the defence, so, between us, we may arrive at the truth."

"It strikes me as a deuced irregular proceeding. But I am curious to hear the defence all the same."

"You are welcome to all of it that there yet is. An alibi, of course."

"Ah!" commented Mr. Carlyle with expression.

"So recently as yesterday a lady came hurriedly, and with a certain amount of secrecy, to see me. She came on the strength of the introduction afforded by a mutual acquainceship with Fromow, the Greek professor. When we were alone she asked me – besought me, in fact – to tell her what to do. A few hours before, Mrs. Dupreen had rushed across London to her with the tale of young Loudham's arrest. Then out came the whole story. This woman – Well, her name is Guestling, Louis – lives a little way down in Surrey and is married. Her husband, according to her own account – and I have certainly heard a hint about it elsewhere – leads her a studiedly outrageous existence: An admired silken-mannered gentleman in society, a tolerable polecat at home, one infers. About a year ago, Mrs. Guestling made the acquaintance of Loudham, who was staying in that neighbourhood painting his pretty unsaleable country lanes and golden sunsets. The inevitable, or, to accept the lady's protestations, half the inevitable, followed. Guestling, who adds an insatiable jealousy to his other domestic virtues, vetoed the new acquaintance and thenceforward the two met hurriedly and furtively in town. Had either of them any money, they might have snatched their destinies from the hands of Fate and gone off together, but she has nothing and he has nothing and both, I suppose, are poor weak mortals when it comes to doing anything courageous and outright in this censorious world. So they drifted, drifting but not yet wholly wrecked."

"A formidable incentive for a weak and desperate man to secure a fortune by hook or crook, Max," said Carlyle drily.

"That is the motive that I wish to make you a present of. But, as you will insist on your side, it is also a motive for a weak and foolish couple to

277

steal every brief opportunity of a secret meeting. On Wednesday, the sixth, the lady was returning home from a visit to some friends in the Midlands. She saw in the occasion an opportunity and on the morning of the sixth a message appeared in the personal column of *The Daily Telegraph* – their usual channel of communication – making an assignation. That much can be established by the irrefutable evidence of the newspaper. Philip Loudham kept the appointment and for half-an-hour this miserably happy pair sat holding each other's hands in a dreary deserted waiting room of Bishop's Road Station. That half-hour was from 4:14 to 4:45. Then Loudham saw Mrs. Guestling into Praed Street Station for Victoria, returned to Euston, and just caught the 5:07 St. Abbots."

"Can this be corroborated – especially as regards the precise time they were together?"

"Not a word of it. They chose the waiting room at Bishop's Road for seclusion and apparently they got it. Not a soul even looked in while they were there."

"Then, by Jupiter, Max," exclaimed Mr. Carlyle with emotion, "you have hanged your client!"

Carrados could not restrain a smile at his friend's tragic note of triumph.

"Well, let us examine the rope," he said with his usual imperturbability.

"Here it is." It was a trivial enough shred of evidence that the inquiry agent took from his pocket-book and put into the expectant hand. In point of fact, the salmon-coloured ticket of a "London General" motor omnibus.

"Royal Oak – the stage nearest Paddington – to Tottenham Court Road – the point nearest Trenion Street," he added significantly.

"Yes," acquiesced Carrados, taking it.

"The man who bought the bhurine dropped that ticket on the floor of the shop. He left the door open and Lightcraft followed him to close it. That is how he came to pick the ticket up, and he remembers that it was not there before. Then he threw it into a wastepaper basket underneath the counter, and that is where we found it when I called on him."

"Mr. Lightcraft's memory fascinates me, Louis," was the blind man's unruffled comment. "Let us drop in and have a chat with him?"

"Do you really think that there is anything more to be got in that quarter?" queried Carlyle dubiously. "I have turned him inside out, you may be sure."

"True, but we approach Mr. Lightcraft from different angles. You were looking for evidence to prove young Loudham guilty. I am looking for evidence to prove him innocent."

278

"Very well, Max," acquiesced his companion. "Only don't blame me if it turns out as deuced awkward for your man as Mrs. G. has done. Shall I tell you what a counsel may be expected to put to the jury as the explanation of that lady's evidence?"

"No, thanks," said Carrados half-sleepily from his corner. "I know. I told her so."

"Oh, very well. I needn't inform you, then." And debarred of that satisfaction, Mr. Carlyle withdrew himself into his own corner, where he nursed an indulgent annoyance against the occasional perversity of Max Carrados until the stopping of the car and the variegated attractions displayed in a shop window told him where they were

Mr. Lightcraft made no pretence of being glad to see his visitors. For some time he declined to open his mouth at all on the subject that had brought them there, repeating with parrot-like obstinacy to every remark on their part, "The matter is *sub judice*. I am unable to say anything further," until Mr. Carlyle longed to box his ears and bring him to his senses. The ears happened to be rather prominent, for they glowed with sensitiveness, and the chemist was otherwise a lank and pallid man, whose transparent ivory skin and well-defined moustache gave him something of the appearance of a waxwork.

"At all events," interposed Carrados, when his friend turned from the maddening reiteration in despair, "you don't mind telling me a few things about bhurine – apart from this particular connection?"

"I am very busy," and Mr. Lightcraft, with his back towards the shop, did something superfluous among the bottles on a shelf.

"I imagine that the time of Mr. Max Carrados, of whom even you may possibly have heard, is as valuable as yours, my good friend," put in Mr. Carlyle with scandalised dignity.

"Mr. Carrados?" Lightcraft turned and regarded the blind man with interest. "I did not know. But you must recognise the unenviable position in which I am put by this gentleman's interference."

"It is his profession, you know," said Carrados mildly, "and, in any case, it would certainly have been someone. Why not help me to get you out of the position?"

"How is that possible?"

"If the case against Philip Loudham breaks down and he is discharged at the next hearing, you would not be called upon further."

"That would certainly be a mitigation. But why should it break down?"

"Suppose you let me try the taste of bhurine," suggested Carrados. "You have some left?"

"Max, Max!" cried Mr. Carlyle's warning voice. "Aren't you aware that the stuff is a deadly poison? One-fifth of a grain – "

"Mr. Lightcraft will know how to administer it." Apparently Mr. Lightcraft did. He filled a graduated measure with cold water, dipped a slender glass rod into a bottle that was not kept on the shelves, and with it stirred the water. Then into another vessel of water he dropped a single spot of the dilution.

"One in a hundred-and-twenty-five-thousand, Mr. Carrados," he said, offering him the mixture.

Carrados just touched the liquid with his lips, considered the impression, and then wiped his mouth.

"Now for the smell."

The unstoppered bottle was handed to him and he took in its exhalation.

"Stewed mushrooms!" was his comment. "What is it used for, Mr. Lightcraft?"

"Nothing that I know of."

"But your customer must have stated an application."

The pallid chemist flushed a little at the recollection of that incident.

"Yes," he conceded. "There is a good deal about the whole business that is still a mystery to me. The man came in shortly after I had lit up and nodded familiarly as he said: 'Good evening, Mr. Lightcraft.' I naturally assumed that he was someone whom I could not quite place. 'I want another half-pound of nitre,' he said, and I served him. Had he bought nitre before, I have since tried to recall, and I cannot. It is a common-enough article and I sell it every day. I have a poor memory for faces, I am willing to admit. It has hampered me in business many a time. We chatted about nothing in particular as I did up the parcel. After he had paid and turned to go he looked back again. 'By the way, do you happen to have any bhurine?' he inquired. Unfortunately, I had a few ounces. 'Of course you know its nature?' I cautioned him. 'May I ask what you require it for?' He nodded and held up the parcel of nitre he had in his hand. 'The same thing,' he replied. 'Taxidermy.' Then I supplied him with half-an-ounce."

"As a matter of fact, is it used in taxidermy?"

"It does not seem to be. I have made inquiry and no one knows of it. Nitre is largely used, and some of the dangerous poisons – arsenic and mercuric chloride, for instance – but not this. No, it was a subterfuge."

"Now the poison book, if you please."

Mr. Lightcraft produced it without demur and the blind man ran his finger along the indicated line.

"Yes, this is quite satisfactory. Is it a fact, Mr. Lightcraft, that not half-a-dozen chemists in London stock this particular substance? We are told that."

"I can quite believe it. I certainly don't know of another."

"Strangely enough, your customer of the sixth seems to have come straight here. Do you issue a price list?"

"Only a localised one of certain photographic goods. Bhurine is not included."

"You can suggest no reason why Mr. Phillip Loudham should be inspired to presume that he would be able to procure this unusual drug from you? You have never corresponded with him, nor come across his name or address before?"

"No. As far as I can recollect, I know nothing whatever of him."

"Then as yet you must assume that it was pure chance. By the way, Mr. Lightcraft, how does it come that you stock this rare poison, which has no commercial use and for which there is no demand?"

The chemist permitted himself to smile at the blunt terms of the inquiry.

"In the ordinary way I don't stock it," he replied. "This is a small quantity which I had over from my own use."

"Your own use? Oh, then it has a use after all?"

"No, scarcely that. Some time ago it leaked out in a corner of the photographic world that a great revolution in colour photography was on the point of realisation by the use of bhurine in one of the processes. I, among others, at once took it up. Unfortunately it was another instance of a discovery that is correct in theory breaking down in practice. Nothing came of it."

"Dear, dear me," said Carrados softly, with sympathetic understanding in his voice. "What a pity. You are interested in photography, Mr. Lightcraft?"

"It is the hobby of my life, sir. Of course most chemists dabble in it as a part of their business, but I devote all my spare time to experimenting. Colour photography in particular."

"Colour photography. Yes. It has a great future. This bhurine process – I suppose it would have been of considerable financial value if it had worked?"

Mr. Lightcraft laughed quietly and rubbed his hands together. For the moment, he had forgotten Loudham and the annoying case and lived in his enthusiasm.

"I should rather say it would, Mr. Carrados," he replied. "It would have been the most epoch-marking thing since Gaudin produced the first dry plate in '54. Consider it – the elaborate processes of Dyndale, Eiloff, and Jupp reduced to the simplicity of a single contact print giving the entire range of chromatic variation. Financially it will scarcely bear thinking about by artificial light."

"Was it widely taken up?" asked Carrados.

"The bhurine idea?"

"Yes. You spoke of the secret leaking out. Were many in the know?"

"Not at all. The group of initiates was only a small one and I should imagine that, on reflection, every man kept it to himself. It certainly never became public. Then when the theory was definitely exploded, of course no one took any further interest in it."

"Were all who were working on the same lines known to you, Mr. Lightcraft?"

"Well, yes. More or less I suppose they would be," said the chemist thoughtfully. "You see, the man who stumbled on the formula was a member of the Iris – a society of those interested in this subject, of which I was the secretary – and I don't think it ever got beyond the committee."

"How long ago was this?"

"A year – eighteen months. It led to unpleasantness and broke up the society."

"Suppose it happened to come to your knowledge that one of the original circle was quietly pursuing his experiments on the same lines with bhurine – What should you infer from it?"

Mr. Lightcraft considered. Then he regarded Carrados with a sharp, almost a startled, glance and then he fell to biting his nails in perplexed uncertainty.

"It would depend on who it was," he replied.

"Was there by any chance one who was unknown to you by sight but whose address you were familiar with?"

"Paulden!" exclaimed Mr. Lightcraft. "Paulden, by Heaven! I do believe you're right. He was the ablest of the lot and he never came to the meetings – a corresponding member. Southem, the original man who struck the idea, knew Paulden and told him of it. Southem was an impractical genius who would never be able to make anything work. Paulden – yes, Paulden it was who finally persuaded Southem that there was nothing in it. He sent a report to the same effect to be read at one of the meetings. So Paulden is taking up bhurine again – "

"Where does he live?" inquired Carrados.

"Ivor House, Wilmington Lane, Enstead. As secretary I have written there a score of times."

"It is on the Great Western – Paddington," commented the blind man. "Still, can you get out the addresses of the others in the know, Mr. Lightcraft?"

"Certainly, certainly. I have the book of membership. But I am convinced now that Paulden was the man. I believe that I did actually see him once some years ago, but he has grown a moustache since."

"If you had been convinced of that a few days ago, it would have saved us some awkwardness," volunteered Mr. Carlyle with a little dignified asperity.

"When you came before, Mr. Carlyle, you were so convinced yourself of it being Mr. Loudham that you wouldn't hear of me thinking of anyone else," retorted the chemist. "You will bear me out so that I never positively identified him as my customer. Now here is the book. Southern, Potter's Bar. Voynich, Islington. Crawford, Streatham Hill. Brown, Southampton Row. Vickers, Clapham Common. Tidey, Fulham. All those I knew quite well – associated with them week after week. Williams I didn't know so closely. He is dead. Bigwood has gone to Canada. I don't think anyone else was in the bhurine craze – as we called it afterwards."

"But now? What would you call it now?" queried Carrados"

"Now? Well, I hope that you will get me out of having to turn up at court and that sort of thing, Mr. Carrados. If Paulden is going on experimenting with bhurine again on the sly, I shall want all my spare time to do the same myself!"

A few hours later the two investigators rang the bell of a substantial detached house in Enstead, the little country town twenty miles out in Berkshire, and asked to see Mr. Paulden.

"It is no good taking Lightcraft to identify the man," Carrados had decided. "If Paulden denied it, our friend's obliging record in that line would put him out of court."

"I maintain an open mind on the subject," Carlyle had replied. "Lightcraft is admittedly a very bending reed, but there is no reason why he should not have been right before and wrong today."

They were shown into a ceremonial reception room to wait. Mr. Carlyle diagnosed snug circumstances and the tastes of an indoors, comfort-loving man in the surroundings.

The door opened, but it was to admit a middle-aged matronly lady with good humour and domestic capability proclaimed by every detail of her smiling face and easy manner.

"You wished to see my husband?" she asked with friendly courtesy.

"Mr. Paulden? Yes, we should like to," replied Carlyle, with his most responsive urbanity. "It is a matter that need not occupy more than a few minutes."

"He is very busy just now. If it has to do with the election – " A local contest was at its height. " – he is not interested in politics and scarcely ever votes." Her manner was not curious, but merely reflected a business-like desire to save trouble all round.

"Very sensible too, very sensible indeed," almost warbled Mr. Carlyle with instinctive cajolery. "After all," he continued, mendaciously appropriating as his own an aphorism at which he had laughed heartily a few days before in the theatre, "after all, what does an election do but change the colour of the necktie of the man who picks our pockets? No, no, Mrs. Paulden, it is merely a – um – quite personal matter."

The lady looked from one to the other with smiling amiability.

"Some little mystery," her expression seemed to say. "All right. I don't mind, only perhaps I could help you if I knew."

"Mr. Paulden is in his darkroom now," was what she actually did say. "I am afraid, I am really afraid that I shan't be able to persuade him to come out unless I can take a definite message."

"One understands the difficulty of tempting an enthusiast from his work," suggested Carrados, speaking for the first time. "Would it be permissible to take us to the door of the darkroom, Mrs. Paulden, and let us speak to your husband through it?"

"We can try that way," she acquiesced readily, "if it is really so important."

"I think so," he replied.

The darkroom lay across the hall. Mrs. Paulden conducted them to the door, waited a moment and then knocked quietly.

"Yes?" sang out a voice, rather irritably one might judge, from inside.

"Two gentlemen have called to see you about something, Lance – "

"I cannot see anyone when I am in here," interrupted the voice with rising sharpness. "You know that, Clara – "

"Yes, dear," she said soothingly. "But listen. They are at the door here and if you can spare the time just to come and speak, you will know without much trouble if their business is as important as they think."

"Wait a minute," came the reply after a moment's pause, and then they heard someone approach the door from the other side"

It was a little difficult to know exactly how it happened in the obscure light of the corner of the hall. Carrados had stepped nearer to the door to speak. Possibly he trod on Mr. Carlyle's toe, for there was a confused movement. Certainly he put out his hand hastily to recover himself. The next moment the door of the darkroom jerked open, the light was let in and the warm odours of a mixed and vitiated atmosphere rolled out. Secure in the well-ordered discipline of his excellent household, Mr. Paulden had neglected the precaution of locking himself in.

"Confound it all!" shouted the incensed experimenter in a towering rage. "Confound it all, you've spoiled the whole thing now!"

284

"Dear me," apologised Carrados penitently, "I am so sorry. I think it must have been my fault, do you know. Does it really matter?"

"Matter!" stormed Mr. Paulden, recklessly flinging open the door fully now to come face to face with his disturbers – "Matter letting a flood of light into a darkroom in the middle of a delicate experiment!"

"Surely it was very little," persisted Carrados.

"Pshaw!" snarled the angry gentleman. "It was enough. You know the difference between light and dark, I suppose?" Mr. Carlyle suddenly found himself holding his breath, wondering how on earth Max had conjured that opportune challenge to the surface.

"No," was the mild and deprecating reply – the appeal *ad misericordiam* that had never failed him yet. "No, unfortunately I don't, for I am blind. That is why I am so awkward."

Out of the shocked silence Mrs. Paulden gave a little croon of pity. The moment before she had been speechless with indignation on her husband's behalf. Paulden felt as though he had struck a suffering animal. He stammered an apology and turned away to close the unfortunate door. Then he began to walk slowly down the hall.

"You wished to see me about something?" he remarked, with matter-of-fact civility. "Perhaps we had better go in here." He indicated the reception room where they had waited and followed them in. The admirable Mrs. Paulden gave no indication of wishing to join the party.

Carrados came to the point at once.

"Mr. Carlyle," he said, indicating his friend, "has recently been acting for the prosecution in a case of alleged poisoning that the Public Prosecutor has now taken up. I am interested in the defence. Both sides are thus before you, Mr. Paulden."

"How does this concern me?" asked Paulden with obvious surprise.

"You are experimenting with bhurine. The victim of this alleged crime undoubtedly lost his life by bhurine poisoning. Do you mind telling us when and where you acquired your stock of this scarce substance?"

"I have had – "

"No – a moment, Mr. Paulden, before you reply," struck in Carrados with arresting hand. "You must understand that nothing so grotesque as to connect you with a crime is contemplated. But a man is under arrest and the chief point against him is the half-ounce of bhurine that Lightcraft of Trenion Street sold to someone at half-past-five last Wednesday fortnight. Before you commit yourself to any statement that it may possibly be difficult to recede from, you should realise that this inquiry will be pushed to the very end."

"How do you know that I am using bhurine?"

"That," parried Carrados, "is a blind man's secret."

"Oh, well. And you say that someone has been arrested through this fact?"

"Yes. Possibly you have read something of the St. Abbots mushroom poisoning case?"

"I have no interest in the sensational ephemera of The Press. Very well. It was I who bought the bhurine from Lightcraft that Wednesday afternoon. I gave a false name and address, I must admit. I had a sufficient private reason for so doing."

"This knocks what is vulgarly termed 'the stuffing' out of the case for the prosecution," observed Carlyle, who had been taking a note. "It may also involve you in some trouble yourself, Mr. Paulden."

"I don't think that you need regard that very seriously in the circumstances," said Carrados reassuringly.

"They must find some scapegoat, you know," persisted Mr. Carlyle. "Loudham will raise Cain over it."

"I don't think so. Loudham, as the prosecution will roundly tell him, has only himself to thank for not giving a satisfactory account of his movements. Loudham will be lectured, Lightcraft will be fined the minimum, and Mr. Paulden will, I imagine, be told not to do it again."

The man before them laughed bitterly.

"There will be no occasion to do it again," he remarked. "Do you know anything of the circumstances?"

"Lightcraft told us something connected with colour photography. You distrust Mr. Lightcraft, I infer?"

Mr. Paulden came down to the heart-easing medium of the street.

"I've had some once, thanks," was what he said with terse expression. "Let me tell you. About eighteen months ago, I was on the edge of a great discovery in colour photography. It was my discovery, whatever you may have heard. Bhurine was the medium, and not being then so cautious or suspicious as I have reason to be now, and finding it difficult – really impossible – to procure this substance casually, I sent in an order to Lightcraft to procure me a stock. Unfortunately, in a moment of enthusiasm, I had hinted at the anticipated results to a man who was then my friend – a weakling called Southem. Comparing notes with Lightcraft, they put two and two together and in a trice most of the secret boiled over.

"If you have ever been within an ace of a monumental discovery, you will understand the torment of anxiety and self-reproach that possessed me. For months the result must have trembled in the balance, but even as it evaded me, so it evaded the others. And at last I was able to spread conviction that the bhurine process was a failure. I breathed again.

"You don't want to hear of the various things that conspired to baffle me. I proceeded with extreme caution and therefore slowly. About two

286

weeks ago I had another foretaste of success and immediately on it a veritable disaster. By some diabolical mischance I contrived to upset my stock bottle of bhurine. It rolled down, smashed to atoms on a developing dish filled with another chemical, and the precious lot was irretrievably lost. To arrest the experiments at that stage for a day was to lose a month. In one place and one alone could I hope to replenish the stock temporarily at such short notice, and to do it openly after my last experience filled me with dismay. Well, you know what happened, and now, I suppose, it will all come out."

A week after his arrest, Philip Loudham and his sister were sitting together in the drawing room at Hazlehurst, nervous and expectant. Loudham had been discharged scarcely six hours before, with such vindication of his character as the frigid intimation that there was no evidence against him afforded. On his arrival home he had found a letter from Max Carrados – a name with which he was now familiar – awaiting him. There had been other notes and telegrams – messages of sympathy and congratulation, but the man who had brought about his liberation did not include these conventionalities. He merely stated that he proposed calling upon Mr. Loudham at nine o'clock that evening and that he hoped it would be convenient for him and all other members of the household to be at home

"He can scarcely be coming to be thanked," speculated Loudham, breaking the silence that had fallen on them as the hour approached. "I should have called on him myself tomorrow."

Mrs. Dupreen assented absent-mindedly. Both were dressed in black, and both at that moment had the same thought: That they were dreaming this.

"I suppose you won't go on living here, Irene?" continued the brother, speaking to make the minutes seem tolerable.

This at least had the effect of bringing Mrs. Dupreen back into the present with a rush.

"Of course not," she replied almost sharply and looking at him direct. "Why should I, now?"

"Oh, all right," he agreed. "I didn't suppose you would." Then, as the front doorbell was heard to ring: "Thank Heaven!"

"Won't you go to meet him in the hall and bring him in?" suggested Mrs. Dupreen. "He is blind, you know."

Carrados was carrying a small leather case which he allowed Loudham to relieve him of, together with his hat and gloves. The introduction to Mrs. Dupreen was made, the blind man put in touch with a chair, and then Philip Loudham began to rattle off the acknowledgment of

287

gratitude of which he had been framing and rejecting openings for the last half-hour.

"I'm afraid it's no good attempting to thank you for the extraordinary service that you've rendered me, Mr. Carrados," he began, "and, above all, I appreciate the fact that, owing to you, it has been possible to keep Mrs. Guestling's name entirely out of the case. Of course you know all about that, and my sister knows, so it isn't worthwhile beating about the bush. Well, now that I shall have something like a decent income of my own, I shall urge Kitty – Mrs. Guestling – to apply for the divorce that she is richly entitled to, and when that is all settled we shall marry at once and try to forget the experiences on both sides that have led up to it. I hope," he added tamely, "that you don't consider us really much to blame?"

Carrados shook his head in mild deprecation.

"That is an ethical point that has lain outside the scope of my inquiry," he replied. "You would hardly imagine that I should disturb you at such a time merely to claim your thanks. Has it occurred to you why I should have come?"

Brother and sister exchanged looks and by their silence gave reply.

"We have still to find who poisoned Charlie Winpole."

Loudham stared at their guest in frank bewilderment. Mrs. Dupreen almost closed her eyes. When she spoke it was in a pained whisper.

"Is there anything more to be gained by pursuing that idea, Mr. Carrados?" she asked pleadingly. "We have passed through a week of anguish, coming upon a week of grief and great distress. Surely all has been done that can be done?"

"But you would have justice for your nephew if there has been foul play?" Mrs. Dupreen made a weary gesture of resignation. It was Loudham who took up the question.

"Do you really mean, Mr. Carrados, that there is any doubt about the cause?"

"Will you give me my case, please? Thank you." He opened it and produced a small paper bag. "Now a newspaper, if you will." He opened the bag and poured out the contents. "You remember stating at the inquest, Mrs. Dupreen, that the mushrooms you bought looked rather dry? They were dry, there is no doubt, for they had then been gathered four days. Here are some more under precisely the same conditions. They looked, in point of fact, like these?"

"Yes," admitted the lady, beginning to regard Carrados with a new and curious interest.

"Dr. Slark further stated that the only fungus containing the poison bhurine – the Amanita called the Black Cap, and also by the country folk the Devil's Scent Bottle – did not assume its forbidding appearance until

288

maturity. He was wrong in one sense there, for experiment proved that if the Black Cap is gathered in its young and deceptive stage and kept, it assumes precisely the same appearance as it withers as if it was ripening naturally. You observe." He opened a second bag and, shaking out the contents, displayed another little heap by the side of the first. "Gathered four days ago," he explained.

"Why, they are as black as ink," commented Loudham. "And the – *Phew!* – Aroma!"

"One would hardly have got through without you seeing it, Mrs. Dupreen?"

"I certainly hardly think so," she admitted.

"With due allowance for Lackington's biased opinion, I also think that his claim might be allowed. Finally, it is incredible that whoever peeled the mushrooms should have passed one of these. Who was the cook on that occasion, Mrs. Dupreen?"

"My maid Hilda. She does all the cooking."

"The one who admitted me?"

"Yes. She is the only servant I have, Mr. Carrados."

"I should like to have her in, if you don't mind."

"Certainly, if you wish it. She is – " Mrs. Dupreen felt that she must put in a favourable word before this inexorable man pronounced judgment. "She is a very good, straightforward girl."

"So much the better."

"I will – " Mrs. Dupreen rose and began to cross the room. "Ring for her? Thank you." And whatever her intention had been, the lady rang the bell.

"Yes, ma'am?"

A neat, modest-mannered girl, simple and nervous, with a face as full, as clear and as honest as an English apple. "A pity," thought Mrs. Dupreen, "that this confident, suspicious man cannot see her now."

"Come in, Hilda. This gentleman wants to ask you something."

"Yes, ma' am." The round, blue eyes went appealingly to Carrados, fell upon the fungi spread out before her, and then circled the room with an instinct of escape.

"You remember the night poor Charlie died, Hilda," said Carrados in his suavest tones. "You cooked some mushrooms for his supper, didn't you?"

"No, sir," came the glib reply.

"'No,' Hilda!" exclaimed Mrs. Dupreen in wonderment. "You mean 'Yes', surely, child. Of course you cooked them. Don't you remember?"

"Yes, ma'am," dutifully replied Hilda.

289

"That is all right," said the blind man reassuringly. "Nervous witnesses very often answer at random at first. You have nothing to be afraid of, my good girl, if you will tell the truth. I suppose you know a mushroom when you see it?"

"Yes, sir," was the rather hesitating reply.

"There was nothing like this among them?" He held up one of the poisonous sort.

"No, sir. Indeed there wasn't, sir. I should have known then."

"You would have known then? You were not called at the inquest, Hilda?"

"No, sir."

"If you had been, what would you have told them about these mushrooms that you cooked?"

"I – I don't know, sir."

"Come, come, Hilda. What could you have told them – something that we do not know? The truth, girl, if you want to save yourself?" Then with a sudden, terrible directness the question cleft her trembling, guilt-stricken little brain: "Where did you get the other mushrooms from that you put with those that your mistress brought?"

The eyes that had been mostly riveted to the floor leapt to Carrados for a single frightened glance, from Carrados to her mistress, to Philip Loudham, and to the floor again. In a moment her face changed and she was in a burst of sobbing"

"O-ho, o-ho, o-ho!" she wailed. "I didn't know. I didn't know. I meant no harm. Indeed I didn't, ma'am."

"Hilda! Hilda!" exclaimed Mrs. Dupreen in bewilderment. "What is it you're saying? What have you done?

"It was his own fault. O-ho, o-ho, o-ho!" Every word was punctuated by a gasp. "He always was a little pig and making himself ill with food. You know he was, ma'am, although you were so fond of him. I'm sure I'm not to blame."

"But what was it? What have you done?" besought her mistress.

"It was after you went out on that afternoon. He put on his things and slipped down into the kitchen without the master knowing. He said what you were getting for his dinner, ma'am, and that you never got enough of them. Then he told me not to tell about his being down, because he'd seen some white things from his bedroom window growing by the hedge at the bottom of the garden and he was going to get them. He brought in four or five and said they were mushrooms and asked me to cook them with the others and not say anything because you'd say too many were not good for him. And I didn't know any difference. Indeed I'm telling you the truth, ma'am."

"Oh, Hilda, Hilda!" was torn reproachfully from Mrs. Dupreen. "You know what we've gone through. Why didn't you tell us this before?"

"I was afraid. I was afraid of what they'd do. And no one ever guessed until I thought I was safe. Indeed I meant no harm to anyone, but I was afraid that they'd punish me instead." Carrados had risen and was picking up his things"

"Yes," he said, half-musing to himself, "I knew it must exist: The one explanation that accounts for everything and cannot be assailed. We have reached the bed-rock of truth at last."

The Ghost at Massingham Mansions

"**D**o you believe in ghosts, Max?" inquired Mr. Carlyle.

"Only as ghosts," replied Carrados with decision.

"Quite so," assented the private detective with the air of acquiescence with which he was wont to cloak his moments of obfuscation. Then he added cautiously: "And how don't you believe in them, pray?"

"As public nuisances – or private ones for that matter," replied his friend. "So long as they are content to behave as ghosts, I am with them. When they begin to meddle with a state of existence that is outside their province – to interfere in business matters and depreciate property – to rattle chains, bang doors, ring bells, predict winners. and to edit magazines and to attract attention instead of shunning it, I cease to believe. My sympathies are entirely with the sensible old fellow who was awakened in the middle of the night to find a shadowy form standing by the side of his bed and silently regarding him. For a few minutes the disturbed man waited patiently, expecting some awful communication, but the same profound silence was maintained. 'Well,' he remarked at length, 'if you have nothing to do, I have,' and turning over went to sleep again."

"I have been asked to take up a ghost," Carlyle began to explain.

"Then I don't believe in it," declared Carrados.

"Why not?"

"Because it is a pushful, notoriety-loving ghost, or it would not have gone so far. Probably it wants to get into *The Daily Mail*. The other people, whoever they are, don't believe in it either, Louis, or they wouldn't have called you in. They would have gone to Sir Oliver Lodge for an explanation, or to the nearest priest for a stoup of holy water."

"I admit that I shall direct my researches towards the forces of this world before I begin to investigate any other," conceded Louis Carlyle. "And I don't doubt," he added, with his usual bland complacence, "that I shall hale up some mischievous or aggrieved individual before the ghost is many days older. Now that you have brought me so far, do you care to go on round to the place with me, Max, to hear what they have to say about it?"

Carrados agreed with his usual good nature. He rarely met his friend without hearing the details of some new case, for Carlyle's practice had increased vastly since the night when chance had led him into the blind man's study. They discussed the cases according to their interest, and there the matter generally ended so far as Max Carrados was concerned, until he casually heard the result subsequently from Carlyle's lips or learned the sequel from the newspaper. But these pages are primarily a record of the methods of the one man whose name they bear and therefore for the occasional case that Carrados completed for his friend there must be assumed the unchronicled scores which the inquiry agent dealt capably with himself. This reminder is perhaps necessary to dissipate the impression that Louis Carlyle was a pretentious humbug. He was, as a matter of fact, in spite of his amiable foibles and the self-assurance that was, after all, merely an asset of his trade, a shrewd and capable business man of his world, and behind his office manner, nothing concerned him more than to pocket fees for which he felt that he had failed to render value.

Massingham Mansions proved to be a single block of residential flats overlooking a recreation ground. It was, as they afterwards found, an adjunct to a larger estate of similar property situated down another road. A porter, residing in the basement, looked after the interests of Massingham Mansions. The business office was placed among the other flats. On that morning it presented the appearance of a well-kept, prosperous-enough place, a little dull, a little unfurnished, a little depressing perhaps. In fact, faintly reminiscent of the superfluous mansions that stand among broad, weedy roads on the outskirts of overgrown seaside resorts – but it was persistently raining at the time when Mr. Carlyle had his first view of it.

"It is early to judge," he remarked, after stopping the car in order to verify the name on the brass plate, "but, upon my word, Max, I really think that our ghost might have discovered more appropriate quarters.

At the office, to which the porter had directed them, they found a managing clerk and two coltish youths in charge. Mr. Carlyle's name produced an appreciable flutter.

"The governor isn't here just now, but I have this matter in hand," said the clerk with an easy air of responsibility – an effect unfortunately marred by a sudden irrepressible giggle from the least overawed of the colts. "Will you kindly step into our private room?" He turned at the door of the inner office and dropped a freezing eye on the offender. "Get those letters copied before you go out to lunch, Binns," he remarked in a sufficiently loud voice. Then he closed the door quickly, before Binns could find a suitable retort.

So far it had been plain sailing, but now, brought face to face with the necessity of explaining, the clerk began to develop some hesitancy in beginning.

"It's a funny sort of business," he remarked, skirting the difficulty.

"Perhaps," admitted Mr. Carlyle. "But that will not embarrass us. Many of the cases that pass through my hands are what you would call 'funny sorts of business'."

"I suppose so," responded the young man, "but not through ours. Well, this is at No. 11 Massingham. A few nights ago – I suppose it must be more than a week now – Willett, the estate porter, was taking up some luggage to No. 75 Northanger for the people there when he noticed a light in one of the rooms at 11 Massingham. The backs face, though about twenty or thirty yards away. It struck him as curious, because 11 Massingham is empty and locked up. Naturally he thought at first that the porter at Massingham or one of us from the office had gone up for something. Still it was so unusual – being late at night – that it was his business to look into it. On his way round – You know where Massingham Mansions are? – he had to pass here. It was dark, for we'd all been gone hours, but Willett has duplicate keys and he let himself in. Then he began to think that something must be wrong, for here, hanging up against their number on the board, were the only two keys of 11 Massingham that there are supposed to be. He put the keys in his pocket and went on to Massingham. Green, the resident porter there, told him that he hadn't been into No. 11 for a week. What was more, no one had passed the outer door, in or out, for a good half-hour. He knew that, because the door 'springs' with a noise when it is opened, no matter how carefully. So the two of them went up. The door of No. 11 was locked and inside everything was as it should be. There was no light then, and after looking well round with the lanterns that they carried, they were satisfied that no one was concealed there.

"You say lanterns," interrupted Mr. Carlyle. "I suppose they lit the gas, or whatever it is there, as well?"

"It is gas, but they could not light it because it was cut off at the meter. We always cut it off when a flat becomes vacant."

"What sort of a light was it, then, that Willett saw?"

"It was gas, Mr. Carlyle. It is possible to see the bracket in that room from 75 Northanger. He saw it burning."

"Then the meter had been put on again?   "

"It is in a locked cupboard in the basement. Only the office and the porters have keys. They tried the gas in the room and it was dead out. They looked at the meter in the basement afterwards and it was dead off."

"Very good," observed Mr. Carlyle, noting the facts in his pocketbook. "What next?"

"The next," continued the clerk, "was something that had really happened before. When they got down again – Green and Willett – Green was rather chipping Willett about seeing the light, you know, when he stopped suddenly. He'd remembered something. The day before, the servant at 12 Massingham had asked him who it was that was using the bathroom at No. 11 – she of course knowing that it was empty. He told her that no one used the bathroom. 'Well,' she said, 'we hear the water running and splashing almost every night, and it's funny with no one there.' He had thought nothing of it at the time, concluding – as he told her – that it must be the water in the bathroom of one of the underneath flats that they heard. Of course he told Willett then, and they went up again and examined the bathroom more closely. Water had certainly been run there, for the sides of the bath were still wet. They tried the taps and not a drop came. When a flat is empty, we cut off the water like the gas."

"At the same place – the cupboard in the basement?" inquired Carlyle.

"No. At the cistern in the roof. The trap is at the top of the stairs and you need a longish ladder to get there. The next morning, Willett reported what he'd seen and the governor told me to look into it. We didn't think much of it so far. That night I happened to be seeing some friends to the station here – I live not so far off – and I thought I might as well take a turn round here on my way home. I knew that if a light was burning, I should be able to see the window lit up from the yard at the back, although the gas itself would be out of sight. And, sure enough, there was the light blazing out of one of the windows of No. 11. I won't say that I didn't feel a bit homesick then, but I'd made up my mind to go up."

"Good man," murmured Mr. Carlyle approvingly.

"Wait a bit," recommended the clerk, with a shame-faced laugh. "So far I had only had to make my mind up. It was then close on midnight and not a soul about. I came here for the keys, and I also had the luck to remember an old revolver that had been lying about in a drawer of the office for years. It wasn't loaded, but it didn't seem quite so lonely with it. I put it in my pocket and went on to Massingham, taking another turn into the yard to see that the light was still on. Then I went up the stairs as quietly as I could and let myself into No. 11."

"You didn't take Willett or Green with you?"

The clerk gave Mr. Carlyle a knowing look, as of one smart man who will be appreciated by another.

"Willett's a very trustworthy chap," he replied, "and we have every confidence in him. Green also, although he has not been with us so long. But I thought it just as well to do it on my own, you understand, Mr. Carlyle. You didn't look in at Massingham on your way? Well, if you had, you would have seen that there is a pane of glass above every door, frosted glass to the hall doors and plain over each of those inside. It's to light the halls and passages, you know. Each flat has a small square hall and a longish passage leading off it. As soon as I opened the door, I could tell that one of the rooms down the passage was lit up, though I could not see the door of it from there. Then I crept very quietly through the hall into the passage. A regular stream of light was shining from above the end door on the left. The room, I knew, was the smallest in the flat – it's generally used for a servant's bedroom or sometimes for a box room. It was a bit thick, you'll admit – right at the end of a long passage and midnight, and after what the others had said."

"Yes, yes," assented the inquiry agent. "But you went on?"

"I went on, tiptoeing without a sound. I got to the door, took out my pistol, put my hand almost on the handle and then – "

"Well, well," prompted Mr. Carlyle, as the narrator paused provokingly, with the dramatic instinct of an expert raconteur. "What then?"

"Then the light went out. While my hand was within an inch of the handle the light went out, as clean as if I had been watched all along and the thing timed. It went out all at once, without any warning, and without the slightest sound from the beastly room beyond. And then it was as black as Hell in the passage, and something seemed to be going to happen."

"What did you do?

"I did a slope," acknowledged the clerk frankly. "I broke all the records down that passage, I bet you. You'll laugh, I dare say, and think you would have stood, but you don't know what it was like. I'd been screwing myself up, wondering what I should see in that lighted room when I opened the door, and then the light went out like a knife, and for all I knew the next second the door would open on me in the dark and Christ only knows what come out."

"Probably I should have run also," conceded Mr. Carlyle tactfully. "And you, Max?"

"You see, I always feel at home in the dark," apologised the blind man. "At all events, you got safely away, Mr. –?"

"My name's Elliott," responded the clerk. "Yes, you may bet I did. Whether the door opened and anybody or anything came out or not I can't say. I didn't look. I certainly did get an idea that I heard the bath water running and swishing as I snatched at the hall door, but I didn't stop to consider that either, and if it was, the noise was lost in the slam of the door and my clatter as I took about twelve flights of stairs six steps at a time. Then, when I was safely out, I did venture to go round to look up again, and there was that damned light full on again."

"Really?" commented Mr. Carlyle. "That was very audacious of him."

"Him? Oh, well, yes, I suppose so. That's what the governor insists, but he hasn't been up there himself in the dark."

"Is that as far as you have got?"

"It's as far as we can get. The bally thing goes on just as it likes. The very next day, we tied up the taps of the gas – meter and the water cistern and sealed the string. Bless you, it didn't make a ha'peth of difference. Scarcely a night passes without the light showing, and there's no doubt that the water runs. We've put copying ink on the door handles and the taps and got into it ourselves until there isn't a man about the place that you couldn't implicate."

"Has anyone watched up there?"

"Willett and Green together did one night. They shut themselves up in the room opposite from ten till twelve and nothing happened. I was watching the window with a pair of opera-glasses from an empty flat here – 85 Northanger. Then they chucked it, and before they could have been down the steps the light was there – I could see the gas as plain as I can see this ink-stand. I ran down and met them coming to tell me that nothing had happened. The three of us sprinted up again and the light was out and the flat as deserted as a churchyard. What do you make of that?"

"It certainly requires looking into," replied Mr. Carlyle diplomatically.

"Looking into! Well, you're welcome to look all day and all night too, Mr. Carlyle. It isn't as though it was an old baronial mansion, you see, with sliding panels and secret passages. The place has the date over the front door, 1882 – 1882 and haunted, by gosh! It was built for what it is, and there isn't an inch unaccounted for between the slates and the foundation."

"These two things – the light and the water running – are the only indications there have been?" asked Mr. Carlyle.

"So far as we ourselves have seen or heard. I ought perhaps to tell you of something else, however. When this business first started, I made a few casual inquiries here and there among the tenants. Among others I saw Mr. Belting, who occupies No. 9 Massingham – the flat directly beneath No. 11. It didn't seem any good making up a cock-and-bull story, so I put it to him plainly – Had he been annoyed by anything unusual going on at the empty flat above?

"'If you mean your confounded ghost up there, I have not been particularly annoyed,' he said at once, 'but Mrs. Belting has, and I should advise you to keep out of her way, at least until she gets another servant.' Then he told me that their girl, who slept in the bedroom underneath the little one at No. 11, had been going on about noises in the room above – footsteps and tramping and a bump on the floor – for some time before we heard anything of it. Then one day she suddenly said that she'd had enough of it and bolted. That was just before Willett first saw the light."

"It is being talked about, then – among the tenants?"

"You bet!" assented Mr. Elliott pungently. "That's what gets the governor. He wouldn't give a continental if no one knew, but you can't tell where it will end. The people at Northanger don't half-like it either. All the children are scared out of their little wits and none of the slaveys will run errands after dark. It'll give the estate a bad name for the next three years if it isn't stopped."

"It shall be stopped," declared Mr. Carlyle impressively. "Of course we have our methods for dealing with this sort of thing, but in order to make a clean sweep, it is desirable to put our hands on the offender *in flagranti delicto*. Tell your – er – principal not to have any further concern in the matter. One of my people will call here for any further details that he may require during the day. Just leave everything as it is in the meanwhile. Good morning, Mr. Elliott, good morning . . . ."

"A fairly obvious game, I imagine, Max," he commented as they got into the car, "although the details are original and the motive not disclosed as yet. I wonder how many of them are in it?"

"Let me know when you find out," said Carrados, and Mr. Carlyle promised.

Nearly a week passed and the expected revelation failed to make its appearance. Then, instead, quite a different note arrived:

My dear Max,

    I wonder if you formed any conclusion of that Massingham Mansions affair from Mr. Elliott's refined narrative of the circumstances.

    I begin to suspect that Trigget, whom I put on, is somewhat of an ass, though a very remarkable circumstance has come to light which might – if it wasn't a matter of business – offer an explanation of the whole business by stamping it as inexplicable.

    You know how I value your suggestions. If you happen to be in the neighbourhood – not otherwise, Max, I protest – I should be glad if you would drop in for a chat.

Yours sincerely,

Louis Carlyle

Carrados smiled at the ingenuous transparency of the note. He had thought several times of the case since the interview with Elliott, chiefly because he was struck by certain details of the manifestation that divided it from the ordinary methods of the bogy-raiser, an aspect that had apparently made no particular impression on his friend. He was sufficiently interested not to let the day pass without "happening" to be in the neighbourhood of Bampton Street.

"Max," exclaimed Mr. Carlyle, raising an accusing forefinger, "you have come on purpose."

"If I have," replied the visitor, "you can reward me with a cup of that excellent beverage that you were able to conjure up from somewhere down in the basement on a former occasion. As a matter of fact, I have."

Mr. Carlyle transmitted the order and then demanded his friend's serious attention.

"That ghost at Massingham Mansions – "

"I still don't believe in that particular ghost, Louis," commented Carrados in mild speculation.

"I never did, of course," replied Carlyle, "but, upon my word, Max, I shall have to very soon as a precautionary measure. Trigget has been able to do nothing and now he has as good as gone on strike."

"Downed – Now what on earth can an inquiry man down to go on strike, Louis? Notebooks? So Trigget has got a chill, like our candid friend Eliott, eh?"

"He started all right – said that he didn't mind spending a night or a week in a haunted flat, and, to do him justice, I don't believe he did at first. Then he came across a very curious piece of forgotten local history, a very remarkable – er – coincidence in the circumstances, Max."

"I was wondering," said Carrados, "when we should come up against that story, Louis."

"Then you know of it?" exclaimed the inquiry agent in surprise.

"Not at all. Only I guessed it must exist. Here you have the manifestation associated with two things which in themselves are neither usual nor awe-inspiring – the gas and the water. It requires some association to connect them up, to give them point and force. That is the story."

"Yes," assented his friend, "that is the story, and, upon my soul, in the circumstances – well, you shall hear it. It comes partly from the newspapers of many years ago, but only partly, for the circumstances were successfully hushed up in a large measure and it required the stimulated memories of ancient scandal-mongers to fill in the details. Oh yes, it was a scandal, Max, and would have been a great sensation too, I do not doubt, only they had no proper pictorial press in those days, poor beggars. It was

299

very soon after Massingham Mansions had been erected – they were called Enderby House in those days, by the way, for the name was changed on account of this very business. The household at No. 11 consisted of a comfortable, middle-aged married couple and one servant, a quiet and attractive young creature, one is led to understand. As a matter of fact, I think they were the first tenants of that flat."

"The first occupants give the soul to a new house," remarked the blind man gravely. "That is why empty houses have their different characters."

"I don't doubt it for a moment," assented Mr. Carlyle in his incisive way, "but none of our authorities on this case made any reference to the fact. They did say, however, that the man held a good and responsible position – a position for which high personal character and strict morality were essential. He was also well known and regarded in quiet but substantial local circles where serious views prevailed. He was, in short, a man of notorious 'respectability'."

"The first chapter of the tragedy opened with the painful death of the prepossessing handmaiden – suicide, poor creature. She didn't appear one morning and the flat was full of the reek of gas. With great promptitude, the master threw all the windows open and called up the porter. They burst open the door of the little bedroom at the end of the passage, and there was the thing as clear as daylight for any Coroner's Jury to see. The door was locked on the inside and the extinguished gas was turned full on. It was only a tiny room, with no fireplace, and the ventilation of a closed well-fitting door and window was negligible in the circumstances. At all events, the girl was proved to have been dead for several hours when they reached her, and the doctor who conducted the autopsy crowned the convincing fabric of circumstances when he mentioned as delicately as possible that the girl had a very pressing reason for dreading an inevitable misfortune that would shortly overtake her. The jury returned the obvious verdict.

"There have been a great many undiscovered crimes in the history of mankind, Max, but it is by no means every ingenious plot that carries. After the inquest, at which our gentleman doubtless cut a very proper and impressive figure, the barbed whisper began to insinuate and to grow in freedom. It is sheerly impossible to judge how these things start, but we know that when once they have been begun, they gather material like an avalanche. It was remembered by someone at the flat underneath that late on the fatal night, a window in the principal bedroom above had been heard to open, top and bottom, very quietly. Certain other sounds of movement in the night did not tally with the tale of sleep-wrapped innocence.

"Sceptical busybodies were anxious to demonstrate practically to those who differed from them on this question that it was quite easy to extinguish a gas-jet in one room by blowing down the gas-pipe in another, and in this connection there was evidence that the lady of the flat had spoken to her friends more than once of her sentimental young servant's extravagant habit of reading herself to sleep occasionally with the light full on. Why was nothing heard at the inquest, they demanded, of the curious fact that an open novelette lay on the counterpane when the room was broken into?

A hundred trifling circumstances were adduced – arrangements that the girl had been making for the future down to the last evening of her life – interpretable hints that she had dropped to her acquaintances – her views on suicide and the best means to that end: A favourite topic, it would seem, among her class – her possession of certain comparatively expensive trinkets on a salary of a very few shillings a week, and so on. Finally, some rather more definite and important piece of evidence must have been conveyed to the authorities, for we know now that one fine day a warrant was issued. Somehow rumour preceded its execution. The eminently respectable gentleman with whom it was concerned did not wait to argue out the merits of the case. He locked himself in the bathroom, and when the police arrived they found that instead of an arrest, they had to arrange the details for another inquest."

"A very convincing episode," conceded Carrados in response to his friend's expectant air. "And now her spirit passes the long winter evenings turning the gas on and off, and the one amusement of his consists in doing the same with the bath-water – or the other way, the other way about, Louis. Truly, one half the world knows not how the other half lives!"

"All your cheap humour won't induce Trigget to spend another night in that flat, Max," retorted Mr. Carlyle. "Nor, I am afraid, will it help me through this business in any other way."

"Then I'll give you a hint that may," said Carrados. "Try your respectable gentleman's way of settling difficulties."

"What is that?" demanded his friend.

"Blow down the pipes, Louis."

"Blow down the pipes?" repeated Carlyle.

"At all events try it. I infer that Mr. Trigget has not experimented in that direction."

"But what will it do, Max?"

"Possibly it will demonstrate where the other end goes to."

"But the other end goes to the meter."

"I suggest not – not without some interference with its progress. I have already met your Mr. Trigget, you know, Louis. An excellent and reliable man within his limits, but he is at his best posted outside the door of a hotel waiting to see the co-respondent go in. He hasn't enough imagination for this case – not enough to carry him away from what would be his own obvious method of doing it to what is someone else's equally obvious but quite different method. Unless I am doing him an injustice, he will have spent most of his time trying to catch someone getting into the flat to turn the gas and water on and off, whereas I conjecture that no one does go into the flat because it is perfectly simple – ingenious but simple – to produce these phenomena without. Then, when Mr. Trigget has satisfied himself that it is physically impossible for anyone to be going in and out, and when, on the top of it, he comes across this romantic tragedy – a tale that might psychologically explain the ghost, simply because the ghost is moulded on the tragedy – then, of course, Mr. Trigget's mental process is swept away from its moorings and his feet begin to get cold."

"This is very curious and suggestive," said Mr. Carlyle. "I certainly assumed – But shall we have Trigget up and question him on the point? I think he ought to be here now – if he isn't detained at the Bull."

Carrados assented, and in a few minutes Mr. Trigget presented himself at the door of the private office. He was a melancholy-looking middle-aged little man, with an ineradicable air of being exactly what he was, and the searcher for deeper or subtler indications of character would only be rewarded by a latent pessimism grounded on the depressing probability that he would never be anything else.

"Come in, Trigget," called out Mr. Carlyle when his employee diffidently appeared. "Come in. Mr. Carrados would like to hear some of the details of the Massingham Mansions case."

"Not the first time I have availed myself of the benefit of your inquiries, Mr. Trigget," nodded the blind man. "Good afternoon."

"Good afternoon, sir," replied Trigget, with gloomy deference. "It's very handsome of you to put it in that way, Mr. Carrados, sir. But this isn't another Tarporley-Templeton case, if I may say so, sir. That was as plain as a pikestaff after all, sir."

"When we saw the pikestaff, Mr. Trigget. Yes, it was," admitted Carrados, with a smile. "But this is insoluble? Ah, well. When I was a boy I used to be extraordinarily fond of ghost stories, I remember, but even while reading them, I always had an uneasy suspicion that when it came to the necessary detail of explaining the mystery, I should be defrauded with some subterfuge as 'by an ingenious arrangement of hidden wires the artful Muggles had contrived', etc., or 'an optical illusion effected by means of concealed mirrors revealed the *modus operandi* of the apparition'. I thought that I had been swindled. I think so still. I hope there are no ingenious wires or concealed mirrors here, Mr. Trigget?"

Mr. Trigget looked mildly sagacious but hopelessly puzzled. It was his misfortune that in him the necessities of his business and the proclivities of his nature were at variance, so that he ordinarily presented the curious anomaly of looking equally alert and tired.

"Wires, sir?" he began, with faint amusement.

"Not only wires, but anything that might account for what is going on," interposed Mr. Carlyle. "Mr. Carrados means this, Trigget: You have reported that it is impossible for anyone to be concealed in the flat or to have secret access to it – "

"I have tested every inch of space in all the rooms, Mr. Carrados, sir," protested the hurt Trigget. "I have examined every board and, you may say, every nail in the floor, the skirting-boards, the window frames, and in fact wherever a board or a nail exists. There are no secret ways in or out. Then I have taken the most elaborate precautions against the doors and windows being used for surreptitious ingress and egress. They have not been used, sir. For the past week I am the only person who has been in and out of the flat, Mr. Carrados, and yet night after night the gas that is cut off at the meter is lit and turned out again, and the water that is cut off at the cistern splashes about in the bath up to the second I let myself in. Then it's as quiet as the grave and everything is exactly as I left it. It isn't human, Mr. Carrados, sir, and flesh and blood can't stand it – not in the middle of the night, that is to say."

"You see nothing further, Mr. Trigget?"

"I don't indeed, Mr. Carrados. I would suggest doing away with the gas in that room altogether. As a box room it wouldn't need one."

"And the bathroom?"

"That might be turned into a small bedroom and all the water fittings removed. Then to provide a bathroom – "

"Yes, yes," interrupted Mr. Carlyle impatiently, "but we are retained to discover who in causing this annoyance and to detect the means, not to suggest structural alterations in the flat, Trigget. The fact is that after having put in a week on this job, you have failed to bring us an inch nearer its solution. Now Mr. Carrados has suggested – " Mr. Carlyle was not usually detained among the finer shades of humour, but some appreciation of the grotesqueness of the advice required him to control his voice as he put the matter in its baldest form. "Mr. Carrados has suggested that instead of spending the time measuring the chimneys and listening to the wall-paper, if you had simply blown down the gas-pipe – "

Carrados was inclined to laugh, although he thought it rather too bad of Louis.

"Not quite in those terms, Mr. Trigget," he interposed.

"Blow down the gas-pipe, sir?" repeated the amazed man. "What for?"

"To ascertain where the other end comes out," replied Carlyle.

303

"But don't you see, sir, that that is a detail until you ascertain how it is being done? The pipe may be tapped between the bath and the cistern. Naturally, I considered that. As a matter of fact, the water-pipe isn't tapped. It goes straight up from the bath to the cistern in the attic above, a distance of only a few feet, and I have examined it The gas-pipe, it is true, passes through a number of flats, and without pulling up all the floors it isn't practicable to trace it. But how does that help us, Mr. Carrados? The gas-tap has to be turned on and off. You can't do that with these hidden wires. It has to be lit. I've never heard of lighting gas by optical illusions, sir. Somebody must get in and out of the flat or else it isn't human. I've spent a week, a very trying week, sir, in endeavouring to ascertain how it could be done. I haven't shirked cold and wet and solitude, sir, in the discharge of my duty. I've freely placed my poor gifts of observation and intelligence, such as they are, at the service – "

"Not 'freely', Trigget," interposed his employer with decision.

"I am speaking under a deep sense of injury, Mr. Carlyle," retorted Mr. Trigget, who, having had time to think it over, had now come to the conclusion that he was not appreciated. "I am alluding to a moral attitude such as we all possess. I am very grieved by what has been suggested. I didn't expect it of you, Mr. Carlyle, sir. Indeed, I did not. For a week I have done everything that it has been possible to do, everything that a long experience could suggest, and now, as I understand it, sir, you complain that I didn't blow down the gas-pipe, sir. It's hard, sir. It's very hard."

"Oh, well, for Heaven's sake don't cry about it, Trigget," exclaimed Mr. Carlyle. "You're always sobbing about the place over something or other. We know you did your best – God help you!" he added aside.

"I did, Mr. Carlyle. Indeed I did, sir. And I thank you for that appreciative tribute to my services. I value it highly, very highly indeed, sir." A tremulous note in the rather impassioned delivery made it increasingly plain that Mr. Trigget's regimen had not been confined entirely to solid food that day. His wrongs were forgotten and he approached Mr. Carrados with an engaging air of secrecy.

"What is this tip about blowing down the gas-pipe, sir?" he whispered confidentially. "The old dog's always willing to learn something new."

"Max," said Mr. Carlyle curtly, "is there anything more that we need detain Trigget for?"

"Just this," replied Carrados after a moment's thought. "The gas-bracket – it has a mantle attachment on?"

"Oh no, Mr. Carrados," confided the old dog with the affectation of imparting rather valuable information. "Not a mantle on. Oh, certainly no mantle. Indeed – indeed, not a mantle at all."

Mr. Carlyle looked at his friend curiously. It was half-evident that something might have miscarried. Furthermore, it was obvious that the warmth of the room and the stress of emotion were beginning to have a disastrous effect on the level of Mr. Trigget's ideas and speech.

"A globe?" suggested Carrados.

"A globe? No sir, not even a globe, in the strict sense of the word. No globe, that is to say, Mr. Carrados. In fact, nothing like a globe."

"What is there, then?" demanded the blind man without any break in his unruffled patience. "There may be another way – but surely – surely there must be some attachment?"

"No," said Mr. Trigget with precision, "no attachment at all. Nothing at all. Nothing whatsoever. Just the ordinary or common or penny plain gas-jet, and above it the what you may call it thingamabob."

"The shade – gas consumer – of course!" exclaimed Carrados. "That is it."

"The tin thingamabob," insisted Mr. Trigget with slow dignity. "Call it what you will. Its purpose is self-evident. It acts as a dispirator – a distributor, that is to say – "

"Louis," struck in Carrados joyously, "are you good for settling it tonight?"

"Certainly, my dear fellow, if you can really give the time."

"Good. It's years since I last tackled a ghost. What about?" His look indicated the other member of the council.

"Would he be of any assistance?"

"Perhaps – then."

"What time?"

"Say eleven-thirty."

"Trigget," rapped out his employer sharply, "meet us at the corner of Middlewood and Enderby Roads at half-past-eleven sharp tonight. If you can't manage it, I shall not require your services again."

"Certainly, sir. I shall not fail to be punctual," replied Trigget without a tremor. The appearance of an almost incredible sobriety had possessed him in the face of warning, and both in speech and manner he was again exactly the man as he had entered the room. "I regard it as a great honour, Mr. Carrados, to be associated with you in this business, sir."

"In the meanwhile," remarked Carrados, "if you find the time hang heavy on your hands, you might look up the subject of 'platinum black'. It may be the new tip you want."

"Certainly, sir. But do you mind giving me a hint as to what 'platinum black' is?"

305

"It is a chemical that has the remarkable property of igniting hydrogen or coal gas by mere contact," replied Carrados. "Think how useful that may be if you haven't got a match!"

To mark the happy occasion, Mr. Carlyle had insisted on taking his friend off to witness a popular musical comedy. Carrados had a few preparations to make, a few accessories to procure for the night's work, but the whole business had come within the compass of an hour and the theatre spanned the interval between dinner at the Palm Tree and the time when they left the car at the appointed meeting-place. Mr. Trigget was already there, in an irreproachable state of normal dejection. Parkinson accompanied the party, bringing with him the baggage of the expedition.

"Anything going on, Trigget?" inquired Mr. Carlyle.

"I've made a turn round the place, sir, and the light was on," was the reply. "I didn't go up for fear of disturbing the conditions before you saw them. That was about ten minutes ago. Are you going into the yard to look again? I have all the keys, of course."

"Do we, Max?" queried Mr. Carlyle.

"Mr. Trigget might. We need not all go. He can catch us up again."

He caught them up again before they had reached the outer door.

"It's still on, sir," he reported.

"Do we use any special caution, Max?" asked Carlyle.

"Oh, no. Just as though we were friends of the ghost, calling in the ordinary way."

Trigget, who retained the keys, preceded the party up the stairs till the top was reached. He stood a moment at the door of No. 11, examining, by the light of the electric lamp he carried, his private marks there and pointing out to the others in a whisper that they had not been tampered with. All at once a most dismal wail, lingering, piercing and ending in something like a sob that died away because the life that gave it utterance had died with it, drawled forebodingly through the echoing emptiness of the deserted flat. Trigget had just snapped off his light and in the darkness a startled exclamation sprang from Mr. Carlyle's lips.

"It's all right, sir," said the little man, with a private satisfaction that he had the diplomacy to conceal. "Bit creepy, isn't it? Especially when you hear it by yourself up here for the first time. It's only the end of the bath-water running out."

He had opened the door and was conducting them to the room at the end of the passage. A faint aurora had been visible from that direction when they first entered the hall, but it was cut off before they could identify its source.

"That's what happens," muttered Trigget.

He threw open the bedroom door without waiting to examine his marks there and they crowded into the tiny chamber. Under the beams of the lamps they carried it was brilliantly though erratically illuminated. All turned towards the central object of their quest, a tarnished gas-bracket of the plainest description. A few inches above it hung the metal disc that Trigget had alluded to, for the ceiling was low and at that point it was brought even nearer to the gas by corresponding with the slant of the roof outside."

With the prescience so habitual with him that it had ceased to cause remark among his associates, Carrados walked straight to the gas-bracket and touched the burner.

"Still warm," he remarked. "And so are we getting now. A thoroughly material ghost, you perceive, Louis."

"But still turned off, don't you see, Mr. Carrados, sir," put in Trigget eagerly. "And yet no one's passed out."

"Still turned off – and still turned on," commented the blind man.

"What do you mean, Max?"

"The small screwdriver, Parkinson," requested Carrados.

"Well, upon my word!" dropped Mr. Carlyle expressively. For in no longer time than it takes to record the fact, Max Carrados had removed a screw and then knocked out the tap. He held it up towards them and they all at once saw that so much of the metal had been filed away that the gas passed through no matter how the tap stood. "How on earth did you know of that?"

"Because it wasn't practicable to do the thing in any other way. Now unhook the shade, Parkinson – carefully."

The warning was not altogether unnecessary, for the man had to stand on tiptoes before he could comply. Carrados received the dingy metal cone and lightly touched its inner surface.

"Ah, here, at the apex, to be sure," he remarked. "The gas is bound to get there. And there, Louis, you have an ever-lit and yet a truly 'safety' match – so far as gas is concerned. You can buy the thing for a shilling, I believe."

Mr. Carlyle was examining the tiny apparatus with interest. So small that it might have passed for the mummy of a midget hanging from a cobweb, it appeared to consist of an insignificant black pellet and an inch of the finest wire.

"Umm, I've never heard of it. And this will really light the gas?"

"As often as you like. That is the whole bag of tricks."

Mr. Carlyle turned a censorious eye upon his lieutenant, but Trigget was equal to the occasion and met it without embarrassment.

"I hadn't heard of it either, sir," he remarked conversationally. "Gracious, what won't they be getting out next, Mr. Carlyle!"

"Now for the mystery of the water." Carrados was finding his way to the bathroom and they followed him down the passage and across the hall. "In its way, I think that this is really more ingenious than the gas, for, as Mr. Trigget has proved for us, the water does not come from the cistern. The taps, you perceive, are absolutely dry.

"It is forced up?" suggested Mr. Carlyle, nodding towards the outlet.

"That is the obvious alternative. We will test it presently." The blind man was down on his hands and knees following the lines of the different pipes. "Two degrees more cold are not conclusive, because in any case the water had gone out that way. Mr. Trigget, you know the ropes. Will you be so obliging as to go up to the cistern and turn the water on."

"I shall need a ladder, sir."

"Parkinson."

"We have a folding ladder out here," said Parkinson, touching Mr. Trigget's arm.

"One moment," interposed Carrados, rising from his investigation among the pipes. "This requires some care. I want you to do it without making a sound or showing a light, if that is possible. Parkinson will help you. Wait until you hear us raising a diversion at the other end of the flat. Come, Louis."

The diversion took the form of tapping the wall and skirting-board in the other haunted room. When Trigget presented himself to report that the water was now on, Carrados put him to continue the singular exercise with Mr. Carlyle while he himself slipped back to the bathroom.

"The pump, Parkinson," he commanded in a brisk whisper to his man, who was waiting in the hall.

The appliance was not unlike a powerful tyre pump with some modifications. One tube from it was quickly fitted to the outlet pipe of the bath, another trailed a loose end into the bath itself, ready to take up the water. There were a few other details, the work of moments. Then Carrados turned on the tap, silencing the inflow by the attachment of a short length of rubber tube. When the water had risen a few inches he slipped off to the other room, told his rather mystified confederates there that he wanted a little more noise and bustle put into their performance, and was back again in the bathroom.

"Now, Parkinson," he directed, and turned off the tap. There was about a foot of water in the bath.

Parkinson stood on the broad base of the pump and tried to drive down the handle. It scarcely moved.

"Harder," urged Carrados, interpreting every detail of sound with perfect accuracy.

Parkinson set his teeth and lunged again. Again he seemed to come up against a solid wall of resistance.

"Keep trying. Something must give," said his master encouragingly. "Here, let me – " He threw his weight into the balance and for a moment they hung like a group poised before action. Then, somewhere, something did give and the sheathing plunger "drew".

"Now like blazes till the bath is empty. Then you can tell the others to stop hammering." Parkinson, looking round to acquiesce, found himself alone, for with silent step and quickened senses, Carrados was already passing down the dark flights of the broad stone stairway.

It was perhaps three minutes later when an excited gentleman in the state of disrobement that is tacitly regarded as falling upon the *punctum caecum* in times of fire, flood, and nocturnal emergency shot out of the door of No.7 and bounding up the intervening flights of steps pounded with the knocker on the door of No. 9. As someone did not appear with the instantaneity of a jack-in-the-box, he proceeded to repeat the summons, interspersing it with an occasional "I say!" shouted through the letter-box.

The light above the door made it unconvincing to affect that no one was at home. The gentleman at the door trumpeted the fact through his channel of communication and demanded instant attention. So immersed was he with his own grievance, in fact, that he failed to notice the approach of someone on the other side, and the sudden opening of the door, when it did take place, surprised him on his knees at his neighbour's doorstep, a large and consequential-looking personage as revealed in the light from the hall, wearing the silk hat that he had instinctively snatched up, but with his braces hanging down.

"Mr. Tupworthy of No. 7, isn't it?" quickly interposed the new man before his visitor could speak. "But why this – homage? Permit me to raise you, sir."

"Confound it all," snorted Mr. Tupworthy indignantly, "you're flooding my flat. The water's coming through my bathroom ceiling in bucketfuls. The plaster'll fall next. Can't you stop it? Has a pipe burst or something?"

"Something, I imagine," replied No. 9 with serene detachment. "At all events it appears to be over now."

"So I should hope," was the irate retort. "It's bad enough as it is. I shall go round to the office and complain. I'll tell you what it is, Mr. Belting: These mansions are becoming a pandemonium, sir, a veritable pandemonium".

"Capital idea. We'll go together and complain: Two will be more effective," suggested Mr. Belting. "But not tonight, Mr. Tupworthy. We should not find anyone there. The office will be closed. Say tomorrow – "

"I had no intention of anything so preposterous as going there tonight. I am in no condition to go. If I don't get my feet into hot water at once I shall be laid up with a severe cold. Doubtless you haven't noticed it, but I am wet through to the skin. Saturated, sir." Mr. Belting shook his head sagely.

"Always a mistake to try to stop water coming through the ceiling," he remarked. "It will come, you know. Finds its own level and all that."

"I did not try to stop it – at least not voluntarily. A temporary emergency necessitated a slight rearrangement of our accommodation. I – I tell you this in confidence – I was sleeping in the bathroom."

At the revelation of so notable a catastrophe Mr. Belting actually seemed to stagger. Possibly his eyes filled with tears. Certainly he had to turn and wipe away his emotion before he could proceed.

"Not – not right under it?" he whispered.

"I imagine so," replied Mr. Tupworthy. "I do not conceive that I could have been placed more centrally. I received the full cataract in the region of the ear. Well, if I may rely on you that it has stopped, I will terminate our interview for the present."

"Good night," responded the still tremulous Belting. "Good night – or good morning, to be exact." He waited with the door open to light the first flight of stairs for Mr. Tupworthy's descent. Before the door was closed another figure stepped down quietly from the obscurity of the steps leading upwards.

"Mr. Belting, I believe?" said the stranger. "My name is Carrados. I have been looking over the flat above. Can you spare me a few minutes?"

"What, Mr. Max Carrados?"

"The same," smiled the owner of the name.

"Come in, Mr. Carrados," exclaimed Belting, not only without embarrassment, but with positive affection in his voice. "Come in, by all means. I've heard of you more than once. Delighted to meet you. This way. I know – I know." He put a hand on his guest's arm and insisted on steering his course until he deposited him in an easy-chair before a fire. "This looks like being a great night. What will you have?"

Carrados put the suggestion aside and raised a corner of the situation.

"I'm afraid that I don't come altogether as a friend," he hinted.

"It's no good," replied his host. "I can't regard you in any other light after this. You heard Tupworthy? But you haven't seen the man, Mr. Carrados. I know – I've heard – but no wealth of the imagination can ever really quite reconstruct Tupworthy, the shoddy magnifico, in his immense

310

porcine complacency, his monumental self-importance. And sleeping right underneath! Gods, but we have lived tonight! Why – why ever did you stop?"

"You associate me with this business?"

"Associate you! My dear Mr. Carrados, I give you the full glorious credit for the one entirely successful piece of low-comedy humour in real life that I have ever encountered. Indeed, in a legal and pecuniary sense, I hold you absolutely responsible."

"Oh!" exclaimed Carrados, beginning to laugh quietly. Then he continued: "I think that I shall come through that all right. I shall refer you to Mr. Carlyle, the private inquiry agent, and he will doubtless pass you on to your landlord, for whom he is acting, and I imagine that he in turn will throw all the responsibility on the ingenious gentleman who has put them to so much trouble. Can you guess the result of my investigation in the flat above?"

"Guess, Mr. Carrados? I don't need to guess: I know. You don't suppose I thought for a moment that such transparent devices as two intercepted pipes and an automatic gas-lighter would impose on a man of intelligence? They were only contrived to mystify the credulous imagination of clerks and porters."

"You admit it, then?"

"Admit! Good gracious, of course I admit it, Mr. Carrados. What's the use of denying it?"

"Precisely. I am glad you see that. And yet you seem far from being a mere practical joker. Does your confidence extend to the length of letting me into your object?"

"Between ourselves," replied Mr. Belting, "I haven't the least objection. But I wish that you would have – say a cup of coffee. Mrs. Belting is still up, I believe. She would be charmed to have the opportunity No? Well, just as you like. Now, my object? You must understand, Mr. Carrados, that I am a man of sufficient leisure and adequate means for the small position we maintain. But I am not unoccupied – not idle. On the contrary, I am always busy. I don't approve of any man passing his time aimlessly. I have a number of interests in life – hobbies, if you like. You should appreciate that, as you are a private criminologist. I am – among other things which don't concern us now – a private retributionist. On every side, people are becoming far too careless and negligent. An era of irresponsibility has set in. Nobody troubles to keep his word, to carry out literally his undertakings. In my small way, I try to set that right by showing them the logical development of their ways. I am, in fact, the sworn enemy of anything approaching sloppiness. You smile at that?"

311

"It is a point of view," replied Carrados. "I was wondering how the phrase at this moment would convey itself, say, to Mr. Tupworthy's ear."

Mr. Belting doubled up.

"But don't remind me of Tupworthy, or I can't get on," he said. "In my method, I follow the system of Herbert Spencer towards children. Of course you are familiar with his treatise on 'Education'? If a rough boy persists, after warnings, in tearing or soiling all his clothes, don't scold him for what, after all, is only a natural and healthy instinct overdone. But equally, of course, don't punish yourself by buying him other clothes. When the time comes for the children to be taken to an entertainment, little Tommy cannot go with them. It would not be seemly, and he is too ashamed, to go in rags. He begins to see the force of practical logic. Very well. If a tradesman promises – promises explicitly – delivery of his goods by a certain time and he fails, he finds that he is then unable to leave them. I pay on delivery, by the way. If a man undertakes to make me an article like another – I am painstaking, Mr. Carrados: I out at the time how exactly like I want it – and it is (as it generally is) on completion something quite different, I decline to be easy-going and to be put off with it. I take the simplest and most obvious instances. I could multiply indefinitely. It is, of course, frequently inconvenient to me, but it establishes a standard."

"I see that you are a dangerous man, Mr. Belting," remarked Carrados. "If most men were like you, our national character would be undermined. People would have to behave properly."

"If most men were like me, we should constitute an intolerable nuisance," replied Belting seriously. "A necessary reaction towards sloppiness would set in and find me at its head. I am always with minorities."

"And the case in point?"

"The present trouble centres round the kitchen sink. It is cracked and leaks. A trivial cause for so elaborate an outcome, you may say, but you will doubtless remember that two men quarrelling once at a spring as to who should use it first involved half-Europe in a war, and the whole tragedy of Lear sprang from a silly business round a word. I hadn't noticed the sink when we took this flat, but the landlord had solemnly sworn to do everything that was necessary. Is a new sink necessary to replace a cracked one? Obviously. Well, you know what landlords are: Possibly you are one yourself. They promise you Heaven until you have signed the agreement, and then they tell you to go to Hell. Suggested that we'd probably broken the sink ourselves and would certainly be looked to to replace it. An excellent servant caught a cold standing in the drip and left. Was I to be driven into paying for a new sink myself? Very well, I thought, if the reasonable complaint of one tenant is nothing to you, see how you like the unreasonable complaints of fifty. The method served a useful purpose too. When Mrs. Belting heard that old tale about the tragedy at No. 11 she was terribly upset. Vowed that she couldn't stay alone in here at night on any consideration.

"'My dear,' I said, 'don't worry yourself about ghosts. I'll make as good a one as ever lived, and then when you see how it takes other people in, just remember next time you hear of another that someone's pulling the string.' And I really don't think that she'll ever be afraid of ghosts again."

"Thank you," said Carrados, rising. "Altogether I have spent a very entertaining evening, Mr. Belting. I hope your retaliatory method won't get you into serious trouble this time."

"Why should it?" demanded Belting quickly.

"Oh, well, tenants are complaining, the property is being depreciated. The landlord may think that he has legal redress against you."

"But surely I am at liberty to light the gas or use the bath in my own flat when and how I like?"

A curious look had come into Mr. Belting's smiling face. A curious note must have sounded in his voice. Carrados was warned and, being warned, guessed.

"You are a wonderful man," he said with upraised hand. "I capitulate. Tell me how it is, won't you?"

"I knew the man at 11. His tenancy isn't really up till March, but he got an appointment in the north and had to go. His two unexpired months weren't worth troubling about, so I got him to sublet the flat to me – all quite regularly – for a nominal consideration, and not to mention it."

"But he gave up the keys?"

"No. He left them in the door and the porter took them away. Very unwarrantable of him. Surely I can keep my keys where I like? However, as I had another . . . Really, Mr. Carrados, you hardly imagine that unless I had an absolute right to be there I should penetrate into a flat, tamper with the gas and water, knock the place about, tramp up and down – "

"I go," said Carrados, "to get our people out in haste. Good night."

"Good night, Mr. Carrados. It's been a great privilege to meet you. Sorry I can't persuade you . . . ."

The Missing Actress Sensation

First nights are not what they were, even within the memory of playgoers who would be startled to hear anyone else refer to them as "elderly". But there are yet occasions of exception, and the production of *Call a Spade* at the Argosy Theatre was marked by at least one feature of note. The play itself was "sound", though not epoch-making. The performance of the leading lady was satisfactory and exactly what was to be expected from her. The leading gentleman was equally effective in a part which – as eight out of twelve dramatic critics happily phrased it on the morrow – "fitted him like a glove", and on the same preponderance of opinion the character actor "*contrived to extract every ounce of humour from the material at his disposal*". In other words, *Call a Spade* might so far be relied upon to run an attenuating course for about fifty nights and then to be discreetly dropped, "*pending the continuance of its triumphal progress at another West End house – should a suitable habitation become available*".

But a very different note came into the reviews when the writers passed to the achievement of another member of the company – a young actress described on the programme as Miss Una Roscastle. Miss Roscastle was unknown to London critics and London audiences. She had come from Dublin with no very great dramatic reputation, but it is to be presumed that the quite secondary part which she had been given on her first metropolitan appearance was peculiarly suited to her talent. No one was more surprised than the author at the remarkable characterisation that "Mary Ryan" assumed in Miss Roscastle's hands. He was the more surprised because he had failed to notice anything of the kind at rehearsals. Dimly he suspected that the young lady had got more out of the part than he had ever put into it, and while outwardly loud in his expression of delight, he was secretly uncertain whether to be pleased or annoyed. The leading lady also went out of her way to congratulate the young neophyte effusively on her triumph – and then slapped her unfortunate dresser on very insufficient provocation, but the lessee manager spoke of his latest acquisition with a curious air of restraint. At the end of the second act Miss Roscastle took four calls. After that she was only required for the first few minutes of the last act, and many among the audience noted with surprise that she did not appear with the company at the fall of the curtain – she had, in fact, already left the house. All the same the success of the piece constituted a personal triumph for herself. Thenceforth, instead of, "Oh yes, you might do worse than book seats at the Argosy," the people who had been, said, "Now don't forget: You positively must see Miss Roscastle in *Call a Spade*," and as The Press had said very much the same, the difference to the box-office was something, but to the actress it was everything. Miss Roscastle, indeed, had achieved that rare distinction of "waking to find herself famous". Nothing could have seemed more assured and roseate than her professional future.

About a week, later Max Carrados was interrupted one afternoon in the middle of composing an article on Sicilian numismatics by a telephone call from Mr. Carlyle. The blind man smiled as he returned his friend's greeting, for Louis Carlyle's voice was wonderfully suggestive in its phases of the varying aspects of the speaker himself, and at that moment it conveyed a portrait of Mr. Carlyle in his very best early-morning business manner – spruce and debonair, a little obtuse to things beyond his experience and impervious to criticism, but self-confident, trenchant, and within his limits capable. In its crisp yet benign complacency, Carrados could almost have sworn to resplendent patent boots, the current shade in suede gloves and a carefully selected picotee.

"If you are doing nothing better tonight, Max," continued the inquiry agent, "would you join me at the Argosy Theatre? I have a box, and we might go on to the Savoy afterwards. Now don't say you are engaged, there's a good fellow," he urged. "You haven't given me the chance of playing host for a month or more."

"The fact is," confessed Carrados, "I was there for the first night only a week ago."

"How unfortunate," exclaimed the other. "But don't you think that you could put up with it again?"

"I am sure I can," agreed Carrados. "Yes, I will join you there with pleasure."

"Delightful," crowed Mr. Carlyle. "Let us say – "

The essential details were settled in a trice, but the "call" had not yet expired and the sociable gentleman still held the wire. "Were you interested in Miss Roscastle, Max?"

"Decidedly."

"That is fortunate. My choice of a theatre is not unconnected with a case I have on hand. I may be able to tell you something about the lady."

"Possibly we shall not be alone?" suggested Carrados.

"Well, no, not absolutely," admitted Carlyle. "Charming young fellow, though. I'm sure you'll like him, Max. Trevor Enniscorthy, a younger son of old Lord Sleys."

"Conventional rotter, between ourselves?" inquired Max.

"Not a bit of it," declared Mr. Carlyle loyally. "A young fellow of five-and-twenty is none the worse for being enamoured of a fascinating creature who happens to be on the stage. He is – Oh, very well. Goodbye, Max. Eight-fifteen, remember."

They were all punctual. In fact, "If Mr. Enniscorthy could have got me along we should have been here before the doors opened," declared Mr. Carlyle when the blind man joined them. "Now why are there no programmes about here, I wonder?"

"I hardly fancy they anticipate their box-holders arriving twenty minutes before the curtain rises," suggested Carrados.

"There are some," exclaimed Mr. Enniscorthy, dashing out as an attendant crossed the circle. He was back in a moment, and standing in the obscurity of the box eagerly tore open the programme. "Still in," he muttered, coming forward and throwing the paper down for the others to refer to. "Oh, excuse my impatience," he apologised, colouring. "I am rather – "

He left them to supply the rest.

"Mr. Enniscorthy has given me permission to explain his position, Max," began Mr. Carlyle, but the young man abruptly cut short the proposition stated in this vein of deference.

"I'd rather put it that if Mr. Carrados would help me with his advice I should be most awfully grateful," he said in a very clear, rather highly pitched voice. "I suppose it's inevitable to feel no end of an ass over this sort of thing, but I'm desperately in earnest and I must go through with it."

"Admirable!" beamed Mr. Carlyle's inextinguishable eye, and he murmured: "Very natural, I am sure," in the voice of a man who has just been told to go up higher.

"Perhaps you know that there is a Miss Roscastle put down as appearing in this piece?" went on Enniscorthy. "Well, I knew Miss Roscastle rather well in Ireland. I came to London because I followed her here."

"Engaged?" dropped quietly from Carrados's lips.

"I cannot say that we were actually engaged," was the admission, "but it – Well, you know how these things stand. At all events she knew what I felt towards her, and she did not discourage my hopes."

"Did your people know of this, Mr. Enniscorthy?"

"I had not spoken to my father or to my stepmother, but they might easily have heard something of it," replied the young man. "Miss Roscastle, although she did not go about much, was received by the very best people in Dublin. Of course, for many things I did not like her being on the stage. In fact, I detested it, but she had taken the step before I knew her, and how could I object? Then she got the offer of this London engagement. She was ambitious to geon in her profession, and took it. In a very short time I found it impossible to exist there without seeing her, so I made an excuse to get away and followed."

"Let me see," put in Mr. Carlyle ingenuously. "I forget the exact dates."

"Miss Roscastle came on Monday, October the 4th," said Enniscorthy. "The piece opened on the following Thursday week – the 14th. I left Kingstown by the early boat yesterday. At this end we were nearly an hour late, and after going to my hotel, changing and dining, I had just time to come on here and bag the last stall. I thought that I would send a note round after the first act and ask Una to give me a few minutes afterwards. But it never came to that. Instead I got a very large surprise. 'Mary Ryan' came on, and I looked – and looked again. I didn't need glasses, but I got a pair out of the automatic box in front of me and had another level stare. Well, it wasn't Miss Roscastle. This girl was like her. I suppose to most people they would be wonderfully alike, and her voice – although it wasn't really Irish – yes, her voice was similar. But to me there were miles of difference. I saw at once that she was an understudy, although 'Miss Una Roscastle' was still down in the programme, and I began to quake at the thought of something having happened to her.

"I slipped out into the corridor – I had an end seat – and got hold of a programme girl.

"'Do you know why Miss Roscastle is out of the cast tonight?' I asked her. 'Is she indisposed?'

"She took the programme out of my hand and pointed to a name in it.

"'She's in all right,' she replied – stupidly, I thought. 'There's her name.'

"'Yes, she is on the programme,' I replied, 'but not on the stage. Look through the glass there. That is not Miss Roscastle.'

"She glanced through the glazed door and then turned away as though she suspected me of chaffing her.

"'It's the only Miss Roscastle I've ever seen here,' she said as she went.

"I wandered about and interrogated one or two other attendants. They all gave me the same answer. I began to get frightened.

"'They must be misled by the resemblance,' I assured myself. 'It really is wonderful.' I went back to my seat and then remembered that I had got no further with my original inquiry, which was to find out whether Una was ill or not. I couldn't remain. I kept my eyes fixed on 'Mary Ryan' every time she was on the stage, and every time I became more and more convinced. Finally I got up again and going round sent in my card to the manager."

"Stokesey?" asked Carrados.

"Yes. I didn't know who was technically the right man, but he, at any rate, had engaged Miss Roscastle. He saw me at once.

"'I have come across from Dublin to see Miss Roscastle,' I told him, 'and I am very disappointed to find her out of the cast. Can you tell me why she is away?'

"'Surely you are mistaken,' he replied, opening a programme that lay before him. 'Do you know Miss Roscastle by sight?'

"'Very well indeed,' I retorted. 'Better than your staff do. The "Mary Ryan" tonight is not Miss Roscastle.'

"'I will inquire,' he said, walking to the door. 'Please wait a minute.'

"He was rigidly courteous, but instinct was telling me all the time that it was sheer bluff. He had nothing to inquire. In a moment he was back again.

"'I am informed that the programme is correct,' he said with the same smooth insincerity, standing in the middle of the room for me to leave. 'Miss Roscastle is on the stage at this moment. The make-up must have deceived you, Mr. Enniscorthy.'

"I had nothing to reply, because I did not even know what to think. I simply proceeded to walk out.

"'One moment.' I had reached the door when Mr. Stokesey spoke. 'You are a friend of Miss Roscastle, I suppose?'

"'Yes,' I replied. 'I think I may claim that.'

"'Then I would merely suggest to you that to start a rumour crediting her with being out of the piece is a service she would fail to appreciate. Good evening.'

"I left the theatre because I despaired of getting any real information after that, and it occurred to me that I could do better elsewhere. Although Una and I did not correspond, I had begged her, before she left, to let me know that she arrived safely, and she had sent me just half-a-dozen lines. I now took a taxi and drove off to the address she had given – a sort of private hotel or large boarding house near Holborn.

"'Can you tell me if Miss Roscastle is in?' I asked at the office.

"'Roscastle?' said the fellow there. 'Oh, the young lady from the theatre. Why, she left us more than a week ago – nearer two, I should say.'

"This was another facer.

"'Can you give me the address she went to?' I asked.

"'Couldn't. Against our rule,' he replied. 'Any letters for her were to be sent to the theatre.'

"I didn't think it would be successful to offer him a bribe, so I thanked him and walked away. As the hall porter opened the door for me I dropped him a word. In two minutes, he came out to where I was waiting.

318

"'A Miss Roscastle left here a week or two ago,' I said. 'They won't give me her address, but you can get it. Here's a Bradbury. I'll be here again in half-an-hour and if you've got the address – the house, not the theatre – there'll be another for you when I've verified it.'

"He looked a bit doubtful. Evidently a decent fellow, I thought.

"'It's quite all right,' I assured him. 'We are engaged, but I've only just come over.'

"He was waiting for me when I returned. The first thing he did was to tender me the note back again – a piece of superfluous honesty that prepared me for the worst.

"'I'm sorry, sir, but it's no go,' he explained. 'The young lady left no address beyond the theatre.'

"'You called a cab for her when she went?' I suggested.

"'Yes, sir, but she gave the directions while I was bringing out her things. I never heard where it was to go.'

"And that is as far as we have got up to this moment, Max," struck in Mr. Carlyle briskly.

"I'm afraid it is," corroborated Enniscorthy. "I got round to the stage door here in time to see most of the people leave, but neither Miss Roscastle nor the girl like her were among them."

"She is off half-an-hour before the piece finishes," explained Carrados. "And of course she might not leave by the stage door."

"In any case it is an extraordinary-enough business, is it not, Mr. Carrados?" said Enniscorthy, rather anxious not to be set down a blundering young idiot for his pains. "What does it mean?"

"So far I would describe it as – curious," admitted Carrados guardedly. "Investigation may justify a stronger term. In the meanwhile, we need not miss the play."

By this time the theatre had practically filled and the orchestra was tuning up for the overture. With nothing to occupy his attention, Mr. Enniscorthy began to manifest an unhappy restlessness that increased until the play had been proceeding for some few minutes. Then Carrados heard Mr. Carlyle murmur, "Charming! Charming!" in a tone of mature connoisseurship. There was a spontaneous round of applause and "Mary Ryan" was on the scene.

"The understudy again," Enniscorthy whispered to his companions.

"Well," remarked Mr. Carlyle when the curtain descended for the first interval, "you are still equally convinced, Mr. Enniscorthy?"

"There isn't the shadow of a doubt," he replied. Carrados had been writing a few lines on one of his cards. He now summoned an attendant.

"Mr. Stokesey is in the house?" he asked. "Then give him this, please – when you next go that way." Before the curtain rose the girl came round to the box again.

"Mr. Carrados?" she inquired. "Mr. Stokesey told me to say that he would save you the trouble by looking in here during the next interval."

"Shall I remain?" asked Enniscorthy.

"Oh yes. Stokesey is a most amiable man to do with. I know him slightly. His attitude to you was evidently the outcome of the circumstances. We shall all get along very nicely."

The second act was the occasion of "Mary Ryan's" great opportunity and again she carried the enthusiasm of the audience. After the curtain the young actress had to respond to an insistent call. In the darkness, Mr. Stokesey entered the box and stood waiting at the back.

"Glad to see you here again, Mr. Carrados," he remarked, shaking hands with the blind man as soon as the lights were up. Then he looked at the other occupants. "My word, I have put my head into the lion's den!" he continued, his smile deepening into a good-natured grin. "Don't shoot, Mr. Enniscorthy. I will climb down without. I see that the game is up."

"What are you going to tell us?" asked Carrados.

"Everything I know. The lady who has just gone off is not Miss Roscastle. Mr. Enniscorthy was quite right. She wasn't here last night either."

"Then why is her name still in the programme, and why do you and your people keep up the fiction?" demanded Enniscorthy.

"Because I hoped that Miss Roscastle might have returned to the cast tonight, and, failing tonight, I hope that she will return tomorrow. Because we happen to have a substitute in Miss Linknorth so extraordinarily like the original lady in appearance and voice that no one – excluding yourself – will have noticed the difference, and because I have a not unreasonable objection to announcing that the chief attraction of my theatre is out of the cast. Is there anything very unaccountable in that?"

Mr. Carlyle nodded acquiescence to this moderate proposition. Enniscorthy seemed to admit it reluctantly. It remained for Carrados to accept the challenge.

"Only one thing," he replied with some reluctance.

"And what is that?"

"That Miss Roscastle will not return to the cast and that you are well aware why she never can return to it."

"I – what?" demanded the astonished manager.

"Miss Roscastle cannot return to the cast because she has never been in it."

Stokesey wavered, burst into a roar of laughter and sat down.

"I give in," he exclaimed heartily. "That's my last ditch. Now you really do know everything that I do."

"But why has she not been in?" demanded Enniscorthy.

"Better ask the lady herself. I cannot even guess."

"I will when I can find her." Not for the first time the young man was assailed by a horrid fear that he might have been making a fool of himself. "Where in the meantime, is she?"

"The Lord alone knows," retorted Mr. Stokesey feelingly. "Don't annihilate me, Mr. Enniscorthy. I don't mean a member of the peerage. But, I'll tell you, the lady put me in a very deuced fix."

"Won't you take us into your confidence?" suggested Carrados.

"I will, Mr. Carrados, because I want a consideration from you in return. I can put it into a very few words. Twenty minutes before the curtain went up on the first night, a note was sent in to Miss Roscastle. She read it, put on her hat and coat, and went out hurriedly by the stage door."

"Well?" said Carlyle encouragingly.

"That is all. That is the last we saw of her – heard of her. She never returned."

"But – but " stammered Enniscorthy, and came up short before the abysmal nature of the prospect confronting him.

"There are a good many 'buts' to be taken into consideration, Mr. Enniscorthy," said the manager, with a rather cryptic look. "Fortunately we had Miss Linknorth, and the first costume, as you know, is immaterial. Up to the last possible moment we hung on to Miss Roscastle's return. Then the other had to go on."

"With not very serious consequences to the success of the play, apparently," remarked Carrados.

"That's the devilment of it," exclaimed Stokesey warmly. "Don't you see the hole it has put me into? If 'Mary Ryan' had remained a negligible quantity, it wouldn't have mattered two straws. But for her own diabolical vanity, Miss Linknorth made a confounded success of the part. Of course it was too late to have any alteration printed on the first night, and now Miss Roscastle is the draw of the piece. People come to see Miss *Roscastle*. Miss *Roscastle* is the piece."

"But if you explained that Miss Linknorth was really the creator of the part," suggested Mr. Carlyle. Stokesey rattled a provocative laugh at the back of his throat.

"You run a theatre for a few seasons, my dear fellow, and then talk," he retorted. "You can't explain. You can't do anything. You can only just sit there. People cease to be rational beings when they set out for a theatre. If you breathe on a howling success it goes out. If you move a gold mine of a piece from one theatre to another, next door, everyone promptly

321

decides to stay away. Don't ask me the reasons. There are none. It isn't a business. It ought to come under the Gaming Act."

"Mr. Stokesey is also faced by the alternative that after he had announced Miss Linknorth, Miss Roscastle might appear any time and claim her place."

The manager nodded. "That's another consideration," he said.

"But could she?" inquired Mr. Carlyle. "After absenting herself in this way?"

"Oh, goodness knows. I dare say she could – agreements are no good when it comes to anything happening. At any rate, here am I with an element of success after a procession of distinct non-stops. If we get well set, whatever happens will matter less. Now I haven't gone to any Machiavellian lengths in arranging this, but I have taken the chance as it came along. I've told you everything I know. Is there any reason why you shouldn't do us all a good turn by keeping it strictly to yourselves?"

"I don't know that I particularly owe you any consideration, Mr. Stokesey, or that you owe me any," announced Mr. Enniscorthy. "Just now I am only concerned in discovering what has become of Miss Roscastle. You know her address?"

"In Kensington?"

"Well, yes."

"74 Westphalia Mansions."

"You sent there of course?"

"Heavens, yes! The various forms of messages must be six inches deep all over the hall by now. Last Friday I had a man sitting practically all day on her doorstep."

"But she has someone there – a housekeeper or maid?"

"I don't think so. She told me that she was taking a little furnished flat – asked me if the neighbourhood was a suitable one. I imagine there was something about a daily woman until she found how she liked it. We've had no one from there anyway."

"Then it comes to this, that for a week there has been absolutely no trace of Miss Roscastle's existence! Do you quite realise your responsibility, Mr. Stokesey?" demanded Enniscorthy with increased misgivings.

The manager, who had turned to go, caught Mr. Carlyle's eye over the concerned young man's shoulder.

"I don't think that Miss Roscastle's friends need have any anxiety about her personal safety," he replied with expression. "At all events, I've done everything I can for you. I hope that you will not fail to meet my views. If there's anything else that occurs to you, Mr. Carrados, I shall be in my office. Good night."

"Callous brute!" muttered Mr. Enniscorthy. "He ought to have put it in the hands of the police a week ago."

Mr. Carlyle glanced at Carrados, who had transferred his interest to the rendering of the last musical item of the interval.

"Possibly Miss Roscastle would prefer a less public investigation if she had a voice in the matter," said the professional man.

"If she happens to be shut up in some beastly underground cellar I imagine she would prefer whatever gets her out the soonest. I dare say it sounds fantastic, but such things really do happen now and then, you know, and why not?"

"You don't know of any threats or blackmailing letters?"

"No," admitted the young man. "But I do know this: That if Una was at liberty, she would never allow another actress to take her place and use her name in this way."

"A very significant suggestion," put in Carrados from his detached attitude. "Mr. Enniscorthy has given you a really valuable hint, Louis."

"I don't mean that Miss Roscastle is really out-of-the-way jealous," Enniscorthy hastened to add, "but in her profession – "

"Oh, most natural, most natural," agreed the urbane Carlyle. "Everyone has to look after his own interest. Now – "

"I don't suppose that you are particularly keen on this act," interposed the blind man. "Are you, Mr. Enniscorthy?"

"I'd much rather be doing something," was the reply.

"I was going to suggest that you might go round to Westphalia Mansions, just to make sure that there is no one there now. Then if you would find your way to our table at the Savoy, we could hear your report."

"Yes, certainly. I shall be glad to think that I can be of some assistance by going."

Mr. Carlyle's optimistic temper was almost incapable of satire, but he could not refrain from, "You can – poor beggar!" on Enniscorthy's departure. "I suppose," he continued, turning to his friend, "I suppose you think that Stokesey may? Eh?"

"I fancy that in the absence of our young friend, he may be induced to become more confidential. He may have some good ground for believing that the missing lady will not upset his ingenious plan. He, at all events, discounts the 'underground cellar'."

"Oh, that!" commented Carlyle with an indulgent smile. "But, after all, what is the answer, Max? Enniscorthy is a thoroughly eligible young fellow and this was the first chance of her career. What is the inducement?"

"That much we can safely emphasise. What, in a word, would induce an ambitious young lady to throw up a good engagement, Louis?"

"A better?" suggested Mr. Carlyle.

"Exactly," agreed Carrados. "A better."

It is unnecessary to follow the course of Mr. Carlyle's inquiry on the facts already disclosed, for, less than twenty-four hours later, the whole situation was changed and Mr. Stokesey's discreet prevarication had been torn into shreds. The manager had calculated in vain – if he had calculated and not just accepted the chance that presented itself. At all events the fiction proved too elaborate to be maintained and late in the afternoon of the following day all the evening papers blazed out with the –

Sensational Disappearance of Popular London Actress

The event was particularly suited to the art of the contents bill, for when the news came to be analysed there was little else to be learned beyond the name of the missing actress and the fact that "*at the theatre a policy of questionable reticence is being maintained towards all inquiry.*" That phrase caused two men at least to smile as they realised the embarrassment of Mr. Stokesey's dubious position.

The conditions being favourable, the Missing Actress sensation caught on at once and effectually asphyxiated public interest in all the other sensations that up to that moment had been satisfying the mental requirements of the nation – a "*Mysterious Submarine*" an "*Eloping Dean*" (three wives), and an "*Are We Becoming Too Intellectual?*" correspondence. Supply followed demand, and it very soon became difficult to decide, not where Miss Roscastle *was*, but where she was *not*. Public opinion wavered between Genoa, on the authority of a retired lime and slate merchant of Hull who had had a presentiment while directing a breathless lady to the docks, when a Wilson liner was on the point of sailing, Leatherhead, the suggestion of a booking-office clerk who had been struck by the peculiar look in a veiled lady's eyes as she asked for a third-class return to Cheam, and Accrington, where a young lady with a marked Irish accent and a theatrical manner had inquired about lodgings at three different houses and then abruptly left, saying that she would come back if she thought any more about it.

Before the novelty was two days, old Scotland Yard had been stirred into recognising its existence. A London clue was forthcoming, apparently the wildest and most circumstantial of them all. A plain-clothes constable of the A Division reported that an hour after midnight three days before, he had noticed a shabby-genteel man, who seemed to be waiting for someone, loitering on the Embankment near the Boadicea statue. There was nothing in the circumstance to interest him, but when he repassed the spot ten minutes later the man had been joined by a woman. The sharp eyes of the constable told him that the woman was well and even fashionably dressed, although she had made some precaution to conceal it, and the fact quickened his observation. As he shambled past – an Embankment dead-beat for the occasion – he heard the name "Roscastle" spoken by one of the two. He could not distinguish by which, nor the sense in which the word was used, but his notebook, with the name written down under the correct date, corroborated so much. On neither occasion had he seen the face of the man distinctly – the threadbare individual had sought the shadows – but he was able to describe that of the woman in some detail. He was shown half-a-dozen photographs and at once identified that of Miss Roscastle. The crowning touch requisite to make this story entirely popular was supplied by an inspector of river police. According to the newspaper account, the patrol boat was off the Embankment near Westminster Bridge between one and a quarter-past on the night in question when a distinct splash was heard. The crew made for the spot, flashed the lights about and drifted up and down several times, but without finding a trace of any human presence. At once the public voice demanded that the river should be dragged from Chelsea to The Pool, and, pending the result, every shabby wastrel who appeared on the Embankment arrested. In his private office, Mr. Carlyle threw down the last of his morning papers with an expression that began as a knowing smile but ended rather dubiously. For his own part he would have much preferred that the disappearance of Miss Roscastle had not leaked out – that he had been left to pursue his course unaided, but, in the circumstances, he carefully read everything on the chance of a useful hint. The Embankment story both amused and puzzled him.

He dismissed the subject to its proper mental pigeonhole and had turned to deal with his most confidential correspondence when something very like an altercation breaking the chaste decorum of his outer office caused him to stop and frown. The next moment there was a hurrying step outside, the door was snatched open and Mr. Enniscorthy, pale and distracted, stumbled into the room. Behind him appeared the indignant face of Mr. Carlyle's chief clerk. Then the visitor extinguished the outraged vision by flinging back the door as he went forward.

"Have you seen the papers?" he demanded. "Is there anything dreadful in them?"

"I have seen the papers, yes," replied the puzzled agent. "I am not aware – "

"I mean the evening papers – just out. No, I see you haven't. Here, read that and tell me. I haven't – I dare not look."

Mr. Carlyle took the journal that Enniscorthy thrust under his eyes – it was the earliest *Star* – glanced into his visitor's face a little severely and then focussed the the column.

"Good Heavens!" he exclaimed. "What is this! '*Missing Actress. Embankment Clue. Body Found*'!'

"Ah!" groaned Enniscorthy. "That was on the bills. Is it?"

"It's all right, it's all right, my dear sir," reported Mr. Carlyle, glancing along the lines. "This is the body of a man . . . the man who was seen . . . most extraordinary . . . ."

"My God!" was wrung from the distressed young man as he dropped into a chair. "Oh, my God! I thought – " He took out his handkerchief, wiped and fanned his face, and for the next few minutes looked rather languidly on things.

"Very distressing," commiserated Mr. Carlyle when he had come to the end of the report. "Can I get you anything – Brandy? A glass of water? – The mere act sipping, I am medically informed, has a beneficial effect in case of faintness. I have – "

"Nothing, thanks. I shall be all right now. Sorry to have made an ass of myself. You have heard – anything?

"Nothing definite so far," was the admission. "But there may be something worth following in this story after all. I shall go down to the mortuary shortly. Do you care to accompany me?"

"No, thanks," replied the visitor. "I have had enough of that particular form of excitement for one morning. . . . Unless, of course, there is anything – "

He was assured that there was nothing to be effected by his presence and half-an-hour later Mr. Carlyle made his way alone to the obscure mortuary where the unclaimed dead hold their grim reception.

An inspector of the headquarters investigation staff who had been put on to the case was standing by the side of one of the shells when Carlyle entered. He was a man whom the private agent had more-than-once good-naturedly obliged in small matters that had come within his reach. He now greeted Mr. Carlyle with consideration and stood aside to allow him to approach the body.

"The Embankment case, I suppose, sir?" he remarked. "Not very attractive, but I've seen many worse in here." He jerked off the upper part of the rough coverlet and exposed a visage that caused Mr. Carlyle to turn away with a "*Tch, tch!*" of emotion. Then a sense of duty drew him round again and he proceeded to note the descriptive points of the dead man in his pocket-book.

"No marks of violence, I suppose?" he asked.

"Nothing beyond the usual abrasions that we always find. A clear case of drowning – suicide – it seems to be."

"And the things?"

The inspector nodded towards a seedy suit laid out for identification and an overcoat, once rakish of its fashion and now frayed and mouldering, put with it.

"Fur collar too, Mr. Carlyle," pointed out his guide. "'*Velvet and rags,*' isn't it? '*Where moth and rust doth corrupt.*' A sermon could be made out of this."

"Very true. Very true indeed," replied Mr. Carlyle, who always responded to the sentimentally obvious. "It is a sermon, Inspector. But what have we here?"

Beside the garments had been collected together a heap of metal discs – quite a considerable heap, numbering some hundreds. Carlyle took up a few and examined them. They were all alike – flat, perfectly round, and somewhat under an inch in diameter. They were quite plain and apparently of lead.

"Hmm, curious," he commented. "In his pockets?"

"Yes, both overcoat pockets. Very determined, wasn't he? They would have kept him down till the Day of Judgment. I've counted them – just five-hundred."

"Any money?"

The inspector smiled his tragi-comic appreciation – the coin embellished the moral of his unwritten sermon – and pointed.

"A halfpenny!" he replied.

"Poor fellow!" said Mr. Carlyle. "Well, well, perhaps it is better as it is. You might pull up the cloth again now, please. . . . There are no letters or papers, I see."

The detective hesitated a moment and then recalled the obligation he was under.

"There is a scrap of paper that I have kept from The Press so far," he admitted. "It was tightly clenched in the man's right hand – so tight that we had to use a screwdriver to get it out, and the water had barely reached it." He was extracting a slip of paper from his notebook as he spoke and he now unfolded it. "You won't put it about, will you, Mr. Carlyle? I don't know that there's anything tangible in it, but – well, see for yourself."

"Extraordinary!" admitted the gentleman. He read the words a second time: "'Fool! What does it matter now?' Why, it might almost – "

"It might be addressed to the coroner, or to anyone who tries to find out who he is or what it means, you would say. Well, so it might, sir. Anyhow, that is all."

"By the way, I suppose he is the man your fellow saw?"

"Everything tallies, Mr. Carlyle – length of immersion, place, and so on. Our man thinks he is the same, but you may remember that he didn't claim to be very positive on this point."

There seemed nothing else to be learned and Mr. Carlyle took his departure. His acquaintance had also finished and their ways lay together as far as Trafalgar Square. Before they parted the inspector had promised to communicate with Mr. Carlyle as soon as the dead man was identified.

"And if he has a room anywhere he probably will be, with all this talk about Miss Roscastle. Then we may find something there that will help us," he predicted. "If he is purely casual the chances are we shall never hear."

His experience was justified and he kept his promise.

Two days later Carlyle heard that the unknown had been identified as the occupant of a single room in a Lambeth lodging house. He had only occupied it for a few weeks and he was known there as Mr. Hay. Tenement gossip described him as a foreigner and credited him with having seen better days – an easy-enough surmise in the circumstances. Mr. Carlyle had been on the point of turning his attention to a Monte Carlo Miss Roscastle when this information reached him. He set off at once for Lambeth, but at Tubb's Grove disappointment met him at the door. The landlady of the ramshackle establishment – a female with a fluent if rather monotonous delivery – was still smarting from the unappreciated honour of the police officials' visit and the fierce light of publicity that it had thrown upon her house. All Mr. Carlyle's bland cajolery was futile and in the end he had to disburse a sum that bore an appreciable relation to a week's rent before he was allowed to inspect the room and to command conversation that was not purely argumentative.

Then the barrenness of the land was revealed. Mr. Hay had been irregular with his rent at the best, and when he disappeared he was a week in arrears. After two days' absence, with the easy casuistry of her circumstances, the lady had decided that he was not returning and had proceeded to "do out" the room for the next tenant. The lodger's "few things" she had bundled together into a cupboard, whence they had been retrieved by the police, in spite of her indignant protest. But the lodger's "papers and such-like rubbish" she confessed to burning, to get them out of the way. Mr. Carlyle spent a profitless half-hour and then returned, calling at Scotland Yard on his way back. His friend the inspector shook his head. There was nothing among the seized property that afforded any clue.

It was at this point that Mr. Carlyle's ingenuous mind suggested looking up Carrados, whom he had not seen since the visit to the theatre.

"Max was interested in this case from the first. I am sure he will be expecting to hear from me about it," was the form in which the proposal conveyed itself to him.

The same evening he ran down to Richmond for an hour, after ascertaining that his friend was at home and disengaged.

"You might have brought Enniscorthy with you," remarked Carrados when the subject had been started.

"Nice, genuine young fellow. Evidently deeply in love with the girl, but he is young enough to take the attack safely. What have you told him?"

"He is back in Ireland just now – got an idea that he might learn something from some people there, and rushed off. What I have told him – well" – experience endowed Mr. Carlyle with sudden caution – "what would you have told him, Max?"

Carrados smiled at the innocent guile of the invitation.

"To answer that I should have to know just what you know," he replied. "I suppose you have gone into this Embankment development?"

"Yes." He had come intending to make some show of his progress and to sound Carrados discreetly, but once again in the familiar room and under the sway of the clear-visioned blind man's virile personality he suddenly found himself submitting quite naturally to the suave, dominating influence. "Yes, but I must confess, Max, that I am unable to explain much of that incident. It suggests blackmail at the bottom, and if the plain-clothes man was correct and saw Miss Roscastle there last Thursday – "

"It was blackmail, but the plain-clothes man was not correct, though he had every excuse for making the mistake. There is one quiet, retiring personage in this drama who has been signally overlooked in all the clamour."

"You mean?"

"I suggest that if Miss Linknorth had been subpoenaed for the inquest and asked to account for her movements after leaving the theatre on Thursday last it might have turned public speculation into another channel – though probably a wrong one."

"Miss Linknorth!" The idea certainly turned Mr. Carlyle's thoughts into a new channel.

"Has it occurred to you what an extraordinary act of self-effacement it must have been on the part of this young unknown actress to allow her well-earned success to be credited to another? As Enniscorthy reminded us, ladies of the profession are rather keen on their chances."

"Yes, but Stokesey, you remember, insisted on keeping it dark."

"I am not overlooking that. But although it was to Stokesey's interest to keep up the fiction, and also to the interest of everyone else about the theatre – people who were merely concerned in the run of the piece – it would have richly paid the Linknorth to have her identity established while the iron was hot, whatever the outcome. A paragraph to The Press the next

329

day would have done it. There wasn't a hint. I am not overlooking the fact that Miss Linknorth's name now appears on the programme, but that is an unforeseen development so far as she is concerned, and her golden opportunity has gone by. With the exception of the first row of the pit and of the gallery, you won't find that one-per-cent of the house now really knows who created 'Mary Ryan' or regards the Linknorth as anything but a makeshift."

"Then what was the incentive?"

"Suppose it has been made worth Miss Linknorth's while? It is not necessarily a crude question of money. Friendship might make it worth her while, or ambition in some quarter we have not looked for, or a dozen other considerations – anything but the box-office of the Argosy Theatre, which certainly did not make it worth her while.

"Yes, that is feasible enough, Max, but how does it help us?"

"Do you ever have toothache, Louis?" demanded Carrados inconsequently.

"No, I am glad to say," admitted Mr. Carlyle. "Have you got a turn now, old man? Never mind this confounded 'shop'. I'll go and then you can – "

"Not at all," interposed Carrados, smiling benignly at his friend's consideration, "and don't be too ready to condemn toothache indiscriminately. I have sometimes found it very stimulating. The only way to cure it is to concentrate the mind so terrifically that you forget the ache. Then it stops. I imagine that a mathematician could succeed by working out a monumental problem. I have frequently done it by 'discovering' a hoard of Greek coins of the highest art period on one of the islands and classifying the find. On Monday night I thought that I was in for a devil of a time. I, at once, set myself to discover a workable theory for everyone's conduct in this affair, one, of course, that would stand the test of every objection based on fact. The correct hypothesis must, indeed, be strengthened by every new circumstance that came out. At twelve o'clock, after two hours' mental sudation, I began to see light – excuse the phrase. By this time the toothache had gone, but I was so taken up with the idea that I called out Harris and drove to Scotland Yard then and there on the chance of finding Beedel or one of the others I know. . . . Why on earth didn't you let me have that 'Fool!' message, Louis?"

"My dear fellow," protested Mr. Carlyle, "I can't beat up for advice on every day of my life."

"At all events it might have saved me an hour's strenuous thinking."

"Well, you know, Max, perhaps that would have left you in the middle of the toothache. Now the message?"

"The message? Oh, that settled it. You may take it as assured, Louis, that although Miss Roscastle's departure from the theatre was hurried, in order to allow her to catch the boat-train from Charing Cross, she had enough time to think out the situation and to secure Miss Linknorth's allegiance. Whether Stokesey knows any more than he admits, we need not inquire. The great thing is that Miss Roscastle had some reason – some fairly strong reason – for not wanting her absence from the cast to become public. We agreed, Louis, that a better engagement would alone satisfactorily explain her defection. What better engagement would you suggest – it could scarcely be a theatrical one?"

"A brilliant marriage?"

"Our minds positively ident, Louis. 'A brilliant marriage' – my exact expression. One, moreover, that suddenly becomes possible and cannot be delayed. One – here we are on difficult ground – one that may be jeopardised if at that early stage Miss Roscastle's identity in it comes to light, or if, possibly, her absence from London is discovered. That sign-post," said Carrados, with his unseeing eyes fixed on the lengthening vistas that rose before his mind, "points in a good many directions."

"The blackmailer?" hazarded Carlyle.

"I gave a good deal of attention to every phase of that gentleman's presence," replied Carrados. "It corroborates, but it does not entirely explain. I would say that he merely intervened. In my view, Miss Roscastle would have acted precisely as she did if there had been no Mr. Hay. At all events, he did intervene and had to be dealt with."

"It had occurred to me, Max, whether it was Miss Linknorth's job to impersonate the other?"

"It may have been originally. If so, it failed, for Hay proceeded with his demand. His price was five-hundred pounds in English or French gold – an interesting phase of your ordinary blackmailer's antipathy to paper – merely an *hors d'oeuvre* to the solid things to come, of course. But he was not dealing with a fool. Whether Miss Roscastle frankly had not five-hundred pounds just then, or whether she was better advised, we cannot say. She temporised, the Linknorth being the intermediary. Then the dummy pieces? Hay was a menace and had to be held off. At one point there may well have been the pretence of handing over the cash and then at the last moment some specious difficulty, necessitating a short delay, is raised. That would account for the otherwise unnecessary detail of the lead counterfeits, for there is no need of them on Thursday. Then, when the danger is past, when the tricked scoundrel has lost his sting, then there is no attempt at evasion or 'Compromise'. Fool! What does it matter now?' is the contemptuously unguarded message, and the five-hundred doits are pressed upon him to complete his humiliation. Why doesn't it matter,

331

Louis? Is there any other answer than that Miss Roscastle is safely married?"

"It certainly looks like it," agreed Mr. Carlyle. "But if there was anything so serious as to have compromised the marriage, surely Hay could still have held it over her, as against her husband?"

"If it was as against the husband before – yes, perhaps. But suppose the chink in the armour was the good grace of some third person whose consent was necessary? This brilliant marriage . . . Well, I don't commit myself any further. At any rate, in the lady's estimation she is safe, and if she had deliberately sought to goad Hay into suicide she couldn't have done better. He read the single line that shattered his greedy dreams and its disdainful triumph struck him like a whip. He had spent literally his last penny on pressing his unworthy persecution, and now he stood, beggared and beaten, on the Embankment at midnight – 'he, a gentleman' . . . It doesn't matter how he took it. He went over, and the muddy waters of the Thames closed over the last page of his rotten history."

"Max!" exclaimed Mr. Carlyle with feeling. "Remember the poor beggar, with all his failings, is dead now. Not that I should mind," he added cheerfully, "but I saw him afterwards, you know. Enniscorthy had the sense to keep away. And, by Gad! Max, that reminds me that this is rather rough on my confiding young client – running up a bill to have a successful rival sprung upon his hopes. Have you any idea who he is?"

"Yes," admitted Carrados, "I have an idea, but today it is nothing more than that. When does Enniscorthy return?"

"He ought to be back in London on Friday morning."

"By then I should know something definite. If you will make an appointment with him for Friday at half-past-eleven I will look in on my way through town."

"Certainly, Max, certainly." There was a note of faithful expectation in Mr. Carlyle's voice that caused his friend to smile. He crossed the room to his most-used desk and opened one of the smaller drawers.

"For this simple demonstration, Louis, I require only two appliances, neither of which, as you will see, is a rabbit or a handkerchief. In other and saner words, there are only two exhibits. That is from *The Morning Mail*. This is from the Westminster street refuse tip."

"This" was a small brown canvas bag. Traces of red sealing-wax still marked the neck and across it were stamped the words:

Banque de l'Union
Clairvaux

Mr. Carlyle looked inside. It was empty, but a few specks of dull grey metal still lodged among the cloth. He turned to the other object, as Carrados had indicated an extract from the daily Press. It was a mere slip of paper and consisted of the following paragraph:

> *From Clairvaux, in the Pas de Calais, France, where he purchased a country estate when he was driven into exile, it is reported that ex-King Constantine of Villalyia has been lying dangerously ill for the past week.*

"Quite so, quite so," murmured Carlyle, quietly turning over the cutting to satisfy himself that he was reading the right side."

"I see that you haven't anything very hopeful to report," said Mr. Enniscorthy – he and Max Carrados had entered Mr. Carlyle's office within a minute of each other two days later – "but let me have it out."

"It isn't quite a matter of being hopeful or the reverse," replied the blind man. "It is merely final to your ambition. You know Prince Ulric of Villalyia?"

"I have been presented. He hunted in Ireland last season."

"He knew Miss Roscastle?"

"They were acquainted, she has told me."

"It went deeper than you imagined. Miss Roscastle is Princess Ulric of Villalyia today."

"Una! Oh," cried Enniscorthy. "But – but that is impossible! You don't mean that she – "

"I mean exactly what I say. They were married within a week of her disappearance from London."

Enniscorthy's pained gaze went from face to face. The fatal presentiment that had always just robbed him of the heroic – the fear that he might be making an ass of himself – again assailed him.

"But isn't Ulric in the line of succession? They couldn't be really married without the king's consent. Of course Villalyia is a republic now, but – "

"But it may not be tomorrow if the expected war breaks out? Quite true, Mr. Enniscorthy. And in the meanwhile, the forms and ceremonies are maintained at the exile Court of Clairvaux. Yet the king gave his consent."

"Gave his consent! For his son to marry an actress?"

"Ah, there was a little sleight of hand there. He only knew Miss Roscastle as Miss Eileen O'Rourke, the last representative of a line of Irish kings. She was a Miss O'Rourke?"

333

"Yes. Roscastle was only her stage name. The O'Rourkes were a very old but impoverished family."

"Royal, we may assume. This business was the outcome of one of the interminable domestic squabbles that the Villalyia Petrosteins seemed to wage in order to supply the Continental comic papers with material. Ex-King Constantine recently quarrelled simultaneously and irrevocably with his eldest son Robert and his first cousin Michael. Robert, who lives in Paris, has respectably married a robust minor princess who has presented him with six unattractive daughters and now, by all report, stopped finally. Hating both son and cousin almost equally, old Constantine, who had fumed himself into a fever, sent off for his other son, Ulric, and demanded that he should at once marry and found a.prolific line of sons to embitter Robert and cut out the posterity of Michael. Prince Ulric merely replied that there was only one woman whom he wished to marry and she was not of sufficiently exalted station, and as she refused to marry him morganatically – yes, Mr. Enniscorthy – there was no prospect of his ever marrying at all. The king suddenly found that he was very ill. Ulric was obdurate. The constitution allowed the reigning monarch to sanction such an alliance, provided there were no religious difficulties, and I understand that Miss Roscastle is a Catholic. Constantine recognised that if he was to gratify his whim he must consent, and that at once, as he was certainly dying. As things were, Ulric would probably renounce and marry ignominiously or die unmarried and the hated Michaels would step in, for, once king, the conventional Robert would never give his consent to such an alliance. Besides, it would be a 'damned slap in the face' to half the remaining royalty of Europe, and Constantine had always posed as a democratic sovereign – that was why his people ran him out. He coughed himself faint and then commanded the lady to be sent for."

"If only Una had confided in me I would – yes, I would willingly have flown to serve her."

"I think that Miss Roscastle was well qualified to serve herself," responded Carrados dryly. "Now you can put together the whole story, Mr. Enniscorthy. Many pages of it are necessarily obscure. What the man Hay knew and threatened – whether it was with him in view or the emissaries of the hostile Robert and Michael that she took the sudden chance of concealing her absence and cloaking her identity – what other wheels there were, what other influences at work – these are only superfluities. The essential thing is that, in spite of cross-currents, everything went well – for her, and perhaps for you. The lady's married and there's an end of it."

"I hope that she will be as happy as I should have tried to make her," said Enniscorthy rather shakily. "I shall always think of her. Mr. Carrados,

I will write to thank you when I am better able to express myself. Mr. Carlyle, you know my address. Good morning."

"A very manly way of taking it and very properly expressed – very well indeed," declared Mr. Carlyle with warm approval as the door closed. "Max, that is the outcome of good blood – blood and breeding."

"Nonsense, you romantic old humbug," said Carrados with affectionate contempt. "I have heard exactly the same words in similar circumstances once before and they were spoken by a Canning Town bricklayer's labourer."

One incident only remains to be added. A month later Mr. Carlyle was passing the Kemble Club when he became conscious of someone trying to avoid him. With a not unnatural impulse he made for his acquaintance and insisted on being recognized.

"Ah, Mr. Stokesey," he exclaimed, "*Call a Spade* is still going strong, I see."

"Mr. Carlyle, to be sure," said the manager. "Bother me if I didn't mistake you for a deadhead who always strikes me for a pass. Good Heavens! Yes, they come in droves and companies to see the part that the romantic Princess Ulric of Villalyia didn't create! I've had three summonses for my pit queue. Didn't I tell you it was a gamble? When I have to find a successor – When, mind, I say – I'm going to put on *You Never Can Tell!* What?"

The Ingenious Mr. Spinola

"You seem troubled, Parkinson. Have you been reading the Money Article again?"

Parkinson, who had been lingering a little aimlessly about the room, exhibited symptoms of embarrassed guilt. Since an unfortunate day, when it had been convincingly shown to the excellent fellow that to leave his accumulated savings on deposit at the bank was merely an uninviting mode of throwing money away, it is not too much to say that his few hundreds had led Parkinson a sorry life. Inspired by a natural patriotism and an appreciation of the advantage of 4½-over-1¼-per-cent., he had at once invested in Consols. A very short time later, a terrible line in a financial daily – "*Consols weak*" – caught his agitated eye. Consols were precipitately abandoned and a "sound industrial" took their place. Then came the rumours of an impending strike and the Conservative press voiced gloomy forebodings for the future of industrial capital. An urgent selling order, bearing Mr. Parkinson's signature, was the immediate outcome.

In the next twelve months Parkinson's few hundreds wandered through many lands and in a modest way went to support monarchies and republics, to carry on municipal enterprise, and to spread the benefits of commerce. And, through all, they contrived to exist. They even assisted in establishing a rubber plantation in Madagascar and exploiting an oil discovery in Peru and yet survived. If everything could have been lost by one dire reverse Parkinson would have been content – even relieved, but with her proverbial inconsequence Fortune began by smiling and continued to smile – faintly, it is true, but appreciably – on her timorous votary. In spite of his profound ignorance of finance, each of Parkinson's qualms and tremors resulted in a slight pecuniary margin to his credit. At the end of twelve months he had drawn a respectable interest, was somewhat to the good in capital, and as a waste product had acquired an abiding reputation among a small but choice coterie as a very "knowing one".

"Thank you, sir, but I am sorry if I seemed engrossed in my own affairs," he apologised in answer to Mr. Carrados's inquiry. "As a matter of fact," he added, "I hoped that I had finished with Stock Exchange transactions for the future."

"Ah, to be sure," assented Carrados. "A block of cottages Acton way, wasn't it to be?"

336

"I did at one time consider the investment, but on reflection I decided against property of that description. The association with houses occupied by the artisan class would not have been congenial, sir."

"Still, it might have been profitable."

"Possibly, sir. I have, however, taken up a mortgage on a detached house standing in its own grounds at Highgate. It was strongly recommended by your own estate agents – by Mr. Lethbridge himself, sir."

"I hope it will prove satisfactory, Parkinson."

"I hope so, sir, but I do not feel altogether reassured now, after seeing it."

"After seeing it? But you saw it before you took it up, surely?"

"As a matter of fact, no, sir. It was pointed out to me that the security was ample, and as I had no practical knowledge of house – valuing there was nothing to be gained by inspecting it. At the same time I was given the opportunity, I must admit, but as we were rather busy then – it was just before we went to Rome, sir – I never went there."

"Well, after all," admitted Carrados, "I hold a fair number of mortgage securities on railways and other property that I have never been within a thousand miles of. I am not in a position to criticise you, Parkinson. And this house – I suppose that it does really exist?"

"Oh yes, sir. I spent yesterday afternoon in the neighbourhood. Now that the trees are out there is not a great deal that can be actually seen from the road, but I satisfied myself that in the winter the house must be distinctly visible from several points."

"That is very satisfactory," said Carrados with equal seriousness. "But, after all, the title is the chief thing."

"So I am given to understand. Doubtless it would not be sound business, sir, but I think that if the title had been a little worse, and the appearance of the grounds a little better, I should have felt more secure. But what really concerned me is that the house is being talked about."

"Talked about?"

"Yes. It is in a secluded position, but there are some old-fashioned cottages near and these people notice things, sir. It is not difficult to induce them to talk. Refreshments are procurable at one of the cottages and I had tea there. I have since thought, from a remark made to me on leaving, that the idea may have got about that I was connected with the Scotland Yard authorities. I had no apprehension at the time of creating such an impression, sir, but I wished to make a few casual inquiries."

Carrados nodded. "Quite so," he murmured encouragingly.

"It was then that I discovered what I have alluded to. These people, having become suspicious, watch all that is to be seen at Strathblane Lodge – as it is called – and talk. They do not know what goes on there."

337

"That must be very disheartening for them."

"Well, sir, they find it trying. Up to less than a year ago, the house was occupied by a commercial gentleman and everything was quite regular. But with the new people they don't know which are the family and who are the servants. Two or three men having the appearance of mechanics seem to be there continually, and sometimes, generally in the evening, there are visitors of a class whom one would not associate with the unpretentious nature of the establishment. Gentlemen for the most part, but occasionally ladies, I was told, coming in taxis or private motor cars and generally in evening dress."

"That ought to reassure these neighbours – the private cars and evening dress."

"I cannot say that it does, sir. And what I heard made me a little nervous also."

Something was evidently on the ingenuous creature's mind. The blind man's face wore a faintly amused smile, but he gauged the real measure of his servant's apprehension.

"Nervous of what, Parkinson?" he inquired kindly.

"Some thought that it might be a gambling house, but others said it looked as if a worse business was carried on there. I should not like there to be any scandal or exposure, sir, and perhaps the mortgage forfeited in consequence."

"But, good Heavens, man! you don't imagine that a mortgage is like a public house licence, to be revoked in consequence of a rowdy tenant, surely?"

Parkinson's dubious silence made it increasingly plain that he had, indeed, associated his security with some such contingency, a conviction based, it appeared, when he admitted his fears, on a settled belief in the predatory intentions of a Government with whom he was not in sympathy.

"Don't give the thing another thought," counselled his employer. "If Lethbridge recommended the investment, you may be sure that it is all right. As for what goes on there – that doesn't matter two straws to you, and in any case it is probably idle chatter."

"Thank you, sir. It is a relief to have your assurance. I see now that I ought to have paid no attention to such conversation, but being anxious – and seeing Sir Fergus Copling go there – "

"Sir Fergus Copling? You saw him there?"

"Yes, sir. I thought that I remembered a car that was waiting for the gate to be opened. Then I recognised Sir Fergus: It was the small dark blue car that he has come here in. And just after what I had been hearing – "

"But Sir Fergus Copling! He's a testimonial of propriety. Do you know what you are talking about, Parkinson?

338

The excellent man looked even more deeply troubled than he had been about his money.

"Not in that sense, sir," he protested. "I only understood that he was a gentleman of position and a very large income, and after just listening to what was being said, Carrados's scepticism was intelligible. Copling was the last man to be associated with a scandal of fast life. He had come into his baronetcy quite unexpectedly a few years previously while engaged in the drab but apparently congenial business of teaching arithmetic at a public school. The chief advantage of the change of fortune, as it appeared to the recipient, was that it enabled him to transfer his attention from the lower to the higher mathematics. Without going out of his way to flout the conventions, he set himself a comparatively simple standard of living. He was too old and fixed, he said, to change much – forty and a bachelor – and the most optimistic spinster in town had reluctantly come to acquiesce.

Carrados had not forgotten this conversation when next he encountered Sir Fergus a week or so later. He knew the man well enough to be able to lead up to the subject and when an identifiable footstep fell on his ear in the hall of the Metaphysical (the dullest club in Europe, it was generally admitted) he called across to the baronet, who, as a matter of fact, had been too abstracted to notice him or anyone else.

"You aren't a member, are you?" asked Copling when they had shaken hands. "I didn't know that you went in for this sort of thing." The motion of his head indicated the monumental library which he had just quitted, but it might possibly be taken as indicating the general atmosphere of profound somnolence that enveloped the Metaphysical.

"I am not a member," admitted Carrados. "I only came to gather some material."

"Statistics?" queried Copling with interest. "We have a very useful range of works." He suddenly remembered his acquaintance's affliction. "By the way, can I be of any use to you?"

"Yes, if you will," said Carrados. "Let me go to lunch with you. There is an appalling bore hanging about and he'll nab me if I don't get past under protection."

Copling assented readily enough and took the blind man's arm.

"Where, though?" he asked at the door. "I generally – " He hesitated, with a shy laugh. "I generally go to an A.B.C. tea shop myself. It doesn't waste so much time. But, of course – "

"Of course, a tea shop by all means," assented Carrados.

"You are sure that you don't mind?" persisted the baronet anxiously.

"Mind? Why, I'm a shareholder!" chuckled Carrados.

"This suits me very well," remarked the ex-schoolmaster when they were seated in a remote corner of a seething general room. "Fellows used to do their best to get me into the way of going to swell places, but I always seem to drift back here. I don't mind the prices, Carrados, but hang me if I like to pay the prices simply to be inconvenienced. Yes, hot milk, please."

Carrados endorsed this reasonable philosophy. Carlton or Coffee house, the Ritz or the tea shop, it was all the same to him – life, and very enjoyable life at that. He sat and, like the spider, drew from within himself the fabric of the universe by which he was surrounded. In that inexhaustible faculty he found perfect content: He never required "to be amused".

"No, not statistics," he said presently, returning to the unfinished conversation of the club hall. "Scarcely that. More in the nature of topography, perhaps. Have you considered, Copling, how everything is specialised nowadays? Does anyone read the old-fashioned unpretentious *Guidebook to London* still? One would hardly think so to see how the subject is cut up. We have '*Famous London Blind-alleys*', '*Historical West-Central Door-Knockers*', '*Footsteps of Dr. Johnson between Gough Square and John Street, Adelphi*', '*The Thames from Hungerford Bridge to Charing Cross Pier*', '*Oxford Street Paving Stones on Which De Quincey Sat*', and so on."

"They are not familiar to me," said Sir Fergus simply.

"Nor to me. Yet they sound familiar. Well, I touched journalism myself once, years ago. What do you say to '*Mysterious Double-fronted Houses of the Outer Northern Suburbs*'? Too comprehensive?"

"I don't know. The subject must be limited. But do you seriously contemplate such a work?"

"If I did," replied Carrados, "what could you tell me about Strathblane Lodge, Highgate?"

"Oh!" A slow smile broke on Copling's face. "That is rather extraordinary, isn't it? Do you know old Spinola? Have you been there?"

"So far I don't know the venerable Mr. Spinola and I have not been there. What is the peculiarity?"

"But you know of the automatic card-player?"

The words brought a certain amount of enlightenment. Carrados had heard more than once casual allusions to a wonderful mechanical contrivance that played cards with discrimination. He had not thought anything more of it, classing it with Kempelen's famous imposture which had for a time mystified and duped the chess world more than a century ago. So far, also, some reticence appeared to be observed about the modern contrivance, as though its inventor had no desire to have it turned into a popular show: At all events, not a word about it had appeared in The Press.

"I have heard something, but not much, and I certainly have not seen it. What is it – a fraud, surely?"

340

Copling replied with measured consideration between the process of investigating his lightly boiled egg. It was plain that the automaton had impressed him.

"I naturally approached the subject with scepticism," he admitted, "but at the end of several demonstrations, I am converted to a position of passive acquiescence. Spinola, at all events, is no charlatan. His knowledge of mathematics is profound. As you know, Carrados, the subject is my own, and I am not likely to be imposed on in that particular. It was purely the scientific aspect of the invention that attracted me, for I am not a gambler in the ordinary sense. Spinola's explanation of the principles of the contrivance, when he found that I was capable of following them, was lucid and convincing. Of course, he does not disclose all the details of the mechanism, but he shows enough."

"It is a gamble, then, not a mere demonstration?"

"He has spent many years on the automaton, and it must have cost thousands of pounds in experiment and construction. He makes no secret of hoping to reimburse his outlay."

"What do you play?"

"Piquet – rubicon piquet. The figure could, he claims, be set to play any game by changing or elaborating the mechanism. He had to construct it for one definite set of chances, and he selected piquet as a suitable medium."

"It wins?"

"Against me invariably in the end."

"Why should it win, Copling? In a game that is nine-tenths chance, why should it win?"

"I am an indifferent player. If the tactics of the game have been reduced to machinery and the combinations are controlled by a dispassionate automaton, the one-tenth would constitute a winning factor."

"And against expert players?"

Sir Fergus admitted that to the best of his knowledge the figure still had the advantage. In answer to Carrados's further inquiry he estimated his losses at two- or three-hundred pounds. The stakes were whatever the visitor suggested – Spinola was something of a grandee, one inferred – and at half-crown points, Sir Fergus had found the game quite expensive enough.

"Why do people go if they invariably lose?" asked the blind man.

"My dear fellow, why do they go to Monte Carlo?" was the retort, accompanied by a tolerant shrug. "Besides, I don't positively say that they always lose. One hears of people winning, though I have never seen it happen. Then I fancy that the novelty has taken with a certain set. It is a thing at the moment to go up there and have the rather bizarre experience.

341

There is an element of the creep in it, you know – sitting and playing against that serene and unimpressionable contrivance."

"What do the others do? There is quite a company, I gather."

"Oh yes, sometimes. Occasionally one may find oneself alone. Well, the others often watch the play. Sometimes sets play bridge on their own. Then there is coffee and wine. Nothing formal, I assure you."

"Rowdy ever?"

"Oh no. The old man has a presence. I doubt if anyone would feel encouraged to go too far under Spinola's eye. Yet practically nothing seems to be known of him, not even his nationality. I have heard half-a-dozen different tales from as many cocksure men – he is a South American Spaniard ruined by a revolution. A Jesuit expelled from France through politics. An Irishman of good family settled in Warsaw, where he stole the plans from a broken-down Polish inventor. A Virginia military man, who suddenly found that he was dying from cancer and is doing this to provide a fortune for an only and beautiful daughter, and so on."

"Is there a beautiful daughter?"

"Not that I have ever seen. No, the man just cropped up, as odd people do in great capitals. Nobody really knows anything about him, but his queer salon has caught on to a certain extent."

Now any novel phase of life attracted Carrados. The mixed company that Spinola's enterprise was able to draw to an out-of-the-way suburb – the peculiar blend of science and society – was not much in itself. The various constituents could be met elsewhere to more advantage, but the assemblage might engender piquancy. And the man himself and his machine? In any case they should repay attention.

"How does one procure the entree?" he inquired.

Copling raised a quizzical eyebrow.

"You also?" he replied. "Oh, I see. You think – Well, if you are going to discover any sleight-of-hand about the business, I don't mind – "

"Yes?" prompted Carrados, for Sir Fergus had pulled up on an obvious afterthought.

"I did not intend going up again," said Copling slowly. "As a matter of fact, I have seen all that interests me. And – I suppose I may as well tell you, Carrados – I made someone a sort-of promise to have nothing to do with gambling. She feels very strongly on the subject."

"She is very wise," commented the blind man.

Elation mingled with something faintly apologetic in the abrupt bestowal of the baronet's unexpected confidence.

"It was really quite a sudden and romantic happening," he continued, led on by the imperceptible encouragement of his companion's attitude. "She is called Mercia. She does not know who I am – not that that's anything," he added modestly. "She is an orphan and earns her own living. I was able to be of some slight service to her in the science galleries at South Kensington, where she was collecting material for her employer. Then we met there again and had lunch together, and so on."

"At tea shops?"

"Oh yes. Her tastes are very simple. She doesn't like shows and society and all that."

"I congratulate you. When is it to be?"

"It? Oh! Well, we haven't settled anything like that yet. Of course this is all in confidence, Carrados."

"Absolutely – though the lady has done me rather an ill turn."

"How?"

"Well, weren't you going to introduce me to Mr. Spinola?"

"True," assented Sir Fergus. "And I don't see why I shouldn't," he added valiantly. "I need not play, and if there is any bunkum about the thing, I should certainly like to see how it is done. What evening will suit you?"

An early date had suited both, and shortly after eight o'clock – an hour at which they were likely to find few guests before them – Carrados's car drew up at Strathbane Lodge. By arrangement he had picked up Copling, who lived – "of all places in the world," as people had said when they heard of it – in an unknown street near Euston. Parkinson, out of regard for the worthy man's feelings, had been left behind on the occasion and in ignorance of his master's destination.

The appearance of the place was certainly not calculated to reassure a nervous investor. The entirely neglected garden seemed to convey a hint that the tenant might be contemplating a short occupation and a hasty flight. Nor did the exterior of the house do much to remove the unfortunate impression. Only a philosopher or an habitual defaulter would live in such a state.

The venerable Mr. Spinola received them in the salon set apart for the display of the automaton and for cards in general. It was a room of fair proportions – doubtless the largest in the house – and quite passably furnished, though in a rather odd and incongruous style. But probably any furniture on earth would have seemed incongruous to the strange, idol-like presence which the inventor had thought fit to adapt to the uses of his mechanism. The figure was placed on a low pedestal, sufficiently raised from the carpet on four plain wooden legs for all the space underneath to be clearly visible. The body was a squat, cross-legged conception, typical of an Indian deity, the head singularly life-like through the heavy gilding with which the face was covered, and behind the merely contemplative

343

expression that dominated the golden mask the carver had by chance or intention lined a faint suggestion of cynical contempt.

"You have come to see my little figure – ? Aurelius, as we call him among ourselves." said the bland old gentleman benignly. "That is right. That is right." He shook hands with them both, and received Mr. Carrados, on Sir Fergus's introduction, as though he was a very dear friend from whom he had long been parted. It was difficult indeed for Max to disengage himself from the effusive Spinola's affection without a wrench."

"Mr. Carrados happens to be blind, Mr. Spinola," interposed Copling, seeing that their host was so far in ignorance of the fact.

"Impossible! Impossible!" exclaimed Spinola, riveting his own very bright eyes on his guest's insentient ones. "Yet," he added, "one would not jest."

"It is quite true," was the matter-of-fact corroboration. "My hands must be my eyes, Mr. Spinola. In place of seeing, will you permit me to touch your wonderful creation?"

The old man's assent was immediate and cordial. They moved across the room towards the figure, the inventor modestly protesting.

"You flatter me, my dear sir. After all, it is but a toy in large. Nothing but a toy."

A weary-looking youth, the only other occupant of the room, threw down the illustrated weekly that he had picked up on the new arrivals' entrance and detained Copling.

"Yes, I had been toying a little before you arrived," he remarked flippantly. "I came early to cut Dora Lascelle off from the idle crowd and the silly little rabbit isn't coming, it appears. I didn't want to play, because, for a fact, I have no money, but the old thing bored me to hysterics. Good God! How he can talk so little on anything really entertaining, like The Giddy Flappers or Trixie Fluff's divorce, and so much about strange, unearthly things that no other living creature has ever seen even in a dream, baffles my imagination. What's an 'integral calculus', Copling? No, don't tell me, after all. Let me forget the benumbing episode as soon as possible."

"Do you wish for a game, Sir Fergus?" broke in Spinola's soft voice from across the room. "Doubtless Mr. Carrados might like to follow someone else's play before he makes the experiment."

Copling hesitated. He had not come to play, as he had already told his friend, but Max gave no sign of coming to his assistance.

"Perhaps you, Crediton?" said the mathematician, but young Crediton shook his head and smiled wisely. Copling was too easygoing to stand out. He crossed the room and sat down at the automaton's table.

"And the stake?"

"Suppose we merely have a guinea on the game?" suggested the visitor.

Spinola acquiesced with the air of one to whom a three-penny bit or a kingdom would have been equally indifferent. The deal fell to Copling and the automaton therefore had the first "elder hand," with the advantage of a discard of five cards against its opponent's three"

Carrados had already been shown the theory of the contrivance. He now followed Spinola's operations as the game proceeded. The old man picked up the twelve cards dealt to the automaton and carefully arranged them in their proper places on a square shield that was connected with the front of the figure. As each fell into its slot it registered its presence on the delicate mechanism that the figure contained.

"The discard," remarked Spinola, and moved a small lever. The left hand of the automaton was raised, came over the shield which hid its cards from the opponent, touched one with an extended finger, and affixing it by suction, lifted the selected card from the slot and dropped it face downwards on the table.

"A little slow, a little cumbersome," apologised the inventor as the motions were repeated until five cards had been thrown out. "The left hand is used for the discard alone, as a different movement is necessary." He picked up the five new cards from the stock and arranged them as he had done the hand. "Now we proceed to the play."

Crediton strolled across to watch the game. He stood behind Copling, while Carrados remained near the automaton. Spinola opened the movements.

"Aurelius has no voice, of course," he said, studying the display of cards, "so I – point of five."

"Good," conceded the opponent

Spinola registered the detail on one of an elaborate set of dials that produced a further development in the machinery.

"Spades," he announced, declaring the suit that he had won the "points" on. "Tierce major."

"Quart to the queen – hearts," claimed Copling, and Spinola moved another dial to register the opponent's advantage.

"Three kings."

"Good," was the reply.

"Three tens," added the senior player, as his three kings, being good against the other hand, enabled him to count the lower trio also. "Five for the point and two trios – eleven." Every detail of the scoring and of the ensuing play was registered as the other things had been.

This finished the preliminaries and the play of the hands began. The automaton, in response to the release of the machinery, moved its right arm with the same deliberation that had marked its former action and laid a card face upwards on the table. For the blind man's benefit each card was named as it was played. At the end of the hand Copling had won "the cards" – a matter of ten extra points with seven tricks to five and the score stood to his advantage at 27-17.

"Not bad for the junior hand," commented Crediton. "Do you know – " He addressed the inventor. " – there is a sort of 'average', as they call it, that you are supposed to play up to? I forget how it goes, but 27 is jolly high for the minor hand, I know."

"I have heard of it," replied Spinola politely. Crediton could not make out why the other two men smiled broadly. The succeeding hands developed no particular points of interest. The scoring ruled low and in the end Copling won by 129 to 87. Spinola purred congratulation.

"I am always delighted to see Aurelius lose," he declared, paying out his guinea with a princely air.

"Why?" demanded Crediton.

"Because it shows that I have succeeded beyond expectation, my dear young sir: I have made him almost human. Now, Mr. Carrados."

"With pleasure," assented the blind man. "Though I am afraid that I shall not afford you the delight of losing, Mr. Spinola."

"One never knows, one never knows," beamed the old man. "Shall we say "Half-crown points for variety?"

"Very good. Ah, our deal." He dealt the hands and proceeded to dispose the twelve that fell to the automaton on the shield. There was a moment of indecision. "Pray, Mr. Carrados, do you not arrange your cards?"

"I have done so." He had, in fact, merely spread out his hand in the usual fan formation and run an identifying finger once round the upper edges. The cards remained as they had been dealt, face downwards.

"Wonderful! And that enables you to distinguish them?"

"The ink and the impression on a plain surface – oh yes." He threw out the full discard as he spoke and took in the upper five of the stock.

"You overwhelm us. You accentuate the tiresome deliberation of poor Aurelius." Spinola was hovering about the external fittings of the figure with unusual fussiness. When at length he released the left hand it seemed for an almost perceptible moment that the action hung. Then the arm descended and carried out the discard.

"Point of five," said Carrados.

"Good."

346

"In spades. Quint major in spades also, tierce to the knave in clubs, fourteen aces – " *i.e.* four aces. "Fourteen" in the language of piquet as they score that number. He did not wait for his opponent to assent to each count, knowing, after the point had passed, that the other calls were good against anything that could possibly be held. "Five, twenty, twenty-three, ninety-seven." Having reached thirty before his opponent scored, and without a card having so far been played, his score automatically advanced by sixty. "That is the repique."

"By Jove!" exclaimed Crediton, "that's the first time I've ever known Aurelius repiqued."

"Oh, it has happened," retorted Spinola almost testily.

The play of the hand was bound to go in Carrados's favour – he held eight certain tricks. He won "the cards" with two tricks to spare and the round closed at 119-5.

"You look like being delighted again, Mr. Spinola," remarked Crediton a little critically.

"Suppose you make yourself useful by dealing for me," interposed Carrados. "Of course," he reminded his host, "it does not do for me to handle any cards but my own."

"I had not thought of that," replied Spinola, looking at him shrewdly. "If you had no conscience, you would be a dangerous opponent, Mr. Carrados."

"The same might be said of any man," was the reply. "That is why it is so satisfactory to play an automaton."

"Oh, Aurelius has no conscience, you know," chimed in Crediton sapiently. "Mr. Spinola couldn't find room for it among the wheels."

The second hand was not eventful. Each player had to be content to make about the "average" which Crediton had ingenuously discovered. It raised the scores to 33-30. Two hands followed in the same prudent spirit. The fifth – Carrados's "elder" – found the position 169-67.

"Only two this time," remarked Carrados, taking in.

"Jupiter!" murmured Crediton. It is unusual for the senior hand to leave even one of the five cards to which he is entitled. It indicated an unusually strong hand. The automaton evidently thought so too. It availed itself of all the six alternative cards and, as the play disclosed, completely cut up its own hand to save the repique by beating Carrados on the point. It won the point, to find that its opponent only held a low quart, a tierce and three kings. As a result Carrados won "the cards" and the score stood 199-79. The discard was, in fact, an experiment in bluff. Carrados might have held a quint and fourteen kings for all the opposing hand disclosed.

"What on earth did you do that for?" demanded Copling. He himself played an eminently straightforward game – and generally lost.

"I'll bet I know," put in Crediton. "You are getting rather close, Mr. Spinola – the last hand and you need twenty – one to save the rubicon." The "rubicon" means that instead of the loser's score being deducted from the winner's in arriving at the latter's total, it is added to it – a possible difference of nearly 200 points.

"We shall see, we shall see," muttered Spinola with a little less than his usual suavity.

Whatever concern he had, however, was groundless, for the game ended tamely enough. Carrados ought to have won the point and divided tricks, leaving his opponent a minor quart and a solitary trio – about 15 on the hand. By a careless discard he threw away both chances and the final score stood at 205-112. Copling, who had come to regard his friend's play as rather excellent, was silent. Crediton almost shrieked his disapproval and seizing the cards demonstrated to his heart's content.

"Ninety-three and the hundred for the game – twenty-four pounds and one half-crown," said the loser, counting out notes and coin to the amount. "It has been an experience for both of us – Aurelius and myself."

"And certainly for me," added Carrados.

"Look here," interposed Crediton, "Aurelius seems off his play. If you don't mind taking my paper, Mr. Spinola, I should like another go."

"As you please," assented the old man. "Your undertaking is, of course – " The gesture suggested "quite equal to that of the cashier of the Bank of England." The venerable person had, in fact, regained his lofty pecuniary indifference. "The same point?"

"Right-o," cheerfully assented the youth.

"I will go and think over my shortcomings," said Carrados. He started to cross the room to a seat and ran into a couch. With a gasp Copling hastened to his assistance. Then he found his arm detained and heard the whisper. "Sit down with me."

Across the room the play had begun again and with a little care they could converse without the possibility of a word being overheard.

"What is it?" asked Sir Fergus.

"The golden one will win. It is only when the cards are not exposed that you play on equal terms."

"But I won?"

"Because it is well to lose sometimes and, by choice, when the stake is low. That witless youth will have to pay for both of us."

"But how – how on earth do you suggest that it is done?"

"Look round cautiously. What eyes overlook Crediton's hand as he sits there?"

"What eyes? Good gracious! is there anything in that?"

"What is it?"

348

"There is a trophy of Japanese arms high up on the wall. An iron mask surmounts it. It has glass eyes. I have never seen anything like that before."

"Any others round the walls?"

"There is a stuffed tiger's head on our right and a puma's or something of that sort on the left."

"In case a suspicious player asks to have the places changed or holds his cards awkwardly. Working the automaton from other positions is probably also arranged for."

"But how can a knowledge of the opponent's cards affect the automaton? The dials – "

"The dials are all bunkum. While you were playing I took the liberty of altering them and for a whole hand the dials indicated that you must inevitably be holding eight clubs and four spades. All the time you were leading out hearts and diamonds and the automaton serenely followed suit. The only effective machinery is that indicating the display of cards on the shield and controlling the hands, and that is worked by a keyboard and electric current from the room below. The watcher behind the mask telephones the opposing hand, the discard and the take-in. The automaton's hand has already been indicated below. You see the enormous advantage the hidden player has? When he is the minor hand he knows everything that is to be known before he discards. When he is the elder he knows almost everything. By concentrating on one detail he can practically always balk the pique, the repique and the kapot, if it is necessary to play for safety. You remember what Crediton said – that he had never known Aurelius repiqued before. The leisurely manipulation of the dials gives plenty of time. An even ordinary player in that position can do the rest."

Copling scarcely knew whether to believe or not. It sounded plausible, but it reflected monstrously.

"You speak of a telephone," he said. "How can you definitely say that such a thing is being used? You have never been in the room before and we've scarcely been here an hour. It – it may be awfully serious, you know."

Carrados smiled.

"Can you hear the kitchen door being opened at this moment or detect the exact aroma of our host's mocha?" he demanded.

"Not in the least," admitted Copling.

"Then of course it is hopeless to expect you to pick up the whisper of a man behind a mask a score of feet away. How fearfully in the dark you seeing folk must be!"

349

"Can you possibly do that?" Even as he was speaking the door opened and a servant entered, bringing coffee and an assortment of viands sufficiently exotic to maintain the rather Oriental nature of entertainment.

"Stroll across and see how the game is going," suggested Carrados. "Have a look at Crediton's discard and then come back."

Sir Fergus did not quite follow the purpose, but he nodded and proceeded to comply with his usual amiable spirit.

"It stands at 137 to 75 against Crediton and they are playing the last hand. Our young friend looks like losing thirty or forty pounds."

"And his discard?"

"Oh – seven and nine of clubs and the knave of hearts."

Carrados held out a slip of paper on which he had already pencilled a few words. The baronet took it, looked and whistled softly. He had read: "'*Clubs, seven, nine. Hearts, knave.*'"

"Conjuring?" he interrogated.

"Quite as simple – listening..

"I suppose I must accept it. What staggers me is that you can pick out a whisper when the room is full of other louder sounds. Now if there had been absolute stillness – "

"Merely use. There's nothing more in it than in seeing a mouse and a mountain, or a candle and the sun, at the same time. Well, what are we going to do about it?"

Copling began to look acutely unhappy.

"I suppose we must do something," he ruminated, "but I must say that I wish we needn't. I mean, I wish we hadn't dropped on this. You know, Carrados, whatever is going on, Spinola is no charlatan. He does understand mathematics."

"That makes him all the more dangerous. But I should like to produce more definite proof before we do anything. Does he ever leave us in the room?"

"I have never known it. No, he hovers round his Aurelius."

"Never mind. Ah, the game is finished."

The game was finished and it needed no inquiry to learn how it had gone. Mr. Crediton was handing the venerable Spinola a memorandum of indebtedness. His words and attitude did not convey the impression of a graceful loser.

"I wish you two men would give me the tip for beating this purgatorial image," he grumbled as they came up. "I thought that he'd struck a losing line after your experience and this is the result." He indicated the spectacle of their amiable host folding up his I.O.U. preparatory to dropping it carelessly into a letter-rack, and shrugged his shoulders with keen disgust.

"I'll tell you if you like," suggested Sir Fergus. "Hold the better cards."

"And play them better," added Carrados. "Good Heavens!"

A very untoward thing had happened. They had all been standing together round the table, Spinola purring appreciatively, Crediton fuming his ill-restrained annoyance, and the other two mildly satirical at his expense. Carrados held a cup of coffee in his hand. He reached towards the table with it, seemed to imagine that he was a full foot nearer than he was, and before anyone had divined his mistake, cup, saucer and the entire contents had dropped neatly upon Mr. Spinola's startled feet, saturating his lower extremities to the skin.

"Good Heavens! What on earth have I done?"

Crediton shrieked out his ill-humour in gratified amusement. Sir Fergus reddened deeply with embarrassment at his friend's mishap. Victim and culprit stood the ordeal best.

"My unfortunate defect!" murmured Carrados with feeling. "How ever can I – "

"I who have eyes ought to have looked after my guest better," replied Spinola with antique courtliness. He reduced Crediton with a glance of quiet dignity and declined Carrados's handkerchief with a reassuring touch on the blind man's arm. "No, no, my dear sir, if you will excuse me for a few minutes. It is really nothing, really nothing, I do assure you."

He withdrew from the room to change. Copling began to prepare a reassuring phrase to meet Carrados's self-reproaches when they should break forth again. But the blind man's tone had altered. He was no longer apologetic

"Play them better," he repeated to Crediton, as if there had been no interruption, "and play under conditions that are equal. For instance, it might be worthwhile making sure that a Japanese mask does not conceal a pair of human eyes. If I were a loser, I should be inclined to have a look."

Not until then did it occur to Sir Fergus that his friend's clumsiness had been a calculated ruse to force Spinola to withdraw for a few minutes. Later on he might be able to admire the simple ingenuity of the trick, but at that moment he almost hated Carrados for the cool effrontery with which he had duped all their feelings

No such subtleties, however, concerned Crediton. He stared at the blind man, followed the indication of his gesture, and all at once grasped the significance of the hint.

"By George, I shouldn't wonder if you aren't right!" he exclaimed. "There are one or two things " Without further consideration he rushed a table against the wall, swung up a chair on to it, and mounting the structure began to wrench the details of the trophy from side to side and up and down in his excited efforts to displace them

"Hurry up," urged Copling, more nervous than excited. "He won't be long."

"Hurry up?" Crediton paused, panting from his furious efforts, and found time to look down upon his accomplices. "I don't think that it's for us to concern ourselves, by George!" he retorted. "Spinola had better hurry up and bolt for it, I should say. There's light behind here – a hole through the wall. I believe the place is a regular swindling hell."

His eyes went to the group of weapons again and the sight gave him a new idea.

"A-ha, what price this?" he cried, and pulling a short sword out of its sheath he drove it in between mask and wall and levered the shell away, nails and all. "By God, if the eyes aren't a pair of opera-glasses! And there's a regular paraphernalia here – "

"So," interrupted a quiet voice behind them, "you have been too clever for an old man, Mr. Carrados?"

Spinola had returned unheard and was regarding the work of detection with the utmost benignness. Copling looked and felt ridiculously guilty. The blind man betrayed no emotion at all and both were momentarily silent. It fell to Crediton to voice retort.

"My I.O.U., if you don't mind, Mr. Spinola," he demanded, tumbling down from his perch and holding out an insistent hand.

"With great pleasure," replied Spinola, picking it out from the contents of the letter-rack. "Also," he continued, referring to the contents of his pocket-book, while his guest tore up the memorandum into very small pieces and strewed them about the carpet, "also the sum of fifty-seven pounds, thirteen shillings which I feel myself compelled to return to you in spite of your invariable grace in losing. I have already rung. You will find the front door waiting open for you, Mr. Crediton."

"'Compelled' is good," sneered Crediton. "You will probably find a train waiting for you at Charing Cross, Mr. Spinola. I advise you to catch it before the police arrive." He nodded to the other two men and departed, to spread the astounding news in the most interested quarters.

Spinola continued to beam irrepressible benevolence.

"You are equally censorious, if more polite than Mr. Crediton in expressing it, eh, my dear young friends?" he said.

"I thought that you were a genuine mathematician – I vouched for it," replied Sir Fergus with more regret than anything else. "And the extent of your achievement has been to contrive a vulgar imposture – in the guise of an ingenious inventor to swindle society by a sham automaton that doesn't even work."

"You thought that – you still think that?"

"What else is there to think? We have seen with our own eyes."

"And – " turning to his other guest " – Mr. Carrados, who does not see?"

"I am waiting to hear," replied the blind man.

"But you, Sir Fergus, you who are also – in an elementary way – a mathematician, and one with whom I have conversed freely, you regard me as a common swindler and think that this – this tawdry piece of buffoonery that is only designed to appeal to the vapid craze for novelty of your foolish friends – this is, as you say, the extent of my achievement?"

Copling gave a warning cry and sprang forward, but it was too late to avert what he saw coming. In his petulant annoyance at the comparison, Spinola had laid an emphasising hand upon Aurelius and half-unconsciously had given the figure a contemptuous push. It swayed, seemed to poise for a second, and then toppling irretrievably forward crashed to the floor with an impact that snapped the golden head from off its shoulders and shook the room and the very house itself.

"There, there," muttered the old man, as though he was doing no more than regretting a broken tea-cup. "Let it lie, let it lie. We have finished our work together, Aurelius and I. Now let the whole world – "

It would have been too much to expect the remainder of the mysterious household, whoever its members were, to ignore the tempestuous course of events taking place within their midst. The door was opened suddenly and a young lady, with consternation charged on every feature of her attractive face, burst into the room. For the moment her eyes took in only two figures of the curious group the aged Spinola and his fallen handiwork.

"Granda!" she cried, "whatever's happened? What is it all? Oh, are you hurt?"

"It is nothing, nothing at all. A mere contretemps of no importance," he reassured her quickly. Then, with a recurrence of his most grandiloquent manner, he recalled her to the situation. "Mercia, our guests – Sir Fergus Copling, Mr. Carrados. Sir Fergus, Mr. Carrados – Miss Dugard."

"Then it is Mercia!" articulated the bewildered baronet. "Mercia, you here! What does it mean? What are you doing?"

"What are you doing, Sir Fergus?" retorted the girl in cold reproach. "Is this the way you generally keep your promises? Gambling!"

"Well, really," stammered the abashed gentleman, "I – I only – "

"Sir Fergus only played a game for a mere nominal stake, to demonstrate the working to his friend," interposed Spinola with a shrewd glance – a curious blend of serpentine innocence and dove-like cunning – at the estranged young people.

"And won," added Sir Fergus *sotto voce*, as if that fact condoned his offence.

"Won indeed!" flashed out Miss Dugard. "Of course you won – I let you. Do you think that we wished to take money from you now?"

"You – you let me!" muttered Sir Fergus helplessly. "Good Heavens!"

"I am grateful that your consideration also extends to your friend's friend," put in Carrados pleasantly.

Miss Dugard smiled darkly at the suavely-given thrust and showed her pretty little teeth almost as though she would like to use them.

"There, there, that will do, my child," said the old man indulgently. "Sir Fergus and Mr. Carrados are entitled to an explanation and they shall have it. The moment is opportune. The work of a lifetime is complete. You have seen, Sir Fergus, the sums that Aurelius – assisted, as we will now admit, by a little external manipulation – has gathered into our domestic exchequer. Where have they gone, these hundreds and thousands that you may estimate? In lavish living and a costly establishment? Observe this very ordinary apartment – the best the house possesses. Recall the grounds through which you entered. Sum up the simple hospitality of which you have partaken. In expensive personal tastes and habits? I assure you, Sir Fergus, that I am a man of the most frugal life. My granddaughter inherits the propensity. In what, then? In advancing science, in benefitting humanity, in furthering human progress. I am going to prove to you that I have perfected one of the greatest mechanical inventions of all ages, and I ask you to credit the plain statement that all my private fortune and all the winnings that you have seen upon this table – with the exception of a bare margin for the necessities of life, have been spent in perfecting it."

He paused with a senile air of triumph and seemed to challenge comment.

"But surely," ventured Copling, "surely on the strength of this you, would have had no difficulty in obtaining direct financial support. Well, I myself – "

Spinola smiled a peculiar smile, shaking his head sagely.

"Take care, my generous young friend, take care. You may not quite comprehend what you are saying."

"Why?"

Still swayed by his own gentle amusement, the old man crossed the room to a desk, selected a letter from a bulky pile, and handed it to his guest without a word.

354

Copling glanced at the heading and signature, then read the contents and frowned annoyance.

"This is from my secretary," he commented lamely.

"That is what a secretary is for, is it not – to save his employer trouble?" insinuated Spinola. "He took me for a crank or a begging-letter impostor, of course." Then came the pathetic whisper. "They all took me for that."

Sir Fergus folded the letter and handed it back again.

"I am very sorry," he said simply.

"It was natural, perhaps. Still, something had to be done. My work was all arrested. I could no longer pay my two skilled mechanics. Time was pressing. I am a very old man – I am more than a hundred years old –"

The girl shot a sudden, half-frightened, pleading glance at her lover, then at Mr. Carrados. It checked the exclamation that would have come from Copling. The blind man passed the monstrous claim without betraying astonishment.

" – a very old man and my work was yet incomplete. So I contrived Aurelius. I could, of course, have perfected a model that would have done all that has been claimed for this – mere child's play to me – but what would have been the good? Such a mechanical player would have lost as often as he would have won. Hence our little subterfuge, a means amply justified by so glorious an end."

He was smiling happily – the weeks of elaborate deception were, at the worst, an innocent ruse to him – and concluded with an emphasising nod to each in turn, to Mercia, who regarded him with implicit faith and veneration, to Copling, who at that moment surely had ample justification for declaring to himself that he was dashed if he knew what to think, and to Carrados, whose sightless look agreed to everything and gave nothing in reply. Then the old man stood up and produced his keys.

"Come, my friends," he continued. "The moment has arrived. I am going to show you now what no other eye has yet been privileged to see. My mechanics worked on the parts under my instruction, but in ignorance of the end. Even Merci, a – a good girl, a very clever girl – has never yet passed this door." He had led them through the house and brought them to a brick-built, windowless shed, isolated in the garden at the back. "I little thought that the first demonstration – but things have fallen so, things have fallen, and one never knows. Perhaps it is for the best." An iron door had yielded to his patent key. He entered, turned on a bunch of electric lights and stood aside. "Behold!"

The room was a workshop, fitted with the highly finished devices of metal – working and littered with the scraps and debris of their use. In the

355

middle stood a more elaborate contrivance – the finished product of brass and steel – a cube scarcely larger than a packing-case, but seemingly filled with wheels and rods, relay upon relay, and row after row, all giving the impression of exquisite precision in workmanship and astonishing intricacy of detail.

"Why, it's a calculating machine," exclaimed Sir Fergus, going forward with immense interest.

"It is an analytical engine, or, to use the more common term, a calculating machine, as you say," assented the inventor. "I need hardly remind you, of course, that one does not spend a lifetime and a fortune in contriving a machine to do single calculations, however involved, but for the more useful and practical purpose of working out involved series with absolute precision. Still, for the purpose of a trial demonstration we will begin with an ordinary proposition, if you, Sir Fergus, will kindly set one. My engine now is constructed to work to fifty places of figures and twelve orders of difference."

"If you have accomplished that," remarked Copling, accepting the pencil and the slip of paper offered him, "you have surpassed the dreams of Babbage, Mr. Spinola."

There was a sudden gasp from Mercia, but it passed unheeded in the keen excitement of the great occasion. Spinola received the paper with its row of signs and figures and turned to operate his engine. He paused to look back gleefully."

"So you never guessed, Sir Fergus?" he chuckled cunningly. "We kept the secret well, but it doesn't matter now. *I am Charles Babbage!*"

The noise of wheel and connecting-rod cut off the chance of a reply, even if anyone had been prepared to make one. But no one, in that bewildering moment, was.

"The solution," announced Spinola with a flourish, and he passed a little slip of metal stamped with a row of figures into Sir Fergus's hand. Then, with a curious indifference to their verdict, he turned away from the group and applied himself to the machine again.

"What is it? Is it not correct?" demanded Mercia in an agonised whisper. She had not looked at the solution, but at her lover's face, and her hand suddenly gripped his arm.

"It is incomprehensible," replied Sir Fergus, dropping his voice so that the old man could not overhear. "It isn't a matter of right or wrong – it is a mere farrago of nonsense."

"But harmless nonsense – quite harmless," interposed Carrados softly from behind them. "Come, we can safely leave him here. You will always be able to leave him safely here. Help Miss Dugard out, Copling. It is better, believe me, to leave him now."

356

Spinola did not turn. He was bending over the machine to which he had given life, brain, and fortune, touching its wheels and sliding rods with loving fingers. They passed silently from his presence and crept back to the deserted salon, where the deposed head of Aurelius leered cynically at them from the floor."

The Kingsbouth Spy Case

"Not guilty, my Lord!" There was a general laugh in the lounge of The Rose and Plumes, the comfortable old Cliffhurst hotel that upheld the ancient traditions unaffected by the flaunting rivalry of Grand or Metropole. The jest hidden in the retort was a small one, but it was at the expense of a pompous, pretentious bore, and the speaker was a congenial wag who had contrived in the course of a few weeks to win a facile popularity on all sides.

Across the room one of the later arrivals – "the blind gentleman" as he was sympathetically alluded to, for few had occasion to learn his name – turned slightly towards the direction of the voice and added a pleasantly appreciative smile to the common tribute. Then his attention again settled on the writing-table at which he sat, and for the next few minutes his pencil travelled smoothly, with an occasional pause for consideration, over the block of telegraphic forms that he had picked out. At the end of ten minutes he rang for a waiter and directed that his own man should be sent to him.

"Here are three telegrams to go off, Parkinson," he said in the suave, agreeable voice that scarcely ever varied, no matter what the occasion might be. "You will take them yourself at once. After that, I shall not require you again tonight."

The attendant thanked him and withdrew. The blind man closed his letter-case, retired from the writing-table to the obscurity of a sequestered corner, and sat unnoticed with his sightless eyes that always seemed to be quietly smiling, looking placidly into illimitable space as he visualised the scene before him, and the laughter, the conversation, and the occasional whisper went on unchecked around.

Max Carrados had journeyed down to Cliffhurst a few days previously, good-naturedly, but without any enthusiasm. Indeed, it had needed all Mr. Carlyle's persuasive eloquence to move him.

"The Home Office, Max," urged the inquiry agent, "one of the premier departments of the State! Consider the distinction! Surely you will not refuse a commission of that nature direct from the Government?" Carrados, looking a little deeper than a Melton overcoat and a glossy silk hat, had once declared his friend to be the most incurably romantic of idealists. He now took a malicious pleasure in reducing the situation to its crudest terms.

"Why can't the local police arrest a solitary inoffensive German spy themselves?" he inquired.

"To tell the truth, Max, I believe that there are two or three fingers in that pie at the present moment," replied Mr. Carlyle confidentially. "It doesn't concern the Home Office alone. And after that Guitry Bay fiasco and the unmerciful chaffing that we got in the German papers – with rather a nasty rap or two over the knuckles from the Kölnische Zeitung – both Whitehall and Downing Street are in a blue funk lest they should do the wrong thing, either let the man slip away with the papers or arrest him without them."

"Contingencies with which I am sure you could grapple successfully, Louis."

Mr. Carlyle's bland complacency did not suggest that he, at any rate, had any doubt on that score.

"But, you know, Max, I am pledged to carry through the Vandeeming affair here in town. And – um – well, the Secretary did make a point of you being the man they relied on."

"Oh! Someone there must read the papers, Louis. But I wonder . . . why they did not communicate with me direct?"

Mr. Carlyle contrived to look extremely ingenuous. Even he occasionally forgot that looks went for nothing with Carrados.

"I imagine that they thought that a friendly intermediary – or something of that sort."

"Possibly Inspector Beedel hinted to the Commissioner that you would have more influence with me than a whole Government Department?" smiled Carrados. "And so you have, Louis. So you have. If it's your ambition to get the Government on your books, you can tell your clients that I'll take on their job!"

"By Jupiter, Max, you are a good fellow if ever there was one!" exclaimed Mr. Carlyle with gentlemanly emotion. "But I owe too much to you already."

"This won't make it any more, then. I have another reason, quite different, for going."

"Of course you have," assented the visitor heartily. "You are not one to talk about patriotism, and all that, but you can't hoodwink me with your dilettantish pose, Max, and I know that deep down in your nature there is a passionate devotion to your country – "

"Thank you, Louis," interrupted Carrados. "It is very nice to learn that. But I am really going to Kingsmouth because there's a man there – a curate – who has the second best private collection in Europe of autonomous coins of Thessaly."

For a few seconds Mr. Carlyle looked his unutterable feelings. When he did speak it was with crushing deliberation.

"'Mrs. Carrados,' I shall say – if ever there is a Mrs. Carrados, Max – 'Mrs. Carrados, two things are necessary for your domestic happiness. In the first place, pack up your husband's *tetradrachms* in a brown-paper parcel and send them with your compliments to the British Museum. In the second: At the earliest possible opportunity, exact from him an oath that he will never touch another Greek coin as long as you both live – '

"If ever there is a Mrs. Carrados," was the quick retort, "I shall probably be independent of the consolation of Greek coins as, also, Louis, of the distraction of criminal investigation. In the meantime, what are you going to tell me about this case?" Mr. Carlyle at once became alert. He would have become absolutely professional had not Carrados tactfully obtruded the cigar box. The digression, and the pleasant aroma that followed it, brought him back again to the merely human.

"It began, like a good many other cases, with an anonymous letter." He took a slip of paper from his pocket-book and handed it to Carrados. "Here is a copy."

"A copy!" The blind man ran his finger lightly along the lines and read aloud what he found there:

"'*A friend warns you that an attempt is being successfully made on behalf of another Power to obtain naval information of vital importance. You have a traitor within your gates.*'"

Then he crumpled up the paper and dropped it half-contemptuously into the waste-paper basket. "A copy is no use to us, Louis," he remarked. "Indeed, it is worse than useless. It is misleading."

"That is all they had here. The original was addressed to the Admiral-Superintendent at the Kingsmouth Dockyard. This was sent up with the report. But I am assured that the other contained no clue to the writer's identity."

"Not even a watermark, '*Jones, stationer, High Street, Kingsmouth*'!" said Carrados dryly. "Really, Louis! Every piece of paper contains at least four palpable clues."

"And what are they, pray?"

"A smell, a taste, an appearance, and a texture. This one, in addition, bears ink, and with it all the characteristics of an individual handwriting."

"In capitals, Max," Mr. Carlyle reminded him. "Our anonymous friend is up to that."

"Yes. I wonder who first started that venerable illusion."

"Illusion?"

"Certainly an illusion. Capitals, or 'printed handwriting' as one sees them called, are just as idiomorphic as a cursive form."

"But much less available for comparison. How are you going to obtain a specimen of anyone's printed handwriting for comparison?"

360

Carrados reflected silently for a moment.

"I think I should ask anyone I suspected to do one for me," he replied.

Carlyle resisted the temptation to laugh outright, but mordacity lurked in his voice.

"And you imagine that the writer of this, who evidently has good reason for anonymity, will be simple enough to comply?"

"I think so. If I ask him nicely."

"Look here, Max, I will bet you a box of any cigars you care to name —"

"Yes, Louis?"

Mr. Carlyle had hesitated. He was recalling one or two things from the past, and on those occasions his friend's unemotional face had looked just as devoid of guile as it did now.

"No, Max, I won't bet this time, but I should like to send across a small box of Monterey Coronas for Parkinson to pack among your things. Well, so much for the letter."

"Not quite all," interposed Carrados. "I must have the original."

The visitor made a note in his pocket diary.

"It shall be sent to you at once. I stipulated an absolutely free hand for you. Oh, I took a tolerably high tone! I can assure you, Max. You will find everything at Kingsmouth very pleasant, and there, of course, you will learn all the details. Here they don't seem to know very much. I was not informed whether the Dockyard authorities had already had their suspicions aroused, or whether the letter was the first hint. At all events, they acted with tolerable promptness. The letter, you will see, is undated, but it was delivered on the seventeenth – last Thursday. On Friday they put their hands on a man in the construction department – a fellow called Brown. He made no fight of it when he was cornered, but although he owned up to the charge of betraying information, there was one important link that he could not supply and one that he would not. He could not tell them who the spy collecting the information was, because there was an intermediary, and he would not betray the intermediary on any terms. And, by Gad! I for one can't help respecting the beggar for that remnant of loyalty."

"A woman?" suggested Carrados.

"Even that, I believe, is not known, but very likely you have hit the mark. A woman would explain the element of chivalry that prompts Brown's attitude. He is under open arrest now – nobody outside is supposed to know, but of course he can't buy an evening paper without it being noted. They are in hope of something more definite turning up. At present, they have pitched their suspicions on a German visitor staying at Cliffhurst."

"Why?"

"I don't know, Max. They must fix on someone, you know. It's expected. All the same, they are deucedly nervous at this end about the outcome."

"Did they say what Brown had given away?"

"Yes, egad! Do you know anything of the Croxton-Delahey torpedo?"

"A little," admitted Carrados.

"What does it do?" asked Mr. Carlyle, with the rather sublime air of casual interest which he attached to any subject outside his own knowledge.

"It's rather an ingenious contrivance. It is fired like any other uncontrolled torpedo. At the end of a straight run – anything up to ten-thousand yards at fifty-five knots with the superheated system – the diabolical creature stops and begins deliberately to slash a zigzag course over any area you have set it for. If in its roving it comes within two-hundred feet of any considerable mass of iron, it promptly makes for it, cuts its way through torpedo netting if any bars its progress, explodes its three-hundred weight of gun-cotton and finishes its existence by firing a twenty-four-pound thorite shell through the breach it has made."

"Umm," mused Mr. Carlyle, "I don't like the weapon, Max, but I would rather that we kept it to ourselves. Well, Mr. Brown has given away the plans." Carrados disposed of the end of his cigar and crossed the room to his open desk. From its appointed place he took a book inscribed "*Engagements*", touched a few pages, and scribbled a line of comment here and there. Then he turned to his guest again.

"All right. I'll go down to Kingsmouth by the 12:17 tomorrow morning," he said. "Now I want you to look up the following points for me and let me have the particular before I go."

Mr. Carlyle again took out his pocket diary and beamed approvingly.

As a matter of fact the tenor of the replies he received influenced Carrados to make some change in his plans. Accompanied by Parkinson, he left London by the appointed train on the next day, but instead of proceeding to Kingsmouth he alighted at Cliffhurst, the pretty little seaside resort some five miles east of the great dock-port. After securing rooms at The Rose and Plumes – an easy enough matter in October – he directed his attendant to take him to a sheltered seat on the winding paths below the promenade and there leave him for an hour.

"Very nicely kept, these walks and shrubberies, sir," remarked an affable voice from the other end of the bench. A leisurely pedestrian whose clothes and manner proclaimed him to be an aimless holiday-maker had

362

sauntered along and, after a moment's hesitation, had sat down on the same form.

"Yes, Inspector," replied Carrados genially. "Almost up to the standard of our own Embankment Gardens, are they not?"

Detective-Inspector Tapling, of New Scotland Yard, went rather red and then laughed quietly.

"I wasn't quite sure at first if it was you, Mr. Carrados," he apologised, moving nearer and lowering his voice. "I was to report to you here, sir, and to give you any information and assistance you might require."

"How are you getting on?" inquired Carrados.

"We think that we have got hold of the right man, sir, but for reasons that you can guess, the Chief is very anxious to have no mistake this time."

"Muller?"

"Yes, sir. He has a furnished villa here in Cliffhurst and is very open-handed. The time he came fits in, so far as we can tell, with the beginning of the inquiries in Kingsmouth. Then, whatever his real name is, it isn't Muller."

"He is a German?"

"Oh yes. He's German right enough, sir. We've looked up telegrams to him from Lübeck – nothing important though – and he has changed German notes in Kingsmouth. He spends a lot of time over there – says the fishing is better, but that's all my eye, only the Kingsmouth boatmen get hold of the dockyard talk and know more of the movements than the men about here. Then there's a lady."

"The intermediary?"

"That's further than we can go at the moment, but there is a lady at the furnished villa. She's not exactly Mrs. Muller, we believe, but she lives there, if you understand what I mean, sir."

"Perfectly," acquiesced Carrados in the same modest spirit.

"So that all the necessary conditions can be shown to exist," concluded Tapling.

"But so far you have not a single positive fact connecting Muller with Brown?"

The inspector admitted that he had not, but added hopefully that he was in immediate expectation of information that would enable him to link up the detached surmises into a conclusive chain of direct evidence.

"And if I might ask the favour of you, sir," he continued, "you would be doing us a great service if you would allow us to continue our investigation for another twenty-four hours. I think that by then we shall be able to show something solid. And if you certify what we have done,

363

that's all to our credit, whereas if you take it out of our hands now – You see what I mean, Mr. Carrados, but of course it lies entirely with you."

Carrados assented with his usual good nature. His actual business was only to examine the evidence before the arrest was made and to guarantee that the Home Office should not be involved in another spy-scare fiasco. He knew Tapling to be a reliable officer, and he did not doubt that the line he was working was the correct one. Least of all did he wish to deprive the man of his due credit.

"I can very well put in a day on my own account," he accordingly replied. "And so long as Muller is here there does not appear to be any special urgency. I suppose the odds are that the papers have been got away before you began to watch?"

"There is just a chance yet, we believe, sir, and the Admiralty is very keen on recovering those torpedo plans if it's to be done. Some of these foreign spies like to keep the thing as much as possible in their own hands. There's more credit to it, and more cash, too, at headquarters if they do. Then if it comes to a matter of touch-and-go, a letter, and especially a letter from abroad, may be stopped on the way. You will say that a man may be, for that matter, but there's been another reason against posting valuable papers about here for the past week."

"Of course," assented Carrados with enlightenment. "The Suffragettes down here are out."

"I never thought to have any of that lot helping me," said the inspector, absent-mindedly stroking his right shin, "but they may have turned the scale for us this time. There isn't a posting place from a rural pillar-box to the head office at Kingsmouth that has been really safe from them. They've even got at the registered letters in the sorting rooms somehow. That's why I think there's a chance still." Parkinson's approaching figure announced that an hour had passed. Carrados and the inspector rose to walk away in different directions, but before they parted, the blind man put a question that had confronted him several times, although he had as yet given only a glancing attention to the case.

"Now that Muller has got the plans of the torpedo, Inspector, why is he remaining here?"

It was a simple and an obvious inquiry, but before he replied, Inspector Tapling looked round suspiciously. Then he further reduced the distance between them and dropped his voice to a whisper.

St. Ethelburga's boasted the most tin-potty bell and the highest ritual of any church in Kingsmouth. Outside it resembled a brick barn, inside a marble palace, and its ministration overworked a vicar and two enthusiastic curates. It stood at the corner of Jubilee Street and Lower

Dock Approach, a conjunction that should render further description of the neighbourhood superfluous.

The Revevernd Byam Hosier, the senior curate, whose magnetic eloquence filled St. Ethelburga's from chancel steps to porch, lodged in Jubilee Street, and there Mr. Carrados found him at ten o'clock on the following morning. The curate had just finished his breakfast, and the simultaneous correction of a batch of exercise books. He apologised for the disorder without justifying himself by explaining the cause, for instead of being a laggard, Mr. Hosier had already taken an early celebration, and afterwards allowed himself to be intercepted on his way back to attend to a domestic quarrel, a lost cat, and the arrangements for a funeral.

"I got your note last night, Mr. Carrados," he said, after guiding his guest to a seat, for Parkinson had been dismissed to make himself agreeable elsewhere. "I am glad to show you my small collection, and still more so to have an opportunity of thanking you for the help you have given me from time to time."

Carrados lightly disclaimed the obligation. It was the first time the two had met, though, as the outcome of a review article, they had frequently corresponded. The clergyman went to his single cabinet, took out the top tray, and put it down before his visitor on the now available table.

"*Pherae*," he said.

"May I touch the surfaces?" asked the blind man.

"Oh, certainly. Pray do. I am sorry " He did not quite know what to say before the spectacle of the blind expert, with his eyes fixed elsewhere, passing a critical touch over the details that he himself loved to gaze upon

In this one thing the Reverend Byam was fastidious. His clothes were generally bordering on the shabby, and he allowed himself to wear boots that shocked or amused the feminine element in the first half-dozen pews of St. Ethelburga's. He might – as he frequently did, indeed – make a breakfast of weak tea, bread, and butter and marmalade without any sense of deficiency, but in the matter of Greek coins his taste was exacting and his standard exact. His one small mahogany cabinet was pierced for five-hundred specimens, and it was far from full, but every coin was the exquisite production of the golden era of the world's creative art. It did not take Carrados three minutes to learn this. Occasionally he dropped a word of comment or inquiry, but for the most part tray succeeded tray in fascinated silence.

"Still Larissa," announced the clergyman, sliding out the last tray.

Under each coin was a circular ticket with written particulars of the specimen accompanying it. For some time Carrados took little interest in these commentaries, but presently Hosier noticed that his guest was submitting many of them to a close but quiet scrutiny.

"Excuse my asking, Mr. Carrados," he said at length, "but are you quite blind?"

"Quite," was the unconcerned reply. "Why?"

"Because I noticed that you held some of the labels close to your eyes and I fancied that perhaps – "

"It is my way."

"Forgive my curiosity."

"I can assure you, Mr. Hosier, that other people are much more touchy about my blindness than I am. Now will you do me a kindness? I should like a copy of the inscriptions on half-a-dozen of these gems."

"With pleasure." The curate discovered pen and ink and paper and waited.

"This *didrachm* of the nymph Larissa wearing earrings. This of Artemis and the stag. This, and this, and this." The trays had been left displayed upon the table and Carrados's hand selected from them with unerring precision

Hosier took the chosen coins and noted down the legends in their bold Greek capitals. "Shall I describe the type of each as well?" he asked.

"Thank you," assented his visitor. "If you don't mind writing that also in capitals and not blotting, I shall read it so much the easier."

He accepted the sheet of paper and delicately touched the lettering along each line.

"I have a friend who will be equally interested in this," he remarked, taking out his pocket-book.

The clergyman had turned to remove a tray from the table when a sheet of paper, fluttering to the ground, caught his eye. He picked it up and was returning it into the blind man's hand when he stopped in a sudden arrest of every movement.

"Good Heavens, Mr. Carrados!" he exclaimed in an agitated voice. "How does this come in your possession?"

"Your note?"

"You know that it is mine?"

"Yes – now," replied Carrados quietly. "It was sent to me by the Admiral-Superintendent of the Yard here. He wished to communicate with the writer."

"I am bewildered at the suddenness of this," protested the poor young man in some distress. "Let me tell you the circumstances – such at least as do not violate my promise."

He procured himself a glass of water from the sideboard, drank half of it, and began to pace the room nervously as he talked.

"On Wednesday last, after taking Evensong at the church, I was leaving the vestry when a lady stepped forward and asked if she might speak to me privately. It is a request which a clergyman cannot refuse, Mr. Carrados, but I endeavoured first to find out what she required, because people frequently come to one or another of us on business that really has to do with the clerk, or the organist, or something of that sort.

"She assured me that it was a personal matter and that no other official would do.

"The lights had by this time been extinguished in the church, and doubtless the apparitor had left. I gave her my address here and asked her if she would call in ten or twenty minutes. I preferred that she should present herself in the ordinary way.

"There is no need to go into extraneous details. The unhappy lady wished to unburden her conscience by making explicit confession, and she had come to me in consequence of a sermon which she had heard me preach on the Sunday before.

"It is not expedient to weigh considerations of time or circumstance in such a case. I allowed her to proceed, and she made her confession under the seal of inviolable confidence. It involved other persons besides herself. I besought her to undo as far as possible the great harm she had done by making a full statement to the authorities, but this she was too weak – too terrified – to do. This clumsy warning of mine – " He pointed to the paper now lying on the table between them. " – was the utmost concession that I could wring from her."

He stopped and looked at his visitor with a troubled face that seemed to demand some sort of assent to the dilemma.

"You are an Englishman, Mr. Hosier, and you know what this might mean in a conflict – you know that one of our most formidable weapons has been annexed."

"My dear sir!" rapped out the distressed curate, "don't you think that I haven't worried about that? But behind the Englishman stands something more primitive, more just – the *man*. I gave my assurance as a man, and the Admiralty can go hang!

"Besides," he added, in petulant reaction, "the poor woman is dying, and then everyone can know. Of course it may be too late."

"Do you mind telling me if the lady gave you the names of her accomplices?"

"How can I tell you, Mr. Carrados? It may identify her in some way. I am too confounded by your unexpected appearance in the affair to know what is important and what is not."

"It will not implicate her. I have no concern there."

"Then, yes, she did. She gave me every detail."

"I ask because a man is suspected and on the point of arrest. He may be innocent. I have no deeper motive, but if the one for whom she is working is not a German called, or passing as, Muller, you might have some satisfaction in exonerating him."

The curate reflected a moment.

"He is not, Mr. Carrados," he replied decidedly. "But please don't ask me anything more."

"Very well, I won't," said Carrados, rising. "Our numismatic conversation has taken a strange turn, Mr. Hosier. There is a text for you – Money at the root of everything! By the way, I can do you one trifling service." He picked up the anonymous letter, tore it across and held it out. "You have done all you could. Burn this and then you are clear of the matter."

"Thanks, thanks. But won't it get you into trouble with the Admiralty?"

"I make my own terms," replied Carrados. "Now Mr. Hosier, I have been an ill-omened bird, but I had no suspicion of this when I came. The 'long arm' has landed us this time. Will you come and dine with me one day this week, and I promise you not a single reference to this troublesome business?"

"You are very good," assented Hosier.

"I am at Cliffhurst."

"Cliffhurst?" was Hosier's quick exclamation.

"Yes, at The Rose and Plumes."

"I – I am very sorry, Mr. Carrados," stammered the curate, "but, after all, I am afraid that I must cry off. This week – "

"If the distance takes up too much of your time, may I send a car?"

"No, no, it isn't that – at least, of course, one has to consider time and work. Thank you, Mr. Carrados. You are very kind, but, really, if you don't mind – "

Carrados courteously accepted the refusal without further pressure. He turned the momentary embarrassment by hoping that Hosier would not fail to call on him when next in London, and the curate availed himself of the compromise to protest the pleasure that it would afford him. Parkinson was summoned and the strangely developed visit came to an end. Parkinson doubtless found his master a dull companion on the way back. Carrados had to rearrange his ideas from the preconception which he had so far tentatively based on Inspector Tapling's report, and he was faced by the necessity of discovering whose presence made The Rose and Plumes Hotel inexplicably distasteful to Mr. Hosier just then. Only two flashes of conversation broke the journey, both of which may be taken as showing the trend of Max Carrados's mind, and demonstrating the sound common sense exhibited by his henchman.

"It is a mistake they often make, Parkinson, to begin looking with a fixed idea of what they are going to find."

"Yes, sir."

And, ten minutes later.

"But I don't know that it would be safe yet to ignore the obvious altogether."

"No, sir," replied Parkinson."

"Not guilty, my Lord!"

That was the link for which Carrados had been waiting patiently each day since his visit to Kingsmouth. Or, more exactly, since the sound of a voice heard in the hotel on his return had stirred a memory that he could not materialise. Parkinson had described the man with photographic exactness and still recognition was balked.

Tapling, who found himself at a deadlock before the furnished villa, both by reason of his want of progress and at Carrados's recommendation, contributed his observation, which was guardedly negative. Everyone about knew Mr. Slater – "a pleasant, open-handed gentleman, with a word and a joke for all " – but no one knew anything of him, as, indeed, who should know of a leisurely bird of passage staying for a little time at a seaside hotel?

Then across the lounge rang the mock-serious repartee, and enlightenment cut into the patient listener's brain like a flash of inspiration.

These were the three telegrams which immediately came into existence as a result of that ray, deciphered here from their code obscurity:

To Greatorex, Turrest, Richmond, Surrey.

Extract times full report trial Henry Frankworth, convicted embezzlement early 1906, and forward express.

Carrados

* * * * *

369

To Wrattesley, Home Office, Whitehall, SW

Will you please have Lincoln Authorities instructed to send me confidential report antecdents Henry Frankworth, embezzler, native Trudstone that County. Urgent.

Wynn Carrados

* * * * *

To Carlysle, 72A Bampton St., WC

My Dear Louis,

Why not come down weekend to talk things over? Meanwhile, make every effort discover subsequent history Henry Frankworth, convicted embezzlement Central Criminal Court early 1906. Beedel will furnish police records. Pressing.

Max

On his way upstairs a few hours later, Carrados looked in at the reception office to inquire if there were any letters.

"By the by," he remarked, after he had turned to leave, "I wonder if you happen to have a room a little – just a little – farther away from the drawing room?"

"Certainly, sir," replied the clerk. "Does the playing annoy you? They do keep it up rather late sometimes, don't they?"

"No, it doesn't annoy me," admitted Carrados. "On the contrary, I am passionately fond of it. But it tempts me into lying awake listening when I ought to be asleep."

The young lady laughed pleasantly. It was her business to be agreeable.

"You are considerate!" she rippled. "Well, there's the further corridor. Or, of course, a floor above – "

"The floor above would do nicely. Not on the front if possible. The sea is rather noisy."

"Second floor, west corridor." She glanced at her keyboard. "No. 15?"

"Is that the side overlooking the – ?"

"The High Street," she prompted.

"I am such a poor sleeper," he apologized.

370

"No. 21 on the other side, overlooking the gardens?" she suggested.

"I am sure that will do admirably," he said, with the gratitude that is always so touching from the blind. "Thank you for taking so much trouble to pick it for me. Good night."

"I will have your things transferred tomorrow," she nodded after him.

An hour later, Mr. Slater, generally the last man to leave the lounge, strolled across to the office for his key.

"No. 22, sir, isn't it?" she hazarded, unhooking it without waiting for the number.

"Good little girl," he assented approving. "What a brain beneath that fascinating aureola. *Eh bien, au revoir, petite!* You ought to be about snuffing the candle yourself, my dear."

The young lady laughed just as pleasantly. It was her business to be equally agreeable to all.

Mr. Carrados was sitting in an alcove of the lounge on the following morning when Parkinson brought him a letter. It proved to be the extract from *The Times*, written on the special typewriter. The day was bright and inviting and the room was deserted. On his master's instruction, Parkinson sat down and waited while the blind man rapidly deciphered the half-dozen sheets of typewriting.

"You have been with me to the Old Bailey several times," remarked Carrados, as he slowly replaced the document. "Do you remember an occasion in February 1906?"

Parkinson looked unnecessarily wise, but was unable to acquiesce. Carrados gave him another guide

"A man named Frankworth was sentenced to eighteen months' imprisonment for an ingenious system of theft. He had also fraudulently disposed of information to trade rivals of his employer."

"I apprehend the circumstances now, sir."

"Can you recall the appearance of the prisoner?" Parkinson thought that he could, but he did not rise to the suggestion and Carrados was obliged to follow the direct line.

"Have you seen anyone lately – here in the hotel – who might be Frankworth?"

"I can't say that I have, sir."

"Take Mr. Slater now. Shave off his beard and moustache."

Parkinson began to look respectfully uncomfortable.

"Do you mean, sir –?"

"By an effort of the imagination, Parkinson. Close your eyes and picture Mr. Slater as a clean-shaven man, some years younger, standing in the dock – "

371

"Yes, sir. There is a distinct resemblance."

With this Max Carrados had to be satisfied for the time. Long memory was not Parkinson's strong point, but he had his own pre-eminent gift, and of this his master was to have an immediate example that outweighed every possible deficiency.

"Speaking of Mr. Slater, sir, I noticed a curious thing that I intended to mention, as you told me to be particularly observant."

Carrados nodded encouragingly.

"I was talking to Herbert early this morning as he cleaned the boots. He is a very bigoted Free Trader, sir, and is thinking of becoming a Mormon, and I was speaking to him about it. Presently he came to No. 22's – Mr. Slater's. They were muddy, for Mr. Slater went out for a walk last night – I saw him as he returned. But the boots that Mr. Slater put out to be cleaned last night were not the boots that he went out in and got wet, although they were exactly the same make."

"That is certainly curious," admitted Carrados slowly. "There was only one pair put out?"

"That is all, sir, and they were not the boots that Mr. Slater has worn every day since I began to notice him particularly. He always does wear the same pair, morning, noon, and night."

"Wait," said Carrados briskly. An idea bordering on the fantastic flashed between a sentence in the report which he had just been reading and Parkinson's discovery. He took out the sheets, ran his finger along the lines, and again read – "*stated that the prisoner was the son of a respectable bootmaker, and had followed the occupation himself.*"

"I know how accurate you are, Parkinson, but this may be of superlative importance. You see that?"

"I had not contemplated it in that light, sir."

"But what did the incident suggest to you?"

"I inferred, sir, that Mr. Slater must have had some reason for going out again after the hotel was closed."

"Yes, that might explain half, but what if he did not?" persisted Carrados.

Parkinson wisely dismissed the intellectual problem as outside his sphere.

"Then I am unable to suggest why the gentleman cleaned his muddy boots himself and muddied his clean boots, sir."

"Yes, that is what it comes to. He is wearing the same pair again this morning?"

"Yes, sir. The boots that were dirty at ten o'clock last night."

"Pay particular attention to Mr. Slater's boots in future. I have transferred to No. 21, so you will have every opportunity. Talk to Herbert about Tariff Reform tomorrow morning. In the meanwhile, – Are they any particular make?"

"'Moorland hand-made waterproof', a heavy shooting boot, sir. Size 7. Rossiter, of Kingsmouth, is the maker."

"In the meanwhile, go to Kingsmouth and buy an identical pair. Before you go, cut the sole off one of your oldest boots and bring me a piece about three inches square. Buy yourself another pair. Here is a note. Do you know which chamber maid has charge of No. 21?"

"I could ascertain, sir."

"It would be as well. You might buy her a bangle out of the change – if you have no personal objection to the young lady's society. And, Parkinson – "

"Yes, sir?"

"I know you to be discreet and reliable. The work we are engaged on here is exceptionally important and equally honourable. A mistake might ruin it. That is all."

"Thank you, sir." Parkinson marched away with his head a little higher for the guarded compliment. It was the essence of the man's extraordinary value to his master that while on some subjects he thought deeply, on others he did not think at all, and he contrived automatically to separate everything into its proper compartment.

"Here is what you require, sir," he said, returning with the square of leather.

"Come across to the fireplace," said Carrados. "There is still no one else in the lounge?"

"No, sir."

"Who would be the last servant to see to this room at night – to leave the fire safe and the windows fastened?"

"The hall porter, sir."

"Where is he now?"

"In the outer hall."

Carrados bent towards the fire. "It's a million-to-one chance," he thought, "but it's worth trying." He dropped the leather on to the red coals, waited until it began to smoke fiercely, and then, lifting it out with the tongs, he allowed the pungent aromatic odour to diffuse into the air for a few seconds. A minute later the charred fragment had lost its identity among the embers.

"Go now, and on your way tell the hall porter that I want to speak to him."

The hall porter came, a magnificent being, but full of affable condescension.

"You sent for me, sir?"

Carrados was sitting at a table near the fire.

"Yes. I am a little nervous. Do you smell anything burning?"

The porter sniffed the air – superfluously but loudly, so that the blind gentleman should hear that he was not failing in his duty. Then he looked comprehensively around.

"There certainly is a sort of hottish smell somewhere, sir," he admitted.

"It isn't any woodwork about the fireplace scorching? We blind are so helpless."

"That's all right, sir." He laid a broad hand on the mantelpiece and then rapped it reassuringly. "Solid marble that, sir. You needn't be afraid. I'll give a look across now and then."

"Thank you, if you will," said Carrados, with relief in his voice. "And, by the way, will you ring for Maurice as you go?"

A distant bell churred. Across the room, like a strangely balancing bird, skimmed a waiter.

"Sair?"

"Oh, is that you, Maurice? I want – By the way, what's that burning?"

"Burning, sair?"

"Yes. Don't you smell anything?"

"There is an odour of smell," admitted Maurice sagely, "but it is nothing to see."

"You don't know the smell?"

The waiter shook his head and looked vague. Carrados divined perplexity.

"Oh, I dare say it's nothing," he declared carelessly. "Will you get me a sherry and khoosh?"

The million-to-one chance had failed.

"Sherry and bittaire, sair." Maurice deposited the glass with great precision, regarded it sadly and then moved it three inches to the right.

"I 'ave recollect this odour, sair," he remarked, "although I cannot give actuality. I 'ave met him here before, but – less – less forcefully."

"When?"

"Oh, one week since, perhaps."

"Something in the coals?" suggested Carrados.

"I imagine yes," pondered Maurice conscientiously. "I was 'brightening up', you say, for the night, and the fire was low down. I squash it with the poker still more for safety."

"Oh, then the lounge would be empty?"

"Yes – of people. Only Mr. Slataire already departing."

Carrados indicated that he did not want the change and dismissed the subject.

374

"So long as nothing's on fire," he said with indifference.

"Thank you, sair."

The million-to-one chance had come off after all.

Two days later, walking beyond the usual limit of the conventional promenade, Carrados reached a rough wooden hut such as contractors erect during the progress of their work. Having accompanied his master to the door, Parkinson returned towards the promenade and sat down to admire the seascape from the nearest bench.

Inside the hut, three men had been waiting. One of the trio, a tall, military-looking man with the air of a personage, had been sitting on a whitewash-splashed trestle reading *The Times*. Of the others, one was Inspector Tapling, and the third a dwarfish, wizened creature with the air of a converted ostler. He had passed the time by watching the Cliffhurst side through a knot-hole in a plank. With the entrance of Carrados, the tall man folded his newspaper and a period of expectancy seemed to have come to an end.

"Good morning, Colonel, Inspector, and you there, Bob."

"You found your way, Mr. Carrados?" remarked the Colonel.

"Yes. It is not really I who am late. I had a letter this morning from Wrattesley holding me up for a wire at 10:30. It did not arrive till 10:45."

"Ah, it did come! Then we may regard everything as settled?"

"No, Colonel. On the contrary, we must accept everything as upset."

"What, sir?"

Carrados took out the slim pocket-book, extracted a telegram, and held it out.

"What is this?" demanded the colonel, peering through his glasses in the indifferent light. "'*Laburnum edifice plaster dark dark late herald same dome aurora dark vitiate camp encase.*' I don't know the code."

"Oh, it's Westneath's arrangement," explained Carrados. "'*The individual with whom we are concerned must not be arrested on charge, but it is of the gravest importance that the papers in question be recovered. There must be no public proceedings even if conviction assured.*'"

There was a moment of stupefaction.

"This – this is a bombshell!" exclaimed the Colonel. "What does it mean?"

"Politics," replied Carrados tersely.

"Ah!" soliloquised Tapling, walking to the door and looking sympathetically out atthe gloomy prospect of sea and sky.

"But I've had no notification," protested the Colonel. "Surely, Mr. Carrados – "

"The wire is probably at the station."

375

"True. You said 10:45. Well, what do you propose doing now?"

"Scrapping all our arrangements and recovering the papers without arresting Slater."

"In what way?"

"At the moment, I have not the faintest idea."

The inspector left the door and came back moodily to his old position.

"We have reason to think that he is becoming suspicious, Mr. Carrados," he remarked. "He may decide to go any hour."

"Then the sooner we act the better."

The stunted pygmy in the background had been listening to the conversation with rapt attention, fastening his eyes unwinkingly on each face in turn. He now glided forward.

"Listen to me, gents," he said, throwing round a cunning leer. "How does this sound? This afternoon . . . ."

That afternoon, Mr. Slater had been for what he termed "a blow of the briny", as his custom was on a fine day. He was returning in the dusk and had crossed the spacious promenade when, at a corner, he almost ran into the broad figure of a policeman who stood talking to a woman on the path.

"That's the man!" exclaimed the woman with almost vicious certainty.

Mr. Slater fell back a step in momentary alarm. Then, recovering his self-control, he went forward with admirable composure.

"Beg pardon, sir," explained the constable, "but this young lady has just lost her purse. She says she was sitting next to you on a seat – "

"And the minute after he had gone – the very minute – my bag was open like you see it now and my purse vanished," interposed the lady volubly.

"On the seat by the lifeboat where I passed you, sir," amplified the constable.

"This is ridiculous," said Mr. Slater with a breath of relief. "I am a gentleman and I have no need to steal purses. My name is Slater, and I am staying at The Rose and Plumes."

"Yes, sir," assented the policeman respectfully. "I know you by sight, sir, and have seen you go there. You hear what the gentleman says, Miss?"

"Gentleman or no gentleman, I know my purse has gone," snapped the girl. "If he hasn't got it, why did it vanish – where is it now? That's all I ask – Where is it now?"

"You've seen nothing of it, I take it, sir?"

"No, of course I haven't," retorted the gentleman contemptuously. "I was sitting on a seat. The woman may have sat next to me – someone

376

reading certainly did. Then I got up, walked once or twice up and down, and came across. That's all."

"What was in the purse, Miss?," inquired the constable.

"A postal order for a sovereign – and, thank the Lord, I've got the tag of it – a half-crown, two shillings, and a few coppers, a Kruger sixpence with a hole through, a gold gipsy ring with pearls, the return half of my ticket, some hairpins and a few recipes, a book of powder papers, a pocket mirror – "

"That ought to be enough to identify it by," said the constable, catching Mr. Slater's eye in humorous sympathy. "Well, Miss, you'd better come to the station and report the loss. Perhaps you'll look in as well, sir?"

"Does that mean," demanded Mr. Slater with a dark gleam, "that I am to be charged with theft?"

"Bless you, no, sir," was the easy reassurance. "We couldn't take a charge in the circumstances – not with a gentleman of respectable position and known address. But it might save you some inquiry and bother later, and if it was myself I should like to get it done with while it was red-hot, so to speak."

"I will go now," decided Mr. Slater. "Do I walk with?"

"Just as you like, sir. You can go before or follow on. It's only just down Bank Street."

The two went on and the gentleman followed at a few yards' interval. Three minutes and a blue lamp indicated their destination. No other pedestrian was in sight. The door stood hospitably open and Mr. Slater walked in.

The station inspector was seated at a desk when they entered and a couple of other officials stood about the room. The policeman explained the circumstances of the loss, the inspector noting the details in the record-book.

"This gentleman voluntarily accompanied us as he had been brought into the case," concluded the policeman

"Here is my card, Superintendent," said Mr. Slater with some importance. He had determined to be agreeable, but dignified, and to enlist the inspector on his side. "I am staying at The Rose and Plumes. It's deuced unpleasant, you know, for a gentleman in my position to have to answer to a charge like this. That's why I came at once to clear the matter up.

"Quite so, sir," replied the Inspector. "But there is no charge at present." He turned to the girl. "You understand that if you sign the charge sheet and it turns out that you are mistaken it may be a serious matter?"

377

"I only want my purse and money back," replied the young woman mulishly.

"We will try to find it for you, but there is nothing beyond your suspicion that this gentleman has ever seen it. Probably, sir, you don't possess a sovereign postal order, or a Kruger coin, or any of the other articles, even of your own?"

"I don't," replied Mr. Slater. "Except, of course, some silver and copper. If it will satisfy you I will turn out my pockets."

The inspector looked at the complainant.

"You hear that, Miss?"

"Oh, very well," she retorted. "If he really hasn't got it I shall be the one to look silly, shan't I?"

On this encouragement Mr. Slater made a display of his various possessions, turning out each pocket as he emptied it. The contents were laid before the inspector, who satisfied himself by a glance of their innocent nature.

"I should warn you that I am going to bring out a loaded revolver," said Mr. Slater when he came to his hip-pocket. "I travel a good deal abroad and often in wild parts, where it is necessary to carry a pistol for protection."

The inspector nodded and examined the weapon with a knowing touch. The last pocket was displayed.

"That's not what I mean," objected the girl with a dogged air, as everyone began to regard her in varying degrees of inquiry. "You don't suppose that anyone would keep the things in their pocket, do you? I thought you meant properly."

The inspector addressed himself to Mr. Slater again in a matter-of-fact, business manner.

"Perhaps you would like one of my men to put his hand over you to settle the matter, sir?" he asked. For just a couple of seconds there was the pause of hesitation.

"If nothing is found, you withdraw all imputation against this gentleman?" demanded the inspector of the girl

"Suppose I must," she admitted with an admirable pose of sulky acquiescence. In less exciting moments, the young lady was a valued member of the Kingsmouth Amateur Dramatic Society.

"Oh, all right," assented Mr. Slater. "Only get it over."

"You quite understand that the search is entirely voluntary on your part, sir. Hilldick!" One of the other policemen came forward.

"You can stand where you are, sir," he directed. With the practised skill of, say, a Custom House officer from Kingsmouth, he used his fingers

378

dexterously about the gentleman's clothing. "Now, sir, will you sit down and remove your boots for a moment?"

"My boots!" The man's eyes narrowed and his mouth took another line. He glanced at the Inspector.

"Is it really necessary?"

"That's it!" came from the girl in a fiercely exultant whisper. "He's slipped them in his boots!"

"Idiot!" commented Mr. Slater. He sat down and slowly drew slack the laces.

"Thank you," said Hilldick. He picked up both boots and with them turned to the table underneath the light. The next moment there was a sound like the main-spring of a clock going wrong and the sole and the upper of one boot came violently apart.

"You scoundrel!" screamed Slater, leaping from the chair.

But the grouping of the room had undergone a quiet change. Two men closed in on his right and left, and Mr. Slater sat down again. The inspector opened the desk, dropped in the revolver, and turned the key. Then all eyes went again to Hilldick and saw – nothing.

"The other boot," came in a quiet voice from the doorway to the inner room. "But just let me have it for a second."

It was put into his hands, and Carrados examined it in unmoved composure, while unpresentable words flowed in a blistering stream from Slater's lips.

"Yes, it is very good workmanship, Mr. Frankworth," remarked the blind man. "You haven't forgotten your early training. All right, Hilldick."

The tool cut and rasped again and the stitches flew. But this time from the opening, snugly lying in a space cut out among the leathers, a flat packet slid down to the ground.

Someone tore open the oiled silk covering and spread out the contents. Six sheets of fine tracing paper, each covered with signs and drawings, were disclosed. The finality of the discovery acted on the culprit like a douche of water. He ceased to revile, and a white and deadly calm came over him.

"I don't know who is responsible for this atrocious outrage," he said between his clenched teeth, "but everyone concerned shall pay dearly for it. I am a naturalised Frenchman, and my adopted country will demand immediate satisfaction."

"Your adopted country is welcome to you, and it's going to have you back again," said the inspector grimly. "Here is a pair of boots exactly like your own – we only retain the papers, which do not belong to you. You are allowed twenty-four hours to be clear of the country. If you have not sailed by this time tomorrow, you will be arrested as Henry Frankworth for failing to report yourself when on licence and sent to serve the unexpired portion of your sentence. If you return at any time, the same course will be followed. Inspector Tapling, here is the warrant. You will keep Frankworth under observation and act as the circumstances demand."

Henry Frankworth glared round the room vindictively, drew himself up, and clenched his fists. Then his figure drooped, and he turned and walked dully out into the darkening night."

"So you let the German spy slip through your fingers after all," protested Mr. Carlyle warmly. "I know that it was on instructions, and not your doing, Max, but why, why on earth, why?"

Carrados smiled and pointed to the heading of a column in an evening paper that he picked up from his side

"There is your answer, Louis," he replied"

"'*Position of the Entente. What Does France Mean?*'" read the gentleman. "What has that got to do with it?"

"Your German spy was a French spy, Louis, and just at this moment a certain section of the public, led by a certain gang of politicians and aided by a certain interest in The Press, is doing its best to imperil the Entente. The Government has no desire to have the Entente imperilled. Hence your wail. If the dear old emotional, pig-headed, *Rule Britannia!* public had got it that French spies were stalking through the land at this crisis, then, indeed, the fat would have been in the fire!"

"But, upon my soul, Max. Well, well. I hope that I am the last man to be led by newspaper clap-trap, but I think that it's a deuced queer proceeding all the same. Why should our ally want our secret plans?"

"Why not, if he can get them?" demanded Max Carrados philosophically. "One never knows what may happen next. We ought to have plans and knowledge of all the French strategic positions as well as of the German. I hope that we have, but I doubt it. It would be a guarantee of peace and good relations."

"There are times, Max," declared Mr. Carlyle severely, "when I suspect you of being – er – paradoxical."

"Can you imagine, Louis, an Archbishop of Canterbury, or a Poet Laureate, or a Chancellor of the Exchequer being friendly – perhaps even dining – with the editor of *The Times*?"

"Certainly. Why not?"

"Yet in the editor's office, drawn up by his orders, there is probably a three-column obituary notice of each of those impersonalities. Does it mean that the editor wishes them to die – much less has any intention of poisoning their wine? Ridiculous! He merely, as a prudent man, prepares for an eventuality, so as not to be caught unready by a misfortune which he sincerely hopes will never take place – in his time, that is to say."

"Well, well," said Mr. Carlyle benignantly – they were lunching together at Vitet's, on Carrados's return – "I am glad that we got the papers. One thing I cannot understand: Why didn't the fellow get clear as soon as he had the plans?"

"Ah," admitted the blind man, "why not, indeed? Even Inspector Tapling bated his breath when he suggested the reason to me."

"And what was that?" inquired Carlyle with intense interest.

Mr. Carrados looked extremely mysterious and half-reluctant for a moment. Then he spoke.

"Do you know, Louis, of any great secret military camp where a surprise fleet of dirigibles and flying machines of a new and terrible pattern is being formed by a far-seeing Government as a reserve against the day of Armageddon?"

"No," admitted Mr. Carlyle, with staring eyes, "I don't."

"Nor do I," contributed Carrados.

The Eastern Mystery

It could scarcely be called Harris's fault, whatever the driver next behind might say in the momentary bitterness of his heart. In the two-fifths of a second of grace at his disposal, Mr. Carrados's chauffeur had done all that was possible and the dent that his radiator gave the stair-guard of the London General in front was insignificant. Then a Railway Express Delivery skated on its dead weight into his luggage platform and a Pickford, turning adroitly out of the mêlée, slewed a stationary Gearless round by its hand-rail stanchion to spread terror among the other line of traffic.

The most unconcerned person, to all appearance, was the driver of the London General, the vehicle whose sudden stoppage had initiated the riot of confusion. He had seen a man, engrossed to the absolute exclusion of his surroundings by something that took his eye on the opposite footpath, dash into the road and then, brought up suddenly by a realisation of his position, attempt to retrace his steps. He had pulled up so expertly that the man escaped, so smoothly that not a passenger was jarred, and now he sat with a dazed and vacant expression on his face, leaning forward on his steering wheel, while caustic inquiry and retort winged unheeded up and down the line behind him.

It was not until the indispensable ceremony of everyone taking everyone else's name and number had been observed under the authority of the tutelary constable that the single occupant of the private car stirred to show any interest in the proceedings.

"Parkinson," he called quietly, summoning his attendant to the window. "Ask Mr. Tulloch if he will come round here when he has finished with the policeman."

"Mr. Tulloch, sir?"

"Yes. You remember Dr. Tulloch of Netherhempsfield? He is on in front there."

A moment later Jim Tulloch, as genial as of old, but his exuberance temporarily damped by the cross-bickering in which he had just been involved, thrust his head and arm through the sash.

"Lord, Lord, it really is you then, Wynn, old man?" he cried. "When your Parkinson came up I couldn't believe it for a minute, simply couldn't believe it. The world grows smaller, I declare."

"At all events this car does," responded Carrados, wringing the hearty, outstretched hand. "They've got us two inches less than the makers ever intended. Is it really your doing, Jim?"

382

"Did ever you hear such a thing?" protested Tulloch. "And yet that wall-eyed atrocity yonder has kidded the copper that if he hadn't stopped dead – Well, I should."

"Was it a near thing?" asked Carrados confidentially.

"Well, strictly between ourselves, I don't mind admitting that it might have been something of a shave," confessed Tulloch, with a cheerful grin. "But, Lord bless you, Wynn, the streets of London are paved with 'em nowadays, paved with them. You don't merely take your life in your hands if you want to get about. You carry it on each foot."

"Look here," said Carrados. "You never let me know that you were up in town, Tulloch. What are you doing today?"

"I beg your pardon, sir," interrupted Parkinson's respectful voice, "but the policeman wishes to speak with you, sir."

"With me?" queried Tulloch restlessly. "Oh, good Lord! have we to go into all that again?"

"It's only the bus driver, sir," apologised the constable with the tactful deference that the circumstances seemed to demand. "As you are a doctor – I think there's something the matter with him."

"I'm sure there is," assented Tulloch. "All right, I'm coming. Are you in a hurry, Wynn?"

"I'll wait," was the reply.

The doctor found his patient propped up on a doorstep. Having, as he expressed it afterwards, "run the rule over him", he prescribed a glass of water and an hour's rest. The man was shaken, that was all.

"Nerves, Wynn," he announced when he returned to his friend. "I don't quite understand his emotion, but the shock of not having run over me seems to have upset the poor fellow."

"I was asking you whether you were doing anything today," said Carrados. "Can you come back with me to Richmond?"

"I'm not doing anything as far as that goes," admitted Tulloch. "In fact," he added ruefully, "that's the plague of it. I'm waiting to hear from a man who's waiting to hear from another man, and he's depending on something that may or mayn't, you understand."

"Then you can come along now anyway. Get in."

"If it's dinner you mean, I can't come straight away, you know," protested Tulloch. "Look at me togs – " He stood back to display a serviceable Norfolk suit. " – all right for the six-thirty sharp of a Bloomsbury boarding house, but – eh, what?"

"Don't be an ass, Jim," said the blind man amiably. "I can't see your silly togs."

"No ladies or any of your tony friends?"

"Not a soul."

"The fact is," confided Tulloch, taking his place in the car, "I've been out of things for a bit, Wynn, and I'm finding civilisation a shade cast-iron now. I've been down in the wilds since you were with me."

"I wondered where you were. I wrote to you about six months ago and the letter came back."

"Did it actually? Now that must have been almighty careless of someone, Wynn. I'm sorry. I'm a bit of a rolling stone, I suppose. When Darrish came back to Netherhempsfield my job was done there. I felt uncommonly restless. I hadn't much chance of buying a practice or dropping into a partnership worth having, and I jibbed at setting up in some God-forsaken backwater and slipping into middle age 'building up a connection'. Lord, Lord, Carrados, the tragic monotony of your elderly professional nonentity! I've known men who've whispered to me between the pulls at confidential pipes that they've come to hate the streets and the houses and the same old everlasting silly faces that they met day after day until they began to think very queer thoughts of how they might get away from it all."

"Yes," said Carrados.

"Anyway, 'Not yet,' I promised myself, and when I got the chance of a temporary thing on a Red Cable liner, I took it like a shot. That was something. If there was a mighty sameness about it after a bit, it wasn't the sameness I'd been accustomed to. Then, as luck of one sort or another would have it, I got laid out with a broken ankle on a Bombay quay."

Carrados voiced commiseration.

"But you made a very good mend of it," he said. "It's the left, of course. I don't suppose anyone ever notices it."

"I took care of that," replied Tulloch. "But it was a slow business and threw all my plans out. I was on a very loose end when one day, outside the Secretariat, as they call it, I ran up against a man called Fraser whom I'd known building a viaduct or something of that sort in the Black Country.

"'What on earth are you, doing here?' we naturally both said at once, and he was the first to reply.

"'I'm just off to repair an irrigation 'bund' a thousand miles more or less away, and I'm looking for a doctor who can speak six words of Hindustani, and doesn't mind things as they are, to physic the camp. What are you doing?'

"'Good Lord! old man,' I said, 'I was looking for you!'"

It only required an occasional word to keep Tulloch going, and Carrados supplied it. He heard much that did not interest him – of the journey inland, of the face of the country, the surprising weather, the great work of irrigation and the other impressive wonders of man and nature.

These things could be got from books, but among the weightier cargo Tulloch now and again touched off some inimitable phase of life or told an uninventable anecdote of native character that lived. Yet the buoyant doctor had something on his mind, for several times he stopped abruptly on the edge of a reminiscence, as though he was doubtful, if not of the matter, at least of the manner in which he should begin. These indications were not lost on his friend, but Carrados made no attempt to press him, being very well assured that sooner or later the ingenuous Jim would find himself beyond retreat. The occasion came with the cigarettes after dinner. There had been a reference to the language.

"I often wished that I was a better stick at it," said Tulloch. "I'd picked up a bit in Bombay and of course I threw myself into it when Fraser got me the post. I managed pretty well with the coolies in the camp, but when I tried to have a word with the *ryots* living round – little twopenny ha'penny farmers, you know – I could make no show of it. A lot of queer fish you come across out there, in one way or another, you take my word. You never know whether a man's a professional saint of extreme holiness or a hereditary body-snatcher whose shadow would make a begging leper consider himself unclean until he had walked seventy miles to drink a cupful of filthy water out of a stinking pond that a pock-marked ascetic had been sitting in for three years in order to contemplate quietly."

"Possibly he really was unclean – in consequence or otherwise," suggested Carrados.

"Help!" exclaimed Tulloch tragically. "There are things that have to be seen. But then so was the sanctified image, so that there's nothing for an outsider to go by. And lien all the different little lots with their own particular little heavens and their own one exclusive way of getting there, and their social frills and furbelows – Jats and Jains and Thugs and Mairs and Gonds and Bhills and Toms, Dicks, and Harrys – suburban society is nothing to it, Wynn, nothing at all. There was a strange old joker I've had in mind to tell you about, though it was no joke for him in the end. God alone knows where he came from, but he was in the camp one evening juggling for stray coppers in a bowl. Pretty good juggling too, it seemed to be, of the usual Indian kind – growing a plant out of a pumpkin seed, turning a stick into a live snake, and the old sword-and-basket trick that every Eastern conjurer keeps up his sleeve, but all done out in the open, with people squatting round and a simplicity of appliance that would have taken all the curl out of one of your music-hall magicians. With him he had a boy, his son, a misshapen, monkey-like anatomy of about ten, but there was no doubt that the man was desperately fond of his unattractive offspring.

385

"That night this ungainly urchin, taking a cooler in one of the big irrigation canals, got laid hold of by an alligator and raised the most unearthly screech anything human – if he really was human – ever got out. I seemed to have had something prominent to do with the damp job of getting as much of him away from the creature as we could, and old Calico – that's what we Anglicised the juggler's name into – had some sort of idea of being grateful in consequence. Although I don't doubt that he'd have put much more faith in a local wizard if one had been available, he let us take the boy into the hospital tent and do what we could for him. It wasn't much, and I told my assistant to break it to poor old Calico that he must be prepared for the worst. A handy man, that assistant, Wynn. He was a half-bred 'Portugoose', as they say in Bombay, with the name of Vasque d'Almeydo, and I understood that he'd had some training. When we got out there he said that it was all the same to him, but he admitted quite blandly that he was really a cook and nothing more. What about his excellent testimonials? I asked him, and he replied with cheerful impenitence that he had hired them in the open market for one-rupee-eight, adding feelingly that he would willingly have given twice as much to qualify for my honourable service.

In the end, he did pretty much as he liked, and as he could speak five languages and scramble through seven dialects I was glad to have him about on any terms. I don't quite know how he broke it, but when I saw him later he said that Calico was a 'great dam fool'. He was a conjurer and knew how tricks were done, and yet he had set out at once for some place thirty miles away-to procure a charm of some sort, the Portuguese would swear from a hint he had got. Vasque – of course by this time he'd become Valasquez to us – laughed pleasantly as he commented on native credulity. He was a Roman Catholic himself, so that he could afford it. The next day the boy died and an hour later poor Calico came reeling in. He'd got a nasty cut over the eye and a map of the route drawn over him in thorns and blisters and sand-burns, but he'd got something wrapped away in a bit of rag carried in the left armpit, and I felt for the poor old heathen. When he understood, he borrowed a spade and, taking up the child just as he was, he went off into the pagan solitude to bury him. I'd got used to these simple ways by that time.

"I thought that I'd seen the end of the incident, but late that night I heard the sentry outside challenge someone – we'd had so many tools and things looted by 'friendlies' that they'd lent us half-a-company of Sikhs from Kharikhas – and a moment later Calico was salaaming at the tent door. As it happened, Valasquez was away at a thing they called a village trafficking for some ducks, and I had to grapple with the conversation as best I could – no joke, I may tell you, for the juggler's grasp on conventional Urdu was about as slender as my own. And the first thing he did was to put his paws on to my astonished feet, then up to his forehead, and to prostrate himself to the ground.

"'Sahib,' he protested earnestly, 'I am thy slave and docile elephant for that which thou hast done for the man-child of my house."

"Now you know, Carrados, I simply can't stand that sort of thing. It makes me feel such a colossal ass. So I tried, ungraciously enough I dare swear, to cut him short. But it couldn't be done. Poor old Calico had come to discharge what weighed on him as a formidable obligation and my 'Don't mention it, old chap,' style was quite out of the picture. Finally, from some obscure fold of his outfit, he produced a little screw of cloth and began to unwrap it.

"'Take it, O Sahib, and treasure it as you would a cup of water in the desert, for it has great virtue of the hidden kind. Condescend to accept it, for it is all I have worthy of so great a burden.'

"'I couldn't think-of it, Khaligar,' I said, trying to give his name a romantic twist, for the other sounded like guying him. 'I've done nothing, you know, and in any case this is much more likely to work with you than with me – an unbeliever. What is it, anyway?'

"'It is the sacred tooth of the ape-god Hanuman and its protects from harm,' he replied, reverently displaying what looked to me like an old rusty nail. 'Had I but been able to touch so much as the hem of the garment of my manlet with it before the hour of his outgoing, he would assuredly have recovered."

"'Then keep it for your own protection' I urged. 'I expect that you run more risks that I do."

"'When the flame has been extinguished from a candle, the smoke lingers but a moment before it also fades away,' he replied. 'Thy mean servant has no wish to live now that the light of his eyes has gone out, nor does he seek to avert by magic that which is written on his forehead.'

"'Then it is witchcraft?' I said, pointing to the amulet.

"'I know not, my Lord,' he answered, 'but if it be witchcraft it is of the honourable sort and not the goety of Sahitan. For this cause it is only of avail to one who acquires it without treachery or guile. Take it, Sahib, but do not suffer it to become known even to those of your own table.'

"'Why not?' I asked.

"'Who should boast of pearls in a camp of armed bandits?' he replied evasively. 'A word spoken in a locked closet becomes a beacon on the hill-top for men to see. Yet have no fear. Harm cannot come to you, for your hand is free from complicity."

"I hadn't wanted the thing before, but that settled me. I very much doubted how the conjurer had got possession of it, and I had no wish to be

387

mixed up in an affair of any sort. I told him definitely that while I appreciated his motives, I shouldn't deprive him of so great a treasure. He seemed really concerned, and Fraser told me afterwards that for one of that tribe to be under what he regarded as an unrequited obligation was a dishonour. I should probably have had some trouble to get him off, only just then we heard Valasquez returning. Calico hastily wrapped up the relic, stowed it away among his wardrobe and, with his most ceremonious salaam, disappeared.

"'Do you know anything about the tooth of the ape-god Hanuman, Valasquez?' I asked him some time later. The 'Portugoose' seemed to know a little about everything and, in consequence of my dependence on him, he strayed into a rather more free and easy manner than might have passed under other conditions. But I'm not ceremonious, you know, Wynn." And Carrados laughed and agreed.

"'The sacred tooth of Sira Hanuman, sir?' said Valasquez. 'Oh, that's all great tom dam foolery. There are a hundred million of them. The most notable one was worshipped at the Mountain of Adam in Ceylon until it was captured by my ancestor, the illustrious Admiral d'Almeydo, who sent it with much pomp and circumstance to Goa. Then the Princes of Malabar offered a ransom of rupees, forty lakhs, for it, which the Bishop of Goa refused, like a dam great fool!'"

"'What became of it?' I asked, but Valasquez didn't know. He was somewhat of a liar, in fact, and I dare say that he'd made it all up to show off his knowledge."

"No," objected Carrados, "I think that Baldseus, the Dutch historian, has a similar tale. What happened to Calico?"

"That was the worst of it. Some of our men found his body lying among the tamarisk scrub two days later. There was no doubt that he'd been murdered, and not content with that, the ghouls had mutilated him shamefully afterwards. Even his cheeks were slashed open. So, you see, the tooth of Hanuman had not protected him."

"No," assented Carrados, "it had certainly not protected him. Was anything done – anyone arrested?"

"I don't think so. You know what the natives are in a case like that: No one knows anything, even if they have been looking on at the time. I suppose a report would be sent up, but I never heard anything more. I always had a suspicion that Calico, with his blend of simple faith and gipsy blood, had violated a temple, or looted a shrine, to save his son's life, and that the guardians of the relic tracked him and revenged the outrage. Anyway, I was glad that I hadn't accepted it after that, for I had enough excitement without."

"What was that, Jim?"

"Oh, I don't know, but I always seemed to be running up against something about that time. Twice my tent was turned inside out in my absence, once my clothes were spirited away while I was bathing, and the night before we broke up the camp I was within an ace of being murdered."

"You bear a charmed life," said Carrados suggestively, but Tulloch did not rise to the suggestion.

"It was a bit of luck. Those dacoits are as quiet as death, but for some reason I woke suddenly with the idea that devilment was brewing. I slipped on the first few things that came to hand and went to reconnoitre. As I passed through the canvas I came face to face with a native, and two others were only a few yards behind. Without any ceremony, the near man let drive at my throat with one of those beastly wavy daggers they go in for. I suppose I managed to dodge in the fraction of a second, for he missed me. I gave a yell for assistance, landed the leader one in the eye and backed into my tent for a weapon. By the time I was out again, our fellows were running up, but the precious trio had disappeared."

"That was the last you saw of them?" asked Carrados tentatively.

"No, queerly enough. The day I sailed, I encountered the one whose eye I had touched up. It was down by the water – the Apollo Bander – at Bombay, and I was so taken aback, never thinking but that the fellow was hundreds of miles away, that I did nothing but stare. But I promised myself that in the unlikely event of ever seeing him again, I would follow him up pretty sharply."

"Not under the wheels of a London General again, I hope!"

Tulloch's brown fist came down upon the table with a crash.

"The devil, Carrados!" he exclaimed. "How did you know?"

"Parkinson was just describing to me a rather exotic figure. Then the rest followed."

"Well, you were right. There was the man in Holborn, and of all the fantastic things in the world for a bloodthirsty thug from the back wilds of Hindustan, I believe that he was selling picture post cards!"

"Possibly a very natural thing to be doing in the circumstances."

"What circumstances, Wynn?"

"Those you are telling me of. Go on."

"That's about all there is. When I saw the man I was so excited, I suppose, that I started to dash across without another thought. You know the result. Of course, he had vanished by the time I could look round."

"You are quite sure he is the same?"

"There's always the possibility of a mistake, I admit," considered Tulloch, "but, speaking in ordinary terms, I should say that it's a moral certainty. On the first occasion it was bright moonlight, and the sensational attack left a very vivid photograph on my mind. In Bombay, I had no suspicion of doubt about the man, and he was still carrying traces of my fist. Here, it is true, I had less chance of observing him, but recognition was equally instantaneous and complete. Then consider that each time he has slipped away at once. No, I am not mistaken. What is he after, Carrados?"

"I am very much afraid that he is after you, my friend," replied Carrados, with some concern lurking behind the half-amused level of his voice.

"After me!" exclaimed Tulloch with righteous indignation. "Why, confound his nerve, Wynn, it ought to be the other way about. What's he after me for?"

"India is a conservative land. The gods do not change. A relic that was apprised at seven-hundred-thousand ducats in the days of Queen Elizabeth is worth following up today – apart, of course, from the merit thereby acquired by a devotee."

"You mean that Calico's charm was the real original thing that Valasquez spoke of?"

"It is quite possible. Or it may be claimed for it even if it is not. Goa has passed through many vicissitudes. Its churches and palaces are now in ruins. What is more credible – "

"But in any case I haven't got the thing. Surely the old ass needn't murder me to find out that." The face he appealed to betrayed nothing of the thoughts behind it. But Carrados's mind was busy with every detail of the story he had heard, and the more he looked into it, the less he felt at ease for his impetuous friend's safety.

"On the contrary," he replied, "from the pious believer's point of view, the simplest and most effective way of ascertaining it was to try to murder you, and your providential escape has only convinced them that you are now the holder of the charm."

"The deuce!" said Tulloch ruefully. "Then I have dropped into an imbroglio after all. What's to be done?"

"I wonder," mused the blind man speculatively, "I wonder what really became of the thing."

"You mean after Calico's death?"

"No, before that. I don't imagine that your entertaining friend had it at the end. He had nothing to look forward to, you remember. He did not wish to live. His assassins were those who were concerned in the recovery of the relic, for why else was he mutilated but in order to discover whether he had concealed it with more than superficial craft – perhaps even swallowed it? They found nothing, or you would not have engaged their attention. As it was, they were baffled and had to investigate further. Then they doubtless learned that you had put this man under an undying

390

obligation. Possibly they even knew that he had visited you the last thing before he left the camp. The rest has been the natural sequence."

"It seems likely enough in an incredible sort of way," admitted the doctor. "But I don't see why this old sport should be occupying himself as he is in the streets of London."

"That remains to be looked into. It may be some propitiatory form of self-abasement that is so potent in the Oriental system. But it may equally well be something quite different. If this man is of high priestly authority, there are hundreds of his co-religionists here at hand whose lives he could command in such a service. He may be in communication with some, or be contriving to make himself readily accessible. Are there any Indians at your boarding house?"

"I have certainly seen a couple recently."

"Recently! Then they came after you did?"

"I don't know about that. I haven't had much to do with the place."

"I don't like it, Jim," said Carrados, with more gravity than he was accustomed to put into the consideration of his own risks. "I don't like the hang of it at all."

"Well, for that matter, I'm not exactly pining for trouble," replied his friend. "But I can take care of myself anyway."

"But you can't," retorted Carrados. "That's just the danger. If you were blind it would be all right, but your credulous, self-opinionated eyes will land you in some mess. . . . Tomorrow, at all events, Carlyle shall put a watch on this enterprising Hindu and we shall at least find out what his movements are." Tulloch would have declined the attention, but Carrados was insistent.

"You must let me have my way in such an emergency, Tulloch," he declared. "Of course you would say that it's out of your power to prevent me, but among friends like you and I, one acquiesces to a certain code. I say this because I may even find it necessary to put a man on you as well. This business attracts me resistlessly. There's something more in it than we have got at yet, something that lies beyond the senses and strives to communicate itself through the unknown dimension that we have all stood just upon the threshold of, only to find that we have lost the key. It's more elusive than Macbeth's dagger: '*I have thee not and yet I see thee still*' – always just out of reach. What is it, Jim? Can't you help us? Don't you feel something portentous in the air, or is it only my blind eyes that can see beyond?"

"Not a bit of it," laughed Tulloch cheerfully. "I only feel that a blighted old heathen is leading himself a rotten dance through his pig-headed obstinacy. Well, Wynn, why can't he be rounded up and have it explained that he's on the wrong tack? I don't mind crying quits. I did get

391

in a sweet one on the eye, and he's had a long journey for nothing. Eh, what?"

"He would not believe." Carrados was pacing the room in one of his rare periods of mental tension. Instinct, judgment, experience, and a subtler prescience that enveloped reason seemed at variance in his mind. Then he swung round and faced his visitor.

"Look here, Tulloch, stay with me for the present," he urged. "You can go there for your things tomorrow and I can fix you up in the meantime. It's safer. I feel it will be safer."

"Safer! Good Lord! what could you have safer than a stodgy second-rate boarding house in Hapsburg Square? The place drones respectability. Miss Vole, the landlady, is related to an arch-deacon, and nearly all the people there are on half-pay. The two Indians are tame baboos. Besides, if I get this thing I told you of, I shall be off to South America in a few days, and that ought to shake off this old man of the tooth."

"Of course it won't. Nothing will shake him off if he's made the vow. Well, have your own way. One can't expect a doctor of robust habit to take any reasonable precautions, I know. How is your room situated?"

"Pretty high up. Next to the attics, I imagine. It must be, because there is a little trap-door in the ceiling leading there."

"A trap-door leading to the attics! Well, at all events there can't be an oubliette, I suppose? Nor a four-post bed with a canopy that slides up and down, Jim. Nor a revolving wardrobe before a secret passage in the oak panels?

"Get on with you," retorted Tulloch. "It's just the ordinary contrivance that you find somewhere in every roof when the attics aren't made into rooms. There's nothing in it."

"Possibly, but there may be some time. Anyway, drive a tack in and hang up a tin can or something that must clatter down if the door is raised an inch. You have a weapon, I suppose?"

"Now you're talking, Wynn. I do put some faith in that. I have a grand little revolver in my bag, and I can sleep like a feather when I want."

"Little? What size does it take?"

"Oh, well, it's a .320, if it comes to that. I prefer a moderate bore myself."

Carrados opened a drawer of his desk and picked up half-a-dozen brass cartridges.

"When you get back, throw out the old ones and reload with these to oblige me," he said. "Don't forget."

"Right," assented Tulloch, examining them with interest. "But they look just like mine. What are they? – something new?"

"Not at all, but we know that they are charged and you can rely on them going off if they are fired."

"What a chap you are," declared Tulloch with something of the admiring pity that summed up the general attitude towards Max Carrados. "Well, for that matter, I must be going off myself, old man. I'm hoping for a letter about that little job, and if it comes I want to answer it tonight. You've given me a fine time and we've had a great talk."

"I'm glad we met. And if you go away suddenly, don't leave it to chance the next time you are back." He did not seek to detain his guest, for he knew that Tulloch was building somewhat on the South American appointment. "Shall Harris run you home?"

"Not a bit of it. I'll enjoy a walk to the station, and these Tubes of yours'll land me within me loose-box by eleven. It's a fine place, this London, after all." They had reached the front door, opened it and were standing for a moment looking towards the yellow cloud that arched the west end of the city like the mirage of a dawn.

"Well, goodbye, old man," said Tulloch heartily, and they shook hands. At the touch, an extraordinary impulse swept over Carrados to drag his friend back into the house, to implore him to remain the night at all events, or to do something to upset the arranged order of things for the next few hours. With the cessation of physical contact, the vehemence of the possession dwindled away, but the experience, short as it was, left him white and shaken. He could not trust himself to speak. He waved his hand and, turning quickly, went back to the room where they had sat together to analyse the situation and to determine how to act. Presently he rang for his man.

"Some notes were taken after that little touch in Holborn this afternoon, Parkinson," he said. "Have you the address of the leading motor-bus driver among them?"

"The London General, sir?"

"Yes. The man who was the first to stop." Parkinson produced his memorandum book and referred to the latest of its entries.

"He gave his private residence as 14 Cogg's Lane, Brentford, sir."

"Brentford! That is fortunate. I am going to see him tonight if possible. You will come with me, Parkinson. Tell Harris to get out the car that is the most convenient. What is the time?"

"Ten-seventeen, sir."

"We will start in fifteen minutes. In the meanwhile, just reach me down that large book labelled 'Xavier' from the top shelf there."

"Yes, sir. Very well, sir. I will convey your instructions to Harris, sir."

393

It was perhaps rather late for a casual evening call, but not, apparently, too late for Cogg's Lane, Brentford. Mr. Fitzwilliam – Parkinson had infused a faint note of protest into his voice when he mentioned the bus driver's name – Mr. Fitzwilliam was out, but Mrs. Fitzwilliam received the visitor with conspicuous felicity and explained the circumstances. Fitzwilliam was of a genial, even playful, disposition, but he had come home brooding and depressed. Mrs. Fitzwilliam had not taken any notice of it – she put it down to his feet – but by cajolery and innuendo she had persuaded him to go to the picture palace to be cheered up, and as it was now on the turn of eleven he might be expected back at any moment. In the meantime, the lady had a favourite niece who was suffering – as the doctor himself confessed – from a very severe and unusual form of adenoids. Carrados disclosed the fact that the subject of adenoids was one that interested him deeply. He knew, indeed, of a case that was thought by the patient's parents to be something out of the way, but even it, he admitted, was commonplace by the side of the favourite niece. The minutes winged.

"That's Fred," said Mrs. Fitzwilliam as the iron gate beyond the little plot of beaten earth that had once been a garden gave its individual note. "Seems strange that they should be so ignorant at a hospital, doesn't it?"

"Hallo, what now?" demanded Mr. Fitzwilliam, entering.

Mrs. Fitzwilliam made a sufficient introduction and waited for the interest to develop. So far, the point of Carrados's visit had not appeared.

"I believe that you know something about motors?" inquired the blind man.

"Well, what if I do?" retorted the bus driver. His attitude was protective rather than intentionally offensive.

"If you do, I should be glad if you would look at the engine of my car. It got shaken, I fancy, in a slight accident that we had in Holborn this afternoon."

"Oh!" The driver looked hard at Mr. Carrados, but failed to get behind an expression of mild urbanity. "Why didn't you say so at first?" he grumbled. "All right. I'll trot round with you. Shan't be long, Missis." He led the way out and closed the door behind them, not ceasing to regard his visitor with a distrustful curiosity. At the gate he stopped, having by that time brought his mind round to the requirements of the situation, and faced Carrados.

"Look here," he said, "what's up? You don't want me to look at no bloomin' engine, you know. I don't half-like the whole bally business, let me tell you. What's the gaime?"

"It's a very simple game for you if you play it straightforwardly," answered Carrados. "I want to know just how much you had to do with saving that man's life in Holborn today."

Fitzwilliam instinctively fell back a step and his gaze on Carrados quickened in its tensity.

"What d'yer mean?" he demanded with a quality of apprehension in his voice.

"That is complicating the game," replied Carrados mildly. "You know exactly what I mean."

"And what if I do?" demanded the driver. "What have you got to do with it, may I ask?"

"That is very reasonable. I happened to be in the car following you. We were scraped, but I am not making any claim for paint, whatever happened. I am satisfied that you did very well indeed in the circumstances, and if a letter to your people – I know one of the directors – saying as much would be of any use to you – "

"Now we're getting on, sir," was the mollified admission. "You mustn't mind a bit of freshness, so to speak. You took me by surprise, that's what it was, and I've been wound up ever since that happened." He hesitated, and then flung out the question almost with a passionate directness: "What was it, sir. In God's name, what was it?"

"What was it?" repeated the blind man's level voice persuasively.

"It wasn't me. I couldn't have done nothing. I didn't see the man, not in time to have an earthly. Then we stopped. Good Gawd, I've never felt a stop like that before. It was as though a rubber band had tightened and pulled us up against ten yards squoze into one, so that you didn't hardly know it. I hadn't nothing to do with it. Not a brake was on, and the throttle open and the engine running. There we were. And me half-silly."

"You did very well," said Carrados soothingly.

"I did nothing. If it had been left to me, there'd have been a inquest. You seem to have noticed something, sir. How do you work it out?" Carrados parried the question with a disingenuous allusion to the laws of chance. He had not yet worked it out, but he was not disposed to lay his astonishing conclusions, so far as they went, before the bus driver's crude discrimination. He had learned what he wanted. With a liberal acknowledgment of the service and a reiteration of his promise to write, he bade Mr. Fitzwilliam good night and returned to his waiting car.

"Back home, Harris," he directed. He had gone out with some intention of including Hapsburg Square in his peregrination. He was now assured that his anxiety was groundless.

But the next morning all his confidence was shattered in a moment. It was his custom before and during breakfast to read by touch the headings of the various items in the newspapers and to mark for Greatorex's later reading such paragraphs as claimed his interest. Generally he could, with some inconvenience, distinguish even the ordinary type by the same faculty, but sometimes the inequality of pressure made this a laborious process. There was no difficulty about the larger types, however, and with a terrible misgiving finger-tip and brain had at once grasped the significance of a prominent heading:

Fatal Gas Explosion
Hapsburg Square Boarding House in Flames

"Are you there, Parkinson?" he asked. Parkinson could scarcely believe his well-ordered ears. Not since the early days of his affliction had Carrados found it necessary to ask such a question.

"Yes, sir, I'm here," he almost stammered in reply. "I hope you are not unwell, sir?"

"I'm all right, thanks," responded his master dryly – unable even then not to discover some amusement in having for once scared Parkinson out of his irreproachable decorum. "I was mentally elsewhere. I want you to read me this paragraph."

"The one about Dr. Tulloch, sir?" The name had caught the man's eye at once. "Dear, dear me, sir."

"Yes. Go on," said Carrados, with his nearest approach to impatience.

"'*During the early hours of this morning,*'" read Parkinson, "'*52 Hapsburg Square was the scene of a gas explosion which was unhappily attended by loss of life. Shortly after midnight, the neighbourhood was alarmed by the noise of a considerable explosion which appeared to blow out the window and front wall of one of the upper bedrooms, but as the part in question was almost immediately involved in flames it is uncertain what really happened. The residents of the house, which is a boarding establishment carried on by Miss Vole (a relative, we are informed, of Arch-Deacon Vole of Worpsley), were quickly made aware of their danger and escaped. The engines arrived within a few minutes of the alarm and soon averted any danger of the fire spreading. When it was possible to penetrate into the upper part of the house it was discovered that the occupant of the bedroom where the explosion took place, a Dr. Tulloch who had only recently returned to this country from India, had perished. Owing to the charred state of the body, it is impossible to judge how he died, but in all probability he was mercifully killed or at least rendered unconscious by the force of the explosion.*' That is all, sir."

"I ought to have kept him," muttered Carrados reproachfully. "I ought to have insisted. The thing has been full of mistakes." He could discover very little further interest in his breakfast and turned to the other papers for possible enlargement of the details.

"We shall have to go down," he remarked casually. "Say in half-an-hour. Tell Harris."

"Very well, sir."

Greatorex, just arrived for the day, and diffusing an atmosphere of easy competence and inoffensively general familiarity, put his head in at the door.

"Morning, sir," he nodded. "Tulloch's here and wants to see you. Came in with me. Hullo, Parkinson, seen a ghost?"

"He hasn't yet," volunteered his master. "But we both expect to. Yes, send him in here. Only one mistake the more, you see," he added to his servant, "And one the less," he added to himself.

"I might just as well have stayed, you know," was Tulloch's greeting. He included the still-qualmish Parkinson in his genial domination of the room, and going across to his friend he dropped a weighty hand upon his shoulder.

"'*There are more things in Heaven and Earth than in your philosophy, Horatio,*'" he barbarously misquoted with significance. "There, you see, Wynn, I can apply Shakespeare to the situation as well as you."

"Quite so," assented Carrados. "In the meanwhile, will you have some breakfast?"

"It's what I came in the hopes of," admitted the doctor. "That and being burned out of hearth and home. I thought that I might as well quarter myself on you for a couple of days. You've seen the papers?" His friend indicated the still open sheet.

"Ah, that one. *The Morning Reporter* gave me a better obituary. I often had a sort of morbid fancy to know what they'd say about me afterwards. It seemed unattainable, but, like most things, it's a sad disappointment when it comes. Six lines is the longest, Wynn, and they've got me degree wrong."

"Whose was the body?" asked Carrados.

Gravity descended upon Tulloch at the question. He looked round to make sure that Parkinson had left the room.

"No one will ever know, I'm hoping," he replied. "He was charred beyond recognition. But you know, Wynn, and I know and we can hold our tongues."

"The Indian avenger, of course?"

"Yes. I went round there early this morning expecting nothing and found the place a wreck. One can only guess now what happened, but the gas-bracket is just beneath that trap-door I told you of, and there's a light kept burning in the passage outside. One of the half-pay men brought me a nasty wavy dagger that had been picked up in the road. 'One of your Indian curiosities, I suppose, Dr. Tulloch?' he remarked. I let it pass at that, for I was becoming cautious among so much devilment. 'I'm afraid that there's nothing else of yours left,' he went on, 'and there wouldn't have been this if it hadn't been blown through the window.' He was quite right. I haven't a thing left in the world but this now celebrated Norfolk suit that I stand up in, and, as matters are, I'm jolly well glad you didn't give me time to change yesterday."

"Ah," assented Carrados thoughtfully. "Still the Norfolk suit, of course. Tell me, Jim – you had it in India?"

"To be sure I had. It was new then. You know, one doesn't always go about there in white drill and a cork helmet, as your artists here seem to imagine. It's cold sometimes, I can tell you. This coat is warm. I got very fond of it. You can't understand one getting fond of a mere suit, you with your fifty changes of fine raiment."

"Of course I can. I have a favourite jacket that I would not part from for rubies, and it's considerably more of an antique than yours. That's still a serviceable suit, Jim. Come and let me have a look at it."

"What d'ye mean?" said Tulloch, complying half-reluctantly. "You're making fun of me little suit and it's the only thing in the world that stands between me and the entire."

"Come here," repeated Carrados. "I am not in the least guying. I'm far too serious. I am more serious, I think, than I have ever been in my life before." He placed the wondering doctor before him and proceeded to run a light hand about the details of his garments, turning him round until the process was complete.

"You wore these clothes when the native you call Calico came to you that night?"

"It's more than likely. The nights were cold." Carrados seemed strangely moved. He got up, walked to the window, as his custom was, for enlightenment, and then, after wandering about the room, touching here and there an object indecisively, he unlocked a cabinet and slid out a tray of silver coins.

"You've never seen these, have you?" he asked with scanty interest.

"No, what are they?" responded Tulloch, looking on.

"Pagan art at its highest. The worship of the strong and beautiful."

"Worth a bit?" suggested Tulloch knowingly.

"Not what they cost." Carrados shot back the tray and paced the room again. "You haven't told me yet how you were preserved."

"How?"

"Last night. You know that you escaped death again."

"I suppose I did. Yes. . . . And do you know why I have been hesitating to tell you?"

"Why?"

"Because you won't believe me."

Carrados permitted himself to smile a shade.

"Try," he said laconically"

"Well, of course, I quite intended to . . . The sober truth is, Wynn, that I forgot the address and could not get there. It was the silliest and the simplest thing in the world. I walked to the station here, booked for Russell Square, and took a train. When I got out there I started off and then suddenly pulled up. Where was I going? My mind, I found, on that one point had developed a perfect blank. All the facts had vanished. Drum my encephalon how I might, I could not recall Miss Vole, 52, or Hapsburg Square. Mark you, it wasn't loss of memory in the ordinary sense. I remembered everything else. I knew who I was and what I wanted well enough. Of course the first thing I did was to turn out my pockets. I had letters, certainly, but none to that address and nothing else to help me. 'Very well,' I said, 'it's a silly game, but I'll walk round till I find it.' Had again! I walked for half-an-hour, but I saw nothing the faintest degree familiar. Then I saw '*London Directory Taken Here*' in a pub. window. 'Good,' I thought. 'When I see the name it will all come back again.' I went in, had something, and looked through the '*Streets*' section from beginning to end." He shook his head shrewdly. "It didn't work."

"Did it occur to you to ring me up? You'd given me the address."

"It did, and then I thought, 'No, it's midnight now – ' It was by then. ' – and he may have turned in early and be asleep.' Well, things had got to such a pass that it seemed the simplest move to walk into the first moderate hotel I came to, pay for my bed, and tell them to wake me at six, and that's what I did. Now what do you make of that?"

"That depends," replied Carrados slowly. "The scientist would perhaps hint at a telepathic premonition operating subconsciously through receptive nerve centres. The sceptic would call it a lucky coincidence. The Catholic – the devout Catholic – would claim another miracle."

"Oh, come now!" protested Tulloch.

"Yes, come now," struck in Carrados, rising with decision and moving towards the door. "Come to my room and then you shall judge for yourself. It's too much for any one man to contemplate alone. Come on." He walked quickly across the hall to his study, dismissing Greatorex elsewhere with a word, and motioned the mystified doctor to a chair. Then he locked the door and sat down himself.

"I want you to carry your mind back to that night in your tent when the native Khaligar, towards whom you had done an imperishable service, presented himself before you. By the inexorable ruling of his class, he was your bondsman in service until he had repaid you in kind. This, Jim, you failed to understand as it stood vitally to him, for the whole world, two pantheons and perhaps ten-thousand years formed a great gulf between your mind and his. You would not be repaid, and yet he wished to die."

The doctor nodded. "I dare say it comes to that," he said.

"He could not die with this debt undischarged. And so, in the obscurity of your tent, beneath your unsuspecting eyes, this conjurer did, as he was satisfied, requite you. You thought you saw him wrap the relic in its covering. You did not. You thought he put it back among his dress. He did not. Instead, he slipped it dexterously between the lining and the cloth of your own coat at the thick part of a band. You had seen him do much cleverer things even in the open sunlight."

"You don't say," exclaimed Tulloch, springing to his feet, "that even now – "

"Wait!" cried the blind man warningly. "Don't seek it yet. You have to face a more stupendous problem first."

"What is that?"

"Three times at least your life has been – as we may say – miraculously preserved. It was not your doing, your expertness, my friend. . . . What is this sacred relic that once was in its jewelled shrine on the high altar of the great cathedral at Goa, that opulent arch-bishopric of the East to which Catholic Portugal in the sixteenth century sent all that was most effective of treasure, brain, and muscle to conquer the body and soul of India?"

"You suggested that it might be the original relic to which Valasquez had referred."

"Not now. Only that the natives may have thought so. What would be more natural than that an ignorant despoiler should assume the thing which he found the most closely guarded and the most richly casketed to be the object for which he himself would have the deepest veneration?"

"Then I don't follow you," said Tulloch.

"Because I have the advantage of having turned to the local and historical records bearing on the circumstances since you first started me," Carrados replied. "For instance, in the year 1582, Akbar, who was a philosopher and a humorist as well as a model ruler, sent an invitation to the 'wise men among the Franks' at Goa to journey to Agra, there to meet in public controversy before him a picked band of Mohammedan mullas and prove the superiority of their faith. The challenge was accepted. Abu-l-Fazl records the curious business and adds a very significant detail. These Catholic priests, to cut the matter short in the spirit of the age, offered to walk through a fiery furnace in the defence of their belief. It came to nothing, because the other side backed out, but the challenge is suggestive because, however fond the priesthood of those times was of putting other people to the ordeal of fire and water, its members were singularly modest about submitting to such tests themselves. What mystery was there here, Tulloch? What had those priests of Goa that made them so self-confident?"

"This relic, you suggest?"

"Yes, I do. But, now, what is that relic? A monkey's or an ape-god's tooth, an iron-stained belemnite, the fragment of a pagan idol – you and I can smile at that. We are Christians. No matter how unorthodox, no matter how non-committal our attitude may have grown, there is upon us the unconscious and hereditary influence of century after century of blind and implicit faith. To you and to me, no less than to every member of the more credent Church of Rome, to everyone who has listened to the story as a little child, it is only conceivable that if miraculous virtues reside in anything inanimate, it must pre-eminently be in the close accessories of that great world's tragedy, when, as even secular and unfriendly historians have been driven to admit, something out of the order of nature did shake the Heavens."

"But this," articulated Tulloch with dry throat, leaning instinctively forward from the pressure of his coat, "this – what is it, then?"

"You described it as looking like a nail," responded Carrados. "It is a nail. Rusty, you said, and it could not well be otherwise than red with rust. And old. Nearly nineteen-hundred years old. Quite, perhaps."

Tulloch came unsteadily to his feet and slowly slipping off his coat he put it gently away on a table apart from where they sat.

"Is it possible?" he asked in an awe-struck whisper. "Wynn, is it – is it really possible?"

"It is not only possible," he heard the blind man's more composed voice replying, "but in one aspect it is even very natural. Physically, we are dealing with an historical fact. Somewhere on the face of the earth these things must be enduring. Scattered, buried, lost perhaps, but still existent. And among the thousands of relics that the different churches have made claim to it, would be remarkable indeed if some at least were not authentic. That is the material aspect."

"Yes," assented Tulloch anxiously, "yes. That is simple, natural. But the other side, Carrados – the things that we know have happened – what of that?"

"That," replied Carrados, "is for each man to judge according to his light."

"But you?" persisted Tulloch. "Are you convinced?"

"I am offered a solution that explains everything when no other theory will," replied the blind man evasively. Then on the top of Tulloch's unsatisfied "Ah!" he added: "But there is something else that confronts you. What are you going to do?" and his face was towards the table across the room. "Have you thought of that?"

"It has occurred to me. I wondered how you would act."

It was some time before either spoke again. Then Tulloch broke the silence.

"You can lend me some things?" he asked.

"Of course."

"Then I will decide," he announced with resolution. "Whatever we may think, whatever might be urged, I cannot touch this thing. I dare not even look on it. It has become too solemn, too awful, in my mind, to be seen by any man again. To display it, to submit it to the test of what would be called 'scientific proof', to have it photographed and 'written up' – impossible, incredible! On the other hand, to keep it safely to myself – no, I cannot do that either. You feel that with me?"

The blind man nodded.

"There is another seemly, reverent way. The opportunity offers. I found a letter at the house this morning. I meant to tell you of it. I have got the appointment that I told you of and in three days I start for South America. I will take the coat just as it is, weight it beyond the possibility of recovery, and sink it out of the world in the deepest part of the Atlantic – beyond controversy, and safe from falling to any ignoble use. You can supply me with a box and lead. You approve of that?"

"I will help you," said Carrados, rising.

A Story From
The Specimen Case

The Bunch of Violets
An Episode in the War-time
Activities of Max Carrados

W hen Mr. J. Beringer Hulse, in the course of one of his periodical calls at the War Office, had been introduced to Max Carrados, he attached no particular significance to the meeting. His own business there lay with Mr. Flinders, one of the quite inconspicuous departmental powers so lavishly produced by a few years of intensive warfare: Business that was more confidential than exacting at that stage and hitherto carried on *à deux*. The presence on this occasion of a third – this quiet, suave, personable stranger – was not out of line with Mr. Hulse's open-minded generalities on British methods: "A little singular, perhaps, but not remarkable," would have been the extent of his private comment. He favoured Max with a hard, entirely friendly, American stare, said, "Vurry pleased to make your acquaintance, Mr. Carrados," as they shook hands, and went on with his own affair.

Of course, Hulse was not to know that Carrados had been brought in especially to genialise with him. Most of the blind man's activities during that period came within the "Q-class" order. No one ever heard of them, very often they would have seemed quite meaningless under description, and generally they were things that he alone could do – or do as effectively at all events. In the obsolete phraseology of the day, they were his "bit".

"There's this man Hulse," Flinders had proceeded, when it came to the business on which Carrados had been asked to call at Whitehall. "Needless to say, he's no fool or Jonathan wouldn't have sent him on the ticket he carries. If anything, he's too keen – wants to see everything, do anything, and go everywhere. In the meanwhile, he's kicking up his heels here in London with endless time on his hands, and the Lord only knows who mayn't have a go at him.

"You mean for information – or does he carry papers?" asked Carrados.

"Well, at present, information chiefly. He necessarily knows a lot of things that would be priceless to the Huns, and a clever man or woman might find it profitable to nurse him."

"Still, he must be on his guard if, as you say, he is – No one imagines that London in 1917 is a snakeless Eden or expects that German agents today are elderly professors who say, 'How vos you?' and '*Ja, ja!*'"

"My dear fellow," said Flinders sapiently, "every American who came to London before the war was on his guard against a pleasant-spoken

405

gentleman who would accost him with, 'Say, stranger, does this happen to be your wallet lying around here on the sidewalk?' and yet an unending procession of astute, long-headed citizens met him, exactly as described, year after year, and handed over their five-hundred or five-thousand pounds on a tale that would have made a common or Michaelmas goose blush to be caught listening to."

"It's a curious fact," admitted Carrados thoughtfully. "And this Hulse?"

"Oh, he's quite an agreeable chap, you'll find. He may know a trifle more than you and be a little wider awake and see further through a brick wall and so on, but he won't hurt your feelings about it. Well, will you do it for us?

"Certainly," replied Carrados. "What is it, by the way?"

Flinders laughed his apologies and explained more precisely.

"Hulse has been over here a month now, and it may be another month before the details come through which he will take on to Paris. Then he will certainly have documents of very special importance that he must carry about with him. Well, in the meanwhile, of course, he is entertained and may pal up with anyone or get himself into Lord knows what. We can't keep him here under lock and key or expect him to make a report of every fellow he has a drink with or every girl he meets."

"Quite so," nodded the blind man.

"Actually, we have been asked to take precautions. It isn't quite a case for the C.I.D. – not at this stage, that is to say. So if I introduce him to you and you fix up an evening for him or something of the sort and find out where his tastes lie, and – and, in fact, keep a general shepherding eye upon him – " He broke off abruptly, and Carrados divined that he had reddened furiously and was kicking himself in spirit. The blind man raised a deprecating hand

"Why should you think that so neat a compliment would pain me, Flinders?" he asked quietly. "Now if you had questioned the genuineness of some of my favourite *tetradrachms*, I might have had reason to be annoyed. As it is, yes, I will gladly keep a general shepherding ear on J. Beringer as long as may be needful."

"That's curious," said Flinders, looking up quickly. "I didn't think that I had mentioned his front name."

"I don't think that you have," agreed Carrados.

"Then how – Had you heard of him before?"

"You don't give an amateur conjurer much chance," replied the other whimsically. "When you brought me to this chair I found a table by me, and happening to rest a hand on it my fingers had 'read' a line of writing before I realised it – just as your glance might as unconsciously do," and he held up an envelope addressed to Hulse.

"That is about the limit," exclaimed Flinders with some emphasis. "Do you know, Carrados, if I hadn't always led a very blameless life I should be afraid to have you around the place."

Thus it came about that the introduction was made and in due course the two callers left together.

"You'll see Mr. Carrados down, won't you?" Flinders had asked, and, slightly puzzled but not disposed to question English ways, Hulse had assented. In the passage, Carrados laid a light hand on his companion's arm. Through some subtle perception he read Hulse's mild surprise.

"By the way, I don't think that Flinders mentioned my infirmity," he remarked. "This part of the building is new to me and I happen to be quite blind."

"You astonish me," declared Hulse, and he had to be assured that the statement was literally exact. "You don't seem to miss much by it, Mr. Carrados. Ever happen to hear of Laura Bridgman?"

"Oh, yes," replied Carrados. "She was one of your star cases. But Laura Bridgman's attainments really were wonderful. She was also deaf and dumb, if you remember."

"That is so," assented Hulse. "My people come from New Hampshire not far from Laura's home, and my mother had some of her needlework framed as though it was a picture. That's how I come to know of her, I reckon."

They had reached the street meanwhile and Carrados heard the door of his waiting car opened to receive him

"I'm going on to my club now to lunch," he remarked with his hand still on his companion's arm. "Of course we only have a wartime menu, but if you would keep me company you would be acting the Good Samaritan," and Beringer Hulse, who was out to see as much as possible of England, France, and Berlin within the time – perhaps, also, not uninfluenced by the appearance of the rather sumptuous vehicle – did not refuse.

"Vurry kind of you to put it in that way, Mr. Carrados," he said, in his slightly business-like, easy style. "Why, certainly I will."

During the following weeks, Carrados continued to make himself very useful to the visitor, and Hulse did not find his stay in London any less agreeably varied thereby. He had a few other friends – acquaintances rather – he had occasion now and then to mention, but they, one might infer, were either not quite so expansive in their range of hospitality or so pressing for his company. The only one for whom he had ever to excuse

407

himself was a Mr. Darragh, who appeared to have a house in Densham Gardens (he was a little shrewdly curious as to what might be inferred of the status of a man who lived in Densham Gardens), and, well, yes, there was Darragh's sister, Violet. Carrados began to take a private interest in the Darragh household, but there was little to be learned beyond the fact that the house was let furnished to the occupant from month to month. Even during the complexities of war, that fact alone could not be regarded as particularly incriminating.

There came an evening when Hulse, having an appointment to dine with Carrados and to escort him to a theatre afterwards, presented himself in a mixed state of elation and remorse. His number had come through at last, he explained, and he was to leave for Paris in the morning. Carrados had been most awfully, most frightfully – Hulse became quite touchingly incoherent in his anxiety to impress upon the blind man the fullness of the gratitude he felt, but, all the same, he had come to ask whether he might cry off for the evening. There was no need to inquire the cause. Carrados raised an accusing finger and pointed to the little bunch of violets with which the impressionable young man had adorned his button-hole.

"Why, yes, to some extent," admitted Hulse, with a facile return to his ingenuous, easy way. "I happened to see Miss Darragh down town this afternoon. There's a man they know whom I've been crazy to meet for weeks, a Jap who has the whole ju-jitsu business at his finger-ends. Best ju-jitsuist out of Japan, Darragh says. Mighty useful thing, ju-jitsu, nowadays, Carrados."

"At any time, indeed," conceded Carrados. "And he will be there tonight?"

"Certain. They've tried to fix it up for me half-a-dozen times before, but this Kuromi could never fit it in. Of course this will be the only chance."

"True," agreed the blind man, rather absent-mindedly. "Your last night here."

"I don't say that in any case I should not have liked to see Violet – Miss Darragh – again before I went, but I wouldn't have gone back on an arranged thing for that," continued Hulse virtuously. "Now this ju-jitsu I look on more in the light of business."

"Rather a rough-and-tumble business, one would think," suggested Carrados. "Nothing likely to drop out of your pockets in the process and get lost?"

Hulse's face displayed a rather more superior smile than he would have permitted himself had his friend been liable to see it and be snubbed thereby.

"I know what you mean, of course," he replied, getting up and going to the blind man's chair, "but don't you worry about me, Father William. Just put your hand to my breast pocket."

"Sewn up," commented Carrados, touching the indicated spot on his guest's jacket.

"Sewn up: That's it, and since I've had any important papers on me it always has been sewn up, no matter how often I change. No fear of anything dropping out now – or being lifted out, eh? No, sir. If what I carry there chanced to vanish, I guess no excuses would be taken and *J. B. H.* would automatically drop down to the very bottom of the class. As it is, if it's missing I shall be missing too, so that won't trouble me."

"What time do you want to get there?"

"Darragh's? Well, I left that open. Of course, I couldn't promise until I had seen you. Anyway, not until after dinner, I said."

"That makes it quite simple, then," declared Carrados. "Stay and have dinner here, and afterwards we will go on to Darragh's together instead of going to the theatre."

"That's most terribly kind of you," replied Hulse. "But won't it be rather a pity – the tickets, I mean, and so forth?"

"There are no tickets as it happens," said Carrados. "I left that over until tonight. And I have always wanted to meet a ju-jitsu champion. Quite providential, isn't it?"

It was nearly nine o'clock, and seated in the drawing room of his furnished house in Densham Gardens, affecting to read an evening paper, Mr. Darragh was plainly ill at ease. The strokes of the hour, sounded by the little gilt clock on the mantelpiece, seemed to mark the limit of his patience. A muttered word escaped him and he looked up with a frown.

"It was nine that Hulse was to be here by, wasn't it, Violet?" he asked.

Miss Darragh, who had been regarding him for some time in furtive anxiety, almost jumped at the simple question.

"Oh, yes, Hugh – about nine, that is. Of course he had to – "

"Yes, yes," interrupted Darragh irritably, "we've heard all that. And Sims," he continued, more for the satisfaction of voicing his annoyance than to engage in conversation, "swore by everything that we should have that coat by eight at the very latest. My God! What rotten tools one has to depend on!"

"Perhaps – " began Violet timidly, and stopped at his deepening scowl.

"Yes?" said Darragh, with a deadly smoothness in his voice. "Yes, Violet. Pray continue. You were about to say – "

"It was really nothing, Hugh," she pleaded. "Nothing at all."

"Oh, yes, Violet, I am sure that you have some helpful little suggestion to make," he went on in the same silky, deliberate way. Even when he was silent, his unspoken thoughts seemed to be lashing her with bitterness, and she turned painfully away to pick up the paper he had flung aside. "The situation, Kato," resumed Darragh, addressing himself to the third occupant of the room, "is bluntly this: If Sims isn't here with that coat before young Hulse arrives, all our carefully-thought-out plan, a month's patient work, and about the last both of our cash and credit, simply go to the devil! . . . and Violet wants to say that perhaps Mr. Sims forgot to wind his watch last night or poor Mrs. Sims's cough is worse . . . Proceed, Violet. Don't be diffident."

The man addressed as "Kato" knocked a piece off the chessboard he was studying and stooped to pick it up again before he replied. Then he looked from one to the other with a face singularly devoid of expression.

"Perhaps. Who says?" he replied in his quaintly-ordered phrases. "If it is to be, my friend, it will be."

"Besides, Hugh," put in Violet, with a faint dash of spirit, "it isn't really quite so touch-and-go as that. If Sims comes before Hulse has left, Kato can easily slip out and change coats then."

Darragh was already on his restless way towards the door. Apparently he did not think it worthwhile to reply to either of the speakers, but his expression, especially when his eyes turned to Violet, was one of active contempt. As the door closed after him, Kato sprang to his feet and his impassive look gave place to one almost of menace. His hands clenched unconsciously and with slow footsteps, he seemed to be drawn on in pursuit. A little laugh, mirthless and bitter, from the couch, where Violet had seated herself, recalled him.

"Is it true, Katie," she asked idly, "that you are really the greatest ju-jitsuist outside Japan?"

"Polite other people say so," replied the Japanese, his voice at once gentle and deprecating.

"And yet you cannot keep down even your little temper!"

Kato thought this over for a moment. Then he crossed to the couch and stood regarding the girl with his usual impenetrable gravity.

"On contrary, I can keep down my temper very well," he said seriously. "I can keep it so admirably that I, whose ancestors were Samurai and very high nobles, have been able to become thief and swindler and – " His moving hand seemed to beat the air for a phrase. " – and low-down dog and still to live. What does anything it matter that is connected with me alone? But there are three things that do matter – three that I do not allow myself to be insulted and still to live: My emperor, my country, and

410

– you. And so," concluded Kato Kuromi, in a somewhat lighter vein, "now and then, as you say, my temper gets the better of me slightly."

"Poor Katie," said Violet, by no means disconcerted at this delicate avowal. "I really think that I am sorrier for you than I am for Hugh, or even for myself. But it's no good becoming romantic at this time of day, my dear man." The lines of her still quite young and attractive face hardened in keeping with her thoughts. "I suppose I've had my chance. We're all of a pattern, and I'm as crooked as any of you now."

"No, no," protested Kato loyally. "Not you of yourself. It is we bad fellows round you. Darragh ought never to have brought you into these things, and then to despise you for your troubles – that is why my temper now and then ju-jitsues me. This time it is the worst of all – the young man Hulse, for whose benefit you pass yourself as the sister of your husband. How any mortal man possessing you – "

"Another cigarette, Katie, please," interrupted Violet, for the monotonous voice had become slightly more penetrating than was prudent. "That's all in the way of business, my friend. We aren't a firm of family solicitors. Jack Hulse had to be fascinated and I – well, if there is any hitch, I don't think that it can be called my fault." And she demonstrated for his benefit the bewitching smile that had so effectually enslaved the ardent Beringer.

"Fascinated!" retorted Kato, fixing on the word jealously, and refusing to be pacified by the bribery of the smile. "Yes, so infatuated has become this very susceptible young man that you lead him about like pet lamb at the end of blue ribbon. Business? Perhaps. But how have you been able to do this, Violet? And you husband – Darragh – to him simply business, very good business – and he forces you to do this full of shame thing and mocks at you for reward."

"Kato, Kato – " urged Violet, breaking through his scornful laughter.

"I am what your people call yellow man," continued Kato relentlessly, "and you are the one white woman of my dreams – dreams that I would not lift finger to spoil by trying to make real. But if I should have been Darragh, not ten-thousand times the ten-thousand pounds that Hulse carries would tempt me to lend you to another man's arms."

"Oh, Katie, how horrid you can be!"

"Horrid for me to say, but 'business' for you to do! How have you discovered so much, Violet – what Hulse carries, where he carries it, the size and shape the packet makes, even the way he so securely keeps it? 'Business' eh? Your husband cares not so long as we succeed. But I, Kato Kuromi, care." He went nearer so that his mere attitude was menacing as he stood over her, and his usually smooth voice changed to a tone she had

411

never heard there before. "How have you learned all this? How, unless you and Hulse – "

"Sssh!" she exclaimed in sharp dismay as her ear caught a sound beyond.

" – Oh yes," continued Kato easily, his voice instantly as soft and unconcerned as ever, "it will be there, you mean. The views in the valley of Kedu are considered very fine and the river itself – "

It was Darragh whom Violet had heard approaching, and he entered the room in a much better temper than he had left it. At the door he paused a moment to encourage someone forward – a seedy, diffident man of more than middle age, who carried a brown-paper parcel.

"Come on, Sim. Hurry up, man!" urged Darragh impatiently, but without the sting of contempt that had poisoned his speech before. "And, oh, Phillips – " Looking back and dropping his voice. " – when Mr. Hulse arrives, show him into the morning room at first. Not up here, you understand? Now, Sims."

After a rather helpless look round for something suitable on which to lay his parcel, the woebegone-looking individual was attempting to untie it on an upraised knee.

"Yes, sir," he replied, endeavouring to impart a modicum of briskness into his manner. "I'm sorry to be a bit late, sir. I was delayed."

"Oh, well, never mind that now," said Darragh magnanimously. "Thing quite all right?"

"Mrs. Sims isn't worse?" asked Violet kindly.

Mr. Sims managed to get his back to the group before he ventured to reply.

"No, miss," he said huskily. "She's better now. She's dead: Died an hour ago. That's why I wasn't quite able to get here by eight."

From each of his hearers this tragedy drew a characteristic response. Violet gave a little moan of sympathy and turned away. Kato regarded Sims, and continued to regard him, with the tranquil incuriosity of the pitying East. Darragh – Darragh alone spoke, and his tone was almost genial.

"Devilish lucky that you were able to get here by now in the circumstances, Sims," he said.

"Well, sir," replied Sims practically, "you see, I shall need the money just as much now – though not quite for the same purpose as I had planned." He took the garment from the paper and shook it out before displaying it for Darragh's approval. "I think you will find that quite satisfactory, sir."

"Exactly the same as the one your people made for Mr. Hulse a week ago?" asked Darragh, glancing at the jacket and then passing it on to Violet for her verdict.

"To a stitch, sir. A friend of mine up at the shop got the measurements and the cloth is a length from the same piece."

"But the cut, Sims," persisted his patron keenly. "The cut is the most important thing about it. It makes all the difference in the world."

"Yes, sir," acquiesced Sims dispassionately, "you can rely on that. I used to be a first-class cutter myself before I took to drink. I am yet, when I'm steady. And I machined both coats myself."

"That should do then," said Darragh complacently. "Now, you were to have – "

"Ten guineas and the cost of the cloth you promised, sir. Of course it's a very big price, and I won't deny that I've been a bit uneasy about it from time to time when I – "

"That's all right." Darragh had no wish to keep Mr. Sims in evidence a minute longer than was necessary.

"I shouldn't like to be doing anything wrong, sir," persisted the poor creature. "And when you stipulated that it wasn't to be mentioned – "

"Well, well, man. It's a bet, didn't I tell you? I stand to win a clear hundred if I can fool Hulse over this coat. That's the long and short of it."

"I'm sure I hope it is, sir. I've never been in trouble for anything yet, and it would break my wife's 'art – " He stopped suddenly and his weak face changed to a recollection of his loss. Then, without another word, he turned and made shakily for the door.

"See him safely away, Katty, and pay him down below," said Darragh. "I'll settle with you later," and the Japanese, with a careless "All right-o," followed.

"Now, Violet, slip into it," continued her husband briskly. "We don't want to keep Hulse waiting when he comes." From a drawer in a cabinet near at hand he took a paper packet, prepared in readiness, and passed it to her. "You have the right cotton?"

"Yes, Hugh," said Violet, opening a little work-basket. She had already satisfied herself that the coat was a replica of the one the young American would wear, and she now transferred the dummy package to the corresponding pocket and with a few deft stitches secured it in the same way as she had already learned that the real contents were safeguarded. "And, Hugh – "

"Well, well?" responded Darragh, with a return of his old impatience.

"I don't wish to know all your plans, Hugh," continued Violet meekly, "but I do want to warn you: You are running a most tremendous risk with Kato."

413

"Oh, Kato!"

"It is really serious, Hugh. You don't believe in patriotism, I know, but Kato happens to. When he learns that it isn't ten-thousand pounds at all, but confidential war plans, that this scoop consists of, something terrible may happen."

"It might, Violet. Therefore I haven't told him, and I am so arranging things that he will never know. Cheer up, my girl, there will be no tragedy. All the same, thanks for the hint. It shows a proper regard for your husband's welfare."

"Oh, Hugh, Hugh," murmured Violet, "if only you were more often – "

Whatever might have been the result – if indeed there was yet hope in an appeal to another and a better nature that he might once have possessed – it came too late. The words were interrupted by the sudden reappearance of Kato, his business with Sims completed. He opened and closed the door quietly but very quickly, and at a glance both the Darraghs saw that something unforeseen had happened.

"Here's pretty go," reported the Japanese. "Hulse just come and brought someone with him!"

For a moment all the conspirators stood aghast at the unexpected complication. Hugh Darragh was the first to speak.

"Damnation!" he exclaimed, with a terrible look in his wife's direction. "That may upset everything. What ghastly muddle have you made now?"

"I – I don't know," pleaded Violet weakly. "I never dreamt of such a thing. Are you sure?"

"Slow man," amplified Kato with a nod. "Fellow who walk – " He made a few steps with studied deliberation

"Blind! It's Max Carrados," exclaimed Violet, in a flash of enlightenment. "They have been great friends lately and Jack has often spoken of him. He's most awfully clever in his way, but stone blind. Hugh, Kato, don't you see? It's rather unfortunate his being here, but it can't really make any difference."

"True, if he is quite blind," admitted Kato.

"I'll look into it," said Darragh briskly. "Coat's all ready for you, Kato."

"I think no, yet," soliloquised the Japanese, critically examining it. "Keep door, 'alf-a-mo', Violet, if please." His own contribution to the coat's appearance was simple but practical – a gentle tension here and there, a general rumple, a dust on the floor and a final shake. "One week wear," he announced gravely as he changed into it and hid his own away.

414

"Take your time, Mr. Carrados," Darragh's voice was heard insisting on the stairs outside, and the next moment he stood just inside the room, and before Hulse had quite guided Carrados into view, drew Violet's attention to the necessity of removing the button-hole that the Americans still wore by a significant movement to the lapel of his own coat. It required no great finesse on the girl's part to effect the transfer of the little bunch of flowers to her own person within five minutes of the guests' arrival.

"A new friend to see you, Violet – Mr. Carrados," announced Darragh most graciously. "Mr. Carrados, my sister."

"Not to see you exactly, Miss Darragh," qualified Carrados. "But none the less to know you as well as if I did, I hope."

"I wanted you to meet Max before I went, Miss Darragh," explained Hulse, "so I took the liberty of bringing him round."

"You really are going then?" she asked.

"Yes. There seems no doubt about it this time. Twelve hours from now I hope to be in Paris. I should say," amended the ingenuous young man, "I dread to be in Paris, for it may mean a long absence. That's where I rely on Carrados to become what is called a 'connecting file' between us – to cheer my solitude by letting me know when he has met you, or heard of you, or, well, anything in fact."

"Take care, Mr. Hulse," she said. "Gallantry by proxy is a dangerous game."

"That's just it," retorted Hulse. "Max is the only man I shouldn't be jealous of – because he can't see you!"

While these amiable exchanges were being carried on between the two young people, with Max Carrados standing benignly by, Darragh found an opportunity to lower his voice for Kato's benefit.

"It's all right about him," he declared. "We carry on."

"As we arranged?" asked Kato.

"Yes. Exactly. Come across now." He raised his voice as he led Kato towards the other group. "I don't think that either of you has met Mr. Kuromi yet – Mr. Hulse, Mr. Carrados."

"I have been pining to meet you for weeks, sir," responded Hulse with enthusiasm. "Mr. Darragh tells me what a wonderful master of ju-jitsu you are."

"Oh, well. Little knack, you know," replied Kato modestly. "You are interested?"

"Yes, indeed. I regard it as a most useful accomplishment at any time, and particularly now. I only wish I'd taken it up when I had the leisure."

"Let me find you an easy-chair, Mr. Carrados," said Violet attentively. "I am sure that you won't be interested in so strenuous a subject as ju-jitsu."

"Oh, yes, I am, though," protested the blind man. "I am interested in everything."

"But surely – "

"I can't actually see the ju-jitsuing, you would say? Quite true, but do you know, Miss Darragh, that makes a great deal less difference than you might imagine. I have my sense of touch, my sense of taste, my hearing – even my unromantic nose – and you would hardly believe how they have rallied to my assistance since sight went. For instance – "

They had reached the chair to which Miss Darragh had piloted him. To guide him into it she had taken both his hands, but now Carrados had gently disengaged himself and was lightly holding her left hand between both of his.

"For instance, Hulse and I were speaking of you the other day – forgive our impertinence – and he happened to mention that you disliked rings of any sort and had never worn one. His eyes, you see, and perhaps a careless remark on your part. Now I know that until quite recently you continually wore a ring upon this finger."

Silence had fallen upon the other men as they followed Carrados's exposition. Into the moment of embarrassment that succeeded this definite pronouncement, Mr. Hulse threw a cheerful note.

"Oh ho, Max, you've come a cropper this time," he exclaimed. "Miss Darragh has never worn a ring. Have you?"

"N-o," replied Violet, a little uncertain of her ground, as the blind man continued to smile benevolently upon her.

"A smooth and rather broad one," he continued persuasively. "Possibly a wedding ring?"

"Wait a minute, Violet, wait a minute," interposed Darragh, endeavouring to look judicially wise with head bent to one side. He was doubtful if Violet could carry the point without incurring some suspicion, and he decided to give her a lead out of it. "Didn't I see you wearing some sort of plain ring a little time ago? You have forgotten, but I really believe Mr. Carrados may be right. Think again."

"Of course!" responded Violet readily. "How stupid of me! It was my mother's wedding ring. I found it in an old desk and wore it to keep it safe. That was really how I found out that I could not bear the feel of one and I soon gave it up."

"What did I say?" claimed Darragh genially. "I thought that we should be right."

"This is really much interesting," said Kato. "I very greatly like your system, Mr. Carrados."

"Oh, it's scarcely a system," deprecated Max good-naturedly. "It's almost second nature with me now. I don't have to consider, say, 'Where is the window?' if I want it. I know with certainty that the window lies over here." He had not yet taken the chair provided, and suiting the action to the word he now took a few steps towards the wall where the windows were. "Am I not right?" And to assure himself, he stretched out a hand and encountered the heavy curtains.

"Yes, yes," admitted Violet hurriedly, "but, oh, please do be careful, Mr. Carrados. They are most awfully particular about the light here since the last raid. We go in fear and trembling lest a glimmer should escape."

Carrados smiled and nodded and withdrew from the dangerous area. He faced the room again.

"Then there is the electric light – heat at a certain height of course."

"True," assented Kato, "but why electric light?"

"Because no other is noiseless and entirely without smell. Think – Gas, oil, candles: All betray their composition yards away. Then – " Indicating the fireplace. " – I suppose you can only smell soot in damp weather? The mantelpiece – " Touching it. " – inlaid marble. The wallpaper – " Brushing his hand over its surface. " – arrangement of pansies on a criss-cross background – " Lifting one finger to his lips. " – colour scheme largely green and gold."

Possibly Mr. Hulse thought that his friend had demonstrated his qualities quite enough. Possibly – at any rate he now created a diversion.

"Engraving of Mrs. Siddons as the Tragic Muse, suspended two-feet-seven-inches from the ceiling on a brass-headed nail supplied by a one-legged ironmonger whose Aunt Jane – "

All contributed a sufficiently appreciative laugh – Carrados's not the least hearty – except Kato, whose Asiatic dignity was proof against the form of jesting.

"You see what contempt familiarity breeds, Miss Darragh," remarked the blind man. "I look to you, Mr. Kuromi, to avenge me by putting Hulse in a variety of undignified attitudes on the floor."

"Oh, I shan't mind that if at the same time you put me up to a trick or two," said Hulse, turning to the Japanese.

"You wish?"

"Indeed I do. I've seen the use of it. It's good. It's scientific. When I was crossing, one of the passengers held up a bully twice his weight in the neatest way possible. It looked quite simple, something like this, if I may?" Kato nodded his grave assent and submitted himself to Mr. Hulse's vigorous grasp. "'Now,' said the man I'm speaking of, 'struggle and your right arm's broken'. But I expect you know the grip?"

"Oh, yes," replied Kato, veiling his private amusement, "and therefore foolish to struggle. Expert does not struggle. Gives way." He appeared to do so, to be falling helplessly in fact, but the assailant found himself compelled to follow, and the next moment he was lying on his back with Kato politely extending a hand to assist him up again

"I must remember that," said Hulse thoughtfully. "Let me see, it goes – do you mind putting me wise on that again, Mr. Kuromi? The motion picture just one iota slower this time, please."

For the next ten or twenty minutes, the demonstration went on in admirable good humour, and could Max Carrados have seen he would certainly have witnessed his revenge. At the end of the lesson, both men were warm and dusty – so dusty that Miss Darragh felt called upon to apologise laughingly for the condition of the rug. But if clothes were dusty, hands were positively dirty – there was no other word for it.

"No, really, the poor mat can't be so awful as that," declared the girl. "Wherever have you been, Mr. Kuromi? And, oh, Mr. Hulse you are just as bad."

"I do not know," declared Kato, regarding his grimy fingers seriously. "Nowhere of myself. Yes, I think it must be your London atmosphere among the rug after all."

"At all events you can't – Oh, Hugh, take them to the bathroom, will you? And I'll try to entertain Mr. Carrados meanwhile – only he will entertain me instead, I know."

It was well and simply done throughout – nothing forced, and the sequence of development quite natural. Indeed, it was not until Hulse saw Kuromi take off his coat in the bathroom that he even thought of what he carried. "Well, Carrados," he afterwards pleaded to his friend, "now could I wash my hands before those fellows like a guy who isn't used to washing? It isn't natural. It isn't human." So for those few minutes the two coats hung side by side, and Darragh kindly brushed them. When Hulse put on his own again his hand instinctively felt for the hidden packet. His fingers reassured themselves among the familiar objects of his pockets, and his mind was perfectly at ease.

"You old scoundrel, Max," he said, when he returned to the drawing room. "You told Kuromi to wipe the floor with me and, by crumbs, he did! Have a cigarette all the same."

Miss Darragh laughed pleasantly and took the opportunity to move away to learn from her accomplices if all had gone well. Carrados was on the point of passing over the proffered olive branch when he changed his mind. He leaned forward and with slow deliberation chose a cigarette from

418

the American's case. Exactly when the first subtle monition of treachery reached him by what sense it was conveyed – Hulse never learned, for there were experiences among the finer perceptions that the blind man did not willingly discuss. Not by voice or outward manner in that arresting moment did he betray an inkling of his suspicion, yet by some responsive telephony Hulse at once, though scarcely conscious of it then, grew uneasy and alert.

"Thanks. I'll take a light from yours," remarked Carrados, ignoring the lit match, and he rose to avail himself. His back was towards the others, who still had a word of instruction to exchange. With cool precision he handled the cloth on Hulse's outstretched arm, critically touched the pocket he was already familiar with, and then deliberately drew the lapel to his face.

"You wore some violets?" he said beneath his breath.

"Yes," replied Hulse, "but I – Miss Darragh – "

"But there never have been any here! By Heavens, Hulse, we're in it! You had your coat off just now."

"Yes, for a minute – "

"Quietly. Keep your cigarette going. You'll have to leave this to me. Back me up – discreetly – whatever I do."

"Can't we challenge it and insist – "

"Not in this world. They have at least one other man downstairs – in Cairo, a Turk by the way, before I was blind, of course. Not up to Mr. Kuromi, I expect – "

"Cool again?" asked Miss Darragh sociably. It was her approach that had sent Carrados off into irrelevances. "Was the experience up to anticipation?"

"Yes, I think I may say it was," admitted Hulse guardedly. "There is certainly a lot to learn here. I expect you've seen it all before?"

Oh, no. It is a great honour to get Mr. Kuromi to 'show it off', as he quaintly calls it.

"Yes, I should say so," replied the disillusioned young man with deadly simplicity. "I quite feel that."

"*J. B. H.* is getting strung up," thought Carrados. "He may say something unfortunate presently." So he deftly insinuated himself into the conversation and for a few minutes the commonplaces of the topic were rigidly maintained.

"Care for a hand at auction?" suggested Darragh, joining the group. He had no desire to keep his guests a minute longer than he need, but at the same time it was his line to behave quite naturally until they left. "Oh, but I forgot – Mr. Carrados – "

419

"I am well content to sit and listen," Carrados assured him. "Consider how often I have to do that without the entertainment of a game to listen to! And you are four without me."

"It really hardly seems – " began Violet.

"I'm sure Max will feel it if he thinks that he is depriving us," put in Hulse loyally, so with some more polite protestation, it was arranged and the game began, Carrados remaining where he was. In the circumstances a very high standard of bridge could not be looked for. The calling was a little wild, the play more than a little loose, the laughter rather shrill or rather flat. The conversation between the hands forced and spasmodic. All were playing for time in their several interpretations of it. The blind man alone was thinking beyond the immediate moment.

Presently there was a more genuine burst of laughter than any hitherto. Kato had revoked, and, confronted with it, had made a naive excuse. Carrados rose with the intention of going nearer when a distressing thing occurred. Halfway across the room he seemed to slip, plunged forward helplessly, and came to the floor, involved in a light table as he fell. All the players were on their feet in an instant. Darragh assisted his guest to rise. Violet took an arm. Kato looked about the floor curiously, and Hulse – Hulse stared hard at Max and wondered what the thunder this portended.

"Clumsy, clumsy," murmured Carrados beneath his breath. "Forgive me, Miss Darragh."

"Oh, Mr. Carrados!" she exclaimed in genuine distress. "Aren't you really hurt?"

"Not a bit of it," he declared lightly. "Or at all events," he amended, bearing rather more heavily upon her support as he took a step, "nothing to speak of."

"Here is pencil," said Kuromi, picking one up from the polished floor. "You must have slipped on this."

"Stepping on a pencil is like that," contributed Hulse wisely. "It acts as a kind of roller-skate."

"Please don't interrupt the game any more," pleaded the victim. "At the most, at the very worst, it is only – Oh! – a negligible strain."

"I don't know that any strain, especially of the ankle, is negligible, Mr. Carrados," said Darragh with cunning foresight. "I think it perhaps ought to be seen to."

"A compress when I get back will be all that is required," maintained Carrados. "I should hate to break up the evening.

"Don't consider that for a moment," urged the host hospitably. "If you really think that it would be wiser in the end – "

"Well, perhaps – " assented the other, weakening in his resolution.

420

"Shall I 'phone up a taxi?" asked Violet.

"Thank you, if you would be so kind – Or, no. – perhaps my own car would be rather easier in the circumstances. My man will be about, so that it will take very little longer."

"I'll get through for you," volunteered Darragh. "What's your number?"

The telephone was in a corner of the room. The connection was soon obtained and Darragh turned to his guest for the message.

"I'd better speak," said Carrados – he had limped across on Hulse's arm – taking over the receiver. "Excellent fellow, but he'd probably conclude that I'd been killed . . . That you, Parkinson? . . . Yes, at 155 Densham Gardens. I'm held up here by a slight accident . . . No, no, nothing serious, but I might have some difficulty in getting back without assistance. Tell Harris I shall need him after all, as soon as he can get here – the car that's handiest. That's – Oh, and, Parkinson, bring along a couple of substantial walking sticks with you. Any time now. That's all . . . Yes . . . yes." He put up the receiver with a thrill of satisfaction that he had got his message safely through. "Held up – " A phrase at once harmless and significant – was the arranged shift-key into code. It was easy for a blind man to receive some hurt that held him up. Once or twice Carrados's investigations had got him into tight places, but in one way or another he had invariably got out again.

"How far is your place away?" someone asked, and out of the reply a time-marking conversation on the subject of getting about London's darkened streets and locomotion in general arose. Under cover of this, Kato drew Darragh aside to the deserted card table.

"Not your pencil, Darragh?" he said quietly, displaying the one he had picked up.

"No. Why?"

"I not altogether like this, is why," replied the Japanese. "I think it Carrados own pencil. That man have too many ways of doing things, Darragh. It was mistake to let him 'phone."

"Oh, nonsense. You heard what he said. Don't get jumpy, man. The thing has gone like clockwork."

"So far, yes. But I think I better go now and come back in one hour or so. Safer for all much."

Darragh, for very good reasons, had the strongest objections to allowing his accomplice an opportunity of examining the spoil alone. "Look here, Katty," he said with decision, "I must have you in case there does come a scrimmage. I'll tell Phillips to fasten the front door well, and then we can see that it's all right before anyone comes in. If it is, there's no need for you to run away. If there's the least doubt, we can knock these

421

two out and have plenty of time to clear by the back way we've got." Without giving Kato any chance of raising further objection, he turned to his guests again.

"I think I remember your tastes, Hulse," he said suavely. "I hope that you have no objection to Scotch whisky, Mr. Carrados? We still have a few bottles left. Or perhaps you prefer champagne?"

Carrados had very little intention of drinking anything in that house, nor did he think that with ordinary procrastination it would be necessary.

"You are very kind," he replied tentatively. "Should you permit the invalid either, Miss Darragh?"

"Oh, yes, in moderation," she smiled. "I think I hear your car," she added, and stepping to the window ventured to peep out.

It was true. Mr. Darragh had run it a shade too fine for once. For a moment he hesitated which course to take – to see who was arriving or to convey a warning to his henchman down below. He had turned towards the door when Violet's startled voice recalled him to the window.

"Hugh!" she called sharply. "Here, Hugh." And as he reached her, in a breathless whisper, "There are men inside the car – two more at least."

Darragh had to decide very quickly this time. His choice was not without its element of fineness. "Go down and see about it, Katty," he said, looking Kato straight in the eyes. "And tell Phillips about the whisky."

"Door locked," said the Japanese tersely. "Key other side."

"The key was on this side," exclaimed Darragh fiercely. "Hulse – "

"Hell!" retorted Beringer expressively. "That jacket doesn't go out of the room without me this journey."

Darragh had him covered before he had finished speaking.

"Quick," he rapped out. "I'll give you up to three, and if the key isn't out then, by God, I'll plug you, Hulse! One, two – "

The little "*Ping!*" that followed was not the automatic but the release of the electric light switch as Carrados, unmarked among this climax, pressed it up. In the absolute blackness that followed. Darragh spun round to face the direction of this new opponent.

"Shoot by all means, Mr. Darragh, if you are used to firing in the dark," said Carrados's imperturbable voice. "But in any case remember that I am. As I am a dead shot by sound, perhaps everyone had better remain exactly where he – or she, I regret to have to add, Miss Darragh – now is."

"You dog!" spat out Darragh.

"I should not even talk," advised the blind man, "I am listening for my friends and I might easily mistake your motive among the hum of conversation."

He had not long to wait. In all innocence, Phillips had opened the door to Parkinson, and immeasurably to his surprise two formidable-looking men of official type had followed in from somewhere. By a sort of instinct – or possibly a momentary ray of light had been their guide – they came direct to the locked door.

"Parkinson," called Carrados.

"Yes, sir," replied that model attendant.

"We are all in here: Mr. Hulse and myself, and three – I am afraid that I can make no exception – three unfriendlies. At the moment the electric light is out of action, the key of the locked door has been mislaid, and firearms are being promiscuously flourished in the dark. That is the position. Now if you have the key, Hulse – "

"I have," replied Hulse grimly, "but for a fact I dropped it down my neck out of harm's way and where the plague it's got to – "

As it happened the key was not required. The heavier of the officers outside, believing in the element of surprise, stood upon one foot and shot the other forward with the force and action of an engine piston-rod. The shattered door swung inward and the three men rushed into the room.

Darragh had made up his mind, and as the door crashed he raised his hand to fire into the thick. But at that moment the light flashed on again and almost instantly was gone. Before his dazzled eyes and startled mind could adjust themselves to this he was borne down. When he rose again his hands were manacled.

"So," he breathed laboriously, bending a vindictive eye upon his outwitter. "When next we meet, it will be my turn, I think."

"We shall never meet again," replied Carrados impassively. "There is no other turn for you, Darragh."

"But where the blazes has Kuromi got to?" demanded Hulse with sharp concern. "He can't have quit?"

One of the policemen walked to a table in the farthest corner of the room, looked down beyond it, and silently raised a beckoning hand. They joined him there.

"Rum way these foreigners have of doing things," remarked the other disapprovingly. "Now who the Hanover would ever think of a job like that?"

"I suppose," mused the blind man, as he waited for the official arrangements to go through, "that presently I shall have to live up to Hulse's overwhelming bewonderment. And yet if I pointed out to him that the button-hole of the coat he is now wearing still has a stitch in it to keep it in shape and could not by any possibility . . . Well, well, perhaps better not. It is a mistake for the conjurer to explain."

About the Author

Ernest Bramah Smith – who wrote under the name *Ernest Bramah* – was born in Manchester, England in 1868, the son of a warehouseman. After having grades near the bottom of his class in every subject, he dropped out of school at age sixteen and spent four years farming before deciding that he wanted to be a writer. He pursued a career in journalism. For a time, he wrote a column for the *Birmingham News*, and then moved to London, where he wrote and held the editorship for a number of small publications.

His first collection of short stories was *The Wallet of Kai Lung* (1900), describing a low-key Chinese storyteller, and he began to transition into writing more pulp-like stories for popular magazines. Further Kai Ling stories followed, and in 1913, he wrote the first Max Carrados tales. It is for these two characters that he is most remembered, although his other stories have been compared to those by Edgar Rice Burroughs, Robert E. Howard, and Arthur Conan Doyle.

At the time of his death, Smith's had accumulated over £15,000 – approximately £900,000 today. His writing, while little remembered today, didn't do too badly.

Smith and his wife, Lucy, led very low-key and reclusive lives, to the point that in 1923, Smith's publisher found it necessary to state that *Ernest Bramah* was a real person. At the time Smith died, his wife asked that his place of death be suppressed.

Smith died in June 1942 in Weston-super-Mare, Somerset, leaving behind a substantial amount of work, including the Max Carrados and Kai Lung series, as well as several other novels and a substantial number of non-series short stories.

The MX Book of New Sherlock Holmes Stories

Edited by David Marcum
(MX Publishing, 2015-2025)

"This is the finest volume of Sherlockian fiction I have ever read, and I have read, literally, thousands." – Philip K. Jones

"Beyond Impressive . . . This is a splendid venture for a great cause!"
– Roger Johnson, Editor, *The Sherlock Holmes Journal*,
The Sherlock Holmes Society of London

Part I: 1881-1889; Part II: 1890-1895; Part III: 1896-1929

Part IV: 2016 Annual

Part V: Christmas Adventures

Part VI: 2017 Annual

Eliminate the Impossible
Part VII: (1880-1891); Part VIII: (1892-1905)

2018 Annual
Part IX: (1879-1895); Part X: (1896-1916)

Some Untold Cases
Part XI: (1880-1891); Part XII: (1894-1902)

2019 Annual
Part XIII: (1881-1890); Part XIV: (1891-1897); Part XV: (1898-1917)

Whatever Remains . . . Must be the Truth
Part XVI: (1881-1890); Part XVII: (1891-1898); Part XVIII: (1898-1925)

2020 Annual
Part XIX: (1882-1890); Part XX: (1891-1897); Part XXI: (1898-1923)·

Some More Untold Cases
Part XXII: (1877-1887); Part XXIII: (1888-1894); Part XXIV: (1895-1903)

2021 Annual
Part XXV: (1881-1888); Part XXVI: (1889-1897); Part XXVII: (1898-1928)

More Christmas Adventures
Part XXVIII: (1869-1888); Part XXIX: (1889-1896); Part XXX: (1897-1928)

2022 Annual
Part XXXI: (1875-1887); Part XXXII: (1888-1895); Part XXXIII: (1896-1919)

"However Improbable . . . ."
Part XXXIV: (1878-1888); Part XXXV: (1889-1896); Part XXXVI: (1897-1919)

2023 Annual
Parts XXXVII (1875-1889), XXXVIII (1889-1896), and XXXIX (1897-1923)

Further Untold Cases
Part XL: (1879-1886), Part XLI: (1887-1892) and Part XLII: (1894-1922)

2024 Annual
Parts XLIII (1874-1888), XLIV (1889-1897), and XLV (1898-1917)

Occupants of the Canonical Realm
Parts XLVI (1861-1889), XLVII (1890-1898), and XLVIII (1899-1924)

The True Mr. Holmes: England's Greatest Hero
Parts XLIX (1880-1888), L (1889--18XX96), LI (1897-1901), and LII (1902-1923)

The MX Book of New Sherlock Holmes Stories
Edited by David Marcum
(MX Publishing, 2015-2025)

<u>*Publishers Weekly* says:</u>

Part VI: *The traditional pastiche is alive and well . . . .*

Part VII: *Sherlockians eager for faithful-to-the-canon plots and characters will be delighted.*

Part VIII: *The imagination of the contributors in coming up with variations on the volume's theme is matched by their ingenious resolutions.*

Part IX: *The 18 stories . . . will satisfy fans of Conan Doyle's originals. Sherlockians will rejoice that more volumes are on the way.*

Part X: *. . . new Sherlock Holmes adventures of consistently high quality.*

Part XI: *. . . an essential volume for Sherlock Holmes fans.*

Part XII: *. . . continues to amaze with the number of high-quality pastiches.*

Part XIII: *. . . Amazingly, Marcum has found 22 superb pastiches . . . his is more catnip for fans of stories faithful to Conan Doyle's original*

Part XIV: *. . . this standout anthology of 21 short stories written in the spirit of Conan Doyle's originals.*

Part XV: *Stories pitting Sherlock Holmes against seemingly supernatural phenomena highlight Marcum's 15th anthology of superior short pastiches.*

Part XVI: *Marcum has once again done fans of Conan Doyle's originals a service.*

Part XVII: *This is yet another impressive array of new but traditional Holmes stories.*

Part XVIII: *Sherlockians will again be grateful to Marcum and MX for high-quality new Holmes tales.*

Part XIX: *Inventive plots and intriguing explorations of aspects of Dr. Watson's life and beliefs lift the 24 pastiches in Marcum's impressive 19th Sherlock Holmes anthology*

Part XX: *Marcum's reserve of high-quality new Holmes exploits seems endless.*

Part XXI: *This is another must-have for Sherlockians.*

Part XXII: *Marcum's superlative 22nd Sherlock Holmes pastiche anthology features 21 short stories that successfully emulate the spirit of Conan Doyle's originals while expanding on the canon's tantalizing references to mysteries Dr. Watson never got around to chronicling.*

Part XXIII: *Marcum's well of talented authors able to mimic the feel of The Canon seems bottomless.*

Part XXIV: *Marcum's expertise at selecting high-quality pastiches remains impressive.*

Part XXVIII: *All entries adhere to the spirit, language, and characterizations of Conan Doyle's originals, evincing the deep pool of talent Marcum has access to. Against the odds, this series remains strong, hundreds of stories in.*

Part XXXI: *. . . yet another stellar anthology of 21 short pastiches that effectively mimic the originals . . . Marcum's diligent searches for high-quality stories has again paid off for Sherlockians.*

Part XXXIV: *Mind-bending puzzles are the highlight of Marcum's fully satisfying 34th anthology, which again demonstrates that multiple authors are capable of giving Sherlock Holmes and Watson innovative mysteries to tackle while staying in character. Marcum's inventory of canonical pastiches shows no signs of being exhausted any time soon.*

Also From MX Publishing

Traditional Canonical Sherlock Holmes Adventures
by

David Marcum

Creator and editor of
The MX Book of New Sherlock Holmes Stories

The Papers of Sherlock Holmes

"The Papers of Sherlock Holmes by David Marcum contains nine intriguing mysteries . . . very much in the classic tradition . . . He writes well, too."
– Roger Johnson, Editor, *The Sherlock Holmes Journal*,
The Sherlock Holmes Society of London

"Marcum offers nine clever pastiches."
– Steven Rothman, Editor, *The Baker Street Journal*

Sherlock Holmes and A Quantity of Debt

"This is a welcome addendum to Sherlock lore that respectfully fleshes out Doyle's legendary crime-solving couple in the context of new escapades . . . ."
– Peter Roche, Examiner.com

"David Marcum is known to Sherlockians as the author of two short story collections . . . In Sherlock Holmes and A Quantity of Debt, *he demonstrates mastery of the longer form as well."*
– Dan Andriacco, Author

Sherlock Holmes – Tangled Skeins

(Included in Randall Stock's, 2015 Top Five Sherlock Holmes Books – Fiction)
"Marcum's collection will appeal to those who like the traditional elements of the Holmes tales"
– Randall Stock, BSI

"There are good pastiche writers, there are great ones, and then there is David Marcum who ranks among the very best . . . I cannot recommend this book enough."
– Derrick Belanger, Author and Publisher of Belanger Books

Also by David Marcum
from MX Publishing

Traditional Canonical Holmes Adventures

The Collected Papers of Sherlock Holmes

Volume I: Tales
Volume II: Records
Volume III: Accounts
Volume IV: Narratives
Volume V: Chronicles
Volume VI: Muniments
Volume VII: Annals
Volume VIII: Documents

*"Among the best I must number David Marcum, who, by this point has written
more Holmes stories than Doyle himself. Characterized by unflagging
imagination and ceaseless ingenuity, along with felicitous prose, these tales
continue to provide what we all crave: more Sherlock."*
– Nicholas Meyer - *New York Times* Bestselling Author

432

Edited by David Marcum
from MX Publishing

The Complete Dr. Thorndyke
by R. Austin Freeman
Volumes I-IX

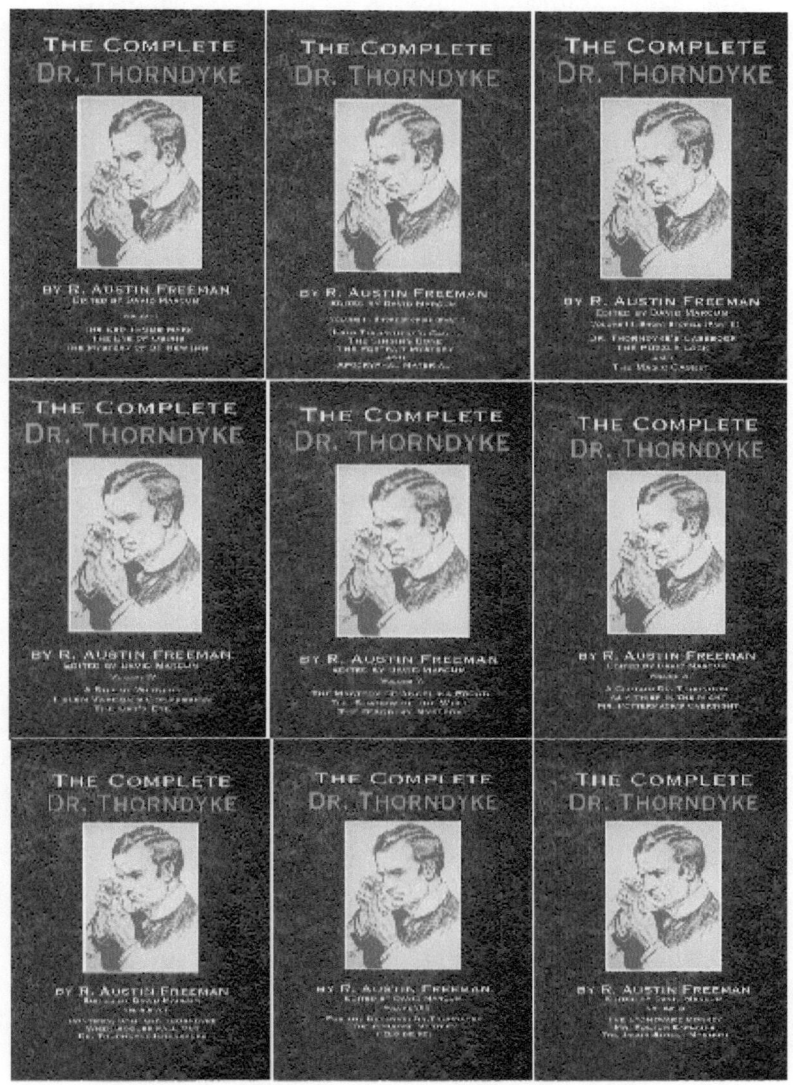

MX Publishing

MX Publishing is the world's largest specialist Sherlock Holmes publisher, with over six-hundred titles and over two-hundred authors creating the latest in Sherlock Holmes fiction and non-fiction

The catalogue includes several award winning books, and over four-hundred-and-fifty have been converted into audio.

MX Publishing also has one of the largest communities of Holmes fans on Facebook, with regular contributions from dozens of authors.

www.mxpublishing.com

@mxpublishing on Facebook, Twitter, and Instagram